The Crescent's Edge

Ms Carolyn Long Silvers

Copyright © 2015 Ms Carolyn Long Silvers
All rights reserved.
ISBN: 1508883459
ISBN 13: 9781508883456

This book is dedicated to the memory of those who survived the sinking of Brother Jonathan, those who perished, and the compassionate citizens of Crescent City who dealt with both. It is also dedicated to the Native Americans who made the Crescent their home before capitalistic interest changed the region, and who, as a people, survived the turbulence it caused.

When you die, you will be spoken of as those in the sky, like the stars." Yurok Tribal Proverb

Introduction

Soon after moving to Crescent City, I was fascinated with the rich history of the town and surrounding area. One-hundred-fifty years ago, one of these historical events occurred. Brother Jonathan, a steamer from San Francisco, sunk off the shores of this community. All but nineteen persons aboard died. While thinking of how this event must have affected the citizens, inspiration came for this book.

The tragedy of Brother Jonathan is historical fact. However, my story is pure fiction. All active characters in the 1865 setting are fictional. Businesses and establishments are as well. In the chapters addressing modern Crescent City, businesses and places mentioned are real and part of the community.

In regard to the natural remedies described in the story; these are researched and are as accurate as I could describe, using incomplete information. However, in no way are they recommended to be used or to replace modern medicine. People of this century utilized what was available to improve their health and lives. Science has made discoveries and developed procedures that have effectively replaced these methods.

I offer a special thanks to the people of this community for sharing their town with me, and the warm welcome I've received while making Crescent City my home. Nestled next to the sea, and framed by the magnificent Redwood forest, it is truly a magical-mystical place.

1

Brother Jonathan
Though men think of ships as feminine, refer to us as she,
They named me Brother Jonathan and sent me out to sea.

Edward Mills commissioned me in eighteen fifty-one
To make his fortune moving gold, his plan had just begun.

Two hundred twenty solid feet between my bow and stern
And eleven meters wide, I was, with lots of steam to burn.

Though steamers aren't too speedy, Mills never had regret.
My first roundtrip to Panama, quite soon a record set.

Within a year, C. Vanderbilt bought me and changed my name.
The Commodore I then became, the Pacific led to fame.

Cornelius added yet a deck, more passengers adorn.
I took them safely many times, around that old Cape Horn.

MS CAROLYN LONG SILVERS

As North and South spilled brothers' blood, the west discovered ore.
I transported it through stormy seas, along the western shore.

The rebel pirates sought my soul, the Shenandoah bold.
I kept my course, my speed prevailed, and she never got my gold.

And then again, I was renewed, my old name was restored
One hundred thousand dollars and my ovens fairly roared.

In summer eighteen sixty-five I left the Frisco scene.
Victoria was my destiny with pauses in-between.

Two hundred forty anxious souls, passenger and crew,
A deadly fate awaited them. That morning no one knew.

A circus family, Portland bound, with camels in the hold,
Grandmother, doctor, cabin boy, Wells Fargo man with gold,

Reporter with his pen and ink, a business man with wife,
A madam with some soiled doves, advised to cause no strife.

A brief stop in the Crescent, we traded bits of freight,
The sky was blue and clear of clouds, no one could know our fate.

Just eight miles from the Crescent, a deep-sea mountain peak,
Uncharted on the Captain's map, soon our demise would seek.

The Nor'wester came from nowhere and spun us in the air,
The Captain yelled his orders, the crew was in despair.

The passengers, all tossed around, hung on with all their might.
The crew worked hard, the crew worked long, two hours in the fight.

"Turn her around, it's back to shore, we cannot hesitate."
The crew complied and almost won, but it was just too late.

That demon wave just picked me up, with little time to fear,
One thousand tons of freight and flesh it dropped on rocky spear.

And now impaled, I couldn't move, cold water filled my hull.
"Load lifeboats up!" the captain yelled, "pass life belts out to all!"

They did their best, those brave young men, "The kids and women first!"
But hungry waves the life boats hit, against the ship they burst.

They tried to fish the people out, with waves and wind at play,
But even as they threw them ropes, the souls were swept away.

One smaller craft at last pulled free, with nineteen barely saved.
Five hours scooping water, to Crescent's shore they braved.

And looking back to watch me, sinking from their sight,
My Captain DeWolf bravely waved, he'd given up the fight.

For weeks the bodies washed to shore, their spirits haunt today,
For lives lost to uncharted rocks, close to the Crescent's Bay.

My grave lies deep, two hundred feet, millions in gold, alone.
What pirates couldn't take from me, the sea claimed for her own.

2

July 1865

"Greed in the end, fails even the greedy." Cathryn Louis

It was drizzling rain in San Francisco at 6:30 AM. Maria DeWolf stirred sugar into her second cup of tea. She didn't usually rise this early. Today however, was steamer day, July 28, 1865. Captain Samuel DeWolf would be leaving soon on Brother Jonathan, and she was always diligent in sending him away with hugs, kisses and smiles.

Maria was two years older than Sam. She adored him. Married now for eight years, she still felt excited for his return from his regular voyages north to Victoria Canada and back again.

Both of them were mid-forties, healthy and attractive. He loved her self-reliant spirit. He knew she would remain occupied while he was away and dutifully attentive when he returned. Fiercely independent, Maria successfully supported herself making hats of her own design before their marriage. Now with him at sea, she kept busy working with charities.

There were many organizations and causes to attend too. San Francisco, once a small town boomed during the gold rush of the forties. It populated faster than housing could be built. The silver boom followed. Now over 100,000 people considered themselves citizens of San Francisco.

The booms did not benefit everyone. Crowded conditions spread diseases; small pox, cholera and tuberculosis moved rapidly through districts of the poor. San Francisco, always generous is spirit had numerous charities to assist the poor and ill. Maria took an active part in it.

California had now been a state for five years. Eighteen counties were formed, and San Francisco was the county seat for one of them. Operating only in gold and silver, business poured in from surrounding communities.

The clock in the parlor struck eight. Maria rose from her chair and returned to her bed chamber. She wanted to dress nicely and fix her hair before Samuel returned from checking the ship. Then they would say their goodbyes.

James Nisbit slipped off his coat and loosened his collar. It was warm even here by the waterfront. He had paid his fare and now waited to board. Boarding was running late. He heard grumbling about freight difficulties. He looked forward to settling into his berth and concluding an article. He was compiling it for The Evening Bulletin, a paper of which he was editor.

He felt some excitement about sailing on Brother Jonathan as he had written about her several times. James, in his mid-forties, was a bachelor and loved being a writer. He spoke his mind in print and always defended the underdog. He cared not who it offended nor did he seek popularity. The unjust deserved exposure and he was dedicated in doing so.

The war was over and now he must find new material. Much about the President's recent assassination remained a mystery. James hoped to have the opportunity to interview Dr. Anson Henery who was known as a personal friend of the Lincolns. Dr. Henery reportedly on board, had recently returned from counseling the president's widow. He might be persuaded to speak about the first family.

Nisbit observed a familiar face also waiting to board. He knew him from a previous interview. Joseph Lord the Wells Fargo agent must be accompanying a shipment of gold, he assumed.

Little did he know that thirty-four year old Joseph was in charge of delivering $140,000 worth of gold. Some would be taken to a bank in Seattle, some to fur traders in Canada, another sum for Indian treaty obligation, and $200,000 US army payroll. Young Joseph Lord was looking forward to a meeting with his lovely wife in Crescent City. It would only be for a few hours but a welcomed reunion.

A bit of dread haunted Minnie Bergman as she boarded with her small son, Albert. She was prone to sea sickness and hoped for calm seas. Having lived in San Francisco for two years while her husband successfully profited from gold mining, she was meeting him in Portland. At last they would return to Illinois where the purchase of a dairy farm would fulfill their dream. Both Minnie and her husband were immigrants from Germany. America had treated them well.

Mrs. Lilly O' Kennan took final inventory of her possessions. The trunk filled with gold bricks from the sale of her establishment, was secured with several locks. The keys were attached to her gold chain belt. A chest filled with jewels was also locked. That key was added to the ring holding the others. Her expensive dresses, shawls, capes, silk stockings, nightgowns and satin slippers filled the two additional trunks to capacity. These, she would keep in her chambers on the ship.

At least a dozen hat boxes were stacked. Each contained one of a kind head adornment, decorated with plumes, feathers, and silk flowers.

Mrs. O' Kennan was humiliated at the closure of her thriving business, Treasure by the Sea. Her establishment in San Francisco far surpassed any other in the city.

It provided a gentlemen's club complete with billiards, poker tables, barbershop, saloon, restaurant, musical entertainment, bedchambers for rent, and the bonus of female attention for a price. She had similar establishments in Portland, Seattle, and Victoria

Canada. But this one, 'Treasure by the Sea' had been her first, and was a model from which the others were designed.

She would walk away from this city with her head held high, her shoulders back, and her gaze straightforward. Being forced to sell and leave the city by the very leaders who had patronized her establishment was worse than insulting.

"They're all weak men who gave in to political pressure," she reassured herself.

Her husband, now in Victoria and occupied with their newest business endeavor, had telegraphed her to behave calmly. Bad press over a closure in one city could sour the reception of the same brothel type establishments in other localities.

The Treasure was known to have the loveliest of women. She referred to them as her jewels. All, very young, had been brought up in upper-middle-class families, spoke several languages, and were musically trained and talented.

Lilly only hired the best of the best. No brash, tactless, rude women need apply. Actually, few of her girls had applied. All had believed they were advancing their hopes for careers in music or acting when applying for jobs with Lilly. Her seducing manipulation soon added prostitution to their resumes.

Bouncers, whom the girls feared and called the strong men, served as heavy-handed brutes when Lilly needed them, either to control drunken customers or runaway jewels. Lily and her husband had a fine tuned plan. All employees owed them more that any could ever repay, or at least were made to believe that they did.

Jewels were traded out among her different establishments every three to six months. This discouraged clients from becoming partial to any one woman, and kept the young ladies a bit unbalanced and insecure with her surroundings.

Ten women had been sent to Portland and Seattle two weeks before as she closed up shop. Several strong men had escorted them. She planned to bring the remaining seven, the youngest of her brothel, and deliver them to the new and thriving 'Ice House', in Victoria.

On this Steamer day she hurried the chattering group along. All nicely dressed, the collection of stylish females could not help but draw attention. Their dresses of fine fabric draped over lace petticoats, hugging waistlines that were tightly cinched by corsets. Colors of navy blue linen, rich green silks and wools, berry red brocades and mustard colored satins were complimented with matching hats. All headwear was accessorized with various assortments of colorful feathers.

These working girls, ages sixteen to twenty, were paid well in San Francisco, though most of the earnings went to Lilly. Some were clever enough to hide tips or swipe loose coins, but their pay from Lilly was very little. She provided them with finery, some jewelry, food and a chamber, all tallied against their earnings.

Any having a personal stash of gold coins would have sewn it into linings of their corsets, the hems of petticoats as well as dresses. They carried with them clothing, jewelry, and accessories in velvet handbags and canvas satchels.

Although many citizens traveled more conservatively, Lilly and her entourage paid for first class with reservations for chambers, meals and fine wine. They gracefully boarded and settled into the arrangements.

Jonas McCain had no ticket. He had grown up an orphan on the streets of San Francisco. He was big and strong of body but weak of mind. Possessing a soft heart and a gentle spirit, the beefy thirty-year-old male had few skills. He had scratched out a living by running errands and working menial tasks.

Sneaking onto the Brother Jonathan he hoped, would be a solution to finding a better life in the lumber mills. He had been told his physical strength would be valued and his mental incapacity ignored.

He hid in the dark shadows of the ever increasing freight being loaded on Steamer Day. In his pocket, he stored a letter that introduced him. A kind widow, for who he had run errands, gave testimony to his honesty and loyalty. A few five dollar gold coins nested in the toes of his shoes.

Captain DeWolf entered his large, Victorian style residence. Maria was waiting. Smiling, she met him at the door. Goodbye must be brief. She felt his tension as she put her arms around him. Looking up into his face she saw concern, or was it anger?

"What is it dear?" she asked.

He shook his head and pulled her close to him. "They've overloaded me again. There's a fire engine and hose going to Portland, large machinery for delivery to the woolen mill in Polk County, and a huge ore crusher. This is in addition to seven hundred tons of freight. Oh, and did I mention the circus animals? There are two camels in the hold. It's caused us delay with departure"

"There are surely limits," Maria protested.

"I complained, and was told to continue with the voyage or be replaced."

He kissed Maria goodbye, leaving her stand at their front door. She would never forget that goodbye and her husband's obvious concern.

By late morning, two hundred and forty-four people were finally loaded. Stewards were setting white clothed tables with china as they arranged seating for the noon meal. As Brother Jonathan navigated into ocean waters, weather conditions greeted them with rowdy waves. Lunch would not be a pleasant experience.

By the time the steamer reached Crescent City, her passengers were a dismal group. Discouraged and sea sick, only a few took small boats to shore. Young Joseph Lord was one who did. He enjoyed a few hours with his wife and her family, the lighthouse keepers.

When he returned to the ship, most passengers were in their chambers or booths attempting to overcome the lingering sickness. One young woman seemed unaffected by the earlier rough voyage and mingled in the lounge.

Elsie Barns, a beautiful teen, was being sent to live with an aunt. Her parents had died and left her a comfortable sum and a guardian to watch over it. Joseph Lord had noticed her earlier drawn to the questionable Lilly and her young women. Now she was occupied with a young crewman named Hayden. He wondered why she had no chaperone. Joseph settled in to wait for Brother Jonathan to commence her journey to Crescent City.

On this summer day in 1865, Thaddeus Barrett walked out of the Redwood Hotel in Crescent City, past two vacant lots and toward the El Sol Saloon. He would have a drink and then saunter down to the waterfront.

The day was chilly for the last of July. Thad buttoned up his woolen jacket and braced his head against the strong wind that rolled in from the sea. He stepped into the front door of the building and blinked, waiting for his eyes to adjust to the dim lighting of the kerosene lamps.

There were no shortages of saloons in town. One was two stories. The Seville had a theater in the upper story that was also used as a dance hall. However, El Sol was Thad's favorite. Older men usually lingered here, exchanging stories.

Thad moved to The Crescent six months before. The town was officially eleven years old and served as the county seat. The first coastal settlement along this northern coastline, it was designed to serve the isolated communities around the mountainous area. Although now settled with more than eight hundred, many open lots remained for sale and half finished buildings awaited new owners.

Having fought for the Union and recovered from a serious battle wound, the twenty-five year old Kansan moved west to heal, clear his head, and to avoid the politics of the reconstruction. He wanted to be far away from reminders of the spoils of war. The screams of dying men still stalked his dreams.

He had worked at various jobs, including lumbering, fishing, and construction within the town. He felt fortunate to now work at

The Print Shop. Three months into his training at setting type, he was content and confident.

The beauty of the area in this pacific pocket provided healing to the former soldier. Nestled into a crescent shaped coastline, surrounded on it's west by the sea with gregarious boulders and jutting rocks, the hamlet's east was backed by mountains that were alive with giant redwoods.

Twenty miles from the Oregon border, the area was first home to the Totowa Nation of indigenous peoples. Eight years before, these people's lives were at great risk as rogue zealots determined to annihilate them in response to an Indian uprising in Oregon. Many had been murdered and some sold into slavery.

Thad chose a table near the front window, as he attempted to straighten his windblown dark hair. The proprietor gave a nod and filled a stein. He knew what his regular customers wanted and wasted no time in providing it. He carried a bottle to Thad's table and set it down. Thad slid a coin in his direction.

"Tomorrow's the day for the steamer," commented Abe Turner, scooping up the coin.

"Tis," replied Thad. "Do you have cargo coming?"

"I do, indeed, and not a day too soon. Can't be letting my customers grow thirsty. I have several crates from the Frisco Brewery"

"I have to pick up some reams of paper for The Print Shop," said Thad. "I'll be at the Harbor."

"Why don't you take my wagon? Pick up your paper and my crates of whisky and beer. I'll pay ya to do it."

"You don't have to pay me, Abe, I'd be glad to do it for you. I'm going anyway. Maybe you can reward me with a shot of that new whiskey."

"Kid, you can have the whole blame bottle," Abe promised, laughing.

Thad left the saloon and walked to Front Street, built near the shore...*Kid, he always calls me kid. I'm five foot eleven, I've fought a war for God'* sakes. I support myself, but he calls me kid...He smiled at himself. In spite of his experiences of being a man, he still felt like a kid.

He looked out over the vast endless shades of blue and grey. Sky, clouds, and water blended together. Only the pointed jagged stones defined the horizon. The wind was intense today. Angry waves beat the rocky shoreline. Gulls called out as they fished the edges.

He cast his gaze toward the lighthouse. The white rock building topped a rocky elevated piece of land called The Point that guarded the entrance to the harbor. Erected ten years before, it served as the only beacon. The keeper and his family lived in the stone building. Children played outside as waves slammed against the rocks that supported it. "I fee l assured Brother Jonathan is having a rough voyage," he thought.

Early the next morning, July 30, 1865, Thad was awakened by the blast of the canon. This was protocol. When the ship was spotted by a watchman the canon warned of its approach. The bi-monthly event was anticipated by the community. It was welcomed for the delivery of needed items and something to divert attention from the mundane. Thad walked to the Saloon and hitched up Abe's wagon and team. He drove the Morgan pair to the harbor. It was a sunny though windy day, far more promising than yesterday. He could clearly see Brother Jonathan in the distance.

A few people soon came to shore on small fishing boats to take a break from the sea. They talked about turbulent waters with several days and nights of sea sickness. They hoped the worse was over.

Thad and crewmen loaded the rolls of paper and crates of liquor into the wagon. He drove back to the El Sol Saloon. Around 10:00 the small boats left the crescent shore with passengers to join the mother ship.

3

2015, Portland Oregon and Crescent City California

"Shattered legs may heal in time, but some betrayals fester and poison the soul."

—George R.R. Martin

Rebecca Cates carefully folded shorts and tops and placed them in the leather Pullman case. Many women would be thrilled to spend the hottest part of summer sailing with her husband and associates, but she was not.

Married barely two years, she was facing the painful reality that her relationship with Philip was on thin ice. She loved their loft apartment in the Pearl District. Her position, teaching kindergarten in the nearby private school was rewarding. She strived to be patient with his long hours at work and frequent trips required by his Insurance Firm. How could things go so wrong? Digging through her box of lotion, she searched for sun block. As a pale skinned red head, she was taking no chances of solar burns...

Darn; I'll have to buy some... I'll also need to refill my birth control script...what else do I need?

As she tossed the last few items into her cosmetic case she scoffed at her mental list... *Like the pills are even needed, Phil has shown no interest in lovemaking for weeks...* She reached into the closet for a windbreaker and red cotton hoodie... *Well, now I know why, don't I? Little Miss Office Tart, Tonya, has claimed my prince.*

She locked the door of the apartment and pulled her case to the elevator...*There's plenty of time to stop by the pharmacy and get to docks in time.* Turning the key in the ignition, she fought tears... *No, I won't cry... I will face this head on. While we're out there in his favorite part of the world, I will tell him I know about Tonya... We will talk this out. A marriage is not disposable like last years stilettos. You don't trade it in like a car. You don't just sell it off like stocks. We can fix this.*

Phillip Terrence Cates locked his Mercedes. He knew it would be safe inside the protective walls of the Pacific Yacht Club. He glanced at his watch. Becca would be here soon. He could wait and walk with her to The Lorelei. That would look more appropriate to Joe and Steve. He was sure they had heard the rumors, like it should matter. They'd probably had their share of office affairs to remember.

He spotted Becca's blue Toyota pull into the gate. Stepping out into her line of vision, he motioned her to the empty space by his Mercedes. Becca didn't mind being outclassed with the vehicles. A successful business man must appear to be a successful business man, Phil reminded her. An economy car is appropriate for a teacher. Such symbols of success weren't important to her. Becca parked, pulled her suitcase out and locked the door.

"I'm really surprised you agreed to go sailing, Becca. You've always been so against going along," he steered her to the boardwalk.

"Well, I'm glad you insisted. I need an adventure." *Not!*

"The Lorelei is ninety-two feet long and has four cabins," he explained as they walked along.

The wheels on the Pullman rattled noisily as it bumped along on the wooden boardwalk. She wished he would offer to carry it, but that wasn't Phil's style.

"There are two crewmen. The other wives stocked groceries and the three of you can plan the meals. We'll stop for some rest and fishing at Crescent City. If anything is needed you women can shop there."

"Super," she answered. *Last time I visited with these women I thought I would die of boredom....* She flashed him a smile," I'm looking forward to seeing them again."

Steve and Joe were board members of Cates & Cates. Every year they rented a sailing vessel and took Phil and his father for a week at sea. Phil loved sailing and looked forward to this trip all year long.

The previous year Becca declined. Water was her least favorite mode of travel. Sea sickness and hours of seeing only sky and water didn't appeal to her. Lesson planning got her off the hook then and could have this year. ..*This time I have no choice...I have to save our marriage.*

The other wives sat on the deck at a small table. Each held a drink. Becca smiled at them. Both were in their mid-forties and obviously pampered women. Becca commented once to Phil that they were superficial. His reply had been that her saying so made her superficial.

"There are many different kinds of snobbery," he reminded her.

At this moment she agreed...*I haven't given them a fair chance; I'm really going to try to fit into their world...at least for these few days.*

"I was very surprised when Steve said you were coming," offered Marsha with a wide smile revealing veneered teeth.

Momentarily Becca was captivated just looking at her face. It didn't move with her smile...Too much Botox.

Straightening up in her seat, she returned the smile. "Yes, it was a bit last minute."

"Too bad Phil's parents couldn't make it, but we're glad you did. Joe said that Phil told him you don't like sailing," commented Peggy.

"I'm prone to get a bit sick from the motion."

"Are you afraid of the water?" asked Marsha.

"Oh no, not really, I swim laps several times a week, and I was on the swim team in high school. It's just bouncing around on endless sea that gets to me." Even as she spoke, she felt wooziness edging in.

"Well, we'll just have to get you up there fishing, and then you'll forget all about being sick," suggested Peggy.

Spoken like a person who has never had motion sickness.

Marsha refilled her glass with daiquiri, and offered more to the other women.

Peggy accepted and Becca declined.

"So, you're a teacher?" asked Peggy, giving Becca a thorough onceover.

"Yes, this will be my second year." *Great we can talk about this, it's my passion.*

Peggy shook her head. "How can you stand being in a room with children all day? I could barely stand my own for more than an hour at a time, Thank God for nannies."

"And thank God for boarding school and summer camp," added Marsha laughing.

OK, so we can't discuss teaching, I guess. Becca smiled.

By lunch, any notion of eating was discarded as Becca avoided watching the others devour rich foods...*If nothing goes down, then nothing comes up.*

"Didn't you say we could spend a bit of time in Crescent City?" she asked Phil.

It was the first opportunity she'd found to distract his attention from incessant talk about business.

"Sure, he answered her, "We can spend the night there and pull away tomorrow. We'll do some crabbing from the dock this evening."

Marsha offered her expressionless smile. "Can you believe how even when they get away from business, they still talk business?"

Becca smiled back acknowledgment. "Yes, it's insurance talk twenty-four-seven," she agreed.

"At least we get the advantage of great coverage on every possible thing we need," said Peggy. "I got my total body makeover, teeth veneers, and new nose, thanks to Cates & Cates."

Marsha nodded toward Steve. "That head of hair he has is all new growth from his transplant. Last year he had a bald crown and wore a hair piece."

Becca processed their comments for a few moments. "I think we only have the basic plan," she said.

"And Life insurance," added Peggy. "Joe said that Phil and his father have million dollar life insurance policies on all family members."

Marsha leaned into Becca. "He may be worth more to you dead, than alive." She giggled and reached for another olive.

The painful ache in Becca's forehead intensified as another tummy roll led her to cover her mouth. She willed control over the churning. "Please excuse me. I' really need to lie down."

"What a sweet little town!" commented Marsha, securing the strap of her handbag over her shoulder?

Becca slipped on her sunglasses, and slid her cell phone into a pocket of her red hoodie. Zipping the pocket to protect it, she pushed her wallet into the other pocket and zipped it securely. Only then did she scope the extended vista.

She was in awe. To the east was an endless forest. She slowly shifted her gaze. The bay was a visual stimulus that took time to process. It contained commercial fishing boats docked in a line, sea lions lounging on the shores and on available piers, and a family playing on the safe beach, protected by the jetty. A small white lighthouse set dutifully on the point. It was a panoramic view.

"What are we going to do while the men fish?" asked Peggy.

"I'd like to check out the museum, "suggested Becca.

"Honey, when you've see one museum you've see them all," responded Marsha. "I would really like to set down and have a bite to eat. We can talk about it over some seafood."

The women decided on a bayside eatery, The Chart Room. Seated by a window, Peggy eyed the menu. "I must have the shrimp, you can't go wrong with shrimp."

Becca suddenly realized that her previous nausea was gone and that food sounded inviting. "I'm going to have the fish and chips, a large coke, followed by the blackberry bliss cobbler," she said handing her menu back to the waitress.

"Goodness dear," said Marsha, looking at her in surprise, "Aren't you worried about all those calories? A few rounds of liposuction and you'll be measuring everything you eat."

Marsha ordered a crab salad and unsweetened tea. "I guess when you are tall, and have a large frame, you can take in more. I've always been so dainty?"

Becca frowned. *Was that a compliment or insult?*

"She didn't mean that in a bad way," Peggy offered, "Did you Marsha?"

"Of course not," said Marsha. "There are some who view large, stout, fleshy women as attractive."

Okay, that does it! Becca turned in her chair and looked directly into Marsha's frozen face. "I'll have you know, that five foot eight and one hundred twenty-five pounds is not out of the average for today's woman." Brown eyes flashed dark with fire at the older woman.

Peggy looked worried. "Now ladies, we're all a bit tired and wind beaten, let's play nice. I think your height and weight are lovely. I wish I looked athletic."

The waitress served their orders and conversation ceased...*I'm messing up big time; I must keep my cool!*

Marsha picked at her salad. "I wasn't trying to offend you, Rebecca, my daughter is a redhead and I understand how overly sensitive..."

"Please, let's just drop it," said Becca, "No harm's done."

The older women discussed possibilities for the afternoon. Peggy suggested they convince their husbands to stay another day. "There's not enough time left for shopping now. Tomorrow, I'd like to find a painting of the lighthouse for my art collection."

"Good idea," agreed Marsha. We can get in some beach time. Did you bring a swim suit dear?"

Becca shook her head, "No, it completely slipped my mind."

"Well I would offer to loan you one of mine but either of them would fit you. Peggy's closer to your height, but neither of her suits would begin to cover your bosom. Have you had implants dear? "

Becca was silent. *I can't believe she's focusing on my body again!*

"She means that as a compliment," said Peggy quickly. "So many young women are going completely overboard these days with the breast augmentation. They actually look abnormal...I'm not saying your breasts look abnormal....I mean they are oversized in a natural way....oh dear."

Becca took a breath. "I guess the difference in our generations is that most women in my age group strive for self acceptance. I realize there are celebrities who draw press attention with goofy makeovers, but most of us believe we should embrace who and what we are."

Both women looked at her in amusement.

"As long as I'm content with my body, I don't care what others think," she added, placing the cloth napkin on her empty plate.

'Well, good for you, Rebecca," said Marsha. "As for my generation, we want to remain beautiful for our husbands. We were chosen to complement them as trophy wives and we could easily be replaced."

"I'll never go under the knife to please a man. And Phil is perfectly happy with my appearance."

"Is he now?" scoffed Marsha.

Peggy shot her friend a warning glance.

Becca felt as though an ice pick had penetrated her heart. *So they know.*

Rising from her seat, she said calmly, "If you'll excuse me, I'll pay for my lunch on the way out; I really intend to see that museum. I'll meet you back at the Lorelei."

Becca paid her bill as the two remaining women huddled together while exchanging some unknown line of information. The waitress provided Becca with the phone number of ABC Taxi.

She was disappointed to hear from Janet the driver, that the museum had restricted hours and wasn't open. Janet suggested she try again in a few days.

"That's disappointing, I love history. What kind of items are on display?"

"There's various things; old relics from the logging and gold rush days. There's clothing, tools and furniture from the mid-eighteen hundreds. They have a large display of Native American baskets. It's set up in the old jail, you know. Oh and there's information about the ship wreck in 1865. You can visit the Brother Jonathan cemetery. Would you like to go there?"

"Yes, I wish I'd brought my camera."

Janet turned and headed toward the coastline and Ninth Street. Becca watched the street signs as they passed.

"All these streets only are named letters and not words or names," she noted.

"I've wondered about that too," Janet replied, smiling at Becca. "You'd thought someone would have come up with names like Red Wood, or Ship Wreck, or Gold Dust, but it's just plain old a, b, c, d, e, f, g, and 1st, 2nd, 3rd, so-on, at least here in the main part of town."

Janet stopped the car and both women walked to the site where a circular arrangement of graves lay, marked with flat stones. Becca read the summarized account of the incident on the sign that listed the passengers. Stars marked the nineteen survivors.

"This can't be everyone that died," said Becca, looking around the circle of stones.

"No, some of the lost were never found, some buried in a mass grave, and others were returned to their families. Many graves that were here in this cemetery were moved to the newer one, some years ago. Others were so decomposed by the time they were discovered; they were buried along the shores where they washed up"

Becca slowly read the names. This is such a sad story...and I can't get over how it affects me... I feel personally connected...

"There are some books about it. If we hurry I can get you to the book store before it closes," Janet offered.

At sunset, Becca returned to the Lorelei with her new bag of goodies. She had two books, picture postcards of Brother Jonathan, Dramamine that was recommended by a pharmacist, and a tee shirt stating her love for Crescent City.

Phil was livid. "I can't believe you abandoned Marsha and Peg and just disappear like that. We've been waiting for you so we could go out for a nice steak dinner. We've had to settle for pizza carry-in. I can't imagine how you be so inconsiderate!"

"I didn't abandon them, I told them I was going to the museum. I said I would meet them back here."

"Marsha told Steve you were rude to her. Don't you realize these are two of the most powerful board members?"

He turned on his heel leaving Becca to board alone. Becca sucked in a deep breath, and prepared for whatever was to come. She approached the group with a smile that she hoped looked sincere.

"Help yourself to Pizza," said Marsha coolly, "Too bad you didn't get here while it was hot."

"She can warm it up in the microwave," suggested Peggy. "Here, I'll do it for you."

"Thank you, Peggy," Becca said.

Looking at her husband she said quietly, "Phil, we need to talk privately, soon."

4

"You may not control all events that happen to you, but you can decide not to be reduced by them."

—Maya Angelou

Philip looked startled at Becca's demand but made no reply. Steve and Joe assisted in cleaning up the debris of the light supper, and Phil idled off to talk to Ike the crewman.

Ike was a burly man. He never made eye contact or changed his facial expression. It wasn't like Marsha's Botox frozen face. Ike's expression was set in deep frown lines. It gave an impression of constant anger or annoyance.

"Steve," began Becca, "The man my husband is talking to...Ike... is he an employee of the yacht club?"

Steve shook his head. "I never met him before. Jorge, the other crewman is with the club. He's been on all our trips. I don't know where Ike came from. Phil seems to know him."

"He certainly isn't friendly," commented Peggy, "whenever I offer food, snacks or drinks, Jorge accepts, but Ike just walks off."

"Maybe he has the good sense to know he should stay in his place as a hired man," responded Marsha.

Joe shook his head. "I've never treated any crewman or employee as less than myself."

"Yes," so I've noticed, said Marsha. "I keep telling your wife she needs to be firmer with her servants. You both spoil your help."

Becca excused herself. She went to the cabin that she and Phil intended to occupy. After reading the label on the box containing the Dramamine, she took two tablets with a swallow of water...*Here we go, do your duty in preventing motion sickness. The pharmacist says you should fix all my woes.*

She showered and combed out her short curly bob. Glancing at the new tee shirt she considered putting it on for sleeping...*No, I brought the black lace nightgown to appeal to Philip. The tee shirt can wait for morning.*

She pushed open the portal a crack and breathed in the salty air.... *All is so calm; if it could just stay like this.*

Giving one last glance at the raspberry colored sunset, she picked up one of her new books and snuggled under the covers...*There may be time to read a few chapters before Phil joins me. Should I talk to him tonight, and tell him what I know? Maybe it would e better to attempt exciting some passion... Maybe he'll confess and I can give him forgiving kisses... Tonya can't really mean anything to him.*

She took a deep breath, slipped on her reading glasses and opened the cover of The Brother Jonathan. She scanned quickly through the first chapters relating the various owners of the ship. It was important, but the technical narrative bored her. She was interested in people and life stories.

By Chapter Four she found herself transported to San Francisco. The variety of people who boarded that day was extensive. There was a military general and his faithful horse...*That makes sense; the civil war was barely over, men like this were returning home...* President Lincoln's personal doctor... *Odd, why would he be all the way out here in California?* ...A circus owner complete with acrobats and camels also boarded.

Becca closed her eyes and imagined the children story, Circus Boy, by Louisa May Alcott. It had been a childhood favorite. She wondered if this circus owner was kind to his workers or cruel like the children's' story...Here's a woman with a three week old baby... *Who would take a newborn on a steamer? A wife who wanted to keep the family together, that's who...* James Nisbit, editor of the Evening Bulletin boarded. *Was he taking a vacation, or was he chasing a story? This says he was known for speaking out against corruption and standing up for the down trodden... Bless him; there are warriors for fairness and humanity in every generation.*

She continued to read about Joseph Lord, agent of Wells Fargo. *He was there to guard 400.000 dollars worth of gold. He was in his early thirties...so young...That was a lot of responsibility for such a young man... and he was just married. That's just too-too sad. The orphan girl just sixteen...she was going to live with relatives.* "Hmm, she was on first class. She couldn't have been penniless.

A Madam and her party of seven soiled doves, mostly teens, boarded first class with a chest of jewels....A madam... *Really... going to Victoria with women so young... that's sex trafficking.*

Becca looked closely at the postcard that pictured the memorial. She squinted, trying to read the names...*Who of these survived and who died?*

Reading the fine print, her eye stopped on July 30, 1865...*July 30th is tomorrow... What-da-ya-know! Its one hundred and fifty years ago tomorrow... imagine that...being at the same place, reading about such a horrid event on the anniversary of the event.*

Noises outside the opened portal drew her attention. "I told you Joe, it's none of you business." Phil was whispering harshly.

The breeze carried his words into the cabin. "Philip, my father and your father started this firm together. They started it with integrity. Employees are more productive when gossip is in check. And you, my man, are creating a lot of gossip." Joe's voice was beginning to rise.

"Shhh, lower your voice or you'll start more gossip! Your father was once a partner, and you own some of the business, but you are not my moral adviser!"

"Give her up, Philip, send her to another department. End this affair or I'll talk with your father. I've had complaints from employees of unfair treatment because of your obsession with that girl. "

"I told you I'd end it when I'm ready, and I will!"

"That was a month ago. You need to work on your marriage and be an example, I mean it. Make this problem go away."

"It's a done deal, drop it already!" answered Phil.

Becca sat stunned…So is it over? Should I even talk to him about it now? …Probably not tonight… maybe tomorrow when he's not so disturbed by Joe's threats.

Becca closed the book, and laid it aside. She flipped out the tiny light on the wall by the bed, and settled down under the comforter… *Maybe Phillip really is over Tonya… Maybe this will all pass… I'll still need to talk to him… We can't just sweep it under the rug. Otherwise, I'll bottle it and eventually have one of my infamous blow-ups… I'll not sleep a wink tonight… I wonder why he hasn't come to bed….*The medication mercifully faded her thoughts into slumber.

Becca awoke shivering as the early misty sea air penetrated her blanket and thin lace gown. *..Burr, I forgot to close the portal…* Looking at her cell she noted the time, 8:00 AM. She hurriedly dressed in white shorts and added black yoga pants. She slipped on the pale blue Crescent City tee shirt and quickly added her red hoodie. Not knowing the morning plans, she checked to be sure her wallet and cell phone were zipped into the pockets.

Carefully applying sun block to her face, she dusted on mineral powder, added a touch of mascara, and finished with a coral lip gloss. She ran her fingers through her short curly hair, leaving it in its natural ringlets…*There, that's about as ready as I can get to confront my bad-boy husband.*

Remembering the Dramamine, she took two more tablets…*As long as this keeps working I'll make it through this…*She heard no voices …*Either the others are sleeping or they had left the Lorelei for the day…*She slipped on her flip flops and moved to the Galley. Coffee was made so she filled a mug and added creamer. As she made her way to the deck, she noticed Jorge heading for the gangway.

"Wait, Jorge where are the others? "

He turned, slipping his sun glasses on he nodded toward the cabins.

"Your husband is still sleeping, ma'am. The other four left about twenty minutes ago to get breakfast and then visit Ocean World. I'm sorry you missed them."

"That's fine, I didn't intend to go, where's my husband sleeping?"

Jorge looked away. He appeared to be embarrassed. "He's in the extra cabin. I'm going now. Mr. Cates said I'm not needed until evening. Good bye, Mrs. Cates. Have a nice day."

Becca sipped her coffee and peered through the fog...*The others will be gone for a while... perfect... now's the time to have a heart to heart with Phil...* Spotting Ike leaning on a rail and smoking a cigarette she called to him.

"Hello, Ike, are you taking shore leave today too?"

The man flipped the cigarette into the water and turned, moving away.

"You should consider running for office, Ike, you have such a nice way with people."

She returned to the cabin area...*Watch it Becca, you're getting cranky with the crewman. He's not what's bugging you... Keep your mind on your mission... who cares if he's a grump.*

Reaching the spare cabin, she attempted to turn the latch. It was locked. She knocked loudly on the door.

"Phillip Terrence Cates, open this door. We're going to talk."

After another round of knocking, the door opened. Phil stood facing her in his boxers. He was short, exactly her height, they were eye to eye. His dark blond hair with cosmetically tipped ends looked like it had been used to scrub the deck. Bags bulged under his bloodshot grey eyes.

"What in Hell do you want, Rebecca?"

"Oh, it's Rebecca, is it? It's been weeks since you've spent time with me and we're on formal terms now?"

She pushed herself past him and jumped on the bed. He sat down and reached for the blanket. She snatched it, wadded it up, and pushed it under her.

"Talk to me and I might give it back," she offered.

Philip looked annoyed. He wasn't particularly handsome, but Becca had first been attracted to him because of his business sense and practicality. She later realized that he measured his manhood on his ability to make money and impress people about making money. His need for material things went against her nature, but he also had a spirit of adventure that she admired. In business he was fearlessly competitive. She settled into loving him just as he was. "Opposites attract, "she always said about their marriage.

Phillip got up and grabbed his terry robe, quickly putting it on and wrapping it around him. He sat in a chair at the end of the bed. She bounced around to face him.

"You have a hangover."

"So, it's my vacation."

"Why didn't you come back to our cabin last night?"

"I didn't want to disturb you. Do you have to talk so loud?'

"Phillip, why did you ask me to come? No, you insisted that I come."

He put his head back and closed his eyes. "Since my parents couldn't make it, I thought you should be the hostess. I didn't expect Marsha to take over like she did."

"That makes no sense. Steve and Joe set up this trip and paid for it. Marsha and Peggy are the natural hostesses for this affair. Why did you want me to come? You have hardly even noticed that I'm here."

He raised his head and looked at her. "Sometimes it looks better for a couple to be seen together. Can't you whisper?"

"Wrong answer... the right answer is, Becca dear, we see so little of each other I wanted us to have quality time together. That's the right answer, Philip."

Philip leaned his head back again. "Are you going to work yourself up into frenzy and cause my head to ache worse?"

"I know about Tonya."

'What about Tonya, she's my assistant."

"She's your adulteress, Phillip, don't lie, work with me here."

"You're allowing your imagination to run away with you, Becca. You're always so dramatic."

"Remember that tennis bracelet you bought me for Christmas? I took it to the jeweler to have the clasp repaired. Mr. Whitaker asked if I wanted to pick up your order that had just come in."

Philip looked up in surprise. "I ordered nothing, he made a mistake."

"I picked it up... The receipt states that you paid $800.00 for a dinner ring... Inside the band it's engraved, to Tonya with love."

"Other people in the firm use Skye's Jewelry Store. Whitaker got confused. You're making something out of nothing, as always."

"I overheard Steve warning you last night. You two stood right by my portal. Was that my imagination? Was Steve confused?"

Phillip kept his eyes closed in silence.

"Don't you want our marriage to work, Phil?" Becca was fighting tears.

"I can forgive a mistake once. I just need to know you love me and want our marriage to work. I need to know I can trust you." Tears now were falling unchecked.

"If you were eavesdropping then you also overheard me tell him I'll end it."

"But do you want to end it? Because if you don't, what's the point? I love you, Philip, and this crushes me, but I won't share. If you can't work with me on fixing this, we might as well get a divorce."

"I said I'll end it, and I will!" He grabbed his head in pain.

"You have until we get back to Portland to convince me that you're truly emotionally invested in this marriage. If I'm not sure of it when we get back, I intend to get a lawyer and hand you over to Tonya, the home wrecker."

She was screaming and he appeared to be receiving her words at their full volume with the intense pain she had hoped he would.

Jumping off the bed, she took the rolled up blanket and threw it in his face.

As he was pawing his way out of it, she slid her arm over his bedside table, knocking off several items including his cell phone, glasses, wallet and a book. She slammed the door as she left.

In her cabin she sobbed... *So much for keeping calm while talking it out... how could I stay calm about something so serious... and he even tried to make me think I imagined everything.*

She went to the bathroom and splashed water on her face. Settling back on her bed she pulled out her phone. She started to call her mother, but decided against it. No reason to upset her. She thought of her older sister Beth. She scrolled to her name in her contact list, and pressed dial.

After the tearful discussion ended, she felt her head clear... *I don't think I want to try anymore. Trust is too hard to rebuild. When we talk again I'll suggest a peaceful divorce. Those two deserve each other...* Becca placed her phone back into her pocket and zipped it up.

I can survive without Phil, but I may never get over him... I can do this. I have my job, my savings, and my family... I'll have to move out of the loft... I won't be able to afford the neighborhood on a teacher's salary... Maybe I can find a roommate... I'll hang onto that dinner ring... good evidence, if I need it... Can't hock it with that personal engraving...I wonder what a divorce will cost...

The tides were rising and the boat rocked gently back and forth. Becca fell into a troubled sleep.

5

"There is no death, only a change of worlds."

—Duwamish Tribal Proverb

Becca awoke from the motion of the rocking bed. She opened her eyes and collected her thoughts. *The motion sickness medication certainly makes me sleep.* She pulled herself up to look out the portal...*Good Lord, we're at sea.*

She slid off the bed and proceeded to the deck. The fog had lifted and the skies were clear. In spite of the wind, it was comfortably warm. She unzipped her hoodie. Looking around, she didn't see the other women. She moved around to the starboard. Philip was talking to Ike. Both men were busy with the sails. Becca braced herself from the increasing motion of the vessel. As she glanced around, she saw Saint George Lighthouse moving nearer...*What possible reason would we have to be out here?*

She knew from her reading that the waters and rocks near Saint George sometimes create precarious conditions. Five light house keepers died in service before it was maintained by controls from shore...*It isn't advisable to get too close in stormy weather or rough seas. Phil has to know that.*

"Philip," she called." Her voice was lost in the wind.

Jonathan Rock ... it's around here close. She shaded her eyes with her hand, and studied the water...*It's invisible except in low tide... I wonder if Dopy Ike even knows about it... He doesn't appear to be one who would read a book... But then again... he seems to know what he's doing with The Lorelei...I hope Jorge is back on board...I trust him more.* Philip was moving in her direction. He appeared to be planning on passing right on by. Becca caught the sleeve of his windbreaker. He tried to pull away, but she gripped her fingers nailing her fingernails tight against the fabric.

"Phil, what are we doing? Why are we out here without the others?"

"I wanted to get a good look at the lighthouse. God, Becca, everything can't always be about you!"

"It's dangerous out here. Why didn't you wake me up? I would have gone a shore. I want to put on a life jacket."

Waves unsteadied both of them, slamming them against the cabin wall. Each struggled to regain balance. This was difficult as Becca clung to Philip and he continued an attempt to free himself.

"Let go of me, Damn It! " He yanked his sleeve from her. "Ike, it's time."

Ike moved in her direction.

"Time for what?" screamed Becca over the tempest.

The burly man focused on her. She tried to make sense of why he was approaching. Suddenly, he was close enough to grab her arm. Becca, jerked away quickly.

"Don't touch me, you thug!"

Philip turned his back, and began making his way to the bow. Ike now had her gripped tightly by both shoulders.

"Phil," she screamed, "Call off your goon!"

As she screamed, she pulled back her right leg, brought up her knee for a hard hit to his groin. Ike yelled obscenities and dropped to his knees. Becca turned to escape, but knew she couldn't run. The sea was too choppy...*Where can I go?" What's happening?*

As she scrambled away from the burley man, he sprang forward on the deck floor and grabbed her ankle. She fell face down and rolled as quickly as she could. Looking back, she aimed a kick with her free foot at his face. Blood shot from his nose. His eyes blazed with pain and rage. His grip still tight on her ankle, he pulled her close enough to scoop her upper body into his other arm as he got to his feet. Pushing her chin into her chest she managed to grasp the skin of his thumb with her teeth. She bit with all her strength. Ike screamed more obscenities as he yanked free. Becca spat the severed skin from her mouth. She tasted blood.

Ike now encased her waist with both arms as he tried to fling her legs over the rail. Becca placed her feet against the metal bar, and pushed back. He backed away and tried a second toss. This time she threaded her legs around the rail and locked her ankles together. As he tried to jerk them free, she reached behind her and clawing anything she could feel, hoping to find an eye. He released his hold on her with one arm and grabbed her thigh. He tried to pull it free from her scissor lock on the rail. She twisted enough to get one arm around his neck.

She felt a blow to her thigh and pain shot up and down her leg. A hard hit from a fist she assumed, but she used the moment to throw her other arm around his neck. She griped her hands around her wrists, and pulled her body as tightly against him and she could. His nose was bleeding on her face. His large hand came to the back of her head and attempted to grab hold of her hair, but it was too short. She flung both of her dangling legs around his hips and locked her ankles behind him. Pushing her face into his neck she sunk her teeth into a mouthful of fatty flesh and clamped down.

More screaming and obscenities escaped the man. Ike slammed her lower back against the rail. Unbearable pain shot up her spine but she held on. The body impact caused her teeth to sever his flesh as they held it in their grip. Blood shot from Ike's neck like a fountain. He turned quickly around in a circle. She tightened her grip. Catching a quick glance of Phil sticking his head out from the other side of the cabins, she noted shock and fear on his face. She was certain it wasn't for her.

Ike now lifted her hips on to the top of the rail and leaned over the water. He yanked at her arms, trying to dislodge them. His blood spurted onto her face. She wondered if she had ripped an artery. He leaned over further. She hung on with all fours. Suddenly, a wave rocked The Lorelei. Ike's weight shifted, taking them both overboard.

The icy water engulfed Becca as she sunk under the salty foam. Her years of training with the swim team kicked in, and she held her breath instinctively. She had lost her flip flops in the fight. Her loose yoga pants were already low on her hips. She kicked out of them, pushing herself to the surface.

Rising into the air, she gulped it in just before a wave slammed her face, taking her under again. She turned around before coming up to be sure her back would be to the onset and struggled out of her hoodie. It was hanging loose and tangling her arms. Up again, she took another breath, glancing around she saw Ike flaying the water. Philip was on deck shouting something to him...*Can't count on him, I'll try to reach one of the rocks...* She spotted one and positioned her body in a way she hoped would wash her in that direction. The next swell took her closer to it...*If only it doesn't crash me against it.*

Then a wall of water lifted her to its lofty height, and propelled her into the stone. With the impact against the rock, blinding pain shot through her. Everything went black. When her eyes opened again, she was floating and tossing on top of the waves. She felt nothing ...*The cold water has numbed my entire body...* She turned her head slightly. A large form developed in her peripheral vision...*What the...?*

Another form, an object bounced toward her. She put out her hand to prevent it from striking her...*Wood...what is this ...some kind of plank?"*

Twisting, with her upper body, she grasped the large elongated piece of wood. Struggling, she maneuvered her arms over it. She tried to kick her feet to swim away from the rock before another wave provided an encore. She couldn't feel her feet or legs....*No matter, the water takes me where it chooses anyway.*

She scanned the horizon. There was no sign of The Lorelei. Ike was nowhere in sight. As she shifted her gaze, the large grey form she saw earlier came into focus. She could plainly see it was a ship. It appeared to be high centered, but waves washed over it intermittently.

She heard two shots. As she drifted closer she heard screaming of women. Men yelled orders. A wave washed over her. She held tight with her arms and tucked her chin into her chest. Popping up again, she saw a life boat lowering...*I can't get to close to that sinking ship or I'll get sucked under. Move legs, move.*"

Another wash of water covered her and spun her around...*Hang on, hang on...*Finally, she was righted up and positioned herself so that she could watch the ship. A wave rocked the vessel against the lifeboat filled with women and children. It toppled over...*Oh God, this is horrible!*

She wanted to stay away from the turmoil, but she couldn't get any paddle motion with her legs. Colorful dresses bobbled like party balloons on the water. Mothers tried to hang on to infants and small children, but they were snatched from their arms. As Becca involuntarily moved closer she saw a second lifeboat lowered. A man dressed in uniform shouted orders. She looked around at the women flaying the water. No one appeared to be able to swim...*Why are they dressed like that? There's too much clothing... why aren't they floating?*

The waves returned some of the confused women back toward the ship. Men on the deck threw out lifelines, trying to retrieve victims. The ship jiggled precariously back and forth. Although impaled on a pointed stone, it appeared to be falling over. Something bumped against the plank and grabbed Becca's arm. She turned her head to see, but a wave engulfed her. As she struggled to breathe, arms wrapped around her neck. She pulled away enough to see the face of a young woman...*Looks like we'll be sharing this plank...*

The frightened violet-blue eyes looked into Becca's face. "Aidez-moi s'il vous plaît, Madame," she said pleadingly.

Great, I understand Spanish but wouldn't you know I'd meet up with a drowning Frenchwoman. Here goes, it's the only phrase I know.

"I know you're speaking French, but mais pouvez-vous parler anglais?" (Can you speak English?")

"Oui," she answered.

"Then speak English. Who are you?" Becca yelled over the noise.

Another sheet of water slammed the women, and they spun around. Becca hung on to the plank as the Frenchwoman hung on to her. When her view cleared again she saw the ship had tipped. Bodies were floating out from under it...*Oh no, it smashed the lifeboat...* Looking around, she now saw bodies everywhere. Some were swimming, some were flaying, while others appeared to be dead or unconscious. Those sank rapidly..."*Why can't they stay up? What's pulling them down?*

She became aware of the stranglehold the tiny woman had around her neck.

"Let go of me, hold to the board," she yelled.

She was able to guide the woman's arms individually to the plank. She grabbed it in sheer panic. Her grip slipped. Becca threw her arms around the girl's shoulders.

"What's this?" she asked, feeling a bundle strapped to her strange looking life preserver. "This life jacket is weird. Did they get this from the Ark? Good grief, woman! This heavy thingy around your waist is pulling us down. It's got to come off!"

She tugged on it, trying to release what appeared to be a carpet bag. Another wave caught her unprepared. Before blacking out, she felt the stranger's arms encircle her neck with a death grip. Suddenly, her eyes opened. She was close to something wooden... men and women's voices excitedly yelled at one another... she heard small children crying...*I can feel my legs... good, that's better... except... something is tangling them up... what's this blob?... It's tied to me.*

She looked up. Men's faces looked over the side...This is a freaking lifeboat...A man leaned over, holding out a rope, dropping it in front of her.

"Grab the line ma'am, hurry!"

She grabbed it. Her fingers were numb and stiff, but she willed herself to hang on. As he pulled her up, another man reached over and grabbed her arm. She tried to help but something wound around her legs and sucked her back into the water...*What in the...is this seaweed?"*

As they pulled her over the side, she worked her body to roll in. Looking up into the man's face, she noticed for the first time that he was African American.

"Thank you, but there's another woman out there, I had hold of her, but we got separated."

"Ma'am, there are lots of people out there. You're fortunate to have floated close enough for us to reach you. We're overloaded. "

"Here," another man said. "Hunker down here with these other ladies, and try to warm up a mite. We're headed for shore."

Becca tried but couldn't fight her way out of the encasement around her legs. Looking down, she saw yards of white lace and green wool bound around her lower extremities...*What's this?* Then she noticed a heavy bundle strapped to her back.

Twisting to look back she yelled, "No this can't be, it's her darn, freaking' suitcase, get it off me!"

"Ma'am, please remain calm," one of the men said sternly. "We need all hands on deck to get to shore."

"Here dear," a woman said softly. "Lie close to me and my son, we'll be all right."

Becca obeyed. The child was tied by cloth straps to his mother's neck, but he was calm.

"My husband tried to murder me." she sobbed.

"No ma'am," said one of the men. "You're confused. You've survived a shipwreck."

"No, I didn't," protested Becca. "My husband's crewman threw me from The Lorelei."

"Delphi dear," said the woman with the child," remember me, Minnie?"

"No, my name's Becca, I don't know you."

The man who had pulled her in, looked into her eyes, "You'll be ashore soon. You're safe now. We're all off the Brother Jonathan and moving towards shore."

The women and children lay as still as possible in the hull of the lifeboat while a man they called Tate, fought the waters with the only oar they had. Other men frantically scooped water out of the boat with a couple of pails. It was an endless task because waves quickly returned the water back to them. The older woman, Minnie, placed a comforting arm around Becca, and cooed comfort to her as though she were her child. Her speech reflected a heavy German accent. The child snuggled between them.

"Elsie's here, Delphi, she's on the other side of me. I know the two of you were friendly."

Becca made no reply...*Everyone's confused. Heck, I'm confused. They think I'm someone else, but what does it matter. I may not get out of this alive.*

"I'm heading for that shore," yelled Tate. "There's less obstructions."

Good, we must be getting close. Maybe I'll make it after all. First thing I'm going to do is get the police notified about Phil and Ike, then call Beth.

"Wait!" yelled a man. "There's Indians on the bank. We can't dock there."

Becca attempted to rise up, but the abominable carpet bag was caught in between other people's bodies and wouldn't budge. "No, go there, they'll help us," Becca called out.

No one paid attention. Turning her head toward Minnie, she asked, "Why are they changing their plan?"

"They're afraid of the Indians, dear. They have no way of knowing if they're friendly."

"That's just nutty," answered Becca, "There's been no uprising from American Natives since the seventy's AIM protests. And they weren't dangerous. Those people might have dry blankets... or... pickup trucks."

"Shhh, remain calm, Delphi, I understand there's been recent Indian conflicts not far from here," the woman answered.

I haven't a chance of survival. Crazies threw me from The Lorelei and other crazies picked me up.

The rough waters subsided and the men traded off with Tate and the rowing. Tate moved his position to check on the survivors.

"There's nothing to fear, ladies. We're moving to another landing area, but it's not far. How are those babies doing?"

The rocking of the craft, fatigue, and the perplexity throbbing in her brain was too much. Becca slipped into unconsciousness.

6

"Everything the power does, it does in a circle."

—LAKOTA TRIBAL PROVERB

Becca heard male voices, but the words didn't register. They were excited. The movement of the lifeboat made one hard bump, and then rocked back and forth several times. She tried to bring her mind to full understanding. She felt only fog and muddled thoughts. She became aware that the wet, soggy people around her were struggling to free themselves from the human cluster.

"We're safe, Delphi," said Minnie, "Elsie, dear, can you help free me from little Albert's harness, so I can hand him out to Tate?"

There was movement in the boat as those around her left, but Becca didn't move. Nothing seemed important except to drift back to that place where there was nothing to fear...*If this is death, it's not so bad...* She felt strong arms lifting her shoulders and other hands hoisting her feet.

She heard Tate call out, "This one's going to need carrying."

She felt her body gently swing into new arms. They were strong, dry and warm.

"Good Lardy," how can a half pint woman be so heavy? The owner of the arms exclaimed.

"It's that carpet bag," said Tate. "Dang thing nearly drowned her. I'm wagering she's got more weight sewn in her clothes."

Becca forced her eyes open. Looking down at her was the most handsome face she had ever seen. Dark straight hair fell in an unruly tumble over his forehead, and hazel eyes with golden flicks looked down at her.

"Well, there you are," he commented with a worried smile. "Everything will be going just fine for you now, little Miss."

"You're an angel?" asked Becca weakly, though she didn't know why.

"Not usually," he replied. "The devil comes around sometimes."

"Where're you taking that one?" a voice called from a distance.

"To the Redwood Hotel, there are open chambers there."

His response vibrated in his chest and she noticed its warmth. He shifted her weight, and began walking up an incline. She was aware of a mild limp in his gait. Then, the fog returned.

Becca heard voices, women's voices. One sounded very young. The older one gave commands to her. "Hannah, get one of your nightgowns. She's small enough to fit into it, I recon."

"Yes", Mrs. O'Shay. I have the kettle of hot water here," the young voice responded.

"Pour some of it in that basin, and then fetch the gown. I'll need you to help me with her corset," responded the older voice.

Becca was aware of hands fumbling with buttons on her bodice. Soon those hands slipped her arms from soggy sleeves. As the older woman wrestled with yards of soppy cloth below her waist, the young girl returned.

"I have the gown, Mrs. O'Shay; I brought her my prettiest one."

"That's very noble of you, Hannah. Unlace her other shoe while I do this one."

She felt her body being turned... *I must be in a hospital. What's all this stuff they're taking off of me? Where's my shorts and tee shirt?*

"Hannah, scurry to the kitchen, and bring back my carving knife,"

What...a Knife? That can't be good... Becca opened her eyes and found flowered wallpaper in front of her. There were tiny wrinkles in it as though moisture had prevented its drying process...*This isn't a hospital.*

"No! Don't get a knife!" she hoarsely gasped.

"So, you are waking up, are you? The woman asked gently. "Miss Castile, we need to cut the cord that you used to tie this bag to your waist."

Who's Miss Castile?

They think I'm someone else...I'll sort it out later... now I'm too tired and cold... The loathsome bundle was now removed. It dropped with a heavy thud on the floor. Mrs. O'Shay pushed it under the bed with her foot.

"Help me with these corset strings, Hannah."

As the layers of wet clothing were pealed off, Becca's bare, moist skin reacted to the air. Her teeth started the chatter and she began to shake.

"Poor dear," said Mrs. O'Shay. She spread a quilt over Becca.

"I'm going to wash the salt water off you, then dress you in a warm gown. "Wrapping a towel around her head she added, "After you've rested, Hanna can comb the snarls from your hair."

Soon, Becca was snuggled under covers. A hot brick, wrapped in flour sacks, lay at her feet. Hot tea in a chipped china cup sat at the bedside table.

"Mrs. O'Shay says that this tea will make your throat feel better," the girl said shyly.

"Thank you, your name's Hannah?" Becca asked.

"Yes," she answered

"My name's Becca. I need to talk with police. Can you get me a phone?"

The girl looked at her in puzzlement, turned and walked out the door.

Becca pressed her feet against the warm brick at the foot of her bed and relaxed as her body slowly stopped shaking from chills. She looked around the room. Dull colored paper defined the walls... *Whoever hung it, didn't know what he was doing. ..The wrinkles and uneven seams look terrible...*

The window had lace curtains. They had an intricate design that Becca had never seen before...*Those are pretty, but that dull rose color isn't the best match for the rest of the room...*The floor made of wood boards, was covered with a large area rug. A few spots here and there indicated spills had occurred...It looks hand braided. *That took a lot of work.*

There was no closet in the small room, but next to the window stood an armoire. A folded quilt lay on top. A chest of drawers stood on the other side of the window. A lace scarf draped across it. A glass lantern sat on top...*Mrs. O'Shay must be an antique enthusiast and a hoarder. This room is way over furnished, and not a modern piece to be seen.*

In the corner, across from the bed, a three paneled screen stood. Next to it was a table holding a large pitcher and bowl. On a hook above it, hung a cloth. Beside the table was an oval standing mirror. Near the door, at the foot of the iron bed, sat a small secretary with chair. A candle, partly burned, was centered on top. Becca looked around the bed. ..*This is a real oldie. It looks like this quilt is also retro. I think its hand stitched. This is like moving into an antique shop... this is one lumpy mattress, I must say.*

Remembering the tea, Becca reached to the tiny bedside table for the cup. She instantly stopped, pulled her hand back and held it up in front of her...*This isn't my hand...*The dainty fingers and short filed nails had no resemblance to the brightly polished ones she had used in self defense earlier today. She looked at the other hand...*My wedding ring is missing. I've never seen this garnet ring before.*

Reaching up, she pulled the towel from her head. Wet locks fell to her shoulders. Pulling a handful of the dark strands in front of her eyes, she caught her breath. Kicking off the quilt, she slid her feet to the floor. Looking down at the small feet touching the braided rug, she gasped... *What's happened to me?*

She stood up. Feeling a wave of dizziness, she steadied herself by grasping the iron bed frame. When she felt her balance return, she walked to the mirror. Looking at the stranger who gazed back at her, she studied every feature. A tiny woman, not more than twenty, faced her with huge blue eyes. Actually, they were more like violet.

Long, dark tangled hair hung over her shoulders, and fell down her back. Her thin frame couldn't be over five foot one or two.

Carefully, she lifted the gown...*Geeez Louise, no muscle tone, girl, you need a cheeseburger... Pulling the gown higher she gazed at the breasts in the mirror... No one will accuse you of enhancements...* She rubbed her hand over the skin revealed in the mirror. Yes, she felt the touch, but how? *This couldn't be the tall, athletic, redhead she knew herself to be.*

There was a knock at the door and Hannah pushed her head in.

"Excuse me, Miss Castile. Mrs. O'Shay says to tell you Doc Conner will be coming up to check on you. Would you like me to help you comb the rats out of your hair?"

Becca walked back to the bed and sat on the edge. Hannah carefully separated strands of hair, and gently worked out the tangles. She braded it in a long braid and tied it with a string.

"How old are you, Hannah?"

"I'll be fourteen in the fall."

"Is Mrs. O'Shay part of your family?" Becca pressed for more information.

"No, I work for her for room and board and a dollar per week."

"I see, "answered Becca, "like a summer job?"

"No, all the time. I finished sixth grade, and it's time I make my way."

"What?" Becca swung around to look at the girl. 'Your parents are all right with that?"

"My parents died, Miss, I'm lucky Mrs. O'Shay took me in to help her with her hotel, else, I don't know what I'd have done."

"Oh, I'm sorry, Hannah. Thanks for helping me with this mop of hair."

"Yes, Miss, I'll leave so Doc Conner can check on you." Hannah left quietly and closed the door.

Becca climbed back under the quilt. She drank the strong tea that had cooled to room temperature. As she set the cup down, a knock at the door announced his arrival.

"Come in," she summoned.

A short slim man with a receding hairline walked in. He pulled the small chair from in front of the secretary, and positioned it beside the bed.

He was dressed strangely. His wool suit seemed inappropriate for summer. The coat sagged across the shoulders. The vest under it strained against its buttons. A chain hung from a vest pocket. Becca assumed it was attached to a watch. What was missing on his head was accounted for with his sideburns. They grew down his face in the shape of mutton chops. The front of his face was adorned with a handlebar mustache. Becca thought it odd that Hannah wore a long, loose dull colored dress, but this suit reminded her of something she saw at a masquerade party.

"Well, my dear, how are you feeling after such an ordeal?"

Becca looked at him as he gazed back at her over the top of his Ben Franklin glasses.

"I must talk to you, doctor. My husband tried to murder me. I think I may have killed a man in self-defense. Well, I didn't exactly kill him, but I'm sure he died because I think I bit through his jugular." The words rushed out with one breath.

Dr. Conner straightened his glasses, "Ah, I see, yes, well, allow me to examine you."

He placed a thumb on her upper eyelid and peered into first one eye, then the other. "Pupils look fine, do you remember bumping your head or receiving a blow to the head, Miss Castile?

Becca shook her head. "Just the waves... my name's not Miss Castile."

"Ah, but the others, who recognize you, say that it is." He checked her neck and shoulders. "Any pain in these areas, can you turn your head both ways?"

"They're wrong. They have me mixed up with someone else. My name is Rebecca Cates. I live in Portland, I'm a teacher, and my husband tried to murder me because he's having an affair with his assistant. I think he wants my life insurance."

Words rolled out in an excited jumbled fashion. Dr. Conner backed up and looked at her quizzically. "Hold out you arms, Miss Castile, can you wiggle all your fingers?"

I'll wriggle them around your neck, if you don't stop calling me Miss Castile!

Pulling the quilt down, the doctor felt her ankles. "Wiggle your toes please. Let's bend your knees. Can you kick out?"

Bend over and I'll show you how I can kick out..."Doctor, why would my appearance suddenly change?" She was fighting tears of frustration.

"Change in what way, Miss?"

"I use to be tall, now I'm short. I use to have red hair and brown eyes, now I'm like this. Why would I change after nearly drowning?" She searched his face for a hint of understanding.

"Miss Castile, or Delphi, may I call you by your first name?"

"That's not my first name, it's Becca."

"Uh huh, Delphi, the mind can take some odd turns when it's been put to the test. It's not uncommon for a person to feel confused after facing possible death, but you're healthy and young. With some rest, you'll be feeling spry in no time."

"What should I do about my husband? I can't let him get away with this. I need to get back to Portland. Is there a way I could fly back tomorrow?"

The doctor sat on the chair and leaned over with his elbows on his knees. "Fly?"

He reached into his medical bag and brought out a leather bound journal and a rustic looking pencil.

"Delphi, dear, I'd like to ask you a few questions. Please don't comment except to answer the questions."

Becca pulled the quilt up to her chest and crossed her arms. She hoped his questions would help unravel the confusion she felt.

"What day of the week is it?"

"Wednesday."

Doc Conner looked at her over his glasses and wrote in his book."Are you sure it's Wednesday?"

'Absolutely sure, we left Portland on Tuesday and..."

"Ah, Ah, Ah, just answer the questions, please," he reminded. "Can you tell me what the date is?"

"July thirtieth, two-thousand-fifteen," she answered with confidence.

"Can you tell me where you are?" he continued.

"Crescent City, I think, since that's the closest town to Saint George Lighthouse. That's where Ike pushed me overboard."

"Saint George Lighthouse?" The doctor raised his eyebrows. "And just where is that?"

"Right out there," Becca, pointing toward the sea. "It's eight miles out from Crescent City."

"Can you name the governor of our state or America's president, either one?"

"Sure, Jerry Brown is governor and Barack Obama is president. He's a democrat and the first black president. He defeated Hillary Clinton, who had she won, would have been the first woman president. There are fifty states in the Union and America was the first country to reach the moon. The climate is changing and unless we get it under control the planet will fry. The world population has reached a whopping...."

"Miss Castile, enough!" said the doctor firmly. "Now lay back and rest. I want you to drink lots of fluids and sleep as much as possible. I'll check on you tomorrow or Tuesday."

The doctor returned the chair to the desk and left, quietly shutting the door. Becca heard voices in the hall. She was sure the doctor was talking to Mrs. O'Shay. She slid out of bed, slipped to the door, and leaned her head against it. She could hear plainly.

"Will she be all right, doc?" asked the woman.

"I can't yet say," he answered.

"The other two women assured me she was mentally sound before the catastrophe, but slight in stature. However, had they not told me that, I would have thought her a moron or lunatic...*What a mean thing to say...and unacceptable labels for use by a doctor!*

"Oh, surely not," protested Mrs. O'Shay.

"If not, she's delusional. She thinks it is Wednesday rather than Sunday. She's confused about the year and all sorts of things. She imagines unreasonable fears and believes she can fly."

"Oh my, poor girl!" replied Mrs. O'Shay.

"At best she has Brain Fever. That wouldn't be unusual after such a horrid event, but if that's her condition, I must say, it's the worse case I've ever encountered."

"What must we do in regard to her care?"

"I have no Laudanum with me, but I'll bring some over. Until then, do you have any Mrs. Winslow's Soothing Syrup?"

"Why, yes, I believe I do."

"Slip some to her every three to four hours. That should keep her resting until the shocks of the events settle in. I didn't tell her about the deaths of her friends. She's too excitable for that."

"Thank you, doctor, I will get some of it to her right now."

"Keep an eye on her, I think she might be a runner, and watch her near the upstairs window. She believes she can fly."

Becca returned to the bed. *Am I crazy? Did I imagine everything? What the heck is going on?*

7

"Wisdom comes only when you stop looking for it and start living the life the Creator intended for you."

—Hopi Tribal Proverb

A tap at the door pulled Becca from her thoughts. "Come in." The door opened and Hannah entered with a tray." Here's some venison stew for your supper, Miss. There's a hot bun too. We have no butter so I spread it with blackberry jam."

Becca swung her legs over the edge of the bed and took the tray. "Thank you Hannah, I do feel hungry."

"Mrs. O'Shay says I must stay with you to assure you eat and drink." She pulled the chair from the desk and plopped down.

Becca scooped a spoonful of soup to her mouth. "This is very good. You don't have to stay if you don't want too, but I like you being here."

Hannah smiled then looked at her hands.

"Hannah, there were others who were on the lifeboat with me. Are they here?"

"Yes, two are here, but the others are staying in people's homes. Mr. Barrett brought you here. Another lady is in a room down the hall."

"Does that lady have a child?" asked Becca, remembering the woman who called herself Minnie.

"No, she's young like you, even younger. Her name is Miss Barns. She's been crying a lot. She's very sad because of all the people who died."

The girl covered her mouth as though she had spoken out of turn.

"You're referring to the shipwreck? Becca asked, needing clarification. "How many died, do you know?"

"Yes. There were over two hundred. At least that's what I heard Doc Conner telling Mrs. O'Shay. Did you lose friends on Brother Jonathan, Miss?"

Becca stopped chewing her bread and looked at Hannah... *That's the second time she heard someone say the name of the sunken ship of eighteen-sixty-five.*

"Hannah, what year is it?" she asked, pushing a hunk of potato around in the brown broth.

"Why, its eighteen-sixty-five, Miss. Everyone knows that."

Becca laid down the spoon, and handed the tray to the girl. "I don't feel hungry now Hannah, I think I need time to think."

"Oh no, Miss Castile, I can't take that back till you eat it clean gone." She shook her head in emphases.

"It would please me very much if you wouldn't call me Miss Castile, Hannah."

She noted the disturbed expression on the girl's face. "Please just call me Becca."

Hannah looked down at the tray and said softly, "I can't Miss."

"Why not? It's my real name. There are lots of things that make no sense to me right now, but that's the one thing I'm sure of."

"Because, "she began shyly, "Doc Conner told us to called you Miss Castile or Delphi to help you remember who you are."

"Oh, he did, did he?" *Well I may need to play along if I plan to get back to my life, wherever I left it.*

"Miss Castile, at least drink your tea so Mrs. O'Shay won't scold me,." Hannah pleaded.

49

Becca took the tea from the tray and gulped down a mouthful. "This is very sweet; I don't usually take so much sugar in my tea."

"Mrs. O'Shay made it, Miss, just please finish it."

Becca finished the sweet liquid, and sat the cup down on the tray.

"There, tell your boss I finished the tea, and don't take any crap off her."

Hannah's eyes grew large, "I mustn't talk back to Mrs. O' Shay, Miss Castile."

"Where are the clothes I was wearing when I was brought here today?" she asked as Hannah turned toward the door.

"They need washing, Miss, and we can't wash them 'til I remove all the coins you sewed into the hems of the frock and petticoats. They're sewn into your corset as well. But, don't be concerned, I'm being very careful not to tear the fabric or rip the seams. It takes time. I'm putting the coins into a poke. I'll bring them to you."

Becca didn't reply and Hannah shut the door behind her. *I have to sort this out in my head...*Lying back against the feather pillow, she thought. *It's not scientifically possible to go back in time. So, either I've done the impossible or the three people I've talked to are crazy and I'm their captive...*She thought of several movies she had seen of such a plot. *It was always about one person locked away from reality and convinced of something that isn't true. It's possible to do this, if the films are based on any fact at all...But why? Are they making a documentary or silly movie?*

She glanced around the room for anything that might suggest a hidden camera...*No, that wouldn't be legal. Could this be a plot Phil thought up? No, he couldn't have predicted that I'd survive...* She wished she had finished the book about Brother Jonathan...*Is this a Reenactment? They do that with Civil War battles.*

Wooziness swept over her. The ceiling began to spin in circles and she felt a drifting sensation. Soon dreams melted together. She saw Ike, looking into her face with rage, and then morphing into a handsome face with hazel eyes. Then, complete emptiness.

She awoke with a start. She was sitting up staring at the foot of the bed. The window was open. A breeze fluttered the rose lace curtain. Moonlight streamed in, making shadows of all Mrs. O'Shay room décor...*What startled me? Was I dreaming? Oh yes, I was holding on to a plank and that girl grabbed on*...Suddenly it was clear to Becca where she had seen the girl in the mirror...*Oh! Dear God no! I took her body, but how? Where's mine?*

She could hear voices. Were they from downstairs or the other rooms down the hall that Hannah mentioned? She had an urgent need to use a restroom. Her bladder felt like it would burst. She tried to remember if she had seen a light switch in the room. Slipping out of bed, she moved along the walls, feeling for one, maneuvering around furnishings. She reached the door and found the knob. It was glass and turned easily. As she pulled it open, she could see that a lantern hung in the hall, lighting the stairs that descended to the lower floor...*There has to be a bathroom in the hall. This is, after all, a Bed and Breakfast sort of thing*...Entering the hall, she started down it, looking at each door for a sign indicating it was a ladies' restroom.

"Oh, no you don't, Miss Castile!"

Becca turned just in time to see a determined Mrs. O'Shay leaving one of the rooms. "I'm looking for a restroom,

"Resting will be in your bed chamber, now back to bed with you."

She took a firm hold to Becca's arm and easily steered her back toward her bedroom. Becca yanked her arm back and moved away, eyeing the stairs as a possible escape.

"Don't ever grab my person; you have no right to do that to someone. Do you understand that? If you ever grab me like that again I'll have to hurt you, real bad."

Mrs. O'Shay's determined face changed to alarm. "Come dear, let's us go back to our bed now."

"Our bed? I'm sharing a bed with no one." Becca backed carefully to the stairs, and placed a foot down to the first step while keeping an eye on the woman.

Mrs. O'Shay looked as though she wanted to lunge, but fearful perhaps of causing Becca to fall. Becca backed down several more steps.

"I appreciate what you have done for me, but I won't be a prisoner."

Suddenly, strong arms surrounded her from behind and gently secured her. He lifted her to the top of the stairs, and then released her. Becca turned her head to see the man with the hazel eyes.

So, what's the disturbance?" he asked pleasantly. "I come up the stairs and walk right into a hen fight."

"Oh, Mr. Barrett, I'm so glad you came up just now. Delphi is attempting to run away. I tried to stop her, but she threatened me. The poor girl's not right in the head."

"I'm not trying to run away, I just need to pee. If you had any darn lights so people could see anything, I'd find the stupid toilet?"

Mr. Barrett laughed. "Why Mrs. O'Shay, I do believe Miss Castile has need of a chamber pot."

Placing a gentle arm around her shoulder, the man nudged Becca back to the door of her room.

"There you are, Miss Castile. Your needs will be met, as soon as my landlady lights a lamp for you."

An hour later, after another cup of sweet tea, Becca was back in the lumpy bed. She was now informed on how to light a lantern and void in a bucket. She tried to remember the passenger names she had read in her book about Brother Jonathan. She couldn't bring to mind any Delphi Castile. Too soon the spinning and drifting sensation took away her thoughts.

Senseless dreams swirled around in her brain. They included Dr. Conner, Ike, then Hannah and the male face with hazel eyes. A patchwork arrangement of images bounced between the Lorelei and the life boat, then back again. The blasts of gunnery from the sinking ship startled her awake. Sitting up, she stared into the darkness. A Grandfather clock somewhere near, struck twelve gongs. Orienting herself from the dream world to her awakened state took several moments...*its mid-night.*

She remembered hearing that clock strike eight just before sinking into that disturbed sleep... *I've only slept four hours, but I'm wide awake...* She felt the pangs of her bladder sending a toilet call. ..*Oh yeah, the chamber thingy...* She fumbled through the process of lighting the lamp, and then padded to the area behind the paneled screen. Wrestling with the long skirt of the nightgown, she attempted to position the proper lady parts over the porcelain container while avoiding tipping it over... *This procedure needs an upgrade.*

She washed her hands in the basin on the small table, and dried them on the cloth hanging above. Since she had at least a dim light, she considered exploring the room... *Why not? They referred to it as mine...* She passed the mirror and avoided looking at it. She moved to the chest of drawers. Opening the top drawer, she saw it was empty. The next drawer was also empty. The third had what appeared to be linens, but nothing like she had seen before. Looking out the window, she saw only darkness. The fog was in, and the moist air coming through the window confirmed it. The moon was invisible now. She could hear sea lions and seals barking in the distance.

She opened the doors on the armoire. It was empty, but had a wooden rod with wooden hangers. Moving to the secretary, she noticed the candle. She lit it to add more light to that of the lamp. Sitting in the chair, she opened the drawer. A stack of yellowed paper, several envelopes, a rustic pencil, sealing wax, and an ink pen lay inside. A small bottle of ink set in a holder on the desk... *Ah, I remember working with this tool in calligraphy class during high school...Placing a paper on the desk, she wrote a statement.*

To Whom It May Concern; On this day, July 30th, 2015, during the afternoon hours, my husband, Philip Terrence Cates, and his hired crewman, Ike, (last name unknown) attempted to murder me. I was thrown overboard, and left to drown near the Saint George Lighthouse. I was rescued by a lifeboat and brought to Crescent City. Signed Rebecca Sawyer Cates, Alias Delphi Castile

I might as well combine these names since I am a bit of both of us.

She set the paper aside to allow the ink to dry, and took a second piece and the pencil. She made two columns and labeled them, *"what I know"* and *"what I don't know."* She wrote the names she had grasped in the hours following her rescue.

Mrs. O'Shay... landlady...business manager...?
Hannah..............hired help
Dr. Conner......medical doctor?.. Maybe
Mr. Barrett...Hot Dude

She folded up the signed statement, and placed it in an envelope. Labeling it, "My statement," she placed it in the drawer. The second paper, she placed back in the drawer to work with later. She pushed the loose strands of hair from her face. They were moist with perspiration. She realized she was overly warm. The flames of the lights made the upstairs room uncomfortable, even with a sea breeze flowing in.

I've had enough of this pesky gown, off with you... Striping off the lace trimmed cotton nightdress, she dropped it on the floor. She lifted the heavy braid off her neck and enjoyed the coolness of nothing against her skin.

Now that I have a bit of a plan, I think I'm getting sleepy. Better make one more perch on the bucket. Mrs. O'Shay's nasty tea is a bladder buster... an alarming thought popped into her head...*The tea...that sickening sweet tea...what's odd about it?... Ahh, it makes me sleep like the Dramamine did, but deeper... No more tea for you, Miss Castile.*

She blew out the candle and lamp, and then lay across the bed. The clock struck three. She wished that she had researched more about how people lived in earlier centuries. As a history lover, she knew about events, wars, federal court cases, but actual life styles weren't part of her interests... *Guess, there's no time like the past to learn something new... or...no time like the present to learn something old...* For the first time since this ordeal began, Becca smiled at the irony, and drifted off into a natural restful sleep.

8

"When you stand with your two feet on the ground, you will always keep your balance."

—Tao Proverb

A rapping on the door blended into Becca's dreams. She and Sister Beth were pranking the neighbors, with nicky-knocky-nine doors, and then running away in a chorus of childish giggles. The rapping repeated and the lovely dream faded. She opened her eyes just as the door gently opened.

"Miss Castile, are you all right? Oooooh! Miss Castile where's your gown?" Hannah's eyes were the size of baseballs.

Becca rolled from her position on her stomach to eye the girl, sleepily.

"What is it Hannah... morning all ready?"

Holding a tray with both hands, Hannah quickly moved through the opening and pushed the door shut with her foot.

"Ma'am, you must know that lying there with no clothes is most improper!"

Seeing the girl was offended, Becca pulled on the disheveled quilt and covered her front.

"Hannah, nothing is improper in a person's private space."

Hannah set the tray on the bedside table by the oil lamp. She walked over to the crumpled gown, picked it up and brought it to Becca. She dutifully put it on.

"Hannah, I'm going to insist that you return the dress I was wearing when I was brought here, I am out of patience with being shut in this room with only this nightgown to wear. I'd like the shoes back as well."

"We have some clothes for you, Miss Castile. Mrs. Walker brought over frocks, stockings and petticoats last evening. Miss Barns is bathing now, and you may use the bathing room next."

"Who is Mrs. Walker?" asked Becca examining the wooden tray. It contained a bowl filled with some kind of gruel and a cup of steaming tea.

"She's Reverend Walker's wife. She's gathered up clothes for all of you. I'm almost finished with sorting out the coins from your other clothing, and I can bring you your shoes."

"That's awesome!" said Becca, taking a bite of the oatmeal.

Hannah looked at her in puzzlement and sat down on the bottom end of the bed. Is that a French word, Miss Castile?"

Becca looked at her in confusion.

"That word...awesooom." she repeated.

"No, it's not French...its slang," answered Becca, sticking a finger into the tea and touching it to her tongue...*Ah-ha, just as I thought, syrupy sweet. Oh no you don't, Mrs. O'Shay.*

"Miss Barns wants to talk to you later. Doc Conner will be by, and Mrs. Bergman requested to meet with both you and Miss Barns this afternoon."

"Sounds like you have my schedule all planned out," Becca smiled at the teen. "I really need to have a talk with Mrs. O'Shay."

"She's very busy. Today is washing day. We always wash the linens on Mondays. Today, I'm allowed to serve you and Miss Barns, so I don't have to help with washing." She smiled, lighting up the usually sad little face.

You have no idea what a pretty young lady you are. Too bad you can't enjoy what's left of your childhood...

"Well, I guess since she's busy, and you're excused from washing, and you're assigned to me and Miss Barns; you're in charge of visitors today, right?"

Becca finished the porridge.

Hannah pondered the remark, but didn't respond.

"So, it'll be between you and me... what my care will be...correct?"

Hannah nodded, "I suppose."

"I want to let you know that I won't be drinking any more of the tea."

Becca nodded at the full cup. She stood up, took the tea, walked to the chamber pot. She emptied the liquid into it. Hannah watched with a worried expression.

"Mrs. O'Shay has been spiking my tea, has she not?" asked Becca.

Hannah tipped her head like a puppy. "She didn't put any spikes in it, Miss. Castile, just soothing syrup."

Becca smiled at the girl's confusion. "Hannah," "I want us to be friends. Please don't call me Miss Castile. It makes me feel like a prim old lady."

"I'll call you Delphi then?"

Becca nodded, "And you'll be sure as my friend, not to serve me tea with soothing syrup."

Hannah looked hesitant. "But Doc Conner....."

"I'll straighten this all out with the doctor," Becca assured her. "A person should never take medicine when it's not needed. Do I look to you as though I need soothing syrup?"

Hannah shook her head. "No Delphi." She gathered up the tray and started for the door. "I'll attend to Miss Barns now. Then, I'll bring your clothing, and prepare your bath."

Becca went to the window and looked toward the sea. The fog was lifting, and people moved along the dirt streets... *No doubt about it, this is a time in the past.*

Women scurried along with long skirts, lifting them to avoid piles of horse dung. Men with slicked down hair, mustaches and sideburns, passed the time of day in front of shops and on corners. A horse drawn wagon delivered water to the businesses along the block. A couple of men in old style military uniforms entered an establishment. She remembered reading that several forts were briefly located near Crescent City. Fort Lincoln and Fort Dick came to mind.

Hannah knocked on the door, and Becca invited her in. The girl carried what appeared to be a robe. She referred to it as a dressing gown.

"The men are all away, Delphi, so this should provide you with respectable coverage to reach the bathing room."

To the end of the hall and then down a back staircase was the bathing room. Becca looked around as Hannah gingerly lifted the large kettle from the small wood burning stove, and poured it into the porcelain tub that already contained cold water.

"Mrs. O'Shay said to put some of the rosewater into your bath, Delphi, it smells real nice."

After Hannah left the room, Becca slipped into the warm water, lowering her head to saturate her now loose hair. Sitting up, she looked into the mirror on the wall near the foot of the tub. The small, thin women looked back with bewilderment on her face. Soaking wet, she appeared even more tiny and vulnerable... *It's going to take some getting use to, being in your body Delphi Castile. I feel like a Rottweiler crammed into the body of a miniature French Poodle. But I'll take care of it, and make the best of things. If you're in my body, I hope you do the same for me...* Becca smiled and the reflection smiled back.

I'm getting the best of it you know; I've never felt so beautiful. If you're in my body, you'll have to deal with big feet, red kinky hair, awkward boobs, freckles, sun-sensitive skin, and a good for nothing husband whose out to get you... Becca's face grew serious as did the reflection in the mirror...*All I can say, Delphi, is if you're now in the twenty-first century, I hope you can find a way to take that creep down.*

After bathing, Becca returned to her room. The bed was made, the room was straightened up, and the surfaces looked freshly dusted...

Hannah must have cleaned... Then she noticed a long flowered cotton dress hanging over the dressing screen. It was light blue with purple buds. White lace trimmed the neck and sleeves. Tiny, cloth covered buttons paraded down the bodice, trailing from the neck to below the narrow pointed waist line.

Becca stepped behind the screen. The pitcher had fresh water and the basin's dirty water was emptied. She peeked into the chamber pot. It was empty and appeared washed and clean... *I must tell Hannah that she needn't clean up after me. I can do these tasks.*

She eyed the under garments hanging behind the screen... *Three petticoats... no way! Not on the last day of July and its summer heat.*

She slipped on the first item. It reminded her of a tank top... *No bra? Hmmm...well that won't be missed...not that this body really needs one.* Next was a pair of white pantaloons... *These look like peddle pushers.*

Stockings hung over the screen but Becca couldn't imagine how they would stay up so she disregarded them. She looked at the three petticoats... *This is certainly over-kill.*

The first one was made of unbleached muslin and in a shade of off white with no trim. The second one was white cotton with a gathered ruffle around the bottom. The last was made of a very lightweight cloth with rows of lace adorning it from its waist tie to the bottom. Hanging beside them was a corset. Becca took the corset and two of the petticoats to the chest of drawers, folded them, and placed them inside... *There, that's a good place for you...* She'd almost finished fighting with the tiny buttons when Hannah's knock sounded at the door.

"Come in Hannah."

The girl entered with a big smile, carrying bundles. "Oh you look so pretty in that frock, Delphi." Her smile changed to a puzzled expression. "Didn't you need help with the corset?"

"I'm not wearing that thing, it looks torturous." Becca secured the last button. "But I do have a question about the hose."

"Hose?" Hannah looked confused.

"These," said Becca, grabbing the long, finely knitted stockings. "What holds them up?"

Hannah covered her mouth and giggled. "Why garters, of course, everyone know that."

Becca rolled her eyes. "Humor me, please, where are the garters?"

Setting the items down on the bed, Hannah walked over to the washing stand, picked up two stretchy, circular shaped ribbons, and handed them to Becca. Becca face lighted up, remembering her bridal garter. She sat on the bed and slipped into the stockings, securing the tops with the garters, and sliding the legs of the pantaloons down over them.

"Here are your shoes. I've had them by the cook stove, and they're dry now."

Becca looked at the narrow, tiny shoes and wondered how she'd adjust to them.

"They won't do for jogging, but I guess I can't be picky."

"Your speech is strange, Delphi," commented Hannah with a shake of her head. "Now allow me to arrange your hair."

The two talked and got better acquainted while Hannah brushed, and then twisted the mass into a bun on top of her head. She secured it with two tortoise picks.

"Hannah, is there some way I can get a toothbrush?"

Hannah stared at her in puzzled silence.

"You do brush your teeth, right?"

"I brush my hair...," stammered the girl.

"How do you clean your mouth?"

"Mrs. O'Shay washed it once with soap when I cussed," she answered looking down.

"Never mind," replied Becca, "I'll think of something."

"I brought you your coins," she said handing Becca a cigar box that she had brought in with her.

Becca opened the box and gasped. "Are these gold coins?"

Hannah nodded. "I worked them all out of your dress seams and corset. That should meet your needs for a while. You must have been saving for a long time"

"Maybe I should take this currency to the bank and exchange it for paper money,".

"Paper money?" Hannah looked confused. "What good would that be?"

Becca looked at her in disbelief. "You've never seen paper money?"

"The only money I know about is gold or silver. Why would anyone want money made of paper?"

The girl walked to a picture that hung above the chest of drawers. As she lifted it from the wall, Becca saw the small safe embedded into the wall. Pulling a key from her apron pocket, Hannah opened the safe and glanced back at Becca. "Put it in there. Wear the key around your neck, under your bodice."

A heavy knock at the door startled Becca. "That's Doc Conner, Hannah said. "I'll leave now and see about Miss Barns."

Hannah opened the door as Becca walked over to sit on the side of the bed. The doctor stepped in and dragged the desk chair over in front of her. He pushed his glasses up on his nose. "Well, Miss Castile, how are we this morning?" he asked as he pulled the small leather book and pencil from his bag.

Why does he use that silly voice that stupid people use when speaking to children? "I have no idea how we are, Dr. Conner, but I'm just peachy," she answered, smiling.

He cleared his throat. "Have you had any headaches, nausea, or confusion?"

"Only when I'm given the soothing syrup, the rest of the time I feel fine, thank you."

"And the lighthouse you described, have you seen it since I last talked to you?"

"What lighthouse is that, Doctor?" she asked using Delphi's most innocent face.

He wrote a sentence in his book.. "The murderous husband, has he bothered you any more?" he asked, not looking up.

"Oh, Sir, you must have me confused with one of the other survivors, I'm not married."

"What's the date, Miss Castile?" he asked.

"Why it's Monday, July thirty-first, eighteen sixty-five, Doctor, don't you have a calendar?" She gave him what she hoped was sweet smile.

He put the book back into his bag. "You seem to have recovered satisfactorily."

Becca stood up, hoping he was preparing to leave, but he continued so she sat back down. "Miss, Castile, now that you're feeling better I would like to collect information from you. I'm attempting to contact relatives for both those who survived, and those who did not." The doctor leveled his gaze over the top of his glasses.

Oh dear, I didn't expect this. I have no idea who Delphi's relatives are.

"I have no one, Doctor...I'm an orphan."

He looked at her disbelievingly. "Miss Barns told me you had discussed with her, relatives in Louisiana."

"No, Sir, she must have me confused with someone else."

"Perhaps, very well, if you don't wish me to inform your family of your whereabouts, I can't help you. I would hope, Miss Castile, You could make changes in your life, now. You'll need to find somewhere to settle down for a new start. If you decide to give me an address, I'll contact your parents, and try to persuade them to help."

With that, Doc Conner left her, closing the door softly behind him.

Well, Delphi Castile, I guess Doc knows more about you than I do. But, thanks to your gold coin savings, I will turn your life around from whatever it is... as soon as I can figure out what I should be turning to.

9

"Discretion will protect you, and understanding will guard you."

—KING SOLOMON

As soon as Dr. Conner left, Becca sighed with relief. She tucked her feet, now sporting high top shoes, under the bed. They bumped something. Leaning over, she raised the quilt, and looked underneath...*That horrid bag!*...She pulled it out, and lifted it up on the bed. She wiggled the clasp but it held fast...*Must be locked.*

Remembering a letter opener in the desk drawer, she hurriedly retrieved it. After a few aggressive attempts at picking the lock, it popped open...*There we go, let's see what you've got in here, for which you were willing to drown...*She opened the case. Everything was wet but tightly packed. A light knock at the door barely drew her attention.

"Delphi?" called Hannah barely opening the door. Mrs. O'Shay wishes you to come to the parlor in an hour to visit with some ladies."

"Huh uh."

Becca had begun lifting items out of the case. Hannah approached, watching with interest. *Ok, everything needs to lie out to dry.*

Becca lifted out some light pink satin slippers. Trimmed with white velvet ribbons, they sported tiny heels.

"Those are pretty, Delphi."

Becca laid them on the bed. Next, she lifted out a black velvet cape, lined in red satin, and trimmed with a large jeweled button at the neck. She shook it out and hung it on the back of the desk chair to dry. Hannah was so excited, she could barely stand still.

"What's wrapped in the package?"

Becca lifted it out and laid it on the bed. It was wrapped several times with oiled cloth. Pealing off the layers, she exposed a wooden jewel box. Becca tried to open it. It was locked. She pushed the end of the letter opener into the tiny keyhole but it was too big.

"Here," said Hannah, reaching into her braided bun and bringing out a hairpin. Becca successfully picked the lock as easily as she had the case. As she opened the lid, Hannah leaned in to see the contents. Becca felt irritation toward the teen but restrained herself...*She doesn't get to see pretty things often. She's as curious as I am.*

Becca picked up a cameo broach and examined it. "Wow, this must have cost a pretty penny."

"You must know, you bought it," said Hannah as she picked up a photograph and looked at it closely.

"Oh, my, my, my!" she covered her mouth; her eyes grew wide as she looked at Becca. "Delphi! You let someone take your tin-type in your under garments!"

Becca took the picture and examined it. It had survived baptism of the sea, and was in great shape. There, straddled a chair backwards, sat Delphi, wearing only her pantaloons and under bodice, white stocking and slippers, the same ones she had just unpacked. Thoughts began to assemble themselves and formed a conclusion.

This picture was obviously a professional PR picture of a 19th century courtesan... That's what Dr. Conner's suggestion was about. He must have heard Delphi was part *of the brothel that boarded the steamer, but how? The other passengers probably knew... So this is how you made all that gold? Holy Cats! Delphi, I'll have to live down your reputation.*

Looking at Hannah's face, that continued to reveal judgment, she said, "There is nothing wrong with undergarments, or our bodies. It's our behavior that matters."

"But, why take a picture like that?" the girl wasn't letting go.

"It was just a joke among friends," she answered, remembering a similar gag picture she and her sister had taken in an old time photo shop in Portland..."*Boy! Am I learning to lie!*

"Hannah, if I let you see what's in my case, you must promise not to tell anyone. These are my private belongings, and you must keep my confidence. Do you understand?"

The girl nodded.

They sorted through more jewelry; a pearl necklace, a ruby brooch, small diamond earrings, an opal ring, a bracelet shaped like a serpent, two white silk handkerchiefs, and a watch on a cord that Becca was sure must be ruined. Spotting a small gold cross on a chain, Becca picked it up and handed it to Hannah.

"Here's a gift for you for being such a good friend to me the short time I've been here."

Hannah smiled and took it. "I've never had a necklace before. Thank you, Delphi. "

Becca fastened the chain around her neck and said, "You must tell Mrs. O'Shay I gave this to you so she won't think you took it."

The last two items in the bottom of the case were removed. A small gold brick now set in Becca hands...*Why would a prostitute have a small brick of gold?* The remaining item was a journal. It was separately wrapped in another piece of oiled cloth. Becca unwrapped it carefully, relieved that it was only wet around the edges. She laid it on the secretary to dry...*That will be my evening reading material. I'll have a chance to get to know me.*

As Hannah admired herself and the cross necklace in the mirror, Becca packed the jewelry and block of gold in the tiny safe, completely filling it up. Locking it and dropping the chained key inside her bodice, she summoned the teen.

"Let's go downstairs and meet the ladies, shall we?"

Becca and Hannah walked down the front staircase, and arrived in a spacious rose colored parlor. The wall covering in this room was neat and tightly adhered to the walls...*This is very pretty; it looks much nicer than my bedroom's wrinkled coverings.*

Becca felt like she had stepped into a museum. A round table occupied space in the center of the room. Against one wall, an upright piano sat. Becca found it amusing how high pictures were hung, each tipped forward to be viewed from below. A couple of couches and chairs were arranged along the other walls, surrounded by small tables, none matching. A wood parlor stove took up one corner. It was not in use in summer, so a vase with wild flowers and sea grass adorned its top. She sat on one of the couches, noting that the furniture in general was much shorter than what she was use to...*A tall, long legged, person like my former self, would have trouble with this sofa.*

Walking into the room, Mrs. O'Shay escorted a young woman into the parlor. The girl sat in the chair nearest Becca. She smiled at Becca like she was familiar with her. Becca smiled back.

"Miss Castile, you've previously met Elsie Barns, I understand," said Mrs. O'Shay, setting down a tray with a tea set and plate of odd looking cookies.

"Good morning, Delphi," Elsie smiled at Becca. "I heard you weren't well, I hope you're better."

"I'm doing fine, how are you feeling?" Becca asked, taking in the beauty of the fair-haired girl before her.

Elsie accepted the cup of tea from their host.

"I've been poorly, I fear, I just can't stop thinking of those poor drowning souls." Elsie's bottom lip quivered. She took a moment to restore her composure.

Becca took a taste of the tea to discern if some of Mrs. Winslow Soothing Syrup might be lurking within. She tasted no sweetness and relaxed, determined to retrieve as much information as possible from this beautiful young woman.

"I've had a bit of trouble with memory Elsie; can you remind me of when and how we met?"

Mrs. O'Shay excused herself, saying she would leave the young ladies alone to visit.

Elsie looked at her questioningly. "I introduced myself to you on Brother Jonathan yesterday morning, right after we were assigned to our berths,"

"Could you please tell me about yourself again? I need my memory refreshed"

"Remember? I told you my parents had died during the past year and my guardian, their lawyer, decided to send me to my spinster aunt in Portland."

"Oh yes, and you were excited about being with your aunt."

Elsie had started to take a bite from a cookie, but took it away from her mouth. Her brow knitted, and she shook her head.

"No, remember? I told you how cross and mean spirited Aunt Mabel is. That's why I asked you if you thought I should accept Lilly's offer for a job."

Becca sat silently for a moment, processing this information. She thought back to her reading the Brother Jonathan book before all this happened *...Lilly and her seven soiled doves... on their way to Canada...prostitution ... My suspicions a few minutes ago, are correct...Delphi worked for Lilly, the madam...Why would a young attractive woman join up with a madam who would traffic her around on a steamer?*

Elsie broke the silence after chewing a small bite of cookie.

"Lilly said she needed girls to serve tables in her new establishment in Victoria. I thought I would rather do that than live with mean, old Auntie Mabel."

"Remind me Elsie, how did I advise you?"

Elsie leaned close and spoke quietly. "You said I shouldn't trust her. You said she would promise a job and a good arranged marriage to a wealthy man, but that she turns every girl who works for her into a harlot."

Good for you Delphi. You can't be too bad if you tried to steer a teen away from a bad choice.

"So, what had you decided to do?" asked Becca in the same hushed tone.

"Right after I talked to you, I met Hayden. We fell deeply in love in just minutes of meeting. He agreed with you. He said not to go with Lilly. He said if I went to Aunt Mabel's, as soon as the return voyage ended, he'd come for me and we'd marry."

Elsie broke down and began to cry, covering her face with her dainty hands.

"How old are you?" asked Becca.

Elsie pulled a handkerchief from inside her sleeve. She dabbed at her eyes and wiped her nose. Catching her breath, she let out a loud sigh.,

"I've just turned sixteen."

Becca reached over and patted her arm. "You've been through a lot in a short time, Elsie, it's all right to cry and work through this."

"But now I can't marry Hayden, he stayed on the sinking ship with the Captain. He was part of the crew."

Becca moved closer and put her arms around the girl.

"I know I can't take your pain away. But I'm older and have had some experience. I can at least encourage you to believe your pain will grow less with time. And you're very young. You'll meet someone, fall in love and marry. Please get to know him first. A few hours isn't enough to know whether someone is worthy of your love."

Elsie turned her face toward Becca.

"Oh but I know I loved him. When the ship first hit that rock, we were together. He'd found a place where we could hide and be alone."

She wiped away a fresh onslaught of tears. "I...I...I... gave him my heart, Delphi, I gave him my love... I knew we'd soon marry...except now we won't. I'll never love anyone again...I'll love him forever."

Becca patted her, thinking back to her early infatuation with Philip. Would she have believed anyone who told her how that love would turn out? *No, I was hard-headed. I was sure it was forever.*

Mrs. O'Shay answered the front door, and entered the parlor with Minnie Bergen and her two-year-old son, Albert. As they walked in, Mrs. O'Shay noticed Elsie's tear stained face.

"Oh my, dear, the melancholies have struck you again. I'll get you some soothing syrup." She headed for the kitchen.

"No!" Becca protested, "She's fine. She has good reason to feel sad. Grief is part of healing, Mrs. O'Shay. I don't want to sound disrespectful, but Elsie must be allowed to think this through."

"I agree with Delphi," said Minnie. "We all must face our sorrows."

Minnie was a short, chubby woman with dark blond hair. It was pulled back into a tight bun at her neck. The grey dress that had been provided to her was a bit tight through the bosom and waistline. Her thick German accent sounded musical, and Becca felt drawn to her immediately.

"Well... all right... but if she becomes hysterical; I'll need to give her the syrup. That's Doc. Conner's orders."

Mrs. O'Shay left the parlor. Elsie immediately threw herself into Minnie's arms. Albert stood silently watching the women. Turning to see Becca, he ran to her making every effort to climb into her lap. Becca picked up the child and placed him on her knees.

"See how he remembers you?" asked Minnie. "He took to you the minute he saw you on the steamer. He's already a fool for a lovely face."

Once Elsie regained control of her emotions, Minnie glanced around and leaned forward, toward the young women.

"Now, my young friends, we must make plans for you both. I won't be in this town for long, so we shall talk about your arrangements."

The younger women listened intently.

"Elsie, if you're still set against living with your aunt, we'll persuade your guardian to arrange for you to come with me. I'll tell him I want you for my governess. My husband and I plan to buy a dairy farm in Illinois. I don't have much to pay a helper, but you'll be well cared for. Mr. Bergen will be happy to have someone helping me."

Elsie nodded. "Thank you Minnie, Doc Conner said he would make recommendations to my guardian. He understands my anxiety of living with Aunt Mabel"

"And now for your future, Delphi. When I was seasick, and you came in to help with Albert...just before we hit that rock... you were telling me how you had been saving, to break away from that woman."

Becca returned her gaze, waiting for more information.

10

"The language of friendship is not words but meanings."

—Henry David Thoreau

Minnie searched her face as though she expected her to understand.

Fill in the blanks Minnie. I surely can't add anything to your memory of this conversation.

"As I see it, Lilly, her strong armed husband, and hired men are not a threat to you now. So we'll keep your connection with Lilly our secret. You're only twenty, dear. There's time for you to change your future. I can't take in both of you, but with your savings, could you not return to Louisiana and make amends with your family?"

Twenty...I'm back to twenty now... I was twenty-five when Ike threw me over board...

"Minnie, I'm forced to rely on your memory. I think I must have taken a bump to the head. I can't remember my family or where they're living. Can you tell me anything about them?"

Minnie's face showed her tender feelings.

"Remember, I asked you if you were from France because of your darling accent... you don't seem to have that now... Anyway, you said you were raised in a Cajun community in Lafayette. You told me you had a disagreement with your family regarding an arranged marriage. That's why you ran away...I was feeling dreadfully ill when you confided in me, so I may have some things wrong."

She studied Becca's face for signs of recognition to her summary. Becca said quietly, "Please go on."

"You got a job with Lilly in San Francisco. You were promised an opportunity to play piano and sing....but she had other plans for you."

Minnie stopped and sipped tea. Becca and Elsie sat silently...*I can't believe all this interaction between perfect strangers occurred in less than five hours on a steamer on a stormy sea.*

"Perhaps it's best you don't remember about all that, dear." Minnie lifted the plate, offering Becca a cookie.

Needing something to do with her hands, Becca took one. Taking a small bite of the treat, she mused at its tastelessness. Its texture was dense and chewy. *Sweetened with honey, and the flour is whole wheat. I guess it's healthy...*

"Minnie, who all knows about this...that I worked for Lilly?"

"Only the three of us, I presume. The men in town have been taking boats out all over. Some bodies are washing up on the shore. It's dreadful. Lilly's body was discovered. Her girls are no where to be found...yet. There'll be none of them around to recognize you."

Becca looked at each of them. "The doctor appears to know something."

Elsie looked at her hands and twisted her handkerchief. "I may have mentioned it to him. He was asking questions about everyone's family."

Thanks a lot for confessing for me, blabber-mouth ... hopefully, the doctor respects confidentiality...

Elsie returned her hanky to her eyes. "I'm sorry, dear, said Minnie, but we have to face our sorrows now. And we must continue with our lives."

Minnie returned her attention to Becca.

"The only other woman to survive is the Chinese lady with her son. She speaks no English and hadn't met you. The crew who helped us get to shore will be leaving soon to return to their work. That leaves Elsie and me, and we can keep our silence regarding the matter. The doctor is bringing some tonic for Albert later. I'll have an understanding with him."

Yeah, I think I'll have an understanding with him too.

"You'll need to ponder on skills you have to earn a living, Delphi. I'm already aware that you sing, play piano, you've passed your eighth grade certification. You're well educated. You'll find useful employment soon."

Eighth Grade...educated... really... sing...I couldn't carry a tune if it were tied on my back... and piano... All I know how to do with a piano is to dust it..."I'll give it some serious thought." *My job skills include life guard, swim teacher, girls' softball coach, teaching school...that's a possibility...hmmm.*

The grandfather clock struck twelve. Several gentlemen appeared, coming from different rooms and walking toward the dining room. The front door opened and Mr. Barrett entered.

"Good Morning, Ladies." He tipped his hat before hanging it on the wall tree. "Or perhaps I should say, good afternoon. I'm delighted to see we'll enjoy our noon meal with a few of the gentler folks, ladies are a rarity here."

Elsie blushed and Minnie smiled. Becca stared; completely stunned...*Puleeez...gentler folk... hat tipping...this'll take some getting use to. I must admit...in comparison to Ike and Phil...it is impressive.*

Becca smiled, "The honor is ours, and I'm sure, Mr. Barrett."

Stepping into the dining room, Becca counted twelve place settings. Hannah, pouring water into goblets, looked a bit disheveled from working in the hot kitchen. Becca felt sympathy for her. *..The girl's responsibilities extended beyond her years...When I figure out how I'm going to survive, I'll try to do something about her situation.*

Mr. O'Shay was introduced to the women before he went to the head of the table. Becca noted that he appeared less stressed and strained than his wife. Molly O'Shay directed the seating, and Becca found herself positioned on Mr. Barrett's left while Elsie sat on his right. Minnie and her son sat opposite with Albert held on his mother's lap.

Three men, new to Becca, were introduced. One, a middle-aged male was seated to Becca's left. They were crewmen who had been on the lifeboat, but Becca hardly remembered what they looked like. Tate was not among them. She wondered where he was. He was one of the heroes in this tragedy...*wonder why he isn't here... I wanted to thank him for fishing me out of the water. I'll have to ask about his whereabouts.*

Everyone stood at their chairs until the hostess sat down before following her example. Becca was happy to see Hannah included in the group and not dining alone in the kitchen. The man on her left pulled out her chair for her. Mr. Barrett assisted Elsie, whose cheeks turned a lovely pink.

Becca struggled to pull her skirts around the chair legs and get her feet in their high-topped buttoned shoes, to cooperate. This resulted in a plopping down and not the graceful set-down she intended...*I see why they have chivalry, it's necessary for women's survival in this killer clothing...*Once seated, Becca surveyed the table. She was famished. A platter held a large baked salmon. Some kind of green herb was sprinkled over its nicely browned skin. Mr. O'Shay cut the fish into appropriate servings, and handed the platter to a guest on his right. Mrs. O'Shay started a large bowl of boiled potatoes around.

"I'm sorry there's no butter," she explained. "At two and three dollars a pound, I just can't see the sense of it, but there's plenty of blackberry jam." She handed a basket of biscuits to Hannah on her right.

Two dollars...that must be a lot in this time period. I'll have to learn how to shop all over again...

"Why is it so expensive?" Becca asked.

"There're not many farmers raising dairy near town," answered Mr. O'Shay. "And it costs a lot to bring it in on the steamer."

"At least fifty pounds of butter went down with the Jonathan, yesterday," commented the crewman on her left.

"I remember a man called Tate. He pulled me out of the water. I wanted to thank him. Is he still around?"

Minnie set her goblet of water down. "We all want to thank him, dear; I owe my little Albert's life to him."

The crewman on her left, Mr. Lynn, replied. "Tate and several other of the ship's crew are with the town's patrol. They're looking for bodies. I was with them last night, and I'll join them again tonight. It'll soon be twenty-four hours, and we're quite sure there can't be survivors, but recovery of the bodies is important to the families."

"We held hope right after the lifeboat arrived," added Mr. Barrett. "The patrol I was with spotted what looked like people hovering on the rocks. We nearly wrecked our small vessel getting there, but the creatures were sea lions."

Becca wondered how Elsie was handling this gruesome conversation. No one else knew her secret about the short love affair with Hayden, and wouldn't understand how insensitive it all must feel to her.

"This jam is certainly delicious, Mrs. O'Shay," she remarked, trying to change the subject. "Did you make it yourself?"

"Yes," she said, brightening up with the praise. "Hannah has picked bushels of these berries and the season is just getting started."

"I heard there were three more bodies that washed up this morning," said Mr. O'Shay, oblivious to the virtues of making jam.

"Yes, answered Mr. Barrett. "Mr. James Nisbit, he had paperwork wrapped in oiled cloth in his coat pocket, so he was easily identified."

Becca, for the moment lost her focus in changing the subject...

James Nisbit, I read about him in the book about Brother Jonathan.

"He was a reporter," she said, not realizing that her thoughts had turned into audible words.

"He was indeed," commented Mr. Lynn, "He was at the top of the news business in the city, and a bit of a troublemaker."

"Because he stood up for the oppressed?" asked Becca, remembering what she had read about him.

Mr. Lynn looked at her and appeared slightly annoyed. "That depends on who you consider oppressed, ma'am. People are either what they are born to be, or destitute because they're too lazy to pull themselves up."

Becca laid down her fork and turned her face toward the man. "Really, Mr. Lynn? Tell me, Sir, have you ever fallen on hard times?"

Molly O'Shay stood up quickly. "I think Hannah and I should bring in the coffee and pie now. Hannah, will you collect the plates?"

"But I'm not finished," protested Mr. O'Shay, "I'd like more potatoes."

"You are quite finished," declared his wife. "Now pass Hannah your plate, please, dear."

I almost got into an argument, I have to watch that. What a stupid thing to say. People shouldn't be destined to hardship because of their birth. Who's he to judge who is or isn't motivated to rise above hardships or setbacks?

As Hannah set the small plate of berry pie in front of her, Becca wiped her cloth napkin across her mouth. Realizing that her bottom lip had protruded itself slightly, she pulled it in. It reminded her of the facial expression of some of her young students...*Where'd that little pout come from? I'm not one to sulk or act passive aggressive; I speak my thoughts and beliefs openly.*

As Hannah stepped to the right of Mr. Barrett to serve his pie, he leaned left and whispered.

"That face is far too lovely to waste itself with a pout."

For the first time since moving from her red-haired, fair-complexioned self, she felt a hot flush move over her light olive cheeks.

"I'll pout if I please, thank you; it's a side effect of tolerance for stupidity."

As the meal concluded and individuals excused themselves, Becca remained. When all had left except Hannah and Mrs. O'Shay, she approached the older woman.

"Mrs. O'Shay, I would be very happy to help with the workload here. If you will assign me some chores, I'll do my best."

"Oh, you mean in exchange for your board?" she asked in surprise. "How long do you intend to stay, Miss. Castile?"

"Would you please call me B...ah...Delphi?" She smiled at her landlady.

"I'm not sure about my plans yet, but I can definitely take part in the work and not someone you have to wait on." That should relieve some of Hannah's responsibilities.

The woman smiled back, the first smile Becca had ever seen on her face... *There, she's not so bad...maybe.*

"Then, you must call me Molly. And, yes, I think we can work something out." She wiped her hands on her apron.

"I'll pay you for whatever I already owe you, if you figure up my bill," Becca offered.

"All right, it can't be much, just a bed for last night and tonight, a bath and a couple of meals." She returned to stacking plates from the table.

"When do I start helping?"

"Tomorrow is the day Hannah sweeps, dusts and beats the rugs. You could help her through the morning with that."

"Super! What time?"

"About eight bells, after we finish with breakfast, straight away." Molly turned and continued with her delivery of dishes to the kitchen.

"Well there you are. I feared you had retired to your room for a nap."

Becca turned to see both Elsie and Mr. Barrett standing at the door that led to the parlor.

"Mr. Barrett offered to escort us on a stroll. I do so need to get out, don't you?"

Becca eyed the two who awaited her answer. Mr. Barrett stood, tall and handsome, while making an intent study of her face. Elsie, smiling broadly, could hardly contain her excitement...*Can it be that this girl, an hour ago, cried her heart out over a lost love... she now reacts in silliness in response to a male's invitation...Than, again, she's only just turned sixteen...a time to be immature and frivolous...*

"Wouldn't the two of you prefer to just go without me?" *The last thing I want is to be a third wheel in a time period full of strange customs.*

"On the contrary," Minnie called. She sat in the corner of the parlor beyond Becca's vision. "Less gossip will be fabricated over a stroll of three young people."

Elsie's eyes pleaded for Becca's agreement.

"I was actually going to request Hannah to accompany me someplace for shopping. Could we include that on our walk?"

"Certainly," answered Mr. Barrett. "We'll drop by The Mercantile. I'm not sure you'll find what you need, but you can leave an order for the next steamer. Mr. Sanders takes orders from suppliers in The City."

"I'll need to gather a few things first," said Becca. "I'll be right back."

She started for the stairs. "Don't forget to take parasols;" reminded Mini. "I noticed some by the hall tree."

Becca ascended the front stairs, walked down the upstairs hall and down the back stairs. Looking into the kitchen she saw Hannah washing dishes in a large pan that set on a long table. Molly was putting jars back on a shelf.

"Please, Molly, I need Hannah's help for just a minute."

Molly nodded her consent to Hannah who quickly dried her hands on her apron, and followed Becca back to her room. Becca opened the safe and pulled out the coins...*Later, I'll need to take time to count these, so I know what I have...*

"Hannah, have you done much shopping?"

The girl stood quietly, watching her with curiosity.

"Only when Mrs. O'Shay sends me on errands."

11

"The quickest way to know a woman is to go shopping with her."

—Marcelene Cox

"Of I want to buy a few things, like a brush, comb, lotion, shampoo... you, know, basic things... how many of these coins should I take?"

"I know what a brush and comb are, but I haven't a notion on what those other things are. Don't you know how to buy things?"

"Ah, I'm not too good at math." This playing dumb is getting old, real fast.

"What's math?" asked Hannah.

"You know, counting money"

Becca retrieved the small beaded purse from the drawer. *Thank goodness Delphi had kept this in the case, or I would have no way to carry money.*

"Oh, you mean arithmetic?" corrected the girl with a giggle. "You never learnt your sums?"

"Please Hannah." Becca's voice grew edgy. "Just advise me. How many gold pieces should I take to The Mercantile.?"

"Not that many, unless you have a wagon to tote it all back. I'd only take one of those coins."

Becca dropped two of the gold coins into the bag, just to be on the safe side. She locked the rest back up in the safe and slipped the chain back over her neck, dropping the key down the front of her dress.

"Thanks, Hannah, I'll bring you something," she promised, directing the girl out and closing the door.

Hannah wore a big smile as she returned to her kitchen tasks. Becca descended down the front stairs. Elsie and Mr. Barrett waited in the parlor. Elsie seemed to be having no problem carrying on conversation, at least not her side of it.

Soon, the three were walking down a wooden sidewalk with each female holding a parasol. Horses with saddles stood idle along the walkway, secured to posts by their reins. Odors of fresh manure hung in the air. A carriage on the other side of the dirt road contained a woman in a grey dress and white bonnet. Her husband walked around to assist her down.

Becca tried to compare this Crescent City to the one she had visited two days ago. Glancing up, she saw a crudely made sign with the letter 'c'. She remembered the taxi driver explaining the street names. *"They're just plain old letters and numbers," she had said.*

"Why are the streets named like that?" she asked the first opportunity she got around Elsie's repeated chatter.

"What do you mean?" asked their escort.

"The letters," she pointed at one of the signs.

"The founders laid out the town lots before anyone settled here. I guess they thought it would be practical, Maybe when the town has had time to make some history, they'll change the names of these streets to names of those events or the people who led them."

"No they won't'" she replied softly.

He looked at her quizzically, "I beg your pardon Miss Castile. I fear I didn't quite hear you."

"Ah, I said I see no reason why they should change them." She scolded herself for thinking out loud.

"There now, we've arrived at The Mercantile." He pointed to a door several buildings ahead.

They closed their parasols, and he opened the door for them to pass through. Inside, Becca glanced around, allowing her eyes to adjust to the dim room. It was large with windows set high, leaving room for shelves to line each wall. Two men were tending the business. One wrapped a woman's purchases in brown paper and string. The other carried out a crate of items to a waiting wagon. While she waited for the clerk to finish, she took stock of the merchandise. Large Barrels lined the front of the counter where the man was wrapping the parcel. One was filled with potatoes; one held apples, another onions, and a fourth had dried beans. On the shelves set tin containers of food...*These are like those old tins Mom collects, how cool.*

She tried to think of what she might need... *Soda is good for a lot of things when you don't have modern conveniences, and so is vinegar. There's some rosewater... that could be useful...*The woman left with her package, and Becca approached the clerk. Mr. Barrett stepped up and introduced her, explaining that he was the owner, Mr. Sanders.

"He'll help you find what you need, Miss Castile, and what he doesn't have, he can order for you."

"Thank you, what I need most is a toothbrush; could you show me where they are?"

Mr. Sanders rubbed his chin. "We aren't asked for those often, but I have them in my gentleman's kits."

People don't often buy them? That's deplorable..."Well, I must have one so let me see the kit please."

He walked to a shelf and retrieved a wooden box. Bringing it over, he opened the highly polished lid to reveal items neatly packed in crumbled dark blue paper. She picked up the toothbrush and examined it. It was a wooden stick. Finely sanded, it curved for easy gripping. On the end were three rows of short coarse hairs, tightly fused to the wood.

"What's this made of?" she asked, touching the brushy section.

"Genuine boar bristle...swine hair," he added seeing her confused look.

"Oh, of course." *I should have known that. It's not my Oral B Power brush... but its something.*

Looking back into the well crafted box, she saw a wooden handled hair brush and carved wooden comb. *These look like finer quality than those Hannah uses when styling my hair.*

"Boar bristles?" she asked regarding the hair brush, hoping she sounded more informed than previously.

He nodded. A long, metal blade knife, sharp on one edge, laid catty-cornered in the arrangement. She looked at him in question.

"It's a razor... shaving." He looked amused.

"Yes, of course it is," she smiled. "It is after all, a gentleman's kit."

Looks like a throat slicer to me. The soft brush is for applying the lather, I remember Grandpa using one of those... A leather strap fitted around the inside of the container. She had no idea what its purpose was, but she had no intentions of asking.

"How much is this?"

"One dollar," he replied.

"No, Sir, I mean all of it."

She sensed Mr. Barrett observing her from a few yards away. Thank goodness Elsie was busy looking at jewelry. She regretted coming with them...*I should have waited and brought Hannah. I feel like an* idiot.

"That's the price for the entire kit, Miss," he said, a bit louder than she preferred.

"Then I shall take two," she said softly.

Mr. Sanders looked surprised. "You wish to buy two gentleman's kits?"

"Yes sir," I'll take two. Unless, you can inform me how else I might purchase two toothbrushes."

"Yes ma'am, I'll wrap up two gentleman kits for you," he announced even louder than his previous volume. The other clerk and another customer were now in the store, increasing her self-consciousness.

"Do you have toothpaste? She asked softly, hoping that by using her inside voice, he would follow the example, as do children.

He looked at her bewildered, than seemed to process that she wanted something to apply to the toothbrush.

"I have tooth powder Ma'am."

"Good I'll take some, now how much do I owe you?"

Mr. Sanders stepped away from the counter. He returned with a small jar of Mackey's Tooth Powder.

"That will be two dollars and twenty-five cents.

Wow, I can't believe these prices... "I'll take a bottle of vinegar and a tin of soda."

After putting the additional items on the counter, he stated, "That's three dollars."

Looking around, she saw no one waiting to speak with Mr. Sanders. The new customer was settling down at a table to play cards with the other clerk. She decided to shop a little more.

"What do you have in the line of lotions, shampoos, deodorants, and skin creams?"

Mr. Sanders stood in silence as though she had spoken to him in Latin.

Guess those luxuries aren't invented yet. What can I use to moisturize?

"Do you have olive oil?" she asked, still keeping her voice low.

"No, but I can order you a bottle, Doc usually wants a few pints." He took a paper from under the counter and wrote something down.

"What's your name, Miss? It'll be a couple of weeks, maybe three. It comes from Southern California by steamer."

"My name is Delphi Castile. Order me two pints, please, and I'll take a jar of that rose water... over there. How much do I owe you now?"

"The olive oil is one dollar each, since I have to send for it, so that brings you up to five dollars and fifty cents. The rosewater is from France." He reached for the large bottle of light pink liquid.

Becca pulled a ten dollar gold piece from her tiny bag and lay in on the counter. Mr. Sanders pulled brown paper from underneath and began the task of wrapping. Becca glanced around. Elsie eyed the silk parasols.

"How much are those?" she asked.

"Two dollars each, they're pure silk." He pulled string from a large spool and wound it around the two wrapped gentleman boxes.

Walking over to Elsie, she whispered, "Pick out one and I'll buy it for you."

The girl looked at her in surprise, "Oh, no, you needn't."

"Please, to celebrate our new friendship," Becca urged.

Elsie picked out a pink one with wide white lace around the edge. Becca selected a light blue with dark blue cord trim. She took them to the clerk.

"You needn't wrap these, we'll use them."

"That's nine dollars and fifty cents." He took the gold piece and handed her a silver half dollar.

Then she remembered Hannah. "Please, give me a sack of that peppermint."

The man nodded and scooped out 10 pieces of candy, placed it in a small bag. He took back the half dollar and handed her two dimes, a nickel and a few pennies. Then she saw the books.

Mr. Barrett gathered up her parcels, and Elsie collected the two new parasols along with the one she had brought. Becca crossed the room where more than a dozen books faced outward on a shelf. "Those belong to James," said Mr. Sander, nodding toward the clerk at the card table.

"He brings those from Frisco to sell."

Becca glanced over the selection. James, realizing he had a customer, excused himself from his game challenger and approached her.

"I just received this shipment last month. They're great books... all of them. I recommend this one, Great Expectations."

"That is a great book, I've read it."

He looked disappointed. "Then you'll like this one. It's also by Dickens. It's even more absorbing than Great Expectations."

"I've read that also, but I don't agree, I liked Great Expectations better."

James looked as though he didn't believe her, "Permit me to show you this one, ma'am, Silas Marner, by George Elliot."

"Oh yes, the linen weaver," I read that one as well. " *It's like my required reading list from high school Classic-Literature class is here on this shelf.*

Then her eyes fell on Lady Audley's Secret, by Mary Elizabeth Braddon.

"Is this one good? It looks like a juicy romance. I love books, so I'll probably be your best customer."

"If the lady likes romance, she might also like this." He handed her Modern Love, by George Meredith. It's a book of sonnets. I've read it and it's both sad and romantic."

"Very well, I'll take that one too. Do you have a children's book here?"

"Only this one, its *Flower Fables* by Louisa May Alcott." James handed her the book with a colorful picture of a girl on the cover.

Becca felt chills move over her... *Louisa May Alcott is alive right now. And she hasn't even written 'Little Women' yet...* "Yes, I'll take this one too."

After using part of her remaining ten dollar gold piece, and placing her change into the small purse, Becca turned to go. Suddenly, she realized the predicament in which she had placed her companions. There they patiently stood, loaded down with her bounty. She had forgotten all about them.

"I'm so sorry. I've been so selfish. Here, allow me to take some of those Mr.' Barrett."

He smiled as he turned toward the door. "All is forgiven Miss Castile, but next time you run errands, I will remember to bring a wheelbarrow."

I must remember...that I can no longer jump into my car and drive away with my loot.

12

"We must consult our means rather than our wishes."

—G<small>EORGE</small> W<small>ASHINGTON</small>

When Becca and her companions returned to the hotel, the clock was striking two. The women returned the borrowed parasols to the holder on the hall tree. Mr. Barrett handed the parcels he had carried to Becca and Elsie. He excused himself, saying that he needed to clean The Print Shop and run a few errands. The young women hurried upstairs where Becca dropped the parcels on her bed, and Elsie retired to her room to take a nap...*Call it a nap if you like, but I'll bet it's an excuse to get free from the bondage of that corset.*

Becca went to the secretary and noticed a folded piece of paper lying on the surface. She had not seen it before and assumed Hannah had brought it. Opening it up, she saw it was the requested bill from Molly.

> Room-$1.00 per day= $2.00
> Meals-$0.50 per day=$1.00
> Bath-$0.25 (only one permitted per week) $0.25

Wash and pressing of dress- $0.35
Total= $3.65

A note added at the bottom stated that the employment agreed upon will reduce future charges 50%

At these prices, it will cost me Ten to twelve dollars per week. At fifty percent off, in exchange for chores, it will still be five to six dollar per week. That's over twenty dollars per month. Although the charges are reasonable, they'll slowly burn through my stash. I can't board in a hotel forever.

She sat at the desk, opened the drawer, and took out the paper she had written on before. She checked off several tasks on the list that she had accomplished. Then, she wrote several new ones; pursue permanent lodging, seek employment, obtain more needed items. She listed what she would need to purchase; a journal, stationary, and several more changes of clothing...*When I find work I'll need more than Delphi's fancy dress and this cotton one...eventually, I'll need a coat.*

On a new sheet of paper, she listed the items she had observed at the mercantile and their prices...*Next time I'll go with a list and know what I'll be spending...*Becca opened the safe and took out the gold coins. She divided the ten dollar coins from the five dollar ones and carefully counted them. The total was two hundred dollars... *I can't believe Delphi stitched so many coins into her garments. I wonder what the gold brick is worth.*

She created a ledger on a fresh sheet of paper and wrote the balance at the top of one column. In another column, she listed the items she had purchased and what they cost, including her room and board for one week. Looking at the jewelry, she tried to guess the worth of each piece, and added them to a column she labeled assets... *I wonder it Delphi bought these pieces or if they were gifts ...maybe Lilly gave her brothel maids bonus gifts in jewels.... a customer may have gifted her as his favorite.... maybe she stole them. No... I don't want to believe that.*

She put the gold and jewelry back in the safe, and locked them up safely, keeping out what she owed Molly and enough to pay ahead for a week. She returned the bill and her paperwork to the drawer and looked at her packages. Opening them, she found places to put everything; brush and comb on the bureau, toothbrush and tooth powder on the wash stand, the vinegar, tin of soda, and rose water on the bottom shelf of the wash stand. She hung the silk umbrella in the armoire with the Delphi's wool dress that Hannah had washed and pressed. She placed the new books on the bedside table and looked around...*This feels real homey... home really is where you hang your stuff... it's the least amount of material things I've ever owned... it feels nice, sort of unfettered.*

A knock at the door reminded Becca that Hannah must be dying of curiosity. She invited her in. The girl wore a big smile.

"Did you have a pleasant stroll, Delphi?"

"Nice enough, Hannah. Tell me, do you like to read?"

"Like to? I reckon that I'm grateful I can." She appeared confused about the question.

"What I mean is, do you ever read books for fun?"

Hannah shook her head, indicating that she did not.

"Didn't your teacher have you read good books in school?"

"Good book? Oh, you mean the Bible? I have my mother's Bible, but I never have time to read it."

"That's a good book too, but there're others full of stories and poems. There must have been some in the school you attended." *We must not be on the same wavelength.*

Hannah shook her head. "We read the constitution, some history, arithmetic problems, the kind you've got to figure out, but not stories, twasn't time for that."

Becca reached for the new book, *Flower Fables*. "See this? I bought it for us to read together."

Hannah took the book and looked at the colorful picture on the cover. She gently turned the pages. "That would be delightful, Delphi, but when?"

"When do you get time off?"

"Only on Sunday."

"What about at the end of everyday? At what time are you finished with your chores?"

"About eight-o-clock."

"Why so late?"

"After the supper dishes are done, I set up things for breakfast. Then I wash out my undergarments and hang them to dry so I can iron them early in the morning."

She shrugged as though nothing was unusual about the arrangement.

"Well, we'll take time every Sunday to read this book, does that sound like a good idea to you?"

"Oh yes, I would so very much like that, Delphi."

The clock struck four and Hannah jumped in alarm. "Oh my...I was supposed to ask you about supper. Guests either eat in the kitchen or have their porridge brought to their rooms for the supper meal. Which would you like this night?"

"What are the others doing?"

"Miss Barns will be eating in her room; Mr. Barrett will be attending a meeting. The crewmen are eating at the tavern. Mr. and Mrs. O'Shay will be taking supper in the kitchen. And I must hurry now to start the prune pudding."

"I'll eat in my room, Hannah, can you join me?"

Hannah hesitated, "I can ask Mrs. O'Shay about it." She closed the door behind her.

An hour later, Becca and Hannah dined on a soup of boiled cabbage with pieces of elk meat, corn bread, and water. Hannah also had prune pudding. Becca declined, not knowing what the consequence would be to her digestive system. Afterward, Becca presented Hannah with the second toothbrush that she had bought and a portion of the tooth powder. She demonstrated the method of dental hygiene, and solicited a promise from the girl that she would continue with the practice daily.

As the clock struck six, Becca slipped into the nightgown, lit the lamp by her bed and picked up the journal written by the woman whose body she now possessed... *Should I read from the beginning or go backwards?* She looked at the last entry.

> **July 27, 1865**
>
> **I finalement accompli the stitchery of embedding the pièces d'or into my corset. It's been difficile to find times of solitude when this effort can be exécuté without notice of Mrs. Keenan. It has taken quatre ans to save so much and it is le plus urgent that I arrive in Portland with all of it in whole...** Becca read through the entry several times... *Why did you write this in part French and part English, Delphi? I guess I shouldn't complain. If it were all in French, I wouldn't be able to read it at all... So, I get from the first part, that you sewed the coins in your clothing in secret. I guess Lilly wasn't into stop and frisk with her doves. "Quatre"... that must mean four... Oh, four years to save this much. That's a long time to work for someone if you don't want to.*
>
> **Sally, being Madam's préféré, is well versed of the itinerary. The remainder of her filles is never informé, but rather to accept and obey sans protestation. Sally informs me that we shall be in Portland pendant la nuit. Madam expects us to gagner money there. This is when I will make my fuite...** *So...there were plans for you girls to make some money in Portland? "Pendant la nuit"... one night? Seems Sally, whoever she is, was the mole. "Madam's préféré"? She was Lilly's favorite...she told you the plan... Fuite... escape, I remember hearing that word. You were planning to escape in Portland. That would have been your next stop... You got so close to freedom...*

The clock struck seven. Becca was startled. It was this time of night she first heard that clock when Mr. Barrett carried her to the hotel. It's been twenty-four hours. *Mom and Beth must be frantic. Or, are they? They aren't even born yet? But I'm born... at least my spirit, my soul, my mind are present? This is so confusing.....*

Becca was in a deep, but troubled sleep when Hannah, dropping in to say good night, turned out the lamp. Becca felt herself sinking. Then a spinning sensation replaced the sinking. She stopped long enough to see a bright light, but sped past it and into a fog. As the fog cleared she saw a bed. Looking around, she recognized that she was standing in a hospital room. *I'm back to my own time. This is a modern room, but why am I here?*

She looked at her hands to see if she recognized them as her own but saw nothing. She moved toward the glass door that looked out at a desk where a nurse sat, facing a computer. The light in the nurses' station was dimmer than the lighting in the hospital room. It shone directly onto a patient. The nurse stood up and walked to the door. Becca stepped back as the woman walked through the door toward the bed...*She didn't even notice me.*

The nurse checked the IV, and took vital signs. She wrote something on a chart that hung on the bottom of the bed frame. She exited the room, passing right by Becca, again without acknowledging her. Becca moved to the bed and leaned over it. The individual had a bandage wrapping her entire head. She was hooked up to a monitor. A body cast held her in a rigid reclined position. She studied the face for a moment and gasped...*That's me! That's my body!*

Becca glanced back toward the glass door. The nurse was now talking on the phone. Becca noticed the reflection of the bed and patient in the glass door...*There's no reflection of me...* She approached the glass and moved her arms...*No, there's no reflection of me. I have no body, but my body is on that bed. How do I get into it?*

A doctor entered the nurses' station, speaking with the woman at the desk for a few minutes. He walked into the room without even a glance at Becca. The nurse followed him and they discussed the patient.

"Her Vital signs have been very strong today, Doctor. Her oxygen level much improved."

The doctor picked up the clipboard that held the chart as he studied her notes. "She's doing better than I dared hope. I'll consult with Dr. Myers in the morning. He may want to move ahead with the spinal surgery."

He lay the clipboard down on the foot of the bed. "I'm leaving after rounds tonight. If she takes a turn for the worse, don't hesitate to call me."

The phone rang in the nurses' station and the woman hurried to answer it. As the doctor headed toward the door, Becca moved in front of him. He passed right through her...*My God, I'm a spirit. Somehow, I've left Delphi's body back in that other time. She must be in mine here*...Becca again moved to the bed and looked at the chart that lay on top of the coverlet. Plainly written on the top of the page; **Rebecca Cates, admitted-July 30, 2015, Head Injury, Spinal Cord Injury. Next of kin; Philip Cates, husband and Martha and Elizabeth, mother and sister...** *So if my body is lying there, alive and breathing, empowered by Delphi's spirit, and if Phil is listed as next of kin, he's alive and well. That's not good. My body's in danger!* Becca hovered over the bed...*Might as well keep an eye on my body.*

Moving closer to the patient she spoke in what she hoped was an audible voice... "You have to pull through, Delphi. You have my body and I want it back. I've been hanging out in your body, and no offense, but it's not a match for my personality. I don't think much of your century either. We need to make a change somehow. I'm betting you have to be conscious for that to happen. When you wake up, you'll need to be aware that the guy named Phil is dangerous. Don't trust him. Beth is my sister and she will do everything she can for you. Trust her. I'll try to hang around and protect you... us."

Becca hovered even closer. The breathing of the sleeping patient was even and rhythmic. She felt herself sinking... then spinning... passing the bright light and falling...She sat bolt right up in the lumpy bed.

The early morning light shinned through the hotel room window, and a breeze fluttered the blue lace curtains. She had sweated so much her cotton gown felt moist. She took it off and tossed it to the floor... *Was that a dream? It was just too real to be a dream...I must have slipped through that thingy...that watcha-ma-call-it...veil...passage... portal... but Why?*

She glanced at the journal lying open on the floor where it had fallen...*I was reading that when this happened...Is that what caused it? Are we able to connect through our words...our thoughts?* Becca got up, lit the lamp, and sat on the side of the bed. She picked up the journal and flipped to the front and to the first entry.

August 4, 1861

Today is my dix-septième anniversaire. My grand-mère présenté me with this lovely journal. I also received a silk fan from Tante Celeste and deux lace handkerchiefs from Materner. Other tantes présenté gifts suitable for my trousseau. If it were not for birthday and Christmas gifts, there would be nothing in that silly chest. I seldom finish the embroidery and fancy work I'm assigned. Materner says a nicely filled trousseau makes evident to the fiancé that the young femme is not shiftless. She also declared that if I'm not wedded by dix-huit, it could become worrisome. My older sisters were married de seize. Pshaw! Such rubbish! I have no hankering to be wed. Men delay marriage until de trente or older, so why not I? I prefer to continue with my musique... *Darn the French and English mixture. Nothing is easy with you Delphi... So this first entry is on your birthday... sixteenth... no...seventeenth birthday. The journal is a gift. Grand-mère must be your grandmother. Looks like you have an Aunt Celeste. Your received a silk fan, lace handkerchiefs, and stuff for your trousseau. That must be*

> *like the hope chest my grandmother told me about… Collecting items for marriage use to be a trend for young women…But, it doesn't look like you cared much for that idea. Wow! Your mother wanted you married by eighteen, and your sisters were married by sixteen? There's nothing like pressure…family pressure. Well, this journal is four years old so we will see what happened to that idea.*

The clock struck six. Becca, remembering this was her first day to work with Hannah, prepared herself for the day, and descended the back stairs.

13

"Laziness may appear attractive, but work gives satisfaction."

—A‍NNE F‍RANK

After a breakfast of oatmeal in the kitchen with Hannah, Becca put on the apron Hannah offered her. "What do I do first?" she asked Molly who was washing dishes in the large metal dishpan.

"You may dry these dishes while Hannah tends to the chamber pots." "Shouldn't I help her with that?"

"No, I preferred that only my hired girl in the private rooms. That way no one can accuse you of stealing or nosing around. Hannah will clean the upstairs rooms, and you can work downstairs." Molly nodded toward a closet that was covered with a curtain.

"There're brooms and mops in there. Hannah will show you the Tuesday chores."

For three hours, the two worked without a pause. Hannah cleaned the bedrooms and Becca cleaned the rooms on the ground floor, sweeping each room then mopping the hallways, kitchen, and entrance way. Hannah demonstrated how they must roll up the large rug in the parlor. They then dragged it outside where they hung it over a wooden rail. There, they beat it violently with large round instruments that reminded Becca of tennis rackets. Hannah called them beaters...*this is a good way to work off some hostility.*

"So, is this the work we will do every Tuesday, Hannah?" Becca pushed a lock of fallen hair from her face.

"Yes, except if we are making jam, or doing something else special."

"And tomorrow?"

"Tomorrow's ironing day. And we polish the silver forks and spoons. With both of us working at it we should finish in a half a day. It usually takes me all day." *Ironing? Oh yeah, that's what they did before electric dryers. Polishing forks and spoons, really?*

"Yesterday, Monday, was wash day. It takes till Wednesday for the sheets to dry enough to iron,"

Hannah continued explaining the chore schedule while never missing a stroke in the rhythm she had set for pounding the rug,

"On Thursdays, we bake all the bread we'll need for the week. Mrs. O'Shay likes to have a cake and some pies baked too. Then Fridays, we clean all the rooms again, but not the rug, unless there's been a lot of rain and trackin' in going on."

Poor Hannah, this is a lot of work for a young teenager... Heck, it's a lot of work for anyone, especially dressed like this... Delphi, you'd better get it together soon... I'm coming after my body and my wardrobe...

After the carpet was returned to the floor, Hannah handed Becca an oiled cloth. They went through the house dusting and polishing the furniture. By eleven thirty, Hannah informed Becca that it was time to prepare dinner. Becca had noticed the mid-day meal was referred to as dinner, and the evening meal as supper.

Becca peeled potatoes while Hannah prepared to fry slices of salt pork and warm up the large pot of beans that had been cooked the day before. Molly placed a large pan of cornbread batter in the oven.

Becca was hot. The long sleeves on her dress were miserable in the steamy kitchen. The braided bun on her neck caused her skin to itch. The woolen stockings held up by garters were torture...*I'd kill for a pair of shorts, a tank top, and some flip flops.*

As they sat down at the table, she looked around. Seated at the table were the two crewmen from yesterday, Elsie, looking fresh and beautiful, both of the O'Shays, and of course Mr. Barrett...Becca suddenly felt disarranged. *I should have slipped to my room and freshened up; I must look like a fright.*

Elsie quickly moved to the chair by Mr. Barrett. He pulled it out for her, and waited until she was seated before sitting down. Mr. O'Shay did the same for Becca who sat on his left. After everyone's plates were filled and table conversation waned, Becca ventured a question.

"I'm going to need to buy some clothing. Where will I go to do this? I saw nothing at The Mercantile that a lady would buy in regard to dresses and such."

"The Mercantile has bolts of calico, wool, and some voiles in the back room," said Molly. "I buy cloth there, and make frocks for myself and Hannah."

I haven't sewn anything since I made that skirt in tenth grade sewing class... it was a disaster... maybe I could do better now... "Do you have a sewing machine?" Molly looked at Becca in confusion...Of course you don't... Singer is probably still working on the invention.

"There are a few women in town who sew for hire," suggested Mr. O'Shay.

"They charge too much," complained Molly. "Their stitches pull right apart. They make loose seams."

Mr. Barrett cleared his throat and began, "I have a tailor in Chinatown. He does excellent work, and charges a fair price. I believe that his wife sews as well."

"Chinatown... is there a Chinatown in Crescent City?"

"Yes, answered Mr. O'Shay. "Some people do business there. It's on Second Street."

"Not a place for a woman to go," Molly shook her head emphatically. "I'd never go there, it isn't safe."

"Why not?"

"It's been said that they steal women and children." She answered in a low tone.

"Have you ever known of an actual case of this happening?"

"It's not happened since I moved here," offered Mr. Barrett. "I've found the merchants there to be fair-minded and pleasant. I also take my laundry there each week. I feel perfectly safe on Second Street."

"Well, I need a seamstress, and you appear to know where one is on Second Street. Mr. Barrett, could I impose on you to accompany me there to meet her? I'm sure that Molly will feel much better about my going if I am dutifully guarded, "

"Certainly, I'm going this afternoon to pick up some shirts I had laundered and ironed. Would you like to come along?" He laid his napkin beside his empty plate.

"Why yes, actually, I would. Is there a fabric store...err...a place to buy cloth on Second Street?" If your tailor's wife will agree, I'd love to get something started as soon as possible."

"Mr. Leng has cloth. He makes suits and shirts. I think he even has some silks from China. He orders a variety of tailoring materials from San Francisco."

Becca could hardly contain her excitement...The thought of shopping is as much a thrill in this century as in my own.

"Molly," Becca began politely. "May I please take Hannah with me? She completed all her work this morning. I promise I will not allow anyone steal her."

Hannah caught her breath and covered her mouth to prevent a squeal.

"I suppose," answered Molly, with hesitation. "But she must be back in time to help me prepare supper."

"Would you like to go with us Elsie?"

"I promised Minnie I would watch Little Albert this afternoon," Elsie sounded disappointed about having to decline.

Mr. Barrett offered to borrow a buggy and horse from his friend, Abe. Within the hour, the three were loaded in the buggy. Hannah squeezed in between the two adults. As the three rode to Second Street, Hannah held the blue parasol to shade them. The conversation turned to clothing.

"So, what do the two of you suggest I have made? I know I need a couple of work dresses," began Becca.

"Two work dresses is all a body needs," said Hannah. "I have two and so does Mrs. O'Shay."

"Do you wash one out every night?" asked Becca, remembering the girl's explanation about washing her underwear each evening.

"Oh no, Delphi, you must know that won't do!" Land sakes! A frock would never last if you washed it every day. Everybody knows that."

"But, Hannah, the dress I worked in this morning is ready for the laundry. I spilled mop water on the bottom of the skirt, perspired in it terribly, and dropped a glob of oatmeal in my lap at breakfast. I can't possibly wear it until Monday. And this wool, dressy outfit isn't suitable for housework."

"Well of course not, you ninny," the girl laughed. "You're supposed to sponge off the underarms and soiled spots each night. That's why I left that sponge in you room by your wash stand."

Becca felt herself blush with embarrassment...*I must look like an idiot! I can't know this stuff.*

"You shant be disrespectful to Miss. Castile," said Mr. Barrett firmly.

"Perhaps she's accustomed to servants. Miss. Barns tells me you came from Louisiana, Miss Castile, before moving the San Francisco."

"Did she?" answered Becca, "and what else did my new friend tell you?"

Maybe you can shed some light on a past I know nothing about.

"She only said that you are from a French community in Lafayette. That you spoke with a lovely accent before the accident. She wondered what happened to it...the accent."

Becca felt flustered. She remembered the few words Delphi spoke to her as they both hung desperately to the floating plank. They were French words and her English phrase was in a heavy accent...*How do I explain this, I wonder? Ahh, Elsie also mentioned that Delphi was a singer and pianist, a performer before Lilly knuckled her under thumb.*

"What Elsie doesn't realize, only knowing me for one day before the ship wreck, is that I came to San Francisco as a performer. Being French by birth, it fit my persona to use the accent." *Ha, the best lie I've ever came up with?*

"What's a persona? Hannah asked.

"It refers to putting on airs," offered Mr. Barrett.

"I prefer to think of it as stage performance...acting...Mr. Barrett." A snarky tone was in Becca's voice that she hadn't intended.

Mr. Barrett looked surprised. "I meant no offense, Miss Castile."

"Could you teach me French?" asked Hannah, "I'd like to do airs."

"Let's get back to discussing my wardrobe. I'm going to get two work dresses, and I need another nice dress, for going out."

"You'll need a church frock," offered Hannah. "Something for summer, that wool will be too hot by next month when the weather warms."

Mr. Barrett offered another suggestion. "There're dances and soirees almost every weekend. Some young ladies order gowns from the city, for those frolics. There are also actors from the city who perform plays at the Theater. Fancy gowns are worn then."

"Only those fuddy-duddy girls from the uppity families," scoffed Hannah. You need a gentleman to accompany you to those, unless you have a brother or uncle, or some kind of family member."

Becca noted that her scoff had morphed into a sad tone...*I'm not even going to ask about the dances or soirees, my ignorance will show.*

"Good...I'll order a Sunday-go-to-meetin' dress and a party dress too. And, I'll get some cooler nightgowns and some more of those... what do you call them... pantaloons."

Hannah startled and covered her mouth with her hand. "Delphi! You mustn't say that!" She leaned into Becca and whispered. "Not in front of a gentleman."

"Oh really...like he doesn't know what ladies wear?"

Hannah gave her an alarmed face. Mr. Barrett looked away, and pretended not to hear the interaction...*Opps! More of the old puritan prudishness, I see.*

"Well, excuse my inappropriate language I'll try to be more careful."

Leaning toward Hannah she whispered, "What should I call them, Hannah?"

Hannah glanced at Mr. Barrett to be sure he was distracting himself and whispered back. "We don't speak of them around men folk. And when we must speak of them, we call them undergarments. Didn't your Mama teach you that, Delphi?"

"It must be something I lost in learning English. The French are very different in their attitudes about such things." Becca spoke loudly enough for Mr. Barrett to hear...*Darn I'm good!*

Mr. Barrett stopped in front of a shop. A hand painted sign, over the door, was filled with Chinese characters.

"Here we are," he announced.

He jumped down, tied the reins to a post. He walked around to assist, first Becca and then Hannah. As he placed his hands on Becca's waist to lift her out, he noticed the lack of the stiff corset worn by all the women he had ever known. His face turned deep red...*What was that all about? This is a grown man, a former Union solder, what did I do to embarrass him?*

As he lifted Hannah down, Becca observed the girl's stiff torso. She looked like a wooden doll being lowered to the ground...*Oh, I get it. That dastardly corset is more than a waist clincher, and breath restrictor. Its armor so no evil warm flesh can be touched, and heaven forbid, tempts a gentleman... I hate this century!*

They walked into the store where a middle aged man sat at a work table. He was sewing a sleeve onto a jacket. Several suits of clothing hung along the wall. On a table, shirts were folded and laid out for easy observation. They had no collars or cuffs. Another table had these, separate from the shirts...*Why aren't they sewn to the shirts? Do the men put those on after putting on the shirts? They must, but why? Must be the laundry issue... they can wash the collar and cuffs without washing the shirt...or visa-versa...She smiled when thinking of Phil dealing with that exercise while getting dressed.*

The tailor stood up and came toward them, bowing and addressing Mr. Barrett. "I help you with suit today?"

Becca and Hannah were introduced, and then the men conversed for several minutes. They were skillful in using both English and Chinese words mixed with signs and gestures. Mr. Barrett motioned to Becca several times.

Finally, Mr. Leng said, "Wait...I bring...Mrs. Leng."

A middle aged woman immerged from a doorway, covered only with a curtain. She smiled and bowed her head when introduced. Her husband explained to her, what Mr. Barrett had told him. Mrs. Leng gestured for Becca and Hannah to follow her into the back room.

"I'm going down the street to get a haircut and a shave," said Mr. Barrett, "I'll also pick up my shirts from the laundry. Take your time; I'll be gone for a spell."

Becca and Hannah followed Mrs. Leng into her shop. Shelves along one wall held bolts of cloth. Glass jars on another shelf had buttons, sorted by color and size. On the opposite wall, hooks held yards of lace in different colors and sizes. A long table stood in the middle of the room,. Fabric pieces lay out, suggesting that Mrs. Leng was in the process of cutting out a garment. A large pair of scissors lay beside the fabric. A long cord hung around the woman's neck with ink spots about an inch apart, marking the entire length. Becca immediately realized this was a measuring tool of some sort.

"There's so much cloth and it's all so grand, Delphi, how ever will you choose?" asked Hannah, with eyes wide in wonderment.

14

"You can never be overdressed or overeducated."

—OSCAR WILDE

Becca looked at Hannah's excited expressions regarding the choices that were available and smiled... *I wonder what you would think of a large shopping Mall...*

Mrs. Leng watched Becca closely as though trying to read her mind.

"What you like?" she asked in broken English.

Might as well start at the skin and work up. "I need pantaloons."

She held up her hand with four fingers, indicating that she wanted four pairs.

"Four?" exclaimed Hannah, "You only need two and you have one."

"Hush, Hannah, you'll confuse Mrs. Leng. We have a language issue here. I need you to be quiet, please."

"Yes, yes," said Mrs. Leng, bowing. She scurried to the other side of the room, pushed a stool in front of a shelf. From the top of the highest shelf, she pulled a large basket and carried it to the work table. Setting it on the end, away from the fabric she had been cutting, she motioned for Becca to look inside. Becca peered into the basket. There, folded and stacked were pantaloons. They were sorted by size, small, medium, and large. Searching through, she found enough of the small size to fill her request of four pairs. Each pair was made of fine cotton and trimmed with wide crocheted lace...*As bad as I hate these rompers, I must admit these are very pretty*...Becca held one pair up. She noted that there was a wide split in the crotch.

"Oh look, it's ripped."

Mrs. Leng shook her head violently. "No, no, not," she insisted, showing Becca the fine stitching around the hem of the opening.

Hannah decided to break the silence Becca had assigned to her and explain. "That's for using the chamber bowl, Delphi. Mrs. O'Shay says only married ladies should have open undergarments. That's why ours aren't like that. "

"Well, remembering the awkward dance that accompanies use of that potty, I think these are an improvement."

She handed the sets to Mrs. Leng, nodding that she wanted them.

Hannah looked as though she would protest, but caught Becca's warning look and restrained herself. Becca was happy to find the chemise tops were also already made, and picked out four that matched the pantaloons. Mrs. Leng motioned to the petticoats. Becca shook her head.

"I have two extra of those in a drawer in my room."

Becca then pointed to her dress, indicating that she wanted one made. Mrs. Leng nodded and went to another shelf, retrieving a second basket. Sitting it where the former basket had been, she lifted out four dolls about twice as big as a Barbie.

Hannah gasped, "Oh Delphi, china dolls, see how lovely they are!"

"They are impressive!" agreed Becca.

The Lady dolls had porcelain faces, arms and legs. High-top black shoes were painted on as was black hair. Asian eyes, pink cheeks and tiny red lips completed their faces.

"Hannah, is she trying to sell me these dolls?" Becca looked at the woman confused.

Mrs. Leng pointed to the dresses on the dolls and then to Becca's dress. "These... what I make."

"Oh, I see. These are her dress pattern samples. They're like little manikins."

"What are manikins?" asked Hannah.

"Big dolls," answered Becca.

She closely examined the dolls. One pattern looked suitable for a work dress. It had sleeves just below the elbow and they were loose enough to roll up. The neck line rounded and had a flat collar rather than stand up décor that would be a nuisance in hot weather. The bustle was removable so it could be left off during strenuous activity.

"I want two of these."

Mrs. Leng smiled. She was obviously very happy as she set this doll aside. Waving her hand toward the shelves of fabric, she encouraged Becca to make a choice. Becca and Hannah moved toward the choices.

"Now I need advice, Hannah, for a work dress, what fabric is best?"

"Cotton cloth is always best for work frocks, Delphi. Everyone knows that. It washes real nice and dries fast. It irons up stiff with starch. You're lucky she has some. Mrs. O'Shay says that the fall of the South and the freein' of the slaves will make cotton real scarce."

"She must have stocked up several years ago to have this selection," murmured Becca.

"She might not have much business to use it up," offered Hannah. "Most white women won't come to Chinatown."

"Really, well ignorance equals lost opportunity, so see how they're missing out?" Becca brushed her hand over the different calicos...*I don't have to pick my colors to compliment my red hair anymore. I wonder what Delphi would choose.*

She picked out a light lavender fabric, covered with tiny dark purple flowers. She chose another in a dark green with scatterings of small white daisies. Mrs. Leng set the bolts aside.

She directed Becca to the lace selection. Becca picked out a white lace to trim the collar and cuffs of the lavender and a light green lace for the other. These were placed in the neat pile growing on the work table.

"Hannah, pick a calico for a new dress," suggested Becca.

"Oh, no, Delphi, Mrs. O'Shay might take offense if I let anyone but her make me a frock. She thinks nobody can sew as well as she can."

"Well, we'll let her sew it. We'll just buy the fabric then," decided Becca.

Hannah could hardly contain her excitement. She picked a pink calico with small green leaves and a white lace for trim. Both women picked buttons for the bodices. Becca chose a set made of blue abalone shells, and another made of light brown bone. Hanna picked buttons made of white shells. Returning to the dolls, Becca selected the doll with a skirt and jacket type top.

"This will work nicely for church and outings."

Returning to the fabric shelf, she chose a brown linen material. Mrs. Leng pointed to the silk and showed Becca, that the doll's outfit was lined with silk. Becca picked a matching silk for lining. She then picked a dark orange to trim the jacket and bottom of the skirt. With her previous coloring, she had avoided wearing orange. This was a new experience. Sit in the chair, Hannah, I'm not finished and may take a while."

As Hannah sat down, Becca looked at the last two dolls. "I need a party dress... which of these works for that, Hannah?"

"I don't know much about party dresses, but my momma always said every woman should have a black dress." Hannah rested her head on one hand.

"Why is that necessary?" asked Becca, closely examining the fancy dress on one of the remaining dolls.

"Because, sooner or later everyone has to go to a funeral," answered the girl.

I could get a party dress made in black and cover it up with a cape or shawl, if a funeral required my attendance. She handed the doll with the ruffled dress to Mrs. Leng. She then selected black velvet and black silk for trim. The dress had short puffed sleeves and scooped neckline...*This will look pretty with Delphi's pearls.*

"You'll need gloves with that," Hannah interrupted her thoughts. "You can't show your limbs without covering them with long gloves."

"Limbs? Trees have limbs, Hannah" Becca answered with a laugh.

"And so do you," answered the girl with a serious expression.

A pair of long black gloves and two pairs of black silk stockings were placed with the other articles. Becca hoped she had brought enough money. She had dropped an entire handful of gold coins in the little drawstring purse before leaving her room earlier.

Mrs. Leng pulled the cord from around her neck and quickly measured Becca from her waist to the length of her dress. She wrote symbols on a paper then measured around her waist. As Mrs. Leng tightened the cord around Becca, she pushed her fingers against her abdomen. Looking surprised, she scurried to one of the shelves and returned with a corset. Handing it to Becca, she waved toward a privacy screen in the corner. Becca shook her head.

"No, Mrs. Leng."

"Why does she want you to put on another support garment?" asked Hannah.

Becca, sighed, "Because, she noticed I'm not wearing one. She probably wants to measure me all sucked up in that beast."

"Delphi!" Hannah stood up, and covered her mouth. "You're out and about with out all of your undergarments?"

"Don't look so indignant!" "This body's already so thin, you didn't even notice."

"But that's not the matter of it, Delphi; the matter of it is what's right... proper... and....and...decent! People will think you're a... reckless...woman!"

Becca smiled at Mrs. Leng, handed her the item back and shook her head. The older woman bowed politely, and returned it to the shelf. After she finished with her measuring she bundled up the readymade items and handed them to Becca. Becca could hear Mr. Barrett talking with Mr. Leng. She was glad he had returned. She needed to ask someone about the prices and payment and she didn't feel up to another lecture from a thirteen year old.

As she walked through the door to the outer shop she noticed several hats...*Hmmm, I wonder why I didn't see these before. I need a hat. I've noticed other women wearing them*...Looking at Mrs. Leng and pointing at the hat, she asked

"May I try this on?"

Mrs. Leng nodded and took it off the stand, handing it to her. Placing it on her head, Becca looked at Hannah.

"So...Whata ya think?"

Hannah smiled, but the look on her face plainly said, "I am so over this trip."

Turning toward Mr. Barrett, she smiled. "Do you think it's becoming?"

As he looked at her, his face lit up like a sunrise. His beautiful hazel eyes crinkled in a big smile. "Why, yes, Miss Castile, it certainly is!"

She turned to Mrs. Leng and confirmed that she would take the hat. While the woman disappeared to collect a hatbox, Becca called her gentleman escort over to the other side of the room.

"I'm having a bit of memory problems, Mr. Barrett, would you be so kind as to assist me in counting out the payment for my purchases?"

"Of course, Miss Castile, how much do you owe the Lengs?"

"I don't know. They haven't told me yet. But I'm not sure I'll understand with the language issues."

Mr. Barrett returned to the counter, and Mr. Leng added up the list of Chinese characters his wife had left him. Mr. Barrett returned to discuss it with Becca just as she opened the silk purse.

"You went whole hog," he said laughing. "You owe them twenty-two dollars now and ten more when the garments are delivered."

Just then he glanced into her open purse that held nothing but the coins. "Good God Woman!" he quieted his voice to a whisper.

"Why are you packing so much gold? It's not safe to carry around more than you need!"

Becca felt her face turning pink...I have to sit down and get a handle on this money thing. I must learn to estimate the prices and plan ahead for what I'll buy...

Soon they were back in the buggy. Hannah was nervous that Mrs. O'Shay might think she was away too long, but she proudly held tight on to her parcel of fabric. Becca held her new treasures securely in her arms. She suddenly felt exhausted.

Back at the hotel, she and Hannah entered the back door. Mr. Barrett left to return the buggy and horse. Becca hurried to her room. She placed the hat, still in its box, on top of the armoire. Placing her new undergarments into a drawer, she glanced at the cast-away corset. She lifted it out of the drawer...*OK, you beasty contraption. Tomorrow I'll encase my boney body into your jaws of death. But, I will not lace you up tight enough to squish my organs!*

Becca sat at the secretary. Taking the papers from the drawer, she listed the items she had purchased with their total cost. She subtracted it from the balance, amazed that two twenty dollar gold pieces paid for such a large order and had plenty to spare. She had just returned the gold from her purse to the safe when Hannah knocked at her door. Becca invited her in.

"I'm here to ask if you'll be eating downstairs or in your room?"

"I think I'll have my meal here, Hannah, what's for supper?"

"Biscuits and gravy and sugared tomatoes," she answered with relish...

How do these people here stay so slim? All they eat is fat and carbs. I never thought I could miss salad so much.

Hannah pushed the door shut and spoke softly. "Miss Barns has already retired. She got bad news today while we were at China town. Mrs. O'Shay said she's quite upset and that I must not disturb her."

Becca looked at Hannah questioningly, wondering if such information should be passed from Molly to Hannah and then to herself. She had little time to make a determination however, as Hannah was rushing on with the report.

"A body was found. It washed up on the beach. Mr. Tate the crewman knew him and said his name was Hayden. I guess he must have been Miss Barn's friend."

"Yes, I understand that she would be upset. Maybe she'll feel like sharing with us tomorrow."

Later, after Becca had eaten, sponge bathed with the warm water Hannah brought to her room, she brushed her teeth and hair and settled into bed with Delphi's journal.

15

Exploring the unknown requires tolerating uncertainty.

—Brian Greene

August 6, 1861,
This is a very triste day. My Papa is gone. He transmis suddenly. The Médecin says it was his heart... *Oh my! Your father died two days after your seventeenth birthday. How horrible!*

Papa travaillé so hard to provide for us. But he had Dettes. Mama won't be able to keep the ferme... *Hmmm...the translation of these words... your father worked hard and provided for the family but died leaving debts....that's sad. Ferme... ahh... that's farm. So not only did you lose your Dad, but your home as well?*

Mama tells me there is no other choice other than to vendre the slave to pay Papa's dettes... *No, no, this can't be true...slaves? I refuse to inhabit the body of a slave-owner. Oh how I wish he was not so appelée to gambling...So your wonderful papa, gambled off the family money did he?*

Poor Zack and Ada, they have been part of our famille since before my soeurs were born. The field hands, George and Louie grew up on this ferme. I want Mama to give them their la liberté, and I said as much...*Ok, now... people have been in your service for years.... la liberte...liberate? Freedom, no doubt... You wanted your mother to free them. Well, at least you're a notch up in human compassion above your parents. But still...brought up like this...how different our childhoods are, even without the difference in time.*

But she says the dettes must be paid. I know she prefers that I be married and not dépendant on her now...*I'll bet the pressure to marry will increase for you now...* **My soeurs' husbands will take the ferme and add it to theirs. That was the accord of their dowries. If only Papa had had a son. He would take care of Mama**...*Dowries... in America? Was this a southern custom of because of your French culture? The farm is inherited by the males apparently. Everything goes to your brother-in-laws except the debts. How nice for them.*

Papa's Funérailles will be tomorrow. Suivant week Mama and I will go to the Ville to live with my Tante Celeste and her husband. La vie is so sorrowful ...*Leaving your home and moving to the city to live with an aunt...after losing your father...no wonder life is sorrowful, Delphi. I must remember as I judge you, that you are merely a teenager when writing this.*

Becca's eyes felt heavy. The clock had just struck eight. She laid the journal on the side table and extinguished the lamp...*I can't believe I'm ready to fall asleep so early... Without television, computer, or my cell phone, there's no reason to drag out the day... I'm surprised I haven't missed them more than I have... Actually, it's a bit nice to have time with my thoughts...*

The sea breeze flowed through the open window. The barking of the sea lions penetrated the silence. Becca watched the lace curtain moving in the draft, back lighted by moonlight. The image began to spin. It seemed to move farther away, she had a sinking sensation. Then, it felt as though she was moving rapidly through darkness, passing a bright light, and finally sinking again into the lighted hospital room.

She hovered in the corner of the room. The bandaged form lay in the bed surrounded by several people. Becca recognized the nurse from last time. A different doctor held the chart. Phil, Beth and Becca's mother stood together, facing the doctor. Becca couldn't see their faces. She moved closer and circled around them.

She glanced at her bruised body. The eyes were open, and appeared to be awake. How confused Delphi must be, surrounded by strangers in a strange place...She merged through Phil's body and placed herself between him and the form on the bed...*Delphi, can you hear me in your thoughts? If you can, blink.*

The brown eyes blinked in a very deliberate manner. *Good, listen to me. You're in my body. I'm taking good care of yours in Crescent City. If you understand me, blink twice*

The brown eyes produced two solid blinks...*This man who is holding your hand, he's bad. He arranged to murder me. We can't trust him. If you understand me, pull your hand away from his...*After several seconds the pale hand slowly slipped away from the grip Phil had on it.

"Look," exclaimed Beth. "She moved her hand."

"Yes" said the doctor, "she has movement and sensations in her upper body. We are worried about the fracture in the lower part of her spine. But, I feel confident we can provide support for the break with surgery. If the spinal cord isn't severed, feeling and movement may return to her lower extremities."

That woman who spoke is Beth, my sister. She'll do everything she can to help us, Delphi. Trust her and tell her what you need. Don't' tell Phil, the man that held your hand, anything. If you understand me, say so

"Oui."

"Did she just speak?" asked Becca's mother.

"She should be able to speak." answered the doctor. "Now that we've allowed her to awaken, it appears her head injury isn't serious enough to prevent speech or responses. However, her memory may be affected for a while. Don't be surprised if she is confused regarding short-term memory."

"Yes," added the nurse," I questioned her when she first awoke. She had no memory of the accident on the boat with her husband. She thought her situation was caused by a shipwreck. She must have had a nightmare."

"Do you think she will ever remember?" asked Phil nervously.

"It takes time for the brain to heal." answered the doctor. "After we get through the spinal surgery, we'll talk about therapies.

Becca leaned close to Delphi...*You must speak English at all times, Delphi. No more French. Also, don't talk about the ship wreck, or Lilly, or your childhood... nothing. We can't have them putting us into a mental institution.*

The brown eyes blinked, even without being asked. *We have to get your and my body through these procedures, but in time I hope to switch our bodies back. I know this is confusing to you, but this mysterious body swap may have, in some crazy way, saved both our lives.*

The doctor continued his explanation about the procedure to the family. Spinal surgery would be tomorrow. He needed signatures.

Phil spoke up assertively, "I don't know if I feel comfortable with this. She's been through a lot. Perhaps we should give her a chance to regain her strength before adding any additional stress."

The doctor looked at him and then to the two women. "Becca is a healthy and strong woman. That's why she is still with us. We need to move forward as soon as possible. The sooner therapy starts the better the results for spinal cord injury."

Beth stepped forward. Looking directly at Phil she said firmly, "My sister texted me about your affair. I still have it on my phone. You two were headed for divorce and you know it. Don't you think for one minute I'll permit you stand in the way of her medical needs!"

The doctor cleared his throat. "I think Becca is coherent enough to decide about her care. We have no legal documents stating that she needs a guardian. Do you want us to proceed with the surgery Becca?"

He's talking to you. You will answer to Becca while you're here. Tell him yes... tell him in English.

"Yes." The voice was low, weak, but determined.

Phil turned and walked out of the room. Beth stared at his back.

"I'm not leaving her alone; I'll stay with you tonight."

So, will I......the room began to spin...Oh no, not yet......I want to stay and look out for my body...

Becca felt as though she had been dropped into her bed. She awakened with a start, and for a few moments thought she had experienced a nightmare. Looking at the window, she noticed that the breeze was no longer flowing into the room. The air was stuffy. She striped off her gown. Getting up, she moved to the window and breathed in freshness. She wondered how much time had transpired.

It's not a dream or nightmare. I was really in Portland. That's the second time that happened after reading the journal... Delphi's thoughts are in her writing ...she hears my thoughts when I'm there...somehow; we'll have to communicate without me making that out of body trip repeatedly. That can't be safe... Something might prevent me from getting back to this body that holds me to earth.

She poured a glass of water from the decanter by her bed, and positioned herself on top of the covers. Suddenly, an idea formed in her mind... *My journal is in the Portland apartment. Hopefully, Phil hasn't found it and destroyed it...Beth could get it and take it to Delphi...if Delphi reads my thoughts; perhaps she can travel my direction...We could take turns. Maybe together, we can figure out how to switch...*

The clock struck eleven. Considering the length of time it took to make the last journey, Becca felt she had time for one more...*I have to go back and arrange for her to read my diary.*

Lighting the lamp, she picked up the journal and opened to the marked page where she had stopped reading.

> August 12, 1861
>
> We are at last établi with Tante Celeste in Lafayette. Her maison is nice enough but not nearly as grandiose as our ferme maison. It is a deux niveaux, clapboard structure, with a large magnolia tree and roseraie in back. It is in the Acadian part of the ville. The gates and stoops are in French mode... *So...you are now at your Aunt's home in the French section of the city. Ok...so it's smaller than you farm house.*
>
> Mama and I must share a chambre. I do so miss having my own! Mama busies herself in réprimande to me all jour long. She will start de travail at Aunt Celeste's milliner boutique tomorrow. Mama made hats for us at home, but none as grandiose as these. Some have real ostrich and peacock plumes... *I get this... sharing a room with your mom...that's got to be difficult for a teenager. .. She's nagging you all day...she will be working with her sister, making hats...*
>
> I could not bring my piano. I will miss it so. I will no longer study musique. For now I am requis to provide care for Tante Celeste's enfants. They are perfectly retched little beings and horribly pampered... *This is sad...giving up your piano and dreams of a music career... Doesn't sound like you think much of babysitting?*
>
> Oncle Anton is most désagréable. I feel he does not want us here. He is often cross with Tante Celeste. I do not feel comfortable when I am alone with the enfants and he is there. His regarder of me is unnerving. I shall pray to the Blessed Virgin to help

us through this procès...*Mmm...Uncle Anton may become a problem...*

I am writing our new adresse so I will not forget it. All couriers, even mine, will come to Mama's nom. I live for the hope my Amis and sœurs from home will écrireto me.
Adele Castile
369 Rue de Belier,
Lafayette, Louisiana

I wonder if your mother is still at this address...she should be notified...but what should she be told? You aren't dead...but...you aren't here...I'll have to give that some thought.

Becca put out the flame in the lamp. She closed her eyes and waited. As before, the spinning began. It reminded Becca of the sensation she had as a child. While sitting in her swing, she twisted the ropes tight and permitted it to rapidly unwind. She tried to relax her body. As she did, she felt herself slip out of it in much the same way a knife slides from its sheath. The fast flight through darkness followed with passing the distant bright light and then in ended the hospital room.

16

"Coming together is a beginning; keeping together is progress; working together is success."

—Henry Ford

No one was in the room but the patient...I thought Beth said she was staying to watch out for her...er... me... Becca looked around the room. Beth's purse sat on the floor beside the bedside chair. A newspaper lay on the chair...She must have stepped out for a moment...Becca moved toward the bed... I hate to wake her, but we need to talk. Her attention was drawn by the headlines on the front page of the paper.

"Coastguard Rescues Couple Near St George Lighthouse"

She scanned the story that followed. "A couple was saved from certain death Sunday, while sailing in the area of St George Lighthouse. Philip and Rebecca Cates were fortunate that a Coastguard patrol spotted the craft moving towards turbulent waters and pursued to give warning. By the time, it reached the sailboat named Lorelei; it had struck the rocks and capsized. Mr. Cates was pulled to safety right away, but it was by chance that Mrs. Cates was spotted floating, some distance from the crash site. She was rescued and given life-saving CPR. She was transported by life-flight to Portland. Captain Fredrick Gale is credited for saving her life. Another passenger of the Lorelei was crewman Ike Mackie. He has not been found. Mrs. Cates is in critical condition at Providence St. Vincent Medical Center. Mr. Cates escaped without serious injury... *So it was the coastguard that pulled my body from death. Ha, without Ike, Phil wasn't able to handle the boat. He didn't plan on me taking Ike overboard with me.*

A large picture of the totaled Lorelei was directly under the headlines and a smaller picture of the heroic captain below the story. Becca studied the image of a man in uniform. It was the typical military formal photograph. He appeared to be in his thirties. His square jaw and chiseled features portrayed a determined personality, if features could be depended upon... *You're a handsome devil...I appreciate your bravery and skills ...but you should have left my no-good cheating husband at the rocks, Captain.*

Becca heard a groan from the sleeping patient. She turned her attention to the bed. The brown eyes opened and looked expectantly from the secured position held in place by a neck brace.

Hi, I'm back.

"I know, I can feel your presence."

Are you in a lot of pain?

"I feel nothing below my waist. My head aches terribly, and I've been held in this position for so long I feel numb. I wish I could move. I feel as though I'm tethered."

Becca surveyed the scene... *You are, actually. The line hooked into your left arm is an IV. That's keeping you nourished, and it's a method of medicating you. The line coming out here is a catheter. That's draining your urine into a bag that's hanging from the bottom of the bed. And that neck brace keeps you from injuring you neck any more before it can heal. I know this is all strange to you, but you are getting the best possible care."*

For several minutes, Becca explained to Delphi the details of their predicament. She was surprised of how quickly the young woman grasped it.

"Then I must know what year is this, to which I've arrived?"

You're now in 2015, one hundred-fifty years from your own time.

"That is, indeed, a mystery."

Yes it is, I had trouble believing it, but it's for real. I have an advantage. I'm not injured so I don't have to concentrate on recovery. But, on the other hand, I have to be responsible and make my own way in a world that's strange to me. You may have to coach me on that sometimes.

"Coach? As in stagecoach?"

No, it means to advise…you may need to advise me.

"Oui… err…yes, of course, and I'll need your guidance as well."

I've been reading your journal, Delphi. I'm sorry, I know it's your personal and private thoughts, but I believe it's why I can visit you.

"So I must request then, that you do not judge me harshly."

I try to not judge others. I don't know what or why you made your life choices, but they're your decisions. I'm reading it so I can know how to live in your body until we can find a way to switch.

"I see."

So I'm here to suggest that you read my journal. I call it my diary. Then you'll understand me, and know more about what you're facing while in my body. Am I making sense?

"Where is this…diary?"

"We have to get Beth to pick it up at the loft and bring it to you."

"It's in a barn?"

"Barn? Oh no, the loft is what we call my apartment, my home."

Becca noticed the brown eyes fixating on something behind her. Turning she saw Beth, holding a mug of coffee.

"I see you're awake, Sis. Do you need me to get the nurse to give you more pain medication? I heard you talking. Who are you talking to?" she asked.

Tell her, you were thinking out loud.

"I was just going over things in my mind," she repeated.

"Ah, and what is making you think so hard tonight? Are you worried about surgery tomorrow?" asked Beth.

Tell her you need her to pick up your diary and bring it to you tomorrow.

Delphi, in Becca's body, followed the instructions.

"Well, of course I'll get it for you. That's a good idea. You can record your experiences through this recovery. That'll be therapeutic. Phil is angry with me for taking a stand against him, so I'll have to sneak into the loft after he's gone tomorrow. But I can do that. You gave me a key when you moved in there, so it won't be a problem. Where is the diary?"

Tell her it's in the bottom drawer of your nightstand, under the picture album. If it's not there, Phil has done something with it.

This information was passed on...Now tell her that Phil tried to kill you and that you are afraid of him.

The entire incident was told to Beth word for word with a French twist, but Beth was more concerned about the information than the speech pattern. Little by little and piece by piece, the two disarranged spirits conveyed the entire story of the struggle on the Lorelei, Ike's demise and the names of the two other couples who might be able to provide helpful testimony.

Beth took her sister's hand. "I'm so glad I stayed with you tonight, Sis. I'm glad you feel strong enough to tell me all this. Now, Mom and I had already decided we didn't trust Philip. We're taking turns for shifts with you until you're out of the hospital. Then, you're going to my apartment, not back to the loft. I'll get your diary while you're in surgery tomorrow. Then later, I'll go to the police. We'll nail his greedy ass, I promise."

Becca felt a strong pull. She knew from previous experiences that she was being drawn back to the body she'd left lying on the bed in the Redwood hotel in Crescent City... *I have to go now, good luck with.........*

Again as before, Becca felt herself spinning. Then the breathless speed passed the distant light. Finally, she experienced the feeling of falling with a collapse into Delphi's body. The clock struck two-o-clock AM as she oriented herself to her room. She closed her eyes and fell into a peaceful sleep.

Becca awoke to the sound of rain on the roof and remembered that her window was opened. She jumped up and rushed to close it.

The curtain was soaked; it had been raining for a while. She used the chamber pot and retuned to bed. The clock struck five-thirty. Hannah would soon be knocking to remind her to get up for another half day of work. Becca settled under the quilt for thirty minutes of thinking while she waited. Her muscles were sore from yesterday's labor... *My own body wouldn't be sore. It was in shape from running and swimming, but Delphi must not have gotten much exercise. Guess I'll be doing her a favor if I shape her up.*

Then she thought of her own body. *It's broken and may never walk again...* The happy mood she had when awakening fell into a new low, the first depression she had felt since the incident. During the quiet of the morning Becca made more plans that would include cooperation from Delphi and Beth, but for now she must concentrate on surviving in Delphi's small fragile body with only her savings. Hannah knocked at her door.

"Come in," she beckoned.

The girl stepped inside with a gloomy face. "It's raining horribly."

"Yes, it is," Becca smiled, even though she didn't feel inclined to do so.

"So what's for breakfast today?"

Hannah smiled. "Its whole-hog today. A farmer brought some eggs and butter into town yesterday afternoon. Mrs. O'Shay bought three dozen eggs and four pounds of butter. She's feeling quite pert about it."

Remembering she had chores, Hannah left quickly. Becca began her morning routine. Her work dress didn't look too bad, she noted. The spot cleaning with soda water had removed the stains and perspiration from the underarms. She retrieved the new undergarments from a drawer. Dressing as fast as she could, she even put on the corset, and laced it to a comfortable tightness.

When she entered the dining room she was surprised to see a full house. A crewman from Brother Jonathan was there. Mr. Barrett was assisting Elsie who appeared to have recovered from her previous grief. Mr. and Mrs. O'Shay were at the ends of the table. A new couple was present that Becca hadn't seen before. They had checked in the previous evening, she was told. Another man, a friend of Mr. Barrett was also present. ..*Word must have gotten around that the Redwood Hotel was serving eggs and butter.*

Becca found herself seated between Hannah and the new male guest. He was in military dress, and the uniform wasn't one Becca recognized. Through conversation, she learned he was from Fort Lincoln. He was a sergeant in town to oversee young soldiers on two-day passes. He stressed how he dreaded the ride back to the fort in the rain.

Becca enjoyed the two eggs and ate heartily. She generously spread the hot cakes with butter and jam. By the end of her second cup of coffee, she wondered if she would have to loosen the corset strings.

The conversation was lively and enjoyable. Several times Becca caught Mr. Barrett looking at her from across the table. When he caught her attention, he smiled. She smiled back, wondering at his interest... *Perhaps, he feels we are acquainted now that he escorted me to Chinatown. I can't help but think that Miss Barns has a crush on him.*

The Sergeant excused himself, saying that he must round up his men. "I'm expecting trouble," he said with a sigh. "They've been mightily liquored up for two days and are probably all-overish."

"Do you want me to come along, in case some of them are contrary?" Mr. Barrett offered.

"Sure. Don't mind some company. Just finding where they've dropped their good-for' nothin' bodies is going to take a spell."

The two men left and so did the ship crewman, explaining that he would continue to search the shorelines for bodies. Elsie moved to the parlor and Mr. O'Shay attended to errands. Hannah and Becca surveyed the table of dirty dishes that would be their first task of the day. As they gathered them, they scraped scraps into a slop bucket; Becca wondered about the surgery in the far off time, in the Portland hospital.

"So, today is ironing, right?" she asked Hannah.

Hannah nodded. "The silver needs polishing. While you wash the dishes, I'll tidy the chambers. Then, we'll start the Tuesday work."

Becca thought the dishwashing would never end. She couldn't remember life without an automatic dishwasher. Hannah demonstrated how to shave off slivers of a bar of lye soap, pour boiling water over the soap pieces, and then cool it down with cold water. She grabbed a broom and dustpan as she headed up the back stairway.

Molly sat at the kitchen table counting coins she had earned for the morning's breakfast. She stacked them and wrote the amounts down in a ledger. She appeared pleased.

Very soon, the dishwater grew cool and greasy. Becca had to start with a new pan of hot water to complete the task. She dried every dish and placed it in the cupboard. The tight fitting seams of her dress made lifting her arms to the high shelf difficult... *If I'm around here for very long I will learn how to sew a comfortable dress.*

When Hannah returned from the chambers, she introduced Becca to the laundry room. A large table was covered with a sheepskin, wool side up. Hannah built fire in a small wood stove, and sat four metal irons on top. Each iron had layers of cloth wrapped around the handles to avoid burns to the hands. She carried over two large baskets of washed and air dried laundry. Demonstrating how to sprinkle water on the various items and follow with the heated iron from the stove, she cautioned about the danger of burning the fabric if one didn't keep the iron moving. As one iron cooled, she replaced it with another. Becca cringed as Hannah, spit on her finger and touched the iron to test it for temperature. If the touch resulted in a sizzle sound, Hannah proceeded... *So thermostats in this century are blistered fingers?*

"How do you tolerate the heat in this room, Hannah? I can hardly breathe." Becca complained after an hour of continuous work.

"I just got used to it, I reckon." She didn't miss a swipe with the iron.

Becca walked to the door that led out to the back yard and ally. She opened it and announced,

"Look Hannah, it's stopped raining, lets leave the door open for fresh air. "

Hannah said nothing, but stacked the folded pillowcases she had completed and set them aside.

"Have you ever ironed a shirt, Delphi?"

"No, is it different from the sheets and pillows cases?"

"Yes, shirts are starched so it's easy to scorch them. I'll iron Mr. O'Shay's shirts, and you can take these ironed linens upstairs to the linen closet."

Becca jumped at the chance to get out of the tiny room. She felt a bit guilty that a teenager could outwork her without a single complaint. *Well, at least I managed to finish two sheets and a pillowcase without burning holes in them.*

After the shirts were completed, Hannah coached Becca through the process of ironing her dress while she ironed Molly's. They then put the irons away, swept the room and returned to the kitchen. Hannah pulled out a silver service, including knives, forks and spoons. She set them on the kitchen table.

Becca felt exhausted, she was certain the corset had turned sideways. The petticoats were hot and uncomfortable ... *Maybe it's my nightlife. .. Darting between centuries is wearing me out...* "At least we can sit down for this, right?" she pulled out a chair.

The task of polishing each item wasn't difficult, but time consuming. By the time they put things away, Molly was stirring the mutton soup, preparing the mid-day meal. As soon as her chores were finished, she escaped to her room. Opening the window, she stripped down to her skin. Remembering that her door had no lock and Hannah's occasional impulsiveness about opening it, she propped the chair under the glass door knob and reclined on the bed. Just as she started to doze off, Hannah knocked on the door.

"Mrs. O'Shay is sending me to The Mercantile to tote notions back for her. Do you want to come along?"

17

"Physical attraction is common, mental attraction is rare."

—UNKNOWN

Becca dressed quickly in her one good dress, tidied up her hair, grabbed the blue parasol, and met Hannah in the parlor. Hannah took an old one from the hall stand. Now that the rain had stopped, the sun was shining. A woman must keep her skin white and prevent tanning whenever possible. This was at least one practice of the century that Becca found agreeable. She enjoyed the walk and took notice of her surroundings. Once at The Mercantile, Becca looked at the books, while Hannah shopped for the items she was sent for. James wandered over and asked if she wish to purchase a book.

"I haven't finished the one I bought from you a few days ago. I'm also reading another as well...*That journal is taking up my reading time.*

James initiated a conversation about 'Great Expectations' that he had been reading. She was enjoying this exchange when Hannah approached her with her bundles. As the women reached the hotel, Mr. Barrett approached in the same buggy he had taken to

Chinatown. Hannah took the parcels into Molly. Becca nodded a response to his greeting.

"I'm taking some newspapers to Second Street. I thought you might want to ride along and check on the orders you have at the Leng's."

"I would like that. Perhaps she has something finished, and I can bring it back."

Mr. Barrett got down and assisted her into the buggy. She wondered if he took notice of her stiff torso, armored in her corset.

As they entered the street Mr. Barrett began conversation immediately. "I want to express to you, my admiration regarding your hard work for Mrs. O'Shay. I know a lady from your background must be unaccustomed to such menial tasks. Taking it on with such dedication is a sign of good character."

I think that's a compliment... "Thank you, Mr. Barrett. I felt it necessary to earn my room and board. I can't afford to pay for it forever, and I would never expect to be provided food and lodging free of charge."

"It must be difficult, after being accustomed to servants," he stated.

"I've never had a servant in my entire life," Becca blurted.

"I used the word servant as a polite reference to the slaves that served most of you in the south," he said.

Becca felt herself ruffle. "Excuse me, Sir; I don't remember ever informing you of taking part in the hideous practice of enslaving another person. Why would you assume anything so dreadful?"

"I beg you pardon Ma'am, I meant no offense." His face reddened. "I was told you were born and raised in Louisiana. That was one of the slave states. I just returned from a war that was, in part, to end the practice. I couldn't help but notice, the other day at the Leng's; you had a good deal of money in your purse. You must have come from wealthy stock."

Becca's mind was racing...*What did I just read in the journal? Oh no, he's right. Delphi's parents did own slaves until they were forced to sell them four years before* the war, to pay her father's gambling bills... Should I admit to that? Maybe I should just makeup my own history... but then I would have to remember everything I said... Or, I could skip that part of her history... I could jump ahead and tell what truth I know, and hope he doesn't ask more questions... I can't know my entire history anyway, until I finish reading Delphi's journal.

Becca took a deep breath. "Actually, Mr. Barrett, my father died when I was quite young, and my mother made hats in a Millinery shop. We had to live with relatives. I have no memories of a privileged childhood, much less one regarding slaves." *There, that's mostly true.*

"I see... I wasn't passing judgment Miss Castile. I was attempting to pay a compliment.".

"I understand," she smiled at him. "And your childhood, Mr. Barrett, where did you call home?" *It's best to move this focus away from me.*

"I grew up on a farm in Kansas. It was raided and burnt by Jayhawkers during the war."

"And why, pray tell, did you come to California? Were you seeking gold?" Becca asked.

"No, I'm not interested in striking it rich. I just wanted to get as far away as possible from the reminders of the war. California was somewhat removed from all that. People here hardly took notice of our president's assassination, so detached were they of the conflict."

Oh my goodness... that did just happen... wow and I hadn't even thought of it... there's been no discussion about it... without cable news, events are less dramatic...I should at least comment.... "That was horrible. I can't believe anyone would feel justified in killing the President."

"He was a good man; it was malice, pure malice." Mr. Barrett's face took on a sad expression.

They stopped at Leng's Shop and Mr. Barrett assisted Becca out of the carriage. Mud surrounded the small shops along the street. Chinatown didn't have the wooden walks like Front Street. She picked her way through the puddles, pulling her skirts up enough to assure they didn't drag. Becca was amazed that Mrs. Lang was almost finished with the black velvet party dress. She had hoped she would make the house dresses first, but she didn't complain. "I have all complete... in two more days," explained the seamstress in her broken English. "You try on?"

Becca followed her into the backroom. Behind the screen, she changed into the new frock.

As she stepped out, Mrs. Lang's face lit up. "Yes, yes, vedy Predy."

The seamstress poked and tugged at the garment until she was satisfied with the fit, and then pinned up the hem to the appropriate length. Becca changed back and returned to the front of the shop where Mr. Barrett stood visiting with Mr. Leng.

"You pick up Fliday?" Mrs. Leng asked.

Becca glanced at her companion. He nodded. "I can pick it up and bring it to you, Miss Castile. Is Friday morning all right?"

"Yes, yes, morning good, yes."

Back in the buggy, Mr. Barrett looked a Becca and smiled. "You look pleased about that new frock. Did she do good work?"

"Yes, lovely work!" *I can't believe anyone could make such tiny, tight stitches by hand."*

"How else could she make them?" he asked in puzzlement

...I can't believe I said that... I have to think before blurting out... Of course there are no sewing machines available yet. "I meant that I couldn't believe she did so much sewing so fast."

"It'd be a blamed shame not to wear your fancy new frock right away."

He directed the horse around the worse of the mud holes to avoid splashing.

"Well, I don't plan to wear a black velvet dress with long black gloves while helping Hannah clean house." She laughed at the image in her mind.

"There's a dance in town Friday night, shall we take your new frock for a frolic?" He glanced at her with a sideway look.

Dance? What kind of dances did they do in the eighteen-sixties? Nothing like what I'm use to, I'll bet... "I would love to, but I must confess, I don't know how to dance." *I hate saying this. I can dance circles around everyone else in my own setting...* "I actually have never been to a dance," *Not your kind, anyway.*

"Well, it's not hard. If a Kansas clod-hopper, with a bum leg can learn, it can't be too hard."

Becca suddenly remembered Elsie and the adoring glances she directed toward Mr. Barrett... *accepting this invitation might cause conflict.*

"Mr. Barrett, I'm sure Miss Barns can dance splendidly. Are you sure you wouldn't prefer to take her?"

He looked annoyed. "If that had been my preference, I would have asked her. Miss Barns is but a child like Hannah. I asked you."

"I accept, thank you." *I can't believe my heart is pounding like a school girl's... I'm a married woman, after all... Or, am I? Philip hasn't even been born yet...I'm in Delphi's body, and she's single... she's going to the dance... So why do I feel so excited... and a bit guilty? This is all so confusing.*

Becca entered the hotel and started toward the stairs. A voice summoned her from the parlor. "Miss Castile...Delphi?"

Stepping into the room, Becca saw Elsie sitting on the sofa, working on embroidery.

"Yes, Miss Barns, did you call me?"

"Please, come and sit for a spell."

Becca wanted to get back to her room, but she sat in a nearby chair and watched the girl push a needle in and out of fabric that was stretched and secured in a small round frame.

"Hannah said the two of you went to The Mercantile with Mr. Barrett."

"Yes, but actually, Hannah and I were on an errand for Molly. Mr. Barrett offered a ride,"

"He has also escorted you to Chinatown thrice, once without a chaperone." *Where is this leading? Am I being chastised by a sixteen-year old?*

"No, not thrice, only two times. And why are you asking Miss Barns?"

"Well, Minnie admonished us, you and me, to begin anew. And, if you're noticed being untoward with Mr. Barrett, people may suspect your past." Elsie continued stitching without looking up.

"May I call you Elsie?" Becca asked.

The girl nodded.

"Elsie, are you worried about my reputation, or are you interested in Mr. Barrett and fearful he might become interested in me?" she asked softly.

Elsie blushed a dark red. She moved her face closer to her work.

"It's all right to have a crush Elsie, but from what you told me, I thought you were grieving for Hayden."

Elsie looked up at Becca. "Yes, I suppose I am, but Hayden is gone, and I have to go on living. I have to find a husband."

Becca took a deep breath... *How horrible, that these girls feel it necessary to marry so young.*

"Elsie, you're barely sixteen. You recently lost your parents and now the man with whom you fell in love." *If it's even possible to fall in love in a few hours.*

She touched Elsie's hand. "The last thing you should be doing now is rushing into a romance. Minnie offered you a home and a job. You've plenty of time to choose a mate."

So, Miss Castile...

"Please call me Bec...Delphi."

"Delphi, so are you and Mr. Barrett courting?"

Courting... is accepting an invitation to a dance considered courting? "I really hadn't thought about it, but he just asked me to the dance on Friday night and I accepted. Is that courting, in your opinion?"

"Why yes, courting it is, ever so much so," Elsie looked both disappointed and annoyed.

"Elsie, do you want to hear a secret? I don't even know how to dance." Becca covered her mouth and forced a coy giggle. *I feel like I'm acting a part in, Gone with the Wind.*

Oh, dancing is ever so simple, Delphi, I can show you."

"That would be perfect. But what would we use for music?"

"Minnie can play piano a bit. She told me that she played for church sometimes. There's sheet music in that cabinet." Elsie nodded toward it.

"Then let's have a dance class tomorrow evening, following supper," suggested Becca.

"Yes let's do, and I'll ask Mrs., O'Shay if we can make it a gathering. Perhaps she'll provide refreshments."

Elsie set her stitch work down beside her. "But, Delphi, I remember you telling me that you are a good dancer. Didn't you dance with your customers while you were working for Lilly?"

"If I told you that, I was teasing or exaggerating. Most of whatever I told you was more than likely not true. Please just forget it all."

Elsie looked back at her. Her expression indicated she was not convinced.

"Good. Then it's decided," said Becca, getting up. "I must rest now. The morning wore me out."

In her room, she thought back on the conversation with Elsie … *There, that may head off some hard feelings… She's leaving with Minnie in a couple of weeks… I hope she doesn't blab whatever information Delphi confided in her before she leaves.*

Picking up her new book, *Lady Audley's Secret,* she settled down to read. Soon, she was engrossed. Hannah's summons at the door pulled her from the story's engaging plot. Becca went to the door and opened it.

"I think I'll eat in my room tonight, Hannah, what's for supper?"

"It's ham and beans, but Mr. Barrett asked me to tell you he would be honored if you'll come down for supper." Hannah's smile was suspicious.

Several strangers were at the table. Elsie took supper in her room. Becca was quickly directed by Molly to set next to Mr. Barrett. She offered an understanding smile…*Geez, there's a lot of assumption going on.* ..Supper was pleasant. Hannah reported to Becca that Mrs. O'Shay had started working on her new pink dress. The crewmen talked about the efforts of locating more of the missing from the shipwreck. Mr. Barrett shared his success in sending telegrams to the families of those who had been identified. Mr. O'Shay explained the progress of burying bodies, now recovered.

"Did you have family or friends traveling with you, Miss Castile?" Mr. O'Shay asked.

"No, I was alone." She quickly asked for him to please pass the butter for her bread... *I'll keep him distracted from more questions.*

After the meal and a half hour talking with those who gathered in the parlor, she hurried to her room. Off came the wool dress, petticoats and corset. Completing her evening hygiene, she grabbed the journal and climbed into bed.

> **September 30, 1861**...*She has skipped over a month, did she tear out pages? Becca examined the binding closely. No, there aren't pages missing.*
>
> **I have been in such désespoir. I have had no will to pen my thoughts. Just as we thought we had paid off all les dettes de papa, we find there are even more. He dû signed so many contrats to repay argent, what was he réflexion? Ma Mère has nothing more to give. She cessions her salaires each week, but there are still dettes. The court has déterminé that I must take an emploi as a serviteur to help pay les dettes de papa. All salaires will be given over to débiteurs. Mère cried all night**...*Oh, my goodness. Your papa was a piece of work, girl. So, even after selling everything, more debts surfaced. Could they force a child to work off her father's debts? Apparently they could. No wonder you ran away. There was no way to know how many more creditors would be popping up.*

The spinning started, the accelerating speed past the bright light and into an undefined passage of time, and finally Becca was in the hospital room, hovering near Beth. She looked at the body, her own body, lying on the bed. The face was ghastly white, the eyes closed. Her mother walked into the room and approached the bed.

"Has she awakened while I was gone?" she asked Beth.

"No, but the nurse checks her often, and her vitals are strong."

"I talked to the surgeon as I came in just now. He was leaving so it was lucky I ran into him. He said everything went very well."

"Yes, he talked to me too. He says Becca's strong and healthy. We should be hopeful. She should respond well to therapy. You know how determined she is, Mom."

"Did you get the stuff she asked for? When she awakes, I want her to have it."

"Yes, Mom, it's in the briefcase under her bed. I also put in a pen and extra paper. I got her a new cell phone as well. I don't want Phil to know I've brought the case, so it's tucked under there, out of sight."

"Did you have any difficulty finding the diary or getting into the apartment, dear?"

Beth shook her head. "No he wasn't there, and the diary was exactly where she said it would be. That tart is staying there with him. Her stuff is all over the loft….You spoke to the police, Mom. Do they believe what you reported to them? Beth asked.

"I think so, but they need to talk with Becca, question Phillip, and speak with those associates who went with them that weekend. There's no evidence, yet."

Beth was thoughtful. "Maybe there's something in the diary…"

The spinning returned. No, not yet…

18

"I've never seen a bird soar without turbulence; adversity lifts him up."

—WILBER WRIGHT

The jolt of the merging of spirit and body was less impacting each time it occurred, Becca noticed. She sighed and resigned herself to fall to asleep. The bells of the striking, grandfather clock awakened her at four-o-clock. *If it wasn't for that dependable old time piece, I'd have no idea what time it is. This is too early to wake up and face the day. What day of the month is it? I wish I had a calendar, I've not noticed one anywhere. How do they keep tract of days and months?*

She got up and sat down at the secretary. Pulling out the drawer, she picked up the papers on which she had written earlier in the week...

Now to make a calendar...while I still have some idea of how much time has passed...Becca selected a clean sheet of paper and picked up a rustic pencil. Using her new book as a straight edge to guide her line-drawing, she created a seven column table. She added five horizontal lines and wrote August 1865 on the top. After adding the days of the week across the top of the squares, her calendar was almost complete...*My rescue occurred on July 30ᵗʰ and that was Sunday in this Century. That makes yesterday August 1ˢᵗ...*She wrote the number one on the fourth top square and added the remaining thirty numbers.

Becca noticed a nail on the wall above the desk...*It must have been used to hang a picture...*She pressed the calendar against the nail, piercing the paper so that it hung securely. She studied it and felt satisfied with its appearance...*Now, I feel oriented... sort of... This is August second... My birthday will be next month... No, wait, that's Becca birthday... I'm not in Becca's body... so I need to find Delphi's birthday. She wrote that in the journal.* Becca retrieved the journal from the bedside table and flipped the page to the first entry. *..Her birthday is August fourth. That's the day after tomorrow. How old is she...am I?*

She referred back to the journal entry...*Delphi wrote this on her seventeenth birthday... so it's dated 1861. That means I'm four years older now... I'll be twenty years old. That feels strange... Not only did I go back in time but back in age as well... I guess it could have been worse. I might have entered the body of an ailing elderly person or of a man... That would have taken more adjustment than this...*Hannah knocked on her door.

"Delphi, are you awake?"

"Yes, come in, Hannah."

The girl entered as lively as always. She started making Becca's bed as she announced the plans for their day.

"You don't have to make my bed, Hannah; I always get to it after I dress," Becca stood at the washbasin where she brushed her teeth.

"I'm just venturing help while you ready yourself, today we bake. Baking day is my most preferred day of all. Since Mrs. O'Shay now has eggs and butter, we can make a cake. We often make pies, since blackberries are so plentiful. Then of course, we'll make bread. Have you ever made bread Delphi?"

Becca, having put on all the inner layers of under clothing was stepping into her work dress. "Yes I have, actually. I've made it many times in my bread maker machine."

"What's that?" asked Hannah, halting her plumping of the feather pillow and looking at Becca with questioning eyes.

"Never mind, could you braid my hair?"

After a breakfast of a hot gruel that Molly called cornmeal mush, Becca took on the chore of dishwashing while Hannah tended to the chambers. Soon they were standing at the table viewing crocks of flour and sugar.

Their first project was the cake. Molly had the cook stove already heated, and the needed utensils and items were setting on the kitchen table. Hannah handed Becca, Molly's cook book.

"Be careful with this. It belonged to Mrs. O'Shay's grandmother, and it's very old. Read the directions to me while I mix it all together."

"Two dollops of soft butter, each the size of an egg," she read... *What?*

Hannah seemed to have no issue with the measuring method, retrieving the large dish of butter from the laundry room where it had been kept away from the heat of the kitchen. She scooped out a blob, looked it over and said. "That's about right." She repeated the process and returned the butter to the adjoining room.

"Two handfuls of sugar," Becca read. *Handfuls?*

Hannah reached her hand into a crock of a light brown raw sugar and dumped each handful into the butter... *I certainly hope she washed her hands after dumping the chamber pots. We will have to have a talk about hand washing. This is scary.* Hannah fiercely stirred these ingredients in the large bowl until the combination was a satin smooth consistency. "Now what?" she asked.

"Four eggs, followed by a scoop of baking powder." *What size scoop?*

Hannah cracked the eggs into the mixture and tipped the baking powder tin. She scooped out baking powder, and stirred it together.

"Now the flour is next, right?"

"Yes, five sifted handfuls," Becca responded, "and enough milk to make it proper... *I guess proper means whatever's needed for the right consistency ... Pretty hard to measure out a handful of milk...*

Becca smiled to herself. She tried to imagine her own mother cooking anything without carefully measuring each ingredient... *These coarse food items are very different. The sugar is brown and coarse and I'm sure the flour is whole wheat.*

Molly had buttered and floured round cake pans and set them on the table. Hannah divided the batter and placed them in the oven.

"Now we'll start the bread. I know how to do this so we can put that away."

Hannah took the cookbook from Becca who was flipping curiously through the pages.

"I can make it," offered Becca, wanting to appear somewhat knowledgeable. "I always start with two cups of warm water, a spoonful of sugar and two packages of yeast."

Hannah looked at her with her usual confused expression and walked to the cupboard. She took out a large jar filled with a gooey substance, and brought it to the table along with another large bowl.

"What in heck is that?" Becca turned up her nose.

"Why it's the sourdough, Delphi, what did you reckon it could be?"

Hannah poured some of the sticky stuff into the large bowl, tossed a handful of sugar in, and added a small amount of warm milk that had been setting in a pitcher by the stove. Stirring it together, she covered it with a cup towel that she referred to as tea towel.

"There, in a while it'll be ready, but now we can start the pies."

Becca watched as Hannah added flour and water back into the sourdough jar. The girl replaced the lid and tightened it. After shaking the container, she placed it back in the cupboard.

"I don't feel that I'm very helpful," complained Becca.

"You can start washing the bowls and spoons we've used. "

While doing this, Becca watched Hannah empty two blue-tinted glass jars of blackberries into a large pan, and add sugar and spices, to prepare the filling for the pies.

"This is the last of Mrs. O'Shay's canned berries. She wants me to pick berries this afternoon. Would you like to help?"

Becca thought about how hot it would be. Picking berries in long sleeves under an afternoon sun would be miserable. She was tempted to decline, but she thought of poor Hannah having to work twice as long if she didn't help. She agreed.

Once the bread, cakes and pies were baked and cooling by an open window, Becca and Hannah cleaned the kitchen while Molly whipped up frosting from egg whites and sugar. Becca marveled how the woman could beat the mixture tirelessly with only a hand-turn beater. Muscles in her forearms revealed themselves from the exertion.

After their noonday meal, they headed for a berry patch. Each carried a large basket. Hannah led them the short way to the shore line. Becca was relieved from the cool sea breeze that constantly blew over the large area of blackberry bushes... *How lucky they are to have so many berries growing wild like this.*

A rustling noise caught her attention and a flash of movement drew her eyes to the outer edge of the patch, nearest the sea. Hannah looked startled and stood perfectly still.

"Is that a bear, Hannah?" Becca whispered.

"No, Hannah said quietly. " It's an Indian."

Becca focused hard to determine if the form crouching in the tall blackberry brush was a bear or human.

"Are you sure, Hannah? What exactly did you see?"

"It wasn't a bear, Delphi, bears don't have long hair."

Hannah looked like she was ready to spring into a rapid retreat. Becca tried to calm her.

"If it's not a bear, it's probably someone picking berries, just like us."

"It's an Indian. They're supposed to stay on the reservation. If he's running around here, he's up to no good. Let's start screaming, Delphi."

"Don't you dare! Don't create an alarm unless something happens to make that necessary. You start walking toward town, and I'll watch from here. If whatever, this is follows you, I'll attack from behind. I really don't think there's anything to fear."

"I can't leave you here to get scalped!" the girl protested.

"It's ok, Hannah. I have a black belt. I know martial arts." Well, at least I did in my own body, unhampered by skirts, corset, and petticoats.

Hannah looked at her doubtingly.

"What's a belt going to do? And where is it? I don't see a belt. And art never saved anyone. Let's just run."

"Never mind that, just start walking back with your berries; I'll follow as soon as I know you're within a safe distance of Front Street."

Hannah started hesitantly, then increased her pace, then broke into a run. Becca watched the dark, shadowy form that had caused their concern. It moved slowly as though to reposition itself, perhaps to see better as Hannah left the area. There was no indication that a chase would follow.

Becca silently set down her basket of berries, and pulled her skirts above her ankles to avoid the noise of dragging them over sticks and twigs. She quietly moved around the perimeter of the large patch to get a better look.

She stopped as the figure came into view. A girl, no older than Hannah, was squatting down, and peering through the bushes in the direction Hannah had gone. Long black hair hung down her back and encircled her on the ground. She wore a skirt of grass and a halter type top, of leather. A large basket of berries sat beside her.

"Don't be afraid of me." Becca said softly.

The child spun around. Terror filled her face. She quickly rose to her feet. She appeared to be preparing to bolt.

"No, don't' leave, I mean you no harm."

The ebony eyes looked at Becca intensely as she halted her retreat.

"Do you speak English?"

The girl nodded, "Yes."

Becca moved a step closer. Her counterpart moved a step back.

"I'm new here," she began. "I have no reason to hurt you. My name is Delphi, what's yours?"

"Your people named me Sarah; my people call me a different name. If you tell others about me, soldiers will look for me. If they find me, they will send me back to the rancher who bought me."

"I won't tell. We can't talk now." Becca eyed Front Street for signs of an unneeded rescue approaching, "But I want to be your friend."

She took off the locket from around her neck. Reaching out her full arm's length, she handed it to Sarah. Sarah gingerly took it and looked at the gold heart.

"For me?"

Delphi smiled, "Yes, as a sign of my good intentions. Let's meet here right after sundown. Is that acceptable to you? I'll bring food."

The girl smiled for the first time. She reached up and took a long leather cord from her neck and handed it to Delphi. Delphi accepted it and thanked her. The girl picked up her berry-filled basket, and quickly slipped down the bank toward the sea... *She'll be invisible, slipping away under the shelter of the sea cliffs, I'm glad it's low tide. But then, I'm sure she planned that out.*

Becca retrieved her basket and moved to the area that the native had been successful in gathering an abundant harvest. As she quickly picked each individual berry and dropped it in the basket, she saw Mr. O'Shay and Mr. Barrett coming rapidly over the bank that separated her from a view of front Street. Each carried a rifle. As they approached she called out.

"I'm over here; did you two come to assist with my task of gathering these lovely fruits?"

Mr. O'Shay's face was a bright red from his exertion. His protruding belly was probably the cause of his breathlessness. Mr. Barrett's face held an expression of concern. Hannah said you were out here alone with an Indian"

Becca glanced around. "Do you see an Indian? I don't see one." She continued to drop the berries in the basket before popping one into her mouth.

Mr. O'Shay walked around the area with his rifle in ready position while Mr. Barrett studied Becca intently.

"What was it then? Something scared that gal? She's plumb streaked right out of her head."

"She's more than likely heard horror stories about Indians like the silly rumors that claim children will disappear in Chinatown," she answered.

"So you're telling me, she saw nothing?" He started picking berries from a nearby vine.

"She saw something, a wild creature, no doubt. But, whatever it was, it's gone now so let's surprise Molly with a basketful of these luscious berries."

Mr. O'Shay wandered back, announcing that he found no trace of a renegade Indian. He then returned to give reassurance to Molly, Hannah, and anyone else she may have alarmed.

"Tell Molly, I'll be back as soon as my basket is filled." called Becca.

"And tell her also," Mr. Barrett added, "I'll stay to guard Miss Castile's safety while she fills the basket."

19

"Sharing and giving are the ways of God."

—Sauk Tribal Proverb

Another hour alone with this interesting man was welcomed by Becca. She couldn't imagine how anyone ever got acquainted during this time period and its extensive supervision.

"Guess what," she began the conversation, "I'm taking a dance lesson from Elsie tonight."

"That's a capital idea, at the hotel?"

"Yes, Minnie is coming over to play the piano, and I guess Molly knows a few tunes as well."

"I'm bringing a young officer in for supper tonight. He has a few days away from the Fort. If we stay for the music, he might ask Elsie to tomorrow's dance."

"That would be nice," agreed Becca. "But if you watch my efforts, you must promise not to laugh."

"Pshaw! I won't watch, I'll teach the lesson. And, if someone laughs, he'll get a dose of this!" He raised a fist and shook it, then laughed.

Thad plopped down and patted a grassy area beside him. Becca dropped to the ground. Her skirts created a nest around her. Becca told him about her morning in the kitchen. Thad shared stories from his childhood. They agreed to address one another by first names. A quick drop of temperature reminded them of the lateness of the day.

Thad stood and held out his hand. Becca took it and held tight as he pulled her up. He didn't release it. Scooping up the basket with his other arm, he gently pulled her in the direction of Front Street.

As they approached the street, Thad dropped her hand and smiled. When they reached the hotel, he handed her the basket and entered the front door. Walking around the building and into the back door, Becca sat the loaded basket on the kitchen worktable.

Hannah busily mashed potatoes in a large bowl as Molly removed a large roasted leg of lamb from the oven. Becca moved over close to Hannah and whispered. "It turned out all right. I'll tell you about it later."

"I don't fancy the way you made a fool of me, Delphi!" she said tersely.

"What do you mean?" Becca asked in surprise.

"Mr. O'Shay came back laughing at how I probably got scared of a silly raccoon. I know I saw an Indian," she pouted.

"Ahh, don't pay attention to him. Men like to joke around about women being scary cats. I'll spin a yarn at supper about a big old bear. We'll get the last laugh."

"Why not just tell everyone it was an Indian? That's the truth, after all."

Molly had left the kitchen, for which Becca was grateful.

"Hannah, were you old enough to remember the Indian War about a decade ago?"

"Yes, just barely," she answered.

"Do you know that before, during, and after that, hundreds of Indians were hunted down and slaughtered by settlers and miners? Most of their population was wiped out with mass murder as well as diseases they caught from settlers and miners"

"How do you know that?" she asked.

"It's written in history." Becca answered, stirring butter into the cooked carrots.

"Well...I never read that during my schoolin," she replied.

"You will...eventually."

Hannah seemed thoughtful and then offered, "That probably happened because they're dangerous, they were bothering folks."

"A few were dangerous because they had been promised things by the government. Those treaties were broken to appease the settlers, lumber companies and gold miners. But most weren't dangerous. They were just people living on land they had occupied for hundreds of years. Then, miners moved in for the gold, settlers moved in for the land, industry moved in for the redwood lumber and salmon fishing. The intruders didn't want to share it with the true owners of the land, they wanted them gone."

"What's that got to do with me?" the girl asked, showing a pouty face.

"Would we wish to be the cause of one more innocent Indian being shot for simply picking berries for food?"

"No, I guess not. Let's just tell them your bear story, then... What's that?"

Becca's eyes followed Hannah's to her apron. The cord, laced with shells and sea snails, peeked from the top of the pocket.

"That's a friendship gift. I'll tell you tonight at bedtime. Let's get supper on the table." She pushed the laced shells deeper into her pocket.

Supper was celebratory. Molly was in rare spirits. She seemed pleased that a social event was being held in her parlor later in the evening. Elsie was in hostess mode since having the dance practice was her idea. Hannah became giddy, having never attended a social gathering of males and females. Mr. O'Shay was thrilled at the hearty meal and with promise of cake later.

Minnie and little Albert were in attendance. She reported that her telegram to Elsie's guardian had been sent, and she looked forward for a prompt reply. Her plan was explained to everyone. Elsie would move East with her family, and become her governess. She'd not need to live with the dreaded aunt.

Becca's mind wandered to another time and the events going on at the Portland Hospital...*I wonder how recovery is going for Delphi in my body... I hope she feels well enough soon to read my diary... I want to discover if it has the same effect as reading hers has for me.*

There was too much continuous conversation for anyone to tease Hannah about her frightening experience, so Becca had no need to fabricate a bear story. She drifted in and out of her thoughts, thinking about Sarah... *Will she come back to meet with me? Maybe she'll fear it's a trap... I'll take some lamb and fresh bread.*

Becca glanced around to those nearest her. They appeared to be occupied with food and talk. She opened the linen napkin onto her lap and slipped her portion of lamb from her plate into the napkin. She then buttered a bun and placed it on the meat. Wrapping it in the napkin, she took a bite of cooked carrots. As her gaze fell across the table, she noticed Thad watching her. His expression reflected a question...*Did he see what I just did?* She smiled at him while scooping up a bite of mashed potatoes. He returned the smile and winked... *I guess flirting styles don't change from one era to another.*

When the meal was over, Hannah and Molly began the task of cleaning up. Minnie and Elsie moved to the parlor so that they could select the sheet music for dancing. Thad and his officer friend left to spend some time in the El Sol before returning to be part of the activities. Becca scurried up to her room and grabbed Delphi's cape that had been washed and pressed since its baptism in the ocean. Running down the back stairs, she quietly left through the kitchen door while Molly and Hannah cleared the table in the dining room.

The western sky framed a sinking sun. The scrubs, bushes, and tilted trees between her and the coastline were silhouettes against the backdrop of orange, pink, and grey. She walked hastily toward the berry bushes where she had met Sarah. Reaching the shrubbery, she circled around just as she had earlier in the day when she first spotted her. Her heart sank when she saw nothing. Then, a thin, brown arm reached through the branches and Sarah crawled from her hiding place.

"I was afraid you wouldn't come," said Becca.

"I hid. I feared you would bring others."

Becca held out the small food bundle. "I brought you something. I hope you like lamb."

Sarah took the offering and looked sadly at Becca. "I have no gift."

"That doesn't matter; eat." Becca's time was short and she hoped to have an opportunity to learn more about the girl. *She is so thin.*

Sarah opened the napkin and smelled the food. She appeared hesitant.

"Some of my people have been poisoned in the past," she muttered.

"That food is safe," Becca insisted. "Here, I'll take a bite of it and eat it right in front of you."

She tore a tiny strip from the large portion of meat and chewed it up as Sara watched. The girl followed her example, and also ate half of the bread. Then, she carefully rewrapped what remained.

"Don't you like it?" asked Becca, knowing the child was hungry by the rapid manner she had devoured the small amount.

"The Grandmother is old. I'll give it to her."

"Are the two of you alone?"

Sarah eyed her suspiciously, but didn't answer.

"I would never cause you or your grandmother harm. Maybe I can be helpful."

"We'll see. I must go. It's dark soon." Sarah turned toward the rocky shore.

"Wait," said Becca, "I want to meet with you again, tomorrow afternoon?"

"Not here." She looked toward the rocky shore and tipped her head to point with her nose toward some jagged rocks.

"Over there."

"When?" asked Becca looking at the boulders, wondering how difficult it would be to climb over the stony natural bridge that connected it. She hadn't felt a desire to go near the water since her drowning experience.

"Not tomorrow... the day that follows."

"Saturday, that's good." *I'm not committed to working for Molly on the weekends.*

"I'll be by the stone that's shaped like a spear as the sun first touches the sky." She pointed to the east to indicated sunrise.

"All right," Becca agreed. "But if I don't show up it is because something stopped me, not because I'm breaking a promise."

Sarah nodded. "As with me." She turned and scampered down the cliff wall.

Becca envied the leather moccasins that gave Sarah the freedom to run and climb. Her own lace-up leather shoes were designed to present a dainty foot and didn't empower her athletically. Darkness was moving in, and with it a thick fog. Becca started back, lifting her skirts to make better time.

"Delphi," a familiar voice startled her. Turning, she saw Thad, standing in the shadows with his hands in his pockets. She placed her hands over her heart.

"Good Grief, Thad, you nearly scared me to death!"

"It's not safe for women to be out alone after sundown." He gently took her elbow and steered her back on course.

"I just needed a little walk and some fresh air to cool down. It's been a full day," she stammered.

"Well, next time request an escort."

Becca looked at Thad intently. "Were you following me?"

Thad waited a few moments before answering. "When Buck and I walked toward the saloon, I saw you come around the building and head for the cliffs. I was worried about you so...yes, I followed you."

Care and concern are not bad things. I can't be angry about that. I'll just have to be more careful. I hope he didn't see Sarah... "I'll remember your advice," she murmured.

He left her at the front door of the Redwood Hotel. She went directly to her room to change into Delphi's wool dressy frock, and to freshen up. Quickly washing up in a basin of cold water, she followed up with a dusting of soda as a deodorant substitute. She splashed rose water on her neck and the sides of her hair. She had never been an overly fussy woman, but she had to admit she missed some of the modern cosmetics and hygiene products to which she was accustomed.

She entered the parlor and walked to the piano. Minnie played a song from sheet music propped up before her. Elsie stood beside her, singing the words. Becca smiled to herself...*This is not much different than karaoke.*

Hannah entered, wearing the new dress that Molly had finished. She proudly spun around as Becca and the other women complimented her. Becca was glad she had bought the fabric for her. Next, Elsie demonstrated dance steps for Becca and Hannah. First she explained the steps and routine of the Quadrille. This would be done in formations of squares and lines. They practiced with the help of Mr. and Mrs. O'Shay filling in for the male roles.

The Polka was livelier and challenging for Hannah, but Becca remembered it from childhood dance classes.

"See, I knew you knew more about dancing than you pretended." Elsie teased.

At last, Thad and Buck arrived. Molly coaxed Leonard, the livery stable's hired boy, to be Hannah's partner. He was no older than Hannah but far more awkward. Becca smiled as they moved around the floor stiff as boards. His hair was parted straight down the middle, but a shock of it insisted on pointing upward. After several hours, Molly announced,

"We all have to rise mighty early in the morning, and you young folk will be dancing all night tomorrow. It's time to wind this down."

"Wait, what about the waltz? Becca asked. "Are we going to practice that one?"

"Oh, I love the waltz," said Elsie. "But some people oppose it."

"Why? What could possibly be wrong with the waltz?"

Thad leaned over and whispered in her ear. "Older people think it's too forward for a couple to dance in an embrace. They prefer the dances that hold partners an arm length. Don't worry; there'll be waltzes tomorrow night, after the older couples retire."

"Where's the cake?" bellowed Mr. O'Shay.

After refreshments, Becca gladly went to her room...*I'm exhausted. Even this lumpy mattress feels good... I'm too tired to read the journal and check on Delphi... I can't even keep my eyes...*

20

"Dance is the hidden language of the soul of the body."

—Martha Graham

Becca awoke early Friday rested but sore. She wiggled her toes and rotated her ankles... *Delphi must not dance much. If she did, her legs wouldn't be killing me now... those narrow, high-topped shoes are torture.*

Her thoughts jumped to Delphi, now suffering in a broken body. She felt a tang of guilt...*I'm at least having some fun... I'll have to check on her, sometime today...* She organized the day in her mind...Cleaning with Hannah all morning is first on the list... *I have my name on the list for a bath. ..Thank God, that will be wonderful...Thad is picking up my dress in Chinatown ... That's exciting.... And finally the dance is tonight... I'll get to Delphi's journal this afternoon, without fail.*

After a breakfast of oatmeal and toast, made in the woodstove oven, Becca worked through her share of the chores without a pause. The routine was the same as Tuesday's so she needed no instruction. Hannah chatted continuously about the night before. Molly agreed to allow her to attend the dance with Leonard, under the chaperoning of Delphi and Thad. The girl was wild with excitement.

Following the mid-day meal, Becca took her bath. She missed shampoo and conditioner, but rinsed her hair with vinegar as Hannah advised. The natural acidity removed all traces of the lye soap. Combing it out would take a good part of her afternoon. During the detangling of one strand at a time with a wooden comb, Hannah knocked at her door.

"Delphi, I have your new frock. Mr. Barrett asked me to bring it to you."

Becca invited her in and she delivered a large flat parcel. As they tore open the packaging, the beautiful black dress with its intricate stitching came into view.

"I've never seen anything so exquisite," said Becca.

"When Mrs. O'Shay sees this, she'll have to change her mind about the skills of Chinatown's seamstress," declared Hannah as Becca hung her newest addition in the armoire. "Mr. Barrett told me to tell you, that Mrs. Leng has another one nearly ready. She'll send it with her delivery boy in the morning."

After the girl left her room, Becca lay on her bed and picked up the journal. She had marked the place where she stopped reading. Rather than turning to the saved page, she flipped the pages to the last entry.

I need to learn more about Delphi's life closer to the time of the shipwreck.... She scanned the late entry she had seen the first day she opened the journal. It described how Delphi hid the coins in her undergarments and skirts hems, but she noticed that it wasn't the final entry after all. She turned the page and saw an entry she hadn't noticed before... *What? How could I have missed this? It looks like a different handwriting and the ink is different. This writing style is familiar...*

August 5, 2015
I am writing this for my sister who continues to recover from spinal surgery. She has always kept

this journal updated and I feel these events should be added. Soon she will be able to write herself but until then, I will assist her. Her injuries were severe but fortunately, because of the quick and correct response provided to her by Captain Fredrick Gale at the time of rescue, and the best surgeons in the country, she will survive. She has weeks of therapy ahead learning to adapt to her disabilities, but there is a small hope that she will regain use of her lower extremities. The doctors advised us that in some cases feeling and movement return in time.

She exhibits odd behavior that can only be explained as part of her head trauma. Her speech is altered. She sounds as though she is speaking with a French accent. Also, her memory is irregular. She contends that Philip and Ike attempted to kill her, but the details about the incident are not consistent. This morning, I read a few entries from this diary aloud to her. I covered the writings about the engagement party, and the love she expressed for Phil before their marriage. She states that she has no memory of that. I worry about her confusion. I fear her testimony against him will not be taken seriously by authorities.

Her loving and devoted sister, Beth

Becca was stunned. Tears filled her eyes...*Oh Beth; you are the best sister ever! I know this journal connects us, so maybe my diary does as well. For now, Delphi and Becca are as one, tethered together in this strange experience, and that tether is our words...*She retrieved a paper from the desk. It was the account she had written shortly after the rescue while all was fresh on her mine. Carefully, she copied it into the journal with a footnote to Beth.

> July 5, 1865
> Dear Sister,
> I know you've heard the explanation of how our spirits (Delphi and mine) were exchanged during our death experience in the waters off Crescent City. I'm sure the tale seems like the confusion of an injured brain, but I hope this writing, appearing in my diary, will convince you that this paranormal incident has indeed occurred.

The person for whom you're caring, in my body, is Delphi Castile. She is a young Cajun woman from the nineteenth century. She is confused about the murder attempt because she only knows what I've tried to convey to her. I have written the entire account here. If you read it to her repeatedly, she will be able to understand the details and relate them accurately. Philip is evil. Do no let him near my body. Be kind to Delphi. I love you so much.

Becca Later, Hannah returned with her own hair still moist from her bath and hanging in a long braid.

"Can we read from the new book?" she asked.

"Yes, let's read. I'd forgotten about our plan to read *Flower Fables*."

Becca sat in the rocker by the window, and Hannah moved the desk chair close by. The light from the afternoon sun shined in as they opened the new book. Becca was surprised at how well Hannah could read. She knew that a school session was only twelve weeks here in Crescent City. Hannah had only completed sixth grade. As they read through the fables, Hannah stopped often to study the illustrations. Becca was just as fascinated... *Can't believe I read "Little Women", "Little Men", and "Circus Boy" as a child and can now read Louisa's books fresh off the press.* When they had finished, Hannah closed the book carefully and stroked the smooth cover.

"You may keep it, Hannah. I do think it's a bit elementary for you. I'm sure you'll find Little Women more suitable for your age.

"Is it at the Mercantile? I've saved some of my wages," the excited girl exclaimed

...*Opps...might not be written yet...* "It will be... eventually. Now we need to have our early supper so we can dress for the dance."

The grandfather clock struck five when Hannah and Elsie joined Becca in her room. Elsie brought in a borrowed dress that Minnie had secured for her. Becca felt a bit guilty about her fancy new one, but she knew Elsie would soon be settled with Minnie's family and her guardian would release her inheritance...*Plenty of new dresses and parties for her then...*

Hannah carried up a bucket containing hot coals. In it were several iron curling tools that resembled Becca's modern curling iron. These, however were kept hot by the coals...*Hmm...we'll do this in the same way we ironed clothing...*

Hannah and Elsie convinced Becca she should allow them to tighten her corset so her small waist would be even narrower. "Good Grief, ladies, how will I breathe?"

"You take little breaths more often," explained Elsie. "If you feel faint, fan yourself rapidly."

"That's what this is for," Hannah handed her the pearl handled fan that Delphi had among her treasures in her bag. "Everyone knows that, Delphi."

"Haven't you ever tightened your corset before Delphi?" asked Hannah. "Sometimes I think you're from a far off land."

If you only knew...

"I think she's acting the silly fool," teased Elsie, "I happen to know Delphi knows quite well how to dress elegantly."

Becca shot her a warning look. Elsie smiled as she busied herself with her dressing. *Why is it I fear you'll spill the beans on Delphi?*

Hannah's gift with hairdressing paid off. All three had bouffant hairdos with curled ringlets, and not one neck burn from the sizzling irons she used to style them.

Becca added a pearl necklace and earrings to her attire and loaned Elsie the cameo locket. They paraded down the front stairs where their suitors awaited them. Hannah and Leonard walked the few blocks to The Dance Hall. The remaining foursome rode in Thad's borrowed carriage.

"I must purchase my own carriage and horse soon," said Thad as he clucked a signal to the bay mare. "I'm beginning to feel like a bum, borrowing this one so frequently."

As they rode along the dirt street, he explained to Becca that The Dance Hall had two stories. The theater held productions on the second story and a Saloon with poker room on the ground floor. Dances were held in the open area of the theater.

"Maybe you'd like to take part in the plays. They have several during the winter," he suggested.

Becca smiled but made no commitment. *If I'm around... can't stay here forever.*

When they arrived, the couples climbed an outdoor staircase up to the theater. Minnie approached them.

"Come along and allow me to introduce you to some of the nice folks I've met."

Becca looked around. The stage was quite large. She could easily imagine a fine play being performed there. Heavy brown velvet curtains were pulled back to reveal smooth wood floors... *Perfect for a ballet performance ... or a concert... even a scene from a Shakespeare classic.*

A grand piano set directly in front of the stage. Seated on the bench was a chubby woman flipping through sheet music. A man, holding a violin, stood on the stage. He talked with another man who sat in a chair while tuning a banjo. On the opposite side of the room was a long table. Assembled refreshments included pitchers of lemonade, without ice, platters of cookies, tarts, and small cakes.

The large area in front of the stage was open for dancing. Theater seats had been moved to line the walls, providing retreats for tired dancers and wall-flowers. Minnie made several introductions and then led them to the serving table. Becca enjoyed a tin cup of lemonade and then a second. She realized how much she had missed fresh fruit. After a few cookies, the couples found places to sit as the musicians practiced a few numbers.

Becca began to feel more comfortable. Even her tight corset didn't distract her. She glanced around to find Hannah. The girl and her young escort were settled on a bench on the opposite side of the room. *Good...she seems safe enough.*

As soon as the first dance was announced, the two couples formed a quadrant. Others followed and the routine began. It was more fun now than during practice. With all the couples skipping in circles, turning, clapping, changing partners, then repeating the process, Becca felt like she was playing a childhood game...*If I ever get back to my own time... I'll teach this to my students.*

After several rounds, she begged to rest. Thad offered to bring her lemonade and she made use of her pearl fan to cool her moist face. When he returned with her cup filled to the brim, she asked.

"Why do so many men keep going in and out? It's like a revolving door."

Thad looked at her in a tilted manner. "Revolving? Is that like... revolution?"

Opps!...wrong word..."Uh, never mind the word. What I'm wondering is, what's causing them to constantly come and go?"

"The saloon," answered Thad. "There's no liquor allowed here among the ladies. They're running down to get drinks, and then coming back for the dance."

Just then, Elsie rushed toward them. "I requested a Polka. Come along, you two. It's an opportunity to show this little town how the polka should be danced."

Thad took Becca's hand and tugged. "I agree, Delphi, let's cut a rug."

Cut what? Cut rugs? What rugs? Becca left her fan and shawl to join Thad as the music started. Round and round the floor they danced. Faces of the others became a blur as she turned and skipped through the steps, and then turned again. Thad guided her, holding her gently but securely. His lame leg didn't prohibit his grace or speed. As the dance ended she breathlessly looked up into his face. His hazel eyes sparkled and he smiled broadly. She only then became aware that they were the only ones remaining on the dance floor.

Everyone else had backed up and allowed them to become the entertainment. Someone started to clap and others followed. Becca felt her face blushing and meekly retired to her seat.

"Another polka," a male voice called out. The stranger who had made the request leaned over Thad who had seated himself next to Becca.

"Mr. Barrett, my friend, I'm sure you'll allow me a dance with your young lady."

Becca looked at Thad in panic. *I've no idea what the acceptable practice about this is... but I prefer not...*

The middle aged man gently took Becca's elbow and pulled her to her feet. She glanced past the gentleman and noticed Elsie was walking to the floor with James from The Mercantile. Hannah was dancing with an elderly bearded man... *I guess changing partners is acceptable... just like in later eras.*

Mr. Mackey's stamina was no match for Thad's so this round was less challenging. When the dance ended, the gentleman walked her back to her seat, gave a bow and thanked Thad for allowing the dance with his partner and initiated more conversation. "Where are you from, Miss Castile? Do you plan to stay in Crescent City, or will you be leaving like Miss Barns?"

"I'm...I'm not decided," stammered Becca. "It's only been a week."

"Delphi is a teacher," offered Thad. It was a small part of the limited information Becca had shared with him.

"Delphi, Mr. Mackey is the school manager. He's the one who hires the teachers in Crescent City and surrounding area. Have you hired one for the country school for the fall term, Mr. Mackey?"

"Yes, I hired a young man who was just mustered out of the army. He had shot himself in the foot and needed a job. He has no teaching experience so if he doesn't work out, I'll let you know."

21

"I find it's usually the bullies who are the most insecure."

—Tom Felton

By nine-o-clock the older couples had left, a few at a time. Hannah and Leonard left with Minnie. This had been the arrangement when Molly consented for her to attend. The table sweets were gone and a bucket of water with a dipper replaced the lemonade. From its taste, Becca determined alcohol was added. A few of the men who had been visiting the saloon appeared a bit tipsy. Becca noticed one tall, balky man watching her. She asked Thad if he knew him.

"I heard someone call him Cain. His last name is unknown to me. He was living with the Indians, I've heard. He showed up into town a few days ago. He probably has a job in the Lumber Mill. Why do you ask?"

"He gives me the creeps," answered Becca.

"Creeps, is that French for shivers?" he asked.

Becca giggled, "It's not French, but you've got the meaning."

"His kind come and goes. I doubt if he'll be around long."

Almost as though the stranger sensed their conversation, he sauntered over and looked directly into Becca's face.

"I would like to dance with the Lady," he said.

"I'm very tired," answered Becca before Thad could answer. "I must graciously decline your offer."

His eyes grew cold; he backed away and left the room. *Probably went down to the saloon...hope he stays there*

Just as predicted, once the elders dispersed, the waltzing began. The original piano player disappeared and a young man from the downstairs saloon took her place. Young couples were soon waltzing around the room in tender embraces. As Becca moved gracefully in Thad's arms, she felt her heart pounding so fiercely she feared he would hear it. Her head found a comfortable place on his chest. He felt warm and alive. His manly scent made her heady. A revolting thought startled her. *I can't be attracted to this man...from another time... what's happening here?*

When the dance ended, Thad gave her a gentle squeeze, and led her back to their seats. "You look flushed; I'll get you some water. You must rest for a while."

When he returned with a tin cup of water, he asked to be excused.

"I'm stepping out to have a cigar, I won't be long."

Becca smiled, 'Of course, you men go ahead. Elsie and I will take a rest and talk for a while."

As the two discussed the evening, Becca noticed Elsie's attention focusing on something behind her. Looking around her, she saw Cain coming in their direction.

"Hello, Sir. Are you seeking someone?" asked Elsie.

"Yes, and I've found her, I have."

He swept his arm around Becca and lifted her to her feet. Elsie's eyes grew wide. Becca looked around and realized the room had only women. *Evidently all males had needed a smoke simultaneously. All except Cain...that is.*

"The music isn't playing sir," she replied with a firm voice. "And I don't wish to dance." She attempted to pull away.

"You otta have danced when it was playin'." He slurred. His breath reeked of whiskey. His body smelled vile and dirty.

Becca slipped into self defense mode. She attempted to bend forward and bring up her knee for a blow to his groin. However, her corset prevented her upper body from mobility, and the layers of petticoats prevented her knee from making contact. He tightened his grip around her waist, and began to spin around in no particular direction. She tried to kick out at him but again, the layers of skirts tangled her feet, putting her more off balance.

"Who are you?" he rasped. "What's happening? I think you know. You know me, don't you?" *The pick-up lines aren't to enticing in this century.*

Becca didn't answer. She now hung on to him for balance. Her feet no longer touched the floor, as the drunken man swung her around aimlessly. She tried to scream, but the tight corset prevented her from filling her lungs with enough air to produce sound. Suddenly, her captor stumbled backwards. Someone had yanked him. Buck caught Becca as she propelled out of Cain's arms. She heard a loud cracking sound followed by a grunt from Cain. Recovering her focus, she saw Thad standing over the fallen man. Blood spurted from his nose and his badly split lip.

"Now, get your filthy, drunken carcass out of here before you get me riled!" Thad demanded.

Becca trembled as Buck steadied her. Elsie put an arm around her waist. "I ran out and got the men folk," she explained. "He won't bother you now."

Several men dragged the subdued man outside. Thad took Becca in his arms. "Did he hurt you?"

"No," Becca answered weakly. "I'm just a little shaken. I'd like to go home now."

Thad retrieved her fan and placed the shawl around her shoulders. "I'll take you home," he said.

Becca leaned against him as they walked to the buggy...*No...you can't...no one can...I want to go home...my home.*

Entering her room, Becca tossed the pearl handed fan, black gloves, and shawl on the secretary. She plopped into the rocking chair. Only then, did she give way to tears. The encounter with Cain had shaken her to her core. .. I felt so helpless... *Even Ike wasn't able to claim such power over me...Ike.*

She thought of the similarities of the two brutish men. It had been a little less than a week since she had fought for her life against the hulky, determined Ike. But she had held her own...*Stupid clothes... stupid...stupid...stupid...*She thought of the hopelessness for any effort in self defense while encumbered in a breath restricting corset, not to mention the immobility of feet tangled in petticoats. ..*Why were women ever put to such a disadvantage...why all the cumbersome layers?*

In an urge to be freed from it, she removed all her clothing and left it lying on the floor. Totally nude, she felt liberated. Sitting on the side of her bed, she tried to think. The lamp gave enough light to catch her reflection in the mirror by the dressing screen. *What a skinny little twig you are...definitely part of the problem...not even a hundred pounds, is my guess...not much muscle...*

Her thoughts turned to solving the problem. She must find a way to empower the fragile body in which her robust spirit had been encased. Lifting weights came to mind. *How? There're no gyms or fitness centers yet....running maybe? ...Right...that would go over...jogging along the streets in those narrow button-up shoes.....skirts dragging through horse poop...bustle flapping behind...* The image made her laugh through her tears. Ideas begin to flow; *modification of clothing would be a must, different shoes would be a necessity, and some way to get exercise...the kind that conditions, strengthens and increases stamina...*

Hannah tapped on the door, opening it to peer in. "Eeek!" she covered her eyes and slammed the door shut behind her.

"I 'm returning the locket, the one you loaned to Miss Barns." She held it out in her free hand, the other still covering her eyes.

Becca grabbed the dressing gown that was draped over the screen and slipped it on.

"You may uncover you eyes, Hannah, my offensive nudity is now veiled. "

"Delphi, you mustn't…"

"Stop right there!" Her sharp tone revealed her annoyance. "If you aren't prepared to be surprised, you should never walk into a room without being invited."

Hannah's expression revealed her hurt. "I beg your pardon," she muttered. "Most people don't sit around without clothes. I have difficulty remembering that you do."

"Never mind, Hannah, I'm not upset with you. I had a bad experience tonight. I'm still edgy."

"Miss Barns just told us about it," said the girl, eyes wide as they always were when she gleaned a bit of gossip.

"I'm not surprised," answered Becca. *Depend on Elsie…the best of the west for news coverage…especially juicy bits about other people…*

"Mrs. O'Shay said to invite you to go to church with us Sunday morning," Hannah said, attempting to change the subject. "We go every week."

"Not this week, I have a lot of personal things to attend to."

"But Sunday is the Sabbath; it's not righteous to miss worship service on the Sabbath."

Hannah's absolutes were getting on Becca's last nerve. "Really… why is that?"

Hannah mulled the question over for a while then attempted an answer. "That's what Reverend Walker says."

"Hannah, worship is a good thing, but not because you're ordered to, or scared not to. It only means something when it's from your heart and when it's of your own choosing. It doesn't have to be in a stuffy church. One can rest and pray anywhere."

"But…not on the Sabbath… the Ten Commandments require that we keep the Sabbath in church."

"The Ten Commandments cover a lot of things; most are disregarded when it's convenient to do so. But to be technically correct,

Hannah, Sabbath as stated in scripture, refers to Saturday, not Sunday. "

"Actually, it starts at sundown on Friday evenings. So when Sabbath began, we were dressing for the dance. It'll continue all day tomorrow and end at sundown Saturday night. So I guess we're already unrighteous, aren't we?"

Hannah's expression was of complete skepticism. "You know what I'm thinking, Delphi? I'm thinking you're all tuckered out. That's why you're talking non-sense and such. You're all huffy because you're tired. I shant wake you in the morning."

She backed her way to the door, and closed it behind her... *Well that was argumentative on my part...poor Hannah...I'll make it up to her tomorrow.*

That thought brought Becca back to the moment. She remembered that she had agreed to meet Sarah at dawn tomorrow. She also needed to write in the journal. Another dress was ready at Mrs. Leng's. It would be a busy day. She sat down at the desk and wrote in the journal. She provided information about what had happened in the five days since her rescue. She explained where she lived and the fact that she was working part time as a housekeeper to help pay room and board. She told about having to hire a dressmaker. She related the experience with Cain at the dance, and inquired if he might be someone who had known Delphi before. Signing her name, she went to bed and drifted into an exhausted sleep.

Something awakened her. She lay quietly, trying to determine what it was. The room was darker than usual. The foggy night prevented moonlight from shining into the window. Someone stood beside her bed. Her thoughts returned to Cain. Had he gotten into her room? She held her body still and tried to control her breathing. Turning only her eyes to the side she searched for a form. A soft blue light, barely visible hovered near the bed...*What the heck?*

"It's me, Delphi." The answer came, not as an audible voice but as a thought in her mind.

Delphi, you've come. Tell me what's happened...how are things going?

Becca remained very still and tried to focus on her thoughts. Delphi's English was clear with a hint of a French accent. Her voice was soft and musical.

"I didn't mean to come. Your sister was reading to me. Then, before I knew what was happening, here I am."

That's good, we need time to talk, to plan, and we're in quite a fix you and me.

"I want my body back."

Yes, I can understand why you would, but I don't know what to do about it, Delphi.

"I'm greatly aggrieved. Your body is broken and painful. I fear your spouse. There must be something we can do to reverse this tragedy."

Maybe, I hope so. Your body doesn't always work out for me either, Delphi. But we have to make the best of it until we figure out how to solve it.

"Let us change it now, I'll take my old body and you go back there...to that place... that infirmary."

That's too risky. One of us might die before reentry. I believe our bodies will have to be in the same location at the same time...like we were when it happened.

"In the sea? I can't even move your body in the bed."

No, not necessarily in the sea... But for now, Delphi, we need a plan... you won't be here long... Do you know a man by the name of Cain? He's large, strong...gross?

"I don't remember. I met many men. Not all of them gave their names to me. Some used false names. Some were as you describe... gross."

There's a man who frightened me tonight. He targeted me for some reason...it was as though he thought he had a right to abuse me... I wondered if you have an enemy that could be trying to settle a score.

"I can't say. So many men...their faces blend into a fog of memories. Enemies... perhaps... when a customer injured us, abused us, or failed to pay, Miss Lilly sent her brutes to give correction. One of them may bear a grudge."

So what would you do if you were here in your body and had to deal with this jerk?

"Tell Lilly? She always advised us in all such matters."

Oh...you don't know do you? Lilly and all the girls with her died. Even their bodies haven't been found...not yet anyway.

"Oh ...that distresses me so... Did any on the steamer survive?"

Nineteen...and most of those were crewmen. You and I are lucky to be alive, even if we are in the wrong bodies and different centuries.

"What must we do then?"

We'll live our lives as safely and sensibly as possible. I'm taking good care of yours. I spent some of your gold, but not much. Anything I buy will be yours when you're back. I have money in my savings account in Portland. Beth can access it for you until you can do the banking alone.

"The fancy gown and under garments on the floor, did you buy them with my gold?"

Yes. And you'll love the dress, Delphi. It's beautiful and the latest style...for this era.

"Why is it cast aside with so little care? Elegant gowns must be hung or folded carefully. There's no excuse for carelessness. Miss Lilly wouldn't take kindly to disregard of an investment."

I promise to hang it up, first thing in the morning. Now tell me what's happening in Portland.

"Your spouse, Peter, persists. He's demanding to be permitted a visit."

It's not Peter. It's Philip.

"Oui, Phel-eep... Your sister and mother have a paper that prevents his coming."

A restraining order?

"Oui and the constables examined me today. I told them all about Peter and Ike."

It's police, not constables and oh, Delphi...you have to remember his name is Philip. Forgetting his correct name won't do."

"Oui, I try to remember all these things, but when I'm in your body my head hurts so. And they give me potions that make me sleep...or dizzy...or confused."

I understand. Just keep reading my diary. It'll become easier to remember if you read it repeatedly. There were others on that yacht trip. Steve and Marsha Ware and Joe and Peggy Redenbacher should be questioned. They might remember something that's helpful. I'll write their names in the journal so you... Delphi....Delphi...

22

*"The world is a dangerous place, not because of those who do evil,
but because of those who look on and do nothing."*

—Albert Einstein

Becca barely slept. Each time she dosed off, disturbing dreams haunted her. She awoke in a cold sweat while running from Ike. In another dream, Cain choked the breath from her. Waking in a fight with the bedding, she realized the end of the sheet was wrapped around her neck. Early in the morning, her nightmare consisted of Delphi reclaiming her body as she looked frantically for her own. Trembling, she heard the clock strike four...*I need to think. What are my commitments today? ...Sarah...at daybreak ....hurry.*

She jumped up and slipped on her work dress. Passing on the corset and petticoats, she hurriedly fought with the hooks and buttons on her shoes. She took a piece of the packaging paper she had been saving from her purchases. Grabbing her cape she quietly slipped down the back stairs. In the kitchen, she scooped up two pieces of pie from the pie safe and wrapped them in the paper. *..Can't keep swiping Molly's napkins...*

She took a basket from the assortment hanging on the wall...*If I bring back a few berries, I'll have an excuse for having been gone...* The clock struck one gong, denoting that it was now four-thirty. Closing the back door behind her, she walked around the front of the building and glanced both ways...*Don't want Thad or anyone else following.*

Even with the sun beginning its ascent above the horizon, the darkness remained intense. A thick fog hovered. Becca was grateful. She wouldn't be seen by any early risers under this cover. She could hear the surf and the sea lions barking their morning chorus. She moved in that direction.

Stepping carefully, she regretted not bringing a lantern. As the distance between First Street and the surf shortened, she peered through the mist. The minus tide exposed a massive amount of flat rippled sand. Spear Rock protruded as a large silhouette. She started toward it...*I wonder if Sarah will be there...*

The natural rock bridge was surrounded by firm, wet sand. She quickly reached her destination without difficulty. Waiting for a while, she sat on a stone on the east side of the large rock...*When the sun burns off the fog, it'll provide heat...*A movement caught her eye. Sarah slipped quietly from around the granite pinnacle. Carrying a basket and a crude small shovel made of wood and shoulder bone of an animal, she smiled.

"You came."

"Of course, and I brought you something." Becca took out the bundle that contained the pieces of pie. She handed it to Sarah.

"I brought two pieces so you can take one to your grandmother."

"Thank you, I must find a gift for you."

"That's not necessary," assured Becca.

"It is. Gifts are exchanged, not taken,"

Holding out her basket she smiled, "I'll give you these."

Half a dozen large razor clams lay in the bottom of her basket. Becca started to refuse, thinking they were needed for her grandmother, but realized it would be rude.

"Thank you. Let's put them in my basket. I'd like to see how you got them. Will you show me?"

For an hour or more, they dug clams. Sarah showed Becca how she spotted where they had quickly buried themselves when the tide receded. Using the custom made shovel, Sarah burrowed deeply into the sand, dropped to her knees, and pushed her hand and arm into the opening. After a moment of feeling around, she pulled out a plump clam. Soon they had two dozen as Sarah dug and Becca reached in and retrieved the prize. Her sleeves were wet and embedded with sand, her skirts tails soaked, and her shoes soggy. She hardly noticed.

"Would you take me to visit your grandmother?"

"Come." The girl answered.

Becca followed the girl who scampered across the sand toward the rocky shoreline. She turned and walked east against the cliffs and out of site from town residents. Becca estimated a half mile eastward, they entered a dense forest. It was not near the area where the lumbering companies harvested trees. She looked around for landmarks...*I want to remember how to get back ...won't do to get lost.* ..The woodland thickened as Becca and her guide picked their way through fallen limbs, vines and undergrowth. Sarah stopped, turned and looked at Becca.

"No one must ever know," she warned.

"I'll never tell where you live, I promise."

As Sarah guided Becca through the thickets, branches grabbed at her, pulling strands of hair from the reckless bun she had assembled. They arrived in a small open area, hidden in a thicket. An elderly woman tended a tiny fire. A metal pot was positioned in the coals. When Sarah approached her, she addressed the woman in her own language. Her grandmother appeared startled.

"Chagutlsri- Hlki"! She looked both frightened and angry.

Sarah gestured Becca to stay where she stood. Alone, she approached the older woman. They discussed Becca for some time...*I wonder if I should just leave....she doesn't appear to want me here.*

Sarah returned and smiled at Becca. "Come."

They walked closer to the fire, and Sarah squatted on the ground. Becca sat down, feeling the dew covered grass push additional moisture through her clothing. It felt cold to her skin. She noticed a small hut made of tall grass and sticks. It had barely enough room for two people to squeeze in.

"The Grandmother has fears," Sarah said. "She told me I should not bring Xvsh- Hlki here."

"What does that mean?"

"It is our word for white humans. Many things happened to make The Grandmother fear your people."

The water in the pot was boiling. Sarah dumped the clams from her basket into the water. Soon the shells popped open.

"Do the two of you live here all alone? Where's your family?"

"Some years ago, before my birth, there was a war, north from here. Tribes grew weary of having their homeland, hunting grounds, and fishing waters taken by men who hungered for gold. They fought back."

After that, there were raids on our people, even those who had nothing to do with the fighting. My grandmother watched the white raiders kill my grandfather and her two sons. She and my mother ran and hid, but she has never forgotten."

"I'm so sorry such horrid things were done," muttered Becca.

"So many of our people were killed, the grasses were stained with blood as far as the eye could see."

The old woman scooped the clams from the boiling water with a forked stick and into a clean basket.

"The ones who ran away joined together. They set about to prepare for the winter, working together. They chose a new Xvsh-xay-yu'. That is what we call our leader, the headman. My mother and my father joined together. Unmarried women took husbands to survive."

Sarah's grandmother began tossing a hot clam back and forth in her hands to cool it before removing the meat.

"Where are you parents?"

"I was born while they lived near the big river and lived with those who gathered together. Your people call it the Smith River. Soon after my birth, the white Xvsh-xay-yu'... uh...leader... governor offered Tr'vt to kill the rest of us."

"Trivet?"

"Tr'vt ... gold... he paid gold to those who would kill as many of my people as could be found."

My God! It was genocide!

"One day my father was fishing. Some of those men...that killed for Tr'vt...they found him...The girl studied her hands and spoke so softly, Becca could hardly hear her. "They chopped his body apart and took his head." Her voice trailed off.

Becca gasped. When she had gathered her nerve she ventured another question.

"And your mother?"

"The Grandmother and my mother began working for a rancher. He protected them. We stayed with his family for about five summers. I learned your talk. The killing got worse. Finally, we were driven, like sheep, to a tiny island...the one where the firelight burns at night."

"The lighthouse rock?"

"Yes, some said it was to protect us, others said it was to protect them...There was little food or fresh water. It was cold and windy ... we had no shelter. Most survived, but my mother died there. She died of sickness...from the cold. After we left, Grandmother took me and we ran away and joined other women and children."

The clams were shelled and steaming in the basket. "Chagutlsri- Hlki."

"What is she saying?"

"She's calling my name. It means White Moon. The rancher's wife named me Sarah. They could not say my name."

She gestured Becca to take a portion of clam meat. As they ate Sarah continued.

"Two winters ago the white Xvsh-xay-yu' gave us land. It had been our home since the creator put us there, but the white leaders believed they gave it to us. They put their soldiers nearby to protect us. They said they were also protecting the white settlers from us.. There are still those around who will pay money for heads and scalps of my people. Killings continue."

"Why are you here and not with your people on that land? Wouldn't you be safer there?"

"After making our home a place of captivity, there were still raids on us when we were discovered alone fishing or gathering food. One day some men caught me and took me away. They sold me as a slave. I knew the grandmother had no one else to care for her in her old age. I ran away and retuned. I fear the man who bought me will come and capture me again...he might even kill the grandmother... It's a white man law that we remain as captives. We are breaking their law so we can stay free."

When they had finished the clams, Sarah offered the old woman the pie. The grandmother sniffed it just as Sarah had done the first time Becca gave her food. Sarah assured her it was safe. The sun rose higher and cast warm rays onto the women in the tiny clearing. It reminded Becca that she had left without telling anyone she was going.

"I must go now," she said. "Is there anything I can get you, food... blankets... clothing?"

"The Grandmother is often cold."

"Next time I come, I'll bring a blanket."

As she got up, Sarah joined her and they walked back the way they had come. "What can I give you?"

"What would I need to get so you could make me shoes like yours?"

"Deerskin...I can get some."

"I have gold coins if you know someone who'd sell me some."

"I know someone who will sell me a deer hide."

"Could you make me shoes like yours?"

Sarah smiled, "I can make them."

As they approached the end of the forest path, Sarah stopped.

"Bring the coins and I will meet you at the cliffs, below the berry bushes."

"When?"

"Following three moons."

"Three nights...? What time of day?"

"When Father Sun first touches Mother Earth." *Guess that's sun-up in three days...*

Gripping her basket of clams she hurried back to town... *It must be close to noon.* Upon arriving, she darted to the back of the building and entered through the back door. As she closed it behind her, she noticed several people in the kitchen. All eyes were on her.

Molly and Hannah looked at her with gaping mouths. She attempted to smooth back her hair and realized it was in total disarray, much of it hanging down her back and over her shoulders. Thad and Mr. O'Shay sat at the work table with cups of coffee. Mr. O'Shay looked amused, and Thad's expression was that of concern.

"We were just planning to start a search for you."

"I checked on you a few minutes ago," explained Hannah. "You weren't in your room."

"Mercy, child, what did you do to your clothing? You look a fright!" Molly exclaimed.

"Uh...I...uh...gathered some clams for you." She handed the basket to Molly.

Molly looked in the basket with surprise. "You gathered all these, by yourself?"

"I was hoping we could make chowder tonight." Becca smiled, very aware that her sandy shoes, sleeves and skirts were the focus of Thad's scrutiny. *I hope chowder's been invented, already.*

"That sounds like a dish I'd hanker for," grinned Mr. O'Shay, always enthused about food.

"We're having Beans and fried potatoes right soon now, so maybe you should tidy up," suggested Molly, carrying the basket to the table.

Becca hurried up to her room... *Close call there old girl, but you pulled through it...* She stripped down to her skin and poured the tepid water from the pitcher into the basin. Grooming herself quickly, she dressed in fresh undergarments and the woolen frock. As she brushed her hair, tiny pieces of stems and leaves caught the bristles of the brush, slowing her progress.

Looking in the mirror to arrange her bun, she observed a deep scratch across one cheek... *How did that happen? I don't remember anything striking against my face ...Oh well... can't do anything about it...* She set the brush down on the dressing table, and observed her nails. Already torn and ragged from her recent housework chores, they looked even worse... *Must have grinded them off digging in the sand.*

Becca could hear voices in the dining room as she descended the front stairs. Elsie's voice, clearer than the others, asked questions. Even without hearing their conversation, she knew her mysterious adventure was being discussed. As she walked into the room, everyone fell into silence.

"We were just informing Elsie of your success at gathering clams, Delphi," explained Mr. O'Shay.

Still feeling full from her clam brunch in the woods, she took small helpings and hoped no one would question her about her early morning escapade. As the meal ended, Thad turned to her.

"I'd planned to drive you to Chinatown this morning. I even borrowed the buggy. Remember, you were to pick up your clothing from Mrs. Leng?'

"Oh, I'm sorry, it slipped my mind. Can we still go?"

"Yes, but we must hurry, I agreed to have the buggy back by two-o-clock."

Front Street was busy. Farmers had come to town to take care of Saturday errands. Soldiers from the Fort assembled on the corners, looking to enjoy some revelry. Town men sauntered down the wooden sidewalks, ready to take advantage of some leisure time by visiting their favorite saloons. Thad reined the horses slowly toward Second Street.

"That's an alarming mark on your face. Did that happen last night at the dance?"

Becca reached up and covered the scratch. "No, I think it occurred in my quest for clams. It'll be fine."

Thad took her hand from her face and held it as he managed the reins with his other. "If you're going to become an earnest clam digger, we must get you some leather gloves."

Nothing gets past this man... In an attempt to change the subject and to obtain useful information, Becca asked a question.

"Where would I purchase a warm blanket or two?"

"Sometimes there's wool bedding at The Mercantile, though I haven't seen any lately. Most families have quilts."

"Then, where would I go to purchase a quilt?"

"I've never bought one, most women make them for their families, or they're given as gifts. Why are you seeking blankets and quilts?"

"I just want some, that's all." *I wonder which Sarah's grandmother would prefer...*

23

"As we express our gratitude, we must never forget that the highest appreciation is not to utter words, but to live by them."

—John F. Kennedy

Stopping in front of Leng's Shop, Thad secured the horses to the hitching post. As Becca waited, she saw an African American man crossing from the other side of the street.

"Look, there's Tate, hello, Mr. Tate."

The man stopped and tipped his hat. "Good afternoon, Miss."

"I've been wondering where you're staying. I've wanted to thank you for saving my life."

"There's nothing to thank me for Ma'am. We were all trying to survive."

"But you fished me out of the water at risk to the rest of you. I'll always be grateful… where are you staying?"

"Some kind people here lent me a room. I'll be going back to San Francisco on the next steamer."

"But, before you go you must come to our hotel, the Redwood, and have a meal. I owe you that much."

Tate was quiet for a moment, smiled and tipped his hat. "I must decline your gracious offer, Ma'am. It's nice to have met up with you, good day."

As the man continued in his direction up Second Street, Becca remarked, "I wonder why he declined my offer?"

"Perchance he's unsure of a welcome at the hotel," answered Thad. "You, being from Louisiana are aware of course, that Negros aren't invited to eat with whites."

Becca's face grew hot. "You've just fought in a war and experienced a severe wound fighting inequality. You of all people should find that to be an unacceptable prejudice. Besides, California wasn't even a slave state."

"I fought a war to prevent the southern states from seceding from the Union and to bring an end to slavery, Delphi. I can't force people to change their social practices by simply demanding that they do. Neither can you."

Why do I forget where I am, sometimes... I'm such an idiot... It'll be years before Rosa Parks and other brave civil rights workers prove change comes by persistence and demand... Oh, how I wish I could tell him what's coming...Thad was still talking, but Becca's thoughts had prevented her from hearing most of it.

"... so that's why you can't compare California to the south. People here might not enslave the Negro, but they don't consider him an equal. There'll always be injustice in some way or the other."

Injustices...yes indeed...like killing thousands of Native Americans or using them as slaves.

Thad dropped Becca off at the Leng's for her fitting and went to the tobacco shop. Becca noticed a handmade new sign written in Chinese characters, hanging in the window.

"What does that say, Mrs. Leng? Are you having a sale?"

The woman studied Becca, trying to make sense of her question. "Everything for sale."

Bargain racks and discounts aren't invented yet...I guess... "Then, what are you posting on the sign?"

"I need helper...too much work."

"Oh, so that's a hiring sign. Is the job only for an experienced seamstress?"

" Can't find one like that...I'll teach helper...you know someone?"

"I can work Saturdays and Sundays, I've only sewn a little, but I learn fast." I'll learn how to make my own dresses, and I'll make them more comfortable... can't beat getting paid while learning... Images of her disastrous experience in high school sewing class flashed through her memory...*That was the stupid sewing machine's fault... running the needle through my finger like that.*

"You work here... in Chinatown?" Mrs. Leng's tone expressed her surprise.

On the way home, Becca smiled as she held the bundle that contained her new work dress. She explained to Thad that she would begin her new part time job the next Saturday.

"Why would you want to do a blame thing like that?" he asked, his brows knitted in puzzlement.

"I'm free on weekends, I could earn a little money, and more importantly, I'll learn to sew."

"Is it because you want a quilt? Mrs. O'Shay could teach you to make one, Delphi. I don't think this decision is wise. It is one thing to do business in Chinatown, but quite another to work there. I've never heard of white folks seeking employment there."

"Well, I guess it's time for the first."

Thad shook his head. "You do the oddest things...fool hearty things. Sometimes I fear for you."

"Well, it's been said that fools rush in where angels fear to tread." Becca smiled.

"Has it?"

"If it hasn't, it will be."

Back in her room, Becca changed into her new work dress and hung the itchy wool dress back in the wardrobe...*It's so different having to make do with only a few things to wear...* She sat down at the secretary and opened the journal. Turning back to where she had been reading about Delphi's life, she picked up on the girl's story. Working through the mixture of French and English phrases, she assembled the story of Delphi's transition from a pampered young woman with dreams of becoming a famous musician to an entrapped prostitute.

Delphi's accounts described the unrest in her aunt's home. Fielding off the advances of her uncle, her mother's irritability, having to care for her aunt's children rather than pursuing her musical dreams, had all led to risky decisions. After reading several posts of complaints from a self-absorbed perspective, typical of adolescents, Becca skipped several pages. Here, Delphi's mood is brighter. A music troupe performed in Lafayette. She expressed exuberance regarding their presentation.

"They have need of La soprano" she penned. **"On the morrow I will go for an audition."** *You've skipped writing for several days...this is scribbled like you are hurried or excited...*"**I will slip away in the night, Mère would never agree and ma soeur would insist the Famille has need of me. I will leave with the Artistes Musicaux. I will learn as I travail. They came from New York and will play in several villes on their way to California. I cannot resist this opportunity."** *So...you ran away to chase your dreams of fame and fortune... I hoped you left a note...Your family must have worried and grieved their entire lives...*

Several days later, Delphi described practice sessions and learning new songs. Several weeks of entries follow before she conveys disappointment.

> "**They assuré me I would have a part in the opérette. But they find other travails for me. I am weary of sewing costumes, painting props, doing errands at the bidding of others. The salaire is much less than they promis. When we arrivée in San Francisco, I will seek another opportunity**" *Ah yes... starting at the bottom takes patience... something of which you seem to have very little at your tender age...so many entries of grumbling and complaining...I will skip those...ah, this sounds positive...*

> "Au dernier! J'adore San Francisco. I have a new position. Mrs. Lilly O' Kennan has hired me to jouer du piano and sing at her establishment. I will perform every evening. She will provide me room and board and clothing. When I am successful, I will write my famille but not before." *This new position didn't work out well for you...did it Delphi...not as you planned?*

Becca closed the Journal. She didn't have the fortitude to read further today. She rested her elbows on the desk and put her face into her hands. She wondered if she should send a telegram to Delphi's mother...*I wouldn't want my mother and sister to worry about me...What would I tell her? Her daughter isn't exactly alive...at least not in this century. What if she'd wish to travel here to see me? She might insist that I return to Lafayette...Would I be willing to do that?...I don't really know them...they'd soon realize I'm not really Delphi...An alarming thought came to her... Delphi wrote these entries before the war. There're lots of changes there from that bloody four year period... Is the family still there? I need to know what Delphi would want me to do...*

The spinning sensation filled her head. She felt as though she had been pole-vaulted into space. She moved at breathless speed toward the distant light...then, a sudden stop in the hospital room. There were only two in the room, a therapist and Delphi in her borrowed body. The sheet was pulled away and Becca had a full view of her lifeless legs. The therapist stood by the bed, rotating her ankles. Becca moved near the bed. Speaking with her thoughts, she announced herself.

Delphi, I'm here.

"*I know.*" Delphi responded, also with her thoughts.

Did you remind Beth to give the police the names I wrote in the journal?

"*I did, and she conveyed your message, but the authorities already had questioned them.*"

What did they learn anything from them?

"*I'm unaware. No one discusses the inquiries with me.*" *She grimaced.*

Is the therapist hurting you?

"No, but she annoys me sorely. Thrice daily, she moves my limbs repeatedly"

It's important to keep the muscles alive and the joints mobile.

"They measured me for a wheelchair today."

That's good. Soon you'll be able to sit up.

The therapist, finished with the ankles, now focused on knees and hips. She lifted each leg separately, bent it at the knee, and straightened it out, only to repeat the process again.

You must ask questions Delphi. No one will speak of the investigation unless you ask for information. They won't wish to upset you, but I can't brief you about what to say or do if I don't have information. You can use your hands; write in my diary after you talk to Beth about it.

"The pens are difficile. I hate writing with them. No one here has a quill"

Do it anyway, I need the information.

"I miss playing piano, I miss music and singing. Your sister brought this thing."

Becca looked at the IPod lying on the side table. *Good, I have some great tunes downloaded on that.*

"It's not music. It's wretched noise. I tried to listen, but it offended my ears. A cotton gin produces a more pleasing racket."

You're not in a great mood, but I believe things will get better. We have to keep our hopes up.

Becca did not hear Delphi's reply. Her own return trip was in progress. She awoke with her face on the desk and the sound of Hannah's knock at the door. "Delphi, are you coming down for supper?"

24

"The most dangerous foe is the one who fears for his life."

—Leslie Allen Long

Becca requested to have supper in her room. Hannah delivered it and asked if she would like company. Becca felt exhausted and needed to think. However, noticing the anxious expression on the teen's face, she smiled and stated that she would. Hanna set the plate and cup of tea on the bedside table. She pulled the wooden rocker over and sat down facing Becca.

"Have you eaten?" asked Becca.

"I set my plate in the warmer," answered the girl, "I'll eat it shortly. Tell me about your visit to the Leng's. Are your clothes almost finished? You promised to tell me where you went this morning."

Becca had just placed the first bite of roast pork into her mouth. Chewing carefully, she delayed answering until she had swallowed. It was evident that Hannah was already thinking ahead to the next question.

"I brought home my new work dress. I'll wear it tomorrow so I can wash the other one. It's filthy. The rest of my order should be ready by Saturday."

She scooped in a forkful of buttered squash. "Hmm... this is good."

"Why were you gone so long this morning?"

"Can you keep a secret?" Becca dabbed the corner of her bun into the brown gravy.

"Yes, I always keep secrets, everyone knows that, Delphi."

"It's critical that you do, Hannah. If you slip up, it could cause harm to someone."

Hannah's eyes were large and questioning. "I'll defend it to my death!"

Becca told Hanna about Sarah and all that had happened, but withheld any information about the location of her new friends.

"I have to get a blanket or two to take to them"

Hannah was silent for a moment. "Why would you want to do that, Delphi? Why does it matter to you?"

"Because there's a girl, a little younger than you, who is also an orphan. Think of what that is like, Hannah. She doesn't have the safety you have. She's trying to take care of her grandmother, avoid being captured, and survive. There's evil people are out there who would kill her for a bounty. Shouldn't that matter?"

Hannah thought about it and finally responded. "I guess it should, but no one else is worried about those people."

"I don't think that's entirely true. There are always voices of compassion. Sadly they're not always as loud as the other voices. These voices must persist until their heard."

"What voices?"

Becca realized she had lost Hannah. Her young mind hadn't developed the ability to understand the abstract.

"Never mind, see the necklace on the desk? Sarah gave that to me. It's made of shells."

Hannah walked over and picked up the item, looking at it closely.

"I wonder how she made the little holes in the shells to string them. I wouldn't let anyone see this if I were you."

"You're absolutely correct. Put it in the drawer, please. I'll stash it in the safe when I finish eating. Do you know where I could get a blanket or quilt? Even a warm cape would be helpful."

"I have a cape that I don't wear anymore. The pastor's wife gave me a bigger one. If Sara is younger and littler than me, it will do."

"That's good, Hannah, but I'm worried about her grandmother too. I need to get blankets for her."

Hannah thought for a moment. Her face lit up with an idea. "The box in the laundry room has clothing in it yet."

"What box?"

"The one Mrs. Walker brought over. The town's women gathered up clothing for the people from the ship wreck. That's where I got the frocks and undergarments I brought up for you and Miss Barns."

"Does it belong to anyone in particular?

Hannah shrugged, "Don't reckon so. Mrs. O'Shay put it back in the corner with the quilt pieces. She figured there'd be more people found that would need clothing, but there hasn't been..."

Her voice trailed off. It reminded Becca that each day more bodies washed to shore all along the coastline. The town's people had collected each one, attempted to identify each person, and when possible informed relatives by telegram. They demonstrated much compassion in regard to this tragedy.

"I'll go eat supper. Then; I'll take a lamp and look at the things in the box. I'll wait until the O' Shays are in bed." She took Becca's dishes and left the room.

Becca slipped into her nightgown. She wanted to retire early. She glanced at the journal. Sitting down at the secretary, she added an entry. Two full pages later, she glanced over the small, tight writing. She had included the dawn meeting with Sarah, digging the clams, Sarah and her grandmother's situation, the Lengs, and her new part time job in Chinatown. So tired was she, that the clock, striking hourly and on the half hour, didn't arouse her. The misty blue form hovering over her did. She jumped and cried out.

"It's only me...why do you carry on so?"

Delphi, you always startle me.

"I read the writing you penned tonight. It pulled me to you."

Have you heard anything about the investigation?

"I asked Beth as you instructed. She said that the names you gave me are with the authorities. They plan to speak to them. She informed me the detective is convinced that Paulo planned to murder you."

Paulo? No, it's not Paulo... its Philip.

"That's what I said, Phil-eep... They want information from your journal...what you call it...diary?"

I don't know how that'll help. I wrote about his affair, but not about being afraid of him. It honestly never occurred to me that he could do something so terrible.

"Nevertheless, Beth said she would take it to them tomorrow. They will copy some pages. You write so much. It will take someone a long time to copy all you write."

Oh no, you don't understand Delphi. They won't copy by handwriting. They have machines that copy documents in just seconds.

"No, how can that be? It must be like the apparatus that took photos of my bones... or your bones."

The pages I've written on since our spirit switch must be removed. Those will make you sound crazy. It's a binder; you can slip them out without tearing pages. Don't forget. I'm glad they're actively working on it.

"I have to tell you, I'm not as enthused about your endeavors, Becca."

What are you talking about?

"My plan, before the horrid demise of the ship, was to break away from Miss Lilly and start a new life... one with music. I wanted to start a school, a lovely academy that teaches young ladies to sing, play piano, recite poetry, and even social dances."

I think that's a great plan, Delphi. You would have to start over someplace where no one knows about your work with Lilly.

"I planned to escape from her in Portland. Her strong men didn't travel with us. I believe I'd have been successful. But we never reached there. If you construct a respectable reputation here, *in my body, I'll start my new life here, as soon as we can change the way things are. However, I'll not be considered respectable if you're discovered chasing through the forest with Indians."*

You could start over here. I think your secret past is unknown. However, I'm not sure there's an economy or interest in a music school, Delphi, The public school is hardly organized. Maybe San Francisco would be a better choice. As far as my friendship with Sarah, no one knows. If it disturbs you, I'll write no more about it.

"No, I want you to be honest. But you must remember, it's my future you are shaping. Meanwhile, you must take better care of my hands. I'm very concerned about your activities. No more digging for clams in the sand. Rather, I need you to practice piano every day, especially scales. I'll need my fingers to be limber and smooth when I return to my body."

Delphi, I don't know one piano key from another. I took two lessons in second grade before my piano teacher quit me. I had flute lessons a year or two, tops. I can't practice what I don't know. Our priority is to get my body well and figure out how to switch back. We need to get free of my husband and he needs to face the consequence. He must pay for what he's done!

"I'm doing my best with your body. I tolerate the nurses sticking needles into me every day. Other people stretch me this way and that way...The divorce is in progress...I signed papers. They tell me Peter protested that the signature wasn't yours."

Philip, its Philip... how did you make it in life with such a bad memory for names?

"In my life, names had no importance. Men preferred that I forgot their names, if I happened to know them. I'll try harder to remember his name..."

Delphi's voice grew more distant..."I meant to tell you... Some fishermen found a man that may be..." *Delphi?*

Becca had difficulty going back to sleep and was relieved to get up when the earliest light of morning streamed into her window. She dressed in the new work dress. Slipping down the back stairs, she noticed the fire was already started in the cook stove...*Great...I can have a pot of tea made and back in my room before everyone else starts fussing around.*

She filled the kettle with enough water to make tea in a small teapot. Slicing a piece of bread, she spread butter on it and set in on the rack inside the oven. After measuring loose tea into the china pot, she poured in the hot water. She lifted one of the stacked trays from the shelf and set the pot, a cup, and the toast on it. Carrying it back up the stairs, she heard someone enter the kitchen...*Whee...just in time. I really want alone time today.*

Turning the rocking chair to face the window, she sat down and poured her tea. Nibbling on the toast, she looked out at the sea. It was a clear day. The fog had lifted early. Gulls flew over the surf hunting for a morning meal. A revolting thought stopped her chewing...*One week ago today, Phil and Ike tried to kill me... In a way, they did... The morning last Sunday looked calm...a lot like this... Can it really be only one week...?* So much has happened in that short time.

She could hear people scurrying through the hall and down the stairs. Elsie, Thad and another guest must be going to church. When she was sure the house was empty, she got up and gathered her laundry. She took it downstairs and into the wash room. Looking around at the various items, she wondered where to start... *If I do my laundry today, it would shorten our time on task tomorrow, when we'll do the regular wash.*

The fire in the cook stove was reduced to embers, but the kettle was filled with hot water. Becca found a bar of lye soap. She had noted that this one cleaning product with occasional vinegar rinsing, was used for everything. She chipped away at the bar with a sharp knife, allowing the pieces to fall in the larger of the two tubs. She then poured hot water over it. After a few moments of watching it melt, she added a bucket of cold water from the rain barrel by the back door.

She dropped in the dirty work dress, a weeks worth of undergarments, and stockings. Swishing them around for a bit she began scrubbing them together as she had seen people do in movies. The stains refused to come out of the work dress...*I'll let it soak while I hang out the rest of these things...* She pulled the other items from the cold water and vinegar rinse, twisted out the excess water, and placed then in a large basket. In an open area behind the kitchen, a clothesline was attracted to an evergreen tree on one end and to a nail in the side of the building on the other. The weeds were almost knee high...*I thought Mr. O'Shay said he was going to cut these down with a sickle...* She tossed each pair of pantaloons over the line, and secured them with a primitive forerunner of the clothespin. Reaching down for the long stockings, she paused and listened carefully.... *That sounded like something moving through grass...* She straightened up and looked around. Seeing nothing, she concluded it was probably a stray animal. She returned to the washroom. Completing the washing of the dress, she turned to place it in the rinse tub. At that moment, something caught her eye. A shadow like movement passed the window.

Becca picked up the knife she had used to cut the soap and grabbed the dress out of the rinse water. Slipping to the door she rapidly pushed it open. A man stood directly in front of her. She swung the sopping wet dress across his face. Its water logged skirt wrapped around his head. He grabbed at it, trying to free himself. Becca threw her body against him, causing him to trip backwards. As he lay on the ground struggling with his entanglement, she dropped to her knees onto his chest. He gasped as the wind was knocked out of him. Placing the knife against his throat, she demanded.

"What do you want and why are you hanging around me?"

He stammered, "I'm not bothering you ma'am, I was looking for the owner. I was gonna offer to cut grass in exchange for a meal."

Oh, oh, I just clobbered an innocent person looking for work... She backed off the man and tugged on her dress. As it slipped from his face, she caught her breath.

"Cain!"

He scrambled to his feet and began backing away. "Who are you?" he demanded. "You aren't who you say you are...I know...I don't know how... but I know." He lumbered away.

Shaking out the dripping dress, she did her best to wring out the water. She hung it carefully over the line and returned to the house. She had just finished cleaning up after her chore when the others filed into the house from church. Hannah appeared in the kitchen first, on her way to her room at the back of the house.

"Delphi, what are you doing, and why are you all wet?"

Becca smiled proudly, "I did my laundry."

The girl shook her head shamefully. And on the Sabbath, too. Mrs. O'Shay will likely pitch a conniption."

Oh, no... not this conversation again... "I have to run and change now." She darted up the backstairs and hurriedly went to her room...*I forgot about the Sunday rule...I can't believe at my age I feel like a kid in trouble*

25

"Any fool can make a rule, and any fool will mind it."

—Henry David Thoreau

Becca changed into the scratchy wool outing dress, straightened her hair and joined the others for lunch; though she was reminded it is Sunday dinner. There was a full house. The doctor was there, as well as Thad's friend Abe Turner, the saloon owner, Minnie and little Albert, and the Reverend and his wife. These, with the regulars, totaled a dozen. Becca took her chair by Thad. It was now accepted that it was her place at the table.

The Reverend was asked to say grace. Becca had never heard a table prayer so lengthy in all her life. Her neck began to ache from bending so long. She raised her head for relief and Thad gently elbowed her. She ducked her head again and shot him a sideward glare. His eyes were closed, but a mischievous smile played at his lips. Little Albert began to fuss. After every imaginable thing in the world was mentioned in thanks, every unfortunate condition on the planet was petitioned, and each person at the table was blessed, the Reverend quoted God a Psalm before concluding his prayer with a smile of pride and accomplishment.

The table was set with china Becca hadn't seen before. She examined it. While browsing through antique shops in Portland, similar pieces had caught her eye, but never a full set. She picked up a saucer and turned it over to see if a company or country was stamped or painted on the back. Austria was inlaid in gold lettering. Thad cleared his throat. Becca looked up to see everyone focused on her. Thad held a platter of cold ham slices in her direction. She had obviously obstructed the flow of food passing.

"Oh, sorry, I was just noticing your china, Molly, it is lovely."

"Yes, thank you. It was my mother's. I only use it on Sundays and Christmas. Nothing's too good for the Lord's Day."

Becca scooped several slices of cold ham and passed the platter to Elsie. She noticed that the meal was all cold foods, obviously cooked by Molly the evening before to prevent work on the Sabbath. A plate of sliced cheese, another of buttered bread, and a bowl of cold roasted potatoes followed the ham. A pitcher of water was at each end of the table. Hannah filled everyone's cup with hot tea. The Reverend tucked his napkin under his chin and looked toward Becca. "Speaking of the Lord's Day, Miss. Castile, we missed you at our morning service. I understand you came close to death only a week ago. You must not be lax in giving thanks for your rescue."

Oh dear...tell me this isn't happening... not a sermon ...I'll be happy to give thanks as soon as the powers that be put me back where I belong.

Becca placed her napkin in her lap and smiled at the Reverend.

"God knows better than anyone, my gratefulness, Reverend. The man who pulled me from a watery grave knows my gratefulness as well. In fact, if he'd been invited to your church or to this meal, I would consider attending a year of Sundays."

"Well, why should he not be invited? Christ says, "Come unto me..." Give me his name and he'll be invited."

"His name is Tate, "offered Minnie, "and Delphi is correct. Without him, me and my little Albert wouldn't be alive, or Elsie either."

"Well, I should like to meet Mr. Tate...."

His wife, Grace, leaned over and whispered in his ear. "Hmm... Yes... I see. Could you please pass the jam this way, Mr. O'Shay?"

The conversation quickly changed and Becca smiled to herself. *Now, I guess the pressure is off, from you, Rev...*The doctor reported about his progress regarding contacts with the relatives of Brother Jonathan's passengers. He had been successful in reaching Minnie's husband by telegraph and received a response.

"Yes, and he'll be here Saturday on the next steamer," beamed Minnie. "And he's agreed that Elsie should stay with us."

Elsie smiled but didn't show the enthusiasm Becca would have expected.

"And, I've received confirmation from Elsie's guardian that he approves as well," said the doctor smiling."

"Did you reach Mr. Nisbit's brother?" asked Mr. O'Shay, who had taken care to keep track of the identities of bodies, washed to shore.

"Yes, he'll be coming Saturday to make arrangements to ship the body back to San Francisco. Mr. Nisbit, you know, had scribbled a will and wrapped it in an oiled cloth before the ship went down. He left most of his effects to a widow, his landlady. We can only hope the brother will respect his wishes. The court might not consider the will, written as it was a legal document."

"He won't. He'll keep everything." Becca gasped. She couldn't believe she had allowed her thoughts to slip out into words. Everyone looked at her.

"I mean, usually, people squabble over wills."

"We must not be judgmental, Miss Castile, God tells us not to judge," reminded the preacher.

Right, as if you don't, you hypocrite! She remained quiet. How could she explain that she had read the history of these exact events long after they occurred, and indeed, the widow would not be given the meager estate?

"Well, I guess it'll be a busy week for us," announced Molly. "We'll need every room readied by Saturday. I must make some arrangements with the farmers for meat and vegetables. We'll do a double batch of baking."

Hannah glanced at Becca as if to say, "We know who the 'we' is she's talking about." Hannah and Becca took care washing the stack of delicate china.

"Hannah, do you think the Good Lord is angry at us for working so hard washing all these dishes, being the Sabbath and all?"

"Don't be such a silly willy, Delphi, who else would wash them?"

"Maybe to please him and to avoid work on the Sabbath, we should just pitch them out," she teased.

Hannah shot her a surprised look, "That's just foolery, Delphi; Mrs. O'Shay would skin us alive. Anyway, it's not really the Sabbath. Remember, you said that was Saturday."

"Oh, so it's the Sabbath when I wash my clothes or don't attend church, but it's not when you need help with the dishes?" Becca laughed at the girl.

Hannah shrugged. "You don't have to help. You're a paying guest. But I sure appreciate that you do."

Becca patted her shoulder. "No problem, you're my friend after all. I think I'll invent plates and cups made out of paper. Then, when it's the Sabbath, people can just serve it up and toss the dishes."

Hannah giggled. "That's the silliest thing I ever heard. People would never agree to eat on paper plates. You get the craziest notions, Delphi."

When the china was put away and the kitchen swept, Hannah directed Becca back to the washroom. She pulled a long deep box from behind a shelf case that stored bars of lye soap, jars of vinegar and cleaning rags. The container had been a wooden shipping crate.

"Here are the things I told you about." Becca began rummaging through the container. As she sorted, Hannah refolded the items.

"We can't choose anything that has bright colors." Becca murmured.

"Sara doesn't like bright colors?"

Becca shook her head. "It's not that, but they need to be camouflaged since they're hiding in the woods."

"What's that mean?"

Hannah refolded the red cape and placed it on the rejection pile. Becca unfolded a grey wool cape and looked it over.

"You know, blend into the forest colors so they aren't noticed."

When the search was complete Becca had salvaged a grey cape for Sarah's grandmother, two pairs of wool socks, a black knitted shawl, and a man's brown jacket. "This should help until I can find a blanket."

"When are you taking them?" Hannah placed the remaining pieces of clothing back into the crate, pushing it back to its place in the corner.

"Wednesday, and you may go with me if you promise to keep it a secret."

Becca, took the items to her room, rolled them up in the knitted shawl, and tied the bundle with twine...*That's taken care of...I hope Sarah and Hannah can become friends... maybe when I leave... or whatever is going to happen to me...Hannah can be her advocate...* She had no more than finished her little project when a knock sounded at her door.

"Come in Hannah."

A male voice spoke. "What if it's not Hannah?"

Becca opened the door laughing, "Sorry Thad, Hannah's the only one to ever knock on my door, when she remembers to knock."

"It's a calm day at the beach. I wondered if you'd like to take a stroll?"

"Yes, I would actually, let me grab my parasol."

They left the house quietly. The Reverend and the Doctor were in the parlor debating some issue concerning science versus religion. The Reverend's bombastic voice was a strong contrast to the Doctor's quiet argumentative tone. The women sat in another part of the room, talking quietly and working of various projects; crochet, embroidery, knitting. No one noticed the couple's departure. The seaside was beautiful. The winds were just strong enough to cool them from the sun, but not brawny enough to be unpleasant. Tides were out. Becca collected several nice shells, and a sand dollar.

"We're ok, doing this, right? Walking and gathering seashells isn't considered work on the Sabbath?"

He smiled, "I would say this could be called rest, not work."

"Good, I wouldn't want to give the Reverend additional material for his next sermon."

"He's not a bad person, Delphi. You should give him an opportunity to prove that. He's a bit loud and quick with his opinions, but he has a good heart."

"Do you know him well?"

"Actually I do. I was raised Baptist. But when I came here I attended his church since there was no Baptist church in town. You see, there were terrible things in my head. I couldn't sleep. The screams and sounds of war rattled around in my mind every time I tried to rest."

"That's called PTSD, it's common after war. Post Traumatic Stress Disorder."

Thad gave her a questioning look and continued. "Doc called it Brain Fever, caused by shock from war. He gave me something to calm me, but it made me feel tired and listless. The sounds were still there, just more distant. I even went to Chinatown to the opium house. I got no relief there, and I didn't feel good about it."

"And the Reverend helped you?"

"Finally, I went to talk to him. I was beginning to think demons had climbed into my brain. He told me that I must push the memories and noises out by replacing them with other things."

"And how did you do that?"

"He came to my room, right there in our hotel, and sat by my bed. He read the Psalms without stopping an entire night. For several nights that man did that, just for me. It must have taken a week, but little by little, my mind could hear his reading more than those horrible noises. Each night I fell asleep a little faster and slept longer. When I awoke and started thrashing around, the Rev started reading right where he had left off"

Becca walked silently along. "Did it cure you? Are you not bothered by it now?"

"I don't think there's a cure. But I have a way to cope now. Some nights I'm not bothered, but on others I am. When that occurs, I quote a few very special Psalms over and over until I fall to sleep. He was right about that. Keeping my mind busy by memorizing the Psalms seemed to crowd out the other. The farther I get from the war, the less intense it is. The Rev. says I need time to build new memories. I think he's right."

"Well then, I'll try my best to not needle him ... but he'd better not pressure me."

When they returned to the Redwood Hotel, the minister and doctor had gone. Minnie and Albert remained. A table was set up outside, and Molly was placing the cold foods on it.

"There you are," she greeted. "You are just in time for a light supper. This is the last of the pies. It's such a pretty day to eat out of doors."

Hannah whispered, "Your clothes were dry so I took them off the line. I put them in the ironing basket."

"Thanks Hannah, I forgot all about them."

After supper was cleared away, they gathered in the parlor. Becca walked over to the piano. She sat down and placed her fingers on the keys. Suddenly, "Chop Sticks" came to mind. She played one round of it, remembering how she and Beth had played this in duet as a game.

"That's interesting, dear. What's that little piece called?" asked Minnie.

"Oh, it's just a kids' tune."

Picking up the sheet music that lay on top of the piano, she studied the notes...Not so different from the flute, just an octave lower. I do remember learning the notes for flute.

Minnie approached and looked over her shoulder. "Why don't you try that one dear? It's not a complicated piece."

"I can't remember the keys," she explained...*Since I never knew them in the first place.*

"It's sure to come back to you. This is middle C. Here is A. You just go right up the scale, A to G and then it starts over. Remember?"

"I was trying to remember how to play the scales," *Considering I didn't even master them on the flute.*

Minnie played the C- scale with her right hand, then with her left hand, and lastly with both together.

"There does that help you remember?"

Becca hesitantly tried what Mini had showed her with her right hand.

"Perfect, see it'll come back to you. Your head is still healing."

Becca tried with her left and then both together. She was stunned. It seemed her fingers had a mind of their own.

"Would you like me to write the others down for you? Minnie asked. "Just to help you remember the sharps and flats in the different keys, until your memory returns."

After working with Minnie for an hour, Becca was amazed...*If I had known piano was this enjoyable, I would have taken lessons and learned it years ago.*

Taking the stack of papers, filled with scales and simple exercises, Becca retired to her room. She had much to write about in the journal.

She wrote about her interaction with the Reverend, about Thad, her practice session with piano, and suggested Beth get a small keyboard for Delphi. She turned out the lamp and went to sleep.

26

"You have to accept whatever comes and the only important thing is that you meet it with courage and with the best that you have to give."

—Eleanor Roosevelt

Becca slept well. She stirred in the pre-dawn hours and wondered why she had awakened. The clock struck Four. Then, she noticed a blue glow in the corner. *Delphi?*

"Oui, it's me. I couldn't sleep so I read your diary. It sent me here...again."

Well, if you read what I wrote, you know that I practiced piano as you advised.

"I'm very happy you practiced. You should also practice singing. My voice will need to be ready when I can use it again."

You must understand, Delphi, it took a lot of courage for me to sit at the piano, with people listening, and attempt to play. I can't carry a tune. Don't expect me to make a fool of myself singing.

"Oh, but you must. My voice requires practice, and for now it's in your care."

Did you notice that I suggested Beth pick you up a keyboard. You can play it while you're in the hospital?

"What does that mean... keyboard?"

It's like a piano but smaller. Some are so small; they set on your lap. I thought it might give you some entertainment while you're in the hospital.

"Ahh, I'll mention it to Beth when she comes in later. Can she purchase sheet music?"

Oh yes, and songbooks too. Ask her to get classic pieces from the 19th century.

"I also read about your remarks to the priest. I met Tate on the ship. He's a fine man I'm sure. He mentioned to me that he has always been a free man. He was educated to the fourth grade and was taught trades useful to working on the steamers He studied with some sort of priest for a while."

Really… I'm glad we agree about Tate. He saved my life and your body.

"That's all very well, but you are making a mistake in scolding the town priest about not asking Tate to church or to dinner with him."

That isn't what I was doing, Delphi. He's a minister, not a priest and I wasn't scolding the Reverend. I was pointing out that with his self-righteousness, he must be aware that he is falling short of Jesus' teachings as much as the people he condemns.

"I was raised Catholic, and heard scripture only in Latin. I know nothing of what you speak …But you must not offend the religious leaders. We need them to approve of you."

We need them? I don't care if the Reverend approves of me or not. Actually, I'm not sure I approve of him.

"Oh, but you must care! It's most important to be respected by the community. That requires acceptance from all community leaders. My secret past must be left behind me. I want you to go to his Mass every Sunday."

It's a protestant church; they don't have Mass, just long prayers and sermons.

"Whatever they call it… do it, please."

Delphi, I appreciate your plans for returning to this time and in changing your life, but you simply can't control everything I do….Delphi…?

Darn! She always gets the last word and fades away…"do this … don't do that"… She has lots of time to sit and think about what I'm doing or not doing, that's the problem.

Becca got up and dressed for the day. She would help Hannah with washday and then go to The Mercantile to buy a blanket. She read from one of the novels until it was time to go downstairs.

After breakfast, she was surprised to see Hannah setting up the washing task outdoors. The girl swung the sickle like a pro, clearing out a large circle of weeds for the huge iron pot. Then she stacked wood, started a fire and set the iron kettle on the flames. Together, they carried buckets of water from the pump and rain barrel until it was filled to Hannah's satisfaction.

"Why are we doing this out here and not in the washroom?" Becca asked.

Hannah shaved a generous amount of lye soap into the water. "We wash inside when it's raining or cold. This works better with so many sheets to launder."

While the pot heated, Hannah sorted the laundry in the washroom. She wrestled one of the tubs from the space, and placed it beside the iron container. While Becca carried water from the pump to fill the rinse tub, Hannah strung another clothesline from the evergreen tree to a live oak. She explained that extra clothesline would be needed.

Hannah asked Becca to bring out a pile of laundry while she fed the fire with more wood. The sheets and pillow cases were placed in the hot water and Hannah poked them under with a long stick. "Now, we need to chop more wood. These pieces are too big to slip under the kettle," she said retrieving the axe from the shed.

"We're going to chop wood?"

"Of course, how else can we make it smaller?" She placed a stick of firewood on its end, raised the axe over her head and buried it into the top. Wiggling the axe, she released the wood's grip, and repeated the assault, splitting the log into two halves.

Becca was amazed. "Hannah, be careful, you could chop off your foot."

Hannah kicked the pieces toward Becca. She picked them up and started a stack near the fire. Hannah split several more.

"Do you want to try?"

Becca started to decline then considered the opportunity... *You never know when I'll need to have this skill...and besides I've wanted strength training.*

"Sure, tell me what to do."

Hannah set up another piece of firewood and pointed to the center.

"Just keep your eye on the wood, stare at the spot you want to hit, then lift the axe and swing as hard as you can."

Becca shifted around in her work dress bodice, thinking how ill-fitted the sleeves felt, she picked up the axe. *..Ok...that's not so heavy...* She lifted and swung, but try as she might, she could not keep her eye on the firewood. She couldn't keep her eyes opened in fact, and the axe came down on the edge of the top of the wood. The wood flipped up in the air, came down several yards away and bounced.

"Nope, that's not how it done, Delphi."

"I realize that, Hannah, I'm going to try again."

"Keep your eyes open and on the wood or you'll cut your foot off. I knew a boy that cut his big toe clean off."

"Thanks Hannah, that's encouraging."

The next swing landed in the dirt. "Mr. O'Shay won't like having his axe hitting the dirt. I'm going to get you a bigger log."

"Why? I haven't split this one yet."

"I'm going to get you one you can hit." She placed another piece of firewood in front of Becca. It had a wider circumference. "There."

Becca backed into position and willed her eyes to stay open. She took a breath, raised the axe and brought it down with all the power she had. She felt the metal contact the wood, but the handle flew out of her hand. The axe sprung from the log and performed its own loop trick in the air.

"Run!" yelled Hannah, heading for the live oak. Becca moved too, but as she backed up she tripped over the log she had previously tried to whack, falling on her bottom. Not knowing where the axe was going to land, she wrapped her arms around her head. It rested in the tall weeds a few feet away.

Hannah looked from behind the tree, than slowly approached.

"I'll take over now, Delphi. You're perilous."

"What did I do wrong? Becca got up and brushed herself off.

"You hit the wood with the side of the axe, not the blade. You didn't have a good grip on the handle. You could've busted the axe head plumb off"

She quickly and expertly split the log into two pieces, and then set each of them on their ends and in two swings had four pieces. Becca looked on frowning, realizing her lips were in a pout, again.

"How did you learn to do that, Hannah?"

"I don't know. Everybody knows how to chop wood."

Hannah set up another piece of wood. She split it with one whack. Give me that axe, Hannah. I'll do this if it kills me."

"Nope, the way you do it, I might be the one you kill."

She smacked another log and kicked the two pieces out of the way.

"Give me that axe, Hannah!"

"Nope, you go stir the clothes, I'll finish here."

"If you don't give me that axe right this minute, I'll not take you with me when I meet Sarah."

Hannah stopped and wiped her forehead with her arm. She handed Becca the axe and took refuge behind the big oak. Several more attempts without coaching and Becca mastered it, though she doubted she would ever be as fast at it as her young mentor.

The sheets were boiling. Hannah pushed the long stick into the pot and wiggled it around until she had positioned it in the middle of the bedding. She lifted the soaking fabric out of the water. She instructed Becca to take the other staff and place it behind the dripping sheet. The two twisted the poles in opposite directions, wringing out the water. Hannah then dropped it into the cold water.

When the items were all out of the wash, Hannah poured another bucket of water in the big pot and some more shavings of soap. In went more sheets and pillowcases. They repeated the process when removing them from the cold rinse and hung them on the line...*I can see why no one feels the need for a lot of clothing changes, this is dang hard.*

They had started at seven-thirty and finished at one-o-clock. They ate their mid-day meal in the kitchen since their work caused them to miss the regular mealtime. Becca scooped the mixture of boiled potatoes, cabbage, onions, and chunks of ham into a soup bowl and sat at the table...*Now to go shopping for a blanket.*

Becca washed her bowl and utensils and put them away. She climbed the backstairs, entered her room and removed the damp work dress. She hung it up to dry. After washing in the basin, she dusted on soda for deodorant, splashed a bit of rosewater on her hair, and smoothed it into a bun. She dressed in the wool outing dress. Leaving her room she moved down the hall and knocked on Elsie's door. *She'll be leaving soon. I'll ask her to go along.*

Elsie, lying in her dressing gown on the bed, asked her in.

"Oh, I'm sorry to disturb your rest. I'm going to The Mercantile and thought you might want to come with me."

"No, thank you. I've been feeling a bit faint today."

"Can I bring you anything?"

"Perhaps a piece or two of peppermint."

I'll get you some. I always bring it back for Hannah, bye now."

Becca left by the front door and turned in the direction of her destination. She enjoyed the sea breeze as she walked the boardwalks down Front Street to The Mercantile. It cooled her from the heat she still felt from a morning of hard work. She passed The Print Shop and thought of Thad. He would be occupied today, organizing the news stories, and setting up the press to print the newspaper...*I'll stop in and visit on my way back.*

As she entered the general store, a cowbell tied on the door rang the announcement of another customer. Several shoppers were looking at items on shelves; one was talking to James in the book area. Two others played a game of cards in the corner. Becca walked up to the counter. Mr. Sanders smiled.

"Well hello, Miss Castile, what can I do for you today?"

"I'd like to purchase a blanket, if you have one."

Mr. Sanders thought for a moment.

"I think I might have one or two used army blankets in the back. No one asks for them in summer." He disappeared through the door behind him.

Becca glanced around at the barrels and crates of fresh produce... The farmers must have brought it in...A crate of cucumbers caught her eye. She picked out two firm ones and set them on the counter. Mr. Sanders returned with a grey, woolen blanket. As he wrapped the blanket and cucumbers up in paper and twine, she pointed to the peppermint candies.

"And, a dozen of those, please."

"Your order will be in with the steamer on Saturday. Stop by Monday. I should have everyone's orders unpacked by then."

He handed her the parcels.

She left the store and strolled toward Redwood Hotel, eating the cucumber as she walked. Stopping at The Print Shop., she entered, Thad's face lit up into a bright smile.

"Good afternoon, Delphi, what a surprise! I'm glad you stopped by, but if you came to buy a paper, they won't be out until tomorrow."

"No, I don't need a newspaper; I just thought I'd see what it is that you do." She laid her packages on the table beside the door.

"Right now, I'm having a rest; will you join me for a cup of coffee?"

She nodded and sat on a straight-back chair beside the table.

As Thad filled a cup with coffee for her, she looked around the shop.

A small woodstove sat in the back left corner. The fire had heated Thad's coffee. It made the room a bit too warm. The window facing the street was open to let in the sea breeze. A table and two chairs stood in front of the window.

To the right was a counter, the height of a bar, and about four feet long. On it, a ledger laid opened, a small container of ink and a pen rested beside the book. Several newspapers were stacked at one end. Becca assumed they were from the week before. A tall shelf on the wall behind the bar held containers of ink and other liquids unidentifiable to Becca...*Cleaning chemicals perhaps*... An opened door at the back, near the stove, revealed the printing press.

"Can I see back there?"

"Of course, but I'm surprised you're interested. I'll show you how it works when we've finished our coffee."

"Does it take you all week to print the paper?"

"There's a Tuesday and Friday paper. Each of them takes an entire day and sometimes part of the night. The rest of the time is filled with writing up news that's turned in, orders for printing from businesses. They pay to print posters for advertisement, menus for hotels and saloons, sale advisements, and such."

"The Reverend has tracts printed sometimes as well as the words of hymns for his services. It's expensive to order enough hymnbooks to go around, so he has me print out the words of his favorite songs. Sometimes I print reading sheets for the school when it's in session. They never have enough books. I've had no requests for that this year."

"Does that keep you busy the rest of the time?"

"The days in between the newspaper printing are less busy, depending on what printing orders come in. The telegraph is here as well. That can use up a lot of time. Especially now, families are responding to Doc's messages concerning their loved ones."

Becca took a drink of the strong brew and willed her face to not reveal the effect it had on her tongue. *This is pure acid...wish I had water to dilute it.*

"Doc Conner was here before you came. He sent another telegram concerning a body that was discovered today. Fortunately, the woman was wearing a locket with initials engraved. He was able to pair those with a name on the passenger list. He sent a telegram to her parents, though we're not sure we have the correct town."

Each time Becca heard another story about an identified body, she searched her memory. Did she see that name or incident in the book she read on her last day in the twenty-first century?

"If he hears nothing, she'll be buried here," Thad continued. "Polina maybe?"

...She was thirty-two. Her husband and children all died, but she was found first.... It was believed that her husband's insistence of strapping their possessions on everyone may have made their survival impossible...

"Polina, why yes, you knew her?

Becca jumped from her thoughts. "No, I know only a little about her. Her husband will be found but not the children."

"How can you know that, Delphi?"

Oh for goodness sake, I must stop speaking my thoughts...Thad will think I'm a witch or fortune teller or something...

"I guess I'm just not very hopeful about small children being found. It upsets me to speak of this, if you don't mind."

"It's not my intent to laden you with troubling thoughts, but there were so few survivors, we must gather what information we can from them. Anything you know may be pertinent."

"I really know very little." *At least not anything I can share.*

"I fear that what I must tell you will aggrieve you."

Then don't tell me.

"Doc said another body was found some miles south. She's a young woman about your age and very beautiful. They say she has the face of an angel and is exquisitely dressed. To have such expensive apparel, she must have boarded first class. Doc can't pair her to any names on the first-class passenger list. He believes she may have been one of Mrs. O' Kennan's girls."

27

"The death of a beautiful woman is unquestionably the most poetical topic in the world."

—Edgar Allen Poe

Becca looked down and fiddled with the blisters on her hands. "I can't identify anyone if that what he's after."

"Doc hoped that perhaps you may have seen her in the group. You were boarded first class as well."

"I stayed to myself and mixed with no one. I can't possibly identify anyone." *Elsie probably could, but if Doc starts questioning her, she might let it slip that Delphi was part of the brothel...Oh dear...what to do...?*

"Would you mind just looking at the corpse? It would mean much to Doc if he could resolve who this girl might be."

"Yes, I'll take a look, and I'll bring Elsie Barns with me. She visited with the O' Keenan party. She may know."

And if she's with me I may be able to keep some control of her loose tongue.

"Thank you, my dear; I know this is distressing for you."

Thad reached out and took Becca's hands in his as he smiled at her. He glanced down at her hands.

'Whatever happened to your hands? These blisters...are you still digging clams?"

"I was chopping wood with Hannah. They'll be fine." She gave him a triumphant smile. "I got pretty good at it."

Thad raised her hands to his lips and gently kissed the blisters. "Is there nothing you won't aspire to accomplish?"

For an hour, Thad demonstrated the techniques of printing as he worked. Becca was fascinated. She finally tore herself away and started back to the hotel. She scurried up the front staircase and into her room. Dropping the bundle on her bed, she selected two pieces of the peppermint before going to Elsie's room.

She knocked on the door and entered when the woman summoned her. Elsie was dressed and sitting in a rocker, embroidery project in her lap. She looked well and smiled when Becca handed her the candy.

"Are you feeling better?"

"Yes, very much so, thank you. Whatever it was that made me feel so faint and nauseous faded away."

"That's good. I'm glad you're feeling better, but you may not when I explain what we must do."

"If you think you can persuade me to dig clams or chop wood, you will be disappointed, Delphi."

"I must persuade you to go with me and look at the corpse."

"And why, pray tell, should I do that?"

"Doctor Conner needs you to identify a young woman. If you know from where she came, you must tell him. Her family needs to know about her death."

Elsie nibbled on the piece of candy. "Does he believe she was with Lilly?"

"Yes, I believe he does. You visited with her girls, you'd recognize her if she was with Lilly."

"But why me...you lived with Lilly's girls and would know her better than I."

"Elsie, I've explained to you several times, I have no memory of being on Brother Jonathan or with Lilly. I have no memory of you or the conversations you've related to me. Besides, I have to keep my association with Lilly secret so I can start over here. I'm keeping a secret for you and you're keeping one for me... remember?"

"Oh phooey. All right, when must we do this?"

"He'll come for us when it's time. Now, let's think happy thoughts. I want you to give me a singing lesson."

Elsie laid her needlework on the side table. "I heard you sing a lullaby to Albert on the ship. Your voice is beautiful already."

"I've forgotten how to sing, Elsie. You must work with me today as you'll be leaving on Saturday."

A few minutes later the two were at the piano in an empty parlor. Elsie looked through Molly's sheet music that was stacked on the side table.

"Here's a new one. I hear they're singing it at all the soirées."

"What's a Soiree?"

"You don't know? I guess Lilly wouldn't have had them at her establishments. They're gatherings, mostly for young people, for the purpose of singing and playing music. Poetry is read as well. They have such frivolity. I know of some girls who met their future husbands at soirees."

She positioned the music sheet on the piano. "Oh My Darling Clementine", it's a sad song with a lovely melody... *"Hey, I know this. We sang this in summer camp around the campfire...at least the others did... I mouthed the words.*

"I wish Minnie was here to play. I can only play the melody, but we can sing to that" Elsie started picking out the tune.

Becca cleared her throat, bracing herself for the obnoxious sound her singing usually produced, and began. To her amazement the sound was not horrid. Her voice lilted into a bell-like clarity of perfect pitch. As Elsie played the melody, Becca finished the song.

"There, silly, I told you that your voice is beautiful. Let's have you sing another."

She laid the sheets of music across the top of the side table.

The Old Clock on the Stairs, Philadelphia Yaller Gals, Old Ironsides at Anchor Lay, Little Rose; Ho! Westward Ho, Uncle Sam's Farm, Glory! Glory! Hallelujah, O Where O

Where Has My Little Dog Gone, Turkey in the Straw... I can't believe some of these songs continue to be sung one-hundred-fifty years after being written.

"Let's try that one." Becca pointed to "Glory, Glory Hallelujah".

After she had sung it as effortlessly as she had the first, she said, "Thank you Elsie. You've helped me regain my confidence about singing."

Which is remarkable....I had none in the first place... Becca took some time to practice the scales, and was thrilled at how quickly she picked them up.

Both young women were in good spirits when the doctor arrived. Hannah answered the door and Dr. Conner walked in. "Good afternoon, ladies," he removed his hat.

"Thad informed me that the two of you will assist me in this most unpleasant task."

They loaded into the doctor's carriage and silently rode to his office on C Street. "Here we are at my Surgery."

He assisted them out of the buggy and led them inside. Becca made a note to refer to Doc's office as The Surgery, and glanced around the room. There was a desk called a secretary much like the one in her room but nicer. It set on one side of the door. On the other side stood a coat rack where Doc immediately hung his black stovepipe hat. A few upholstered chairs were positioned by one wall with an ornate table between them. A scattering of flyers, explaining different maladies, set on top... *He probably had Thad print those...* On the opposite wall, a bookcase containing a large number of medical journals collected dust. A spider busily guarded a web she had secured to its corners... *He spends most of his time with house calls and not here, it appears.*

A wood parlor stove set against the back wall connected to a chimney that appeared to be shared with the adjoining room. No fire was in it. All windows were open, keeping the building cool. Doc opened the door and led them into the room on the other side of the partition. On an examining table, a covered form rested. The windows were opened in this room as well, keeping it as cool as possible.

"The deceased are usually kept at the undertaker's, but his rooms are overfilled at this time. I hope to make a quick identification of this young lady. There'll be burials both tomorrow and the next day. The coffin maker is working day and night."

Becca felt a bit guilty. She had remained secluded from the tragedy, but some in the town were consumed with the daily responsibility of addressing death and burial, and with no end in sight. She felt more respect for Doc Conner than before. He walked over and carefully pulled the light muslin sheet back from the face of the girl. Becca and Elsie stepped forward, maintaining as much distance away as they could.

"Charlotte," whispered Elsie.

The girl appeared to be no more than fifteen or sixteen. Her long blond hair nestled around her face like a halo. Her clear skin, now light gray from death, had escaped bruising or injury. Long blond lashes swept her cheeks. A delicate nose and heart shaped lips adorned an angelic face.

Doc addressed Elsie, ""Charlotte? Do you know her last name or from where she came?"

Elsie shook her head.

"No, she said her name was Charlotte, and she ran away from her home to avoid being married. Her father had arranged a match with a wealthy widower. He was much older. She was with Lilly's group, though I'm sure she was new."

Elsie broke into tears. Becca put her arms around her and led her from the room.

"There, that's all we have to do, Elsie, we can leave now."

Elsie sobbed for a moment and then contained herself.

"Charlotte was the one who begged me to join them. She was the youngest of the seven and wanted a friend her age to accompany them to Victoria. Remember, I talked to you, Delphi, and you advised me not to."

Becca shook her head slightly and touched her finger to her lips as warning to Elsie to say no more. Elsie understood and wiped her eyes with a handkerchief she had pulled from the inside of her sleeve. Becca made note of the convenience of keeping it there.

The doctor stepped from the room and shut the door. He walked over to the counter and dipped water from a metal bucket. Filling two glasses, he asked the women to sit in the green patterned chairs.

"I'll give you opportunity to calm yourselves before leaving," he explained.

He sat down in front of the secretary, picked up a pen, and wrote something on paper that already contained a list. Becca assumed it was Charlotte's name and the bit of information he'd obtained from Elsie.

"If she hadn't run away, she would be alive," he muttered.

"A bad marriage can be as bad as death," responded Becca. "We have no way of knowing from what she was trying to escape."

"Yes, that's true." Doc sighed, and then looked at Becca. "There's a man about town who calls himself Cain. What do you know about him?"

"Nothing, except he's dangerous, I'm quite sure of that."

Becca described the incident that occurred at the dance, and Elsie chirped in with added comments. Becca related the Sunday episode.

"He may not have intended harm on Sunday, but he was cagey. He frightened me."

"I visited the reservation last Wednesday," said the doctor. "They've had some cases of malaria. I was told by the husband of my patient that Cain, as he calls himself, was discovered on Sunday evening by Indians who were fishing. They believed he survived the shipwreck."

"I never saw anyone who looked like him on Brother Jonathan, did you Delphi?"

"I have no memories of Brother Jonathan," she answered. "But how could that be? We barely made it in a lifeboat with life preservers. He wasn't with us. That's impossible."

Doc shook his head. "It appears to me to be impossible, but the Indians insist that they pulled him out of the surf, over by Pebble Beach and revived him. They took care of him for two days. He then had the strength to get himself to Fort Lincoln where the soldiers gave him some clothing. His were ruined."

The women were silent. Doc seemed to be sorting through his thoughts.

"He came to me Saturday to be treated for a broken nose. It became acquainted with Thad's fist, I understand."

"Did he tell you he was from the ship?" asked Becca.

"No, he seemed confused about where he came from. He had discovered a water damaged letter in his original jacket. Most of the writing couldn't be discerned, but at the top of the paper was the word Cain and in another place one could almost make out the word Jones. It might have been the first part of Johnson. He concluded that his name must be Cain Jones, though he appears to be bewildered by that as well."

"Perhaps he's a lunatic," offered Elsie. "Maybe he's trying to be noticed by claiming to have survived the wreck. Some folks seek notoriety."

"Perhaps," replied the doctor, tugging at the curl of his handlebar mustache. "But his confusion reminded me of the same that you experienced, Miss Castile."

"In what way, doctor?"

"He stated that he had been on a smaller boat and someone attempted to kill him. He had been banged up on the rocks and received some gashes. A medicine woman treated his wounds by burning them. It's a method they've practiced for years. It seals off an open wound and prevents infection. They then treat the burn with herbal mixtures made from cactus, barks and such."

Becca felt her blood turn cold. *No, it can't be Ike's spirit...he couldn't have made it to shore...But it must be ...His spirit must have pulled a switch like mine...This place must be a vortex of some kind!*

The doctor continued. "He made the same remarks as you... confusion about dates and time...reference to a nonexistent lighthouse ... and... Miss Castile, you're so pale... are you all right?"

A strong ammonia odor brought Becca back to consciousness. She opened her eyes and turned her head to avoid smelling the obnoxious bottle the doctor was holding under her nose.

"Ah, now you are waking. How do you feel, Miss Castile?"

Elsie supported her head as she slumped in the chair.

"I'd like to go home now."

"And that's where I'll take you straight away, as soon as you feel strong enough to walk to the carriage."

Soon the women were seated in the buggy with Doctor Conner taking them slowly toward the hotel.

"Miss, Castile, I'm concerned about your peaked appearance. I understand today is troublesome, but fainting may also mean you're not well. I'll stop by tomorrow afternoon to check on you."

The women entered The Redwood Hotel quietly. Neither felt like answering questions that Hannah or Molly might have. As they climbed the stairs, Elsie spoke.

"Seeing your old friend Charlotte like that disturbed you all to pieces, didn't it, dear? You must lie down and rest. I'll tell Hannah to bring supper to your room?"

28

"Do not judge and you will not be judged. Do not condemn, and you will not be condemned. Forgive, and you will be forgiven."

—Jesus Christ in Luke 6:37

Once inside her room, Becca undressed. She slipped into the nightgown, dropping the woolen street dress on the floor in a heap mingled with petticoats, stockings, and the corset. Reclining, she stared at the ceiling... *So, did Ike, in Cain's body, recognize me? How could he? I look nothing like my real self... he can't understand the dynamics of what's happened to us... yet he asked me at the dance who I really am.*

She climbed under the covers....*Is he still determined to kill me? Maybe he wants revenge for taking him overboard with me... maybe he doesn't really know that I'm Becca... he could just be a mean evil person behaving the way bad people do... Either way, I need to be ready if he attacks me... I never thought I would need or want a weapon, but I do wish I had something.*

After eating a bowl of broth and dumplings that Hannah brought, she picked up the journal and opened it... *I must check to see if Delphi had added anything to the diary.*

> The authorities took the greater part of the Diary to copy some sheets. I removed the recent entries as advised. They will return it on the morrow. Today, the woman that moves and stretches my limbs attached a bar to the top of my bed. She insisted that I lift myself with my arms, over and over again. It was so wearisome. I even cried and begged her to cease in her demands. I do so want these experiences to end... *Oh Delphi, you must do the exercises. They're getting you ready for a wheelchair. You'll need strong arms and chest muscles for that.*

Moving to the desk, Becca wrote her events of the day. She described in detail the experience of seeing the dead girl, Elsie's information concerning Charlotte and the discovery that Ike was in the body of an unknown man, whose name might be Cain Jones. She blew on the ink until it was dry, and then closed the journal. As she slid under the quilt and extinguished the lamp, she saw her, the pale blue shimmering mist.

Delphi?

"Oui, only just now, I read your entry, your mood appears to be low."

Yes, I am. It was a shock hearing about Ike. That may also mean another poor soul is wandering around in 2015, wearing Ike's body, and wondering what's happened.

"Oui, that's what I must tell you. Remember I mentioned that a man was discovered on the beach in Crescent City?"

No, you didn't, you started to, but you left too soon. Tell me now.

"Well, Beth told me a man was discovered on Puddles Beach..."

That's Pebble Beach.

"Oui, that's what I say...and he's in hospital there. He was unconscious for a time and awoke not knowing who he is. ...so I heard"

So he must be the real Cain Jones.

"I believe his name is Jonah McCain. If so, I met him on the ship quite by accident. He had stowed away, and I gave him some bread. Poor man, he was a simpleton ... child-like.

I felt sorry for him. He had no one to look after him. He said he hoped to find work in the mills."

How do you know it's the same man?

"His picture and the story was placed in newspapers all around asking if anyone knew him since he seems confused. Your sister has insisted I read the paper every day to acquaint me with the times I find myself in. It is helping...I must say. His manner of speaking...as described...it reminds me of him."

Wow, poor fellow.

"Oui, they took his fingers to try to find who he could be."

They took his fingers? Oh, you must mean fingerprints.

"Oui, I said that...but whatever they learn in that way will not be the truth."

Oh dear...well there's not much we can do about him at this point... But I also want to encourage you to work hard with the arm exercises you wrote about. To manage the wheelchair, you'll need upper-body strength.

"I don't want to manage the wheelchair, I want my body back. I want my life."

That's not possible right now. I'm practicing the piano and even singing like you asked. You can do those darn exercises for me.

"You don't understand how demanding the theorist is."

Therapist, you mean therapist.

"Oui, I don't like her much."

You will work with her or I won't practice.

"Very well, I will try more, but you must promise to take better care of my wardrobe. Frocks should be hung or folded and put in their place. I'll need them when I am back in my body."

Say what? You don't have the right to govern every part of my ...Delphi?

Becca tossed on the lumpy mattress. After reading a few chapters in the novel, she fell into a troubled sleep, tormented by dreams that mixed all the experiences and information of the day into one nightmare. She was still tired when forcing herself to rise at six to start the day. *Tuesday's ironing...Yuk... it'll be hot and stuffy work all morning.*

After a breakfast of pancakes and jam, Hannah started the fire to heat up the irons, while Becca washed the stack of dirty dishes. Molly had served more than the usual number of guests, creating more cleanup time. Becca could hear the Reverend's loud voice in the parlor.

"Mercy, mercy, mercy....what grief and sorrow...what grief and sorrow. "

Glad I decided to eat breakfast in the kitchen...don't think I could start the day with his booming voice of doom and gloom... She moved to the laundry room. Hannah was testing the iron by touching it with her finger, moistened with spit. The sizzling sound confirmed the iron was at the proper temperature. She pushed the iron across a sheet and glanced up at Becca.

"You're very quiet, Delphi, are you ailing?"

"Just tired, I guess."

"I piled the pantaloons on your table. You can iron all the undergarments and pillowcases. I'll iron the outer-garments and sheets."

Becca picked up the iron and cringed as she tested it. *There has to be a better way that doesn't risk burning my finger.*

As she started on her own pantaloons, she grumbled. "It's so silly to iron clothing no one sees. Why do we iron underwear, Hannah?"

"Because...only lazy women wear wrinkled garments, Delphi, everyone knows that."

"Is there a book of rules somewhere that you take all these proclamations from, Hannah?"

"Nope, doesn't need to be, everyone already knows what's proper and right."

By the end of the morning, Hannah's concern that Becca would scorch something, resulted in her being reassigned to deliver the completed items to their proper places. Hannah finished the ironing. Becca dropped her own clothing off in her room, and moved on to Elsie's. When she knocked on the door, the young woman invited her in. Elsie was in her dressing gown and lying in bed. She was very pale.

"I have your clean, pressed clothing, would you like me to put them away or set them down for you to arrange later?"

"You may lay them on the chair, and thank you."

"Are you sick, Elsie?"

"Yes, just the same as yesterday, I couldn't maintain my breakfast."

"You vomited?"

"Yes."

"Maybe it's nerves. It was upsetting for both of us yesterday...the dead body...the news about that strange man..."

Tears emerged and streamed down Elsie's cheeks. "Yes, I'm sure that's what's causing it."

"Doc is coming over this afternoon. You must tell him what you're experiencing."

"Yes, I shall."

"Is there anything I can bring you before I return to my duties?"

"Delphi, do you think this could be because... I'm with child?"

Becca gasped. "I hadn't thought of that Elsie. I think it would be too early to know, unless you had a lover long before Hayden."

"No, there's been no one but him."

Becca sat on the side of the bed.

"Have you missed your cycle?""

Elsie looked at her quietly for a few moments.

"You're referring to Eve's curse?"

"Curse... I suppose you call it by a different name, but skipping it is a symptom of pregnancy."

"It's not quite time for my monthly curse...Oh, Delphi, what will I do if I'm with child? I'm not married...Minnie won't want me to be her governess if I'm disgraced. I'll never find a husband..."

She started to sob.

Becca put her arm around the girl and tried to sooth her. "I think you're jumping to conclusions."

"Sob... jumping...sob...over what?"

"I mean, you're letting yourself believe the worst without even knowing if you're pregnant. This could be a bit of bad food, or nerves. Let's wait until you see the doctor to decide if you should be concerned."

"When we were on the ship, and I talked to you about me possibly working for Lilly, you told me all the reasons I should not. Do you remember?"

"No, I remember nothing about it"

"One of the things you disliked about Lilly's treatment of her girls was that she forced one of them to destroy the babe when she ended up in the family way. She gave her no choice in the matter, remember?"

How many times must I tell her, I know nothing about Lilly and her business? Becca shook her head.

"You said that Lilly had a woman, working in her business, who could make the problem disappear."

"I don't know what Lilly did, Elsie, I do know there's a way to medically end a pregnancy. However, if not performed correctly it can cause death or serious health problems. It's against the law...*At this time, anyway...*

"I thought you might tell me how...what they did to...you know...to end it."

Footsteps in the hall reminded Becca that she needed to finish her work with Hannah. *She's probably bringing up the rest of the clean laundry... Becca excused herself and left the room...*

"I'm sorry, Hannah, I was helping Elsie, I'll get the rest."

"No need, it's finished. Mrs. O'Shay has potato soup ready. Is Miss Barns coming down?"

"Not right now, I'll bring her lunch up after we eat. "The two started down the back staircase.

"Why is Miss Barns staying in her room so much of the time?"

"She'll tell us if and when she wishes us to know."

Becca and Hannah assisted Molly with carrying the serving bowls to the dining room table. Molly carried the large urn of potato soup, Hannah delivered the platter of sliced bread and bowl of butter, and Becca completed the service with a large pitcher of tea. She missed having ice, but no one else seemed to mind.

"Mercy, Mrs. O'Shay, you continue to amaze us with your fine cooking," offered the Reverend, tucking his napkin into his collar...

...Great, if I knew he was here, I would have eaten upstairs with Elsie...

The table was crowded. The Rev and his wife sat next to Mr. O'Shay. Minnie and Albert were placed opposite of them. Thad and several men, new to Becca, sat near the other end and three chairs remained empty.

Hannah and Molly took two of the seats and Becca circled the table as she poured tea. She was aware of everyone's silence as they waited for her to complete the task so that the Reverend could pray. The table grace wasn't said unless the Reverend was present, which amused Becca. She took her seat. Rather than asking the preacher to pray, Mr. O'Shay bowed his head and began.

"Heavenly Father, please bless this food and the hands that earned it, and the hands that prepared it, and those who partake of it. Amen. Have some soup, Rev."

Becca resisted a smile. *I must not be the only one who doesn't enjoy the Reverend's long table prayers...* Molly shot a disapproving glance at her husband, who ignored her as he buttered his bread.

"Well, the funeral service went well this morning, don't you think Rev?" he asked.

"Yes it did, yes it did. I feel so sorrowful that some graves will never be marked, so sorrowful. But the Heavenly Father knows who they are and which direction to send their souls."

Minnie blew on Albert's soup to cool it. "Will the young lady be part of the burial this afternoon doctor?"

Doc nodded. "Yes, we must wait no longer for her burial. I now know all I'll be able to find out about her. I have no known relatives to contact for her."

"In normal situations, began the minister, " these poor souls wouldn't be buried in the same graveyards. The righteous would be placed in the cemetery by the church, while those of less reputation would be placed elsewhere. With so many unidentified, we can't make that discernment."

The preacher passed his bowl for a refill. Becca laid down her spoon. Hannah and Thad both looked at her with concerned faces.

"And if they were known, who would decide who are righteous or unrighteous, Reverend?"

The minister looked at her with amusement. He enjoyed debate.

"Well, church members in good standing are always buried among the righteous, Miss Castile. The town cemetery is divided into four sections; Masons, Catholics, veterans, and Odd fellows. I set up a private cemetery by the church for committed Christians who didn't belong in any of those categories."

His face revealed his pride of having accomplished something noble.

Becca could not hide her astonishment. "No way...you're telling me people in this town are sorted out like buttons for burial?"

No one answered, but all eyes were on her.

"So, what if a person isn't a joiner and doesn't belong to those groups, then what? You can't die without having a membership card? Who decides if the deceased person is a committed Christian and if he is suitable for the church cemetery?"

"I do, and occasionally I allow others who are people of good standing in the community; Spouses of church members and other relatives... financial supporters of The Lord's work. "

Mr. O'Shay chuckled. "That's what I'm hoping for, my passing on Molly's good works." He buttered a second piece of bread.

"We'll get you into the fold yet, my friend," declared the pastor.

"And the unrighteous...by your judgment...they're all the people who are non-church members, or not related to church members?" Becca persisted.

"Yes, but that takes in a smaller number of people. Most of those who are excluded are those who don't belong among the righteous. They have demonstrated complete disobedience to God by continuing to break his laws. They are murderers, thieves, prostitutes, adulterers, drunkards, the usual evil sorts. They are also rejected by the town cemetery unless their included in the other four categories."

"So it means, dear, the girl Charlotte can't be buried in the public graveyard, but the mass grave." said Minnie. She looked directly at Becca, guessing her concern.

"As those of you who attended this morning's service know, two Christians were buried by the church. Four unknown souls will be buried this afternoon in a mass grave on Ninth Street. We don't know their names, but I believe at least one of them belonged to a brothel. I could not, with my suspicion, legitimately lay her to rest this morning."

"Do you believe in a final judgment, Reverend Walker?"

"Mercy yes, the Lord will separate the sheep from the goats."

"I guess he won't have to...you'll have already done it."

The pastor was thoughtful for a moment. "I understand your accusation, Miss Castile. You feel I'm making myself the judge of souls, but the burial practice is just an additional reward for those who live righteous lives."

"Dead people don't know where they're buried, Reverend."

"But their families and friends do, Miss Castile."

"So the reward is for the family and friends?"

"Yes, I suppose that is the case."

"Then, that means, those not allowed in the church cemetery are being punished...except they don't know they are punished. So...you are punishing their families and friends because the deceased didn't meet your standards of living?"

Becca could feel Thad's eyes boring holes in the side of her head. She refused to look at him. *No, you won't silence me.*

"I'm having difficulty picturing Christ giving this kind of instruction regarding burial."

She placed her napkin beside her plate and excused herself.

"Elsie is ill, Doctor, would you please come up and check on her when you're finished?"

29

"Panic causes tunnel vision..."

—Simon Sinek

Becca left the dining room and went into the kitchen. She scooped soup from the pan on the stove and assembled a lunch tray. Carrying it up the back stars and to Elsie's room, she knocked on the door. At Elsie's summons, she entered and set the food down on the bedside table.

"Are you feeling better?"

"My stomach is no longer distressed." It appeared that Elsie had not moved since Becca had last seen her.

"You look lower than snake shoes. Cheer up, the doctor will be up shortly and you may find you have nothing to dread."

"I feel so distraught. Life seems so difficult, don't you agree?"

"You have no idea how much I agree with you about that. Now, please try to eat something."

Elsie had finished her lunch and had freshened up behind the screen when Doc knocked at the door. Becca opened it for him and started to leave, but Elsie halted her.

"Please stay, Delphi, I have need of your presence."

Becca closed the door and took a seat in the small chair by the window. Doc approached the bed where Elsie reclined against two plumped pillows.

"Now, young lady, what ails you?" He adjusted his Ben Franklin glasses and peered down at her.

Elsie explained that for three days she had experienced intense nausea and dizziness. She complained that outbursts of crying were frequent. Doc checked her pulse, looked into her eyes and down her throat. He asked a few questions. Finally he advised her.

"You're a healthy woman, Miss Barns. I think you're merely nervous about leaving on the steamer. That's understandable, considering you survived a shipwreck the last time you boarded one."

"See, I told you there are no worries." Becca piped from the sidelines.

The doctor removed a small bottle from his bag. Mrs. Winslow's Soothing Syrup was printed on the label along with the inventor's picture. Becca remember reading about the heroin laced concoction.

"Take a sip of this when ever you feel nervous, keep busy, and you will be fine," he advised.

"No! She shouldn't take that, Doctor Connor."

Both Doc and Elsie looked at her with surprise. Becca calmed her voice and directed her attention to Elsie.

"If you think there's a chance that... you know...you shouldn't take drugs err... medicine. It could cause horrid consequences?"

Elsie burst into tears. Doc looked back and forth at the two women.

"It appears I may be uninformed about matters. Would someone please enlighten me as to why my advice is being questioned?"

Becca looked at Elsie who cried into her hands. Finally she raised her head and whispered, "I fear I may be with child."

"What? But, how could that happen?" Doc sat on the side of her bed and adjusted his glasses that persisted on sliding to the end of his nose.

"Doctor, you know how it happens," offered Becca believing the story of Hayden didn't need to be shared.

Elsie, however, was now ready to bare her soul and confessed the brief love encounter on the ship and the agreement she and the young crewman had to meet in Portland to marry. She also told of Hayden's heroic efforts to save her life, giving her his coat, fishing her from the sea twice, before finally getting her onto a life boat. She related how he bravely waved from the sinking ship as he went down with the Captain and other officers.

The doctor was thoughtful.

"The ailment, as you've described it, sounds like pregnancy. However, it's too early to know for sure. Would you permit me to examine your abdomen?"

Elsie nodded. He directed her to lie flat on her back without a pillow under her head. She complied. He carefully peeled back the layers of her dressing gown, exposing her pantaloons. Elsie, embarrassed, covered her eyes with her hands. Becca moved to stand by her, and placed an encouraging hand on her shoulder. *Poor girl... If you had any idea what women will endure for exams in the future; stirrups, forceps, ultrasound probes...*

Doc pressed his hands on Elsie's lower stomach, massaging it as Hannah might work a lump of bread dough. "Yes, I do detect a small enlarged spot in the area of your uterus. But I can't declare it's pregnancy until you've missed your monthly time. When is that to occur?"

"About two days from now," she answered.

"Yes, well we do have a problem don't we, young lady? Yes, we do, but, I don't understand Miss Castile's objection to you taking the syrup... It'll keep you calm until you're relocated."

Becca addressed the doctor. "I can assure you, without any doubt, opium can affect the development of the fetus. That medication has an opium base. Read the label"

Doc glanced at the label before giving Becca a quizzical look. He handed the bottle to her.

Becca examined it. *Nothing is written on it except the title and the inventor's name...Ahh...so this stuff is handed out like aspirin because no regulations are in place yet... No laws have been passed to protect a patient regarding ingredients...or the doctor for that matter... No warnings... no patient rights have been established yet.*

"What did you expect to discover on the label, Miss Castile? Why are you convinced it's made from an opium base? And even if it is, why, pray tell, do you think that small doses would have diverse effects on a developing infant?"

Oh great... shall I tell him I took a college class that addressed drugs and their connection to learning and physical disabilities...or what will be discovered about addicted newborns...? He thinks I'm only twenty, and few women even go to college yet...Can't tell him I read about the formula of Mrs. Winslow's Soothing Syrup in a book one-hundred-fifty years from now...

"Because...I've read a lot about medications and their effects on births and newborn addiction. Please, just trust me on this one."

"Well, it is up to Elsie what medicine she takes, so I'll leave it with her. I would be interested in reading the medical journals to which you refer."

"I wish I could provide them, Doctor."

"But I don't want to have this child," whined Elsie, annoyed that the conversation had drifted from her personal concern.

Oh dear...you're living a century and a half too soon to consider that, Elsie.

Doc returned his focus to the distressed patient. "It's my responsibility to provide care that aids the health and survival of my patients. I can look after you and advise you through the carrying of your child, and I can deliver your baby, if you're still here when he's born. I can't assist you with alternatives."

"But, there are ways..." Elsie glanced at Becca. "Lilly had ways..."

The doctor glanced at Becca, who faked a confused look, and shrugged her shoulders.

"There are those who can provide help to women who have reason to be relieved of female problems. Most mid-wives are knowledgeable."

Becca gasped as images of coat hangers and knitting needles flashed through her mind.

"If your monthly time is delayed you may want to visit a local mid-wife. There's an herbal tea mixture that's effective. It causes delayed bleeding to occur. I'll leave the names of two trustworthy mid-wives. If you're still experiencing these maladies by Thursday, have Miss. Castile fetch one of them. You may choose to stay with the woman throughout the treatment, or she can visit you here. You'll need her assistance for a full day and night. However, if this is what you decide, you must do it this week. If you wait longer then a few weeks, the effects are more perilous, and the procedure will produce more discomfort."

"Can't you just provide it for me Doc? What will a mid-wife charge me? I have no money until my guardian arrives on Saturday, and then it will be time to leave on the ship."

"No dear, I cannot." He pulled a small writing pad from his case and wrote several names on it with a stubby pencil. Standing, he ripped off the page and handed it to Becca. He picked up his bag and left the room.

Becca looked at the names. One surprised her.

'Delphi, will you find that woman and bring her here?" Elsie asked with urgency.

"The doctor stated that you must think about it for a few days. No decision should be made without careful thought, Elsie, especially one you might regret."

"I've been thinking of nothing else. That's why I asked the doctor about it."

Becca sat on the bed next to the distraught girl. "This is a decision that should be yours alone. I'll assist you in contacting the mid-wife; I'll even help you with her fee, if that's your choice, but, I insist that first you speak with Minnie. You need to factor in all options."

"But if Minnie knows about this, she won't want me to be the governess for Albert."

"I think you underestimate her wisdom, Elsie. She gave both of us good counsel after the tragedy that landed us here, remember? She thought of a solution to keep you from having to live with a cranky aunt, and gave me advice about starting over with my life. She'll be more understanding than you think."

Elsie toyed with the edge of the quilt.

Becca continued." I couldn't help but notice the tenderness in your voice as you told Doc about Hayden and how he worked so hard to save your life. Are you sure you want to end a pregnancy, if you are pregnant, that began with the affection the two of you felt for one another?"

Tears again started to flow freely down pale cheeks.

"It's not that I want to, but that I must. The child and I would be shamed and shunned our entire lives. That's not the sort of existence I can force upon a child."

"Can you please just talk with Minnie? She's offered you a new life. Don't you owe her your honesty?"

"Very well, but if she rejects me, I'm moving in with you."

"It's a deal."

Becca left Elsie, encouraged her to rest, took Mrs. Winslow Soothing Syrup with her, and stepped out into the hall. The clock said two-fifteen. *I'll go and talk with Mrs. Leng... I owe that to Elsie... This really must be her choice. Either way...she's the one who has to live with the consequences.*

She stopped by her room to grab her purse and parasol. Slipping down the back stairs, she cut through an alley and connected with Second Street. The sun was bright. A few people stood outside businesses. Several glanced at her curiously. She walked the seven blocks swiftly until she reached Leng's Shop. Stepping inside she nodded at Mr. Leng who was hanging several new shirts in the window. 'I need to speak with your wife, please."

He directed her to the backroom. She pushed aside the paisley curtain hanging in the doorway. Mrs. Leng sat at a table, sewing furiously on one of Delphi's new dresses. She looked up.

"Hello, no, not ready now. Will be ready Saturday,"

Becca smiled. "I'm not here about the dresses. I'd like to speak with you about a different matter."

The woman nodded toward a chair beside her, and Becca sat down.

"Doc Connor gave me your name for mid-wife services. He recommended you, in fact."

Mrs. Leng laid down the sewing and looked a Becca. "You need mid-wife?"

"My friend might. She's late with her period... her... her monthly curse?"

"Oh, she needs tea?"

Becca nodded.

"Why she, not you, come for tea?"

"I offered because I know you."

"I see."

Mrs. Leng stood up and went into a small area behind another paisley curtain in the back corner of the room. As she opened a silk panel and walked through, Becca saw shelves holding jars filled with leaves and powders. Soon she returned with a folded paper and sat down in the chair next to Becca. The paper was folded four ways. A cotton cord secured it and was tied in a bow. She handed it to Becca.

"This is special tea mixed with poppy, Cyclamen, and vedy special herb from China...many kinds...this one best.... Makes two pots... drink four cups first day, four cups first night.... Add much sugar or honey, and a spoon of ginger. Ginger helps. Sugar alright...make less bitter. ..Stay with friend all night. She feel sick...may vomit... bowels move much."

"Is there any danger? Can this make her sick or cause any health risks?"

"What I say already...Little headache maybe... stomach pain, sure...then bleeding start...all better... throw extra out." She shook her head and posed a serious expression. "Must not leave it out... cause mistakes."

"What do I owe you?"

The woman picked up the sewing, "Not worry, I put on bill...I call it lace."...*Ahh... its lace is it? That's a good cover. No one can trace that I purchased special Tea...I wouldn't want to end up in a 19th century jail...wonder if I could get hung for this?*

As Becca stood to go, Mrs. Leng added, "Drink tea tomorrow, so you come work Saturday..."?

"It really is for a friend and not me," assured Becca, "and I'll be here Saturday."

Stepping out into the sunlight, she tucked the packet into her purse and opened her parasol. As she raised it above her head, she caught her breath. Cain stood directly in front of her.

30

"Providence has its appointed hour for everything. We cannot command results... we can only strive."

—Mahatma Gandhi

For several moments Becca and Cain looked at one another. His eyes held a wild, confused expression. She could feel her heartbeat increase, thumping in her ears. Stepping to one side, she attempted to pass. Cain moved to block her.

"Please excuse me, Sir, I need to pass."

"I'll let you pass when you tell me who you are."

Glancing around Becca could see that the few people entering various shops were taking no notice on her situation. *Darn, I doubt if most of these possible witnesses can speak English...* She took a moment to calm her voice. "I'm Delphi Castile, though I don't understand why you're interested." She stepped to the right of the man but he again, moved to block her. Becca considered returning to the Leng's Shop but decided that Cain might follow...*I would never want to bring harm to the Lengs.*

"I feel I know you." Cain looked at her with an expression of confusion.

I'm sure you do...I know you...that's' for sure...

"You're mistaken; I've never met you before the dance. Maybe we should begin with you introducing yourself to me."

Does he know who he really is?

Cain blurted out, "I'm not sure. I...nearly drowned...some Indians pulled me out of the surf. I found a paper in my pocket that has the name Cain written on it. If you know me...I need help. I don't know how I got here."

He doesn't seem to get it... hasn't he noticed he's in a different body?

"I see. What's the last thing you remember before...nearly drowning, Cain?"

"I was on"...he stopped, and suspicion filled his eyes. "Why do you want to know?"

"You asked for help, if you don't wish me to assist you, please step aside."

"A woman tried to kill me...then I ended up in this place...I don't feel the same...it changed me."

I can't believe you survived...it must have been pure evil that sustained you..."Why did she try to kill you? Were you hurting her?"

"Why do you ask that?"

"Because, she was probably defending herself...."

"It doesn't matter...I need to know how to get back to Portland." He shook his head. "You remind me of someone."

Oh, no...he's on to me...

"Really, n what way?"

"Mrs. Cates...you remind me of Mrs. Cates. The way you tip your head when you talk...the things you say...The way you look right into people's eyes...she did that."

I didn't know I did that..."I'm not Mrs. Cates, sorry."

"I watched you...at the dance...walking, talking...you remind me of her."

"Well, if I come across her, I'll tell her that you're looking for her. Would you like me to deliver a message?"

He shook his head. "No I guess not."

"Good day, Sir."

Just then the door opened and Mr. Leng stuck his head out.

"Miss. Castile, please come in."

Becca walked back inside the shop, pulling the door shut behind her. Cain turned and crossed the street.

"You all right… that man…bother you?" the tailor asked.

"Yes, thank you for providing a distraction. He's bothered me before. I'm very afraid of him."

Mr. Leng locked the shop door. He set a closed sign in the window and pulled the blind down.

"Come…I show you…"

He approached a locked cabinet behind the counter and looked through the shelves. Whatever is he looking for…show me what?

"Ahh…is here…"

He took out a small box. It appeared to be overlaid with ivory. Becca was tempted to educate him about the future outcomes of killing elephants for tusks, but restrained herself. He set the box on the counter and opened it.

"This help you, maybe?"

Becca looked at the treasure in the box. It was a cylinder a little larger than a magic marker and at least an inch longer. The brass casing was engraved with ornamental designs.

"What is it?"

Mr. Leng twisted the item and it separated. Becca was fascinated. One end was a twist on cap, and the other a thin, sharp dagger. He handed it to her.

"Vedy old…deadly."

"It is for sale?" she asked, turning it in her hand.

"I make it gift."

"A gift… to me? Oh, but it's very expensive looking. I must pay you."

The elderly man shook his head. "Have daughter... live in San Francisco. Bad man kill her...we move here." He looked very sad. "No more children...that's all."

"I'm so sorry, Mr. Leng."

"That man...bad. You fearful...take this."

He took the weapon and returned it to its tiny sheaf. Reaching for her arm, he slid it under the cuff of her sleeve....*Just like Elsie's handkerchief. I wonder what else women have up their sleeves?*

She thanked him, left the shop, and turned in the direction of the hotel...I'll *figure out a way to tie it to my arm*...She didn't open her parasol but carried it, ready to use it as a weapon if Cain or Ike, whoever he was, approached her again. Reaching the hotel, she remembered that Molly and Hannah would be cooking supper.

Mustn't go in the back door...a hundred questions will meet me there... She entered the front door and scurried up the front stairs. She noticed the Grandfather clock at the end of the hall; four-forty-five...*That took less time than I thought*...She heard Hannah coming up the backstairs and waited. She addressed the girl before she had time to ask questions.

"Hannah, I'll take supper in my room at 5:30 please. Just make it tea and toast, I'm really tired."

Hannah nodded and moved toward Elsie's room to address supper issues with her. Becca slipped into her own room and shut the door. She placed the packet of tea in the drawer of the secretary. She laid the dagger on her bedside table. Stripping down to her skin, she slipped into her gown and reclined on the bed. Rotating her ankles, she noted how intensely they ached....*Those tight, narrow shoes and the fast walking...not a good way to travel.*

She examined her toes and saw they were very red...*Blasted shoes... either they don't know how to make shoes yet, or Delphi* didn't know how to buy ones that fit...*I must get to the cobbler and have some made for me that don't pinch everywhere.*

Then, she remembered the planned meeting with Sarah. ..*That's at daybreak, tomorrow. Good. I'll take her money and she'll arrange to make* moccasins. Goodbye, achy feet...I wonder how I'll explain them when people notice what I'm wearing...hmmm...that'll take some thought.

She picked up the journal. There was a new entry.

> **The authorities returned the diary. I returned the pages to the journal. Beth told me they copied pages that décrire your suspicion your époux... Ahh...now don't start using the French Delphi... enough, already. Also a page upon which you scribed that you believed he no longer vous aimé...** What?...oh... aime...love...I did write that I feared he no longer loved me... **They told Beth the other personnes were interviewé...Wait...what are you saying here?** Joe, Steve and wives were questioned? **They confirmé that Patrick has assurance on your décès...What?...** assurance...you mean insurance on my death. And his name's not Patrick...it's Philip. Yes, **I suspected that.**
>
> **They have motif but not évidence. ..Beth brought me the petit piano. The tone is impair to my ears, but I will accustom to it. Your fingers are difficile to use. I will practice until they obey me...** Yeah, well...they never worked for me either...especially with anything musical... So, they have a motive but no evidence.... As long as Philip denies everything, it's his word against mine; rather his word against a woman who seems less that competent by slipping into French and forgetting her husband's name all the time.

She closed the journal and was placing it on the bedside table when the spinning began. When the usual transition was complete, she found herself in the Portland hospital room. A therapist stood in front of Delphi who sat in a wheelchair. Becca watched in dismay as her body tipped back and forth, unable to balance in a sitting-up position. The therapist, a gruff woman, fairly shouted at the struggling patient.

"Stop your crying and whining! Recovery is not for wimps! You will teach your body to balance without the use of you hips and legs. Concentrate. I have no patience with spoiled babies. Your sister may spoil you, but I won't."

Delphi was sobbing; continuing to tip over each time the woman pushed her up into a straight position.

Delphi, I'm here. Try to calm yourself. I'll help you with this bitch, but you have to stop crying so you can hear me.

Delphi slowly stopped crying, but the woman continued to bark "Concentrate."

Now, look at her and yell for her to back the hell off, now!

"I can't yell. It's not proper for a lady to yell, it's not good breeding."

In this century women do anything men do to defend themselves. This person is a bully. We won't allow this.

"You'll never learn to sit up if you don't focus and try!" The therapist roughly pushed the leaning body upward again.

Do it, Delphi, yell at her. Yell, "back off, Bitch."

As the therapist gripped her shoulders again, Delphi yelled, "Bitch off, bully."

The woman stepped back. "Oh, you're going to be a smart-mouth are you? Well, I'll leave, and the nurse can get you back to bed. Call me when you're serious about therapy."

She marched out and shut the door.

Delphi, you don't deserve to be treated with disrespect. Never put up with it. But she's right about one thing, you do have to learn to balance. Think hard about holding up your head... Good... now try to position yourself by using your arms and hands....yeah, like that. See...you're upright...now hold yourself...awesome.

The door opened and Beth walked in with an armload of music books and sheet music. She looked surprised.

"What? You're in the wheelchair alone? You aren't even strapped in! Who left you like this?"

"I told that spiteful woman to leave ...to...bitch off!"

"There's the Becca I know," laughed Beth. "You're getting your old fire back."

If Becca had eyes to cry with, she would have. *Poor Beth…you forget I'm not in that body.*

"Becca told me to yell. And, she's here right now."

Beth looked around. Becca wished she could hug her. "Where?"

Delphi pointed at her own head. "In here, that's where she speaks."

Tell her I want to talk with her.

"She wants to talk to you, Beth."

Beth set the music down and took a chair.

"OK, I'm listening."

Tell her I said that the therapist must be replaced; I'll not have her abusing you or my body.

Delphi related the message, though a bit scrambled.

Tell her I witnessed disrespect and verbal abuse towards you.

Delphi repeated Becca's statement. Beth looked worried.

"We were warned that Ms. Ross has a direct and firm bedside manner, but she's highly praised by many who have suffered sports injuries."

Tell Beth, you're not an athlete. You're a woman who has been abused for four years. You need gentle handling.

Delphi was thoughtful. "What do you mean athlete?"

Never mind, just repeat what I said.

Delphi complied.

Tell her to request a replacement therapist. If one's not provided we'll complain to the hospital administration.

"How will we do that?"

Delphi, don't ask questions, just repeat my words.

When Delphi had finished conveying the message, Beth nodded.

"You're right. You and Ms. Ross are not an appropriate match. I'll address this first thing tomorrow. But now we must get you back into your bed. I'll call the nurse."

Delphi, do you realize, you've maintained your balance through that entire conversation?

Delphi smiled, *"Oui, so I did."*

Beth spoke softly, "please thank my sister, and tell her I love her."

Delphi looked at her "You just told her, Beth, she heard you."

Becca felt the spinning begin then heard Hannah's voice.

"Delphi, Delphi, wake up."

She shook Becca vigorously. Becca opened her eyes to look directly into the face of the scared girl.

"You frightened me all to pieces, Delphi, You slept so soundly, I thought you were... were...dead."

"I'm fine, Hannah."

"I brought your toast and tea." Hannah pointed to a small tray sitting on the bedside table.

"Take a sip; it'll help you wake-up. Did you have a bad dream?" She sat at the foot of Becca's bed.

"You could call it that, I guess." Becca took a sip and organized her mind.

"You were gone for a spell today. I always worry when you go for a stroll and tell no one of your departure."

"Hannah, someday you'll make a splendid mother."

"Did you meet with Sarah?"

"No, but I will at sunup tomorrow. Do you want to come? It has to be a secret. We'll be back before time for you to start preparing breakfast."

"Yes, I do so want to go with you." Excitement was shining in her eyes.

"Now eat your toast before it turns limp."

Hannah left and Becca slipped into her house dress, forfeiting the corset. Quietly, she padded barefooted to Elsie's room. She tapped on the door.

"May I come in and talk to you?"

At the young woman's consent, she entered, closing the door behind her.

"Did you get a chance to speak with Minnie?"

"No, I haven't left this room. Did you visit the mid-wife? Hannah said you left for a while this afternoon."

I wish Hannah would stop spying on me. That girl doesn't miss a thing.

"I did."

"Did you get the remedy?"

"Yes, I have it."

"Then, give it to me."

"Doc stated you should give it one night's thought. I requested that you speak with Minnie. After you've done both, if you still want the remedy, I'll explain the instructions, and give it to you to use."

"I fear telling Minnie, but you leave me no choice."

"Choices are what I'm providing. Right now, you feel you have no choice but one. After talking to Minnie, you may learn of others. I'll arrange for her to come here tomorrow."

Elsie sighed. "As you wish."

After bidding her goodnight, Becca left Elsie's room and descended the back stairway. She wrote her name down for a bath the following evening...*Meeting with Sarah in those secret places always covers me with sand or forest dirt.*

She opened the metal tin that held biscuits and day old bread. She took out portions for Sarah and her grandmother. She noticed a covered pan on the back of the stove. Opening it, she discovered a partial pot roast...*Looks like supper was roast elk and potatoes...*

She cut two hefty slices and added it to the biscuits... *I don't know why we don't get food poisoning without refrigeration... There must be some kind of immunity to it from so much exposure. Or...maybe modern bacteria got stronger with time...*

She returned to her own room, wrapped the food tightly in brown paper saved from her own shopping, and placed the bundle by the opened window where the cool ocean breeze would flow over it. She brought her ledger up to date and praised herself on how little gold she had actually spent, considering she had needed to set up a life in a strange era. Opening the small safe, she took out two five-dollar gold coins and placed them in her purse. She placed the packaged tea remedy into the safe and locked it securely. She thought about reading some past chapters in Delphi's journal but decided against it.

I'm not up to another out of body flight. I never know when reading her writing will draw me to her... Instead she read from her new novel before falling to sleep. She was sleeping soundly when she awoke to Hannah's whispers and prodding.

"Delphi, it'll be sunrise soon."

She jumped up. "I didn't hear the clock strike at all last night or this morning. I usually do."

Hannah was wearing a cape. "It's chilly out," she explained.

Becca quickly dressed. Opening the drawer of the secretary, she discretely picked up the dagger and slipped it into her sleeve. She gathered up her shawl, grabbed her purse and the food parcel.

"Here, carry this, Hannah; I have to pack the blanket bundle." She extinguished the lamp Hannah had lit before waking her up. They tiptoed down the hall, down the stairs, and stepped into a chilly fog.

"We should have brought a lantern," Hannah complained. "I can't see my feet."

"Then, others would see us."

"How do you know the way?"

"Listen, hear the sea lions? We'll walk in that direction until we see the silhouette of Spear Rock. But watch your step so you don't trip on something."

"What if following the barking of the animals leads us into the sea?"

"We'd feel water on our feet, silly." Becca laughed at Hannah's persistent questioning.

"But the rogue waves...they hit the shore so fast. I've always been warned to stay away from the rocks."

"Yes, and that's good advice. However, Sarah knows the tides. She arranges these meetings when the tides are far out. That's when she digs clams."

"So you trust her to tell you the truth about that?"

"Hannah, Hannah, do you ever run out of questions?"

"No," the girl answered honestly.

"Shhh," Becca silenced Hannah's next question. "Did you hear that?"

"No, Hannah answered, "hear what?"

Becca listened for a moment then started walking again. "Sounded like someone following us. I thought I heard the sounds of footsteps crunching the sand."

"Why would anyone want to follow us to the sea in the fog?"

"I don't know...lets be quiet so I can hear."

As they trudged along, Becca listened intently, but heard nothing. She strained her eyes to see the rocks. Soon the pointed, spear shaped, formation appeared.

"There, Hannah, that's where we're going.'

They proceeded toward the pinnacle, and stopped on the beach's packed sandy surface.

"Where is she?" asked Hannah, pulling her cloak tighter around herself.

"Shhh, wait and watch."

After several moments, the bronzed skinned girl slipped from a deep crevice in the stone. She looked at Hannah suspiciously.

"This is my friend Hannah. I want to introduce you to one another. You're near the same age."

Both young women remained silent. Becca tried again to break the ice.

"She has a gift of food for you and your grandmother."

She nudged Hannah to hand over the food package.

Hannah held it out. Sarah reached out to receive it.

"Here, a gift back to you." Sarah handed Hannah a small basket of freshly dug clams.

Hannah looked reluctant so Becca coached her.

"It's her custom to give a gift back to the person who gives one to her. Take it Hannah."

Hannah took the basket and smiled, "Thank you."

"How's your grandmother?" Becca asked.

"She coughs much...always cold. We must keep our fire low. Someone might see a large one."

"Here's a blanket and a few items of clothing. Maybe these will help keep her warm." Becca held out the large bundle containing the items. Sarah appeared excited and smiled her appreciation.

For the first time Becca could remember, Hannah was speechless. She was thankful. Sarah was too jumpy for an invasion of questions. Becca retrieved the gold coin and held it out.

"Will this be enough for you to obtain the deerskin for moccasins from the hunter you know?"

Sarah set down the bundles and looked closely at the coin.

"This is too much." She attempted to hand it back. "It would buy many skins."

Becca refused to take it.

"Can't you use the extra to get something for you and your Grandmother? Maybe the hunter who provides you the skins will add some meat for the extra value."

Sarah didn't comment. She dropped the coin into a small leather bag tied by a cord around her waist. She pushed her fingers into the bag and wiggled out a short stick burned black on one end. She then untied a roll of thin bark from the other side of her belt. Becca and Hannah watched curiously. Sarah squatted down and smoothed the two pieces of bark flat on the moist sand. She looked up at Becca.

"Put foot there."

She pointed to one of the pieces. Becca moved her foot in the direction she had pointed, but Sarah pushed it back.

"Not with shoe."

Becca plopped down on the sand and begin to unlace her shoes. She also slipped off her socks and garters. Standing up, she placed her bare foot on the soft aspen bark. Sarah traced around her foot with the burned wood. The same procedure was completed with the second foot. Carefully, Sarah rolled the bark and retied it to the cord. She stood up and gathered the bundles.

"The waters are returning. The light is near. We must go."

Indeed, the fog was lifting and Becca glanced back at the town. The images of the store fronts on Front Street were dimly visible.

"When do we meet again? When will the moccasins be finished?"

"Seven sunrises... come to us. Come to our camp."

"May I come with her?" Hannah asked.

31

"Your own soul is nourished when you are kind; it is destroyed when you are cruel."

—King Solomon

Becca and Hannah hurried across the vast area of rippled sand. Becca carried her shoes and stockings and Hannah clung to the small basket of clams. Hannah had found her tongue.

"Why would you want to get yourself Indian shoes?"

"They're more comfortable."

"How do you know?"

"Because anything would be more comfortable than these stiff, narrow, boots.

"If you don't wear tight shoes your feet will spread out awful, everyone knows that, Delphi."

"Is that why all the women's shoes I see are so terribly narrow?"

"I suppose."

"Well, I don't care if my feet spread out to their natural shape. I want to be comfortable."

"What will people say about you wearing Indian shoes?"

"I don't know. I won't wear them all the time, just for long walks or when I want to run."

"Why would you want to run?"

"Running is good exercise. I guess you've never heard of people running for health?"

"Running is what you do when you're scared."

"Don't you think you would be able to run faster when you're scared if you practiced a little every day?"

Hannah giggled, "You say the silliest things Delphi."

The sun was now up and a breeze moved in from the sea.

"Let's hurry," suggested Hannah, "Mrs. O'Shay will be up soon. What will I tell her about these clams?"

"I'll think of something."

Using their hands to assist them, they started the climb up the sandy, grass covered bank. Becca's eyes fell on a pair of men's boots directly in line with her gaze. She didn't need to look up. She knew those boots belonged to Cain.

"Hannah, hurry back home now, you mustn't be late."

Hannah had set the basket down to use both hands to climb the sandy ridge.

"You want me to go on ahead of you? She asked, eyeing Cain fearfully.

"Yes, I'll be coming, but I need to put my shoes on. Go now, hurry!"

I want her out of here ...if I have to use this blade, she shouldn't have to watch...

Cain had stepped back to allow Hannah space to climb to her feet. Becca tossed her shoes on the bank, and pulled up quickly. As she stood up, her heart pounded like a drum. Putting her hands behind her back, she manipulated the dagger from her sleeve and into her hand. With her other hand, she twisted off its sheath.

"What are you doing out here so early, Cain?"

"I might ask you the same question."

"I came for clams." She slowly brought the blade to her side, hiding it in the folds of her skirt. She edged her way around him and away from the ridge...*The shoes may have to stay...I'm not wasting time to grab them.*

"Why is it, that everywhere I go, you seem to pop up?"

"I need your help...that's all. You always get away before I can talk to you."

"Help? How could I help you? Why would I help you?"

"I think you're Mrs. Cates. I don't know why you're here looking like you do or why I'm here and like this."

Cain walked a few feet away and sat on the sand. Folding his arms around his knees, he gazed out at the incoming tide.

Becca sheathed the dagger and pushed it back into her sleeve. She sat down and began the process of putting on stockings and shoes.

"I know you hate me," he said. "I don't blame you for that. I've been a rotten person all my life, but I never tried to kill anyone before. I got myself in a mess with some loans. I was threatened. Your husband said he would pay me enough to free myself from the goons. All I had to do, he said, was toss you overboard."

Becca didn't answer. Her brain was twirling trying to think of what to say. She focused on lacing her shoe, keeping her side vision alert to the man. Seagulls began their morning hunt, squawking at one another in their pursuit for sea life that had been tossed ashore by waves.

"I thought I was going to drown, you really injured me, you know," he continued. "But I woke up in a lean-to with Indians pounding me on my back. I couldn't understand them. I couldn't figure out where I was. I thought maybe I was in Hell. I even thought it might be Purgatory. I had deep gashes on my face and arms from rocks. They needed stitches. When they held me down and burned the wounds shut, I knew I was in Hell."

Becca had completed the task of lacing her other shoe and stood up.

"An old woman put some kind of snotty goo on the burns and they healed real fast. When I got to the Fort, I saw myself in a mirror, except it wasn't me. It was someone else. I've lived on blackberries and some foods I could steal. There's one place where there's a lot of Asian people. One of them gave me some food and loaned a shed to sleep in."

"That's Chinatown. That's why you saw me there?"

"Yeah, couldn't believe I ran right into you like that. You know what's strange is that I found some funky coins in the toes of the shoes I had on. I used them, but they didn't last long. I don't even know what their worth was. They looked like antiques to me."

The morning light was breaking through the clouds. Becca's thoughts raced... *Should I tell him he was right about my identity. There isn't much time. I'll be missed soon...What should I do about him...? Ike tried to kill me, but the body he's in is guilty of nothing... If something happens to this man, the real Cain won't have a body to come back to...but maybe the real Cain died already...*

The man continued to mutter on. "Then when I figured out who you are, I knew this couldn't be Hell. You were a good person so you wouldn't have gone to Hell... but this sure as hell can't be heaven."

Becca interrupted him. "If I explain to you what's going on, will you leave me alone?"

"I've no intention of hurting you, Mrs. Cates. I won't bother you."

"What I think happened, Ike is this. You and I were drowning one-hundred-fifty-years to the day...to the minute... that the steamer Brother Jonathan sunk. We were in the exact same location as well."

The man looked at her puzzled, "So?"

"So, have you ever read or heard how someone coming close to death, and feels his spirit leave his body. Then, the person sees his own body lying there?"

"Yeah, I've heard of that happening."

"Well, I think that's what happened. Except our spirits somehow, passed through a portal or veil... or some kind of time passage. Our spirits, rather than returning to our bodies, entered other people's emptied bodies."

She could see him processing the theory as she watched his pondering expression.

"Those who drowned from the ship wreck had the same experiences that we did. In fact, my body is in a hospital in Portland, thanks to you. But a different woman inhabits it now, a woman from this century."

"Then, where's mine? It's probably at the bottom of the ocean or inside a shark."

"Maybe, or running around in two-thousand-fifteen wondering what the heck happened."

"Can we fix this?"

"I don't know. I'm thinking on it. I hope so. But, Phil is now being investigated for attempted murder, and I'll bet he lays all the blame on you. You'll likely serve time if you get back to our era."

"I've been in the big house before. I know how to survive there. I can't here. I want to be where I was born to be."

"Well, in the meantime, you have to survive. You should check at the lumber mill for a job. The blacksmith might hire you. You could possibly find a job on a fishing boat. But remember, you'd better stay right with the law. They have no issues about hanging people in this century."

Cain stood up. "Thank you, Mrs. Cates."

"Don't call me that or refer to me by that name. Stick with your new alias too. I'm Miss Castile."

"Right, I'll remember if I meet up with you again."

"I shouldn't help you at all, but I find I'm happier when I take the high road. If you'd like those clams, you may have them,"

She picked up her purse from the ground and removed the extra five dollar gold piece.

"Take this, its worth quite a bit. You can get a few nights in a hotel, a bath and a couple of hot meals. Use it to get started. Find a job and don't drink. You get really stupid when you drink, as I remember"

"Thank you, I appreciate it...I really do."

"And don't come around the Redwood Hotel or me."

She turned and walked as fast as she could through the loose sand toward Front Street. A male form in the distance stood looking in her direction. He started walking toward her. She could tell by the slight limp, it was Thad. When Becca reached him, she was breathless.

"Hello, great morning for a stroll. Are you taking one too?"

Thad looked at her quizzically. "I had hoped you would follow my advice."

Darn...another lecture...people are certainly bossy in these times...

"Oh, but I have. I haven't put more than two coins in my purse since you warned me about packing too much gold around."

"I'm referring to you gallivanting around all alone. There're ruffians, vagabonds and rogue Indians in these parts. The law and order you were accustomed to in Louisiana before the war hasn't taken root here in California yet."

"But, I took my walk very early in the morning, Thad, before ruffians, vagabonds and rogue Indians are up."

Thad's serious expression slowly melted into a smile. "That's the biggest blamed foolery I've ever heard. You think a b'hoy doesn't look for mischief early?"

"Even bad guys have to sleep sometime."

She slipped her hand through his arm and leaned against him. They pushed through the loose sand toward the boardwalk.

"To whom were you talking?"

Oh no...he saw Cain..."When?" she looked up at him in as much innocence as she could muster.

He nodded toward the beach. "There, I saw you walking away from someone. It looked like a man."

"Oh...just someone down there looking for clams... he had a basket full."

Thad walked her to the front door of the hotel.

"Aren't you joining us for breakfast?" she asked.

"No, Abe will prepare something for me. Doc requested I open The Print Shop early. He's sending out more telegrams. I'll see you at supper, perhaps?"

"Yes, of course." I must remember to go down for dinner tonight.

Once in her room, Becca freshened up, harnessed herself into the abominable corset, and hurried down the back stairway for breakfast. Hannah was seated at the small kitchen table finishing a hotcake. She looked at Becca with a questioning gaze.

Becca was famished. She served herself a pancake, doused it with blackberry syrup, and set the plate on the table. Glancing into the dining room, she made sure Molly was busy tending to guests. She poured a cup of coffee and sat by Hannah.

"It's all ok; I gave that man the clams. He was hungry and homeless. Did you get here before Molly came to the kitchen?"

Hannah finished chewing a mouthful and nodded.

"I did, but nary a minute to spare."

"So what's my job today, boss?" Becca chirped.

"We're preparing for the steamer. There'll be someone coming for every chamber. Mrs. O'Shay said she wants the guests to notice that she has a well-ordered household. We have to sweep and dust all the rooms, and make up the beds."

"Well, that'll be fun. I've wanted to see in those other rooms."

Hanna gave her a doubtful look. ..*Guess she doesn't think it'll be all that much fun.*

"When the Hotel is full of guests, it can be interesting," she offered.

"In what way?"

"The guests gather in the parlor. Some talk about the war and who's running for governor... things like that."

"You find that interesting?"

"No. But the uppity ladies from the city have nice clothes. I get to see the new kinds of frocks, and the different ways to fix hair."

"Ah, and you're so good with hair styling. You should do that for a living someday."

Hannah placed her fork on her plate. "You mean become a lady's maid? There isn't anyone around here that highfalutin."

"No, I mean like a beauty shop."

Hannah gave her a tilted look. "There's shops that sell beauty?"

"No, a shop that fixes hair."

"Who's hair?"

"Why ladies who want their hair fixed up pretty and in the latest styles."

"Why in Sam Hill would I want to do that?"

"For money, of course."

"Ladies would pay money for that?"

"Are there no hair salons here?"

"What are hair salons, do they sell hair?"

Becca rubbed her temples. *Sometimes talking with Hannah makes me dizzy...I suppose hairdressers haven't emerged into the business world yet.*

"Actually, Hannah, these guests are coming to claim their loved ones. Any conversation will probably be dismal."

"Yes," Hannah agreed. "The ladies will be in black."

Molly entered the kitchen with a stack of dirty dishes.

"Come along girls, no dawdling. There's too much to do to sit and chatter."

Hannah jumped up and gathered their plates. Molly filled the large dishpan and began scraping off lye soap into the hot water.

"A farmer is bringing me a bushel of cucumbers this morning. I'll make pickles for the weekend. Hannah, you wash these dishes while I clean the dinning room. Clean the kitchen when you've finished that, and start boiling the canning jars."

Becca tied on an apron. "Delphi dear, would you please clean the empty rooms. They quite dusty, I'm sure. The bedding is in the upstairs hall closet. Use it to make the beds up fresh."

Becca returned to the upstairs and collected a broom and duster.

32

"The oldest tree produces the sweetest fruit"...

—Old German Proverb

After collecting a stack of sheets and pillowcases, she walked down the hall...*I have to get in touch with Minnie today. Elsie needs to talk with her before we start the remedy.* She entered the first room and looked around. It was indeed neglected. It smelled stale and musty. She walked over to the window and opened it. *.. Might as well start by refreshing the air.*

An odd hacking sound caught her attention. She leaned out and looked down. A teenaged boy was whacking down the grass and weeds with a long handled tool containing a blade. It looked different than the sickle Hannah had used. "Excuse me. Hey...young man," she called down to him.

He looked all around for a few moments then returned to his task. "Yoo-hoo, up here."

The lad stopped. He took off his straw hat and looked up at her. "Do you have time to run an errand?"

He wiped his face on his sleeve. "I'll be done with this in a spell. Then I can."

"Do you know where the Walker house is? It's on the corner of H and Third."

"Yes Ma'am, I know the Walkers."

"Good, could you take a letter to a woman named Minnie? She's staying with them."

"I reckon so."

"Great, I'll write it." She hurried to her own room and sat down at her desk. Pulling out the stationary she had bought from The Mercantile, she penned a message to Minnie.

> **Dear Minnie**
> **It is imperative that you come today to talk with Elsie and me regarding an urgent matter. Please come as soon as possible.**
> **Sincerely, Delphi.**

Placing it in a matching envelope, she wrote Minnie's full name and the Walker's address on its front. She sealed it with a drop of hot wax. Opening the safe, she took out the sack of coins. She sorted through finding what she believed to be one with the least value. She locked the safe and ran back to the room she had first entered. Pushing her head out the window, she looked for the young man. He was at the water pump, splashing his face with water, drinking from his cupped hands.

"Excuse me..."

He walked back and looked up at her.

"Are you finished weed whacking?"

He remained silent as though he expected her to elaborate.

"Are you finished with that sickle thingy? She pointed to the tool, now leaning against a tree.

He turned his head and looked at it. "That's a scythe, Ma'am."

"But you're finished, right?

He nodded.

She held the envelope out the window. "Please don't get it wet. Are your hands dry?"

He looked at his hands and wiped them on the seat of his trousers.

Becca dropped the letter. It fluttered to the ground. The teen stooped and picked it up. He read the name on the front and looked up at Becca.

"Get ready," she warned, "I'm going to drop a coin for your trouble."

She held out the coin and he held up his hand, waiting to catch it. She let go and he snatched it from the air. The boy looked at the coin and back at Becca with a wide smile.

"Thank you, Miss, I'll run it over right now, Ma'am. Thank you."

He took off in a dead heat...You needn't be in that much of a hurry...I wonder if I overpaid him?

Returning to her work, Becca cleaned and aired out the six extra rooms. Discovering that none of the sheets were fitted confused her at first. She stuffed all the ends under the thin mattresses. She was proud of her productive morning when she returned to the kitchen for the mid-day meal of beans and biscuits. Just as she finished, Minnie walked in to the kitchen.

"Now what's all the fuss about?"

"The fuss is me getting ready for the Steamer," replied Molly as she fastened tops on the blue tinted canning jars.

"Some plan to stay a fortnight. They'll be searching for their loved-ones, you see. It's pickles today and jams tomorrow."

Minnie situated Albert on a chair and handed him a buttered biscuit that remained on a serving platter. She nodded and smiled to Molly in response to her explanation, then turned to Becca. She asked in a quiet voice.

"Now where's Elsie and what's so urgent that you sent a letter to summons me?"

Becca stood, removed her apron and hung it on one of the several pegs. "Come with me."

She turned to Hannah. "Could you please keep an eye on little Albert? When he's finished with the bread, you may bring him up. We're going to visit with Elsie."

Upstairs, she tapped on the young woman's door. Elsie opened it and invited them in. Her face was the image of gloom. She pulled over the desk chair and a wooden rocker for her guests. The three had sat quietly for several moments before Minnie broke the silence.

"Well someone needs to start the telling, or I'll never understand the quandary."

Elsie started to cry, placing her hands over her face. Becca cleared her throat and asked, "May I tell her, Elsie?"

She nodded and pulled a handkerchief from her sleeve. "Elsie has just missed her menstrual cycle...er... I mean the monthly curse."

"I know what it means, dear, I don't need you to explain. Why are you having a conniption about it? That's going to happen every now and then." She patted Elsie's hand.

Becca continued. "I've met with a mid-wife and purchased a remedy... a tea. It'll start her period, but I feel she needs advice from you before using it."

Minnie got up from the rocker and sat down on the bed by Elsie. She placed a comforting arm around her shoulders.

"Did that crewman leave you with child, my dear? That lad that hung around you every moment he could steal... Henry... Harry... Harvey?"

"Hayden, it was his last name, but he went by it" Elsie corrected. "Doctor Conner believes I'm with child, but it's very early. You knew about Hayden?"

"Oh Shaw! Anyone could see it all over your face and his too. The both of you fell head over ears in love. Neither of you could see anyone or anything but each other. People can't fall in love like that without others taking notice."

"Yes, we did fall in love. Even though we only knew each other for that short time, it felt like we were meant to be together forever." Elsie wiped her eyes.

"Well, let me tell you something, dear girl. There're a host of folks that never feel a love like that. Maybe you will again someday, and maybe you won't, but you should thank the Good Lord that you loved a man that much, and knew he loved you just as much."

Elsie glanced at Becca. She was clearly surprised at Minnie's reaction. The older woman continued.

"In fact, he may have loved you more than you loved him. He knew he would go down with the ship, but he fought to save your life. It was something to see. How many times did he fish you out of the sea and put you right back on another boat, only to have to do it all over again? Trice, if I remember right."

"Yes he was very brave." Elsie had calmed herself, but fresh tears tumbled down her cheeks. "He asked me to marry him. I had to get off in Portland and stay with my Aunt for a while, but after the steamer had returned to San Francisco, he was going to collect his wages and come to get me."

"Is that so? Then, I reckon your two are married," Minnie concluded.

"Married? Elsie's eyes grew large. "Why no, Minnie, that was the plan but..."

Oh Shaw! Sweet girl, what in heaven's name do you think marriage is?"

Elsie looked at Becca in hopes she would present an offering. Becca shrugged her shoulders.

"It's...it's a ceremony with a preacher.... and you wear a ring... make vows..."

Minnie looked at Becca, rolled her eyes and shook her head.

"There, you see. I knew she was all confused about that. Now, Elsie, Do you think Adam and Eve had a preacher and a ring?"

"No..."

"And Noah, Abraham, and thousands of couples were married before some pompous man decided it had to be a big frivolity. Do you think my husband and I are any more married that Abraham and Sarah?"

Elsie shook her head.

Minnie held up her left hand. "Do you see a ring?"

"No."

That's because we couldn't get one when we got married. We didn't have six-pence to our name. Do you know what makes us married?"

Elsie stared at her; waiting for the answer she knew was coming.

"Love and promises, vows you called them, and a lot of determination. That's what makes people married."

"So...you believe our promises are like that?" she asked Minnie.

"Did you two promise to love each other forever?"

"Yes," Elsie answered firmly.

"And you promised to remain true to him until he came for you?"

"Yes, of course."

"And he told you, he would be faithful to you?"

Elsie nodded. A bright smile formed on her pretty bow-shaped mouth.

"So you're married, Mrs. Hayden."

Elsie and Becca looked at each other in astonishment.

"I see no need to discuss all this with the people here. They're all very busy dealing with sorrow. When we get home, we'll get you into some black frocks. A widow must mourn properly. Now shall we talk about the remedy?"

Becca started to offer her opinion but restrained herself.

Elsie looked at Minnie in disbelief?

"No, I don't want the remedy."

"Oh but dear, you're very young... a babe takes a lot of lookin' after."

Elsie vigorously shook her head. "No."

"Are you very sure that you don't wish for Delphi to prepare the remedy?"

"I don't want the remedy!" Elsie's voice grew testy.

"Very well dear, it is your decision, after all. Now, I really must check on Albert."

Minnie quietly left the room and Becca rose to follow. As she looked back she saw Elsie, staring into space, hands on her stomach, and smiling mysteriously. After Minnie had a cup of tea with Molly, Delphi offered to stroll along as she and Albert walked back to the Walkers. She really wanted to talk with the woman privately. Each of them held one of Albert's hands, pacing their steps to his tiny strides. The breeze was light and the sun warm.

"I must say, Minnie, you surprised me."

"In what way, dear?"

"You know, your suggestion that Elsie pretend to be married. I think its an excellent idea."

"I didn't suggest that she pretend, Delphi. I advised her to accept her informal marriage. In my mind, she and that young man met the requirements God sets for marriage."

"I see." *A church wedding and diamond ring didn't keep Phil committed to me...that's for sure.*

"If a couple wants the commotion of a wedding that's fine. If a preacher is handy, that's a blessing. If it's possible to do it all up legal with the fancy paper, it's best. But things don't always work like that."

She stopped walking, turned and looked into Becca's eyes. "I wasn't going advise that young woman to have a babe that would cause her and the child to be shunned for the rest of their lives, nor would I tell her to take the remedy. I knew she was just scared of people's judgment. She needed to see she had a way to do what she truly wanted to do. She needed a plan to protect herself from the fuddy-duddies."

"She's very young and immature," commented Becca.

"She'll get older," replied Minnie.

"If she had insisted that she wanted the remedy, would you have tried to prevent it?"

"No, we can try to lead people to a decision, but in the end they have to make it on their own. Everyone has to make their own mistakes and earn their own successes. They're the ones who have to live with the choices. They'll live with the regrets or the rewards"

After a moment she began again. "When I birthed Albert three years ago, I nearly died. There's something not right with my pelvic bones. The doctor said I should never have another. Well, my husband and I love one another, and we aren't going stop our affections, though we try as best we can not to cause another child. About six months ago, I realized that I was with child again. I had to choose whether to take a chance of leaving Albert without a mother, or to seek the help of a mid-wife. I used the remedy."

Becca walked Minnie and Albert to the door and said goodbye. She slowly returned to the hotel, giving herself time to think through the day's events... *I guess women have always been problem solvers... Oppress them and they'll find a way to work around society's restraining rules and judgments... even in this century... Who would have known?*

33

"The art of medicine consists in amusing the patient while nature cures the disease."

—Voltaire

Becca strolled leisurely back toward the hotel. She turned right to walk a block out of her way. The day was too pretty to be inside. She took a deep breath...*I'm growing fond of this town.*

Thinking about the bustle of Portland, Becca listened to the noises around her. A horse tied in front of the saloon, whinnied...*Maybe I should get a horse ... Then I'd have to pay his board at the stables... guess not.*

A man with a mule and wagon drove down the middle of the dirt street. He stopped every few yards while a large boy shoveled horse manure into the wagon...*Guess that's no worse than exhaust fumes...*A couple of young boys played marbles in the dirt, while men stood on the wooden sidewalks behind them and talked. Cigar smoke encircled their heads. A few houses nestled in lots between the stores. One had flowers, and roses filling the small front yard. The other's yard was filled with children, at least five. They waved at Becca. A tabby cat sunned herself on the boardwalk. Becca walked around her...*This is not so bad really...not so bad at all.*

She was glad she had looped around the block. She hadn't walked this street before. She eyed a church as she neared it. A homemade sign announced its name in uneven letters.

Crescent City Church, Pastor The Reverend Titus Walker.

Becca stopped and looked at the building. It wasn't as large as she expected. There was a small cemetery on one side. She smiled, remembering her discourse with the preacher regarding burial... *I can't see that it's preferable to the other graveyard. That one looks over the sea...actually, I think I like the other one better.*

"Hello, Miss Castile. Did you just stroll by, or are you in need of counsel?"

Becca jumped and turned around. The Reverend had approached from behind. Under his arm was a rolled newspaper.

"Good afternoon, Reverend. I'm just strolling."

"I'm glad that we chanced to meet today. I wasn't sure Mrs. O'Shay would remember to tell you that Friday afternoon we're providing a supper. It's to honor the survivors of the...the horrible event. Most will be leaving us soon, and we wanted to pay our respects and give thanks. I hope to send each on their way with a blessing."

It wouldn't be polite to refuse such an invitation..."Where will this be? What time?"

"Right here at our lovely place of worship. We have bring-in suppers each month. We meet at three-clock and have a sing along. Then, the women lay out a bountiful meal under the trees. Of course a preaching service will follow."

"Of course." *I'm not going to get out of this unless I get very ill...Then Doc would provide treatment...might not be a healthy option.*

"Thank you, Reverend, I'll be there. Thank you for inviting me." *I swear, there's an evil, triumphant look in his eye.*

She turned to proceed and again noticed the sign.

"Reverend, the sign says Crescent City Church. So, which faith is it?"

He tilted his head as he prepared to present more than she wanted to know.

"This is a church that has passed through the hands of clergy of several faiths, Miss Castile. This hasn't been the kind of town that draws men of the cloth, nor do they stay long."

"And now...what Faith is it?" she repeated.

"I came here last year and the doors were nailed shut. I opened it up. It's what I make it. This sign is what people have been familiar, so I haven't changed it."

Isn't easy to get a straight answer from this man...

So...what do you propose it to be?"

I converted under the ministry of a preacher who called himself, Methodist Episcopal. He explained that after the War of Independence, the Episcopal faith wasn't in good standing with Americans. It went through some reforms. The American Anglicans adopted methods indorsed by John Wesley, thus the name, Methodist Episcopal. My mentor followed the teachings of John Wesley, an Anglican priest in England. Another denomination has now formed called Methodist. But The Most Reverend Wesley was always Anglican."

Hmm...There may be an answer in there, somewhere...

"So...you, and now this church, are Methodist Episcopal?"

Not officially. My mentor sent me to Seminary, at Newbury Bible Institute in Vermont. I completed one year before the war began. I volunteered as a chaplain for several years with the Union army. I was ordained for that purpose. Official ordination and an assignment will come later. While in my duties as chaplain, I met my lovely Grace. She was a nurse, working with the wounded. We married, and moved here. This is my first church."

"So you will become fully Episcopal."

"Perhaps...the war caused a split in almost all the churches. Congregations tend to hold the beliefs of the locality. They are as divided about slavery as the nation. It will take a few years for religious leaders to bridge the differences. Maybe the separation will result in new denominations. I'm waiting to see where I'll fit in... waiting to see." Hmmm...I never thought how this war would affect churches...that must be a real problem... Everyone thinking God is on their side...

"Are you from a Christian home? Do you usually attend worship, Miss Castile?"

"Yes, my parents are...were... Episcopal." *Oh dear, I think I remember reading in the journal that Delphi is Catholic...*

"Do you usually attend worship, Miss Castile?"

"Sometimes." *Usually, Christmas and Easter...*

"Very well then, we'll look forward to our little gathering. I assure you, you'll be pleasantly surprised."

The spring was out of Becca's step as she walked back to the hotel...

I must learn to keep my mouth shut... If I have to be Delphi, I need to be her... I just allowed my own history to filter into my persona...

Not knowing who might be in the parlor and wishing to avoid conversation, she entered through the kitchen. Taking the backstairs, she went to her room and sat in the rocker. Looking out at the surf, she reflected on the day. There had been some anxious moments with Elsie and some happy ones with Minnie. The Reverend had unnerved her. She thought back on her elective college course, History of Religion...

That had covered early Rome through the Dark Ages... *Now I wish I had followed up with the next religion class. It covered the Reformation and beyond...* A knock at her door jarred her from her thoughts.

"Come in, Hannah."

The door opened.

"It's not Hannah." Elsie stepped in. "I'm going down for supper. Do you wish to join me? Hannah told me that Mrs. O'Shay has baked a salmon. It smells wonderful."

The two young women descended down the front stairs. The parlor had several guests waiting for the meal. Doc, Minnie, Little Albert, and Thad looked up as they entered the room. The good pastor wasn't there for which Becca was relieved. As she glanced at Thad, he smiled broadly. Her distress of the afternoon vanished. Everyone at the table chattered happily. In spite of the past two weeks being tainted by the recovering and burying of bodies, spirits were brighter than usual. Molly explained the planned church supper to everyone seated around the table. She stressed that all were invited.

Elsie's gloom had dissipated. She talked of her excitement of buying needed items when her guardian arrived with money. He would be arranging her monthly allotments for the future... *Elsie will be giving herself some retail therapy...Can't blame her for feeling happy about that...*

"Don't forget, Delphi," Thad reminded. "You have items to pick up. I doubt if Sanders will get everything unpacked and sorted out right away. We could check late Saturday afternoon, just in case."

Becca buttered her bread and tried to remember what she had ordered.

"There's no hurry on my account, I'm working for Mrs. Leng Saturday until four."

Silence replaced chatter. After a few moments Doctor Corner asked, "What kind of work are you doing for Mrs. Leng?"

"Sewing, she needs help for a few weekends to catch up on orders. I expect to learn a lot."

"You will," agreed the doctor, dabbing his napkin against his moustache.

"The Lengs are good honest people. He makes my suits. Mrs. Leng is a skillful nurse. I'd employ her services more, but people aren't receptive to my having a Chinese woman assist me. She does much of the doctoring for me in Chinatown. She's knowledgeable with herbs. I've learned a few things from her."

Ahh... Doc... I'm proud of you. You do have an open mind after all.

"I must say," began Molly," There are plenty of godly women among your own kind who would teach you to sew. You needn't traipse off to Chinatown to learn how to sew on a button."

"And what kind is my kind, Molly?"

"Could someone please pass the salmon this way?" requested Mr. O'Shay.

"Why, people like you," answered the older woman.

"Well, when I was there I noticed she had two arms, two hands, and two feet, just like me." Becca teased her landlady as she forked another piece of fish onto her plate.

"Someone hand over that fish platter, please," repeated Mr. O'Shay.

"I'm sure she has a brain and soul just as Delphi does," added Minnie.

"Oh for goodness sakes, you know what I mean. She doesn't even speak the same language, or worship the same God." argued Molly. "Why, I've heard that those people have little altars with sacrifices burning in front of them."

"If someone doesn't pass that salmon this way, I'm going to offer all of you in sacrifice right on this here table!"

Molly reached for the platter, and Becca handed it to her. "Here, Charlie, all you think of is food."

"You shouldn't eat too heartily tonight. You might feel ill with the bleeding," Doc warned.

"Bleeding?" Becca asked, concerned that Charlie was ill or had been injured." Are you all right, Mr. O'Shay?"

"He's fine," Doc answered, since Charlie's mouth was too full of fish and bread to reply. "We bleed him every month. It helps to keep his weight down and his stamina up."

No...no...no...I just gave you points for being smarter than I first thought...now I have to take them back.

Looking at Molly, Becca said, "I didn't see any altar at the Lengs' but if I see one, I'll ask her to explain her beliefs. I think you've received misinformation. Regarding language, we understand each another. People really are more alike than they are different, Molly."

"Molly, save my pie until after Doc tends to me. I'll have it with coffee then," Charlie instructed.

"Well, if God wanted us working among one another he'd have made us all the same," Molly concluded, placing her napkin on the table.

Now that's nutty logic...

Thad pushed his chair back. He leaned over toward Becca.

"I'll drive you to work on Saturday. I bought the horse and buggy from Abe. He has a new carriage coming in on the steamer."

Later, as Becca carried a stack of dishes to the kitchen for Hannah, she noticed Doc and Mr. O'Shay sitting at the small table by the window. Charlie's arm lay on the table much as one would for a blood draw in a lab. Doc placed a small pan under his wrist that extended off the edge. To her dismay, he slid a small incision and tipped Charley's arm to allow the blood to flow into the container. Molly and Hannah continued with dish washing, paying no attention to the atrocity occurring a few feet away. Becca wanted to protest but she was speechless. Her knees grew weak and her vision blurred.

She awoke on the floor. Molly held a small bottle of smelling salts under her nose, and Hannah fanned her with a tea towel. Charlie sat at the table holding a bloody cloth against his wound. Doc stood over her wiping his hands on a towel. He peered down at her over his glasses.

"Have you never seen anyone bled before, Miss Castile?"

Becca slowly sat up. "If ever I'm ill, unconscious, or even near death, don't you dare do that to me!"

"My, my, Miss Castile, you do work yourself into a tempest, don't you?"

34

"In all debates, let truth be thy aim, not victory, or an unjust interest."

—William Penn

Becca went immediately to her room and prepared for bed. Although there was still light filtering through the lace curtained window, she lit the lantern by her bed, and the candle on the desk. She totaled the numbers on her ledger. She added the five dollar gold piece for the moccasins and the coin she had donated to Cain. This week's room and board were also added to the expense column. ..*Even earning half of my room and board and working for a few Saturdays at the seamstress shop, I'll still be spending more that I wish to...After all, it's not my gold...*

"That's true, it isn't."

The words in the form of a thought, invaded Becca's mind. She spun around. A blue mist shimmered in the darkened corner.

Delphi, you startled me. How and why are you here? I didn't read from your journal yet.

"I was writing in your diary and it transformed me unexpectedly."

Well, I'm glad... there's something I want to discuss with you.

"As I with you...a man sent flowers. They were delivered to my room. I'm not sure how to respond correctly in that time and place. In my experience, a bouquet conveys that a gentleman is interested in beginning an acquaintance. It's the first initiative for courting, but I scarcely know this person. What's the proper response?"

Uh... it only means that the person is sending best wishes. It's often done when someone is ill or injured.

"Oui, I see."

Who sent you flowers? It' wasn't Philip, I hope. The divorce process will begin, and you must not accept gifts from him.

"No, it wasn't him. There was a card. It stated only his name, Captain Frederick Gale. Your sister wasn't there today, so I could not inquire about him. Is he perhaps a relative?"

No...I have no relatives by that name...no friends either...Wait, I do remember seeing the name. It was in a newspaper in your room. I read it while you were still unconscious. Captain Gale is the coastguard officer who rescued you and Phil... Beth said he stopped in to check on you the following day.

"So what should be my proper reaction to the flowers?"

Enjoy them...You should thank him... You could call him on your cell, or send a note. Beth will help you get a phone number or address.

"I see. Very well, I will write a nice note. I don't like much...the cellar thing."

Cellar...you mean cell phone...When writing Captain Gale; try to remember to write all the words in English...

"Oui, I always do. I'll be going home to Beth's house on Friday. Your husband and his mistress are still in your barn."

Barn...? Oh, you mean my loft.

"That's what I say. I've met my new therapist. I like him, he's gentle. I'm working hard, rolling the chair myself. I'm getting more adept"

That's good news, but I need to ask you something before you suddenly vanish. What do you think of my using some of your gold to buy you a house? I feel I'm wasting it by paying for this hotel room.

"Oui, please do. The gold brick will afford a large abode. I'll need one to start my music school."

All right... But I must know Delphi, in case someone asks me to explain why I have so much gold, where and how did you get that gold brick in the first place?" ...Delphi?...Darn!

The next morning Becca began her day by helping Molly in the kitchen. When she entered the room, she was amazed at the fresh vegetables spread out on the table.

"Wow, where did all this come from?"

"The farmers are in town today with wagonloads of bounty. They've stopped by all the establishments. They always do this before a steamer arrives."

Becca picked up a cucumber, went to the water bucket, poured a dipperful of water over it and to.ok a big bite... *Hmmm...I've been craving fresh food.*

"No! What are you doing? You can't eat that!"

"I'll pay for it." Becca mumbled through her crunching of the juicy, delicious, dose of fresh vitamin C.

"No, I care nothing about your paying for it, but you'll be ill. Don't take another bite!"

"Why? How can it make me ill?" She sunk her teeth into the second bite.

"They must be soaked in vinegar first or made into pickles. They're not fit to eat, without precaution."

"Molly, I've eaten raw vegetables all my life. That's the healthiest way to eat them. You destroy the nutrients when you cook them."

Molly watched Becca finish the cucumber. Her face revealed her deep concern.

"Many have died from eating vegetables directly from the garden."

"Really, who? Have you really known anyone, or have you just heard stories from others?"

"You may ask Doc Conner. He'll tell you. Uncooked food causes stomach complaints. That's why the Good Lord created fire."

"Why didn't he just create the veggies already cooked?"

Becca soon realized her argument wasn't going to persuade the woman from a belief she had held a life time... *Perhaps the lack of washing the produce caused illness at times, and they assumed it was the raw food. Maybe contaminated water used to wash it was the culprit.*

By lunch time, Becca was ready to escape the hot kitchen. Jars of green beans, tomatoes, and carrots cooled on the table. Cucumbers soaked in a brine to ferment into sour pickles, Molly and Hannah carried winter squash, onions, potatoes, and several pumpkins to a small cellar. There, they'd remain cool until needed for roasting or stews.

Upstairs, Becca slipped out of the work dress, washed up, and put on the wool outing dress. She made her way to The Print Shop. A small bell rang as she opened the door. Thad stepped from the back room.

He wore a long tan apron that had ink splotches splattered is several places.

"Good afternoon, Delphi, this is a pleasure. Are you out shopping today?"

"No. I'm out for one purpose, to talk with you. I need advice."

"Advice from me... that's a tad extraordinary, you seeking my advice.

"His smile and twinkling eyes revealed that he was teasing.

"Do you have the time? It may take a while."

"Yes, I do. Yesterday I was behind-hand, but I worked into the night, and the papers are now printed. I'll fold them presently, when the ink has dried."

"I've decided to buy a house."

Thad looked surprised. Then a broad smile followed. "You plan to settle here in Crescent City?"

"Yes." ...until Delphi and I can switch ourselves around.

"Allow me time to warm up the coffee, and we'll discuss this notion you have."

As he poured her a cup of what appeared to be crude oil, Becca opened up the subject. "You see, I have a bit of savings. I've been careful with it, but I prefer not to dwindle it away on renting a room and paying for meals.

Thad took a drink of his coffee. "I agree. I've arrived at the same opinion."

"Really, you're buying a house too?"

Thad shook his head. "No, but I've been working on a large room above this shop. I have it livable now, and I'll move in very soon. Mrs. O'Shay may need my room. There'll be a lot of people on this steamer."

"I'm surprised. You've said nothing about moving out of the hotel."

"Perhaps that's because you're a very elusive lady, wandering here and there. When could I have told you?"

Becca smiled as she stirred sugar into the chipped cup of black liquid.

"That's true, I've been very busy."

"And where is this house you wish to own?"

"I haven't picked it out yet. I was hoping you might know of one for sale."

There are houses for sale. What's your intent? There're several small flat board houses near the shoreline. They won't cost you much, but they aren't tight. One has canvas covering on its inner walls, but the others don't."

"Are they big?"

Each has two rooms. There's one log house at the edge of town on the south. I was in it once. It has two rooms and a loft. There's a wood shed and chicken house with the log house."

"I need something bigger."

Thad was thoughtful for a moment. "The Crouch farm is for sale. That house has a second floor. It'd cost a lot of gold. The barn is new."

"I need a big house, without the farm."

Thad pushed his chair back from the table. "I'll get the ads. As I remember when I set the type, there is one like that."

He returned with an open sheet of newsprint. Pushing the coffee cups out of the way, he spread it on the table. Becca quickly glanced over the page. There was a mercantile ad announcing products that were expected on the steamer. Animals were listed for sale; milk cows, breeding bulls, horses. Several wagons and other item were advertised. Thad moved an ink-stained finger down the page.

"There," he tapped a small block of print. "I thought I remembered this. It's the Callaway's house. Mr. Callaway died in an accident at the mill several months ago. Mrs. Callaway is selling their house. She's moving their children back to Ohio, near her parents."

Becca started to ask if there was a phone number, but remembered her place in time. "Does she want a lot of gold for it? How can I contact her? I'd like to see it."

"I'll see her before the weekend. She always comes in on Fridays for a paper,. She checks for telegrams from her family."

"Could you arrange something?"

Becca was feeling excitement swell up inside her chest... *What's this about? I'm buying this for Delphi, not for myself.*

"I'll ask her if I can bring you out to see it Saturday. I' can pick you up at the Leng's and carry you over there. It's on the north-east end of town. You'll need a horse to live there. It's a bit far to be tramping back and forth on foot to Front Street. Also, it's on the edge of the woods. Would you be frightened living there?"

"No...should I be?"

"It's disconcerting to me. I'd worry about you being there all alone. Perchance you won't be alone for much longer."

After leaving The Print Shop, Becca walked to The Mercantile. She purchased a packet of needles and two spools of thread, one black and one white. She also bought a pair of scissors and a package of pins... *Since I'm learning to sew, I'll want to have my own tools.*

Wandering over to where James sat at a small desk, she greeted him. "Hello, James, are you writing a book?"

He looked up and smiled. "I'm writing a letter to my family in San Francisco. I'll send it to them on the steamer."

"Do you have new books coming in on the Steamer?"

"I ordered several. There's a new writer, Mark Twain. He's growing popular in the East. His commentary articles are published in papers and magazines. He's living in California now, and he wrote a story called The Celebrated Jumping Frog of Calaveras County. It's printed in pamphlet form. It's short but very funny; I ordered a stack of them."

Mark Twain? *I can't believe I'm hearing this. His first published writing... this is amazing. And he wrote it here in California.*

"I'll be sure to stop in and get one. I've read several chapters of Lady Audley's Secret. Have you finished it yet?"

James nodded. "I have, and the vixen deserved all she received, in my opinion."

Becca laughed and put her hand up to restrain him. "Say no more, or you'll give away the ending."

"We must have a discussion when you've completed it," he suggested.

"Do you have a Bible for sale among your stock of books?" *If I must be around Reverend Walker, I'll need to prepare myself on his subjects of debate.*

James stood up and walked over to the bookcase where Becca stood scanning the leather and cloth bound selections of novels and poetry. He reached the top shelf and retrieved a black book, brushed off the dust, and handed it to her. The Bible was bound in black leather. Designs, inlaid in the cover, were filled with gold. A latch secured the smooth covers. Becca pressed the tiny latch button and released it. The pages were of thin parchment, bound by strong string sewn into the spine. It was larger than the bibles she had seen people carry around in the twenty-first century... *More like one to adorn a coffee table.*

She laid it opened on the table. The first page depicted a multicolored drawing of an angel. Under the picture, gold letters declared, THE HOLY BIBLE, translated under the authorization of KING JAMES VI.

"Ahh, this is the King James Version."

James looked at her, tipped his head and asked.

"Did you want one in the German translation? They're difficult to obtain."

"No English is fine."

"I once had one that was written in Greek. A priest who passed through purchased it."

Becca carefully turned the pages. ...*Silly, me, there is no other English translations yet, only King James's English...Well, I'll just put my Shakespeare thinking hat on.*

In the middle, dividing the Old Testament and New Testament, were heavier pages. They were designed for family history to be recorded.

I wonder whose family names I should record...Delphi's or mine. I'll just leave it blank.

"I'll take this James."

She closed the book carefully and stepped back so that he could wrap it in brown paper. Taking her sewing items to the counter, she smiled at Mr. Sanders. He returned her greeting.

"Your order will be in on the steamer, Miss Castile, would you like to charge these purchases and pay for all of it when you return to collect that order?"

Becca gave it a moment of thought. She had already paid James for the Bible and decided that charging these small items until Saturday was suitable.

"Did you notice the sewing boxes?"

The store owner pointed to a shelf behind him. There were three boxes similar in size to a boot box. Covered in upholstery cloth, each sported a carved wooden handle. Mr. Sanders retrieved the blue one, set it on the counter, and flipped open the lid.

Becca peered inside. Secured to the padded inside of the lid was a pin cushion. Next to it, a fabric loop held a silver thimble. Another cloth loop secured a small pair of embroidery scissors...*I can't believe how much detail is put into everything...* The light blue linen lining covered the sides and bottom, with a ruffled pocket on one side. She peeked into it. A ball of waxy substance nestled inside.

"Its beeswax," Mr. Sanders answered her questioning expression, "It's to lubricate the needle and smooth the thread."

"Yes, of course it is." *I have no idea what you're talking about, but I will after Saturday.*

Soon she was walking back toward the hotel with the sewing box under one arm and the Bible under the other.

35

"The ache for home lives in all of us. It's the safe place where we can go as we are and not be questioned."

—M<small>AYA</small> A<small>NGELOU</small>

As she passed The Print Shop, she saw Thad locking the door.
"Hello again, are you finished for the day?"
"The newsboys picked up their papers. I'm going to start moving my things from the Redwood. I've hitched up the buggy; do you want a carry back?"

He took her parcels assuming the answer would be, yes. They rode the few blocks while Thad related that he had spoken to Mrs. Callaway. She approved the Saturday afternoon visit.

"She's leaving her furniture. She doesn't want to take a wagon back East. With so many children, she prefers to travel by stagecoach and train. You won't need to buy much to settle in, but that'll cost you more. Her wares are valuable. She brought some by wagon train and had other things shipped after they moved here. It all goes with the sale."

"Thad, I have a gold brick. Will that be enough? I was advised that it should be more than enough." If Delphi's opinion can be relied upon... concerning real-estate.

He looked over at her in surprise. "You have a gold brick? How did you get a gold brick from the ship to land?"

"It was in the carpetbag that was tied to me. It nearly drowned me, as a matter-of-fact."

"No wonder you were so heavy when I lifted you from the lifeboat that night. Your surprises never cease, Delphi."

"So...will that be enough?"

"There's not much land with that house. It should be more than enough, even with the added furniture. You'll have to get the brick melted by a smelter, and the correct amount made into coins. I'm sure you know that."

"Where is the smelter in town?"

"The closest smelter shop is in Eureka, The Murphy Brother Smelter Co. I could take it for you. I'm not hankerin' to interfere in your affairs, but please tell me how you came about owning a gold brick."

They were pulling up to the hotel, for which Becca was grateful. "It's a real long story. I'll explain it all later."

As soon as Delphi explains it to me...

Thad looked at her intently. His hazel eyes tried to search the deep blue ones that were avoiding direct contact.

"Could you answer me one question? Why are you set on a large house?"

"I plan to start a music school."

"But you said you knew nothing of music. That was why you had Mrs.O'Shay teach you scales on the piano. You had Miss Ware to teach you to dance. I've heard you practice, and there is promise, but you are yourself a scholar. I hope not to cause you doubt, but would it not be preposterous to invest a large hunk of gold for a music school that you're not yet prepared to teach?"

"Becca, not waiting to be helped out, climbed from the carriage.

"Thanks for the confidence Thad. I asked for your help in buying the house, not a lecture on wise business practice."

She grabbed her bulky parcels.

Thad jumped out of the buggy and quickly looped the reins over a post. He hurried to catch up with her as she scrambled to the door, skirts swishing around her ankles. He grasped the knob before she was able to reach for it.

"Wait, Delphi. I didn't mean to lecture you. I worry about you. You appear to be wise at times. Then, others times, you baffle me with your lack of understanding, especially about money...gold, and such. I just don't want you to get honey-fuggled by a decision made hastily."

Becca took a deep breath and looked up into his sincere face.

"I'm sorry Thad. Of course, you can't possibly understand from where all my ideas come. All I can say is that I hope that I'll soon be able to explain everything. Let's just say that I must buy a large house for a music school to keep a promise to someone. Can you trust me that I have my reasons?"

He took her hand and pressed it against his lips.

"I'll trust you. But, I can't promise to not worry. You mustn't get huffed at me when I worry. I do so because I care about you."

Becca smiled. "I want you to know that I appreciate everything you've done to help me. It would've been more difficult getting through all this without you."

Thad smiled and squeezed her hand. He opened the door, and they entered the parlor. Upstairs they parted as Thad went to gather his belongings to move to his new apartment above The Print Shop.

In her room, Becca removed the woolen dress...*I'll be so glad to get the cotton ones. I hope Mrs. Leng has them finished Saturday.*

She slipped into a clean cotton work dress. Sitting at the desk, she wrote her name in the front of the Bible. She set it aside, and removed the wrapping from the sewing box. Placing the purchased items into it, she slid it under the desk. Pulling her ledger from the drawer, she entered the prices of the bible, the sewing box, and the other items. After totaling the expenditures, she placed it back in the drawer. Picking up the journal, she opened it to an empty page. She added an entry.

August 9, 1865

Today, I can report that I will be looking at a house that is for sale. I'll see it day-after-tomorrow. I hope it will be suitable for the music school.

Thad, his actual name is Thaddeus Barrett, has been very helpful. I fear he is falling for me, or should I say for your petite, slim body and enormous blue eyes that I temporarily possess. Without him, I would not have located this house. I hope when you are here, you will be kind to him. He would make a wonderful husband.

He fought in the war for the Yankees. I understand that may be an issue since your family was part of the south, and were owners of slaves. I hope you will move on from that to the future. Society will eventually condemn the practice of slavery, and you will be better served by moving with the changing attitudes.

He is an upright, honest, patient, and caring man. He's very nice looking too, with hazel eyes that seem to be always smiling. In finding a mate, you could do much worse.

I have had a conversation with Ike. He is more fearful than dangerous now. Somewhere in time his body is now inhabited by a human spirit named Cain Jones, at least we believe that to be his name. The poor man must be terribly confused.

I must insist that you explain to me the history of the gold brick. It seems to be an oddity for a single young woman to own one.

Give Beth my love,

Becca closed the journal and lay down on the bed... *I have just enough time for a brief nap before supper...*She closed her eyes and started to fade. Sounds mingled in her brain. Footsteps in the hall faded, as spinning sensations scrambled her thoughts. Speedily, she whirled past a tunnel that led to an ethereal light, and then to new sounds. Voices from a TV blared, a car horn sounded outside. She opened her eyes to view Beth's living room. Beth was curled up in a recliner and reading a book. Delphi sat in a wheelchair fumbling with a remote.

"Why must this contraption be so difficult?" she complained.

Just push the arrow button, if you want to change channels.

"Beth, your sister is here," she announced.

Beth closed the book and straightened up. "What is she saying?"

Did you read my diary today?

"She requests that we read the journal."

Beth jumped up and retrieved the diary from a bookcase, and handed it to Delphi.

"You read it please," Delphi requested.

Beth opened the book to the last entry, and read Becca's words. When she finished, she dabbed the tears from her eyes and said, "I love you, sis."

"She loves you too," responded Delphi.

I didn't even have a chance to say it.

"But you would have, so it's all the same."

Are you pleased about the house?

"Oui, it sounds most agreeable. But it must be nice, nothing rickety will do."

What about Thad? I think he would make you an excellent husband.

"With the life I was forced to lead, there are no reputable men who would wish to marry me."

No one knows about your life with Lilly.

"Oui, but better it is to live alone than to deceive a good person. In time, he might learn the truth. Then he would hate me. It's best if you discourage his interest."

Tell me about the gold brick.

"It's called a gold bar, tis smaller than a gold brick. Several weeks before we left the city, a man came to the establishment. Lilly assigned me to him even though it was to be my evening to sing for the guests. I was instantly fearful, and told her as much. She said she would assign one of her strong men to remain close to the chambers."

Did he hurt you?

"Oui, he was a beastly man. He had hidden a gun. Lilly never allowed guns in the establishment. I was wearing some jewels she had provided, since I was the entertainer of the night. I had an emerald necklace and an opal ring. I also wore a serpent bracelet with a ruby eye. Lilly called it, the Cleopatra."

That bracelet is still in your jewel box.

"Oui, she forgot to ask for the jewelry, and I never returned it. This evil man entered the chamber with a small satchel. As I was slipping out of my frock, he pulled out the gun. He demanded I remove the jewels, and place them in his bag. While I was trying to unfasten the necklace, he slapped me, knocking me down. He was hissing at me to hurry. I screamed."

What happened?

"The strong man ran in, and grabbed him. He took him out into the hall, and beat him soundly. I wasted no time. I looked in the satchel. It had a bag of coins and jewels that I'm sure he had stolen from other people. I saw the gold bar. I grabbed the bag and ran to my private chamber. He lay bleeding in the hall. I never saw him again."

No one ever found out?

"I took it to my chamber and hid it. Later, when we planned the trip, I sewed all coins into my clothing. I packed the jewels and bar in the carpet bag. Now I knew I had enough to escape."

So...you have wealth that's stolen from others?

"My life was stolen! Lilly took my life for her own gain. And what I took from that horrid man was already stolen. A thief is a deceiver. He does not deserve honesty from others."

Do you think I should fear this man finding me?

"I doubt if he'd have purpose to wander into the wilderness. He's a thief by trade. The city presents more opportunity for him."

"Tell my sister about the man in Crescent City," prompted Beth from her silent corner.

Delphi reached over and picked up a newspaper from the coffee table. She held it up so the headlines faced the direction she had determined Becca to be.

Becca read the words. **"Do you know this man?"** *That picture...my word...its Ike.*

"He was found about the same time that we were rescued. Fisherman near Crescent City brought him to the hospital there. He was...how you say... unconscious. Once he was able to speak, he claimed his name to be Jonah McCain. They think he has measles."

Measles... do you mean amnesia?

"Oui, all the same thing."

Well...now we know where Ike's body is...

The return trip had begun, and in the distance Becca heard Hannah's voice, "Delphi...Delphi...please wake-up."

Becca opened her eyes. Hannah leaned over her, grasping her shoulders. Her eyes were wide with concern.

"You scare me all to pieces when you sleep so soundly. I knocked and knocked on your door, and called your name. You were so still... like...death."

Becca sat up and rubbed her eyes. "Sorry, Hannah, did you need something?"

"Supper will be ready soon. Miss Barns requested that I persuade you to come down. Mr. Barrett also asked that I assure that you do. Mrs. O'Shay has baked a salmon and an applesauce cake."

"It seems my presence is in demand this evening," Becca chuckled. "I'll straighten myself up first."

"Come and sit by the looking glass and I'll arrange your hair?"

"Yes, I'd like that." Becca smiled at her. Hannah retrieved the brush from the wash stand.

36

"God gives us each a song."

—UTE TRIBAL PROVERB

A few minutes later Becca descended the stairs with a tidy thick braid coiled around her head. Elsie, Minnie and little Albert sat on one sofa. Doc and Thad conversed in the far corner of the parlor. Becca sat on the single chair facing the women.

Elsie looked well, and smiled at her. "I'm glad you didn't retire early. I've convinced Minnie and Mrs. O'Shay to have a music gathering tonight. We'll sing, dance, and enjoy one last evening before so many new guests arrive on Saturday."

I'm exhausted, but... I guess this is important...maybe I'll feel better after eating...

"That's a great idea, Elsie." Becca tried to sound enthusiastic.

"I also reasoned that we should practice a duet. Minnie will accompany us on the piano. We could sing it at the Church's Sing Along, tomorrow."

Darn, I forgot about the church dinner and that sing thing...

"Ah, no... I don't think I'm ready to debut my voice...I..."

Mrs. O'Shay entered the room, wiping her hands on her apron. She announced that the meal was ready to serve. The food was exceptional, and Becca enjoyed second helpings. Thad leaned toward her as he passed her a platter.

"I need to discuss something with you."

After dinner, Becca and Minnie helped with the clean up so that Hannah and Mrs. O'Shay could join the activities. After Minnie played several music pieces, Elsie dragged Becca up to sing *Glory, Glory, Hallelujah*. To her amazement, they harmonized very well.

I'll never get used to this feeling that my voice makes music...that'll be something I'll miss when I return to my body...

"There, I knew we'd do well," Elsie chimed. "We'll sing that at church tomorrow."

"Is there more cake, Molly?" called Mr. O'Shay from his distant position across the room.

"There'll be refreshments later, but let's dance a few rounds," Molly crossed the room and tugged at her husband's hand.

"Play a waltz, Minnie."

Thad immediately approached Becca and took her hand. Minnie shuffled through the sheet music, and soon the melody of Johann Strauss's, From the Mountains, filled room. Elsie and Doc joined up, and the three couples moved gracefully around the large parlor. Hannah turned pages for Minnie.

"What did you need to discuss?" Becca asked.

"Ever since you spoke of the gold brick, I've been troubled."

"Actually, I misspoke, it's not a gold brick it's a gold bar."

"Gold is bringing thirty dollars an ounce here in California. A gold bar is far too valuable to have hiding under the mattress."

"It's in a small wall safe in my room."

"I have one of them in my room as well. Those are intended to provide protection for valuables to overnight guests. They aren't reliable for large amounts of gold. A determined thief could pry it from the wall and take the safe and all."

"What do you suggest? I've seen no banks here in town."

"There are none nearby. There're only a few in the state. Those haven't proved trustworthy. At The Print Shop, there's a large safe. Your gold would be protected there."

He gently turned her around as they passed Mr. and Ms O'Shay.

"Sunday I can go to Eureka to the Smelting Shop. I'll take your bar then. Abe will go with me for extra protection. We both have new Winchester rifles coming in on the steamer Saturday."

"You ordered a gun?"

"Yes. They're the newest and most dependable available. We'll return Monday after I've completed your affairs at the smelters. We'll be back Tuesday. You'll be able to purchase the house after that."

"This sounds like it could be dangerous." Becca's brows knitted in a worried expression.

"We mustn't tell anyone the purpose of our journey. If no one knows we're carrying gold, there'll be less danger. This is untamed land. There's thieving and murder around, when opportunity allows. That's why I'm always so concerned about your carelessness regarding gold."

"So maybe I should put it all in your safe at The Print Shop."

"The hotel will be filling up with strangers, Saturday. The chambers don't have dependable locks. I've warned Mrs. O'Shay that she should provide her guests more security in this regard. I suppose when someone is harmed or robbed, she'll see the need."

"I hadn't thought of that. How do we get it from my safe to The Print Shop without being noticed?"

"I'll be going there shortly. I've one more trunk to move. If you place your valuables in a bag, and pass it to me in the hall, I'll tuck it into my trunk. It'll be safely locked away immediately."

The waltz ended, and Elsie picked up her fan, vigorously fluttering it around her face. Doc sat down, announcing that he preferred to watch any additional dances.

"Now, let's have some of the applesauce cake, Molly," insisted her husband.

As the others moved to the dining room, Becca took the opportunity to scurry upstairs. Once in her room, she fished the key from her bodice, and opened the safe. The bar was still there. She lifted out the jewel box and opened it. *Taking out the opal ring and the serpent bracelet, she set them aside...I'll give the ring to Elsie to use as a wedding ring... I'm sure Delphi will understand... This serpent bracelet fascinates me, now that I heard its history and how she got it... I just might want to wear it to the sing-along tomorrow.*

She placed jewels, coins, and bar into the carpet bag. She was closing the bag when her eye caught the photograph. She quickly snatched it up, and tossed it back into the safe...*I sure don't want Thad to see Delphi's professional PR picture, wearing nothing but her pantaloons...*

She closed the safe but didn't lock it. Taking the bracelet, ring, and key, she moved to the secretary. Opening a secret drawer she had recently discovered, she placed them inside.

A light tap sounded at her door. She opened it. Thad stood there expectantly. She handed the carpet bag out, and he took it to his room. She hurried to join the others in the dining room.

"Well, there you are," said Minnie. "You'd better eat your cake before Mr. O'Shay descends upon it."

"I never take food from women or children," defended the man.

Becca poured cream into her coffee, and took a bite of the moist cake. She heard the door in the parlor open and shut...*There goes Delphi's gold to the big safe.*

Becca entered the kitchen Friday morning, to discover Molly and Hannah were already planning the day. While she ate a small bowl of oatmeal, Molly gave her and Hannah assignments. The parlor and dining room rugs needed to be beaten; all ground level floors mopped, and all furniture dusted. The upstairs rooms must be mopped and dusted as well. While they completed that, Molly would bake bread, pies and cakes.

As she drained the last of the coffee from her cup, she wondered how they could possibly complete everything in time to attend the church singing and supper...*We'll need to start getting ready by two-o-clock.*

When the clock struck one PM, the three women had worked seven straight hours, not even stopping for lunch. Exhausted, Becca dragged herself to her room. Peeling off the sweat-soaked cotton frock, she washed thoroughly, using the water basin. She brushed her teeth, and combed out her hair. Grumbling to herself, she put on the hated corset and an extra petticoat. While fastening the buttons of the wool dress, Hannah knocked on her door. "Come in, Hannah."

"I came to fix your hair; I just finished with Elsie's."

The girl carried a small bucket of red hot coals on which rested a metal curling iron. While Becca sat in front of the mirror, Hannah styled her ringlets, using the heated tool.

Becca, Hannah, and Elsie walked to church, shading their faces with parasols. Elsie carried the sheet music they needed for their duet. Molly and her husband took their buggy. Inside it were foods; cake, a blackberry pie, and several loaves of fresh bread.

As they approached the church, Becca was surprised at the amount of horses and buggies outside the building. Long redwood boards stretched across logs to make temporary tables. Women arranged bowls and pans of food as they were delivered by the parishioners....*This are a bigger affair than I expected. And to think I'm going to sing...* Butterflies fluttered in her stomach. Hannah led the two young women inside the church. As they followed her towards a pew, Becca noticed several people she had met briefly. They were survivors of the shipwreck. The young Asian woman with her infant, the crewmen who had eaten at the hotel several times, and a cabin boy occupied one bench. Minnie, holding Albert, motioned the women to join her on her pew. They turned away from the one they had first selected, and slid into the open space by the woman and child. Looking forward, Becca noticed that directly in front of her sat Tate and two other African American males...

Well, what do you know? I'm glad this service isn't segregated...I'm pleasantly surprised...But since it's a special service for survivors, it's only reasonable...

Her thoughts were interrupted by a bell's loud ringing at the back of the church. Reverend Walker's booming voice caused her to jump. Albert puckered up as though he would cry. The old pump organ started to play a mournful tune Becca had never heard before, and everyone stood. She leaned over and addressed Elsie. "There's no piano...do we sing our duet with that dilapidated organ?"

Elsie nodded and smiled. The butterflies in her core grew into eagles. The procession ended at the front of the church, and the Reverend opened in prayer, a very long prayer. James from The Mercantile approached the pulpit and led the congregation in the song, Amazing Grace. Becca was amused at the slow tempo they sang the hymn. Once seated, all ladies wrestled with skirts and petticoats, arranging themselves in the crowded pews.

The Reverend replaced James at the pulpit, and talked about the protection of God, and how thankful all must be for the nineteen survivors. He then said a prayer for the grieved relatives and friends of those lost at sea. Even with all windows were opened, it was hot.

The crowded conditions limited any relief the breezes could provide. Elsie looked pale, and fanned herself with one of the cardboard fans available in a small cubby attached to the back of the pew in front of them. Minnie fanned Albert, who was becoming increasingly restless.

"And now, it's my pleasure," announced the minister," to introduce two survivors who will bless us with a song. Miss Barns and Miss Castile, please come forward."

Becca could feel sweat dripping over her skin under the woolen dress. Elsie appeared shaky. They shuffled out of the tight space between the pews, and walked to the short stage. Elsie handed the sheet music to Mrs. Walker at the organ. Standing there and facing the crowd, Becca fought to steady her knees that insisted on shaking. Elsie held her arm in a death grip...*Either she thinks I'm going to run away, or she needs to hold on to me to keep her balance.*

Becca would not remember singing with Elsie, but from comments later she assumed they did well. Following the last verse, Elsie fainted. Someone began fanning her while another provided smelling salts. Doc quickly made his way to the front, and requested that Elsie be taken outside where she could breathe fresh air. Becca stayed with her under a shade tree.. They relaxed and enjoyed the sea breeze.

"I'm sorely shamed," the young woman stated.

"Don't be. It's very uncomfortable in that building. You can't be blamed. I won't be surprised if a lot more people pass out in that hot confinement."

Looking up, she saw Minnie coming out of the building with Albert. The woman took the tot into a nearby wooded area where the child relieved himself. Joining them she smiled brightly.

"That song was nicely done. I saw people nodding. I feel they enjoyed it."

Since it appeared that Minnie planned to stay with Elsie, Becca got up and returned to the church. As she took a seat in the back, she saw Tate approach the podium.

"Mr. Jeremiah Tate is a minister as well as a first mate crewman," Reverend Walker announced. "He often preaches in a Negro church in San Francisco, I've asked him to share a scripture."

Mr. Tate opened a worn Bible, and read a passage about Jesus calming a storm. He compared the ocean tempests to life, and admonished the listeners to allow Jesus to be their captain. Becca considered his metaphors to be meaningful. After another dozen hymns and two presented solos, they were dismissed to return to the outdoors for the meal. Becca felt hunger pangs and relief to have something to eat.

Molly scurried across the grass with a basket, her chubby cheeks were red from exertion, and confinement in the hot building.

"I have plates and spoons for all of you, "she huffed, "and a cup for lemonade."

Becca, Elsie, and Hannah sat together eating, fried chicken, baked beans, boiled squash and buttered bread... *I'll bet this is all fixed with lard, and is settling into Delphi's arteries at this very moment...Well, she's the one who will have to deal with that outcome.*

"May we join you?"

The women looked up to see Tate and his two friends holding heaping plates.

"We would be honored," replied Elsie.

They sat in a semicircle. The conversation was lively, and Becca was amused at the laughter that filled the circle. She returned to the table to refill her cup, and scoop up a piece of cake. Reverend Walker approached her.

"I enjoyed your musical presentation. I hope we will be privileged to more of your talent in the future."

"I'm not sure...."

"Oh, but you will at least be attending services?"

"Well, you see..."

"Now, now, remember your promise."

"Promise? I made no promise, Reverend."

"At the O'Shay table, you stated that if I included Negros in our services and meals, you would come to my church."

"Oh, no...that's not quite what I said...I was making the point that a true Christian church should be Christ-like and include all people..."

And a valid point it was, Miss Castile. It's taken me a full week to locate Jeremiah Tate and his Negro crewmates. I told our church deacons that as long as I'm pastor of this church, all people will be welcomed. Now, you won't disappoint me by breaking your promise, will you?"

37

"You can learn new things at any time in your life if you're willing to be a beginner."

—Barbara Sher

Becca opened her eyes before dawn on Saturday morning. Jumping up, she dressed in her clean work dress, braided her hair, and wound the braids around her head. She opened the hidden drawer in the secretary, and selected coins to pay for the frocks that would be finished at the shop today. She placed them into the small beaded purse and then placed the purse into her new sewing box. Collecting her shawl to shield against the morning chill, she descended down the back staircase. In the kitchen, Hannah was in the process of making coffee.

"Why are you up so early, Delphi?"

"It's my first day to work for Mrs. Leng."

"Oh yes, I forgot. We have nothing made for breakfast yet, are you in a hurry?"

"Yes, I'll just grab a cold biscuit with jam and a glass of water."

"You won't be here to see the steamer in," the girl lamented.

"I'm only a few blocks away, Hannah. I'm sure I'll hear the excitement."

Molly entered the kitchen, and put on her apron. "Oh, so you're up and dressed to go out. That must be why Mr. Barrett is waiting in the parlor."

"Yes, he's driving me there in his buggy."

"You won't be here for dinner at noon. Shall I pack you something to tote with you?"

"I'll be content with one of those apples and a cucumber." Becca helped herself to each of the items from baskets setting on the table.

"Be sure to have Mrs. Leng soak the cucumber in vinegar," prompted Hannah.

Becca smiled her goodbye and joined Thad in the Parlor. As they rode through the fog, Becca watched the town come to life. Merchants busily opened their shops and stores. Not all shops opened on Saturday, but on Steamer Day there was too much opportunity to remain closed.

"What will you do today?" she asked Thad.

I haven't much required of me for the morning. I'll get a shave in China town, pick up my laundry, meet the steamer when it arrives, and help Abe load his liquor to take back to his saloon. I have print paper and ink coming in for shop. I'll pick you up at four. We'll ride out to the Callaghan house."

"I'm so excited; I can hardly breathe."

Thad smiled. "You are an easy lady to amuse, if that excites you so."

He left her at the Lengs', and disappeared in the fog. She walked into the shop as Mr. Leng placed the open sign in the window. Its message was written in both English and Chinese characters. He nodded at her as she hurried to the backroom.

Mrs. Leng smiled at her and pointed to a teapot. "You want?"

"Yes please."

Becca removed her shawl, and set her things on a table and out of the way. They enjoyed tea in tiny cups as Becca tried on the new work dress and outing dress that Mrs. Leng had finished...*Now I won't have to wear that hot, scratchy wool dress everywhere.*

Mrs. Leng circled her as she checked the fit of the shoulders and hemline. "Yes, yes, good...all good."

This still cramps me in the upper arms. If I have to stay in this century, I'll figure out how to change patterns...that's for sure.

Becca paid what she owed and then asked, "Now, what is my first task?"

Mrs. Leng brought her a square piece of cloth.

"See?" She pointed at a hand stitched buttonhole. "I show you."

She carefully measured a button by laying it on the fabric, stuck in a pin a few centimeters on each side.

"See? All straight...no crooked."

Becca nodded.

Using small scissors, she carefully cut a tiny slit between the pins. She threaded a needle, pulling enough thread through that once doubled; it measured from her thumb to her elbow. Looking at Becca, she explained,

"Enough thread...finish buttonhole."

Makes sense to not have to rethread halfway through.

She picked up a ball of wax and rubbed it once down the thread. "No knots...knots vedy bad."

Becca smiled...*Now I know what the blob of wax in my sewing box is for.*

Mrs. Leng made three tiny looped stitches at the corner of the slit, and then carefully worked around with tiny perfectly matched looped stitches, placing three in the opposite end.

"Do...two times," she explained.

Becca nodded and repeated her comment. "Stitch around the buttonhole two times."

The woman pushed the practice material toward Becca, "You do now."

Becca carried out the task satisfactorily until time to stitch.

"No...no" Mrs. Leng looked over her work. "Crooked...not straight."

She pointed out how several stitches were longer than others.

So they have to be perfectly even...Ok then, I'll try another.

By the third practiced buttonhole, she had one that pleased her mentor. Mrs. Leng then brought a stack of folded items including a woman's bodice, not yet sewn onto the skirt, a man's shirt, a nightgown, and baby's frock. Each had a collection of buttons attached, held together by a looped string. She showed her where to place the buttonholes on each one. Becca decided to start with the baby frock and work her way to the velvet dress. She set her goal to make each one perfect. Mrs. Leng returned to the work table and began cutting new pieces for a frock. Becca had finished the baby gown and shirt when she noticed her employer stirring a mixture in a small cooker that set over a tiny flame.

"You like rice?" she asked.

Becca nodded and smiled. "I brought an apple and cucumber," she offered.

"Yes...vedy good."

Mrs. Leng cut them into thin slices. Becca began on the buttonholes on the nightgown. When the rice was ready, Mrs. Leng added some herbs from a jar, and some small slivers of fish from a crock of salty brine. She filled three small blue patterned bowls, and laid pieces of apple and cucumber on top. After ladling in a small amount of the mixture into a very tiny china bowl, she placed it on a shelf by a small statue. She placed her hands together and bowed her head...*I guess that's like saying grace.*

Soon the couple and Becca were sitting at a table, sharing a rice entrée. Becca was thankful she had learned to use chopsticks. ...*It's so much easier using them with Delphi's dainty hands than my own...*

It was one-thirty when Becca called her teacher over to inspect her finished work. Mrs. Leng smiled and nodded.

"Yes...Learn fast...all good"

She then demonstrated how to sew on a button correctly. In and out of the buttonholes with the thread, no less than four times, five or six for men's clothing. Then, wrap the thread around the button twice, push needle to back side of cloth, tack it down and tie off with a knot on the back. She taught Becca to make a finishing knot that was almost invisible...*No wonder the buttons in the twenty-first century always fall off.*

It took the remainder of the afternoon to sew on all the buttons. Her neck ached, and she had a number of stab wounds in her thumb from needle jabs. She smiled happily as Mrs. Leng counted out coins for her first day's work.

"You come tomorrow?"

Becca started to agree, and then remembered her conversation with Reverend Walker. *He thinks I promised to go the church.*

"I can work in the afternoon, from one-o-clock until four."

The woman nodded. "Yes...good...you learn to hem."

Becca left her sewing box, and gathered her packages of new frocks, her purse and shawl. Walking out into the front of the shop, she saw Thad smiling.

"Looks like I arrived at the correct time. Are you ready to see the house?"

Becca tucked her parcels in the floor of the buggy, and wrapped her shawl tighter around her shoulders. An afternoon fog was moving in with a chill. The clicking of the horse's hoofs set a rhythm to the movement of the carriage. She was developing a fondness for buggy rides. They rode down Second Street, turned away from the coast and toward the redwood forest. No stores lined this sparse, dirt road. The Mill took up one entire block. Houses, widely spaced, represented different residents' financial status. Some were shabbily built with rough cut boards, no porches, and windows without curtains.

Others had two levels, wood siding, and stoops. One even had a picket fence complete with a tabby cat lounging by the gate. Each had an outhouse in its back yard; some had gardens, and several had chicken pens. Becca could hardly contain her excitement.

"I want to raise chickens."

Thad, lost in his thoughts, looked at her. "Chickens, have you kept chickens before?"

"No, but I'll learn, and I want a garden too."

"I know a man who has a cow for sale. Do you want a milk cow as well?"

"Perhaps, I could..." Catching the twinkle in his eye, Becca realized he was teasing her.

"You could get those music students to milk her for you."

He's right...this house isn't for me; it's for Delphi, and somehow I can't imagine her pulling weeds, raking out a chicken coop, or churning butter...much less milking a cow.

She remained silent, and soon he turned onto a bumpy road. The fog lingered behind and the warmth of the sun made her feel cheerful. Peering ahead, she hoped to see the house, but tall redwoods blocked it from view. The rutty lane halted the previous tempo, replacing it with a very slow pace. She gripped the side of the carriage to brace herself against jostling... *I feel like jumping out, and running the rest of the way.*

A sharp curve soon brought them in view of her prize. The two-story farmhouse stood proudly in a large clearing. On the far end of the property, a small barn was situated. It had a slanted roof and open front. Against the outer wall, a farm plow set propped. A clothesline and outhouse inhabited the backyard. On the other side of the home, what remained of a garden, was overtaken by weeds. There was no visible evidence of farm animals...*She must have already sold all of them...*A porch swing hung on a porch that adorned the entire front of the building. Several children sat on the swing. Thad halted the horse. Becca scrambled from her seat, not waiting for assistance. They walked together through a gate.

As they approached the porch, she scanned the outer condition of the house. The white paint was in fair condition, especially for a coastal home that is subjected to salt air and ocean winds. The structure wasn't fancy, but a few pieces of trim over the doors and windows reminded Becca of the Victorian houses she had seen in Portland. Mrs. Callahan stood at the opened door. It was propped open with a large rock.

"Come in," she smiled brightly.

As Thad introduced the women, the young child in Mrs. Callahan's arms shyly hid his face in his mother's neck.

"Please call me Delphi," Becca offered.

"And you may call me Betsy," she replied.

Betsy stood back and the couple walked into the parlor. Becca was surprised at how small it was. *This isn't much larger than my bedroom at the hotel... but it's much nicer...* The windows were draped in muted coffee colored velvet. A large rug designed in a floral pattern of copper, gold, and dark green, covered most of the smooth wooden floor. *It looks new.*

In the corner directly in front of the window set a piano, slanted so the window light could shine on the ivory keys. A small round parlor stove claimed the wall that connected to another room. At the back of the room was a small table with claw feet gripping glass balls. On its top lay a round, lace doily, and an ornate lamp. On each side of this arrangement were matching dark gold-colored chairs. They were Victorian style, and covered in coarse upholstery. A door, covered by a heavy tapestry, provided an exit on the back wall. Opposite the chair arrangement, set a small sofa. A close match in style to the chairs, its covering was in a green leaf pattern. Large silk throw pillows with fringe dominated all the delicate pieces.

On the wall, a large painting hung high, tipped forward for viewing. It depicted a country scene. It reminded Becca of an old French painting she had seen at an art museum in her own time. Wallpaper covered all four walls in a fern pattern... *There's so much patterning here... it makes me dizzy.*

"Everything in this room is quite new. I had them shipped from San Francisco this past year. The children are not permitted in this parlor, except to practice their music."

Betsy smiled in pride as she surveyed her treasures. Guiding them through the tapestry covered door, she announced.

"Now here's the drawing room. It's where our family spent our evenings."

Another parlor stove shared the wall and chimney of the previous room. It wasn't as elaborate as the first. The wall paper was sprayed with red rosebuds. A rocking chair set nearby with a small red velvet footstool. A basket of mending rested close at hand. The window was framed by white lace curtains. A wooden parson's bench set in front of it. Fluffy pillows lay on the seat. A homemade braided rug adorned the floor. A tea table with two straight back chairs completed the seating arrangement. The only wall decoration was a shelf that supported a wooden clock with roman numerals. As if on cue, it chimed the half hour.

"I brought this rug with me from the east. It's well worn, but I've kept it very clean."

Becca eyed the large area rug, displaying multicolor of red and green.

At least it matches the walls... sort of.

"We ordered the wallpaper last summer. My late husband...may he rest in peace...hung it..." She appeared to be fighting tears.

"Is the kitchen through there?" asked Thad, hoping to lead her away from the sad memory.

"That's the dining room. Come and see. It's exquisite. That surely makes me sound sinfully proud."

As she walked in, Becca had to agree with Betsy's assessment of her dining room. This room had three windows, and all viewed the majestic woods. Airy lace curtains draped gracefully, while letting in an abundance of light. Pale-blue wallpaper covered the walls. A picture of Betsy and her late husband looked over the room from an oak frame.

"I'll take the picture; it's our wedding portrait, but the furniture remains."

"You're right, this room is exquisite. This is Jacobean style furniture, isn't it?" *I remember Beth telling me that in an antique shop.*

Betsy took no notice of Becca's observation as she explained that the large table, eight chairs, and china hutch had been handed down for generations in her family.

"We brought them here by wagon, but I shan't pay the price required to ship them back by rail."

Becca walked over to the hutch and viewed the delicate china in a blue hue.

"I'll leave those as well. They'd be broken all to pieces by the time we reached Iowa. There's a set of silver in the drawer."

They passed to the next room. The kitchen walls, covered with white canvas, were slightly yellowed from the process of cooking. A wood cook stove, wall shelves, and work table indicated that Betsy was a well organized and efficient home manager. A pump, attached to the counter top, connected the well to a large porcelain sink. Amply equipped, the room contained a wooden churn, large bowls, crocks, and every kind of kitchen tool Becca had observed in this era. There were some she hadn't seen before hanging on the walls. Connected to the backdoor was a lean-to. Washtubs, irons, ironing table and a bathtub indicated it was a washing room, much like Molly's. A shelf held stacks of yarns and folded fabric, remnants of Betsy's sewing and knitting projects.

They moved back through the kitchen and Becca realized they had made a complete circle as she found herself back in the formal parlor. After a quick tour of the upstairs and its four bedrooms, Becca easily made up her mind.

"What are you asking for this property?"

"Since I'm leaving the furniture, I must request Three-hundred-fifty dollars."

"Consider it sold," Becca replied, attempting to suppress the eagerness in her voice. "I'll be able to pay you Wednesday. Will that be acceptable?"

"Oh, yes. That's splendid. I'll be able to settle my family in Iowa before the harsh winter arrives there."

As Thad assisted her into the carriage, he asked, "Miss Castile, would I be presumptuous to assume that my assistance in directing you to this opportunity shall result in my being your first dinner guest?"

"She smiled at him. "Yes, Mr. Barrett, you are presumptuous, and you shall be my first dinner guest."

38

"A woman is like a teabag—you can't tell how strong she is until you put her in hot water."

—Eleanor Roosevelt

Becca ate supper in her room and went to bed early. She dreaded attending church the following morning, but at least she could wear her new dress. It seemed only a few moments passed after closing her eyes before Hannah tapped on her door. She barely called out to her when the girl bounced in. " Mrs. O'Shay said you wanted to be summoned in time for church."

"Hmmm, can't you please do it a bit quieter?"

"Are you going to sing today?"

"Absolutely not."

Hannah looked disappointed.

"I'm only attending to keep my promise to Reverend Walker... though I'm not sure it was actually a promise."

"Oh, I'm certain you promised. I heard you. Everyone knows you promised, Delphi. "

Becca sat up and swung her feet to the floor. She stood up and retrieved her new outing dress.

"Remember when we ordered this. You helped me pick out the fabric and lace."

"That's dashing, turned out real nice. I'll wear my new pink one."

She headed for the door and turned. "I'll return to style your hair. Would you like tea and toast?"

Later Elsie, Hannah, and Becca walked out of the hotel just as Thad with his buggy stopped in front of the steps.

"Do you lovely ladies prefer to walk on this fine day, or ride?" As Thad nudged the horse to move forward, he glanced at the new bible in Becca's lap.

"I see that you're going, armed with the sword."

"Actually, it's more like a shield." Becca smiled, and he laughed.

The small building wasn't as over-crowded as it had been for the previous service, but Tate and several visitors from the Steamer were there. It didn't seem as long and torturous as before. Becca's thoughts wandered to the Callahan house and her anxiety about completing the purchase.

After the service, the dining room was filled with extra guests, including the Reverend, his wife and Doctor Conner. Becca didn't take time to join them. She hurriedly changed into her new work dress. Since she would be walking, she slipped the dagger into her sleeve. Grabbing a buttered bun from the kitchen, she headed to China Town.

Mrs. Leng unlocked the door for her. The shop wasn't opened, but work was in progress. Her husband sat by an opened window, stitching a sleeve onto a man's suit coat. The women went into the back room where Becca sat in the same chair as the day before.

The woman showed Becca a small piece of fabric. One end was turned up and pressed flat. Several pins secured it. She demonstrated how to sew a hem. After Becca proved she could duplicate the tiny hem stitch, she was given the task of working her new skill on a child's frock... *Sewing is relaxing; I can't believe I didn't like it when I first tried it years ago... I'm excited to start my own projects.* At three-o-clock, a loud knock sounded at the shop's front door. Becca heard Doc's voice as Mr. Leng let him in.

"I need to speak with your wife."

As he walked into the back room, Mrs. Leng stood up expectantly. "Yes?"

"I have two birthings occurring at the same time. Mrs. Martin is having twins. I must be there with her. Sybil Ferris is having her sixth. That will move quickly; I need you to go there. One of my mid-wives is ill and the other visiting with friends in Eureka."

As he talked, Mrs. Leng filled a large carpet bag with a roll of white fabric, scissors, twine, a jar of dried tea leaves, and a bottle of liquid.

I recognize that bottle...it's Mrs. Winslow's Soothing Syrup.

"Do you want me to stay here and sew, or to just leave?"

Before Mrs. Leng could answer the doctor spoke.

"Go with her, Miss. Castile. Mrs. Farris will be more trusting with a Chinese mid-wife if you're there. I can't seem to rid some of these people from their foolery about the Chinese. And another thing, Mr. Farris always has a conniption during a birth. Don't let him start drinking...he gets plumb crazy when he's drunk."

Becca grabbed her shawl and purse...*This could get wild...I must try to remember what I learned about childbirth in my first aid classes.*

They moved quickly toward the Farris home in Dr. Conner's carriage. He reined the horse in, and the women climbed out of the carriage. The house had three rooms; connected in line...*This is what I've heard called a shotgun house...a shot through front door passed through the back...* The Farris place was located several empty lots away from the area designated as Chinatown.

The wooden house had no foundation. The siding appeared to be loose and drafty. Becca counted four children in the yard, around the rickety stoop. The oldest, a girl, around eight years-old, held a toddler on her tiny hip. The skinny child couldn't have been more that three years-old. Identical twin girls sat in the sandy yard stacking sticks, pebbles and shells. One had a runny nose. A wood pile provided a scattering of logs and limbs...*I wonder if I'll need to chop wood to boil water.*

The axe was balanced precariously on a stump, and too close to small children in her estimation. Mr. Farris paced back and forth in the yard. He was a scrubby man, very thin and of medium height. His short unkempt beard was multicolored, blond and grey and streaked with brown tobacco stains.

He stopped when Mrs. Leng spoke softly. "All will be fine...all good...will be good soon."

A loud moan rolled out the open door, sending the distressed man back to his pacing. As they stepped inside, Becca glanced around. The floor made of rough-cut lumber, displayed splinters and an uneven surface. A simple wood cook stove sat at one end of the room with only a stovepipe to take the smoke from the house. A table with two long benches was positioned under a small window on the opposite side. Stacks of dishes and pans were piled in a wooden box at the corner.

"Put wood in." Mrs. Leng pointed toward the stove. She picked up the kettle and observed it was filled with water. "Good...make it hot."

Becca was relieved to see the wood box filled, and immediately followed instructions. There were hot coals, so starting a fire was quickly accomplished. She moved to the center room. This room was filled with cots...*Here's where the children sleep... there's little room to walk...where will they put one more?*

Stepping into the back room, she allowed her eyes to adjust. There were no windows. The only door led outside. A small lantern provided dim light. A woman lay on a bed at one side of the room. On the other side sat two tubs and a washboard...*This room obviously serves as master bedroom and laundry room.*

Mrs. Leng gently lifted the woman's gown to observe the stage of her progress.

"Get bucket, please."

"Bucket?"

She looked around. There were two large tubs but no bucket.

"Need bucket... placenta... Ask Mister.

The midwife began dragging items out of the large bag. Becca could see the roll of fabric was a pad that had been made of many layers of cloth quilted together. Mrs. Leng slid it under the woman's buttocks.

She turned to search for a bucket, but stopped in her tracks. As the bright sunlight shined through the front opened door, she saw a silhouette. The form of Mr. Farris filled the space. He carried the axe with a sense of purpose.

Becca caught her breath. Placing her hands behind her back, she eased the dagger from inside her sleeve and into her right hand. Tied to her wrist with a ribbon, it had just enough length to allow her to grip the handle, but prevented it from being dropped or knocked from her grasp. She carefully removed the narrow sheath, holding it tightly in the other hand...*It's not a fair match with an axe, but I can at least try to prevent a massacre.*

The man stood for a moment, seemingly to adjust his eyes. Becca spoke over her shoulder.

"Axe...he's got an axe!"

Mrs. Leng had dragged a wash tub over to the end of the bed, turned it upside-down, and sat on it. She was positioned to complete the delivery. She looked up and saw the dagger in Becca's hand.

"No... all good...not problem!"

At that instant, Sybil Farris released a scream that curdled Becca's blood. With that, Mr. Farris rushed through the tiny room knocking Becca out of the way as he pushed the axe under the bed.

"There...all good now..." cooed Mrs. Leng. "All be better now... over soon."

The patient reached her hand out to her husband. "Thank you, Harry, I plumb forgot about the axe."

Becca's hands were shaking so badly, she had difficulty placing the dagger back into its narrow sheath.

The man kissed his wife on top of her head. "There you go, Sybil, that otta make a powerful difference."

Mrs. Leng stood up and shooed him out the room. She handed Becca the jar of tea. "Make for him...water hot now... calm him."

"What is it?" Becca asked, remembering the power of Mrs. Leng's Female Remedy Tea. "Chamomile ...help calm...go now."

Becca hurried to the kitchen. Sybil's groans continued, and Harry's pacing was beating a path across the sparse grass in the front yard. She dug through the boxes of dishes and pans. Finding a dented metal teapot, she measured in tea as she had watched Hannah and Molly do countless times. Glancing out at the distressed man, she added an extra amount and poured boiling water into the pot. Finding no lid, she placed a saucer on the top to hold in the steam. She proceeded to look for a cup...*I don't see any sugar... there must not be any.*

A jar of sorghum caught her eye. It set on a shelf beside a salt box, sack of flour and a few other items. She added a dollop of the sticky goo, and poured the mixture through a tea strainer and into a cup.

Pulling the only chair in the kitchen out on the stoop, she beckoned Harry to sit and have tea. He responded like an obedient child. Even sitting, the man could not hold still. His right leg bounced up and down, nearly causing him to splash the hot liquid over the cup rim. Becca patted him on the shoulder.

"It's all going to be over soon, Mr. Farris. We must stay calm. Mrs. Leng is a fine mid-wife."

The man looked at her, and smiled through a paltry assortment of yellow teeth. "Thank ya, Miss."

His wife's cries intensified. He sprang up. Becca rushed back to the room to assist, if needed. Mrs. Leng looked up, revealing concern by the frown on her face.

"Babe not right...back come first...vedy not right."

Becca was aware of Mr. Farris pressing against her back as she stood in the door. Mrs. Leng took the bottle of soothing syrup. She gently assisted Mrs. Farris, in gulping a considerable dose. She then handed the bottle to Becca while nodding toward the man standing behind her.

"Give to him...calm...need him calm."

"Drug him?

"Go now...calm him...must be calm."

Becca turned and gently guided the man back to the kitchen. She set the bottle on the table, and searched in the box for a spoon. As she turned around, Harry set the empty bottle on the table. She looked at him in alarm as he wiped his mouth on a grubby sleeve... *My God, He drank it all. I wonder if it's possible to overdose on that stuff.*

His wife's cries were now screams. Becca rushed to the back room again. Mrs. Leng said quietly, "I turn babe..."

"Is the head is coming first now?"

"No... his foots. Lift...lift up."

She pointed at the woman's upper body that was straining in a backward bow.

Becca slid under Sybil's upper back, gripped her shoulders, and pushed her forward. The woman released a loud laborious groan and a new life, feet first, slipped into the world. Becca slipped from beneath her and arranged the uncased pillows under her head. As she looked at Mrs. Leng, she saw concern still etched on her face. Moving to the foot of the bed, she viewed the blue lifeless body of the tiny baby boy. The mid-wife gently spanked his buttocks and rubbed his feet. She turned him over and patted his back, but he remained limp. Becca's CPR training kicked in.

"Please, let me try."

Without waiting for a reply, she reached for the infant. Laying him on his mother's abdomen, she turned him sideways and scooped a finger through his mouth. This removed a ball of mucus and cleared his throat. Becca quickly turned him on his back and checked for a pulse. She could feel a tiny but weak heart beat. Supporting his head she covered the tiny nose and mouth with her own, and breathed in a small short breath. The little chest rose ever so slightly. She waited a few seconds and repeated with a second breath. The baby suddenly gasped and sucked in air. He began to cry. Mrs. Leng's worried face broke into a wide smile.

"Ahh, its good...all vedy good."

The new mother started to weep with relief as she reached for her new son. Mrs. Leng pulled a cloth coverlet from her bag, and wrapped him, leaving the cord exposed. She placed him at his mother's breast. Looking at Becca she prompted. "Need bucket soon."

Becca ran back to the kitchen. Harry was sitting on the bench with his head leaning against the wall. His glassy eyes peered out from behind lids at half mast. Drool dripped onto his stained beard...*Oh my goodness...hope he's not dead!*

39

If you want others to be happy you must practice compassion. If you want to be happy you must practice compassion.

—Dalai Lama

She hurried out the front door. Looking at the eldest child, she stated, "We need a bucket, now."

The girl gave the younger sister a command, and she ran to the pump where a large pail lay on its side in the sandy dirt. Grabbing it, she scurried on bare feet back to Becca. As Becca returned with the bucket, she passed Harry. He now had shifted over with his upper body sprawled on the table...*At least he's moving.*

Mrs. Leng placed the bucket on the floor at the foot of the bed. She took scissors from her bag and cut a long length of twine. Becca watched as she carefully wound it around the infant's umbilical cord and tied it tightly. She handed the scissors to Becca.

"You cut... you make him breathe...you cut."

Becca took the shears with hesitance. *She's honoring me... I'm being paid respect...*Clipping through the cord as the mid-wife instructed, she handed the scissors back and smiled. Tears surfaced as she realized she had just released this tiny human from his mother and into the world. His new world would be with a family that lived in poverty.

Mrs. Leng swaddled the infant and returned him to his mother's arms. She began massaging her stomach. Sybil groaned with discomfort, but not in the same desperation she had before the birth.

"Time now for washing...Bring pan... water."

Back to the kitchen, Becca stepped over Harry, who now lay on the floor. Spotting a dishpan hanging on the wall, she grabbed it. Pouring in hot water from the kettle and cold from a pitcher, she returned to the bedroom.

Several hours later, Mrs. Leng and Becca had bathed baby and mother with wet washcloths, cleaned the area, and buried the placenta in a deep hole they team-dug in the back yard. They poured boiling water over the scissors, pan, bucket and the stained floor. Becca took several pillows from the children's cots and repositioned Harry. His pulse and breathing seemed normal relieving her worry.

As the three women enjoyed tea, Doc arrived in his buggy. The children ran to meet him, excited to have a man they admired stop by. He teased them a bit, then, walked in. Stepping over Harry, he moved through the crowded middle room to the back.

Sybil spared no words as she told the story of her baby's near death. She praised both Mrs. Leng and Becca, while insisting that Miss Castile had resurrected her child as sure as Christ had brought Lazarus from the tomb. Becca wanted to object, saying it wasn't really the same thing, but held her peace. Doc listened to their report, examined mother and child, and complimented both women. He examined Harry and stated he would soon sleep it off.

Becca approached him quietly. "Doc, there's nothing in this house to feed these children. What do we do about that?"

He smiled. "I was just going out to get the biscuits from the buggy. Reverend Walker's wife sent them."

He returned with a checkered cloth that had been made into a bag by tying the four corners together.

"I had to stop and tell the Reverend about the Martins' misfortune. They lost their twins. They were too dang early. I told him the Farris' were birthing as well. Mrs. Walker quickly gathered up biscuits, butter and jam for both families. She's a compassionate woman."

On the ride home, Becca related her experiences with Mr. Farris. Doc laughed but then grew serious.

"Harry is an honorable man...but a broken one. He worked for years in the lumber mill. He fell from a height that should have killed him. His back is injured, and deals him pain. I believe his brain suffered from the accident as well. Since then, he's just plain whipped. He can't work to support his family, except for small jobs that don't take a lot of strength. Life has dealt him the little end of the horn."

"So he drinks to kill the pain?"

"He's abated his drinking over the past year. It results in him acting all possessed like. But on occasion, when all fired up over worries, he'll take a nip. Mostly though, when he gets a hankering for something, he goes to the opium den. He finds relief there."

"So he's addicted?"

Doc didn't answer. Becca wondered if that was the wrong word for this generation. Soon he spoke thoughtfully.

"As I see things, the man is in pain. I can do nothing to change that. I can't fix him. If he finds relief that harms no one, why should I judge or object?"

All three were quiet in the moonlight ride. After dropping off Mrs. Leng, Becca pursued another topic.

"Why did Harry put an axe under Sybil's bed, Doc? That's the silliest thing I ever heard."

Doc laughed loudly. "It's a custom that originated in the South and Midwest. I haven't a notion how the idea got started. But, for those who believe, it's a sure way to reduce the intensity of the labor pains, like the saying... cuts the pain."

"But, does Mrs. Leng believe that? She insisted on allowing him in the room with the axe."

"Mrs. Leng knows that Harry would never hurt his wife. He worships that woman. He might chop a hole in a wall, or some other wild-spirited destruction, but he'd never harm a hair of the head of his family members. Mrs. Leng believes in allowing people to believe how they may. If the axe brings comfort, so be it."

"I guess you're right, but it is such superstition."

"The foolery that doesn't hurt anyone isn't what rankles me. It's the nonsense of meanness and pure lack of compassion that gets my dander up," said the doctor.

Later, a tired Becca settled into her lumpy bed. She remembered that tomorrow was wash day with Hannah. As she drifted off, her thoughts were filled with the tender actions of Mrs. Leng and the wise words of Doc Conner. They had earned her respect.

She awoke to the chiming of the clock. The first thing *that popped into her mind was the new baby and the Farris family... I think I'll try to get over and check on them this afternoon...*After making use of the chamber pot, she began her morning hygiene. Then she remembered that Thad was in Eureka today... *He'll be here tomorrow with the coins made from the gold bar...I can complete the house purchase...*She rinsed her mouth from tooth brushing, and splashed water on her face...*I must keep Tuesday afternoon open for house business.*

Patting the moisture from her face, she noticed how dry her skin felt. I'll also go to The Mercantile and pick up the things I ordered... Mr. Sanders has surely gotten everything unpacked by now... *I need that olive oil...That's a task for this afternoon.*

Dressed in a new housedress and her hair pinned into a bun, Becca sat down to lace up the narrow, high top shoes...*Moccasins... they should be ready by now...I'll have to visit Sarah this week sometime...with all this walking I'll need comfortable shoes....Ok, I'll do that Wednesday.*

She picked up the chamber pot to take it to the outhouse for emptying ...*So much to do this week...how did I manage to get Delphi's life on the fast track like this?*

By the time Hannah knocked on her door. Delphi was ready for the day and eager to begin.

"You must have risen early...it's only seven-o-clock," the girl observed.

"I have much to do today. I have a very busy week, actually."

She and Hannah descended the front stairs together. Becca had her breakfast in the dining room with the hotel guests. As introductions were made, she tried to pair names with what knowledge she had of the victims of the shipwreck. Polina's father ate with them on this day, as did several other families. In spite of their mission being grim, conversation was pleasant and informative. Polina's parents had never seen their five grandchildren. Her father, now giving up on knowing if any of the unidentified children were hers, paid for the burial of five of the children who remained unclaimed.

"My daughter was a devoted mother," he explained. "She would approve; these young souls will be buried next to my daughter."

Conversation then turned to a more political theme. A Captain Wiles, there to claim bodies of crewmen, explained that the death of William Logan could have negative consequences for California and the new north-western states.

"Mr. Logan was superintendent of the newly designated United States Mint. It was planned for Dalles, Oregon,"

He forked another pancake onto his plate. "He was on his way to get it established. "

"A mint in Oregon?" Molly walked in with the coffee pot to refill empty cups. "That's good sense, considering so much gold is mined and dredged here in the west."

"I just hope the government will continue with the plan, and not get detoured. All the reconstruction from the war is making progress very slow. Some mint equipment, a lot of gold and the mint's plans went down with the ship and Mr. Logan. I hope they get it going soon. That ought to make the rest of the country set up and take notice of us."

Mr. O'Shay held up his cup to his wife.

Nope, it will end up in Denver...*They'll take notice of you all right... You have no idea what's coming...later they'll try to harvest all of the redwoods ...that'll take a fight to prevent...*

Becca became aware of Molly calling her name, and looked up to see the women offering to fill her cup. "You are a bit idle minded today dear, are you ill?"

"No, I just got lost in my thoughts...yes, please, I'll have more coffee."

"That's because you worked on the Sabbath, Delphi. It's not good for a body to go whole hog, every day of the week. The brain can't find time to do its thinking' when you don't rest it some. That's why the Good Lord told us to rest on Sundays. I've never set store on going against scripture. You'd be better off resting than working for that heathen woman."

Becca felt her irritation start to rise ...*No, I won't let her ruin this lovely day for me.*

"In truth Molly, most of the afternoon was involved in helping Doc. He was overwhelmed by emergencies, yesterday. I'm quite sure God didn't mind."

"Is that so?" Molly looked surprised. "Doc told me yesterday that he was on his way to the Martin home, but he didn't mention that he was taking you to help."

"No, it was at another emergency. Everything worked out fine, but it took up the afternoon."

I hope she leaves it at that...I can't violate confidentiality...wonder if that's become an issue yet...in 1865?

"Well, where then?" Molly's eyes were wide with curiosity. "Was it in Chinatown?"

"I'm sorry Molly. I don't think I can reveal the name or condition of one of Doctor Conner's patients."

"Laws sakes, there's no secrets in this town. We're all neighborly."

"It was the Farris family," piped up Mr. O'Shay, pushing his chair back. "I was outside Reverend Walker's house and talking to him when Doc stopped by. He said that the Martins lost their twins and that he was on his way to the Farris house."

Guess that answers my question about ... confidentiality...there is none.

"You were at the Farris house?" Hannah looked alarmed. "Why, I heard Harry Farris is as crazy as a loon."

"That's not true, Hannah, you're misinformed."

"Everybody knows it, Delphi," the girl insisted.

"Hannah, whatever health problems Mr. Farris has, he's not crazy."

"He's gotten the name of being a bad egg," added Molly. "Sybil could have done a lot better. He's shiftless and daft."

Becca took a deep breath... *I must be fair...I thought he was crazy too, until Doc. explained... I'll keep my voice calm.*

"Mr. Farris was injured and he suffers from extreme pain. I saw him show love and devotion for his wife yesterday. He's not a bad egg, nor is he shiftless."

Mr. O'Shay stood and pulled up his trousers that hung precariously below his belly. "Old Harry is a good enough man, just gets rambunctious when he's liquored up. I saw him chop a gate down once. He got mad at it when he ran into it drunk." He chuckled. "But, he has his row to hoe."

As he and the others moved out of the room, Hannah and Molly begin to clear the table. Becca decided to speak up for some help for the Farris family.

"You know, Molly; I agree that this community is neighborly. They've been wonderful about the shipwreck. They aided the survivors, buried the dead and are now hosting the families."

Molly nodded. "Yes, people here have always been like that."

"So, I was wondering...could we cash in on some of that neighborly love to help the Farris family? Those poor children have nothing to eat."

Molly set the stack of dirty plates she carried back on the table. "What do you have in mind, dear?"

"When I was there, heating water and helping Mrs.... the midwife, I noticed that the kitchen is as bare as Mother Hubbard's Cupboard. If Doc hadn't brought bread and butter from the Reverend's home, there wouldn't have been any supper for those children."

"Oh my!" Molly pulled out a chair. "I know they're poor, but Sybil has always managed with her garden and a few chickens. She takes in ironing for a little bit of pay...."

"She's just had a baby...breech. I don't think she'll be ironing for a few weeks."

"Oh, Doc insists on six weeks of bed-rest for a new mother, nothing less. Harry cuts grass for people, and chops firewood now and then. I just never thought of them being in such dire need."

"Doc says that Harry's back causes him constant pain. Even when he does these menial tasks, Molly, it's limited to what he can endure on any given day. I'm sure he's been busy helping his wife through these last weeks of pregnancy."

"You shouldn't say that word, Delphi; it's vulgar to say a woman who's in the family way is ....well what you said."

Both women looked up to see Hannah entering from the kitchen... *Wouldn't you know the etiquette cop would show up when I'm making progress on my plan?*

"You must not correct your elders, Hannah," scolded Molly. "Delphi is young, but she's still older than you. Delphi wouldn't have used that word if our men folk had been present."

Its medical terminology for goodness sake...ok... calm down... I'm not going to get distracted.

"Sit, and help us think, Hannah." Becca pointed to a chair, "You would just love that new baby. Do you want to go with me to visit this afternoon?"

Molly returned to her tasks. "I'm helping plan some meals to take to the Martins. I'll give the Farris family some thought too."

40

"People will forget what you said, people will forget what you did, but people never forget how you made them feel."

—Maya Angelou

Hannah pondered Becca's invitation regarding the Farris family. "If Mrs. O'Shay can spare me..." she glanced at Molly.

"I think all three of us should go," the woman declared. "With so much cooking this week for the extra guests, I'll have food I can take over. But...we mustn't insult them."

"What do you mean?" asked Becca.

"Because, it hurts people's pride to have others bring them charity," piped Hannah.

"Why should it hurt anyone's pride for others to care?"

"Because it's like saying you aren't smart enough or tough enough to do things for yourself. Everyone knows that Delphi."

"That doesn't make sense to me. Those children are suffering."

"Sybil was from a proud family out east and she must feel shamed. People look down on other people who let themselves get poor. Even if it isn't their fault, they don't want people noticing." Molly explained.

"When I was orphaned, I felt like that," added Hannah." I didn't want to be a burden to someone else. That's why I was lucky the O'Shay's let me work for my keep." She looked at Molly with gratitude.

Right...and she works your tail off. The honorable act would have been to adopt you and let you finish your childhood and schooling...It's a good thing I discussed this...I could have blundered ...

"So how do we help without them knowing we're helping?" *I hate dishonesty for the sake of public opinion!*

"Well, I'm starting a big pot of mutton stew. I'll make a bit extra. We'll have Charley set us up for a wagon ride. You can explain that you're following up for Doc by checking on the babe. I'll tell her that with the steamer passengers in town, I've overcooked." She looked very pleased with herself.

"So we're doing what I wanted to do, but using words that make it seems like that's not what we're doing?"

"We're simply making what you want to do acceptable." Molly disappeared through the kitchen door.

"So, they won't mind charity, as long as everyone pretends that it isn't charity, even though it's charity?"

Hannah giggled. "You say the silliest things, Delphi. We better start on that washing."

Since the beds were all made up for guests, there were no sheets to wash. Molly had paid a youth to chop enough wood to meet the needs of a full house, so Hannah and Becca didn't have to take time to do it. The laundry chore moved along rapidly. Tea towels, bath towels, tablecloths and napkins were on the line by ten-thirty, and the two began washing Becca's, Hannah's and the O'Shay's personal clothing.

Hannah showed Becca how to sponge her wool outing dress with cold rosewater and then press it dry with an iron. Becca had nearly plopped it into the hot vat of soapy water when Hannah intercepted it.

"You never wash wool in hot water. Everyone knows that, Delphi. That would shrink it all to pieces."

"Silly me, I forgot," Becca muttered.

By noon, both were ready to freshen up for the mid-day meal. They then returned to the kitchen to assist Molly in serving a table filled with guests. A few new faces were gathered and introductions were made. Becca took a seat beside George Hanson. Mr. Hanson was introduced as the Superintendent of Indian Affairs, usually referred to as Indian agent. After mutton stew and hot crusty rolls had been passed around, conversation turned to the local events.

"How's everything on the reserve, Mr. Hanson?" asked Charley O'Shay.

Mr. Hanson buttered his roll before placing the knife on the side of the butter dish.

"Everything was in a bit of an upheaval for a while. The gold and rations for the tribe went down with the ship as you know. Fortunately the Indians are resourceful with fishing. Other staples couldn't be bought and distributed."

"It came in with this steamer, I hope," offered Molly." We wouldn't want them to go plundering and raiding our town."

"There's not any likelihood of that, Mrs. O'Shay. Our tribes are peaceful enough, but we have rendered them dependent on our rations by confining them to such a small acreage."

"So, they can't leave the reservation for any reason?" asked Becca.

"There are arrangements that can be made," he answered, "for particular situations."

"Like, what kind of situation?" she prodded.

Mr. Hanson smiled at her, conveying he was pleased with her interaction.

"Well, for instance, when Brother Jonathan went down, the army payroll was lost. Now, those men at The Fort get pretty restless out there. There's no Indian trouble to keep them busy, so they look forward to the monthly payday. They can go into town and get liquored-up at the saloons."

Molly circled the table with a coffee pot. "I haven't noticed the usual crowd of men coming into town this month."

They couldn't because they didn't have their gold. So a boodle of them took off. Guess they thought without pay, they didn't want to work for the government anymore. But, you can't run off from the army."

"Did they catch them?" asked Charley.

Mr. Hanson stirred sugar into his coffee. "The problem that arose was that if half the men are runners and the other half is chasers, there's no one to man the Fort."

"So, how did they manage?" asked Becca.

"The Captain hired Indian guides to go with several soldiers to gather up the runners so the remaining soldiers could stay at the Fort and guard the other Indians." Mr. Hanson looked at Becca with this conclusion. He had a merry twinkle in his eyes. Becca burst into laughter.

"How ironic," she managed to say as she gathered her repose.

"So, to answer your question, Miss, regarding arrangements for extraordinary situations; someone responsible makes the request and I decide if it warrants an arrangement."

Hannah, sitting across from Becca looked up as though she had been struck by an idea.

"Can arrangements be made for children to leave?"

Becca shot her a look of caution.

"I mean... I always wondered about that," the girl explained.

"Why, sakes alive, Hannah, why would you wonder that?" demanded Molly.

Mr. Hanson continued. "There are occasions that I have granted arrangements; one for a child and one for an adult. The first was to be employed off the reserve with a rancher, and the other was a child with serious illnesses that can only be treated in another location."

Becca and Hannah exchanged glances, and Hannah nodded slightly, letting Becca know she had curtailed her tongue... *She scared me there for a moment...but she did help me get some important information...I'll keep that in mind for Sarah's issues...*

By two-thirty the kitchen was cleaned, and the three loaded into the wagon. Charley O'Shay sat holding the reins, while Molly climbed to the wagon seat to sit beside him. As Becca and Hannah settled onto the board seat behind them, Becca fondly remembered how gallantly Thad always assisted women in and out of the buggy...*I have to admit; I find myself liking his chivalry... to some extent.*

As Charley stopped in front of the Farris house, children spilled out of the door. Harry Farris came out onto the stoop.

"Hello, Mr. Farris," greeted Molly, "I brought Miss Castile over to check on Sybil, and thought you might be willing to relieve me of this extra stew. My rooms are all filled and I must have overestimated what I needed."

Harry stepped aside, allowing Molly to enter. Hannah followed with buns. Becca carried a blackberry pie.

"It's right kind of you to think of us, Mrs. O'Shay. Since you've got extra...wouldn't want it to go to waste."

"Good," answered Molly, setting the pot on the stove. "Waste is a sin. That's what the good book says."

*Well, if it doesn't say that, it should...*Becca placed the pie on the table. She asked, "Is it alright if I go back to see your wife?"

He nodded, "She'll be glad to see you, but Doc checked on her about an hour ago."

"Yes, I'd like to be sure the newborn is still breathing as he should." *I feel like such a liar.*

She moved through the middle room filled with cots. None were made up, and items lay of the floor. *Yesterday, it was crowded but not messy... Sybil is going to need some help here...*"Hi, Mrs. Farris, how are you and your new son feeling?"

"I'm feeling very tired and sore, dear. Please call me Sybil."

"What did the doctor say? Does he think you and baby are as well as you should be?"

"He said that I'm bleeding more than the usual. It's probably because of the difficult birth. He hopes I won't have anymore children."

"Are you eating and drinking enough?"

"Some tea and bread, mostly water."

"Molly brought over some extra stew. I'm going to get a bowl of it for you; I'll bring it with some tea. You must get plenty of fluid."

When Becca returned to the kitchen, she saw that Hannah and Molly had the family seated at the table. Molly was filling bowls with mutton stew while Hannah washed little faces and hands with a partially clean cloth. Harry sat at the end of the table, buttering rolls for his brood. Becca found a flat pan to use as a tray. Placing a bowl of stew, a roll, and a slice of pie on it, she turned to Hannah.

"The kettle is hot; would you please make tea for Sybil? It's on the shelf: teapot is in that box, and Molly brought sugar."

Placing a fork and spoon on the pan, she returned to the back room. She borrowed a few pillows from the middle room, and propped the woman up. She set the pan down on a wooden crate that served as a table.

"Let me hold that little fellow while you eat." She reached out her arms.

Sybil handed her the bundled baby. Becca pulled back the thin blanket and looked into the tiny pink face. She remembered how blue it was when she blew breath into his mouth. His eyes were closed, and he pushed out his lips, causing his cheeks to dimple.

"He's beautiful, Sybil, what did you name him?"

Sybil finished chewing a bite before answering. "We're naming him Delford, after you."

"After me?"

"I had to ask Doc what your name was. Neither Harry nor I could remember. When Doc said it was Delphi, I had to figure out how to turn it into a boy's name."

"I'm much honored." Becca lifted the infant to her face and kissed his head.

"Hello, Delford, we'll have to become good friends, me and you."

"More than friends, Miss Delphi, we want you to be his godmother."

Oh oh, what do I do about this?...I'm not going to be around...wonder if Delphi will be agreeable in taking this on?

"We clean stopped going to church when Harry got hurt. I just couldn't manage to get us all there without his help. He was so mad at God after that. But now...with the way you raised little Delford from the dead...we think we ought to get back to worshiping again."

"Sybil, what I did for your baby was to fill his lungs with air. He wasn't dead; his heart was beating...it's called..."

"So, I sent word with Doc to tell Reverend Walker to stop by. I'll tell him we want to baptize Delford and that you'll be his godmother, if your willing."

On the other hand...as a godmother to their child, I'll have a good excuse to help the family..."I'd be honored to be his godmother, Sybil."

Molly and Hannah appeared at the door. "Hello, Sybil, I can't wait to see that youngin'."

Becca passed the baby to Molly, and left to make more room in the tiny space. In the kitchen, she poured a cup of tea, and sent it back to Sybil with her oldest child. She poured herself and Harry cups and set at the table. Harry was finishing up his stew. He thanked her for the tea. He wiped his beard on the cloth Hannah had used for dirty faces. Then he and smiled at Becca.

"Did Sybil tell you what we want to do about Delford?"

"The baptism?"

He nodded. "Is that agreeable to you Miss Castile? We'd be honored if you became his godmother."

"Yes, I'd love that, but you and Sybil must call me Delphi."

He smiled and reached out his hand. She took it, and they shook.

"And as godmother and baby nurse, I plan to take appropriate responsibility. I'll be over here at least once a day for a while to help out with the house, children, meals, and baby as long as Sybil is bedbound."

He nodded and smiled...*Ah-ha, I'm catching onto this game...*

The women had the dishes washed and kitchen swept by the time Charley returned. As they started home, Molly looked over her shoulder and smiled.

"I arranged for us to provide winter sweaters to the children."

"That's wonderful, Molly, how did you manage that?" Becca asked.

"She told a lie," whispered Hannah.

"I heard you, and it isn't a lie," argued Molly. "I told Sybil I'm starting a knitting bee to teach young women wifely skills. She agreed to allow us to use her children to measure for our patterns. Naturally, we'll give the sweaters to the children when they're finished."

"Sounds like a good plan to me," said Becca. "Who are you students?"

"You and Hannah, of course."

"I already know how to knit," pouted Hannah.

"Well, I don't, and I'll need your coaching. If we get started before Elsie and Minnie leave, they can help. Elsie is very good at those kinds of things."

Then she remembered the rest of her plan for the day.

"Could you please drop me off at The Mercantile? Mr. Sanders has an order for me. And… would you mind if Hannah comes with me? There may be a lot to carry home."

Hannah brightened as she looked expectantly at Molly.

"As long as she's back in time to help me make supper," agreed Molly.

41

"Rebellion to tyrants is obedience to God."

—Benjamin Franklin

Becca and Hannah walked into The Mercantile. "Are you figuring on getting some candy today, Delphi?"

"Ah yes, several kinds."

Mr. Sanders was busily wrapping up a purchase for a woman in a large hat. He smiled at them.

"Good afternoon, ladies. I have your order already wrapped, Miss Castile."

"Thank you, Mr. Sanders; I'd like to look around at your new merchandise first."

"I have some new cloth, yarn and sewing notions." He nodded to shelves in a far corner.

Becca scanned the new wares. A bolt of soft blue muslin caught her eye...I wonder if I could sew a gown for little Delford?

"Would you like me to take that down for you?"

Delphi turned to see Mr. Sanders approaching. "Yes, please, I'd like to feel the fabric."

He lifted it down, and she stroked the material. "This is soft enough for a baby, don't you think?"

"This is the best quality we can get right now," he assured her...

I wonder how much I'd need...where's Hannah?

Glancing around, she saw her young friend talking with James and scoping the books shelves.

"I'll take three yards of this soft blue. Also two spools of matching thread, and do you have tiny buttons?"

"Here are all the buttons I have."

The clerk pointed to stacks of buttons sewn to pieces of cardpaper and displayed inside a glass counter. Reaching in, he took out a card of eight tiny abalone shell buttons. Becca turned them in the light. The radiant blue reflected different hues.

"Yes, these are perfect."

"Would you like some ribbon?" He pointed to large spools of various colored silk strands.

"Yes, four yards of the baby blue."

Mr. Sanders took down the spool, laid it on the counter, and cut the requested amount.

"It's called robin-egg blue. In case you send someone to get you more, you'll want the correct color name."

"Now, I'd like to see the yarn."

Moving further down the same counter, they arrived at a shelf with wooden boxes lined up side by side. The yarn was sorted by weight, the largest and heaviest first and graduating down to the small fine, more delicate skeins. There were no bright colors. Shades were equally divided among black, grey, brown, tan, navy and white. She settled on a white lightweight one that she deemed suitable for an infant...*how much to get...well...I can always use any extra.*

She took four skeins, and then looked over the knitting needles. Not knowing what size she would need, she selected a kit that had multiple sizes.

"I'm joining a knitting bee. I don't know how to knit, but I soon will."

"A knitting bee? The man looked interested. "Where is that starting?"

"Mrs. O'Shay is organizing it at the Redwood Hotel."

"I wonder if I might persuade Ruthie to go...that's my daughter... she and her mother don't work well together. Lottie was complaining just yesterday that Ruthie still hasn't mastered wifery arts. She hasn't even completed her sampler, and most girls have finished that by the time they start to school."

"She's certainly welcomed to join us. Maybe working with Hannah would be more fun for her. To be truthful, Mr. Sanders, I was a brat when my mother tried to teach me to sew, and now I love doing it."

They both laughed. A familiar, irritating voice pulled her from the revelry. Turning, she saw Reverend Walker talking to James and Hannah. The girl hung her head and James looked like he had just witnessed a hanging.

"Excuse me, please package these items, I must check on Hannah."

Crossing the long room, she moved toward the books. "Hello, Reverend, how are you this afternoon?"

Hannah stood deathly still, holding a novel. She looked at Becca with a mortified expression on her face.

"Good afternoon Miss. Castile." He held a new hymn book in his hand and stood before a box of a dozen or more identical hymnals. . Becca assumed he previously ordered them, and came to pick them up.

"Are you going to introduce some new songs to your congregation?"

He ignored the question. His face contorted into a scowl.

"I was giving counsel to Hannah and to James as well. I don't want to see any more of these novels made available to our women and young folks. They're inspired from the pits of hell!"

Becca reached out and took the book from Hannah. She opened it up.

"Not to worry, Reverend. This was published in London, not Hell, see."

"Don't be impertinent with me, young lady. It is my duty and calling to provide spiritual leadership to the people of this town."

Becca was aware that the bombastic voice was drawing attention. .. *Keep calm...quiet voice...pretend he's a sassy kindergartener...*

"Excuse me, Reverend; I'm speaking calmly with my inside voice to show respect. It's as important that you respect others as it is for you to expect it. From the looks of my friends, James and Hannah, you've also served up some impertinence; I dare say?"

He cleared his throat. "As a pastor, I have need at times, to chastise when I see it due."

"Do you know in what country you reside, Reverend?"

"Why of course, don't be absurd, America."

"Correct, where we are guaranteed freedom of certain choices. Which means, Sir, you may choose your religion and form your opinions, but you don't have the right to choose for James, Hannah, me or the rest of the town."

"And Behold, it is prophesied that in the last days they shall turn their ears..."

"Ahh, Mr. Walker, hiding behind memorized snippets of scripture doesn't empower you, or give you license to tell James what he may or may not sell, or Hannah what she can read."

"This is preposterous. You don't know your place, woman. I shall have a talk with Mrs. O'Shay about you. How dare you speak to a minister like that! How dare you contradict a man of God!"

Becca looked at the novel in her hand. "David Copperfield... ahh ... this is a great story. I've read it several times."

Holding it up, she looked around the store.

"I highly recommend this book. Wrap it up for us, James. Do you have Great Expectations?"

James looked stunned, but reached into an unpacked box and found the requested book.

"Great! I'll take that too."

Hannah was as pale as if she'd been given a one-way ticket to Purgatory...*I hope this old fuddy-duddy hasn't intimidated her from ever reading* *again...*As Becca scanned the newly stocked books, her eyes fell on another book, *Incidents in the Life of a Slave Girl.*

"That looks educational; I'll take that one as well, James."

James scrambled to retrieve it from the shelf. Reverend Walker stood in stone silence, glaring.

"*My Lost Love,* by Georgiana Meriwether, that might be a biography. I'll take that as well. Oh, and one more, grab that other new one, *The House by the Churchyard.* That should keep me busy for a while."

Becca was aware that the customers in the store had watched in deathly silence, though a few spoke in whispers behind gloved hands. Smiles and smirks appeared on some faces...*I hope that means they approve of me and aren't planning to burn me at the stake.*

James stacked the books on a large piece of brown paper and pulled the ends around to wrap them.

"I'll be moving soon, James. I plan to start a reading circle. Once a month, members will meet at my house. Over refreshments, we'll read to one another, discuss literature, and even try writing poetry. Would you help me get it started?"

If a knitting bee worked for Molly, maybe this ill work for me.

Looking at her, he smiled broadly. "Oh yes, Miss Castile. It would be like a soirée, but with books rather than music."

"Exactly, we'll set it up to start in October. Could you make a... poster...or a..?"

"An advertisement...yes, I can do that."

The man in black laid the hymn book on the table.

"I've decided not to buy the box of hymnals from you, James. I won't need your services anymore."

"I'll take the hymn books, James; I'm getting a piano and need some music to practice. I'll take one with me today, but I'll need you to deliver the box later. Now what do I owe you?"

Smiling sweetly at the preacher, she added, "Thank you, Reverend, you've saved me from having to order music."

"This is all an abomination... sin, sin, sin! The Bible is the only good book."

"And you have the right to believe that, Mr. Walker, because you live in America. And at church, where you're in charge, that's what is read. Outside of church, people are in charge of their choices because they also live in America."

She plopped the packaged books into Hannah's arms. The girl looked as though she was handed a python. After paying James, while wondering if Delphi would resent her splurge, she moved to the counter and paid Mr. Sanders for the items he had packaged for her there.

"I'm very sorry, Mr. Sanders, I fear we've made quite a disturbance in your store."

He counted out her change and smiled.

"You are always welcomed in my store, Miss Castile. I'll talk to Lottie and Ruthie about the knitting bee, and I'll mention the reading circle to them too. Lottie loves reading novels, though she seldom dares to admit it to anyone but me."

As Becca led the way out of The Mercantile, Hannah trailed like a whipped pup. Reverend Walker waited outside.

"You made a fine spectacle of yourself today, Miss Castile. I'll be speaking with Mrs. O'Shay about the detrimental influence I saw you have over her young charge."

Becca stepped very close the man, and looked directly into his eyes.

"Mr. Walker, I was just beginning to believe you might be a man of God. I had started to respect you. But I see that you are clearly a Pharisee. For you it's all about rules...not God's love. And the rules you impose are your rules, not God's. Shame on you! I'm so disappointed! I am placing you in Time Out until you have reflected on your disrespect of others."

His face turned grey and slowly morphed from anger to what appeared to be remorse. He reminded her of a five-year-old caught stealing someone else' milk money.

"Good day, Sir."

They turned right. With arms loaded, they walked briskly...*I hope I got that right. It's been several years since that Bible class in college. Was Pharisee the right word...the rule keepers...the perpetual challengers of Christ's behaviors and teachings? ...Or was it Sadducees...or Maccabeus...or Applebee's...no, that's an eatery...*

A sobbing sound interrupted her thoughts. Looking around, she saw that Hannah was in total melt-down.

"Sweetie, what's wrong? Don't let that old buzzard upset you!"

She wanted to put arms around the girl, but there wasn't anywhere suitable to set all the packages.

"He's going to make, sob, sob... Mrs. O'Shay stop me from being with you...sob."

"No, I will talk to her first. Besides, he's just a big bully, and bullies bluff. Darn, I forgot to buy candy. Shall we go back and get it?"

"No!" The girl answered quickly. "I shan't be late to help with supper."

Becca struggled to retrieve the handkerchief from her sleeve. Balancing the packages on a raised knee and holding them with one hand, she wiped Hannah's nose and face.

"No more tears, my little friend. Everything is going to be just fine." *If only I knew that to be true.*

The two entered through the backdoor. Hannah hastily grabbed her apron as Becca collected the packages, and prepared to go up the back staircase. Then remembering Hannah's upsetting afternoon, she turned towards the girl.

"I'm very tired and will eat supper in my room. You may bring your plate up to my room and eat with me, Hannah."

"I will, if Mrs. O'Shay doesn't need me."

"Don't worry about Reverend Walker talking to Molly. I'll talk to her first."

Hannah didn't look reassured as she started peeling potatoes. After getting the parcels to her room, Becca put the items away, and sat down at the desk. Taking the paper that she used for a ledger, she listed the items she had bought along with the prices. She tallied the total. Reaching for the journal, she moved to the bed to relax. She wrote about her experience with Mrs. Leng, her being asked to be a godmother and her excitement in completing the house purchase on the morrow. She laid the pen and journal on the bedside table and reclined back on her pillow.

Almost instantly she sensed the spinning. Relaxing into the transition, she soon found herself in Beth's home. Both Delphi and Beth sat at the table eating dinner. Becca moved toward them... Hmmm, pizza, I really miss pizza.

"Hello, Becca, we were just speaking of you," Delphi stated.

"My sister is here?" Beth's voice sounded excited.

"Oui, she's here, coveting pizza."

"We must update her on the divorce before she slips away," Beth urged.

"Your husband's attorney spoke with my...your attorney this morning." Delphi began. She spoke aloud so that Beth would hear at least one side of the conversation.

And, what is the offer?

"He will cooperate completely with the divorce. It will be fast and easy, if you will refute the accusation that he tried to kill you."

I absolutely will not! He's not getting away with what he tried to do. Don't sign anything that agrees to backing down from the truth. He has to pay!

"That's what your sister said you'd say. But you must know that he will give you the barn...I mean loft, all the furniture, and one half of his savings, stocks and bonds that were bought during the marriage, if you agree."

No, I do not agree. He arranged my death, and as a result upset all our lives. He has to pay. I'll never forgive him.

Beth frustrated with hearing only Delphi's side of the conversation, asked, "What is she saying?"

Delphi looked at Beth. "She is saying what you said she would, no agreement on her part."

"Good, tell her about Ike Barker."

"Oui, the authorities matched his fingers, they say the poor confused man in Crescent City is Ike Barker."

'Don't you mean fingerprints?"

"Oui, same difference. Philip says that Monsieur Barker was the one who wanted to assassiner...no...murder you. He wants you to agree with that."

I heard Phil tell Ike to do it. I've talked to Ike's spirit that it is now in Jonah's body. He was hired by my husband to kill me. I won't back down.

"The authorities will be questioning the man this week. They said he has a long report. He's not a good man."

Report? You mean record...a long police record?

"Oui, that is the word."

Oh no, Ike's no longer in his own body. Jonah won't know what they're talking about. They'll think he's lying. Poor Jonah is innocent. What can I do to straighten this out?

"This is driving me crazy...tell me what my sister is saying," demanded Beth.

"She said..."

But all Becca could hear was Hannah's voice calling her name.

42

"Three may keep a secret, if two of them are dead."

—Benjamin Franklin

"Delphi, wake up. I have potato soup for you."

"Oh, is supper here already? I must have fallen asleep."

Hannah sat the tray on the desk top, placed a spoon into the bowl of steaming brew, and handed it to Becca.

"Hmm, it smells really good. I must be very hungry."

"I put extra ham in it. Mrs. O'Shay said to put a cupful into the pot and I put two. All the guests complimented it."

"The guests have finished eating? It must be later than I thought." Becca blew on the hot liquid in her spoon.

"Yes, it's past six. I finished cleaning the kitchen before bringing up your supper. When I checked on you earlier, you were sound asleep."

"That's good; I need to talk to you. If you aren't rushed to get back to your chores, we'll have more time for my explanation."

Hannah looked worried.

"Its good news, Hannah, so don't feel concerned. But it's also a secret until everything about it is completed."

"I keep secrets, everyone knows that I do."

"You won't need to keep it for long. When Thad returns from Eureka tomorrow, I plan to buy the widow Callahan's house and property. I'll be moving there by the end of the week. I hope to have it settled by tomorrow night. Then I'll announce it at supper"

Hannah appeared stunned.

"It really is good news, Hannah; I'll have my own house."

Tears welled up in the girl's eyes.

"I want to be happy for you, Delphi, truly I do, but it's not good news for me...not one bit. I'll never see you. You're my only friend. I'll miss you all to pieces."

"No, Hannah, I'll make arrangements for you to come over often, I will. I promise."

"It's so far." The girl now gave into sobs. "I could never walk that far, Mrs. O'Shay wouldn't allow it."

"I'll also get a horse." *I think.* "I can come and pick you up."

Hannah looked skeptical through her tears. "You can handle horses?"

"Sure, how hard can it be?"

Hannah wiped her face with her sleeve. She looked down at her hands. "Maybe you should get a buggy. Two of us riding sidesaddle on one horse will be difficult."

Side saddle...no way... I forgot about that custom...Well, that's not going to happen...But even if I break the rules and ride straddle... I can't encourage Hannah to do so...

"You're so right, clever girl. A buggy it will be. I'll go the The Mercantile tomorrow and order one in on the next steamer. I'll get us one of those fancy ones with the top on it, decorated with fringe."

Hannah giggled. "That's silly. Then people will think you're all uppity."

"And when have you seen me care about what people think?"

Hannah covered her mouth and laughed for several seconds.

"You'll be wearing your Indian shoes and riding in a fancy lady's buggy."

She sobered and said quietly, "I'll still miss you ever so much."

"Now that you mentioned my moccasins, I need to remind you that we'll go pick them up on Wednesday afternoon. We must get started on our work early so you'll be free to go with me to Sarah's camp. It'll be a long walk."

"I'll get up an hour earlier to start the cleaning," she promised.

After Hannah left with the dishes, Becca changed into her gown, completed her hygiene, and picked up a novel. She read several chapters...*How can anyone think it wrong to read these stories? They awaken the reader's minds to the thoughts and feelings of others. I guess that's why they worry. Some people resent thinkers...they want only followers.*

She turned out the light and thought about the problem regarding Ike and Jonah. Plans began to form in her mind...*It just might work...*

A blue glow formed at the foot of her bed. She blinked.

Delphi?

"Oui, I was in process of writing in your journal, but again...here I am."

Good, I need to discuss something with you.

"You must withhold your remarks. I have need to give you report. When you were with us, I had to tell you about your husband's offer. But, I have more to say."

Becca waited for Delphi to form her thoughts into English.

"Beth assisted me in a purchase from your money."

It must be needed, or my sister wouldn't have helped with it. What is it?

"I purchased a piano. It is wonderfully grand. It will be deliberated on the morrow."

I think you mean, delivered?

"Oui, as I said. Beth told me we should inform you, so I wrote it in your journal."

That's fine with me; practice will pass the time for you. I'm going to buy a horse and buggy with some of your gold.

"Oui, I'll need one when I return. Be assured that the creature is gentle, the carriage good quality, and obtain, selle de côté. I ride very well."

What is that?

"Selle de côté...it's...oh how do you say? A lady's seat...riding seat."

Saddle...side saddle? God help me...

"You will need to have the seamstress make a riding skirt...I'd like that in bleu clair..."

Blue? Light Blue?

"Oui, and the trim...I prefer noir...uh...black."

Never mind that. I have to tell you something. I'm trying to think of a way to switch Ike and Jonah back. But first, they have to be able to communicate, as we do.

"I don't comprehend...by writing in journals?"

That works for us. So I'm going to get Jonah, he thinks his name is Cain, a journal and convince him to write in it.

"I see...but how will you do that for the poor man in Crescent City?"

I can't, but Beth can. She must find out where he is, and take him a journal. He'll need to write everything he can think of about himself. If it works like it did for us, they should start visiting one another.

"So this is your instruction...I'm to tell Beth this?"

Yes, and as soon as possible. Once the authorities start questioning him, he may not be available....Delphi...?

After thinking about her busy day, Becca fell into a deep sleep. She didn't hear the clock's chimes through out the night, or its early proclamation of seven bells. Hannah aroused her by announcing breakfast. She hurried though her routine, dressing in a house dress and Delphi's velvet slippers. Pulling her hair back, she tied it in a ribbon at her neck and scurried down the front stairs.

Thad stood by the hall tree, hanging his top hat. She hurried to him...*My heart's in a flutter. I must be feeling excitement about buying the house today...* "I'm so glad you came here for breakfast," she said, smiling.

"I needed to report to you." He smiled back. "I was successful, but we were followed for a time. I was glad I had my new Winchester with me, even though I didn't need it after all. Perhaps, just seeing both Abe and me toting new rifles discouraged any no-accounts from trying to rob us."

"You were followed? Did you see who he was? How would someone know you were carrying gold?" Becca spoke is soft tones.

"The clerk at the smelting shop warned us that there are some rascals who stand on the streets and watch men come out of the shop. They figure there's only one reason to be there, so they trail you around like a hound after a rabbit."

"That's terrible! Did the man follow you all the way back?"

"We were aware we were being tracked by a lone rider for the first part of our return. Then we got into dense forest and we kept on the ready. We never got a good look, he stayed too far back. Once we hit the clearing, we rode full chisel back into town. Your gold is in the safe at The Print Shop."

"Thank you, ever so much for doing that for me, Thad, I couldn't pull this house deal off without you. I hope you realize how grateful I am."

He smiled broadly, placed his hand on her back as he nudged her toward the dining room. "We better get to the vittles before Charley starts on seconds. Otherwise, we won't get any."

His hand remained on the small of her back. His touch shot of electric current through her core...*Stop it, Becca! You're out of your time-zone. You can't fall for this man...you're still married to Phil for the moment. What's wrong with me?*

They took their places at the table. It was filled to capacity, again... *Molly must be raking in the money while all these people are here. And it'll be another week before the steamer returns to pick them up...She should have profited enough by then to give Hannah some time off...Hannah would love a few days with me in my new home...*

There was a generous bowl of oatmeal at each setting. A pitcher of cream, a container of soft butter, and a bowl of sugar sat available. Molly circled the table with a coffee pot, filling cups.

"You look mighty perky today, dear. You must be pleased to have your young man back at the table."

Becca felt her face flush and imagined it to be bright red. *Dang that woman!*

"I'm perky every morning, Molly. And Mr. Barrett is not my young man, he's a free agent."

"Is Mr. Barrett helping you...?"

Hannah stopped in the middle of her question, filled her mouth with bread, and looked down at her bowl...*What the heck...might as well tell them about my plans.*

"Mr. Barrett will be assisting me this afternoon. We're meeting with Mrs. Callahan. I expect to purchase her house and land."

Silence fell across the table.

"Well, I knew you were working some," muttered Charley "I didn't know the Chinese woman could pay those kinds of wages."

I find that rude on so many levels...I'm not going to respond.

"Now Charley," scolded his wife, "We have no business wondering about Delphi's money affairs." She pushed the platter of biscuits toward him.

"Shaw, I meant no offence." The man took two biscuits and reached for the butter.

"I'll miss your working half days," said Molly. "You're a good hand. Hannah will miss you, for sure."

The girl pushed her chair away from the table and ran from the room.

"See? She took to you like gravy on bread."

"I think the world of her too. Surely she can visit me often?" Becca gave Molly a pleading look.

"If I didn't allow her to visit you, she would be pining all over the place. She'd be as worthless as buttons on a dishrag. We'll work something out."

Mr. Hanson stacked his drained cup onto his empty bowl, and laid his napkin beside it.

"I must say, Miss. Castile, you're the most industrious young woman, I have ever met. A few days ago, I heard you raised the dead, I hear you stood toe to toe with the preacher, you took on a job in Chinatown, and now you're buying a house. I've known you less than a week, but if you were a man, I'd recruit you into the army."

"I don't think your army is ready for Miss. Castile." Thad offered. "She'd have the troops regrouped before you knew what hit."

Laughter filled the room, but Becca's thoughts had turned to Hannah...*I have to tell her that Molly's going to let her visit...At the front door, Becca and Thad made their afternoon arrangements.*

"Mrs. Callaghan always comes in for a paper on Tuesdays. I have it all set to print. I worked on it since two this morning. I'll go and print them off now. When you come over this afternoon, we'll run out there."

He placed his hat on his head, and reached for the doorknob. Turning he asked, "What's the chatter about raising the dead and fighting with the preacher?"

"I'll tell you later. Both are long stories. We have some catching-up to do."

"I've only been gone three days."

"I'll see you later." She placed her hand on his arm. "All is fine. I must go comfort Hannah."

Hannah was pleased that Molly agreed to visits, but it didn't completely lift the dark cloud that hovered over her. After sweeping, dusting, and straightening the rooms, they dragged the parlor rug to the clothesline. As they were beating it with rackets, Hannah focused her attention over Becca's shoulder.

"What are you looking at, Hannah?"

"A man across the street has been watching us. I've never ever saw him before."

Becca turned. The man was walking away. He turned the corner

"Maybe he never saw women beat a rug before."

Once the rug was placed back in the parlor, Becca hurried upstairs. Grabbing her outing dress, she moved to the chest of drawers to retrieve a petticoat. Glancing out the open window she saw the same man. Leaning against a hitching rack, he gazed up at her window. Becca shivered. .*OK, now that's spooky...he does seem to have an interest in this hotel or someone here...*She pulled the curtain closed...*No doubt about it...this will be a dagger in the sleeve kind of day.*

43

"Go confidently in the direction of your dreams! Live the life you've imagined. As you simplify your life, the laws of the universe will be simpler."

—Henry David Thoreau

Opening the secretary, Becca pressed a tiny lever under the bottom shelf. A small secret drawer slid out...*This is so awesome. I don't understand why these aren't in modern desks...* She took out the dainty dagger and the blue ribbon she always used to tie it to her wrist. She noticed the serpent bracelet and picked it up. As she turned it in her hand, she reflected on Delphi's story about it. She pushed the dagger into her sleeve, and slipped the bracelet over the top of her cuff...*Well go figure...this is more secure than the ribbon...I can easily remove the dagger without jiggling the sheath. And it's decorative as well...*

After she pushed the drawer back into its hidden space, she closed the desk. Looking in the mirror, she adjusted her hat...*I'm buying a house. I want to look business like...*She gathered her purse and parasol and exited her room, closing the door securely behind her. As she stepped outside the hotel and descended the steps, she opened her parasol. The distraction caused her to abruptly bump into a tall stocky man who was preparing to ascend.

"Excuse me, Sir, I didn't see you."

He didn't answer her as he passed her and walked into the hotel. His head was tipped, his eyes hidden under the rim of his hat... *Molly will have to tell him she's out of rooms...if he waits a few days, mine will be available...*

She breathed in the fresh autumn air as she walked the few blocks to The Print Shop. The first thing she saw after she walked in was Thad folding papers. A tall stack was piled on the counter, and a shorter pile of unfolded sheets on the table.

"I'm almost finished. I had to let the ink dry before folding them. Abe is coming over to keep the shop until we get back."

"Allow me to help," offered Becca as she laid down her purse and parasol.

"Take care with your sleeves. If you brush them across the print, they may get blackened."

"I will, thanks for the warning." She picked up a news print sheet, folded it in the middle and used a finger to press the seam flat.

"That's a lovely dress. It's one of your new ones."

"Yes, I picked it up Sunday when I worked for Mrs. Leng. It went well last weekend. I learned to sew seams, stitch hems, and sew buttons and buttonholes."

As they finished the papers, Becca told in detail, the story of her midwife work with Mrs. Leng. Thad laughed heartedly about Harry and his axe incident, and then looked at her in amazement about the resuscitation of the new born. He shared her concern about the family's poverty.

"I wish there was some way Harry could work with his injured back," she muttered.

"Since I've mastered the press, my employer has suggested I take on a part time apprentice. He was thinking of a boy. I need someone a few hours, two or three days a week. An apprentice cleans the press, removes the stamps and returns them to their proper place.

I also need someone in the front to sell papers while I operate the telegraph, on occasion."

"Oh Thad, that could be the answer. Do you think it's possible?"

"I'll check with Ben. It wouldn't be a lot of money, but it would help out. It would teach him a new trade. He'd have to leave the liquor alone and not bring his axe."

Becca threw her arms around him. "How do you always manage to come up with the solutions to my problems?"

Thad, being aware of the black ink on his hands stood quietly without returning the embrace. Becca became aware of her overexuberance. She pulled back and laughed at herself.

"I'm so sorry; please forgive my impulsive reaction."

His eyes twinkled. "I assure you that your reaction is forgiven. However, giving into your impulse while my hands are inked is unforgivable, Miss Castile. That's entirely unfair."

He locked the front door and moved to the washstand. There he soaped and rinsed the blackening from his hands. Drying them on a towel, he motioned for her to follow him to the backroom. He opened a large safe. Pulling out a parcel wrapped in brown paper, he untied it. Becca looked at the gold bar.

Thad explained, "This is two pounds. The bar I took to Eureka for you was three pounds. Gold is worth thirty dollars an ounce. I had the price of the house made into twenty dollar gold coins. I paid the smelter and had one hundred dollars in various coin values made for you. You should easily live for a while with that. He molded the remaining gold into this. It's worth around a thousand dollars or more, depending on gold prices."

He then removed a cigar box from the safe. He untied it and lifted the lid. Shiny new gold coins glittered in the sunlight that streamed in from the window. He counted out the amount needed for the house. He dropped them into a small canvas bag.

"Here, hang onto this."

He took out a one dollar coin and handed it to her. "Put this in your purse. You'll need to pay the assessor for his time and his writing up the document. He'll give you each a copy of the deed and agreement."

"Will he be there at the house?" she asked, as she placed the coin in her purse.

"Yes, Mrs. Callahan dropped in this morning to say she had asked him there to save time. He's acted as her lawyer in the past. She's anxious to complete her moving plans."

"Do you know him? Is he trustworthy?"

"Yes, he's my employer, Ben Harris. He's an honest man."

"The same employer you must ask about Harry working for The Print Shop?"

"Yes, the same, but we'll not discuss that with him today. You must be patient and allow me to work that out with him. Today, business is about buying your house."

On a small piece of paper, he wrote; Property of Delphi Castile, and locked the bar and box back up in the safe.

"If anything ever happens to me, Ben will know that it's yours."

*I must remember to tell Delphi that...she may need to know...in an emergency...*The thought of anything happening to Thad caused her to feel panic. A knock at the door drew Thad's attention. He hurried to open it.

Abe came in with a wide grin. "So there's reason for the two of you to lock out the world?"

"Mind your tongue in the lady's presence, Abe," Thad cautioned his friend. "We opened the safe. I always lock the door when it's opened."

"No offense intended, Miss." Abe took off his hat and hung it on the rack.

Only a bit later, while riding to the house, did Becca process what Abe had suggested. She smiled quietly... *It must be terribly easy to offend a woman in these times.*

Becca gripped her purse and the bag as they moved toward the outskirts of town. Now that she was used to dealing with gold and understood the value of things, she was mindful about protecting it.

"I'll need a horse and buggy very soon."

"I suggest you order a new one through Mr. Sanders. There may be some old ones for sale, but you might have to repair them. If you buy one that's new, it'll be more dependable and last longer."

That's what Delphi said too...I must get in and order one right away.

"I'm not aware of anyone who's selling a gentle horse," Thad continued. "But if we check at the Blacksmith Shop, Mac would know. He shoes lots of horses, so he's privy to which are gentle and those that are cantankerous."

I need to do that anyway. I recommended Ike...er...Cain to get a job there... That's where I'll start my search for him...

They turned into the Callahan property. Thad pulled back on the reins. Becca waited until he climbed out, and came around to lift her to the ground. They exchanged smiles.

"I see Ben is already here," Thad pointed out. "That's his bay mare tied to the post.

As they stepped up on the porch, the door opened. Mrs. Callahan greeted them. Becca looked around. The room was in perfect order. A tea service arrangement set on a small table positioned next to the piano. An older man sitting at the table stood and smiled at them.

"Ben, this is Delphi Castile," Thad began introductions. "Delphi, this is Ben Harris."

The old gentleman reached for her hand and shook it gently. "I'm honored to meet you Miss, I've heard so much about you."

Becca noticed his smiling eyes were of the lightest blue she had ever seen. His partially gray hair was thinning. A lonely tuft on the top of his head, and a rim surrounding the sides were all that remained... *I hope he's heard good things from Thad, and not bad things from the Reverend.*

They settled into chairs provided as their hostess poured each a cup of tea. Becca, anxious to complete things, silently wished they would hurry it along. This wasn't the bustling twenty-first century however, so she calmed herself as the four exchanged pleasantries about weather, coming winter, and local politics. Finally, Ben pulled a leather bound folder from a case that set at his feet. The papers he laid out impressed her. Each page, written in a scrolling even handwriting, maintained perfect alignment. The first letter of every sentence was a work of art. Glancing back and forth between the two sheets, she could see the scribe had handwritten two exact copies.

"This is exquisite penmanship. Did you write this, Mr. Harris?"

"Why yes, it's my job to write legible documents." His tone was matter-of-fact.

How and why did we ever lose this wonderful calligraphy skill? Ben Harris read the simple document aloud. It stated the price of the property, the size of the house and barn, and stated the well water was adequate for drinking. It listed each piece of furniture and several items in the barn. Becca took note of a plow, 2 saddles, a cart and a few other things she hadn't noticed when they viewed the property. At last, each woman took the pen and signed her name. Becca signed Delphi's... *Well, my friend, I just bought you a house.*

Thad and Ben signed as witnesses. Becca opened the bag and counted out the gold, then returned it to the canvas container. Mrs. Callahan took it and left the room... *She must be taking it to a safe or at least a hiding place...* When she returned she smiled at Becca.

I was confident in your promise to complete the purchase today, so I arranged to leave with the children tomorrow morning by stage. We're only taking a few trunks of clothing. The stage should get us to the train by Friday. I'm grateful for your promptness in this matter."

Becca couldn't conceal her surprise. "That's much earlier than I expected, but I'm excited to move into this lovely home, so I'll not complain."

Mr. Harris, after blowing on the signatures, carefully folded each of them, and placed them in separate envelopes. Handing one to each woman, he placed his hat on his head.

"I hate to hurry off, but I do have another meeting. So, if you will excuse me."

He left abruptly and Thad stood as he passed. Becca rose from her chair, gathering her purse and parasol. She said goodbye.

Mrs. Callahan remarked, "Oh, I mustn't forget to mention, I'm leaving several trunks of clothing the children have out grown, as well as some of my own. I meant to deliver them to the Reverend's wife, Mrs. Walker. Perhaps you can see that these items are dispersed among the needy."

On the way back, Becca smiled so wide her cheeks hurt.

"You must be finding immense satisfaction in purchasing a house." Thad commented as he looked into her face.

"I'm smiling because I believe Mrs. Callahan has unknowingly clothed Harry's family, you may be providing Harry with a job...and because I bought a house."

As they turned on Front Street, Becca asked, "Could you drop me off at The Mercantile? I'm going to pick up a journal."

"I have to return promptly to The Print Shop. Abe can't stay much longer."

"That'll be fine. I can walk back to the hotel."

"The afternoon is passing. Please don't linger too long," he cautioned.

"I promise to be back at The Redwood before dark."

44

"I have spent many years of my life in opposition, and I rather like the role."

—Eleanor Roosevelt

T had stopped in front of The Mercantile and assisted Becca out of the buggy. She hurried into the store as he went on his way. The store was empty of customers. Moving back to James's book nook, she asked in a quiet voice.

"Has the preacher been around to harass you?"

James looked up from his work. He was painting a poster advertising her Book Gathering. He smiled mischievously.

"No, and my sales are increasing. People come in and ask for the same books that Miss Castile bought."

They both laughed. "Well, what do you know," she said.

Looking over his bookshelves, her eye found several journals. She chose one that had sturdy binding. After paying James, she returned to the front of the store to select a pencil. When

Mr. Sanders met her at the counter, she had him fill several small paper bags with candy.

"I'll take a bag of the peppermint, the horehound drops, and the rock candy."

"Either you're hankering for sweets or celebrating," commented the storekeeper as he scooped the pieces into the sacks.

"Celebrating," announced Becca. "I just bought the Callahan house."

"Is that right? That's a big house for one lady. Maybe I'll receive a wedding invitation soon?"

Becca didn't answer his inquiry...*That will be up to Delphi.*

She hurried on to her next request. "I need to order a carriage. It must accommodate seating for more than two."

He looked at her with wonderment... *I guess he isn't accustomed to single women ordering such large items.*

"Perhaps we should ask Mr. Barrett to come in and advise you before you make a final selection."

What? Do I look like an idiot? "Mr. Barrett is busy managing his own affairs. I'd like to see pictures of what's available, please?"

"Yes, of course." Mr. Sanders thumbed through a pile of papers that advertised various merchandise. He laid out three sketched pictures.

"This is a nice one. I've heard it called a Victoria. It's low and open so ladies can easily get in and out. It has four wheels that give balance. It's light enough to be pulled by one horse. This one costs twenty dollars, and I can have it here in two to three weeks."

"Becca looked at it and shook her head. "No, it's too small. I'd want a covered carriage. I'll need protection from rain and sun."

Mr. Sanders pushed another picture forward. "This one has a hood, also called a calash. You can fold it back when you want an open carriage. It's a bit wider. You could seat two adults and a child in this one. It's still light enough to..."

"I want that one." Becca reached across the paper sketches to the one farther back. She pulled it forward... *This man would never make it as a car salesman; he's determined to sell me the cheapest...*

"There, see?" She pointed to the picture under the words, Wagonette. "It has a seat that holds two to three in the front and another seat the same size in the back. I like the covering... the calash. It's perfect. Order this one please."

Mr. Sander leaned over and focused on the picture. "The seats are leather...it will require two horses...it's more expensive."

That's what Delphi wants..."Then I'll be shopping for two horses. Order that one please."

"I must request a sum of ten dollars. It'll cost me if I'm required to send it back on the next steamer."

Becca looked into the man's face. She spoke softly.

"Mr. Sanders, do you really think I would order something from you and not pay you for it?"

His pale complexion reddened. "No, Miss, I have a concern that you may be buying more than you need. Without a husband or father to advise you, I must..."

Becca smiled at the troubled man. "Well I have no husband or father, and I need that carriage. What is the total cost?"

Mr. Sanders cleared his throat and looked as though he would choke on the answer. That carriage, Miss Castile, is forty dollars, one dollar for freight and a dollar for my handling the order."

Becca took the total amount from her purse. "Here you go; I prefer to pay for the order now, rather than when it arrives. I trust you, Mr. Sanders."

"Thank you, Miss Castile; your order will leave on the steamer Sunday. The carriage should be here two weeks after that."

Becca picked up the journal, pencil and candy, said goodbye to both men as she left the store...*Now... two blocks to The Blacksmith, and I'll have a talk with Cain.*

The mid-day sun cast shadows. It was warm, and Becca crossed the street to walk in the shade of the buildings and shops. She estimated the time to be three or three thirty...*There's still plenty of time before sundown.*

Spotting the Blacksmith Shop, she crossed the street. Fresh horse manure cluttered her path. She lifted her skirts, and picked her way through to the wooden sidewalk. As she approached the building, she noticed its wide, opened door. Even with a sea breeze blowing through the shop that was opened at both ends, the large room was hot. A blazing fire burned at one end of the structure. A large man in an apron held a long fork-like tool. With it, he positioned a horseshoe over the flame.

"Excuse me, Sir, it's my understanding that Cain Jones works for you."

The man turned slowly and glanced at her. Placing the hot curved metal onto a stone ledge, he began tapping it with a hammer. She was preparing to repeat the question when he responded.

"Yes, Cain works here."

He turned around and pushed his project back into the flames. *He's not a talkative sort, I guess.*

"Then, may I please speak to him?"

"No," he answered turning again and hammering the metal. "He's not here." He dipped the horseshoe into water. A hissing sound and steam resulted.

"Where might I find him?"

The man turned and leveled his gaze at her. Sweat rolled down his face. "Are you a friend? He's never mentioned a lady friend. What do you want from him?"

"Uh...I've known Cain for a long time. I have a gift for him." She held up the journal.

"He went for a shave... won't be back today." Laying down the cooled horseshoe, he walked past Becca to the open door. Outside, he stood breathing in fresh air.

"And where would that be? Where does he go for a shave?"

The man looked at her with a bit of mockery in his expression. "At the barbershop."

"Right, of course." *Dummy, I should have figured that out. Duh!*
"Over there?"

She pointed at a small shop. It was several stores down on the other side of the street. A red and white painted pole stood by its door and large glass window.

Nodding, he walked back into the building.

"Sir, I'm not trying to be a nuisance, but I need information from you. I was informed you might know of horses for sale. I need two gentle ones."

He stopped and appeared to be thinking. Since his previous responses had been slow in coming, she calmed herself to wait.

"I might know of one, maybe two. I'll talk to Clem. I'll let you know." He turned and walked back to the fire.

"But Sir, how will you find me? Should I come back and check?"

He didn't appear to hear. He busily pumped the bellows over the flames. She started toward the barbershop.

45

"Never allow a person to tell you "no" who doesn't have the power to say "yes.""

—Eleanor Roosevelt

Reaching the barbershop, she opened the door, walked in, and scanned the room. Three chairs lined one wall and two men sat reading papers. An empty chair was between them. It looked inviting. Two barbers served men in barber seats. One, cutting hair looked up and his eyes grew wide. Having just finished a man's shave, the other wrung out a rag in a pan of hot water. He froze in place, still holding the dripping rag. On closer inspection, Becca recognized the customer as Cain. The men waiting glanced up and dropped their papers. Everyone stared in silence. Cain looked to see what had drawn the attention.

"Mrs. Cat..uh...Castile...Miss Castile. Why are you here?"

"I need to talk to you, Mr. Jones. I'll wait until your shave is finished."

His barber regained his focus and re-dipped the rag, wringing it out completely. He turned and placed it over Cain's face. His peripheral vision remained aimed at Becca.

"I'll meet you outside." Cain's voice was muffled through the steaming towel.

"That's ok, my feet hurt. I'll just wait in here."

She plopped into the empty chair between the two waiting men. They jumped up in unison and moved to the other side of the room.

Cain tossed the towel off, digging for a coin from his pocket. After paying the barber, he hurried toward her. The barber took his payment in one hand while holding a bottle of men's cologne in the other.

"Come," said Cain, as he approached her.

"I'm fine. Don't hurry. Finish your shave...get the full treatment."

He reached out and lifted her by her elbow.

"Excuse me, I'm capable of rising."

She yanked it away. He gently nudged her out the door.

Outside she turned to face him. With her hands on her hips, she stamped one foot.

"Why are you manhandling me?"

"Women aren't allowed in barbershops," he hissed.

"Says who?"

"How do I know who made the stupid rules in this nightmare. All I know is that women are never in there. I've heard it said they aren't allowed in barbershops or saloons."

"Oooh, that burns me! I can deal with rules that have a purpose, but there's no good purpose for that one!"

He continued to nudge her toward a rustic bench nearby. As she passed the window, she looked in, tossed her head back and squared her shoulders.

"I guess they think it's a good place for men to run their mouths without having to censor what they say," he offered.

They sat down and Becca opened her parasol.

"What do you want?" he asked.

"First, how's your employment working out?"

"It's hard and it's hot, but he pays me enough to survive. I also sweep the livery stable every night in exchange for a cot in the tack room. It's not all that bad, I guess."

"Are you staying out of trouble?"

"From the looks of things just now, I'm doing better than you." He chuckled.

"The investigation is moving in on the real Cain. Actually his name is Jonah McCain. They've matched fingerprints from your old police records to him."

He studied her, "And...?"

"I've learned that I can spirit travel back and forth, as can Delphi. We do it by writing in our journals. It seems that our words and thoughts are somehow connected with our spirits."

She handed him the journal. "I want you to take this home with you, and write a few paragraphs, sentences, whatever comes to your mind. Write something very personal about yourself."

She handed him the new pencil. He looked at the book, opened it, and then looked back at her.

"And then what happens?"

"My sister is taking a journal to Jonah McCain. He's now known by your name Ike. If it works for you like it did for me, when he writes in it, you may have a visitor. Or you may find yourself in his hospital room."

"And then what? It sounds scary."

"It is, at first, but you'll get use to it. In time I hope we can switch you two out."

"Which means... I'll go straight to prison."

"Not necessarily. Phil is denying that he had anything to do with the attempt to murder me. If you offer the prosecutor a deal...like plead to a lesser charge to share everything about Phil, you might serve no more than a year, if that long. Phil must pay for what he tried to do, Ike!"

"I'm really sorry for letting him talk me into that. I made a major mess of our lives."

"So, help me fix it. Will you do as I've asked? Will you go back and tell the authorities the truth?"

He stood up and faced her. "I'll take it a day at a time. I'll write in this book and we'll see. That's all I'm committing to."

She stood and brushed out her skirts. Cain placed his hat on his head and turned to go. He looked back.

"Please don't search me out at the barbershop again. I don't want my new reputation besmirched."

Becca's eyebrows knitted into a frown as she watched him walk away.

I can't believe it…He's strutting like a dandy… She opened one of the candy sacks and popped a horehound drop into her mouth…*Hmmm, that's a weird flavor…next time I'll take a peppermint.* She turned toward the hotel.

She entered by the back door. Molly stirred a large skillet of fried potatoes. She looked up.

"Open your mouth and close your eyes," Becca instructed.

Molly gave her a questioning look. She placed a lid on the skillet and laid down the spatula.

"What are you telling me, child?"

"Quick, do as I say. Close your eyes and open your mouth."

When the older woman complied, Becca tossed a peppermint into her mouth. Molly opened her eyes, and closed her lips over the spicy sweet nugget. Pleasure lit up her face.

"I see you've been spending your hard earned coins on folly," she chided.

"Everyone needs a little folly in their lives. Where's Hannah?"

"She's cleaning all the lamps. We'll need plenty of light for our knitting bee after supper."…*Oh no, not tonight. I need to contact Delphi…and I planned to go to bed early.*

"I didn't realize you were having the bee tonight."

Molly pulled a large pan of cornbread from the oven, setting it on top of the stove.

"We must be prompt. Elsie and Minnie will leave Sunday. They're both fast knitters. I've gathered up all my leftover yarns."

"I bought some too. I also bought fabric for baby gowns. Do you have a pattern?"

"I can quickly cut one out for you from newsprint. I'll do that while you're learning to knit."

Becca hurried to her room to freshen up. As she grasped the glass doorknob, she noticed the door was not completely closed...*That's odd...I always make sure the door is tightly shut...*She slowly pushed it open. She scanned what she could see of the room. The narrow bed was turned on its side, pillows, quilts and sheets were dumped into a heap on the floor. Looking toward the bureau, she saw drawers pulled open. Pantaloons and stockings hung over the sides. She stepped in and turned to view the safe. Its door was opened...*Lucky I didn't have anything in there... I need to get Molly...or maybe Charley.*

She turned to leave but the door shut behind her. A rough hand grabbed her arm...*Stupid me...he was behind the door...*As she struggled to free her arm, the hand moved to grip her waist and held it tight. She opened her mouth to scream. A hard cold metal object pressed against her head.

"You scream and I'll blow your head off," a gruff voice whispered.

Her mind raced. There could only be one shot from the black powder pistol, but it would be deadly. She tried to calm herself. She moved her eyes to the side, trying to see her attacker. She was sure it was the same man she had bumped against when leaving earlier.

"What do you want?" she could barely squeak out the question.

"Everything you took from me, Wench."

"Who are you?" *He must be the man in Delphi's bad experience.*

"You know who I am. You had your brutes beat me. They broke my nose and ribs while you ran off with my bag, that one."

He nodded at the carpet bag that lay opened by the tossed covers on the floor.

"I'm not who you think. The bag was given to me."

She concentrated on moving her hands together in effort to grasp the dagger in her sleeve.

"Liar... You've hid it. Get it...all of it! I want the gold bar and the jewels."

Becca heard Elsie's door open....*No, don't come out now...a wild shot might hit you....please, please don't knock on my door...*Hot, moist, whisky breath blew on her neck. Her right hand felt sweaty as she gripped the dagger's handle.

"How can I get your treasure while you hold onto me?"

He released her but watched warily. Taking slow deliberate steps, she moved herself around her assailant. This positioned her and the point of the gun away from the hall and other chambers. She pretended to focus on the wardrobe and glanced up at her hat boxes.

"I can't reach it."

He moved to the wardrobe, and reached to retrieve the round box. Becca lunged forward, driving the dagger into the back of his right shoulder. He screeched and dropped the gun. She ran from the room.

Elsie, walking down the front stairs, was halfway to the bottom. Hearing the noise, she turned to look up to the landing. Becca reached her.

"Hurry, get to the dining room now!"

As the women ran across the parlor, the man staggered from the landing and stumbled down the stairs. Guests were seated at the table. When the women rushed in, Becca gasped.

"There was a man in my room. He held a gun on me. "

Male guests jumped up from their chairs and ran to the parlor. Becca heard the front door slam. The men pursued. Molly coaxed the shaken Becca back to her room. She, Elsie, and Hannah restored the room to order. Hannah gasped when she saw the opened safe. She covered her mouth and looked at Becca.

"Nothing important was in there," Becca assured her. "He took nothing, but he threatened to kill me. I hope they catch him."

"Why is there blood everywhere? Did he hurt you?" Molly looked at her in alarm.

"No, I stabbed him with my dagger."

Becca broke into tears as her mind accepted the shock of all she had experienced.

Hannah threw her arms around her.

"Don't cry, Delphi. It's not sin to stab someone who's trying to kill you, everyone knows that."

As Becca looked over Hannah's shoulder, her eyes spotted the gun under the oak wardrobe. She patted Hannah's back in response to her attempt at comfort. She pushed her gently away, and moved to the closet...*He dropped it when I stabbed him ...it slid under here... I thought he took it...*

She stooped and gingerly dragged it into the open. Picking it up, she assured the barrel pointed away from everyone in the room... *No reason to preserve fingerprints...their use in forensics hasn't been discovered yet...too bad...*The front door closed and the men's voices alerted the women they had returned from their pursuit of the villain.

"Let's go see if they caught him," blurted Hannah, leading the departure of the women from her room. Becca followed with gun in hand. The self appointed posse all talked at once until Molly silenced them.

"Please, we can see that you didn't detain him. Charley, tell us what occurred."

"That varmint got clean away. I don't know how he could move so fast. He left a blood trail for a while, but that ran out. He just faded into thin air, I reckon."

"Delphi stabbed him with a dagger," Hannah bragged.

"Is that so?" marveled Mr. Hanson. "Now I'm certain you should be in the army. What are you planning to do with that gun?"

Becca handed it to him. He took the firearm and examined it.

"This pistol isn't loaded. Is this the gun he used to threaten you?"

Becca nodded. "It's not loaded?"

"No, ma'am, either your thief is too poor to afford lead and powder, or he's too cowardly to shoot someone. It appears that he was bluffing. What did he want?"

"He believes I have gold and jewels" she explained. "If I'd known his gun wasn't loaded, I wouldn't have used the dagger"

Tears swelled up in her eyes and spilled onto her cheeks. "I was so scared."

Mr. Hansen placed a fatherly arm around her shoulders.

"There, there, dear, don't you fret one bit. You had every right to protect yourself and your possessions. You had the courage to fight with only a dagger. That's remarkable. He deserved it, even if his pistol wasn't loaded. It's a matter of time until he gets himself hanged anyway."

"I guess we might as well get on with eating supper," announced Charley.

"I wonder why he chose your chamber?" asked Elsie. "Mine is the next room, and he didn't come in there.

"He probably realized you were inside," reasoned Hannah. "Maybe he was rummaging through all the empty chambers."

With that thought, guests started toward the stairs to inventory their rooms. Charley looked toward the dining room in disappointment.

"Seems to me all this fuss could wait until after supper," he muttered.

It was a cold meal of fried potatoes, sliced ham, and pickled beats, when the group reassembled. All reported that their rooms were untouched. Charley passed the ham after selecting two large pieces for his own plate. Mr. Hansen took the platter and offered it to Becca before forking a slice.

"It seems peculiar that he selected a young lady's room. For what might he have been searching?"

Molly passed the large bowl of fried potatoes to Elsie. "It's probably gotten around that Delphi bought that house. It makes people talk. He thought she had more on hand. That's my thinking."

"But how would he know which room was hers?" questioned Minnie.

"I looked out of my window today. He was standing on the street, gazing up at the building. He saw me," explained Becca.

"That was before you bought the house," reasoned Molly, passing the cornbread. "He wouldn't yet have reason to believe you had something to steal."

"I believe he's a professional thief." Becca took a sip of water to relief the dryness in her throat." Thad conducted some minting business for me in Eureka several days ago. He was convinced someone followed him back to Crescent City. This thief may be the same individual. He could have trailed him here. Thad ate supper with us, after all. I passed this person walking into the hotel this afternoon."

Molly looked surprised. "I didn't see him come in. He must have slipped right upstairs."

"Did he break into the safe?" asked Charley. He held his cup out for Molly to fill with coffee.

"She left it opened. She had nothing in it," Hannah offered before Becca could answer.

"I had a few unimportant papers and a bag of medicinal tea in the safe. He might have taken them, or just knocked them out. I'll look when I clean the room."

She noticed that the mention of the tea caused Elsie to become more interested in the contents of her plate. Hannah's face wore the expression it always exhibited just before an outburst.

"And the tintype, I saw you put it in there, Delphi."

Becca's blood turned cold. She shot a censoring glance at the girl. Hannah diverted her attention to buttering her cornbread... *That stupid picture! The hurdy-gurdy picture of Delphi in her underwear...I hope he didn't take that...*

Through the remainder of the meal Becca could think of nothing but the picture...*Why on earth didn't I destroy that picture when I discovered it? I didn't feel it was mine to throw away...Delphi may want it when she's back...she kept it after all.*

Following supper, she rushed to her room. After a half an hour of probing everything in her space, she collapsed onto the bed...*It's not here... He must have taken it and the abortion tea. Why would he bother with those items? They're worthless to him...* Hannah's knock reminded her that it was time for the knitting bee. Grabbing her new yarn and needles, she opened the door.

46

"Nobody ever did, or ever will, escape the consequences of his choices."

—Alfred A. Montapert

Following Hannah down the front staircase, Becca wondered how she would manage to concentrate on learning a new skill. Molly, Minnie and Elsie sat in the back parlor. The front parlor contained the men who enjoyed after supper time as they smoked cigars and shared conversation. She settled on a sofa as Hannah poured her a cup of tea. Lamps lit up in all four corners of the room. The largest one set on a center table. Even with autumn sun setting, the room was bright.

"Now," began Molly, "I borrowed these patterns from a friend. She knitted them for her son years ago. We can look at these as we follow the steps she penned down for me."

Becca examined the items that lay on the table. An infant sweater, a cap, booties, and what appeared to be short pants were knitted in fine white yarn. She held out her new yarn.

"Is there enough of this blue yarn for all these pieces?

Molly looked at the skeins. "Yes, if we trim with the white I have. We'll need to wind new skeins so we can divide the yarn. Hannah, come sit by Delphi. Show her how we wind a ball from a skein. Make four balls of the blue and four of the white."

Hannah placed a stool next to Becca. "Hold up your hands like you're praying, please." The girl pushed Becca's hands closer together and began pulling the yarn from the skein while wrapping it around her hands.

"Is this the cloth you plan to use for the babe's gown?" asked Molly.

"Yes" answered Becca, watching Hannah's fast movement. "I bought a lot. I wanted to be sure to have enough."

"There's plenty here," responded Molly, as she unfolded the fabric. Holding it out, she measured it between the ends of her fingers and her nose. "Yes, we can make several baby frocks from this."

"Frocks as in dresses? But Delford is a boy. I was thinking nightgowns or pajamas."

"That's why we make them large. They'll be nightgowns now, and as he grows, they'll be his frocks."

Molly lifted a hand-made pattern, and held it up to the light. It was cut from newsprint and yellowed with age... *It looks like it was cut out years ago.*

"Boys don't wear frocks," Becca protested.

Hannah now slipped the wound yarn from her hands and started winding yarn around it, shaping it into a ball.

"Of course they do. Boys don't get their britches until they're three or four, everyone knows that, Delphi."

"Perhaps Delphi hasn't been around children." defended Minnie. "Little Albert barely got his trousers before the shipwreck"

Becca was silent as Hannah started a second round of yarn around her hands. Thinking back to the first day she saw Harry's children, she remembered that little Ben wore a dirty dress-like garment. Molly moved the lamp to the side of the table, removed the knitted items, and laid down the fabric. She bent one end over. Folding the pattern in half, she aligned the folded edge with that of the cloth. Becca watched carefully. The pattern reminded her of paper doll cut-outs she did with her class. This one, unlike the craft, didn't have a head. Molly carefully cut around the paper. She then repeated the process, making two identical pieces."

"There, you'll sew up the sides, and cut a slit here to enlarge the neck. After hemming the bottom, the neck opening and sleeves, I'll teach you to crochet a trimmed border around them."

Molly continued to cut more frocks from the cloth. Minnie looked over the hand-written knitting instructions.

"Elsie, you're a skilled knitter. You can make the sweater. You must cast on fifty stitches with small needles. Hannah can make the cap. Since Delphi is just learning, I'll show her how to make the booties. I'll make the soakers."

"Soakers? Becca looked up at the older woman.

Minnie held up the knitted bloomers. "These, dear, they hold the baby's diaper in place, and soak up some of the wetness."

Soon Elsie was clicking her needles as she added rows of the soft blue yarn. Becca picked up a pair of wooden ones and Minnie laughed.

"Not those, Delphi. If you knit booties with that size needles, they'll be big enough to fit Charley. These small ones are just right. Now allow me to show you how to cast on twenty stitches."

By the time the women disbanded, the men had left the front parlor. As Becca walked through the room and headed for the staircase, she covered her nose. The offensive odor of cigar still lingered... *What can they possibly get out of puffing and breathing something so obnoxious?*

She opened the door of her room and glanced around in the darkness. Pushing the door all the way to the wall, she vowed to never be caught off guard again. Then she saw the dim blue glow... *Delphi?*

"*Oui, I went to you in that other place but you were too occupé to take notice.*"

You were in the back parlor? You saw us knitting?

"*Oui, I have new rapport for you. Your counselor gave your reply to Philip's counselor. We must wait to apprendre his décision.*"

The divorce will take time. Is there new information about the investigation? Has the investigator communicated with you or my sister about it?

"Oui, his business associate will testify that on the day of the incident, he advised Philip to end the affair. Deux femmes from his office will also testify about his indiscrétions with her...uh...Tonka?"

"Tonya."

"Oui, that one. They have moved from the stable."

"Loft"...

"Beth récupéré the rest of your clothing and shoes. I have it all now. Your épouse can't get out of the agreement until after the divorce. So you may wish to keep it, when you return."

Maybe... I love that loft, and Phil has a two-year lease... I can't afford it on a teacher's salary...I may not have a teaching job now...school started several weeks ago.

"That's another rapport I have for you... The school prince called..."

School prince? ... Do you mean principal?"

"He told your sister, he'll hold the position temporalité: in case you...I...recover enough to teach."

And the doctors... do they believe my body will recover, Delphi?

"Ah...la plus importante rapport..."

Stop! Speak English. We don't have enough time for me to translate your words...

"I am doing that...with the English. News is good...I have sensation in the toes and finger tips. That means good things."

Really...that is great news...Delphi....Delphi? Darn! I wanted to ask about Cain or Ike and if Beth can get a journal to him. Oh well. I'll make contact tomorrow...wait...I have to visit Sarah tomorrow...and pick up my moccasins. ..I just need to sleep now...

As she closed her eyes, Becca reviewed the happenings of the last few days. Soon she drifted into a kaleidoscope of dreams. Images of Thad, Hannah, Sarah, her new house and her godchild blended into nonsense.

The ringing clock announced the six-o-clock hour as she slipped from her bed. There was baking to do this morning. *That shouldn't take long.* She loved baking with Molly and Hannah. From them she had learned many new skills.

Thad and Doc arrived for breakfast. Thad's presence for meals occurred less now that he'd moved to the apartment above The Print Shop. She greeted him with a warm smile as she placed the platter of hot biscuits on the table. Doc appeared tired.

"What are your plans today, Delphi?" Thad asked as he ladled gravy over his bread.

"I'll help here this morning. Then Hannah and I'll check out the house."

I hate deceiving him, but I can't tell him that we'll walk past the house and into the woods to Sarah's camp.

"Would you like a ride over in the buggy?"

Hmm…I wish I could accept… it's a long walk…but he might want to linger…

"No, but thank you. We may wander a bit. I know you're busy with the paper today. Tomorrow, I could use your help to move my things over to my new home."

"Delphi, Charlie told me about the robber. I believe he's the same fellow who trailed me back from Eureka. I fear I may have led him to you. I don't want you wandering around without an escort while he's on the loose."

I hope he doesn't get over-protective today. I have to visit Sarah…

"What robber?" asked Doc.

Charley tucked his napkin into the neck of his shirt.

"I have to drive by there to pick up a load of fire wood. I'll drop them off as I go past. No reason for you to leave your printing, Thad."

"Thanks, Charley, that's perfect." Becca accepted the favor before Thad could make a counter offer.

"Who was robbed?" Doc repeated his question."

"We'll make an extra loaf of bread and a special pie. You can drop them off at you godson's," offered Molly.

Thad's brows knitted, revealing his lingering concern. "You'll still be walking back. I'm coming to pick you up, as soon as I close the shop."

"That sounds good, so it's all settled." She gave him a grateful smile.

"I can't say all is settled. I'm very distressed about this stranger, Delphi. Have you thought about the possibility of him being a danger to you once you've moved?"

"Thad, I appreciate your concern, but I'll not hide in fear. I'll continue with my plans."

Doc pounded a fist on the table, rallying everyone's attention.

"Would someone please tell me who got robbed and by whom!"

Becca related the story while Molly and Charley interjected opinions. Hannah proudly added that Delphi stabbed him with a dagger.

"A dagger?" Doc looked at Delphi. "Was it in his right shoulder?"

"Why, yes it was. He had a gun and I..."

"You stabbed him with a dagger?" Thad looked startled. "I'd heard a man entered your room and tried to rob you, but no one mentioned a dagger."

"Was it a Chinese dagger?" asked Doc.

"Yes, how did you know?"

"A chap came to my house last night. He was in such pain his wits were distorted. A dagger was imbedded in his right shoulder joint and crazed him. He told me that an Indian stabbed and robbed him. I knew when I removed the dagger that it was a Chinese dagger, and not the sort of knife used by Indians. I mentioned this, and he changed his account. He then said he was robbed by a Chinese man. I have the dagger at my surgery. I assumed his delirious state confused him"

"Where is he now?" asked Thad. "Did he give you his name? The man is a ruffian. Delphi, you must talk with the sheriff."

"He didn't do well answering questions," Doc explained. "He didn't offer a name or reply when I asked for one. I remained occupied in removing the blade and closing the wound. I can't see inside his shoulder, but my conjecture is that the joint has severe damage. He may not regain full use of it."

Molly watched Becca closely. "Don't you fret, dear; he deserves whatever becomes his lot."

"Where did you get a Chinese dagger?" asked Thad, his face revealing his puzzlement.

"Mr. Leng gave it to me as a gift. The Lengs' daughter was murdered in San Francisco. He wanted me to have it for protection."

Thad shook his head." You amaze me Delphi, You certainly fixed his flint."

"It'll be his misfortune if Gangrene sets in. If it's in a foot, leg or arm, I can amputate. A shoulder can't be removed."

Becca felt nauseous. She laid her napkin by her plate...*How can he keep stuffing his mouth and explaining such gruesome medical issues... no one else is bothered either...So many things about women and their clothing can't be mentioned without offending someone, but Gangrene and amputation during breakfast, creates no disturbance.*

"He had a terrible stomach upset," continued the doctor. "He had severe dysentery and couldn't keep even water down for hours. He said he thought a new tea he had tried poisoned him. I was up with him until daybreak when he insisted on leaving."

Becca and Elsie exchanged glances. Elsie smiled and Becca giggled.

"I guess that will teach him not to steal medicinal tea from other people's safes.

"Thank goodness, he didn't show Doc the picture...maybe he lost it in his distress...

The doctor glanced at Elsie and Becca. He nodded his head.

"I see, yes, medicinal tea, when it's not prescribed correctly, or when it's used by a person for the wrong ailment, can have dire effects."

Molly stood up and began collecting dirty dishes. "Come, ladies, our baking is waiting for us in the kitchen."

47

"Compassion is not weakness, and concern for the unfortunate is not socialism."

—Hubert Humphrey

By eleven-thirty, with the baking complete, Becca felt drenched in sweat. Even with door and windows opened, the heat of the woodstove was overpowering. She placed a fresh loaf of bread and an apple pie for the Farris family in the window to cool. She also wrapped four hot rolls up in brown paper...*Hannah and I will share these with Sarah and her grandmother*...Taking a jar of jam, she dropped coins into Molly's money jar...*I must pay for what I take for them...it's only fair*...She selected a large basket from the shelf and packed it full with the items... *I'll bring candy down from my room to add to this.*

She and Hannah hung their aprons up before going to their rooms to freshen and change. Becca stepped out of the soiled dress, and slipped into her clean work dress...*No reason to damage my outing dress, thrashing through the thickets...What I would give for a pair of jeans...* She quickly braided her hair, wound it around her head, and secured it with a decorated comb. As she rode along with Hannah and Charley, the cool sea breeze blew against her back. It felt good to Becca, in spite of the September chill.

"It won't be long until I must start a fire in the parlor," Charley mused.

Becca noticed several children playing near the street. "Why are these children not in school, Charley?"

"It hasn't started yet." He muttered, talking around his cigar.

"It won't start until late in October," added Hannah.

"Why so late?"

"No reason to go to school in good weather," answered Hannah. "Families need everyone working when the weather's nice. When the rains come, school will begin."

"How long is the rainy season?" *I'm sure it's not as long as in Portland.*

"Three or four months," offered Charley.

"Is that the duration of the school term? That's not long."

"It lasts eight to twelve weeks. It depends on how much time the schoolmarm can spend teaching, or how much money there is to pay her," Charley explained, tossing the cigar to the ground.

"There's a new three-room school in town with regular teachers, but the one-room country-school out on the edge of town has trouble keeping opened."

"Sometimes there's not a teacher for that school," added Hannah. "Then there's no school there at all."

Charley pulled on the reins in front of the Farris house. "Whoa Dolly."

Becca sorted through the basket. She took out the pie and bread. This won't take long," she explained as she climbed out of the wagon.

Harry stood in the front yard chopping wood. He grimaced in pain each time he raised the axe. Becca kept her distance as she greeted him... *I don't want to startle him...that's for sure.*

"Hello, Harry, I came to visit my godchild."

He turned and smiled. "Good afternoon, Miss Castile. Walk right on in."

She tapped on the door, and opened it slowly. The room smelled of fish. The oldest child, Emily, stood by the table, washing dishes. A piece of fried fish lay in a skillet on the stove...*Good... they've had something to eat, at least.*

"Is your mother in the bedroom?" she asked as she set the bread and pie on the far side of the table.

"Yes...oh...you brought pie?" The girl smiled as she threw wet hands and arms around Becca in a hug.

Becca laughed and pulled free. "I must see Delford," she said as she moved to the back room. "Sybil?"

She gazed into the dark room, and allowed her eyes time to adjust. A faint odor of mildew hung in the air. The woman sat on the side of the bed, folding articles of clothing.

"Oh, hello Delphi, come and sit."

She patted the bed. As Becca sat down she noticed the bundle in the middle of the mattress. A cloth lay across his face.

"Why is his face covered, Sybil?"

The woman looked at her in astonishment. "It must be covered as much as possible for six weeks."

"Whatever for? He needs to see your face, look around and learn to focus. His brain is developing"

"But his eyes aren't ready for light," Sybil explained.

"Who told you that? Did Doc find something wrong with his eyes?"

"No, it's the custom with all new infants."

Oh dear, I just bumped into another Victorian custom. I'll leave this alone...better to pick my battles...

"I can't stay but a moment. Charley and Hannah are waiting. There's pie and a loaf of bread in the kitchen. Molly sent them over. Have you talked with Reverend Walker about Delford's baptism? I'll plan a reception for him in my new house."

Sybil looked at Becca. "I think we won't be taking Delford to church. But you are still his godmother. Nothing can change that."

Becca could see that the woman was distressed. "What happened, Sybil?"

"Reverend Walker stopped by because Doc asked him to." She paused, choosing her words. "He said since we haven't been to church for more than a year, Delford can't be baptized, yet...We have to prove to him we can be committed members."

"What?' I can't believe that."

"We don't have the right clothing for church. Ben and Ivy don't even have shoes."

"We can get shoes and clothing, Sybil, if that's all that's holding things up."

The woman looked down at her lap. "There's more, isn't there?" Becca prodded.

"He also said he won't baptize Delford if you are the godmother. He says you are worldly."

Becca allowed a pause while she planned her response.

"I understand. I'm not surprised. He and I don't agree on things."

The woman raised her head and looked defiant. "Harry told him that if you can raise the dead, you can be a godmother."

"If you need to choose someone else, Sybil, I'll understand. I'll still be your friend. But I must go now. Here's a sack of candy for your family to enjoy later. And when my carriage arrives, I'll arrange to pick up your family for dinner in my new home."

She kissed the woman on the cheek, and hurried out to the wagon. Smiling at the two waiting, she handed them each a peppermint.

"Let's go, I'm ready to show Hannah the house."

Her smile was stiff. Inside she was boiling with anger. Charley left them in front of Becca's house. He took the wagon on to a woodland area where he planned to gather downfall. Hannah stared at the house and smiled.

"I love it, Delphi. I wish I could move here with you."

"Let's take a quick look inside, and then we must hurry to see Sarah," Becca urged.

They walked through the rooms on both floors. Becca took inventory of the pantry. It delighted her to discover jars of jams, pickles, sauerkraut, canned berries and pumpkin on the shelves...*This should last until I can make a garden next spring....wait I won't be here next spring...or until Delphi has to get more.*

Soon the two started through the woods in the direction Becca remembered visiting the camp. Before, she came from the coastline to visit, but she was sure if she walked south-east she would connect with the path Sara showed her.

"We must be quiet, Hannah," she advised. "If there're woodmen in the forest today, I prefer they not hear us and follow."

"But if we don't make noise, we might scare up a bear or mountain lion," reasoned Hannah. "Everyone knows that, Delphi."

"Perhaps you're right, but I want us to be quiet."

She has a valid point. I wish I still had my dagger. But I'd rather face a bear than lead a bounty hunter to Sarah...

After a half-hour of walking, Hanna whispered, "I hope we aren't lost, Delphi."

"Of course we aren't. There should be a deer trail around here close...ahh, there it is." *I think*

They followed the narrow, grassy path. Soon, Becca pointed to an opening in the thicket. Without speaking, she stooped over and pushed through the tangling vines. Hannah followed. Berry bushes grabbed at their hair, and pinecones crunched under their feet. A whiff of smoke assured them a camp was near by. Emerging into a small clearing, they saw a cone-shaped, bark and grass dwelling.

"They live in that? Why that's no bigger than an outhouse," muttered Hannah.

"Shhh... let me do the talking at first."

"Sarah?" Becca called. "It's me, Delphi. I brought Hannah. I came for my moccasins."

They waited at the edge of the thicket. Becca noticed movement in the small lodge. In a few moments, the grandmother came out of the short door. Her back had a curve bend in it. Becca thought must be a painful position. She shuffled toward them. Becca searched the area for Sarah...*I hope she's here.* ..The grandmother stopped a few yards away and motioned for them to come to the camp. They followed her. The grandmother pointed to the doorway of the lodge. Becca approached, dropped to her knees, and looked inside the rustic enclosure. Sarah lay on the blanket she had given them. Her face looked sallow.

"What's wrong, Sarah, are you sick?"

The girl lifted her right arm a few inches above the coverlet. Becca gasped. A large cluster of blisters covered the inner part of her upper and lower arm.

"Burned," she said.

"How did it happen?"

"I carried a pan of boiling water... dropped it... it splashed on my arm."

Becca felt nauseous. She had never seen a burn so serious...*She should see a doctor...but I don't know if the treatment in this century is good or damaging.*

Sarah pointed to a small lump in the shadows. "Shoes," she whispered."

Becca reached over her carefully to retrieve them. "These are beautiful."

She backed out of the tiny door and explained Sarah's accident to Hannah. The grandmother looked on as though listening. Becca wondered if she understood English. Hannah's face revealed her alarm.

"We can't leave her here, Delphi; we must take her to your house."

Delphi's mind rushed through possible options...*Could I get arrested for harboring them?... but then, who would know?...in time someone would find out... Grandmother can't hunt and gather food...they'll starve...*She opened the paper parcel of rolls, handing one to the grandmother and one to Sarah. The girl accepted her roll with her left hand and ate hungrily.

"Sarah, are you in pain?"

"Grandmother put the cactus poultice on the burns. She says I must move my arm so it won't grow useless. That causes pain."

"How are you getting food?" Becca asked.

"The coin you gave me...it bought meat from a hunter, but now it's gone. I can't fish, hunt or gather acorns now."

"Sarah, I now have a house. Will your grandmother consent to stay at my home until you're healed from your burns?"

"I believe she will agree. She said we may have to return to the tribe for help. I fear I will be sent away if we do."

"All right then, it's settled. Now I have to figure out how to get you there."

"I can walk. I may have need to rest often."

"Good, let's get started soon. It'll take an hour or more to get back to my home. Explain all this to your grandmother."

Sarah scooted, on her bottom, out of the lodge. She cradled her injured arm. There was a brief discussion between the two in their native tongue. Becca could see the relief on the old woman's face as Sara explained the plan.

"She wants me to tell you she is grateful and considers you a friend," Sarah related.

"Great, is there anything we need to take with us?" Becca asked.

Sarah thought for a moment. "Grandmother will take her medicine basket of plants. She'll need them to treat my burn."

The girl then directed a question to the old woman. The grandmother looked at the lodge, and answered her granddaughter. She shuffled to the small campfire, pushing sandy dirt over it with her foot.

"She says we must push down the lodge and bury the fire pit," explained the girl. "We must make the camp appear to have been desolate for a long time."

"Why?" asked Hannah?"

"If scalpers find a camp recently abandoned, they will follow our trail. It will lead to your house."

*I hadn't thought of that. We mustn't leave any of the clothing I gave them either. That would definitely point to me...*Becca dropped to the ground. Taking off her shoes, she unlaced them. She then put on the moccasins. She crawled to the lodge door and pulled out the blanket, cape and few items of clothing. Folding the blanket into thirds, she placed the items and her shoes on it, and rolled it into a tight bundle. Tying her shoestrings together, she wrapped the combined length around the roll... *There, I can use the laces as a handle...*

"Hannah, bury the fire pit completely, and then we'll knock down the shelter."

Sarah watched Hannah's unsuccessful attempt, and picked up a large piece of bark. "Here," she offered, "use it like a shovel."

While Hannah covered the fire pit, Becca retrieved several baskets from the small structure for the grandmother. One basket contained hunks of dried cactus and a variety of leaves. The other held bundles of bark, roots and a round rock. Becca assumed the stone was used to pound the plants. The old woman tossed the rock, and arranged everything into the larger basket. She dropped the smaller basket, and ground it into the dirt with her foot.

"Oh! That was a lovely basket, why is she doing that?" Becca asked.

"She can make new baskets," answered Sarah. "She wants this place to look long abandoned."

After emptying the dwelling, they all stood at its back and pushed. It tumbled into a heap... *I think these wise ones invented disposable houses long before society came up with paper plates and throw-away diapers.*

In less than twenty minutes, the former camp revealed no indication of recent habitation. The grandmother handed Hannah the basket to carry, and picked up a branch. She motioned them to leave. Becca led the way, looking back to see what the old woman was doing. The grandmother dragged the leafy branch around the area, erasing all tracks. She then shuffled backwards, pulling the branch and eliminating their departing footprints. Becca took off her cape as they entered the blackberry passage. She wrapped it around Sarah, tying it securely around her neck and at her waist.

"Keep your injured arm inside so it doesn't get scratched or poked. We can't have that getting infected."

Once they were through the thicket's opening, the old woman stuffed the branch into the entrance, making it all but disappear.

Becca led the way westward, through the woods. Except for several reminders to hush Hannah, the trip back was uneventful.

Sarah appeared pale. The pain radiated on her features, but not once did she accept an offer to rest. They approached Becca's property from the back where it joined a redwood forest. Becca felt relief that Thad had not yet arrived... *Or, maybe he has come and left... No, he wouldn't drive away ...if he came and we were missing...He'd still be tearing up the place, looking for us.*

48

"No man has a good enough memory to make a successful liar."

—Abe Lincoln

She glanced at the position of the sun. "It must be close to four, don't you think, Hannah?"

"Yes," the girl replied," maybe even after four."

They entered the house by the kitchen door, and set down the basket and bundle. Becca's mind was swirling with organizational plans.

"Hannah, pump a fresh bucket of water and wash your face and hands. Pull the twigs out of your hair. You look a fright. I don't want Molly asking questions when she sees you. I'll have Thad take you home and I'll stay here to get these two settled."

Hannah picked up a bucket.

"Sarah, I'm taking you both upstairs to a bedroom, where you'll be staying. You'll need to lie down and relax. Explain this to your grandmother."

Becca watched Hannah pump water from the small hand pump at the sink.

"Hannah, if Thad pulls up in the buggy, do not allow him inside the house. Run out to meet him, and explain that I've found things to do and wish to spend the night. Don't tell him or anyone about my guests...ANYONE! Then climb into the buggy and insist that you must get home immediately."

Hannah stopped pumping water. She looked at Becca in alarm.

"You want me to lie to him for you?" He's your fella. It's not honorable for a girl to lie to her fella, Delphi. Everyone knows that."

"I'm not lying. I'm prolonging the truth...misleading a little... Oh, for God's sake, Hannah. These women's lives are at stake!"

Hannah's eyes grew large. "You shouldn't curse Becca. It's not God's fault you're gotten yourself into this predicament!"

Becca rolled her eyes. "You suggested we bring them here, and that was good. Now, you'll help me conceal their presence, young lady!"

Hannah stood her ground. "I shant tell a soul about Sarah and her grandmother, but I won't lie to Thad for you. You'll have to do your own sinnin'!"

Grrr...I can't deal with her morality now...I have to get them hidden safely...

"Come ladies, I'll show you to your room. She led the way up the stairs. Sarah followed, looking back to check on her grandparent. The old woman gripped the banister and slowly ascended the steps. Becca opened the door to the first bedroom...*The two small beds in this room will be perfect for them.*

She opened the window, and pulled back the curtains to allow a breeze to freshen the room...*It was so thoughtful of Mrs. Callahan to leave all the beds freshly made...*She turned back the quilt and helped Sarah remove the cape and her moccasins. The girl lay down on the bed, and closed her eyes. Becca arranged a small pillow to support the injured arm.

"Tell your grandmother to rest too, and we'll fix your medicine as soon as I take care of this little situation." Becca turned and started down the stairs.

"He's here," Hannah called.

Darn, just a few more minutes would have worked out better...

"Hannah, go out and tell Thad I'll be staying here tonight. Tell him that you need to get back to the hotel to help Molly with supper."

Hannah glanced at her friend. Her face revealed her disapproval. She walked outside, closing the door behind her. Becca descended the stairs, and moved to the parlor window. Peeking out between the curtains, she watched Hannah deliver the message. Thad, already out of the buggy, tied his horse and walked through the gate.

Becca, rushed to the door, opened it, and forced a smile.

"Hello, I sent Hannah out to save you from having to come in. She's late for her chores."

Thad studied her face, and then looked over her shoulder as he scanned the room.

"I'm to blame. I'm late in coming for you ladies. I'll explain her tardiness to Mrs. O'Shay. I'd like to come in and discuss some things with you."

Hannah, following Thad back, mounted the porch. Her look said, "I told you so."

Becca stepped back, and the two passed by her. Thad sat on the sofa in the formal parlor. He laid his hat on the floor beside him and crossed his legs. It appeared he planned to stay for a while. Hannah sat on the piano bench, and watched the scene with curiosity. Thad's hazel eyes gazed over Becca's form. She felt uncomfortable and followed his gaze to the bottom of her skirts. The light calico print was stained brown from her trek through the forest with its dusty floor. Then she remembered the moccasins. They were so comfortable; she had forgotten all about them. The brown buckskin shoes hugged her feet and peeked out from under her skirt. Tiny snail shells outlined a flower blossom on the toe of each one. Thad was now focused on them. He raised his eyes to hers and lifted his brows in question.

Becca sat in a chair, and tucked her feet back under her skirts. "We went berry picking today. We soiled our clothing."

She placed her hand on her head to smooth her hair and felt a prickly blackberry twig anchored in her braids. At that moment, a thud noise drifted down from the upper story. Thad's eyes moved to the staircase.

"Who is here?"

Becca remained silent. Her stare at Hannah was threatening. Thad stood and walked toward the staircase. Becca rushed a head of him, and blocked his entrance to the stairs.

"Delphi, something is peculiar. I intend to search your upstairs. A few days ago, a man with a gun attempted to rob you. Today, you tried to prevent me from coming in, and now I clearly hear a noise in your upper story. I believe there's someone here that makes you feel fearful. I won't leave until I get this unraveled."

I guess I must tell him about Sarah… I can't allow him to go charging up there. It'd scare her to death. But…how to I explain this…I need him on my side.

Thad turned and faced Hannah…*No, don't go after the weak link…*

"Hannah, you know who is upstairs, don't you?"

Hannah's bottom lip protruded and trembled. She was on the verge of tears. Thad turned towards Becca, placed his hands under her elbows, and easily lifted her to the side. He stepped on the first step. Becca threw her arms around him.

"No, I'm trying to explain. Please sit down and listen."

Thad led her to the sofa, and they sat together. It took some time to relate the story of Sarah. Becca started with their first meeting, the developing friendship, the reason the girl and her grandmother lived away from the reserve, and Sarah's burns. She concluded with the arrangement for her moccasins. Thad listened without uttering a word. At times his face reflected his thoughts. Assembling curious incidents during the last several weeks, he understood what had happened.

When she had finished, he cleared his throat.

"You're wise to be secretive. It's unlawful to harbor Indian runaways. There are ruffians who would have no qualms in bursting into your house to kill or abduct them, especially if one was already sold to service. We should take them back to their reservation. They'll be more safe there than here."

"Sarah's burns are serious. They could cripple her arm or become infected and cause her death. Her grandmother is old and not well. I think she's going blind. I want to keep them here until the girl is well and I can advocate for her. Remember, Mr. Hanson, the Indian Agent? He said he can give written permission for Native Americans …er …Indians to leave the reserve. I need time to write a request to him."

Thad stood up and pulled her hands. She stood and faced him.

"How did you plan to bring that about, Delphi? Were you going to traipse eight miles to the Fort in search of him?"

"I…well…I haven't had opportunity to think that through yet."

"Did the thought of asking for my help ever once find a place in you mind?"

Tears tumbled down her cheeks. "I didn't want to involve you in something dangerous."

Thad pulled her into his arms, and she surrendered to his comforting embrace. She encircled him with her arms, and hugged him with all her strength.

"Such nonsense, Delphi, I care for you. Anything that concerns you involves me. How can I be of help to you if you won't trust me?"

"I told her she shouldn't lie to her fella," Hannah chided.

The couple laughed, and Thad picked several more twigs from Becca's hair. "I must meet the fugitives. I need to know what they look like, and they must understand they can trust me."

"Let me prepare them. I'll explain you to them first." Becca started up the staircase. Thad slowly followed.

Hannah took a deep breath and muttered, "The truth is always best, everyone knows that."

Becca reached the landing and noticed Sarah's closed door. The breeze caused the door to shut, that's what made the noise. She gently knocked.

"Sarah, I'm coming in to speak with you."

She opened the door. Sarah's face continued to show her discomfort. Her grandmother sat beside her on the small bed.

"I want to introduce you to my friend. You needn't be afraid of him. He'll keep our secret and help us. But please help me learn to pronounce your grandmother's name. Its awkward calling her 'your grandmother' all of the time."

"When she and my mother worked for the rancher, he called her Annie. She won't mind if you call her Annie," Sarah replied.

When Sarah said the name, the old woman smiled in recognition.

The two showed no fear when Becca introduced Thad. "I'll be back up very soon," Becca promised, and she and Thad returned to the parlor.

Thad picked up his hat. "I'll take Hannah back to help Mrs. O'Shay, but I'll request she be allowed to return to spend the night with you. I'll explain that you need her help to make your new home livable. You shouldn't be here alone until we get official permission for the two ladies to stay with you. Meanwhile, if you pen the letter of request to Mr. Hanson, I'll deliver it tomorrow. We'll need his written permission to assure safety for all of you."

He opened the door for Hannah, and she walked out. Thad turned and smiled at Becca.

"Try to find time to rest; you look a mite tuckered out."

Becca smiled back. She went to the drawing room and looked through the drawers of the oak desk...*I wish I had my stationary here... maybe Mrs. Callahan left some paper...*She found a bottle with a small amount of black ink. A quill pen rested beside it. Another drawer contained a few sheets of stationary. Violets trimmed the upper right corner of the paper which was tinted a delicate pink... *This isn't right for an official letter... I need plain white paper...*Her extended search proved fruitless... *This will have to do...*She sat at the desk and penned her request.

Delphi Castile
Crescent City, California
September 20 1865

To George M. Hansen
Superintendent Indian Affairs
Dear Mr. Hansen,

I so enjoyed meeting you at dinner at the Redwood Hotel. Your interaction was informative and appreciated. I have recently purchased a house, and have established my residency in Crescent City.

It has been my privilege to meet two wonderful individuals. A young woman named Sarah and her grandmother, Annie. Annie is elderly, nearly blind, and in poor health. Sarah, a child, has met with an accident, causing severe burns to her right arm. I am compelled to help these people, and house them until they are restored to good health.

During our conversation at dinner, a few days ago, you explained that you have authority to grant tribal members leave from the reserve for various reasons. Sarah and Annie are tribal members.

I am requesting that you approve my humanitarian request and provide written permission for them to reside in my home. I am open to any advice or instruction you wish to provide concerning this matter.

Sincerely,
Delphi Castile

She blew on the writing, and then folded the sheet. Placing it in a matching pink envelope, she lit a candle and dropped a dollop of wax for a seal. As it cooled, she pressed her thumb onto the wax, leaving her thumb print...*There, that's done. Now to sort through the clothing box, Mrs. Callahan left. I'll find suitable clothing for my guests before Hannah returns to help me with their baths.*

49

"We are all one child spinning through Mother Sky."

—Shawnee Tribal Proverb

Becca hurried upstairs and checked on her guests. Both were lying down and appeared to be sleeping. She moved to the larger bed chamber...*This; I would consider the master bedroom*...She walked to the window. Pulling back the curtains, she looked out at the view...*Perfect...I can observe the road from here...I'll be aware if anyone approaches from either direction. I'll use this room*...She glanced around. The wall paper had shades of light brown in its autumn leaf pattern. The posted bed and dresser were of dark wood. A large mirror set above the drawers. A pastel quilt of bright calicos lay over the bed. Two ornate lamps promised ample light for evening reading. An oval wooden frame displayed an arrangement of pressed orange poppies; under a glass pane...*This is much cozier than my room at the hotel.*

Becca focused her attention back to her errand. ..*The trunk should be in here...there it is*...The large curved top trunk sat in a corner, hidden by the opened door. She pulled it from the wall and lifted the lid. Seeing it packed with folded clothing, Becca silently blessed

Mrs. Callahan. It didn't take her long to sort out nightgowns for Annie, Sarah, and herself. She dug deeper, finding one for Hannah...*She can keep it here for when she stays with me.*

As she left her new room, she carried an armload of frocks that included a several housedresses for each of her guests, pantaloons and stockings. She slipped into Sarah's and Annie's room, and hung the dresses on pegs that lined one wall. She placed the undergarments into drawers. Once downstairs, she peeked into the pantry...*Ah... there are the laundry tubs and bathtub...*Becca searched out every kettle she could find. Filling each with water, she started a fire in the kitchen stove, and set them all on its top. She opened the windows to prevent overheating the house. It was then she heard the approach of a horse...*Thad and Hannah are back much sooner than I expected.*

She rushed to the door to greet them. Each entered the house, their arms filled with her possessions.

"We brought some of your clothes and things," offered Hannah.

"I'm so grateful. It will make less to do tomorrow." She stacked them at the bottom of the stairs.

"I'll go back to the buggy for the mutton stew and hot bread," said Thad as he walked out.

"Mrs. O'Shay wouldn't hear of me returning without your supper," said Hannah. "She sent a dozen eggs for tomorrow's breakfast. She and the others will be knitting this evening, but she'll explain our absence."

I'm so lucky to have these friends.

Becca set the dining room table with the lovely china in the cabinet. The five of them sat around it, and celebrated her first day in her new home. While she spread her bread with the warm butter Molly had generously shared, movement from the side caught her eye. She looked to her right and saw the blue glow shimmering in the corner. A glance around at the others assured her they hadn't noticed. Thad interacted with Sarah, trying to break the ice, and Annie ate hungrily. Hannah picked at the food in her bowl.

Delphi, how did you find me?

"How do I know how it all works…I end up where you are when I read or write in your journal. I have news for you, but first…Is this my new maison?"

Yes, but what is the news?

"Who are these people? Why are there Indians at my table?"

They are my friends…They need a bit of help so I invited them…

"Ah…they are vagabonds."

No, they are friends who need help…tell me the news.

"Why are you choosing friends for me from among the heathens? How will I founder a respectable école de musique if you lower my status so?"

If you insult them again I won't communicate with you. I'll have you know I am well respected in this community. You should be grateful… If they knew your occupation, I would not have been allowed to purchase this house for you…

"You needn't be harsh…I meant no offense…I speak the truth. But, Oui, your point is well taken… I fear when I replace you, I will be expected to run a poor house."

What is the news?

"Your sister sojourned to Crescent City. She located the l'homme…er…man. He is quite daft, poor fellow."

It would be better to say that he is mentally challenged.

"Oui, that too."

Did my sister get a journal to him?

"Oui. But he can neither read nor write."

Oh, I hadn't thought of that.

"Beth instructed him to draw pictures of his past. That he can do. He sketched a large ship…The Brother Jonathan, I'm sure…He penned his name…sort of."

That might work. I must find Ike, I mean Cain…I'll find out if it appeared in his journal.

"There's more…the authorities gave him a lie protector exam."

Lie protector…polygraph?

"Oui, that's what I say. His story of being shipwrecked, and having the name Jonah McCain proves true with that test, but we know that."

Poor fellow, he must be so confused.

"His insistence of never knowing your spouse proves true, as we well know it should. Beth believes he'll be announced insane and not blamed in court"

Yes, and when he's diagnosed incompetent and not charged, Phil will get away with it, unless someone testifies against him. We must get Ike back into that body. I refuse to let Philip get away with what's he's done!

"She sees me."

Who?

Becca looked at the others around the table. Annie, with her dim eyesight, stared at the corner as though she saw Delphi. The other three watched Becca with silent interest.

"That old blind woman sees me, I shall leave now."

"Becca, are you feeling poorly? You appear distant." Thad reached across the table and took her hand.

Sarah and her grandmother exchanged comments. "Grandmother says there is a spirit here," the girl reported.

Thad chuckled. "Maybe you've gone and bought yourself a haunted house."

"No, we're all very tired, that's all." Becca scooped up a spoon of food that was now lukewarm.

It took three hours to draw and heat enough water to provide four baths. Becca was appreciative that Thad stayed to carry the heavy buckets. When all was complete, she and Annie attended to Sarah's treatment. Thad sat in the drawing room with Hannah and Sarah and enjoyed cups of sweetened-creamed coffee.

Becca watched Annie with interest. The old women pounded one fist into her other opened hand. Becca understood she needed a mortar and pestle. Searching through the pantry shelves, she found a small one and gave it to her. Annie put in a few blue flax roots, several dried cactus pads, a handful of willow leaves, birch leaves, and two juniper twigs into the small pan of boiling water. In a cup of steaming water, she pushed in more willow and birch leaves.

Finally, she added leaves that Becca didn't recognize. After allowing the plants to soften, she ladled them out a few at a time and crushed them with the mortar and pestle. Soon, the mixture became a drippy pulp. She glanced around and pointed to a tea towel hanging over the workbench. Becca understood her need for a cloth and found a clean one. Annie then strained the leaves from the willow tea and carried both concoctions into the drawing room. The grandmother applied the herbal pulp to the girl's blistered arm and palm, wrapping it loosely with the clean towel. After the burned skin became pliable, she instructed Sarah to stretch out her arm and move her wrist and fingers. It was obvious by the girl's expressions that this exercise was painful. After this, she encouraged Sarah to drink all of the tea.

"What is the purpose of these plants, Sarah? Can you share with us?" Becca inquired.

"The willow and birch leaves and bark makes the hot pain go away," she replied." It makes the swelling less."

It works like aspirin. It's an anti-inflammatory and fever reducer...what do you know?

The guests returned to their room, and Becca showed Hannah the small room she would use when visiting.

"Consider it yours, Hannah. This is your other home."

Will Delphi take care of these people of whom I've grown so fond?

Descending the stairs, she saw Thad waiting at the bottom.

"You've been ever so helpful. You must be exhausted. You can go home and get some rest. We'll be fine."

"I'm here every night until you're holding the letter of consent in you hand. I'll sleep on the sofa, and be gone at sun up. I'll take your letter with me. Now up to bed with you,"

"What about gossip?"

"With Hannah here, it should appear less dishonorable. However, my horse and buggy are in your barn. Anyone passing won't notice my presence. Now to bed with you or I'll tuck you in myself."

At sunrise, true to his word, Thad left. Becca stirred as she heard his horse neigh. She got up and looked out the window. Watching him ride away in the early fog, her heart warmed. Trying to mesh her growing affection for him and her knowledge that they were of two different times rattled her nerves. She climbed back into bed, pulling the quilt up to her chin.

Thoughts flooded her mind... *must move the last of my belongings here, today... need to purchase food and staples ... have to get everyone settled in today... tomorrow is work at the Lengs...need to take the clothing to Harley's family...but how?... hope Thad has no problem finding Mr. Hansen... What if he can't be found? This is when I really miss telephones...What if he's found, but won't approve the request? What will I do then? I won't throw them out, that's for sure.*

She sat on the bed and thought about trying to go back to sleep... *Oh, for goodness gracious sakes alive! I won't sleep while thinking like this...* She dressed and tiptoed to the stairs. The aroma of coffee reached her nose. Entering the kitchen, she smiled. Annie stood at the stove. There was a crackling fire and a pot steamed on the hot surface. She smiled when she heard Becca approach. Before Becca could reach the cupboard, Annie lifted a cup down and filled it with coffee.

Becca sat at the table. "Thank you. Do you always rise so early?"

The elderly woman continued to smile...*How are we going to communicate without Sarah's help...*Remembering sign language, she stood and signed hungry with large motions. Recognition lit up Annie's face... *Good. Sign language may work for us if I do the signs large enough for her to see. I'll fix her some eggs.*

As Becca started to rise, Annie shook her index finger back and forth.

"No, no, no," she said.

Becca sat back on her chair, puzzled. The woman took a fry pan from a hook behind the stove, and set in on the stove. She shuffled into the pantry, and brought back a large crock. As she opened it up, Becca realized it was salt pork...*I must have missed that when I inventoried the pantry.*

Annie sliced the pork into small slivers and stirred it around in the pan. After allowing it to fry for a few minutes, she reached for a bowl on the work space. Dipping out thick batter with a spoon, she dropped small globs of mixture into the grease and flattened them... *I can't believe how well she does with those cataracts. She seems to have memorized my* kitchen and pantry...The woman shuffled back to the pantry, and returned with the basket of eggs. After cooking the bread on both sides, she fried two eggs and scooped them onto the plate with the three small pieces of fried bread. Placing it in front of Becca, she retrieved a fork from a cut glass vase that held spoons and forks. She handed it to her.

"Thank you, but you needn't wait on me, you're my guest."

Annie smiled and pointed to the food and then to Becca. As soon as she finished, Annie quickly picked up her dishes and moved to the sink.

"No, Annie, I won't allow you to clean up after me."

Becca gently nudged her from the sink, and signed that she herself would wash dishes. She pointed to the basket of herbs, to her own arm and then to the upstairs.

"You take care of Sarah."

Annie obviously understood, and set about preparing the treatment. As soon as everyone was fed and dressed, Becca explained the day's plans.

"Hannah and I will walk back to the hotel. I must gather up the last of my belongings, and Hannah has to work there today. I'll also purchase some provisions, and have James bring me back with them. Under no circumstances will you or Annie answer the door while I'm away. Keep it locked and don't allow yourselves to be seen looking out of the windows."

Sarah agreed from her propped up position in her bed. Annie settled into a rocker nearby and hummed softly. "Let's go, Hannah, while it's yet cool."

The two started out on the long walk to town. "I really wish I could stay with you."

"I wish so too, Hannah. But you have commitments to the O'Shay's. How long are you promised to them?"

"I don't know, till I'm married, I reckon."

"What if you were given opportunity for more education, or a chance to start a business, would Molly release you?"

"You mean like apprenticeship? Nobody, I know will take girls for that."

"What about starting your own business, without completing an apprenticeship?"

"Women don't start businesses, Delphi, everyone knows that."

That's a problem for solving on another day...After firmly reminding Hannah to keep the guests a secret, Becca entered the back door of the hotel, and took time to have a cup of tea with Molly.

50

"Man is kind enough when he is not excited by religion."

—Mark Twain

Molly showed her the completed items from the knitting bee the night before.

"Elsie and Minnie finished their projects and I'll have mine done by Sunday. Elsie will complete the booties for you, dear, and Minnie's working on Hannah's task. You can deliver them soon. The babe can wear them for his baptism."

Becca stared at her cup, planning her words. "The Reverend has deemed me unworthy to be the baby's godmother, and he set stipulations for Delford to be christened. I'm not sure now that it will occur."

Molly refilled both their cups with tea. "Yes, he visited me. He said that he feared you would soon lead our Hannah astray. He also mentioned that he didn't feel the Farris family were committed enough to have their babe honored with baptism. Well, I told him what I thought about that!"

"I'm sorry if I've gotten you crossways with your pastor, Molly."

"I'm not crossways with him, he's crossways with God. Minnie said so too. She was here. She told him that he was making it harder to get to Heaven than The Good Lord ever intended!"

Becca searched the woman's face. "What did he say to that?"

"He just stuck his self-righteous nose into the air and said that as long as he's the pastor it is gonna be his deciding that matters."

Both were silent. Finally, Becca spoke. "Well, guess I'll collect my things and go. I've a lot to do today."

Molly blurted out. "I told him that I never saw a harder worker than you. Though you do have some peculiar ideas about stuff, your heart's pure, in my way of thinking."

"Thanks for sticking up for me, Molly." Becca stood and pushed the chair under the table.

"I told that man I'd be proud if our Hannah turned out just like you, because there's not a mean thought in your head."

"You told him that?"

"I did. Then Minnie said that we should find that Tate fellow. He's a preacher. We'll have a christening right in my parlor or yours."

Becca stood silent. This had turned into a larger battle than she ever expected...I wonder if Harry and Sybil would agree.

"Well, that made him huffy, mind you. He said, baptism doesn't count unless it's in a church, and it's conducted by an ordained minister."

"Oh dear...maybe..."

"Minnie shook her finger right in his proud face, and then asked him if Jesus was baptized in church. She said she had no memory of anyone moving the Jordan River into a church house. Then she asked him if anyone checked John's ordination credentials before he baptized Christ."

I really must read that new bible... if I'm going to be up to these debates...Molly was tuned up and waving her hands for emphasis. "He jumped up, grabbed his hat and rushed out." She demonstrated his actions. "But he turned to say that he wouldn't serve communion to either of us until we repented for our disrespect."

Becca moved around the table and hugged the woman. "Molly, I can truly say, I love you like family."

Molly swiped away a tear. "We love you too, Delphi. As far as Charlie and I are concerned, you're like our own daughter... if we'd ever had one."

Becca climbed the back stairway to empty her old room. She entered the chamber and looked around. The bed was stripped to the mattress. The washstand, pitcher, and bowl were cleaned to a shine. Her things lay in a neat stack on the bed and desk top. She packed everything into the carpet bag. Opening the secret desk drawer, she took out the serpent bracelet, string of pearls, the cameo necklace, several rings and some coins. Noticing the dainty opal ring, she thought of Elsie... *She spoke of needing a ring to authorize her claim to widowhood....Well, Delphi; you're gifting Elsie with a wedding ring...* She slipped it on her finger and glanced around. The only item that remained lay on the dressing table... *The pistol... forgot about it...Well it's mine now...* She plopped it into the bag, and closed the clasp. As she left, she shut the door behind her.

Moving down the hall to Elsie's room, she tapped on the door. The young woman summoned her into the chamber.

"Delphi, I was fearful I wouldn't have opportunity to say goodbye. We're leaving with the steamer Sunday. I know you'll be working at Mrs. Leng's that day."

"I walked here this morning for several reasons. Saying goodbye to you was one of them."

She embraced Elsie. The teen returned the hug.

"I shall always remember the ways you've helped me. I'll write a letter as soon as I'm settled."

"Please do. I promise to answer. I want to know all about your baby's birth."

Elsie's face lit up with excitement. "I plan to name her after you and Minnie...if it's a girl.

Hmm...another namesake for Delphi...I must remember to tell her...

She slipped the ring off her finger and handed it to Elsie. "I want you to have this. You might want to use it for a wedding ring."

The young woman examined it carefully. "It's lovely, but are you sure you wish to part with it? It appears to be valuable."

"I want you to have it. You need a ring more than I."

Elsie gave Becca the finished knitted articles. She tucked them into the carpet bag, under the pistol. Later she walked to The Mercantile, and went to the back of the store to speak with James. The young man agreed with her request to deliver her and her groceries, and left to hitch the wagon.

Becca gathered the items on her mental list. A ham, bacon, beans, oats, rice, potatoes, a cabbage, apples, onions, a squash, a pumpkin, coffee and tea were soon piled on the counter.

"Do you have cream and butter?" she asked the store owner.

He busied himself wrapping the items in brown paper. "I will tomorrow. I'll send some to you with Thad."

She paid for her purchase just as James returned. He carried the groceries out, and piled them into the wagon.

"This is a big load of vittles for one woman," he commented.

"I plan to have guests from time to time."

"Yes, our book gathering is planned for next week," he reminded her.

Yikes! I forgot about that.... What'll I do about Sara and Annie...must give that some thought...

James rattled on about a novel for the group to share. Becca tried to listen, but her thoughts juggled from one concern to another. She felt a presence at her shoulder....*Delphi?*

"Oui, Is this the gentleman you tell me I must learn to love? He's debonair."

No, this is James. He's a nice person, but he's not Thad. This isn't a good time to talk to me.

"The time I visit is not my choosing...I must speak with you."

James voice cut into the mental conversation. "I was wondering if a book of poetry would be better than a novel for our first meeting. I'll need to prepare an order for whatever you decide. I'll send it on the steamer Sunday."

"Poetry would be fine, James."

Delphi, can you come back this evening?"

"Each trip leaves me exhausted. Your body is not strong yet. When I depart from it, it weakens."

Then I'll come to you...tonight.

"I'll order some books of poetry then," James concluded. He guided the horses toward her gate. Becca looked at the house. A curtain moved.

"Is there someone in your house?" James voice revealed his concern.

"No, just place the bundles on the porch, please."

"I'm sure I saw a curtain move."

"I left windows opened; a breeze must have moved it."

"This is a lot for you to carry in. I'll tote it all to your kitchen."

They reached the porch, and Becca opened the door slightly. She peeked in. No one was in sight. She opened the door for James whose arms were full of parcels and the pumpkin. He followed her to the kitchen where he sat everything on the work counter. He hurried back to the wagon for the rest. Becca's eyes scanned the room. Her eyes fell on Annie's native basket filled with herbs. Quickly, she snatched it up, and pushed it under the table. James returned and placed the remaining packages on the kitchen table where the basket had previously set. He looked around.

"Are you going to show me your lovely home?"

"I'll start some water for tea. While it's heating, we'll tour. "

Becca hoped her voice projected to Sarah. *She must know someone is here and is keeping out of sight.*

"I'll show you the ground floor, even the barn if you wish, but the upstairs is a mess. I must get organized before anyone sees it."

After walking James through a tour of the downstairs' rooms, she invited him to sit in the parlor. They had tea and talked while Becca secretly wished he would hurry on.

*He's done me a favor... can't just rush him off...*Suddenly, the sound of horses at the front of the house caused her to startle.

"Perhaps Thad is back." She stood and rushed to the window. She saw Cain dismount from a horse.

Becca stepped out on the porch. James followed. "That's the man from the Blacksmith and livery stables, isn't it?"

"Yes," she answered.

"It appears that he's delivering a horse. Is that your horse?"

Cain indeed not only arrived on a horse, but led another. He tied both to the railing.

"No," she answered James "I have no horses."

Cain approached, taking off his hat. "Good afternoon, Miss Castile. I was told to bring these animals over for you to have a look. The boss just shoed them and said you might want to buy them. Clem O'Leary is selling out."

"How did you know where to find me?" Becca tried to keep a suspicious tone from her voice.

"Wasn't easy," he answered. "I took them to the Redwood Hotel first. The woman there told me where you'd moved. She said to tell you there's a knitting party or something going on there tonight."

"Oh, well thanks for the message, and for bringing by these beautiful horses. I'm not qualified to judge one horse from another."

She introduced the two men and each nodded. "I'm shopping for horses for my new carriage, James. Come have a look and advise me."

The three walked toward the railing. "I don't know much about horses, "Cain began. "Never rode one till I got...till I came here. But I wouldn't give a plug nickel for that grey one. He's pure meanness."

"Why do you say that, mean in what way?" asked Becca.

"We had to hobble him and put on a muzzle just to get him shoed. He's a biter and a kicker."

Becca looked at the grey horse. He was pale grey with black specks. You're beautiful...why are you mean?

"Maybe he just doesn't like having his feet bothered. Maybe someone's hurt him in that way before."

"Well, he must not like riding either. I was going to ride him here today and he threw me. I had to change to the mare," Cain grumbled.

"He does appear a mite skittish," observed James. "He's a gelding and he shouldn't behave like a stallion. He may have a bad temperament. You might want to wait for a calmer steed."

"Clem said he and that bay mare were trained together for wagon and carriage. Guess he doesn't give much trouble if you keep them paired," Cain explained.

"How does the mare ride?" asked James.

"She's a sweetheart," answered Cain. "If you don't buy the mare, I will." He patted the mare's nose. "That dapple needs to be shot."

"No," protested Becca, "he just needs understanding. What does Clem want for them?"

"He's asking ten bucks for the pair. He won't split them up. He says the dapple is worthless without the bay."

"You can put them in the barn, Cain. I'll take the money into town tomorrow. I don't keep any here at the house."

That's not entirely true...I do want for folks to think that.

Cain led the horses to the back. Becca turned toward James.

"Thanks again for delivering my groceries, James. I don't wish to rush you off, but I have some pressing issues to which I must attend."

James said goodbye, promising to order the poetry for the gathering.

Becca made her way to the barn. Cain had put each horse into separate stalls, and fed them hay he had taken from a stack of hand bound bundles at one end of the barn.

"This is the right amount to feed them twice a day," he explained. Twice daily you'll need to give them a bucket of water. You have to give them each a bucket. If you have them share, old Dublin kicks it over before Bonnie can drink."

"Well if he's so attached that he won't cooperate without her, why would he deny her opportunity to drink?"

Cain shrugged. "He's just ornery like that. Clem should've named him Satan"

As they walked back to the front of the house Cain muttered, "I wrote in that book, like you said."

"Did any replies appear in response?"

"Some strange looking scribbles...nothing that makes sense."

"Keep writing, make an entry each day."

"I may be moving to San Francisco.' I wanted to tell you that. There're more varieties of work there. The livery stable arrangement will end soon. That was temporary.

"No, Cain, you can't leave. We have to make the switch. Give me a few days to think about it."

When Cain had gone, Becca rushed up to check on Sarah and Annie. Sarah's arm had been redressed...*Anna was finishing up when I returned...that's why the herbs were on the table...*Becca examined the girl's arm.

"That's amazing! It looks much better. I've had less severe burns from the sun that took longer to heal. You should patent that treatment."

Sarah looked at her in question. "Pat it?"

"Never mind, if you're tired of these four walls, you can come down stairs and we'll get something to eat."

The three of them sat around the kitchen table and feasted on slices of ham, cold fry bread and tea. Becca set up a pot of beans to cook on the stove, and mixed up yeast bread. She covered it with a damp tea towel, and set it on the table to rise.

"Someone's here," announced Sarah, peeking around the kitchen curtain.

"Don't allow yourself to be seen, Sarah."

"It's your man friend, Thad."

51

"An unjust law is itself a species of violence. Arrest for its breach is more so."

—Mahatma Gandhi

Becca rushed to the door and pulled it open wide. Thad dismounted and tied his horse to the rail. She noticed an envelope in his hand... *I sent a pink one and that's white...must be a reply.*

He approached the porch with a big grin, waving the letter. "I had to look several places, but I found him."

Becca moved toward him, and they embraced so naturally she didn't give it a thought. Thad kissed her forehead and pulled away enough to hand her the document. Becca broke the seal and slipped out a white paper. She scanned the bold writing. Smiling, she looked at Thad.

"He approved my request. I can house them without breaking the law." *Dumb, unjust law that it is...*

"You'll need to place that letter with other treasures, like your land deed. Keep it safe in case someone challenges your word."

"I'll do that right away. Now come in and have something to eat. I also have some horses for you to assess, later."

She pushed a loose strand of hair behind her ear. Thad followed her into the house.

"What? I'm gone part of one day, and you've managed to acquire horses?"

The dining room table provided the setting for the second supper in her new house. Thad expressed amazement at the improvement of Sarah's burns. Annie smiled as Sarah explained to her that Mr. Hansen approved their lodging. Thad shared stories about his perils of the day.

He patted the white cloth napkin on his lips and mustache. "I must say that gentleman admires you greatly. He appeared flattered that you wrote him on your delicate, personal stationary. He also spoke at length about your courage and Christian character."

"Really... Christian character... perhaps I should ask him to send a letter of recommendation to the Reverend."

Becca explained all she had learned about the Farris baby and his blocked baptism. She also told Thad about Minnie's idea of hosting the baptism at her house with Tate officiating.

Thad was quiet and appeared thoughtful. He stirred sugar into his second cup of coffee.

"I think this is Harry and Sybil's matter. You can't fix everything for everyone, Delphi."

"But his attitude is unjust and harsh..."

Thad reached across the table and took her hand. "He's the appointed leader for this church. It's not your place to dictate how he does his job. That babe belongs to the Farris family. They must sort it out."

His words stung. She pulled her hand away. The stern tone in his voice stirred the hurt she had felt at Sybil's news. It now rushed to the surface...*Why do people in this time think they have to lie down and take a kicking?*

Thad noticed the hurt on her face. "Delphi, dear, I'm only guiding you away from trouble. It appears that you're always in opposition with someone or something."

"That's not true! The Reverend is the only person with whom I've had disagreements." Her voice trembled.

Sarah looked up with concern. Annie's perpetual smile morphed into a frown. Becca stood and began gathering empty dishes. As she carried them to the kitchen, she heard Sarah quietly translating to her grandmother...*I don't want them to become uncomfortable...I must pull myself together.*

Thad approached her from behind, and put his arms around her.

"It was not my intent to offend you. But you move full chisel from one thing to another. I can't keep up. I fear for your safety and reputation. I would be most at peace if you could settle down and be content."

Becca turned and shared his embrace. "I'm sorry, Thad. You gave up a day of work to help me, and I must seem ungrateful. My only causes right now are little Delford's baptism and lodging for Sarah and Annie. I know my decisions always drag you into solving problems. I'll try to avoid anymore conflicts."

It would be better for Delphi; as well...

He bent and brushed a gentle kiss across her lips. "I have news that will lift your spirit."

She searched his face. "What is it? Tell me, I need some cheer."

"I have permission to offer Harry an apprenticeship at The Print Shop. He must sign an agreement to abstain from drinking until after his training and while working."

"Oh Thad, thank you. I can't wait for you to give him the news. You're wonderful. Their lips met and Becca relaxed into the experience. *Time seemed to halt...This feels so right...but how can it be...I'm not yet born...not really.*

The sound of rattling dishes interrupted her moment of bliss. The couple turned to see Annie standing at the door. She gave them a knowing smile, and carried the dishes to the work table. The elderly woman prepared to wash dishes.

Thad suggested, "Take me to see the horses. Are they in the barn?"

A few minutes later, they stood before the stalls. Becca carried two carrots and handed one to Thad. He offered it to Bonnie. She nibbled at it and nuzzled his hand.

"She's a gentle mare. I think she's quite suitable for you."

He moved to Dublin. The horse tossed his head and snorted.

"He's not a friendly sort. See his ears? When a horse lays his ears back like that, he's plotting something rambunctious ...even dangerous."

Thad took the second carrot and held it out. Dublin smelled it, and then in a flash seized teeth into Thad's wrist. Thad thumped his nose with his other hand. The horse released his grip and stepped back.

"This isn't a horse for a lady! He's as savage as a meat axe. I'd advise you to keep the mare, and send this rogue back to whoever sold him to you. Have you paid for him yet?"

Becca examined Thad's wrist. The skin wasn't broken, but a bruise already defined the bitten area. She started to explain that Dublin would most likely be shot if separated from Bonnie. Then she remembered her promise about avoiding causes.

"Thank you for checking them out. I know nothing about horses so your advice is most appreciated...But...*Dublin is staying. I'll figure out some way to gentle him.*"

Thad stepped into the tack room. "You have two saddles," he called out, "and reins, halters, and plenty of rope."

Becca glanced into the small room. "That's a strange looking saddle. Is it unfinished?"

Thad walked to the wall at which she pointed. "It's a side saddle. Surely you've seen a lady's saddle before." He tipped his head and studied her.

"I've never been around horses or saddles."

"There must have been horses on the plantation. Your mother must've used a saddle like this?"

I can't explain myself out of this...change the subject...I've actually ridden only once." A pony ride in the park....

"But I used a saddle like that." She pointed to the saddle propped against the opposite wall.

"That's a man's saddle...not appropriate for a lady. You'll need some guidance since you know so little, so don't try to ride until I'm with you. In the meantime, you'll need to make a riding skirt. Mrs. Leng will help you.

Pointing to her long ruffled skirt he added, These frocks can tangle up your feet."

Exactly...that's the reason women will eventually change to pants...Now I remember... Delphi told me to get a riding suit...

As they returned to the house, they smiled at Annie and Sarah who sat on the back porch in rockers. A cool breeze blew across the landscape and both appeared content. Becca hurried upstairs to change her dress, and tidy up for the knitting bee. Thad offered to take her to and from the hotel, but he must first ride back to town to get the buggy. *As soon as I get back, I'll write in the journal. I have to find out what Delphi wanted to tell me.*

Becca collected her sewing basket and materials and went downstairs. Annie and Sarah's voices drew her to the kitchen. As Sarah looked up and smiled, Annie applied a new dressing to her arm.

"The pain is less. I can move it more."

"I'm so glad. I hope the scaring isn't too bad?" Becca replied.

"Scars shows bravery," answered the girl. "If people have no scars, they've never been tested."

Her words made an impact as Becca applied them to her own concerns... *That holds some wisdom...Should a scar be something we treasure? ... Is it the same with emotional scars?*

Becca explained to them that she would be out. She cautioned them to keep the doors locked, and not open them to anyone.

"We have permission for you to stay here, but I prefer it not be challenged while I'm away."

As Thad assisted her into the buggy, he noted her shoes. "Did you intend to wear those?"

She glanced at her moccasins.

"I forgot to change them, but I don't care. I walked miles today, and my feet refuse to be cramped into those tight shoes. Don't worry. I'll tuck my feet under my skirts. I plan to tell the ladies about my approved houseguests anyway."

Thad chuckled. "Your houseguests will turn you into a squaw before you can civilize them."

Becca looked at him sharply. "Don't ever refer to them as squaws, not ever! They're as civilized as anyone else"

Thad's brows knitted in confusion. "I said nothing wrong. Why are you cross?"

"That's a derogatory word. They're my friends and I won't stand for it!"

He sat quietly for a moment. "And who determined that it's derogatory and why? Do you believe I'd spend a day assuring their safety only to insult them?"

"No," Becca softened her tone. "I believe you spoke in ignorance and didn't mean..."

"Ignorance? You know nothing of horses or saddles... barely understand the value of gold, and you call me ignorant?"

Thad's hazel eyes snapped. Becca had never seen him look at her in this way. She reached out and touched his arm.

"I didn't mean to say that you're ignorant, Thad. I believe you're the smartest and most capable man I know. I meant the use of that word, is in a general sense, ignorant. That term reduces Native American women to a lower status...it has meanings that derives from a time that Natives were treated less than human..."

Thad studied her like one might evaluate an alien from space.

"Why do you call them natives? They're Indians, that's what they're called."

Oh dear... I lost my place in time again...the time of their oppression is now...that's why they're hunted for bounty...

"I'm sorry if I sounded testy. I care so much for those two; I want them treated with respect. No one would call me, Hannah, or Mrs.

O'Shay a squaw, would they? Women are women regardless of creed or race. Do you understand what I'm saying?"

Thad clucked at his slacking horse who jerked to attention. "No one will call you a squaw, but they will call you touched in the head if you insist on getting riled over every nit pickin' thing."

He turned the buggy toward town. Becca's mood fell. *I must think before I speak....I can't force twenty-first century philosophies on nineteenth century people... scars show bravery ...how? They remind us of the mistakes that caused harm... The ugly history of this time...slavery...Indian massacres...women's oppression...they're scars...lessons learned from pain...America's scars ...except now I'm experiencing them as fresh wounds...*

"So, Miss Castile, what would you have me call your friends?" Thad's cold tone interrupted her thoughts.

"Call them women...or by their names. Please don't be angry with me."

The buggy bounced as Thad attempted to avoid a rut.

"I have a difficult time trying to figure how you can be so committed to the welfare of two Indian women when you grew up on a plantation that built it's wealth from sweat and oppression of Negro slaves."

Oh no...we're on an uncharted course again...how can I defend something that I didn't experience...Delphi should have to answer this...but...she wouldn't give a snap about Sarah and Annie... I must seem like a real paradox to this poor man.

"Delphi Castile was born into the plantation life, she didn't choose it."

I can't keep misleading him about living where I didn't...

"In fact, she protested her family selling the few slaves they owned when her father died. She wanted her mother to free them."...*I'm sure I read that in her journal...*

Thad looked at her. The twilight shadowed his face, but she could see his troubled expression.

"Why are you speaking of yourself as though it is someone else?"

"Because, I feel it is someone else. I don't feel like I am Delphi Castile, raised on a plantation, and served by people held against their will."

He pulled the reins, bringing the buggy to a stop. "And who do you feel you are?"

52

"Hypocrisy is the mother of all evil and racial prejudice is still her favorite child."

—Don King

Becca studied his face. Her blue eyes were solemn as she chose her words.

"I'm not sure who I am at this moment, Thad. I feel that somehow, I was reborn the minute Tate fished me out of the sea. I believe that life is precious. No one should have it wasted in needless pain. I'm referring to the pain of emotional and mental agony caused by prejudice, hate, and the misuse of religion. Everyone has the right to happiness."

His hazel eyes grew tender. He pulled her into his arms. "I understand your words. I felt that way when I was wounded in battle. They talked about taking off my leg. I remember pondering about how much blood was shed because some people thought it acceptable to enslave other people."

Becca cuddled closer. "The passion that sent you to war...it's the same that drives me into conflicts."

Thad kissed her cheek. "When I went to war, the government and thousands of soldiers backed me, and I still nearly got myself killed. You're like a tiny woman warrior running into battle, armed with nothing but your words."

"I'm not alone. I have Hannah, Molly, Annie and Sarah, the Farris family, Mr. Hansen, the Lengs, and most importantly, you."

Thad laughed. "That's a bedraggled assortment to take to war." His tone sobered, "Just remember, my darling, it took a hundred years of good men speaking against slavery, and a bloody war before it ended. Slow your pace. Save your strength. Survive to see the victory. Don't die in the first battle because of too much zeal."

A lingering kiss and embrace put the subject to rest except in Becca's mind. As Thad silently held the reins in one hand and encircled her with the other arm, she processed his words...*I have to tell him soon...feelings are deepening...if only fair to tell him...can he understand the truth?*

Thad kissed Becca's cheek after he lifted her from the carriage. "I'll be back to take you home in a few hours. Meanwhile, I'll be at The Print Shop. I'll clean the press and catch up on some of the work I missed today."

Becca entered the hotel, and made her way to the drawing room. Four strategically placed large lamps lit the room, and added warmth against the evening chill. Becca glanced around. Elsie furiously knitted a row on a brown scarf. Becca envied her skill. She looked up and smiled.

"This is for Harry; I must finish it tonight since I'm leaving Sunday"

Hannah rushed in to give Becca a hug. "I miss you all to pieces. Especially mornings, I miss your help."

"I miss you too, Hannah. Perhaps Molly can release you to visit me Sunday."

Molly stood at the round tea table in the center of the room. "I've cleared this area so we can cut out the infant's gowns. I'll help you piece them together."

Becca's eyes swept to the other side of the room. She caught her breath. "Sybil, I didn't expect to see you here, but I'm so glad you are."

Sybil smiled as she held the sleeping newborn close. "Mrs. O'Shay sent her husband to gather me and Delford. Harry is with the other children."

Molly spread out the paper patterns on the table. Becca set her sewing basket on the floor as she removed the black shawl.

"I wanted Sybil here tonight to discuss the babe's christening," Molly explained.

Oh no...Thad thinks I run full chisel...this woman's planning faster than I do.

"Mr. Tate will drop by later, "Molly continued. "I visited Harry and Sybil today and explained that we wish to host a baby christening at your new home. We can make it a house blessing as well. They're in agreement. Mr. Tate leaves on the Sunday steamer, so we must plan it for tomorrow night."

*Becca was stunned...Now I know how Thad feels...Molly's thrown this together before I've decided if it's a good idea...*She crossed the room and sat by Sybil. The mother placed the baby in her arms. Delford didn't awaken. She slipped the cloth from his face and studied his tiny features...*All of Sybil's children are beautiful, but he's an absolute angel...*

With his eyes closed, his lashes swept his cheeks. Tiny lips pursed out and made a sucking motion. Becca placed her finger in his diminutive hand and it closed around it.

Quietly she spoke. "You needn't feel pressured to do this, Sybil. There's plenty of time to christen Delford. After a few months you will have worked things out with Reverend Walker. Then you can have it in the church."

Sybil shook her head. "Harry feels shamed, and he already blames himself for his inability to support his family. The Reverend's words of condemnation hurt him deeply."

Becca basked in the warmth of the baby in her arms. She thought back to her conversations with Phil about planning a family. *He always refused to discuss it....That was for the best...as things turned out...*

"I believe that religious decisions should never be made under pressure," she replied.

Sybil placed her hand on Becca's arm. "My sweet babe's alive because of you. We want you to be his godmother. I'm grateful to Mrs. O'Shay and Minnie for finding a way to bring it about."

Molly brought two pieces of the blue fabric to Becca. "Now pass that darling back to his mother and stitch this seam. Make the stitches short and tight, but not too tight or it'll cause a pucker.

"I'm crocheting a blue and white lace to sew on the sleeves and hem," Minnie added.

Becca threaded a needle...*I can't have a gathering at my home without explaining about Sarah and Annie...*She cleared her throat. "I have something to tell all of you."

She glanced at Hannah who stopped knitting and returned her gaze, expectantly.

"I now have house guests. They'll be with me indefinitely. They're from the reservation, and I have Mr. George Hansen's written letter of consent."

All busy work ceased. "You have Indians in your home?" asked Molly.

"One's a young girl near Hannah's age. She suffered a terrible burn on her arm, and she is recovering from it. The other lady is her grandmother. She's lost most of her sight. Mr. Hansen and I concluded they need care that's not available on the reserve."

She checked the knot at the end of her thread and began sewing the seam, pulling it tight as Mrs. Leng had taught her.

"This will not in any way prevent the christening service being held in my home. They'll attend our celebration, and I hope we'll make them welcomed."

"Well...I suppose, "Molly stammered, "I suppose...you'll need to Christianize them. This would be a beginning...you know...to show them the right way...away from their heathen ways."

Becca's face grew hot. She took a deep breath...*Do as Thad suggested... focus on the victory...take it easy with the battles...*She smiled at Molly.

"I'm so glad you understand. They're generous, loving, and compassionate women. I'm proud to have them as friends, and I can't wait for you to meet them."

Minnie chuckled, "I think this'll be an interesting service."

Sybil had been thoughtful, but she now offered a suggestion. "What about the midwife, Mrs. Leng? Do you think she would come? She was so comforting at the birth."

"I'm sure she and her husband would be honored to take part in a gathering at my home," Becca replied. "I work there tomorrow, so I'll invite them."

She focused on her sewing, but she watched Molly from the side. The woman held the scissors in midair. Her knitted brows revealed an inner struggle.

"But they worship idols."

"No, I think not," insisted Sybil. "When I was in such pain from the breach birth, Mrs. Leng stroked my temples and murmured something. I'm sure she was praying. There were no idols to be seen and I instantly felt more relaxed."

Becca smiled as she made a knot, and bit off the thread. She re-threaded her needle...*Keeping my mouth shut is working... they're sorting it out...*

"Well..." Molly returned to cutting the fabric. "It's your christening, and you should have whoever you wish to invite. But...won't it be awkward...having Indians, Chinese, a Negro preacher, and white folk all together? I mean...Mr. Tate is at least a Christian..."

Minnie laid her work in her lap. "Why, Molly dear, do you not know there'll be people of every race and tongue in Heaven? Did you think God was going to have separate heavens for peoples of different countries?"

"I hadn't thought about it like that." She folded the fabric pieces. "I'll invite Doc, is there anyone else that we should include?"

The next few minutes continued with suggestions regarding foods to bring, and the plans for a meal to follow the service. Becca wondered how she would fit everything into one day. Later as Hannah served tea,

Tate arrived. He borrowed a Bible. As the group sipped the hot beverage, he read the passage of Christ inviting the children to him, and summoning his disciples to, "Forbid them not to come to me."

Then, he addressed Sybil personally.

"Mrs. Farris, there's a few things I want you to understand before you decide about the dedication of your child."

Sybil gave her full attention.

"I was born in Philadelphia, a free man. I belong to the Free African Society that began there. From that group a number of Negro churches branched and now they fellowship with one another. They ordain ministers. I'm ordained through this organization. I've worked for several years in ministry under the training of a lead pastor."

Everyone in the room was silent. "Preachers in our churches are not paid. I came west to earn and save money so I can return, and work full-time in ministry."

Sybil smiled, "I'm not concerned about your credentials, Mr. Tate. I can feel a kind spirit in your words."

He smiled. "In the churches I serve, we don't baptize babies, we dedicate them. We request the Lord's blessings and protection over the child. We ask for wisdom for his parents. We leave baptism for the child to choose for himself when he's old enough to understand."

Sybil was thoughtful. "So, the only difference is the water? The prayers and intent are the same?"

Tate smiled. "There's no scripture that sets an age for baptism, Mrs. Farris. Religions have different interpretations about age and methods, but the important thing is the intent of the heart. If your intent is to commit yourself to raising your child in the fear of the Lord, and to provide instruction to him in following his teaching, you meet the requirement to christen this little one."

"We also want to christen little Ben. He's just turned three. Harry's accident happened while Ben was yet a babe. That's when we had to cease with our attendance to church."

"That'll be fine. I'm honored to share this with you."

Later, on the ride home, Becca snuggled up to Thad. She shivered under her shawl. Thad held a firm grip on the reins as the horse stumbled, then found his footing in the moonlight. The usual fog didn't hover, and stars were visible.

"You're tired, my darling warrior, did you slay a dozen dragons tonight?"

"No," she giggled. "I did however; stab my thumb several times with the needle."

"Self wounds are always possible when one is reckless with a weapon."

"You'll be free and willing to attend Delford's christening at my house tomorrow night?"

"So, you decided to go ahead with it?" His tone reflected concern.

"No, the others decided. I merely agreed to allow use of my home."

"The Farris family wants this?"

"Yes, and Mr. Tate has met with Sybil to discuss it."

"What about your house guests? Won't their presence cause a problem?"

"They're invited, and so are the Lengs."

"And this wasn't your idea?"

"Nope, I swear. I have a favor to ask of you."

Thad gave her a sideways glance. He appeared hesitant.

"Could you find time tomorrow to print two certificates? I'm sure you know how to format a baptismal certificate, but it must be titled dedication certificate."

"I will do that. I've made certificates for Reverend Walker several times."

"We'll need two, please. Little Ben will be dedicated too"

Thad pulled his horse to a halt. As he helped Becca to the ground, he cupped her chin, raising her face to look at him. "I'll pick you up early for your ride to Chinatown, so off to bed with you. You need your rest." He kissed her forehead.

"Yes, I agree." *And as soon as I visit Delphi... I'll gladly drop into bed.*

53

"Life is what happens while you are busy making other plans."

—John Lennon

J had walked Becca to the door. He didn't turn to leave until she unlocked it and walked in. She lit the candle that always set on the small table by the entrance. After walking through each of the downstairs rooms, she ascended the stairs...Everything appears to be safely locked down...She moved quietly down the hall. Annie and Sarah were silent...They must be resting well in soft beds after sleeping on the hard ground all summer... Lighting a lamp, she slipped out of the restrictive clothing and into her dressing gown. Retrieving the journal, she sat at the small table and began to write.

> **September 21, 1865**
> It's been a busy week. I moved in and stocked the pantry. Two Native Americans are in a spare bedroom, and I've obtained legal permission to keep them here indefinitely. I will have the doctor

see Annie, and inform me if anything can be done about her cataracts.

The girl experienced a serious burn. In the few days that her grandmother treated her with herbal poultices, amazing improvement occurred. Her arm will be scarred but regain full use.

In two weeks, I'll have the new carriage I described to you earlier. I've already bought a team of horses. One is a darling, the other, not so much, but I'll explain when we talk.

Our first open house will be tomorrow night. A christening will be held for the baby whose birth I assisted. He's named after you Delphi, you will feel honored, I'm sure. You are his godmother. Also Thad is growing quite serious, and I'm hoping we've switched before *he decides to propose.*

*Heaviness moved through her chest...Do I really hope that? How will it feel to be home and wonder how another lifetime's love might've developed?...This is crazy...we have to switch...I don't belong here, and Delphi doesn't belong there...it's a mistake of nature...history is what it is already...switching people around in centuries...that would mess it up...*He is a wonderful, wise strong and sexy man, Delphi. You will never find a husband more tender, honest, and upright.

The pen fell from her hand as the room whirled around her. She caught her breath as she felt the pull of a vacuum carry her through a wind tunnel...past the light...and to Beth's apartment.

As she collected herself, she looked around. She watched Beth lock the door and turn off the living room light. As her sister walked to her room, Becca craved to hug her. Darkness didn't limit her own vision, she noted. She moved around the room. A new piano set in the corner. Lesson books arranged on the bench revealed the titles, Teaching Little Fingers to Play, and Thomson

Piano Book 1...*Oh yes, I remember those. I butchered of a few those little songs during my failed piano lessons.*

She willed herself to hover by Beth's desk. A filled-out form lay open and she read, Application, Request for Guardianship. Remembering that Beth often volunteered to serve as temporary guardian for disadvantaged adults, she read no further.

As she floated to Delphi's bedroom she observed that Beth's apartment felt cramped now that it housed two women and their belongings...*It's a good thing Beth isn't fussy about roominess.*

She moved through the entrance. Delphi's room was meticulously in order. The young woman sat in bed, and her wheelchair set waiting nearby. A pink ruffled lamp cast light on the diary in her hands. She wore a frown.

Is my writing too poor for you to read, or do you feel displeased with what I wrote?

The young woman looked up. "There you are. I was readying myself to write in your diary when I saw your words appearing."

Well if you read my latest entry, you're pretty much caught up about me in your world.

"Oui, we must discuss your entry, but first I shall tell you what I tried to relate earlier."

Good news I hope.

"Perhaps... perhaps not. The persecutor will not press charges against Ike Barker. He says there's no evidence that he did what you had me say he did."

You do mean prosecutor, don't you?

"Don't correct me, I must consecrate."

Concentrate? Sorry!

"One more interruption and I shant speak English to you ever again!"

I'm just trying to help you improve...I'm a teacher...after all...

"As I was saying...Ike, he insists his name is Jonah McCain, is being mustered out of the infirmary in Crescent City. He has no family. Beth is working on a plan."

Guardianship... that's what those papers are on her desk...

"Oui, We can't have him disappear before we switch them. Anyway, Beth is fearful he will end up trying to live on the streets with no understanding how to exist here."

Beth, bless her. She's always compassionate, but what about the fingerprints? They identified him as Ike Barker. He, well his body, has a prison record and connection with the mob. He probably has warrants out for his arrest.

"The authorities say the warrants are petty things and the prison sentence was served. They feel it may have been a miscarriage of justice. His special doctor reported that he has the mind of a twelve-year-old child. He also said he is not violet."

Violent...sorry...continue.

"So there is doubt about your words. I am having difficulty holding to a histoire I've not myself endured. They are aware that your head was injured, you realize."

And Phil, what does he say? Do the investigators suspect him?

"Oui, he is the problème. His comparions spoke against him regarding his affairé. His employés did as much, but the authorities say poor business management and bad morals do not provide évidence for attempted murder."

But... the million-dollar life insurance policy he recently purchased on me....that proves a motive.

"Oui, well, we've discovered he also placed the same policy on himself, so it appears less suspect."

That no-good rat! I might have known he'd cover his tracks! The only way to convince them is to bring the real Ike back. If he told the truth, it might help. I won't give up until Phil is punished.

"I said that as well. Your sister reasoned it continues to be one's word against another."

He simply can't get away with it...it's not right!

Becca wanted to cry, but without a body to utilize, she could only feel the deep sorrow and hot anger that follows defeat. ..*I won't give up.*

"I must inform you that I spent a large amount of your money for the piano. But usability checks will start soon. That will pay for my basic needs."

It's called disability, and it won't pay much. I don't care about the money...

"I am giving piano lessons to three scholars. They live here in the building. I expect to have more soon. I'll build you a business to earn your living. And you'll get something... a settlement from the divorce."

I appreciate your efforts, but I can't give piano lessons. That's not my gift. But since you enjoy it, go ahead. I can sell the piano later.

"I understand the difficulty for you with these large hands, but I'm training them. If you continue to practice while you're there, you'll be ready."

Becca, still caught up in her disappointment, was unprepared for her departure. When she awoke, she was lying on the floor...*I fell out of the chair...feels like I bumped my head...* She crawled to her bed. Climbing on top of the quilt, she faded into sleep.

Becca awoke shivering. She sat up and looked around. The room was dark and she needed the chamber pot. As she attempted to light the lamp, a breeze blowing from the window hindered. The curtain fluttered and she realized why the room was so cold. After shutting the window and relieving herself, she wrapped up in a quilt. The journal caught her eye. It laid sprawled opened on the floor... *I remember...I fell and bumped my head...* She caressed her forehead. *Ouch! Next time I plan a spirit flight, I'll lie in bed...* She picked up the book and started to close it when fresh writing drew her attention to the opened page... *Delphi must have written an entry after my visit...*

> I wish you had remained long enough for me to discuss important matters with you. I understand that departing is out of your control.
>
> Here are the concerns I must stress:
>
> Do not commit me to marriage. Once married, the husband owns all you have. I will not have a spouse taking all I have travaillé so hard to obtain.
>
> Best to send the suitor away before he becomes persistent.
>
> I am not pleased at being a godmother. I'm not fond of children in general. I teach them piano because I love musique and the lessons pay well. If you can reverse this arrangement, it would be best.
>
> You said in your entry that of the two horses, one is gentle and the other is not. Discard the wild one. I'll have no time or patience for breaking a wild horse.
>
> The houseguests may remain until the child has recovered. Then they must make other arrangements.

> **The exchange of our bodies will undoubtedly be difficile without obligations supplémentaires. We must each be diligent in preparing a simple transition.**

She closed the journal. The chill she had been feeling moved inward...*We're so different... Delphi is organized...has long term plans...thinks in an orderly way...I fly by the seat of my pants, and react from my heart...I can't do as she asks...* A shuffling sound of moccasin feet in the hall let Becca know Annie was on her way to the kitchen...*She's starting breakfast...bless her heart...I could never send her away.* Then she remembered her day's plan...*Working at Lengs today... christening tonight...*

She took the last bite of fry bread as a knock came at the door. She hurried to welcome Thad and they embraced. Delphi's words ran through her mind...*I can't send him away either...my best friend. Perhaps the best friend I've ever had,,,*

"Thad, I have a question."

"What is it?"

"Is it true that when a couple weds, the woman's property and money is then owned by the husband?"

"Yes." He answered frankly. "Are you planning to wed?"

"No, I heard that's the case and wondered if it's true. That doesn't seem fair."

"Did your mother own her own property? Of course she didn't. How would you not know that this is the law?"

There he goes again...asking about Delphi's situation... "Couldn't that be changed if the husband signed a contract that forfeited his claim to her possessions?"

His face showed his puzzlement. "I've never heard of such foolishness. The law is made to protect the wife from being swindled, or from her squandering the wealth away."

Guess there's no prenuptial agreements in place yet... "Why is it assumed that women can't handle money?"

He raised an eyebrow and she remembered her confusion with the gold system and her need for his assistance..."This argument is lost for the moment."

He held open the door. "Charley came by to tell me he's bringing Hannah to your house today. He wanted me to assure you that she will clean house for the christening tonight. Molly thought you'd need the help"

"That takes a big load off my mind."

Thad dropped her off at the Leng's and returned to The Print Shop.

54

"Encourage children to come to me and forbid them not..."

—Jesus-New Testament...

She wasted no time in relaying the information about the christening to Mrs. Leng. The couple was honored to accept her invitation. She sketched a simple map that would guide them to her home over town and country roads.

"I bring duck," the woman declared.

"Duck?" I've never eaten duck.

"I make duck...vedy good...I bring gift...I made coat for child." She hurried to a shelf and pulled out the item, holding it up.

"That's lovely!" Becca exclaimed.

The green wool jacket was lined with black silk. The matching hat proudly sported a black, silk bow. It was large enough for him to wear through the winter. Mrs. Leng then retrieved the china dolls. She explained that new frocks needed to be designed for them. The day passed quickly as they looked at a fashion magazine, drew patterns, cut out cloth, and sewed the miniature dresses... *This is a priceless experience...I've just learned how to make a dress by doing it on this small scale. I'll experiment with making looser armhole and sleeve.*

Over lunch of rice, fish, and tea, Becca ordered a blue riding skirt and jacket. Mrs. Leng already had her measurements so picking out the fabric was all that was necessary. During the afternoon, the mentor left Becca to work alone while she prepared the duck for the oven.

Thad was on time, and Becca excitedly shared all she had learned that day. They slowly ambled over the dirt roads.

"Mrs. Leng won't need me for a while. She's caught up now. I'm going to miss working with her."

"Then you'll be able to attend church with me tomorrow?"

Becca's forehead creased into a frown. *I forgot how my Sunday job excused me from church...darn!*

"The Reverend doesn't think I'm worthy."

"Then your attendance will prove him wrong. After the service we'll go to the dock and watch our friends leave on the steamer."

"All right...but he's likely to be ripping mad about the christening."

"I knew my little warrior wouldn't run from a duel."

I'm not a warrior, Thad. I'm a woman who believes everyone should have a chance, and I abhor cruelty in any form."

He smiled at her. "Yes, my darling, and that's why I'm growing so fond of you."

When Becca entered the house, her mind was whirling through a list of things she knew must be accomplished. Hannah met her, smiling.

"I swept the entire downstairs, dusted the piano, beat the parlor rug, and baked two apple pies. I intended to make bread, but Annie is cooking a big platter of some kind of new bread. I hope the others like it; I find it pleasing."

"Thanks so much, Hannah. What would I have done without you? So now we only need to get ready. I guess I should feed and water the horses. Then we can dress for the christening."

"I'm sure Thad is tending to them," the girl replied.

Becca passed through the kitchen on her way to the back door. Annie dropped a piece of dough into hot grease. A platter piled high with golden pieces of fry bread set cooling. Becca took a piece as she greeted Annie, and started for the barn. Thad had let Bonnie and Dublin into the opened area. He was filling a bucket at a pump as she approached him.

"We'll need to take two buckets of water at the same time. Dublin dumps Bonnie's if he doesn't have his own," she advised.

"Blame horse, you'll regret buying that scoundrel."

The two walked around the small area. Thad assured her the fencing was secure enough to allow the team to be free of the stalls. He brought in his own horse, Susie. He fed and watered her. Dublin gave the visiting mare an evil eye.

"Stay away from that beast, Susie, he's as crazy as a March hare," Thad patted her neck.

When they returned to the kitchen, Annie greeted them with cups of tea and saucers of fry bread spread with jam. Becca encouraged her to sit and eat with them, but she indicated she would take a treatment to Sarah. Hannah stood ironing near the stove where she had several irons heating.

"Why are you ironing?" Becca asked.

"Sarah showed me the dresses you found for them in the Callaghan trunk. I thought they'd look more suitable if I pressed them. "

She dipped her fingers into sugared water and sprinkled the liquid evenly. The hot iron hissed as she pushed it across the homemade starch.

"Sarah allowed me to arrange her hair, but Annie refuses any styling but braids."

"Grandmothers can wear their hair however they wish." Becca chuckled, remembering her own grandmother's blue hair rinse.

"I appreciate your help with their wardrobe."

Several hours later the household waited in anxious anticipation. Thad moved the parlor furniture around so that all seating faced the same direction. He carried in dining room chairs for extra accommodations.

Becca pulled a small Victorian table to the front of the room and placed a lamp on it. She laid her new Bible beside the lamp... *This can be the pulpit ... Hannah polished and filled the lamp...perfect.*

Doc was the first to arrive. Thad took charge of his horse, turning him into the fenced pen. Becca took his hat and cane. The older man nodded at Sarah and Annie.

"Doc, could you take a look at Sarah's arm? She burned it with boiling water several days ago. Her grandmother treats it with an herbal remedy, but I'd like your opinion."

Becca led him to the two who were settled on kitchen chairs in a back corner of the room. Doc took the girl's hand, adjusted his spectacles and looked closely at the scabs.

"Those were horrid, bloody blisters, just a few days ago," Becca explained.

"I've long known that these people have skills in treating burns," he responded. "This was very serious. It could have turned into gangrene. I've had to amputate limbs that were injured less severely. It's necessary after infection develops."

Sarah glared at the doctor and pulled her arm away.

"You've nothing to fear from me, child," he spoke softly. "Your wounds are healing superbly."

He looked at Becca. "Does she show signs of Brain Fever? Nightmares... distorted wits... lymphatic... memory loss... fits...? Those are the symptoms of Brain Fever. Bad accidents can lead to it."

Becca shook her head...*He must be referring to seizures ... shock ...depression...post traumatic stress...*

"No, she's the same as she's been since I first met her. I'm also concerned about her grandmother's eyes. She sees a little but they look murky, do you think she has cataracts?"

He reached out a hand and Annie permitted a handshake. He looked into the old woman's face.

"She may be losing sight from several ailments, but the cataracts are advanced. Blindness can't be cured or abated."

As he sat in an upholstered chair near the piano, he reached into his coat pocket and retrieved a bundle.

"This belongs to you. I'm returning it."

Becca opened the folded white handkerchief. "It's my dagger."

"It's been in my surgery since I removed it from that vagabond. I thought it might be useful as evidence, but it appears the Sheriff considers it a small concern, a picayune affair. I suppose he thinks the ruffian got what he deserved. I thoroughly cleaned it."

I'm glad there's no investigation...They might find out that Delphi stole hot gold from him...could turn out bad...She placed the dagger on a shelf above the piano.

The O'Shay's are here," announced Hannah from the window. Thad went out to help Charley with his horses. Hannah assisted Molly with baskets and pans of food. An elk roast, a large bowl of mashed potatoes, and a pitcher of brown gravy soon sat on the table with the pies and fry bread. One guest after another arrived. Mrs. Leng brought the roasted duck as she promised...*I think this is called Peking duck, in Portland.*

Becca placed it on the table. "That looks very good," commented Molly. "You must get the recipe," she whispered to Becca.

"I think you should ask her for it," suggested Becca. "I'm sure I won't remember."

Good opportunity to get all of them talking to one another.

Once the Farris family arrived, Molly and Becca took little Delford to the drawing room. Molly dressed him in the new blue gown. Then Becca threaded his tiny arms through the knitted sleeves of the sweater. Once the matching hat and booties were added, the infant looked like the perfect model for a christening portrait...*I wish I had thought of making arrangements with a photographer.*

Becca carried her godchild back to his mother and noticed the parlor was filled with guests. All who had been invited were in attendance, and several unexpected who were brought by invited guests. Minnie sat at the piano, and Elsie stood beside her. The new hymnal Becca bought from James set opened to Amazing Grace. Tate gave an opening prayer. Elsie led the group in singing the hymn. When they finished, Elsie addressed Becca.

"Delphi, you must sing something... a song for your godchild."

Becca was stunned. *No, Elsie...don't start pressuring me to sing again.*

"You sing, Elsie, you know more songs than I."

All eyes were on her. Sybil smiled. Suddenly an old Sunday school tune popped into her head...*I can't sing that, I'm not sure it's been written yet.*

Thad nudged her with an elbow. "I've heard you sing, you must do this," he whispered.

She stood and walked to the front of the room. Glancing around, she noticed Annie and Sarah at the back, in kitchen chairs. Mr. and Mrs. Leng sat on the loveseat near the front door. Doc, James, and the O'Shay couple shared the couch. Others sat dispersed among them. The room was filled. Tate stood at the makeshift podium where he held her Bible, opened to a passage. She cleared her throat and hoped Delphi's melodious voice would save the day since Becca's would be a disaster.

>Jesus loves the little children,
>all the children of the world.-
>Red brown, yellow, black and white,
>all are precious in his sight.
>Jesus loves the little children of the world.
>Jesus came for all the children,
>all the children of the world.
>Every nation, every race,
>Jesus gives them all his grace.
>Jesus came for all the children of the world.

She returned to her chair. Thad squeezed her hand. Murmurs circled the room indicating surprise and approval. Tate smiled.

"It's a blessing that you sang that song, Miss Castile. It sounds like it's taken from the scripture I'll now read."

He raised the Bible and asked God for a blessing of the word. Then, he read from Matthew. "**Then there were brought unto him little children that he should put his hands on them, and pray: and the disciples rebuked them. But Jesus said, Suffer little children, and forbid them not, to come unto me: for of such is the kingdom of heaven. And he laid his hands on them.**"

He spoke for a few minutes regarding the scripture, and the importance of raising a child to live as The Lord taught. He stressed how the parents, the church, and the community must be an example of righteousness. Then, he called the Farris family and Becca to join him. Tate reached out his arms. Sybil placed the infant in them.

Positioning the sleeping baby firmly in his hands, he lifted him level with his head...*Careful...don't drop him.*

"Heavenly Father, we present this child to you and we ask for a blessing. Just like those little ones you blessed so long ago, we ask a blessing for Delford Farris. And just as you rebuked those who discouraged those little children, please protect Delford from discouragement, and from anyone who would stand between him and you. Protect him and teach him your path."

He carefully handed the baby to Becca.

"There's another child?"

Sybil reached behind her and untangled Ben from his refuge in the folds of her skirts. She lifted him and he hid his face in her neck. Tate prayed a similar prayer for Ben, but left him in the security of his mother's arms. He offered prayers of blessings and protection for the other children, Emily, Rose, and Ivy. He prayed for wisdom for Harry and Sybil... *This is moving right along... Reverend would still be on the first prayer...*

Tate turned toward Becca. He laid a hand on her head and prayed.

"And we ask a blessing for this lady whom you raised from a watery grave. Everything you do is for a purpose. Lead Miss Castile to that purpose for it is why you saved her."

Becca felt a chill...*Might I really be here for a purpose?...but what?...all that is happening is already history...except this part...this part in which I'm involved... or is it?*

55

"Money has the power to alter human personalities, and reveal their true natures."

—U<small>NKNOWN</small>

Becca watched Annie wash a pan as she finished her coffee and eggs.

"I don't know what I'd do without you, Annie."

The woman turned and flashed a grin. *Sometimes I think she understands me...*Hannah and Sarah entered the kitchen. They had giggled late into the night. Becca had no doubts a strong friendship would develop.

"Oatmeal or eggs?" she asked.

"Oatmeal for me." replied Hannah. Annie went directly to the stove and scooped some into a bowl.

"Sarah, does Annie understand English?" She addressed the girl who now sat across from her at the table.

"I'm sure she learned a lot when she worked at the ranch. She refuses to make it her language. I speak your words, but the Grandmother refuses."

"Why would she refuse?" asked Hannah as she stirred sugar into the porridge.

"She believes that surrendering her language is to surrender the spirit of our people."

"But she uses a type of simple sign language, isn't that the same as speaking English?" Becca asked.

Annie turned and placed Sarah's bowl of steaming oats before her. Looking at Becca, she shook her head. "No," she responded.

Sarah reached for the sugar. "The hand talk has been with us for many years. The Great Spirit gave it to the tribes so they could speak to one another with understanding. But English is the white mans' tongue. He used his words to lie and deceive us. The Grandmother, and many of the elder ones refuses to speak in that tongue until it's used for truth."

"Well, I'm glad she understands me. Now I know I can talk to her when you're not around. The sign language she uses is easy to figure out. There's no problem."

Annie smiled and refilled Becca's cup.

" I wish you didn't feel you have to serve everyone. You're the elder here."

"The Grandmother has always taken care of all around her. She's grateful to have people who she feels need her."

A knock at the backdoor drew their attention. Becca rose to respond. Thad removed his hat and jacket.

"It's a mite cold this morning. I fed Bonnie and that Beast. I was hopin' I'd find a hot cup of coffee."

Annie was already pouring a cup as he pulled out a chair.

"Who's going to church? Do I need to make two trips to carry everyone?"

Becca glanced at Sarah and Annie. *I couldn't bear it if people were rude to them...But...he's right...I should ask.*

"Hannah and I will be leaving for church in a few hours. You're both welcome to come, if you wish."

Sarah spoke to her Grandmother in their native language and Annie answered her.

"She asked if the dark man will speak." Sarah explained.

"No, he might be there, but the pastor, Reverend Walker will speak."

Annie looked disappointed. More interaction occurred between the two before Sarah added.

"The Grandmother wants to know if you will be singing the Great Spirit song."

Becca tipped her head, trying to understand the question.

"The one that tells how the Great Spirit loves children," the girl clarified.

"Oh, I see, no... but, I'll sing it for you here any time you'd like."

"She said she will remain here." Sarah said, "But I'll go with Hannah."

"Then one trip will be enough, as long as we set tight together," concluded Thad.

The fog was cleared and the sun had warmed the air by the time the women loaded into Thad's buggy. Hannah's skills with hair were displayed in the stylish braids and curls each of them wore. Becca thought Sarah stunning in the yellow calico. A yellow ribbon wove through the braids, and contrasted against the black strands. Hannah had secured them on top of her head. Hannah and Becca opened parasols. Becca positioned her new bible and small purse securely between her and Thad...*I'm not looking forward to this...That's for sure.*

When they arrived, most of the congregation were scattered around outside. As Thad assisted each of them out, Minnie and Molly started in their direction.

"Why look at this beauty," Minnie exclaimed. "I'm so glad you came to service, Sarah."

Before Becca could suggest how to approach the building, each of the older women placed an arm around one of the girls, and walked them toward the church. Thad and Becca followed. Reverend Walker stood at the door. A large bell rang the call to mass. Mrs. Walker stood beside her husband smiling at each member entering the fold. Molly and Hannah reached him first. He shook hands with them and smiled.

"I'm looking forward to that Sunday dinner, Mrs. O'Shay."

Minnie and Sarah followed close behind.

"Mrs. Bergman, we shall miss your playing the organ after you leave. I'm sorry to say, we'll have no accompaniment today. The poor old instrument isn't working. I fear she's doomed to silence. God will need to accept only our voices this Sabbath."

His eyes moved to Sarah. "And who is your young friend?"

Minnie hugged Sarah reassuringly. "This is my friend Sarah. I want her to see what a welcoming congregation you lead, Pastor."

"Yes, well... are you new to the area, Sarah?"

"No Sir, my people have lived here for hundreds of years."

Elsie approached and the clergyman forced another smile. Then his eye caught Becca's and his lips formed a thin straight line.

"Well, Miss Castile, I'm so pleased you have chosen to return to worship."

Before she could respond Thad stepped forward and pumped the hand of the older man.

"Yes, she's finally settled in, and can fall into a routine. We're so pleased you're pleased."

They moved through the door and Becca whispered, "I don't think he knows the christening already occurred."

"Good," Thad answered as he directed her to an empty seat behind the O'Shay's'.

From the pulpit the Reverend announced. "We no longer have an organ. Today, we must sing acappella. Our building fund was used to paint the church, and for the purchase of the new wood stove. We'll take a special offering at the end of the service, but if anyone has an organ or piano that could be spared, we'd appreciate your loaning it until we can collect enough funds."

"Is this the church I must attend?"

Delphi?

"Oui, I must talk to you. This doesn't look like a church. Where's the crucifix?

This isn't Catholic, its Methodist Episcopal…sort of.

"But I'm Catholic."

Well I'm not…besides there's no Catholic Church in town right now. I can't talk at the moment.

"Then, I must come here I suppose…that's regretful. That priest, I don't think I like him much."

On that we agree … this is where most people attend. He wants a piano, shall I donate yours?

"Never! I'll need that piano. Why do you ask foolish questions? However, I'll also need approval of the clergy for my école de musique to succeed. Give him gold for a new piano or organ. Be sure he knows it's from me. That will buy his approval and provide me with power when I need it."

I can't believe you want me to bribe the preacher.

"Men and money, money and men… pas de différence"

That's not true about all men…but it might be with this one.

"Four hundred is more than enough…not a schilling more. Don't permit him to fool you regarding the price."

Four hundred! That's more than I spent on the house. I won't give that bigot that much!

"I don't see a big gut but his face is quite sour. Nevertheless, Clergy can do harm to one's plans if they feel you're of no use to them. Instruments musicales are very expensive. Trust me…this is important. Don't place it in the offering. Give it to him directly, and explain you are doing it because of your love for musique and the church."

Well…that's an outright lie…I 'can't say I love either.

"I've been lying for your cause regarding your spouse."

Very well then, I'll do it….

Becca became aware of her head nodding and everyone looking at her.

Thad smiled, "Go ahead sing the song, everyone wants you to."

What?…Did I agree to sing?…Delphi! See what you got me into…

Leaning toward Thad, she whispered, "What song?"

"The children's color song," he whispered back.

Becca stood, maneuvered her skirts and pinching shoes, she stepped into the aisle. She felt the many eyes following her to the platform. She wished she could zap herself back to her own century. She turned and faced the congregation.

"I would like to dedicate this song to all children in this room and everywhere in the world. All are created by God and are his very own."

She cleared her throat and began. Just as the evening before, Delphi's trained voice chimed out the words and melody that Becca had learned as a child. She could see faces smiling up at her and children beaming. Hannah mouthed the words and it occurred to Becca to take it a step further. When she had finished the last verse, she made a request.

"Those are very simple words. I know you can sing them right along with me this time."

She was amazed at the reaction. Everyone belted out the song with enthusiasm. Then, taking a sidelong glance at Reverend Walker she observed a pouty expression.

She smiled and said, "That was wonderful. I'm surprised you have no choir, Reverend. There're so many talented voices here. Let's sing it one more time, and this time lets each pledge that we'll show God's love to a child this coming week."

After leading them through one more round, she gracefully walked back to her pew.

"What are you doing?" Delphi hissed into her ear. *"I advised you to buy an instrument, not take over the programme musical... I fear you will commit me to direct the chorale in a church that is not to my liking."*

Go away...my body needs you...I'll visit you later.

"Don't forget. It's of great importance...."

She felt Thad squeeze her hand. She squeezed back. The minister took his place in the pulpit. "I am beginning a succession of sermons. These will cover the Ten Commandments. Today we shall begin with the first."

He raised his voice and loudly proclaimed "Thou shalt have no other gods before me."

For forty minutes he expounded on what he perceived to be idol worship of most other religions including pagans and heathens. The air became stuffy. Odors of perspiration mixed with a faint mildew smell drifted by her nose. Becca felt nauseous as they stood for his lengthy benediction...*I can't believe God ever intended worship to be this miserable....it's painful.*

On the outside Molly approached her. "A large number are coming to the hotel for dinner. You're invited, as always."

Becca thanked her but responded that she must get home and check on Annie. ..*Hannah has one more day this week at my house, I won't short-change her*...Once home, they dined on leftover duck and roast.

Later, when they prepared to go to the docks, Hannah chose to remain at home with Sarah and Annie. Becca changed into a lighter dress of calico, and exchanged the button up shoes for her. moccasins. She and Thad rode back into town.

"Your carriage should be coming on this steamer," Thad reminded her.

"That's right, I'd forgotten about it with all the excitement of the christening."

"Harry will be starting at The Print Shop tomorrow. Training him will take most of my time. I must take opportunity to teach you about handling those horses."

"So much is happening so fast, "Becca exclaimed.

"I sent the trunk of clothing home with the Farris family last night. I can't wait to learn from Sybil if the items are useful"

As they found a place among the crowded Front Street to tie Thad's horse, Becca noticed the Reverend and his wife strolling toward the dock. Thad assisted her out of the buggy and she headed for them. Thad watched her, puzzled.

"Reverend Walker, I have something to discuss with you."

The man turned to face her. His wife smiled. He glowered.

"If you are going to apologize for your impertinence in my church this morning, I don't think this is the proper place."

Becca was momentarily stunned. Mrs. Walker shuffled nervously.

"Why no, sir, I've done nothing for which I'd apologize...I only sang a song that was requested. If you didn't want me to sing, you shouldn't have asked me to come forward and do so."

"It s not the singing to which I refer!"

His voice level raised a few notches. "Speaking directly to the congregation is not a woman's place. Women are to remain silent in God's house. You criticized me for not having a choir. You disrespected my authority."

Thad approached from behind. "What's the dispute here?"

Becca looped her arm through Thad's.

"The pastor's offended that I spoke a few words to the congregation. I suppose he'll now have to refuse my donation of a new piano or organ. After all, it would be scandalous to accept a gift of four hundred dollars from a woman who disrespects his authority."

Mrs. Walker's head popped up, and her eyes grew wide. Becca could feel Thad's body tighten. The clergyman stood speechless.

"That's settled then. If you wish me to be silent, I shall, and I'm sure my money will be more useful where I have a voice. Good day, Mrs. Walker, Reverend."

As they walked toward the dock Thad looked into her face.

"Are you becoming mindless? Why would you give so much to a man you find disagreeable? I must advise against this, Delphi. You're a woman alone, and you can be quite foolish with money."

Becca bristled. "I was just scolded by Mr. Walker for having a voice, now don't you start harping about money."

Calm down...don't take this out on Thad...it's hard to defend a decision that I didn't make nor agree with...It's Delphi's request...I personally wouldn't give that jerk a lead penny, a wooden nickel, of a three dollar bill...

"I'm sorry for snapping at you, Thad. I want us to enjoy the day. Let's forget the nasty preacher and say goodbye to our friends."

56

"If you have men who will exclude any of God's creatures from the shelter of compassion and pity, you will have men who will deal likewise with their fellow men."

—Francis of Assisi

Becca spotted the Farris family. All were neatly dressed in the donated clothing she had provided. They looked happy as they waved back at her. Moving through the crowd, the couple located Molly, Charley and their passenger friends. Elsie and Minnie shared a trunk of items they had obtained since the shipwreck when they lost everything. Minnie displayed visible excitement about seeing her husband again. Elsie was radiant, her loosened corset revealed a thicker waist, but she proudly wore her opal wedding ring. She hugged Becca.

"I'll write you as soon as the babe is born. If it's a boy, I'll name him for his father, but if a girl is birthed, she'll be called Delphi Miette, after you and Minnie."

Minnie noticed Becca's quiet mood. "Are you feeling melancholy with our parting, dear, or is something troubling you?"

Before Becca could think of an answer, Thad responded.

"The Reverend was unkind to her, unduly so. I've always paid him proper respect, but I must say he riled me today."

Minnie placed a motherly arm around her. "Now don't you fret about Pastor Walker. He can be an old fuddy-duddy. He's good at heart, just baffled at what's really important."

Becca felt tears fill her eyes. "I don't think he's good at heart. He's mean-spirited; he cares nothing about the feelings of others. He's a power monger in my opinion."

Minnie pulled a lace handkerchief from her sleeve and handed it to her.

"In the old country, my father was a pastor. Lutheran, he was. But Papa had a tender heart. He taught his children to look at each situation through the eyes of Jesus. There were other ministers around that viewed life as does Mr. Walker. Papa said that those who readily judge others are angry because of their own shortcomings."

"I'm sure your papa was a wonderful man of God. But I don't think he knew anyone like Reverend Walker. This man thinks his own words are God's words."

"Oh, but Papa did encounter clergy like him, often. If Papa were alive, he would tell us to not judge the pastor. What he does is wrong and unwise, but only God can see his heart. He needs a missionary to bring him to the light. Perhaps, that will be you, dear. No one else is as courageous."

"Me? I have no intention of speaking to him ever again, or going to his church. He's a jerk!"

Minnie took both of her hands and held them lovingly.

"Dear Delphi, it's not his church. Mr. Walker is a lost shepherd leading a flock of innocent sheep. Look how harshly he treated the Farris family. Now they want nothing to do with attending. Someone must help him find his way. Could it be that your coming to The Crescent was for such a purpose?"

Becca shook her head. "Are you kidding? He doesn't even think a woman is worthy to speak one word in church. He won't listen to me."

"Yes, I understand your provocation. That belief is another misinterpretation of the scripture. There are no males or females in God's eyes. Papa always said that anything can be proven, disproven or approved by misinterpreting scripture, even murder. That's why a Christian's focus should be on the teachings of Christ. He took all the complication and confusion and turned it into simplicity."

Becca was thoughtful. "I can remember hearing that in Sunday school. I recall the teacher saying that the Ten Commandments are summed up in the golden rule."

"That's exactly right, and so is all the rest of the instruction in the Old Testament. It's important. It shows us the lineage of Christ, the long struggle of man, the rise and fall of leaders and kingdoms. But it's the teachings of Jesus that sorted it out, and summed it up for a way to live life. I heard Papa tell a cranky minister once that he made getting to Heaven harder than did the Heavenly Father."

"I wish you were staying, Minnie. You're so skilled in working good deeds around Reverend Walker's obstruction."

"Any skill I may have, I learned from Papa. What you must do, Delphi, is read the word for yourself. It's your sword. Read the gospels over and over. Memorize the beatitudes. Study the parables. When you have these in your heart, you'll have an answer to all Mr. Walker's errors of judgment. Don't use scripture for debate, but for instruction and guidance."

"Thank you Minnie, I'll always remember you... *Even when I get back to my time, I'll remember this woman.*

The cannon blasted from Battery Point, announcing that the steamer had anchored. "I'll write..." shouted Minnie over the roar of the cheering crowd.

Passengers climbed into fishing boats that would take them out to board. These boats would return with freight. Becca and Thad moved away from the docks and strolled toward the beach. It was a balmy day and Becca was glad she had dressed in light cotton. The wind picked up and tugged strands of her hair from the cascade of curls, Hannah had styled on her head. She pushed them back from her face.

Looking down the beach she saw a large crowd of men gathered in a circle.

"Thad, what are they doing?" Thad raised his hand to shield his eyes from the sun.

"Oh that's the dog men; they're down there every Sunday afternoon. Look, Delphi, if you watch intently, you'll see your friends climb aboard."

Becca was not distractible. "Why do you call them dog men? They're jumping up and down...They're cheering."

"See, Delphi, Minnie and Elsie's boat reached the ship... where're you going... Delphi?"

"I'm going to check this out," she called over her shoulder.

Thad hurried to catch up. He took her arm and pulled her to a stop. "Delphi, women aren't permitted there."

Remembering the ruckus caused when she entered a barbershop, she asked. "Really...why not? Is it a meeting of the Esteemed Order of the Barbershop Brethren?"

"Delphi, some of men like to fight dogs. Only men attend these gatherings. They do some betting. Language isn't suitable for the gentler sex. Besides, I can assure you that you aren't missing anything you'd want to see."

Becca studied his troubled face.

"Are you telling me those men are running a dog fighting ring? That's barbaric! Isn't that against the law? I'm going to find the Sherriff, I saw him a few minutes ago."

Thad shook his head. The wind ruffled his dark hair and scattered it over his eyes.

"It's not against the law. What a person does to animals is not under control of law. Why would you think so?"

She looked at him with disbelief. "It's cruel and inhumane. Surely you don't condone this!"

"It's not a sport I'd take part in, but it's not my business if others do."

"Well, shame on you! How do you expect society to improve, if you never speak up against wrongdoing? Forcing animals to fight is not a sport! It's bloodlust!"

"Pulling her arm from his grasp, she lifted her skirts enough to run, and proceeded toward the crowd. Thad followed, his limp more pronounced by his increased gait.

"Delphi, stop..."

I'm glad I wore these moccasins... those button-ups would have caused me to turn an ankle in this sand...

"Delphi, stop!"

Delphi was now close enough to hear the uproar. Some curse words filtered though the excited yelling of the rowdy observers. She approached the outer edge of the circle. Thad was close behind.

"Excuse me, what are you doing?"

No one paid attention to her inquiry. Thad took hold of her wrist. She twisted free. She pushed hard on the back of a man.

He turned to face her. He looked surprised. "Why, hello, Little Miss. You need to return to your family. This is no place for a lady."

She elbowed between him and another taller male. She gasped. A dog with blood dripping from his mouth was being pulled back by a rope tied around his neck in a choke knot. He howled frantically. Another dog lay on the ground; his cheek was torn and hung from his face. Blood pooled around his head. His breath shook his body in jerks. The eyes stared blankly forward. Becca sensed the pain and shock in the animal's being.

She squatted by the defeated gladiator. Pulling her shawl from her shoulders she covered him. She gently pushed the torn skin back in place. She looked up into the faces of a dozen stunned men.

"All of you are pathetic excuses for men! You are the lowest examples of humanity I've ever seen! What right do you have to find amusement in causing pain to an animal?"

Her voice was unrecognizable to her. It pushed out forcefully and at a pitch she had never heard before.

One man pulled a pistol from his belt.

"Stand back, Miss, I need to put him out of his misery. Becca jumped up and lunged for his arm. The gun fell on the sand. Becca quickly kicked it in the direction of the sea. It miraculously took flight and landed at the water's edge as sand peppered the faces of those who watched.

"His misery is caused by you, you idiot! You will do no further harm to this animal!"

She could hear Thad beckoning her with reason, but she ignored him. Never had she ever felt so angry. She grabbed the man's sleeve and the wrist of another male close by.

"Here we go," she screamed. "How about round two? Only this time it'll be between the two of you. Everyone call your bets. Do you think Skinny Arms here, or Fat Face there will win this fight?"

The group was silent.

"What are you waiting for? Let see some blood and teeth fly. No, better yet, it'll be a fight to the death. Or, are you both too cowardly to have a go at it?"

She felt Thad's arms encircle her, lift her, and turn away from the group. He started walking back to the dock. Becca kicked and swung her arms.

"Put me down, I'm not finished."

"Yes you are," he replied calmly. "I'm not in the mood to fight all of those men, and you're not big enough to back me up."

She laced her feet around his legs, tripping him. They both fell to the ground. Skirts and petticoats encircled both their heads. As Becca tried to free herself from the tangle, she realized Thad was hopelessly encumbered by her hooped petticoat. She reached under her skirt and pulled loose the tie that secured it around her waist. Kicking free, she left Thad to escape the ruffles, wire and whalebone.

Running back, she was aware that her hair was now completely released to the wind and her stockings had fallen to her ankles, but she didn't care. Dropping down by the dog, she checked his breathing. It was a bit more regular. ...*Annie will know how to doctor him*...She contemplated how to get the damaged animal home.

The crowd was dispersing. She watched them walking away. One mumbled as he passed.

"Some men can't handle their women."

She threw her arms around his knees, and brought him to the ground. Slipping the dagger from her sleeve, she pressed it to his neck.

"Would you like to repeat your insult about my friend?"

His eyes grew wide. "No, Ma'am."

"Get out of my sight, you slime ... you disgust me!"

He scrambled to his feet as Thad approached, dragging the petticoat. Thad dropped to the ground, pushed his fingers through his hair, and then rested his head in his hands.

"Delphi, Delphi, Delphi, What happened to you? It's as though you took leave of your wits."

Tears were now flowing freely down her cheeks. "I know, I didn't even recognize myself. I hate cruelty, be it against humans or animals. I can't tolerate it."

"So in your rage, you kicked a man's valuable pistol into the sea, goaded two men to fight to the death, revealed your undergarments, disgraced your suitor, and threatened a man's life with a dagger."

"Are any of those offenses cause for arrest or hanging?"

"No, but calling men cowards could lead to my being challenged to a duel."

A chill moved through Becca's body. "They shouldn't challenge you. You tried to stop me. I'm the one who offended them."

He looked at her intently.

"That's not the matter at hand. A man is expected to either control or defend his woman. Since I couldn't control you, I may have to defend your honor as well as defend mine."

"Well, that's pure rubbish! If there's any dueling to be done, I'll do it."

He shook his head, and gave her a look of hopelessness. Glancing at the dog he said, "This animal is suffering. We should end its life."

"I'm taking him home, Annie will know how to save him."

"Even if he can be saved, he won't be a suitable pet. He's been trained to fight, to mistrust man; he'll become vicious at unexpected times, especially around other animals."

"Sorry, Thad. I know I sound unreasonable, but I have to try. Please help me get him home."

"I'll go and return with the buggy," he answered in a defeated voice.

As he left Becca began the task of maneuvering her discarded petticoat under the animal to serve as a stretcher. He opened his eyes and their gaze met. His pain-crazed stare appeared to focus on her face.

"Don't you worry, Warrior, I'll take care of you. No one will ever subject you to that again."

He whined a reply, from deep in his throat. Soon the animal was placed in the carriage and Thad quietly held the reins as they rode home in the warmth of the late afternoon. Becca squirmed in the buggy seat. She worried about Thad's feelings. She may have unintentionally caused more problems for him than she could have imagined.

"What are you thinking Thad?"

"I was trying to figure how the angel that sang so beautifully in church this morning, could become the demon who challenged twelve men this afternoon."

"I wish I had an answer for you, Thad."

He took a deep breath. "I don't wish to offend you, but there's a matter I must address."

She watched him closely, trying to anticipate what would come next.

He looked at her. "Is there any madness in your family?"

She wanted to giggle. The tension of the day now played reckless with her nerves. Suppressing the urge, she answered with a serious tone.

"No, there's no insanity in my family, none." But you'll think I'm completely crazy when I tell you all I must relate."

57

"Your own soul is nourished when you are kind; it is destroyed when you are cruel."

—King Solomon - Old Testament

Once the battered dog was in the house, Annie, Hannah, and Sarah gathered around with expressions of shock.

"Where did you find him, Delphi?" Hannah asked, as she responded to Becca's request to get a sheet.

"We'll lay him on the table," instructed Becca. "That way, Annie can attend to him easer."

Hannah arranged a folded sheet on the table. "Where did you find him?" she repeated."

"She forcibly took him from his owner." replied Thad, dryly.

"His owner doesn't deserve to own an animal," spat Becca. "He subjected him to a fight for sport."

Annie leaned over the animal. She moved close to focus her failing eyes on the wounds.

"Take care... that dog may attack you if tending his wounds causes pain," Thad warned.

He left through the back door to unhitch Susie and put her in the pen.

"Can you save him, Annie?" Becca whispered.

Annie carefully pressed the torn cheek. Warrior flinched and whined. She looked up at Becca. Using her hands, she made a sewing motion. She spoke to her granddaughter in their Indian tongue.

"Grandmother says we must sew his mouth or he will never be able to eat. She asks for a needle, small is best."

Annie examined the dog, moving carefully over his body and looked at a deep gash that left an open gapping wound on his back. She spoke again to Sarah, who answered her promptly.

"She requests that I go to the sea and get a stinging creature from the tide pools. It's needed before she can continue with healing the animal. If I may ride your horse, I'll return swiftly."

Becca rushed out to the barn where Thad was watering the horses. She explained to him that Sarah needed a horse.

"I'll need Dublin and Bonnie to go and pick up your new carriage, but she can ride Susie. I'll saddle her for you."

"I won't need a saddle." Sarah replied. Soon girl headed toward town. Skillfully planted bareback on Susie, she tapped the mare's sides with her toes and broke into a gallop.

Becca returned to the kitchen. Hannah brought the sewing box and Annie used scissors to carefully cut away the blood drenched hair and fur from the animal's wound. She sang a soft, slow chant. The dog seemed to calm and closed his eyes.

"Don't you think he should be shot?" asked Hannah. "He's suffering so. It would be merciful, everyone knows that, Delphi."

"He has as much a right to live as any of us, Hannah."

Annie washed the wounds, flushing out sand. She then selected bark from her medicine basket. Becca recognized it as the same she had used to calm Sarah after her burn. She placed a selection in a pan of water to boil. Soaking a clean rag in fresh, cool water, she squeezed small amounts of the liquid into the dog's partially opened mouth. Becca could see Warrior's throat move as he attempted to swallow as sand and blood was rinsed from his mouth. When the bark reached a boil, Annie took it off the stove and set it aside to cool. Becca paced the floor. She worried about Sarah... *I hope no one sees her... Lots of people are at the seashore today... Someone might harm her...My impulsiveness may have placed those I care about in danger...*

Hearing the sound of an approaching horse, she ran out the front door. Sarah dismounted even before the horse completely stopped. She held a bundle under her arm. Tying the horse, she scurried up the steps, past Becca, and into the house. Becca followed closely wanting to ask a question but knowing too little about anything to form it into words. Sarah opened the bundle as she approached her grandmother.

"That's what you mean by a stinging creature? That's a sea anemone... what good can that do?" questioned Becca.

"Watch," answered the girl.

Annie scooped out the hairy looking tentacles onto a plate. She mashed them with a fork. A gel like substance oozed out. With her fingers, she scooped it up and pushed it into Warrior's gapping mouth, making sure to saturate the flesh on the torn cheek.

"Why is she doing that?" asked Hannah.

"It will stop the pain while she sews his mouth," answered Sarah. "He won't feel the needle pricks."

Annie threaded a small needle with thin sinew. She touched the torn flesh. Warrior didn't flinch as he had before. The medicine woman pushed the needle through the skin, pulling the separated pieces into place and carefully tying a knot. She repeated the process twice more.

Not the neat stitching a surgeon would make, but it holds it in place.

Becca suddenly noticed a poker lying on the top of the heated cook stove. Annie instructed Sarah and Hanna to hold the animal securely.

"What are you doing?" She cried in alarm as Annie picked up the poker with its red hot tip. "No, don't burn him!"

"Annie looked up. Her face was stern. "Stand back!" she demanded in perfect English.

Becca dropped to a chair, covered her eyes, and started to sob. She heard Warrior yelp with pain. Annie began singing the chant. Becca peeked out from behind her hands. The opened gap was now fused though seriously burned.

"The Grandmother can heal the burn," explained Sarah. "But the wound was so large; it could have caused sickness to enter his body."

Becca remembered Cain complaining how the Natives who took care of him had burned his wounds. She took a deep breath and moved closer to the table. Annie was already applying the same cooling poultice to the burn that she used with Sarah's arm.

Becca stroked Warrior and spoke softly to him. Annie took the cooled bark broth and a large spoon. She motioned for them to turn Warrior over. The three of them worked together to shift his body. Annie carefully spooned the tea into the uninjured side of his mouth. Warrior swallowed each dose as though he was thirsty.

"That tea will calm him, make him sleepy, and prevent his wounds from swelling." explained Sarah.

Ahh, aspirin from the birch and willow barks...now I remember...As Warrior dozed, they sat around the table, drank tea and observed him.

"You must explain to me how the sea anemone numbed his pain," insisted Becca. "I've touched them before; I didn't feel any sting."

Sarah sat down her cup and began.

"My people have used them for years for pulling teeth that cause pain. The part Grandmother scooped out has a poison. It stings smaller creatures and paralyzes them for its food. It doesn't sting hard enough to hurt us, but when chewed or ground and placed in the mouth, its stinging parts cause the flesh and tongue to feel nothing."

It numbs...like Novocain...what do you know...

Becca was chopping cabbage, potatoes, and onions for supper, when Thad returned from having slipped off to town. Hannah ran into the kitchen.

"A new carriage is here," Her voice revealed excitement.

Becca wiped her hands on her apron, and moved to the window. In the excitement, she had forgotten her new carriage had arrived on the steamer. Thad moved around it, checking her purchase from top to bottom.

"Hannah, will you place these vegetables and a piece of salt pork in a pot with water, please? Annie will make the fry bread, soon."

She hurried out to view her new means of transportation. Thad looked up and smiled.

"It's a nice carriage, Delphi. I had no idea you were getting one so grand. It must have cost you a boodle."

"Yes, well, I received some advice that I should spare nothing up front to assure it provides reliable service for a long time." *Not to mention...the gal that advised me owns the gold that bought it...*

"Ride with me around to the barn. You can feel how it carries. I'll show you how to unhitch Bonnie and the Beast. But you must not attempt to hitch them or use the carriage until I have time to show you how to do so safely."

She giggled. "Please don't refer to Dublin as Beast. He'll begin to think that's his name."

"When he reforms his ways, I'll cease calling him Beast. For now, my concern is for you to remember my precautions. If you attempt to hitch this team and make an error, it may cause a serious mishap. I knew a young lad that died from such a blunder."

Thad opened the large barn doors and directed the horses to move through. He helped Becca out. She noticed the fine worked leather on the seats...*I can't wait to describe this to Delphi... she'll be really pleased...*

"Come around here, Delphi; don't move too close to Dublin's backside. I think we should start with Bonnie. Dublin will be better behaved because he'll want to follow her."

"Did they give you any trouble?"

"Not as a team, but on the way to town, Dublin tried to bite me on the leg a few times. I whacked his nose with the whip. You can't allow him to dominate you, Delphi. Once they were hitched to the carriage, their movement was as smooth as molasses."

Becca watched closely as Thad completed the task. "I'll get two buckets of water," she offered.

Thad measured out a bundle of hay for each of them. Becca returned with water. "Can you come back tomorrow for a riding lesson?"

"I'll come after I close the shop."

Glancing around to assure they were still alone, he pulled her to him. She looked up into his hazel eyes and saw his desire. He leaned in and lowered his head. She felt his breath touch her hair, and sensed his heartbeat. She closed her eyes and relaxed in his embrace. As his lips pressed against hers she felt electrified...He jerked away.

"Ouch!"

Startled, she looked to see what had broken their moment of magic. A loud snort from Dublin and Thad's curses solved the mystery. Rubbing his shoulder he snarled.

"The devil bit me. If he were mine I'd have shot him already. He deserves to be fed to the buzzards."

"I'm so sorry, Thad. He is naughty. He's probably getting even with you for smacking his nose. I think he'll get use to you... eventually."

Thad was still scowling as they walked toward the house. "Look, Thad, isn't that cart the one Mr. Leng uses for deliveries?"

They hurried around the side of the house and to the front gate.

Mr. Leng stopped and hopped out. He made a short bow and shuffled quickly to the back of the cart. Retrieving a brown paper bundle he returned to the couple and handed it to Becca.

"The wife work two days. Finish just for you." He smiled.

"Oh how nice of her, but she didn't have to rush with the order. I must send her a note. Please come in for tea, Mr. Leng. It's my riding skirt, Thad."

As the group sat around the dining room table drinking tea, Becca penned a note of thanks on soft blue stationary. Paying little attention to Thad and Mr. Leng's conversation, she placed her note in the matching envelope, added gold coins for payment, and sealed it with wax. Then, she caught a comment from Thad.

"There've been some killings further north; I hope the unrest doesn't spread."

She looked up at the two men. Mr. Leng's face held a sad expression.

"What killings, Thad? What are you two talking about?"

"Take nothing to heart, Delphi. It's just men's talk."

Mr. Leng took the blue envelope and left, promising to bring Mrs. Leng back for a visit. The sounds and smells from the kitchen gave promise of a hearty supper. Hannah brought a stack of plates to the table. "Thad, come with me to the drawing room, please."

The two stepped through the door, and Becca pulled the tapestry curtain closed. She placed her hands on her hips. "Now men's talk or not, you will tell me what you meant about killing!"

Thad studied her face. "Delphi, I don't want you worrying about something that might not happen."

"Well, I'll worry more if you don't tell me."

"There's been some trouble in some other places...trouble with the Chinese. People get all kinds of notions. They think the Chinese take their jobs...the best land ... complete with their businesses... You know folks...they blame them for all kinds of things. They're too blind to see that the same people they resent are also spending money in their town, and providing services they need. We're just hoping that kind of thinking doesn't commence here."

"What did you mean about killing, Thad?"

"There've been some run-ins in other places. Up north...further east... Mr. Leng's cousin was beaten badly. He'll be coming here. He got word to the Lengs, that some shop owners were burned alive in their stores."

Becca could feel the shock that Thad saw on her face. She placed her hand over her mouth.

"Now, Delphi, that's in other places. Don't get all disturbed thinking it's here. We don't want to say or do anything to get trouble started."

They talked no more about it, but it haunted Becca through supper. After Thad left, she climbed the stairs. Sinking into bed, she closed her eyes. Then they opened wide...*Darn...I have to visit Delphi...I promised.*

58

"The greatest conqueror is he who overcomes the enemy without a blow."

—CHINESE PROVERB

Becca lit her bedside lamp and propped up her pillows. Taking Delphi's journal and a pencil, she turned to where a ribbon held her place. Holding the book to the light she focused on Delphi's latest entry...

> Today we I received a message from your family attorney. He reports that Philip and his mistress have parted. Remember, I reported to you that she left her job in his company to dispel gossip after the accident. She soon commenced a romantic relationship with her new employer...*Ah ha, so she cheated on you too, Phil... deserves you right.*
>
> Since it is Sunday, it was unusual to hear from your representative, but he want to forewarn that Philip's attorney is ready with a new proposition and will call me on the morrow. He suspects that

your discarded spouse may want to propose reconciliation...*Oh no, I won't fall for that. He's just worried about splitting his recourses with me in a divorce...for all I know he'll try to kill me again.*

I must state my opinion. If you so choose to reconcile, we will need to resolve our intent to return to our own times. I have no attraction to this man or any man. I could not fill your position as wife. We must discuss what your desire will be in this regard...Delphi.

Becca aggressively wrote her reply. **My choice in this matter is a resounding no. I want no part of reconciliation. He tried to have me murdered. Even if the investigation could not find needed evidence, I know the truth. He believes because of your injuries, or rather the injuries to my body, there is mental weakness as well. Tell my attorney that my answer is no! ...Becca**

Becca blew out the flame and rested back on her pillows. She didn't feel the usual dizziness and spinning...*I wonder if I'm going to visit Delphi. This communication usually results in an out of body experience...*

She awoke in the early morning light, still in her propped-up position. She climbed out of bed and moved to the wash table. Splashing water on her face, she looked in the mirror...*You look a bit haggard, girl.*

She combed her hair, brushed her teeth, and then dressed in a fresh work dress. After slipping into her moccasins, she descended the stairs. The smell of coffee assured her that Annie was already in the kitchen. At the bottom of the stairs lay Warrior on a sheet. He looked up and whined a greeting. Becca sat on the bottom step and petted him, being careful to not touch his wounds. She went to the kitchen and poured herself coffee. Annie stirred her mixtures for Warrior's treatment.

One bowl contained the pulpy substance for his burn, and a cup held the cooling tea that would be spooned into his sore mouth

"Thanks so much for what you're doing for this poor animal, Annie." Becca patted her arm.

The older woman smiled. Becca put on her apron and stepped into the pantry. She selected several large carrots and two apples. Cutting the apples into quarters, she left the house through the back door. As she walked toward the barn, Bonnie walked to the gate that led into the fenced area. Becca stroked her face, scratched behind her ears, and spoke softly to her. She offered her one of the pieces of apple. Bonnie retrieved it carefully from her hand. Dublin, who stood at a distance, snorted. He laid his ears back and gave her a suspicious glare....*I wonder how I'll ever get you to trust me...*

As she studied him she remembered a documentary she had seen as a child...*Horse Whisper...that's what they called it...He trained horses gently without having battles with them...*

She pondered on his methods as best she could remember. Dublin kept his gaze focused on her. Becca ignored him as she pumped two buckets of water and set them inside the pen. She fed each of them an allotment of hay. As they ate and drank she slowly circled the fenced area, checking it for security. She explored the barn and wondered how she might make use of it for chickens...*Stop it! You won't be here long enough for chickens...*

Leaving the barn, she crossed the penned area. Bonnie walked up to her and nuzzled her shoulder. She gave her a carrot, speaking to her in gentle tones. Remembering Thad's experience with Dublin's biting, Becca kept him in her peripheral vision. She leaned on the fence and looked out toward the woods. She sensed Dublin watching her every move. The dappled horse sauntered in her direction and stopped a few feet away. She walked away, keeping her back to him. He approached her again. This time he made a snorting sound. It didn't sound aggressive. She walked away and stopped by the gate. He followed. As she passed Bonnie, she gave her a piece of apple. Sneaking a peek at Dublin, she noticed his ears were up and positioned forward.

She placed an apple chunk on the gate post and turned her back. Dublin stepped gingerly toward the gate, and stretched his neck to remove it. With his nearness, she could hear his munching. She placed a carrot on the post. This time she remained partially turned in his direction. Dublin stepped closer and took the carrot. She could hear his breathing and smell the horse flesh. She calmed herself...*I can't have fear...he'll sense it*...She felt his warm breath on her neck. She remained still, refusing to look at him. Dublin nudged her shoulder ever so slightly. Taking a risk, she lifted her last carrot, still not looking in his direction. Dublin carefully took it from her hand. She opened the gate and secured it behind her...*Maybe next time, we can talk...for now that will do.*

When Becca returned to the kitchen, Hannah and Sarah were eating oatmeal. She joined them as Annie placed a bowl on the table for her.

"Charley should be here soon to pick you up, Hannah" Becca reminded.

"I know," she replied, pretending to pout. "I wish I could stay here forever. Today, I have to do all that laundry. There'll be linens and towels from all the chambers used by those who came and left with the steamer."

"We need to do laundry here too." Becca mused, scooping up her last bite of porridge.

Annie turned her ear toward the open window as they heard Charley's carriage pull to a stop.

"Quick, Hannah, gather your things." Becca urged, " I'll offer him coffee, but you mustn't doddle. We want them to let you come every weekend."

Hannah rushed up the stairs to get her bag. Annie poured a cup of coffee for their guest. Becca led Charlie into the kitchen. He took off his hat and sat at the table. Stirring in two spoons of sugar, he helped himself to a piece of Annie's fry bread.

"Molly told me to bring you back with Hannah." He took a bite.

"Why? I just saw her yesterday. We have a lot of work to do around here today," Becca protested.

"Mrs. Walker is there. She came over very early this morning, and remains there talking to Molly. She wants to talk with you, but she feared she might not be welcomed here."

"The Reverend's wife wants to talk to me? Are you sure Molly isn't just trying to play peacemaker?"

Charlie shook his head. "I heard Mrs. Walker express her need to talk with you...heard it with my own ears." He dunked fry bread into his coffee.

I promised myself not to ever talk to the Walkers again...but Molly's my friend...I can't let her down...

Becca changed into a cream voile tea dress and the button-up shoes. *Thanks to Betsy for leaving this frock behind.*

She chattered cheerfully on the ride with Charley and Hannah. She wanted to cheer Hannah who dreaded the workday ahead of her. She was pleased that Annie and Sarah offered to do all the laundry. She wouldn't feel the need to hurry home. As she entered the hotel, she braced herself for Mrs. Walker...*What could she possibly want with me?*

She placed her parasol and shawl on an empty peg in the hall tree before walking into the parlor.

"I'm sure the ladies are in the kitchen," said Charley." Go on back and have a cup of coffee. I'll take you home when you're ready."

As Becca stepped into the kitchen, both women looked at her and smiled. Mrs. Walker sat at the table with a cup before her. Molly stood at the stove. She poured Becca a cup of steaming brew.

"Have a seat, Delphi. I'll get us a plate of cookies from the pantry."

She set the cup on the table opposite the minister's wife. Becca poured cream from a tiny pitcher. I need cream at the house. I must remember to ask Molly where she gets it.

"I'm so pleased you agreed to come and speak with me." Mrs. Walker attempted to break the tension.

"I came at Molly's request. She's been like a mother to me since I arrived in The Crescent. I want to assure you that I have no quarrel with you. Any conflict I've had is with your husband."

The woman looked down at her cup. She fussed with a teaspoon. Finally, she looked up. Her gray eyes looked troubled as she searched Becca's face.

"I want to apologize for my husband's behavior yesterday. He's... I'm sure you've become aware... he's unduly tense...at times."

Becca tried to think of an appropriate response. "Yes, I agree that your husband is both tense and intense."

Molly returned with a plate of oatmeal, raisin cookies. She placed them between the women and pulled up a kitchen chair.

"I feared Charley might have found them. We're fortunate that he didn't search the top shelf."

"I don't hold you responsible for your husband's rude behavior, Mrs. Walker. You needn't apologize to me for him."

"Please, call me Grace. I'd like to think we might become friends."

"And what would the Reverend say to that?"

Grace shrugged her shoulders. "You're like a light...a sunrise. Your thinking is fresh and new. New thinking frightens him, but I believe he'll grow accustomed to you if you can be enduring."

Becca shook her head. "I can endure a certain amount of meanness toward me, but I have no tolerance of his cruel and controlling behavior toward people I care about."

"Tell her about the beatings," coached Molly.

Grace cleared her voice. "I haven't shared this with anyone but Molly and Doc. I implore you to tell no one. Titus is shamed by the memories of his childhood."

Becca felt uncomfortable. "Perhaps you shouldn't tell me..."

"No, Molly is wise in advising me to do so. Then you may understand why he's intense. Titus's father died when he was a young child. His mother married his stepfather when he was eight-years-old. This man was cruel to both Titus and his mother."

Becca remained silent as she waited for the women to continue. Glancing out the window, she watched Hannah by a large kettle of water that heated over an open fire. The girl dropped several sheets into the iron pot, and poked them down with a stick.

"When Titus's mother married George, he took ownership of the farm she had with her first husband. He forced Titus and his mother to do all the heavy work that kept the farm productive. He beat them both regularly. Titus was allowed to attend school only a few months during the winter. George wouldn't allow his mother to even send a lunch with her son."

"This is sad, but why should he be mean to others?"

She watched Hannah drag the sheets from the scalding hot water with the stick. She placed them into a tub of cold water... *I wonder how she'll wring them out without my help.*

"Titus promised himself that he would take his mother away as soon as he was old enough. But she died when he was fifteen. He ran away after her funeral. He has always been angry about her death. He blames George. George often...well...he spent time with bad company in town...women."

"Prostitutes?"

Grace nodded. "He contacted Tuberculosis at the brothels. Once Titus's mother contacted it from him, she grew seriously ill. To Titus, George represents evil. He drank heavily, swore constantly, lied, and lived a life of sin, and his sin killed his mother. Titus hates sin or anything that reminds him of George or his youth."

"I understand that Reverend Walker had a painful childhood. But why did he become a minister? Ministers are called to reach out to sinners, not judge them. And his need to control everyone, that's just wrong!"

"Perhaps, it wasn't a wise choice for him...the ministry. He was an army chaplain when I met him. After leaving the farm, a clergyman hired him to clean the church, maintain the churchyard, and church cemetery. Remembering all the hard work farming, he thought the clergyman's job appeared to be quite trouble-free. I feel his regrets of having no control in preventing the death of his mother...I feel it causes him to be over controlling now."

Becca nibbled on a cookie, and glanced out at Hannah. She was struggling to hang a wet sheet on the line. A strong wind made her efforts more difficult than usual...*Poor Hannah; I wish I could help her. I'd rather do that than hear the Reverend's sob story.*

"The employer agreed to teach Titus reading and writing as part of his wages. Later, the pastor found a sponsor who helped him pay for him to attend seminary."

"So you see, dear, he is fighting a battle inside his head," Molly added.

Hannah was walking toward the boiling kettle with more sheets. The flames were licking the sides of the large iron pot as the wind whirled around it.

"I sympathize with you, Grace. It can't be easy to be married to an angry man who chose the wrong profession because he thought it would be easy. However, it doesn't give him a pass to browbeat the people he is supposed to help and love...**Oh! My God! Hanna's on fire...!**

59

"Wherever the art of medicine is loved, there is also a love for humanity."

—Hippocrates

Becca jumped up and rushed out the back door. Hannah jumped up and down, screaming. As she twisted and turned, her flaming petticoats became swirling rings of flame.

"Hannah! Drop to the ground!" Becca screamed.

The frantic girl could not process the command, and continued to fan the blaze with her movement. As Becca passed the clothesline, she grabbed a wet sheet and yanked it free from the wire. Hannah, in her aimless motion, tripped over the wood pile and fell. Becca reached her as she crumbled to the ground and threw the wet sheet over her body.

Dropping beside her, Becca pushed the wet sheet around the panicked teen, patting out flames with her hands. Molly and Grace were soon close by.

"Oh my, oh my, oh my," screamed Molly. Looking around, she spotted a fresh bucket of cold water fresh from the well. Becca saw her from the corner of her eye...No...don't throw the cold water on her...you'll cause shock...

The flames were out and Hannah lay sobbing. Becca turned as Molly came running with the bucket, water splashing from both sides. "No! Stop Molly! The fire is out!"

Molly paid no attention and gripped the handle with purpose in her eye. Becca lunged and blocked her attempt, catching the force and water with her torso. Grabbing the bucket she yanked. Molly held tight. Becca wrestled her to the ground.

"What are you doing?" the women screeched. "We have to cool her down!"

"No, not that way, it's too much too fast."

She looked up just in time to see Grace running from the kitchen, carrying Molly's lard jar...*Oh, no, not grease*...She tried to scramble to her feet but her wet skirts insisted on wrapping around her legs. On hands and feet, she scurried to Hannah's side just as Grace reached her. Hannah's burned skirts blew in the breeze, revealing horrid burns on her legs, from the tops of her button-up shoes to her thighs. Her pantaloons were charred.

"Here," Grace held out the jar. "Smear this on those burns."

Becca took the jar from her and set it on the ground. Then she noticed the burns on her own hands.

"No, Grace. That's the worse possible thing to do. We need to get her into the house and out of this wind."

She took the sheet off Hannah, folded it double, and spread it on the ground, next to the girl.

"Quick, help me lift her onto the sheet."

Molly now joined them and the three women gently lifted the whimpering girl onto the makeshift stretcher. Grace gripped the bottom of the sheet and Molly grabbed the top. Becca slipped her arms under the wet cloth to support Hannah's back. They inched their way to the house. As they laid her on the cot in her tiny room off the kitchen, they heard the front door close.

"That's Charley," said Molly. "I'll tell him to get Doc." She rushed from the room.

Becca carefully lifted the layers of burned petticoats...We can't have fabric sticking to her burned skin...She noted the burns were mostly on the front parts of her legs but some burns were blistering on her calves. Becca ran to the linen closet and grabbed two clean towels. She dunked them into the kitchen water bucket and rung them out. Her hands throbbed with pain.

Back in the little room, Grace sat beside Hannah and held her hand. Becca folded the wet towels and slipped them gingerly under the girl's burned calves. She carefully peeled off what was left of her long stockings. She cut off the garters.

Grace looked up and exclaimed, "Delphi, dear, your hands are burned."

"I'm fine for now."

"Delphi," Hannah rasped, "I want Annie. She can help me."

Molly entered the room. "Charley is going for Doc, Hannah. He'll know what to do. Meanwhile, let's get some of this into you, child."

Molly poured a spoonful of Mrs. Winslow Soothing Syrup into a large spoon. She pushed it toward Hannah who looked imploringly at Becca.

"I'll bring Annie here, Hannah." Becca assured her. "Doc respects Annie's burn remedy."

As Hannah opened her mouth to say thank you, Molly shoved the spoon of liquid in.

"Perhaps, I should hurry home and fetch Titus," suggested Grace.

"No," protested Hannah. "He was harsh with me in The Mercantile. He shamed me to tears. He'll bring me no comfort."

"But darling," soothed Grace. "He can pray."

"So can I," answered Hannah.

Grace proceeded to argue but caught Becca's disapproving eye. She silenced her debate.

Hannah had calmed by the time Doc arrived.

"What happened?"

Her skirts caught on fire from the flame under the wash kettle," explained Becca.

Doc looked around the room. "It's stuffy in here. I must ask everyone to leave the room so the child can breathe."

Molly and Grace moved out of the space and Becca followed.

"No, not Delphi," the girl protested. "I want her with me."

Becca returned to the wooden chair by her side. Doc made no objection. He examined her burns and shook his head.

"These are quite serious...quite serious, indeed." He opened his bag and took out a tin. I'll treat these wounds with salve. It'll be painful for her as I apply it. A dose of Laudanum will be required."

Becca reached across the bed and laid her hand on the doctor's arm.

"Please Doc, can't we have Annie treat Hannah's burns the way she treated Sarah's? The poultice she uses doesn't stick to the damaged skin...it allows air to heal the wound while protecting it."

Doc was quiet for a moment. "There's no doubt the old woman knows much about herbs, but this is a more serious burn and covers more area than that of her grandchild."

"I want Annie to treat me," insisted Hannah.

"Will the woman come here?"

"I'm sure she will."

"Can't I go to Delphi's house?" Hannah begged.

Doc pushed his spectacles up on his nose. "With her treatment, there's constant changing of the poultice, is there not?"

"Yes, every two hours at first and every four hours once healing begins. She keeps the wounds moist and clean with frequent exposure to air."

"This could be better tended at your house, but getting her there will present difficulty."

"In my new carriage, there's room to lay her down in the back. It's covered so she won't be exposed to sun or wind."

"We'll need to move her quickly. These wounds need to be tended. I'll go to The Print Shop and summons Thad. He can ride to your place and return with the carriage."

"That's a good idea. See, Hannah, I told you Doc would agree with Annie's treatment."

Doc reached out and took Becca hands in his. "Your burns are serious too, young lady. Be sure you get Annie's attention for these hands."

"I will, please hurry now and tell Thad the plan."

Doc placed the tin back into his bag, and handed Becca a bottle of Laudanum. "She'll need to be calmed when she gets past her numbness from the accident. One spoonful every few hours should suffice."

He stood up and moved toward the door. Then he turned around.

"Annie may be a doctor among her own people, but she is not a doctor under the law. Treating her own grandchild is a different matter than treating a white child who is not her relative. If something turns bad with Hannah, and it could...everyone will blame the old woman. That could have a serious outcome." *I hadn't thought of that.*

"Therefore, I'll observe Annie's treatment; learn the ingredients of the poultice. I'll take responsibility for the treatment. As far as anyone else will know, Annie is only assisting me."

He looked directly into Becca's eyes, searching for understanding.

"Gotcha," Becca assured him. Seeing his puzzled expression, she clarified her response to, "Yes sir, I understand your meaning."

After Doc left, Becca's attention turned to her painful hands. She examined them carefully. They were bright red, and the palms had large blisters. She felt nauseous... *I can't imagine how poor Hannah must feel. Her burns are much worse.*

She leaned back and concentrated on taking even breaths. Molly entered the room.

"Doc's gone to fetch Thad, dear. It shouldn't take long. Oh my, but you're pale, Delphi. You should take a dose of calming syrup."

"I mustn't fall asleep. I have to be awake to settle Hannah into the carriage and my house."

"Allow me to give you only a half spoonful, Delphi. It'll make the pain less intense."

She opened the bottle of Laudanum as she spoke. Filling the same spoon she had used for Hannah, she pushed it toward Becca's mouth.

Not sure about this...there's such a lack of medical knowledge...I guess if this didn't kill Harry when he drank an entire bottle... a spoonful won't hurt me...

After swallowing the sticky, bitter substance, she tried to get comfortable by repositioning herself in the chair.

"Delphi, you should lie down, dear. I fear you'll faint."

"I'll stay with Hannah."

"Hannah's sleeping. See; look at her calm, sweet face. She won't miss you if you rest on the sofa in the parlor."

Becca turned her head to view the girl. She was indeed resting calmly.

I won't leave her...someone will get a crazy notion to use grease, butter, or who knows what on her legs

She felt lightheaded. Leaning over in the chair, she placed her head on the pillow by Hannah's. She felt as though the throbbing in her hands, her heartbeat, and the sound of Hannah's breathing blended into oneness.

Then, strong arms pulled up from under her knees and another arm supported her back. She opened her eyes. She knew the chest in front of her face was Thad's. She recognized his shirt and his scent. Looking up she tried to protest.

"I can walk...only my hands are injured."

"Shhh, my darling. I'll have you safely home very soon."

"But Thad, we must move Hannah first."

"Doc and Charley will move her on a plank. Quiet now, you needn't fuss."

Thad left her on the front seat of her new carriage. He turned to return to the hotel. "Thad don't allow them to bundle her legs. I want nothing unsterile touching those burns. We must tent a sheet over her" she called.

It seemed to Becca that eternity passed before at last they reached her home. As they approached the property, she saw two long lines of laundry flopping in the wind. "It looks like Annie and Sarah have been busy," Thad commented.

Thad carried her into the house in spite of her dissent, and set her on the sofa. Annie and Sarah rushed into the room, both wide-eyed and questioning. Becca used minimal time and words to explain the accident.

The men carried Hannah in. She moaned. The ride disturbed the calm she had previously achieved and Becca knew her pain must be severe. They laid the board plank carefully on the floor.

Shall we take her upstairs?" Charley asked.

"I think they both should be situated downstairs," stated Doctor Conner. "It'll make treatment less complicated. Let's bring a mattress down to the drawing room."

Thad and Charley started for the stairs. Thad took the steps two at a time. Charley panted, his sweaty forehead testifying to the excursion he had just endured. Annie rushed to the kitchen to prepare tea and potion. Sarah hurried to the pantry and collected clean linens. Soon both Hannah and Becca were settled on the mattress that was covered with clean white sheets and pillows.

"Now we must put our patients into more comfortable clothing," ordered Doc.

"I'll take my leave," said Charley heading for the door.

Thad looked at Sarah, "Could you please gather some gowns for them?"

The girl ran upstairs. Doc removed scissors from his bag and gently cut off what was left of Hannah's burned skirt ...*Poor Hannah...she's so modest*...Sarah soon returned with a gown for each of them.

"Come. Sarah," summoned the doctor, "Help me remove this frock and underclothing."

Hannah appeared distressed. Becca noted that Sarah had no reservations in assisting with disrobing her friend...She has fewer inhibitions...She's lucky to have missed all the intimidation regarding modesty that Hannah has had...Doc quickly slipped Hannah's gown over her chemise and plumped up her pillows.

"You must avoid pushing the gown over your limbs, Hannah. It could stick to the skin when the blisters weep or break."

"But my limbs can't be out for all to see," the girl whined. "It's not decent."

"We'll tent the sheet to cover you after your treatment," he assured her.

Annie entered the room with a bowl of her herbal poultice. She knelt down by Hannah and began carefully applying the moist mixture. Hannah moaned. Annie began softly singing a native song. Although they could not understand the words, it resonated like a prayer. The repetitive, rhythmic, mournful melody calmed the girl.

Doc came around the mattress and squatted by Becca. Thad was besides her stroking her hair. "We must get you free from that corset, young lady. Those cussed things prevent women from breathing properly. You need to breathe deeply to prevent the duress from settling into your brain."

"I couldn't agree with you more about the corset... Wait, what are you doing?"

Thad had begun to unbutton her bodice and doc was removing her moccasins. "Darling, be sensible. You can't use those burned hands to undress."

"I agree," asserted Doc, pulling off one shoe and starting to untie the other. "You mustn't cause further injuries to those burned hands. I've known of people who required amputations for gangrene in such cases."

Sarah stepped forward. "I'll help Delphi into her gown. I had a burn; I know how to avoid injuring her hands."

Doc and Thad accepted their dismissal and moved to the parlor. Annie loosely wrapped Becca's hands in strips of wet cotton cloth filled with the poultice. Hannah watched as she drank the calming tea Sarah gave her. Annie gently tipped a cup of the brew to Becca's mouth. When the treatment was completed, Annie pulled the window shades and left the room.

"Delphi?"

"Yes, Hannah?"

"Do you think I'll be able to walk again?"

"Yes, Hannah. I have total confidence in Annie's treatment and your determination."

"Do you think your hands will be useful again?"

"Yes, let's think positive thoughts."

Feeling movement next to her, she looked to see Warrior crawling onto the mattress. "Well, there you are. I guess we'll all recover together."

He gently sniffed her bandages and laid his head on her arm. Annie's tea made Becca drowsy. Its effect was not like the Laudanum, causing a more natural relaxation. The throbbing eased in her hands and she closed her eyes. Hannah's regular breathing suggested that she had fallen asleep. She could hear Annie in the kitchen. The two hour treatment regimen would keep the older woman busy all day and night. Becca began to drift...

"What in mercy's name have you done to my hands?"

She startled, and opened her eyes. *"Delphi?"*

60

"Humankind has not woven the web of life. We are but one thread within it."

—Chief Seattle (1780 - 1866)

The pale, blue, vapor hovered over her. "My hands...they're bandaged."

I burned them patting out flames. Hannah's skirts caught fire. I don't feel like explaining more...did you bring news?

"Not good news. It's was the most distressful day."

What happened? Is Beth alright?

"She is well in regard to health. I believe her fondness for the Captain grows stronger. I've concluded that the interest I thought he had in me was really for her. But she's greatly grieved about today's meeting."

Oh that's right...the attorneys met today.

"Not only did the attorney meet, but Phil, Beth and I as well."

You were firm, I hope. I want a divorce, end of story.

"Well, I attempted to convey your feelings but...Phil and his attorney presented the argument that I...well you... that I'm not compliant enough to make such a serious decision."

Compliant? I don't understand...

"Ahh...In regard to your thinking...you mind."

Competent?

"Oui, they pointed out that the examination with one doctor revealed a very low QT. They say scores show a serious decline. I don't understand to what they are referring."

It's IQ not QT. It's an evaluation given by a psychologist. It was necessary to apply for disability benefits. You must remember someone asking you a lot of questions?

"Oui, it was foolish. He asked me if I knew who the president is. I told him Mr. Lincoln was recently murdered. He frowned. What other answer did he expect? Now I know the correct answer, but I did not at that time."

That experience must have been frustrating. There's no way someone from another century could pass an IQ test in the twenty-first. Especially, with English being your second language.

"They are using my French and my playing piano as issues as well. The attorney asked Beth if I...you, of course...If I had had ever taken French classes or had spoken the language before, or if I played piano. She had to say, "No.""

Beth could never lie.

"They insist such changes of behavior and personality are connected to brain trauma or personality disorder. I believe they were saying I'm a lunatic. He now says he believes you deliberately jumped from the boat, and that it proves you are a danger to yourself."

Phil is such a jerk! He's looking out for himself, as always.

"He's going to seek a power of the court to handle all your affairs unless you agree to reconciliation."

Oh...this is bad news...I'll have to give it some thought...

"He frightens me... I want to change back to my time...If you were back in your body, you could prove you are in your right mind. I've been thinking about it much."

I thought I had Cain talked into making the first attempt by changing with Jonah. But that's not working out. He doesn't want to return to his century. He may now be in San Francisco for all I know. Jonah will receive better care there, there's no one for him here.

"Beth is taking me with her to Crescent City on Thursday. We'll bring Jonah back to Portland. Beth was awarded custody and wants to place him in a group home where he'll be safe and provided with care and training."

What's your idea?

"Since The Crescent is where this began, we will place ourselves at a chosen location, at the same time of day. We'll carry our journals, I'll post in your diary and you'll read my message from my journal. One of us should become disembodied. Perhaps we both will. At that moment, we can exchange bodies, just as we did before."

That does seem possible, though it may result in death to one or both of us. I'm not sure how I can travel to another location. I can't use my hands, or rather, your hands. Sarah will help me if we don't have to go far.

"I could come here, to this house. You're already here."

I'm not sure this house is standing in the twenty-first century. There'll be several Tsunamis between now and then. The Brother Jonathan cemetery would be better. Beth will be able to drive you there, and push your wheelchair right up to the edge.

"That is a splendid idea. I'll plan it all with Beth. She'll be enraptured to have you back."

Tears filled Becca's eyes. Not being able to wipe them away, they rolled down her cheeks. She looked at Hannah, sleeping.

You must promise to take care of Hannah, Annie, and Sarah. And, you must be kind to Thad. You must take good care of Warrior, he's suffered so much.

"Oui, I promise. I'll agree to anything to avoid living with your retched spouse."

The darkness in the late afternoon lightened as Annie, with a candle and a bowl of fresh poultice, entered the room. She set both on the desk and approached Becca. Stopping, she looked directly at the blue vapor. She frowned.

"I think she sees me."

She's a medicine woman...she's spiritual and wise...

Annie looked closely at Becca in the dim light. The woman gently brushed the tears from her patient's cheeks. Turning toward Delphi, she spat out.

"GO! Leave this dwelling now."

"No, Annie, don't send her away, you don't understand."

Delphi vanished.

"The spirit made you sad...not good."

"Annie, you're speaking English."

Annie smiled.

"I need to talk with someone. Will you hear me out and advise me in English?"

The old woman nodded. "But I must tend your wounds first."

Hannah stirred and groaned.

"Its okay, Hannah, Annie is dressing our burns. The pain will be less when she's finished."

"The spirit that comes... who is it?" The old women rasped as she folded clean strips of cloth around Becca's hands. She moved to the other side of the mattress. She gently raised the sheet that tented the girl's legs.

"Annie, have you ever heard of a spirit leaving a body and entering another?"

The medicine woman nodded.

"Our spirit leaves our body when we go to Father Spirit. Our bodies return to Mother Earth."

"But I mean, while the person still lives, have you heard of that?"

Annie gently lifted the poultice from Hannah's burns. "The fever is less."

Becca waited. She knew from her talks with Sarah that rushing the story wouldn't bring faster responses from either of these women.

Annie focused on her task and didn't look up. "Some... only a few, those very powerful with medicine...they can do it."

"They can? Do they do it on purpose? Why would they choose to?"

"They do it for reasons...sometimes to protect another...sometimes to find knowledge they need to learn...sometime to chastise themselves...it's called shape-shifting."

Becca processed Annie's brief explanation. "I've heard of that. A person turns into an animal and then back again?"

Annie moved to treat Hannah's other leg. "A person wills his spirit to enter an animal...it might be an eagle so that he can fly over another place and learn what is happening. Sometimes a relative wills himself to enter the body of a dog to follow and protect a grandchild or spouse. Sometimes, a person who has harmed others punishes himself by entering an animal and surviving alone until he has reformed his ways."

Annie's voice was in a harsh whisper as though by not speaking aloud, she could believe she wasn't speaking English, or maybe in reverence to the subject at hand. Becca strained her ears and peered through the dim light to be sure she caught all of what the woman said.

"Does that happen among your people often?"

Annie shook her head and positioned the sheet over Hannah. "No, only for good reason, though some do it for evil and greed. Bad medicine will come to them."

Becca sensed that the woman preferred the conversation end, but she needed to know more.

"I'll get tea for both of you." Annie stood and shuffled to the kitchen.

I'm not sure if I believe her. I always thought shape-shifting was superstition...but then I'd never believed one could go back in time...

Annie returned with two cups of warm calming tea. She handed one to Hannah and brought the other to Becca. After Becca had allowed her to scoop a spoonful into her mouth she continued.

"Have you ever done this, Annie? Have you entered an animal's body?"

The woman spooned in more tea. "No, I have never had good reason. When I need to hear...or learn...I pray. The Spirit Father sends me dreams. Why are you asking these questions?"

"The spirit you saw...she is the real Delphi...this is her body. That's why she came...she wants it back."

"It is bad medicine...someone has cursed you...it's a trick. You must chase her away with your thoughts. Never, never talk to her. It gives her power."

"No listen please...I am really Rebecca Cates. I first lived one-hundred-fifty years from now. ..in the future. I was in an accident... well, actually an attempted murder...and I think I may have died for a moment."

Annie looked into her face with her black filmy eyes. Becca wasn't sure how clearly she could see, but the woman had seen her tears so she met her gaze.

"This event was one-hundred-fifty years to the very hour of when Brother Jonathan went down. Another young woman named Delphi Castile was on that steamer. I believe she also died for a brief moment. Our spirits switched bodies. Now she is there and I am here."

The old woman sat back on her bottom, and pulled her legs up. She placed her arms around her knees and stared for a while at the candle.

"Annie, you're one of the wisest people I know. Can you tell me how that could happen and why? Why would we cross time...?"

Annie cleared her throat. "To my people, there is no such thing as time. That is a word of the white man. We do not make calendars or clocks. We follow the seasons and our lives move in harmony with them. Yesterday...tomorrow...today...what does it matter? We are now...you are now...the spirit that was here...she needs to be in her now."

Becca was quiet. *I don't think she understands...she can't help me...*

Annie's voice broke the silence. "What happens can not happen without the Spirit Father willing it. It can't happen without Mother Earth giving her blessing... You are here and the other woman is there because of Father Spirit and Mother Earth. They have made it happen for a purpose."

"But it's so hard to live in a time...well...another life...when it isn't what or like you're use to living."

"Yes...my people are learning too... We must learn to accept the ways of the white man and his government while remembering our ways...The Spirit Father wants us to learn. White people must learn from us as well. Life is about changing."

"What could possibly be the purpose for what happened to me?"

"You are here...now... to learn... here to teach...you are here for a purpose."

"If Delphi and I try to force our spirits to change back...do you think it'll work?"

"If the Spirit Father wants you to change, you will. It can not be your plan. It's never wise to go against his wisdom or that of Mother Earth."

She took the cups and candle back to the kitchen. Becca cried into her pillow...I'm not sure what to do.

61

"Cherish her and she will exalt you; embrace her and she will honor you."

—King Solomon

Becca dozed off but awoke when Sarah and Annie assisted Hannah in using the chamber pot. "What time is it?" she asked.

Both Annie and Sarah looked at her without answering...It's time for Hannah to use the toilet, I guess...She smiled at herself. She had already forgotten what Annie had explained about her feelings regarding clocks.

"I need to use the pot too," she announced. "And I must feed and water the horses...some how."

The women helped Hannah back onto the mattress. "Thad is doing that," said Sarah.

"Thad's here now? Becca's mood brightened.

"Yes, and he said Doc will be over after supper," explained Hannah, grimacing as Annie repositioned her.

"Grandmother says for you to wiggle your toes often," said Sarah." It'll prevent your skin from growing tight and useless."

Becca finished using the chamber bucket. She needed Sarah's help with pantaloons and nightgown. She walked into the kitchen where a basin remained available at all times'. *..Silly me, I can't wash my hands.* Annie returned to the kitchen, and reached for the small bar of lye soap.

"I'm feeling less pain, Annie. Do you think I could disperse with these bandages?"

The women dried her hands and signed a half circle conveying after sunrise... *Guess we're back to sign language...* Annie moved to the stove where a good smelling stew simmered.

"The stew smells like chicken, Annie. Did someone bring us a chicken?"

The women shook her head. She made a motion that meant bird and pointed toward Sarah, who had just entered the room.

Becca voice showed surprise. "With her spear? Her arm is still healing."

"With a snare," informed Sarah. "I hunted most of the afternoon and caught two quail."

Thad walked in the backdoor. He carefully cleaned his boots on a mat. Seeing Becca caused him to break into a smile.

"You appear to feel better," he offered as he approached her. "Are you still in dreadful pain?"

"Not so much now," she accepted his embrace though her bandaged hands prevented her from returning it properly.

"I need to talk with you about something very important. I have something to explain."

"As do I, but, it must wait. Annie is setting the table for supper, and we won't keep her waiting."

As they sat around the table, Becca looked around at her friends. Thad sat across from her and Sarah next to him. Annie remained in the drawing room assisting Hannah with her meal...*I should just blurt it out. Annie had no difficulty believing me... he might not either.*

Thad ladled stew into her bowl. Tiny pieces of white meat, onions and turnips floated in a milky liquid.

"Now, I've never fed anyone before, so I plead for your patience," He lifted a spoonful, blew on it until the liquid cooled, and put it to her mouth.

She swallowed the soup, "Salt...it needs salt."

Thad reached for the shaker. "Thad, there's a lot you don't know about me..."

Another spoonful found its way to her mouth. "We have a lifetime to learn each other's secrets, my dear."

Swallowing, she responded, "I might not have a lifetime here... that's why I need to explain something."

Another scoop of warm liquid filled her mouth. "Now dear, your burns were painful, but not life threatening. We'll both live long healthy lives. My father is still alive and he's reached the ripe old age of fifty-five."

Fifty...that's not old...

"I haven't always been me...like this...I used to be someone else. What are you searching for in your pocket?"

"Since you're so persuaded to talk rather than eat, I'm going to confess my secret."

Sarah stood up and picked up her bowl. "I'll start washing the dishes," she announced.

Thad laid his closed fist on the table. Watching Becca's face, he slowly opened his hand and released its contents. Becca caught her breath. A gold ring with a mounted pearl glistened in the lamplight. A blue ribbon looped through to allow it to be worn as a necklace.

She wanted to reach for it and remember she couldn't. "Thad, it's so pretty, is it for me?"

"I want you to wear this as a symbol of our betrothal. On our wedding day, I'll place it on your finger. Your hands will be healed by then."

Becca fought back tears. She looked into Thad face. His hazel eyes had gold flicks from the lamp light. She focused on the sensuous smile beneath his well trimmed mustache. It revealed white, even teeth...

This man is the nearest to perfect that I'll ever meet. I would love to say yes. Delphi doesn't want to be married...I can't say no...it's against my heart...but...do I have a right to him? Will I be here?

Thad stood and slipped the blue ribbon over her head, and positioned the ring on her chest.

"Now, my lady, don't look worried. I've told you my secret, and I'll pay full attention to yours. But, there's nothing you can tell me that will assuage my affection for you."

Leaning over, he kissed away a tear that had cascaded over her lashes.

"There, there, my darling. Please tell me these tears are for joy."

The door in the front parlor opened and closed. Becca remembered that Doc was stopping in to check on them...*I can't tell him now...I'll have to have privacy ...I must pull myself together first...*

Doc stopped in the drawing room. Becca could hear his voice speaking with Hannah. She stood and excused herself.

"I want to see what Doc has to say about Hannah."

Thad stood and announced, "I really need to get back to The Print Shop. I trained Harry today, and I'm behind-hand. I'll work late tonight."

He pulled her to him and kissed her. She felt no passion, only anxiety.

She settled into a rocking chair and watched Doc. He carefully looked at Hannah's burns while Annie held a lamp.

"Is the pain dwindling, dear?" he asked the girl.

"It still hurts dreadful."

"The burned skin remains pliable. Don't do anything to break the blisters. It will happen, but as long as they're in place, the flesh under them is safely healing. The redness around the serious wounds is less."

"Annie says I should wiggle my toes often."

"As well you should, Hannah, it will keep the blood flowing through your limbs. As soon as you can tolerate moving your feet and ankles, you should do so. We want your skin to remain pliable. "

The doctor stood and walked over to Becca. He unwound her hands and examined them. "The pain, is it still severe?"

"Only when I move them, do you think I can leave off the wrappings except for when the poultice is applied?"

"No, you're a rambunctious young lady. The blisters on your palms have broken. The burns are less serious than Hannah's. However, the wounds are open and gangrene could settle in. Especially the way you're so hardihood in all things you do."

He looked at her and smiled good-naturedly. "I see Mr. Barrett has offered you his hand. You're wearing the ring. I'm pleased you accepted. He's a dashing fine man ... in the mind of a young woman, I should think."

"You knew he was planning to propose?"

"I was in the store when he ordered the ring. He forced me to take a vow of silence."

"Doc, could I talk with you privately in the parlor?"

"Certainly, Delphi, and perhaps Annie will provide us with some tea."

In the parlor, Doc lit two lamps and carefully placed them to provide adequate light for interaction. Sarah carried in a tray with two cups or tea; regular for Doc and Annie's calming tea for Becca.

Becca whispered a request to the girl. She scurried up stairs to Becca's chamber. Doc stirred sugar into his steaming brew.

"So what is so troublesome to you that you need a private conversation, dear Delphi?"

"What I'm going to tell you is complicated, Doc. I plead with you to withhold snap judgment and keep an opened mind."

Doc looked concerned. "If you are inclined to reveal that you are with child, I wouldn't condemn you, Delphi. Many of my women patients are with child when they marry. At the birth I simple report that the babe is a bit premature. Reality and people's expectation are not always aligned. "

"Oh no, Doc, I'm not pregnant. Thad and I haven't become that intimate. This is a more serious matter than that."

The older man raised his brows in question.

"Doc, do you believe the human spirit can leave the body in which it dwells?"

The doctor took a sip of his tea, and placed the cup back on the saucer.

"I am a scientist, my dear. I prefer to say I believe what can be proven. However, I could not have practiced the arts of healing this long without being witness to things I can't explain."

Becca silently studied his face.

"There have been two instances I could not explain, and in consultation with other physicians, I've learned that they also have made the same observation."

He took another drink of tea...Oh get on with it, for goodness sakes.

Sarah returned and handed Becca an item. Doc straightened his handlebar moustache and pushed up his spectacles.

"In one instance, my patient was a girl-child, and in the other a grown woman. These events were years apart from one another. In both situations my patients died. I have no doubt of this. I could not find a pulse, and the looking glass under their noses showed no vapor, or breath."

Hmmm...That's how death is determined ... a bit disconcerting...

"I have no idea how long their death trance lasted as I was occupied with the grief of the family. The child's mother began to wail. She then rushed to the bedside, grabbed up the child and shook her violently. To my astonishment, the child gasped and coughed."

"She was alive?"

"She is now a married woman with six children of her own. The other case was similar."

He repositioned himself on the sofa, crossed one leg over the other and gazed upward, as though drawing from distant memories.

"The other instance was many years ago in my early practice. I was called to the bedside of a middle-aged woman who had mistakenly eaten poisonous mushrooms. My mentor was her doctor. He was occupied with a birth. He sent me in his stead. He advised me that nothing could be done to intercept the poisons; death was certain. I went with the intention of providing comfort as best I might."

At this rate we'll take all night to get to my story...but I have to ease him into it...don't want him thinking I have brain fever.

"A few minutes following my arrival, the woman passed. I found no pulse and no vapors on the looking glass. I turned to offer my condolences to her husband, and to offer setting with the corpse through the night. As soon as he left the room, the woman opened her eyes and demanded a drink of water."

"I don't understand how these stories, though very interesting, answer my question about body and spirit."

"I'm approaching the conclusion, Delphi. What a restless soul you are. In both of these cases, each patient later related similar testimony. They claimed to have left their bodies, hovered at the top of the room, and to have watched the occurrences from that perspective."

"Interesting...why do you think that happened?"

"Well, here again, in regard to science, I can prove nothing. My personal belief is that God, in his wisdom, determined the outcome. The illness of the child, and the poison in the woman could have ended their lives, but the higher power intervened. The child is still alive and involved in all matters of charity. The woman lived another fifteen years and raised an orphan-child who grew up to be a clergyman. Does that answer your question?"

Becca nodded. "Now imagine, if you will, that both patients are in the same room when their deaths occur. Then picture the spirits becoming confused, and each entering the wrong body."

Doc Conner finished his tea. He shook his head. "I can't imagine it, as I've seen nothing like that."

"But, if it is possible that the spirit could go in and out as you described, what I described would also be possible...don't you agree?"

"He was thoughtful...I suppose...but why does this interest you?"

"It interests me because I experienced it."

The man straightened and sat forward. "Recently?"

"At the time of the ship wreck."

His eyes were focused on her face with keen attention. "Tell me more."

"On July thirtieth, almost four months ago, I was thrown from a yacht...er...boat. It was a murder attempt by my husband, but I tell you that part later..."

Doc's eyebrows knitted. "You're married?"

"Does that date mean anything to you?"

After a brief ponder he responded. "Yes, Brother Jonathan sank."

"Correct, and I was in the water, fighting for my life while passengers from the steamer fought for theirs. I found myself sharing a wooden plank with another desperate woman... a young lady with a French accent."

"You believe that you left your body?"

"I know I did. I believe that I died from the abuse the waves gave us. I believe she died from drowning. She had a heavy bag tied to her waist."

She studied his face; He didn't appear to have doubts so she continued.

"When I was again conscious, I was no longer in the body that is mine but in this one...here...instead."

Doc remained silent in anticipation.

"Doc, I was born a freckled, red-head. I was tall, taller than you. I was athletic, educated...I was a teacher in Portland. Now my spirit inhabits a tiny, body with olive skin and dark brown hair. What else could have happened?"

Doc pushed his spectacles up on his nose and looked away, in thought.

"That is extraordinary...yes indeed."

"My name is really Rebecca Cates, and I was born and raised in Portland. This woman is Delphi Castile who was raised in Louisiana."

Doc looked back at her. "Yes, I was bewildered when I heard that. You have no manner of speaking that indicates a southern belle."

"When you first examined me...you though I was babbling from shock...remember? But I was telling you the truth. I didn't yet know that my spirit was misplaced"

"The other woman...she died?"

"No, she is very much alive. She inhabits my body...my original body."

The doctor's expression brightened. "That's wonderful, I must meet her."

Becca shook her head. "No, you see........."

He rushed on. "Can't you foresee what a revelation this will be to science? With both of you to testify and witnesses the experience... we can open the door to the death mystery."

Oh dear, now he's gone scientist on me.

62

"The best thing about the future is that it comes one day at a time."

—Abraham Lincoln

"Doc, there's more to this...and here's where it gets complicated."

He brought his attention back to her.

"Perhaps you haven't heard of this, but in the future there'll be those who believe that time is a continuous spiral, separated by a veil...opened by a portal. ...Try to imagine that, just for the sake of hypotheses."

His eyebrows knitted again. He rested back, as he placed an arm over the back of the sofa.

"I, Rebecca, lived in the twenty-first century, one-hundred-fifty years from now. On July thirtieth, two thousand and fifth-teen, I was thrown from a boat. My theory is that I passed through the portal to eighteen sixty-five. Delphi's spirit is in my body there...far away in time."

He shook his head. "I'm not sure there's science or observation to endorse that theory."

"Remember the man you treated soon after the wreck, he told you his name was Cain? He also passed through the veil. He is really Ike, the man that pushed me overboard. I held to him so tightly, I took him over with me."

Doc frowned. "That's your husband?"

"No, he was hired to kill me. His spirit exchanged with another drowning victim, Jonah McCain. Jonah's spirit is in Ike's body in the later era. Ike has completely changed; the experience was good for him. Jonah is faring better as well."

The doctor laid his head back, and rubbed his forehead. "This is bewildering, Delphi. If I didn't know you well enough to believe in your integrity, I would think you insane."

OK, it's time to bring out the evidence... She handed him the journal Sarah had retrieved for her. "Read the last ten or so entries. You'll see that they are in different handwritings and clearly written by different people. You'll also read my fist entry where I explained my situation, and you'll note her responses."

Doc leaned over to cast light on the pages. He adjusted his glasses and read silently. He handed it back to her. "It's very convincing, but scientifically one would argue it could be an improvised deception."

"Remember, when I saved little Delford? I used a method I learned in my own era. It hasn't yet been discovered in yours."

Doc raised his head and looked into her face...*Good I got him back...*

"It's called CPR and rescue breathing but don't worry about the labels. In my time all teachers, medical professionals... most people actually, learn these procedures."

Doc's eyebrows were again forming a uni-brow. "Tell me more..."

"And Hannah's burns...my interference with you're treatment... that's because I've learned in First Aid training what's best."

"Just in the pretense that I can accept your hypotheses, tell me what other discovers will occur in medicine."

"Well, for one thing, they'll determine that bleeding a patient is not a cure for anything, and can be harmful."

"Blood letting will cease?"

"Yes, and hand washing will become most important in preventing infection and illness."

"Will there be cures for small pox, cholera, diphtheria, measles...?"

"Yes, both cures and preventions...."

"And leprosy and tuberculosis?"

"Drugs will be discovered that stops leprosy in its tracks, and TB will be controlled, but new diseases will develop that are just as deadly."

"Delphi," he said with excitement in his voice. "Think of all you can teach me...I can write articles...teach others...we can save lives..."

Oh no, we're off track again..."Doc, what I really need to ask is this; do you think it's possible to change my spirit back to my birth body?"

Hi eyes widened. "Why ever would you want to do that? You have everything here that a woman could want, and a man that loves you."

"The other spirit wants her body back. I got the best deal in the bargain. She's stuck in my body that is recovering from a broken back. It may never walk again...that's yet to be seen. She lives with my sister who is falling in love, and will probably marry. She may relocate...who knows. My husband from that era is threatening to seek power of attorney over her...he thinks it's me...she wants her life back."

"Goodness, all the more reason why you should wish to remain here."

"Yes, well, we've always...more or less... had an understanding we would change back. I worry that it will result in one or both of us dying."

"As well you should worry. I'd advise you to put that notion out of your mind."

Becca explained the plan Delphi had proposed. "So... I wondered if you think it's possible, and if you'll assist me in getting to the cemetery Thursday...if I decide to go through with it."

"I will not. It would be to me like assisting in your death for which you know, I took a vow to preserve sustainable life."

His expression and voice softened. "Delphi...Rebecca... dear, There are two kinds of death. One is of natural causes when disease strikes or the body or parts wear out. The spirit is forced from the body because it loses its place of habitation."

He took a deep breath. "The other form is not natural. Murder, accidents, and suicide take lives before their bodies are ready to surrender the spirit. In the cases I witnessed, the passing of the spirits, in and out, was smooth and not forced. "

He reached out and took her bandaged hand. "In your experience of unnatural death, something mysterious intervened to preserve your life. To orchestrate something so spiritual...I feel you would enter an unknown, one quite perilous. I implore you to accept your lot. The other woman should do likewise."

"Thank you Doc. I'll give your advice serious thought. Please don't tell anyone of what I shared with you."

"Your secret is safe, my dear." He stood and collected his hat and bag. Becca walked him to the door. As he opened it he turned.

"I was thinking as you spoke. Perhaps this has happened many times. Think of the many masters whose wisdom progressed civilization. They seem to be far ahead of the knowledge of their day. Aristotle, Galileo, Leonardo, and many others that come to mind, might they not have drifted from another time?"

Becca smiled and placed a bandaged hand on his arm. "Then, you believe me?"

He gently laid his hand on hers.

"As a scientist...never... as a friend...most certainly."

Becca locked the door and returned to the drawing room. Annie sat on the floor by Hannah, dressing her burns...*It's unbelievable how that old woman gets up and down from the floor...her' mobility is amazing...* Several lamps gave the room a cozy feeling.

"How's our patient? Becca asked.

Annie looked up and smiled... *Guess that suggests a good prognosis.*

Hannah smiled at Becca. It was the first smile Becca had seen from her since before the accident.

"The constant burning is not so severe," she said.

Becca sat in the rocker. She struggled with the decision she must make. Sarah sat by a lamp and looked at the pictures in the children's book, Flower Children. She noticed one of her own novels, Lady's Audly's Secret, laid on the mattress by Hannah. ..*I didn't know she was reading that one...It's racy for a teen to read in this era...well, they expect her to work like an adult...I'm not taking it away from her...she's had very little time to practice reading skills...*

Annie stood up and approached Becca with the poultice. "I could have come to you, Annie."

Annie removed the bandages. She sponged the burns with the special tea, patted the skin dry and applied the poultice. As the woman loosely wrapped her hands, Becca looked around the room. The evening was absorbing a chill from the dropping temperature outside. The lamps added some heat, but the wood stove would be needed in the near future...*I'll need to arrange a delivery for fire wood... Hannah, Sarah, and I aren't up to chopping and stacking it, that's for sure... I'll talk to Thad about it... it feels so cozy...the girl's both reading...Annie mothering all of us...I should take advantage of our recovery time and provide schooling for them...I could include the Farris children... Wait, what am I thinking? I have a decision to make by Thursday...*

Warrior crawled to Becca's feet and nudged her bare feet. She spoke soothing words to him, and then thought of his future.

"I wonder if he'll ever walk on all fours again," she said aloud.

Hannah looked up from the book. "I spoke of it to Doc. He examined his legs and said nothing is broken, just chewed up badly. He believes he has a few broken ribs. He said ribs mend themselves, and Warrior will start walking when it ceases to cause him pain or discomfort."

Becca sighed relief. Then her eyes fell on the Bible that set on the table by her chair... *I could use this down time to read the passages Minnie suggested...I'd never be able to turn the pages with these bandages...*

"Hannah, I see you're enjoying my novel, but I wonder if you'd mind reading some Bible passages aloud."

Hannah looked up and nodded agreement. A few minutes later Becca laid by her on the mattress. Hannah leafed through the Bible to the book of Matthew.

"Do you think that's where we should start?" Becca asked as she eyed the colorful picture depicting the babe in a manger...*This bible has such lovely pictures. I don't remember such beautiful art in the bibles in my previous life.*

"You said you wished to hear about Jesus, Delphi. This is where we start for it, everyone knows that."

Becca smiled as she thought back to how much the phrase once annoyed her. Now it was a part of Hannah that was endearing.

Hannah read surprisingly well. The Shakespearian language smoothly flowed over her tongue...*She's conditioned from listening to all those long sermons in church...no doubt...*

When Hannah placed the attached ribbon between pages to mark her place and closed the book, Becca noticed Sarah had laid aside her book to listen. Annie was relaxed in a rocker, and appeared to have been listening as well.

"He was such a gentle person and he taught such wonderful things, I wonder why some people try to make religion so harsh?"

She received no answer. Annie stood and moved around the room, blowing out the lamps. Sarah followed her out. Becca settled her head into the feather pillow. Suddenly, Warrior raised his head and growled. Becca peered through the darkness.

"Is that cantankerous old woman gone?"

Delphi?

Becca sit up. She spoke reassuringly to Warrior. *Annie's not cantankerous.*

"Oui, but she is. She chased me away, last time I visited."

She mistook you for an evil spirit.

"I wanted to inform you that Beth's working on a plan. She called the special doctor... the one with the silly test.

The psychologist?

"Oui, we'll meet with him tomorrow. Beth will go with me. Her plan is to have him recommend Philip be prohibited any contact or control of me. We'll stress that my fear of him, whether founded or not, is my...well...your reality."

It's a well- founded fear, but I understand how everyone around you may see it as paranoia.

"So...if our plan to change bodies succeeds on Thursday, your defense will be in place."

Have you given thought to the possibility that one or both of us might not make the change and could die?

"No, but Beth's concerned. What else can we do? The longer we prolong the decision...the more difficult it'll be to adjust into the lives each of us reshaped for the other. Beth says she prefers keeping things the same if it means we could all live happily. She fears one of us will not survive."

We've both already died, Delphi. But our spirits failed to move on and returned to bodies that were not their own. Both of us, through no power of our own, defeated fate... once. We're tempting fate to attempt this switch.

"Why do you both think in that way? We don't die when we visit one another."

Because one of us still occupies a body. When we both depart the bodies simultaneously, we may move on to our afterlives.

"But what happened...what kept us on earth...it must have been caused by God."

If so, then where he placed us where he wanted us to be.

"I understand your reasoning, but I can't bear living a life in your world. It's far too difficult. Beth advises me to take a class to learn how to use the...the contraption she calls computer. The stinging sensation moves up my limbs now. I can hardly get sleep."

You'll learn computer skills easily, Delphi, you're a smart woman. And the sensation in your...my legs is good...it's healing. You'll soon have use of your...my legs.

"Oui, that reminds me of another trial. I'll be starting a new therapy next week, or you will if we succeed with the change. I don't look forward to it."

What kind of therapy?

"Allow me to remember...its exo ...exoskeleton...it'll be difficult...but helpful."

I remember learning about that. It's like a robot walking machine that forces the patient's legs to work. It's been very successful. I once saw a woman in a Portland park walking with one.

"Oui…because the doctor believes your spine is healing, and the spinal cord is transferring feeling and impulses to your legs, it's most important to retain and prepare the muscles and joints."

I'm impressed. Your English has improved greatly as well as your understanding of the twenty-first century. You'd now find it as difficult to adjust to this time if you were to return.

"Perhaps, but I have no hope for a future in your world. The income I'll receive will be very low. I can teach music, but not earn enough to support myself. Everything is so expensive, and it seems people need so much more of everything. I'm sure Beth and Captain Gale will soon want to marry, and I don't want to be a burden to her. I fear Philip dreadfully, and I'm weary of struggling with your body's pain and disrepair."

So…if the choice is between continuing as you now live, or dying in an attempt to change us back…you would want to take that chance?

"Oui…I will take the chance."

I see. Well I have fifty-percent of the decision, and I'm not willing to die for the change. It's not because of a fear of Philip…it's not because I'm reluctant to fight through the therapy. I'd will myself to recover completely because that's how I roll. I've invested a lot of emotion in people and situations here. If my fate is suppose to be here…then this is where I must be. However, I'm not saying I'll never be willing to try to change…just not now. Life and death are too important to make snap judgments or high-pressured choices.

"So…we won't make an attempt to exchange our destinies?"

Someday, perhaps, but not Thursday. I'll visit you soon, and explain my decision or a new plan based on a lot of thought and advice from various wise sages.

"I'm sorely disappointed…but Beth will be pleased…Oh have mercy…the old woman is back."

Sure enough, as Delphi faded, Annie walked into the room. She carried fresh bandages and a large bowl of poultice.

63

A gentle answer turns away wrath, but a harsh word stirs up anger."

—King Solomon

Following Annie's treatment Becca slept soundly. She felt relieved that she had more time to think and decide about the body switch.

Her hands looked much improved when Annie cleansed them after breakfast the next morning. The redness and swelling were much reduced. Annie partially wrapped her hands, allowing her fingers and thumbs to remain free. She wiggled them. The pull it had on her palms was uncomfortable, but not unbearable.

Sarah's arm was now bearing hard scabs and she wore no bandage. Annie applied cactus juice three times daily to keep her wounds pliable. Hannah asked to sit up and Thad carried her to the rocker when he came for breakfast. A footstool assured her legs were positioned correctly, and a sheet tented them.

Sitting together, Thad, Becca, and the others enjoyed morning coffee in the drawing room. Thad assured them he and Abe would cut and haul firewood on the weekend. "We'll take our guns. We might be fortunate and see an elk or deer. The weather's cool enough now to hang game for cooling."

Becca gave him a list of needed groceries and a few gold coins when he left for The Print Shop. He assured her he would shop for her, returning in time for supper. Becca and Warrior moved to the front porch. She positioned her rocker in the early morning sunlight. Warrior crept to the edge of the porch and offered Becca an adoring gaze. Sarah stood in the doorway. Becca felt relaxed and content.

"Someone's coming," Sarah announced.

Warrior raised his head and whined. His mouth and tongue was not yet healed enough to bark. Becca stood and opened the door.

"Come, Warrior, you must go inside." *I don't want him injuring himself trying to bark...* He obeyed and crawled to the door that Sarah held opened.

Becca looked at the approaching rider. She didn't recognize him. As he dismounted and turned in her direction her memory was refreshed.

The man at the dog fight...She positioned herself in front of the door and faced him. As he walked to the porch she looked at him with an unwavering stare.

"Can I help you?"

He stepped onto the porch and moved uncomfortably close to her. She couldn't back away; her back was against the door.

"You stole my dog, Mike. I want him back."

"That's absurd; you were preparing to kill him. Now, I want you off my property."

"Well, I heard Mike's doing just fine, so I want him back."

"That's not happening. You're wasting your time and mine. Now go!"

"Or what... you gonna send for the Sheriff? Maybe I should talk to him about you stealing Mike, and throwing my gun in the ocean."

"I didn't throw it; I kicked it out of your hand before you could shoot the dog you say I stole. If you want your gun replaced, I'll do that. First, I'll need to know your name."

"Tom Wilkins, the Sheriff's my cousin. Just thought you might be interested."

"Well, isn't that special, Mr. Wilkins. Just a minute please."

Becca cracked the door and stuck her head in. Sarah stood, frozen in her moccasins with brown eyes wide. Becca smiled, hoping it reassured her.

"Please get a piece of stationery and pencil from the desk."

The girl complied. "Now, hand me that pistol on the shelf by the woodstove."

Sarah looked at her in disbelief, but retrieved the gun. Becca took it, closed the door, and turned to the sneering man. Although it pained her hands, she quickly wrote on the paper; one pistol was given to Tom Wilkins by Delphi Castile on this date____. and one dog, Mike, was given to Delphi Castile by Tom Wilkins., on this date_____.

"Sign and date this, and this gun is all yours." He complied and handed the paper back.

She handed him the gun, handle outward. He examined the pistol carefully. "Is this your pistol?"

"It's yours now. I've no need for it. I took it from the last man who attacked me...right after I stabbed him...just in case you're interested."

Tom Wilkins' expression changed. He studied her as though he was recalling the scene at the beach.

"Do you have gun powder?"

"'No, and I wouldn't give it to you if I did. I owe you nothing more."

He turned and retreated slowly. Looking back, he tipped his hat. "Good doin' business with ya, ma'am."

"Just don't expect any more communication with me, Mr. Wilkins. Don't show yourself on my property without first obtaining my permission. I find men like you disgusting."

He mounted his horse. Becca felt herself shaking. She wasn't sure if it was anger or fear. She felt both...*I'm really not comfortable with him knowing where I live…it's a small town…guess everyone knows where I live…* She opened the door. Sarah still stood there.

"You didn't shoot him?"

Becca shook her head. "No, did you think I was going to shoot him?"

The girl nodded. Becca laughed and placed an arm around her.

"I can't see myself ever shooting anyone, I actually don't like guns."

But then, I never thought I would stab someone either…guess it's all about how scared I feel…

Becca didn't feel like sitting on the porch after the incident. She and Sarah took carrots and turnip slices to the back, and interacted with the horses. Dublin reacted much as he had before though eyeing Becca in a friendlier manner.

"Someone's coming," Sarah announced for the second time that day.

I hope it's not someone else with an axe to grind… Sarah went into the house through the back door, and Becca walked around to the front. She soon calmed when she saw it was the Lengs in their small delivery wagon.

The couple approached the porch with arms filled. "I hear you be injured. I brought duck," the woman smiled.

"It's glazed duck, you like?"

"I adore your glazed duck, please come in."

She held the door for the couple as she called to Annie. "We have a wonderful surprise for supper."

With everyone sitting around the drawing room with tea, Becca explained the accident to the Lengs. They expressed sincere concerns, and then Mrs. Leng explained another reason they had come.

"Work grows more and more. I brought work for you. Need buttonholes and hems on frocks."

She looked at Becca's hands. "But, not necessary…your hands…."

"I can sew," announced Hannah.

Becca glanced at her and then at the seamstress. "I'll bet she could do this work for you. She might even be available to be you're apprentice, if you liked."

That would keep her from Molly's hard labor.

Mrs. Leng and Hannah were both enthused as the woman observed the girl work her skill with a buttonhole and hem stitch. She offered some instruction, and Hannah took her guidance respectfully. The seamstress explained what she would pay for the tasks and Hannah's eyes shined brightly.

"That's powerful more than I get working at the hotel."

Mrs. Leng admired Annie's baskets and offered to pay for a dozen. Annie agreed to make them. Sarah immediately rushed to gather reeds and sea grass.

"You make them...I sell them in shop." Mr. Leng offered. "I pick them up here when ready."

The man then looked at Becca. "Wife say you say you like chickens."

"Yes, I do remember telling her that I'd like to have some, but I know nothing about them."

Mrs. Leng smiled. "Our chickens vedy good. They hatched... very good. We bring you chickens."

Oh my...chickens...where will I put them?

Mr. Leng stood up and motioned. "Come see."

Becca followed him to the wagon. There, in a cage were six hens. In a separate cage was a brown rooster.

"I thought you meant baby chicks, but these are adult poultry."

The man nodded. "Yes...they lay eggs."

He pointed at the rooster. "That is Crow." He leaned his head up and mimicked the sound of a crowing rooster. Neighbors not like Crow."

Becca laughed. "Well no one will complain here, I have no neighbors."

Also in the wagon were tools, a bucket of corn, various sized boards and scrap lumber. "I make chicken coop," he declared.

Becca and Mrs. Leng sat on the back porch, and watched the construction of the small chicken coop. The older woman explained that she must keep them penned up for a few days and then they could run free. However, they must be locked up at night or animals would kill them. Becca listened to all the instruction about the chickens, filling in the blanks caused by the woman's broken English. Finally she opened a new subject.

"Mrs. Leng, do you believe a human spirit can leave its body?"

The woman was silent for a moment, her black eyes boring into Becca's.

"You ask that, why?"

"I asked you the question because I feel you're a wise and spiritual woman. I have disturbing concerns."

"I see. You ask about death?"

"Well, not just death, but the experience of dying, and the possibility of a spirit entering another body."

"Yes, in a new born...reborn to learn lessons."

"That's reincarnation. I'm speaking of a spirit entering an adult body that has lost its own spirit in death."

The woman pondered the question for a moment. "I'd say...if Creator sends spirit...it goes."

Becca explained the entire experience, choosing her words carefully to accommodate Mrs. Leng's limited English. The woman listened intently. Becca could not discern any expression of judgment in her features. When she finished she waited for the woman's response.

"Do you understand?" Becca asked.

The woman nodded. "Yes... what is problem?"

"The problem is another woman and I have switched bodies. We're like opposites in every way, and also in different times...we planned to switch, but I fear it might end our lives."

The woman reached across the small outdoor table and touched Becca's arm. "No, no, no...life must be in harmony. "She moved her hands in a circular motion. "Be in harmony with opposites...with same...with nature...with self...that is right way."

I don't think she gets it..."But that doesn't answer my question... do you think it's dangerous or wrong to exchange back with her?"

Mrs. Leng closed her eyes and smiled. She opened them and patiently asked, "If you be in harmony...why do that?"

"I see...by harmony you mean acceptance?"

The woman shook her head, "Acceptance...that say...I will do it...but harmony say...I like it."

Becca thought about the words the woman had said. *Try selling that idea to Delphi...*

Mrs. Leng again reached out and grasped Becca's forearm. "A happy life...healthy life...need harmony....struggle is bad...live in harmony with all things ... all work out fine......all good."

"So you believe I'm here for a reason?"

"Without reason, you not be here."

Mr. Leng stepped on the porch. He wiped perspiration from his forehead. "All fine now... gave corn and water. We go now..."

Mrs. Leng stood. Becca thanked them warmly, and walked with them to their wagon. The couple climbed in, and Mr. Leng took hold of the reins. Mrs. Leng smiled down at her.

"Happy life...it leaves no tracks...walks in harmony."

Becca stood watching them ride into the distance. As she turned to enter the house, she saw another rider coming down the country road.

Squinting, she made out the form of a well dressed man. James?

James rode up to her entrance and dismounted. He smiled as he took a saddle bag from the back of his horse. "I heard you couldn't come to town so I came to you. I have the books for the reading group meeting."

"Oh yes, remind me again. When's that to be?"

"It was announced for Friday, remember? The advertisement is hanging in The Mercantile, The print Shop, and Post Office."

"That's this coming Friday...right...come in, James. I'll get us something to drink, you must be parched."

Inside they set in the drawing room so Hannah could see the books. Annie and Sarah looked on in interest. Opening the bag he took them out and laid them on the tea table. "I ordered six of each, just as you requested. They can either buy one or borrow it. If many attend, some may have to share."

Becca picked up one from each of his selections. "The Song of Hiawatha...and... Life of a Slave Girl... have you read these, James?

"The Song of Hiawatha is a lovely poem by Longfellow. It was published ten years ago. I've read it several times. It's perfect for our first few gatherings. Have you read it?"

Becca smiled, gently flipping through the book...I can't believe I'm buying one of these editions...Longfellow must still be alive..." I've read it, he was writing about a character of the Iroquois Tribe."

"And this one has been out a few years." He pointed to the other book."*Life of a Slave Girl,* by a woman author, Linda Brent.

I've heard that it isn't her real name. Since it's a biography of a woman in our time, I think it's relevant."

"I agree, I bought that one, remember? Let's allow the members to decide which book to read first."

Finishing the afternoon tea, James excused himself. Becca walked him to the door. As they stepped out into the fresh air, James noted.

"Someone's coming in a buggy."

Becca took a deep breath. "Yes, indeed, it's the Reverend and Mrs.

Walker. "

64

"Grief can be the garden of compassion."

—Rumi

After the Walkers were seated in the front parlor, Becca dashed into the drawing room. Annie was dressing Hannah's burns while Sarah flipped through The Song of Hiawatha.

"We have more guests and we'll need more tea," she announced.

Sarah laid down the book, and hurried to the kitchen. Becca reluctantly returned to the parlor...*I'd rather do anything today than deal with him...*

"How have you both been?" She feigned a cheerful voice.

The Reverend appeared serious but not angry. Grace smiled weakly and toyed with her lace handkerchief.

"We're fine but concerned, Delphi. I told Titus...Mr. Walker about the accident. He finds your deeds most heroic, don't you, dear?"

"Your quick decision in the situation was fortunate for the girl's sake; she might have been burned alive. Where is she? I want to speak to her, and offer a prayer."

"You may visit with her in a moment. Annie is changing the bandages."

"Remember, Titus, I told you about Annie helping Doc with Hannah's treatment?" Grace reminded her husband.

Sarah entered the room with a tray. On it were three cups of steaming tea and a bowl of sugar. She passed them out and the Reverend scooped in two heaping spoons of sweetness. Grace took a sip and appeared baffled. Becca gingerly picked up her tea with her bandaged hands and tasted it...*This is Annie's birch and mystery herb tea. Sarah must have confused the kettles...if I say anything, Sarah will be embarrassed...*Mr. Walker was taking his second drink...*Well...if he hasn't noticed by now, he won't.*

"How are your hands," asked Grace.

"They're healing rapidly. I hope to have the wrappings off completely in a few days."

"That's wonderful. You see my husband has something to ask of you."

Oh no you don't, I'm doing no favors for you, Mr. Grumps!

The man emptied his cup. "Could I bother you for more?"

"Of course, Sarah, please bring more tea." The girl stepped into the room and the pastor handed her his cup.

"Be sure to pour his tea from the same kettle as before, Sarah." *Can't switch on him now or he'll notice the difference.*

The girl nodded and left the room. Grace had returned her tea to the tray. *She must have thought it tasted odd.*

"Are you finished with that Grace?" he asked.

"I'm not terribly thirsty."

He took the cup, stirred in sugar, and emptied half of the liquid in one gulp.

"Titus," Grace said in a quiet but determined voice. "Tell Delphi what you'd like her to do,"

He cleared his throat, took a deep breath and forced himself to look into her eyes.

"It's the Christmas service. It's now late October and it'll be upon us soon. Your singing voice is pleasant...we...I...thought you might consider putting together a choir for that service."

Becca muddled through the mental paralysis that stunned her brain.

"You're inviting me...no requesting me... to lead your church choir? Did you not just inform me last Sunday that I was out of line speaking words in the service?"

The Reverend finished Grace's tea. Sarah returned with his cup brimming full and he sweetened it.

"Yes... well... but that..."

"Do I not remember you saying that as a woman I must remain in submission in the church? Organizing and leading a choir takes leadership qualities. I think you should look for a man to do this."

Grace's hanky looked like it might shred apart from her twisting.

"There're no men available who can do it, Delphi. We have some men members who can sing, but not read music." Grace offered.

Read music...neither can I...

The Reverend drank more tea. "I've pondered this, Miss Castile, and since the leadership is with music, I see no sin in it. Moses' sister Miriam led the people in songs of praise and thanksgiving."

So ask Miriam to do it...no...I won't say that...

"I'll give it some thought, and I'll look through those hymn-books I bought from James, and let you know."

The Man focused on the teacup...*You're remembering the scene in The Mercantile when you rejected the box of hymnbooks you had James order...I hope you're ashamed of yourself.*

"Titus regrets his harsh behavior last Sunday, Delphi."

Becca looked at Grace. "I haven't heard him say that, Grace."

After one more gulp of tea, the Reverend looked into Becca's face. "I should have held my tongue. I admonished you without considering that you might be ignorant of Church ethics."

Was that an apology? It didn't feel like an apology...."strive to live in harmony with both the opposite and the same".... Ok, Mrs. Leng, I'll give it a try...

"I'll make a deal with you, Reverend Walker. I'll do this choir thingy, if you'll use your influence to put an end to the dog-fighting. They're doing it to gamble, you know. That must be sinful."

"Whose doing that?" His face that had looked stressed now grew stern.

"One is Tom Wilkins, cousin to the Sheriff, or so he says. I caught them at it myself. Last Sunday I rescued a dog that had be torn up and condemned to death. I think it's deplorable."

"Well, it certainly is. I knew nothing about this. I'll talk with the Sheriff and with this Wilkins fellow. That's not the kind of carryings-on we want in our town."

He gulped the last of the tea. Leaning back, he stretched his legs and almost smiled... *He's feeling the effect of the calming properties...*

Grace studied her husband, curiously.

She looked at Becca. "The choir would sound splendid if only we had an organ or piano."

Ah ha... you two came to butter me up so I'd my repeat my earlier offer...

"As you know I offered to purchase a new piano for the church... if you feel I'm worthy enough...."

"It would be most appreciated, Miss Castile," the minister blurted out before she had finished.

"Order the one you want from Mr. Sanders, and I'll stop by and pay him." Becca instructed.

The man's face broke into a big smile. Becca couldn't remember seeing him smile before, and was surprised it didn't break the skin.

"Everything is arranged then, wonderful, now take me to that sweet child, Hannah."

Becca led them to the drawing room. She was relieved to see the novels were hidden from sight. As the pastor walked over to Hannah, Grace tugged on her sleeve. Becca leaned toward her.

"Can you please tell me how to get some of that tea you served my husband? It relaxed him so."

Becca nodded. "We'll keep you supplied."

"Our little secret," the woman cautioned.

"Of course." *In another century, he'd be prescribed an anxiety medication...we'll just jump things forward a bit...thanks to Annie.*

As the Walkers climbed into their buggy, Thad arrived. He hopped from his carriage and eyed the Reverend suspiciously, then glanced at Becca's face, searching for a hint of distress. She smiled to reassure him. He tipped his hat to them, and began unloading items he had bought at The Mercantile. As they departed, Becca rushed up to him. His arms were full, but he leaned down so she could plant a kiss on his cheek.

"Was he offensive toward you today?"

" I was asked to lead the choir, and Reverend Walker is going to help me stop dog fighting... Tom Wilkins came by and tried to intimidate me. I gave him that pistol in exchange for the one that washed out to sea...The Lengs brought chickens that lay eggs and a noisy rooster...and oh yes, we're having glazed duck for supper..."

"Delphi, breathe." Thad coached as he laughed at her breathless onslaught of words. His face revealed his astonishment.

"I've only been away for eight hours."

"I know...it all just kept happening."

Thad set his bundles on the porch and embraced her. The setting sun was creating a beautiful red sky. She relaxed in his arms and enjoyed the beating of his heart.

"Now tell me about your day."

"Mine cannot compare to yours." He chuckled.

"How's Harry doing?"

"He's a good worker, especially with the pain he suffers. He was given a small advance, so I took him to The Mercantile before coming home. He bought some bacon, beans, coffee and lye."

"Lye? Is Sybil going to make soap?"

"No, it's for their outhouse. I got some for yours as well. Sanders just got it unpacked and everyone will need some. Harry said they haven't had any for a long time and their outhouse is ripe."

Oh yeah, I remember the bucket of lye Molly had in the toilet. A scoopful down the hole after each use keeps odors and flies under control... I hadn't even thought of getting any for here...

He picked up a heavy cloth sack. "I'll take this on out there. It's not advisable to keep it in the pantry or around food."

Becca scooped up the butter, bacon, and coffee. She hurried to the kitchen. "We have butter for the mashed potatoes," she announced.

Thad tended the horses, coaxed the poultry into their little coop, and closed the door. Becca and Sarah set the table for their feast of glazed duck. Coffee in drawing room, with lighted lamps ended the day. Sarah listened to Hannah read aloud from the novel. Annie sat on the floor before a bucket of soaking reeds and sea grass, and began her basket work for the Lengs. Becca and Thad flipped through hymn books and discussed possible selections for the choir.

"Do you sing, Thad?"

"I do, front porch singin'. I use to play a romping fiddle, but I haven't picked one up since before the war."

"You can play a violin? You never told me that. I want to hear you play."

Thad grinned. "I'll need practice before I play for your ears, my dear."

I know what you'll be getting for Christmas...if I'm here at Christmas.

Thad held up the opened hymnal. "Here's Silent Night, Delphi. We sang this every Christmas in Kansas."

"Put a bookmark in that place. Here's one recently written by Longfellow." *I'm so glad I bought these new hymnbooks.*

"I heard the Bells. I wonder if the Rev would think it's religious enough. I'll mark it."

Thad read aloud more chapters in Matthew and then prepared to leave. Becca walked him to the door. On the porch he kissed her tenderly and held her close. She snuggled into his arms. *Mrs. Lee said to not struggle with the path...*

"We need to plan our marriage," he whispered. "I want to be here...not always leaving to return to that little room above the shop...we belong together."

"I still need to tell you something important."

"We'll allow time for that, but now you need rest. Sleep well, my darling." With a departing kiss, he left her standing in the chilled night air, and walked to his buggy.

From a deep sleep, Becca awoke to Thad's desperate voice. His hands grasped her shoulders, shaking her frantically.

"Delphi, wake up, the Farris family needs you."

She sat up; stunned that Thad was in her bedroom. "What?"

He pulled off the quilts with a sweep, placed an arm behind her, and assisted her to her feet."

"Why are we hurrying?" she asked sleepily.

"Harry's boy Ben ate lye. Doc's on his way, but Sybil is demanding that you come too."

Thad grabbed the housedress from where Becca had tossed it on the rocking chair. He began tugging on her gown, attempting to pull it over her head.

"Thad, what are you doing?"

"Helping you dress...your hands...."

He tossed the gown on the *floor, and plunked the dress over her head. Becca was stunned... Guess there's no corset today...* He helped her thread her arms through the sleeves, and began fastening the bodice buttons. "Where's the others?" she asked.

"Sleeping, I didn't wake anyone. We have to hurry. Where are your shoes?"

Becca nodded toward the moccasins. Thad grabbed them and slipped them on her feet. Hannah had braided her hair the night before. She glanced in the mirror. *Doesn't look too bad.*

"You'll need a wrap, it's quite cold."

"In the wardrobe," she directed.

He opened the oak doors, surveyed the clothing items, and grabbed the cape. Placing it around her shoulders, he nudged her out the door and toward the stairs. Outside she observed it was yet predawn. Thad lifted her into the buggy, and covered her lower body with a lap robe. As he climbed in, a cold breeze shocked Becca out of her foggy lethargy.

"Now, what happened to little Ben?"

Thad shook the reins and clucked to his horse. "Harry filled the lye bucket for their outhouse, but he left a half sack of lye in the kitchen corner. Lye should never be left out like that."

"So Little Ben ate it? Why would a child do that?"

"I've heard of it before. They think its sugar. It poisons a child rapidly."

Panic swelled in Becca's chest. What to do… remember … think …mustn't make him vomit.…milk…make him drink milk to dilute it…"Hurry, we have to hurry."

"I know. That's why I dressed you."

He popped the reins. Their accelerated speed jerked Becca backwards. When they arrived at the Farris house, Becca saw Doc's horse tied to the fence. They ran into the house without knocking. Sybil sat on the floor holding Ben. She cried as she rocked her body back and forth.

Emily, the eldest, held baby Delford. Little Rose and Ivy huddled in a corner crying. Harry thrashed around, cursing himself, hitting walls, yelling at God. Doc leaned over the child and tried to find a pulse, scowling at all the commotion.

"That dang Harry goes berserk every time there's ordeal with his family. I've a half notion to knock him in the head to keep him down until this is over."

"Do you have Winslow's Calming Syrup?" asked Becca.

"There's some in my bag, but it won't help this child; I'm not sure he's even alive."

"Not for Ben, for Harry." Becca located the medication. She handed the bottle to Thad. "Make him drink this."

"How much?" Thad asked.

"All of it." She turned toward the doctor. He gently shook the child.

"He convulsed and vomited blood. I don't think I can save him."

"If we could give him milk to dilute the lye..." She glanced around the shelves hoping to see a pitcher of milk.

"He was past that when I arrived," Doc muttered.

He looked into Becca's face. "Can you do it? Can you do that... RPC ...PRC...?

"CPR," Becca corrected. I can breathe into him, but if his esophagus and airway are clogged or collapsed, it may not help."

She felt his neck and thought she detected a weak pulse. Wiping his mouth, and clearing his airway, she covered his mouth and nose with her mouth. She breathed gently into the small body. Sybil ceased her crying. The room grew silent. Becca watched Ben's abdomen and chest. There was no rise or evidence of air intake. She attempted gentle compressions to his chest. Her healing hand wounds broke open. They bled onto Ben's nightshirt. The boy's body remained limp and lifeless. Finally, she collapsed into tears.

"I can't save him."

Sybil released a loud, mournful wail from the very depths of her core. Doc scooped Ben from his mother's arms, and took him to a bed in the backroom. The children huddled, now weeping loudly. Thad restrained Harry, trying to coax him to drink the tranquilizing fluid. Becca felt her heart rip apart. She folded her body and sobbed into her hands. Doc returned.

"It's not your fault, dear. He removed clean bandages from his bag and proceeded to wrap Becca's hands.

"You did what you could," he whispered. "Every family loses a child or two. I'm surprised any of these children are yet alive. Now we move on to comforting. Stay strong, Delphi girl, this family will need your wisdom."

65

"In poverty and other misfortunes of life, true friends are a sure refuge."

—Aristotle

Becca wiped her eyes and glanced around the room. Harry had transitioned from the wild man to a sobbing boy. Sybil sat silently, her arms wrapped around herself. Emily, in the corner, tried to embrace her younger sisters while holding the newborn. Becca rose and went to the children. She took the baby, sat down on a bench, and pulled the girls to her. Doc stood and picked up a tea-towel. Waking over to a small mirror that hung above the wash basin, he draped it, covering it completely. No one said anything to him. They seemed to understand his action as he moved to the small adjoining room. He pulled a blanket from a cot and covered a larger mirror. Becca watched him through the door...*What's this all about?*

"Sybil, is there a looking glass in the back room?" he asked.

She shook her head. Becca stood. Carrying Delford, she joined him in the middle room. Ben lay on one of the cots like a sleeping child. She deliberately didn't look at him.

"Doc, what are you doing?" she whispered.

"Many people believe a spirit can be trapped in a looking glass on its way to the afterlife." He walked to the window above Ben's cot and opened it several inches. "They also believe the spirit can become trapped within the walls of a house... if an escape isn't available."

"You surely don't believe that."

"I believe in providing whatever comfort and assurance I can. It's not my place to dictate their beliefs."

He looked at her over his spectacles. "You of all people shouldn't doubt the mysteries of the human spirit, Delphi."

"I suppose you're right about that. What do we do now?"

"I'm going to the Leng's. I'll bring her here to sit with the deceased and help out. The babe must stay with Sybil since she has to nurse him. I'd like to place the little girls somewhere until after the funeral. Do you think you could keep them a few days?"

"Certainly, I have plenty of room. Who'll arrange the funeral?"

"I'm a bit worried about that. Harry is still riled up at Titus over the baptism ruckus. We've a shortfall of ministers here. The Reverend and Harry will have to sort it out. I'll get Molly to get things arranged."

Doc left to retrieve Mrs. Leng. Becca handed Delford over to his mother for feeding. She hurriedly gathered changes of clothing for the girls, and was ready to take them when Doc returned with the mid-wife.

The sun was up and the day warm when they arrived home. Annie made breakfast for them. Thad left for The Print Shop and Becca prepared a bath for the girls. Afterwards, they sat on the floor by Hannah and she styled their hair, complete with bows. Sarah entertained them with the pictures in the children's book. At mid-day, Doc dropped in. He carried his case into the house.

"Doc. you look beat. You need to take time for some rest," Becca noted.

"I napped for an hour. There's so much to do. Molly went over to dress the body." He kept his voice low to be sure Emily and her sisters didn't hear.

"I sent Mrs. Leng home to sleep. Harry went for the photographer. I wondered if you'd come and help with the post-mortem photographs."

"I'll ask Annie if she minds watching the girls. Hannah and Sarah can keep them occupied. They're well behaved."

Doc checked Hannah. "These limbs are healing, young lady. Now I'd like you to put weight on your feet for a few minutes several times a day. I'll get some crutches here tomorrow. You must start moving your limbs a bit at a time."

Soon Becca was in the buggy with Doc. As they clopped along the dirt road, she asked, "Why is Harry getting a photographer?"

Doc glanced at her in surprise. "They must not do that in your time...photographing the deceased is part of the final arrangements."

"That's what their doing? Goodness sakes, no. That's just plain creepy."

"It's the family's last opportunity to have a portrait of the person they loved and lost. Ben's portrait will be hung in a place of honor in their home. Why is that....what did you call it...creepy?"

"I'd rather have a picture of my child alive. This'll be a reminder of sadness. However, I suppose Harry and Sybil haven't had recourses to photograph their children alive."

"Most families manage to take at least one family photo, but Harry has had hard times," the doctor replied.

"Who'll pay for this?" I think it's morbid, but if it's what they want, I'll pay.

"There'll be an offering taken at the funeral. Expenses will be paid from that. Folks aren't always kind in life, but in death they'll look after each other."

When they approached, Becca noticed the Reverend's carriage. Titus Walker stood outside, his head bent. He rubbed the toe of his shoe over a tuft of grass. She stepped onto the stoop.

"Reverend, did the family send for you?" She tried to sound pleasant.

He shook his head and looked out at the street. "No, Harry will have nothing to do with me. Grace brought a fried chicken and a cake. She's inside. I'd like to pray with them, but Harry said if I didn't care about them when they wanted their children baptized, then they don't need my concern now."

For a moment, Becca thought she spotted a tear creeping onto his lower lashes. If it was, he soon blinked it back.

"They were very hurt about that. There must be some way to sooth Harry's feelings. They need comfort right now."

He looked into her eyes. "Can you speak with him? Tell them that you and I are at peace. Encourage him to allow me to assist them with this. They'll listen to you."

At peace...hmm...you assume a lot...

"If the Farris family listens to me, it's because they know I'll always listen to them. That's necessary you know."

He looked away. "I realize I should have had more compassion when they approached me. I just wanted their commitment for church attendance and wholesome living."

"At that time, they didn't even have shoes for their children. They needed your spiritual guidance and compassion without demands. Their commitment would have followed."

"But if they had done as they should, this child might not have died."

Becca felt anger rise from her core to the top of her head. She moved close to the man and poked a finger into his chest. Her voice rasped and startled her, but she didn't waiver.

"Don't you dare hand any blame to these grieving parents... don't you dare! This child died from an accident, nothing more. It could happen to any family. God doesn't punish people in this way... he doesn't turn his back on them, like you do. If you're planning to toss that kind a crap at them, you can leave right now...it's not happening!"

"Miss Castile, you needn't turn vile. I hadn't planned to tell them they were at fault, just guide them in the right direction."

"As long as that thought is stuck in that block head of yours, it'll eventually roll out of your mouth. I won't speak to Harry about you until you change your attitude."

"But they'll need a minister."

"They'll need someone to read scripture, sing a song, and say a prayer...do you think you're the only person in the Crescent that can do that?"

Another carriage stopped in front of the house. A man dressed in black got out, and began unloading a camera, tripod, and a case. Becca pulled herself out of her rage and took a deep breath.

"They'll be busy with photographs now. You take some time and think what Jesus would say to these parents. Then think how he would feel for them, seeing their pain. Then think of how he feels about you for turning them away. When you get it sorted out, come back. I might let you talk with them."

She started into the house and then turned. "I'll tell Grace you're waiting for her."

When Becca entered the house she first noticed Harry. He huddled in a kitchen chair in the corner of the room. With elbows on his knees, he laid his face in his hands. Becca patted his shoulder as she passed. Grace sat in another chair holding the baby. Becca reached out for Delford and Grace released him to her. The minister's wife stood up and gathered her shawl.

"I'll go now. I guess it's not the right time for Titus to visit."

"Thanks so much for the food you brought, Grace. I think it's best to give them some time to deal with their loss. I'll keep in touch."

Grace left and Becca walked to the entry of the adjoining room.

I'm not sure I can go in and see that poor child...but I have to... She walked through the door. Molly was fussing with a doily on top of the small chest of drawers. The room was cleaned, cots made up, and Ben was dressed in a clean nightgown. His blond curls were dampened and arranged around his face. To Becca, he looked like an angel. She walked to the cot, and sat beside him. Reaching out slowly, she touched his pale cheek. The overwhelming grief that had lingered in her heart lightened

...I feel no life here...his spirit is gone...this is a shell..."I know where you are, Ben. I've passed by that portal in my visits to Delphi. You're just fine."

"What's that, dear?" Molly asked turning in her direction.

"Nothing."

"Sybil is almost dressed. I arranged her hair. Ben is ready. I'll have Mr. Baines come in to set up now."

She left the room. Sybil entered from the other door. She was dressed in the nice frock Becca had provided her from the trunk of donated clothing. Her hair was styled. *..She's beautiful...face a bit puffed and tearstained, but she has a new resolve...*

"Harry refuses to be in the photograph," she whispered. "He won't eat or sleep. He blames himself for leaving the lye in the house. But Ben never gets out of bed before we rise...rather; he had never done so before."

"No one's to blame, Sybil. I hope he accepts that, eventually."

The photographer stepped into the room and glanced around. "I believe the best lighting is over here, Mrs. Farris."

Becca left the room with Delford. Molly was cleaning the kitchen. Harry hadn't moved.

"Charlie and a carpenter are making the coffin right now," Molly told Becca in low tones. "Mr. Sanders provided satin for lining. Enough ladies promised to cook, and bring in meals so that Sybil won't have to cook for several days."

"I'm impressed with everyone's kindness. It is true community spirit."

"Sybil mentioned that she wants you to sing that song, Delphi, the one about the children."

"I can do that, but Molly, where will this take place? Who'll speak, if they refuse to allow Reverend Walker?"

Molly hung up the tea towel and looked at her. "Why you, dear, of course, it'll be at the graveyard."

"Me?" Oh dear...She walked over to Harry,

"Molly's making you tea. You must drink something. She's preparing a plate for you, Harry."

The man shook his head, "I don't want nothin'."

"Harry, I need you to hold Delford so that I can help Molly."

Molly turned to protest, but Becca shook her head in warning. Harry straightened up and looked at her. She handed the infant to him. The baby looked up, fixing his blue eyes on the man's face. Harry sniffled and looked back at him.

"You have four beautiful children that need you, Harry. You're their Papa. Sybil needs you too. You're going to eat now, and be strong for your family. All this thinking through stuff is going to take time."

"I don't deserve to be their Papa. I killed my son."

"I can't make you stop blaming yourself. I hope you'll come to realize that no one's to blame. But for now, you have to take hold of the reins and be their Papa. There's no one else to do it."

Molly set a filled plate and cup of tea on the table. Becca took the baby and Harry turned his chair to face the task of eating. The photographer passed through on his way out. Becca followed him. He eyed her curiously.

"I already told the Missus I'd have these done in a few days."

"I'd like to pay for them. But I don't want anyone to know. Can we arrange that?"

"Yes, ma'am. I'm Robert Baines, we weren't properly introduced."

He stuck out his hand, noticed her bandages and retracted it.

"I'm Delphi Castile, a close friend of the family. I'm looking after the Farris girls in my home. I'd like to make arrangements for pictures of them as well. I think Harry and Sybil should have photographs of all their children."

"Is tomorrow morning acceptable, ma'am?"

"Yes, that would be perfect. I'll pay you for all your work then." Becca provided directions to her home.

When she returned to the kitchen, Sybil was sitting by her husband. Her arm draped around him and his head lay on her shoulder. He had partially finished his portions, and his tea cup was empty.

"I might suggest that the two of you lie down and rest. Delphi and I will look after things." Molly's voice held a tone of authority.

"Molly's right, dear," Sybil said. "Let's take a rest, tomorrow will be a trying day."

Harry meekly followed his wife to the backroom. Becca pondered all that was going on around her. The few deaths in her family had been so different. *The bodies were quickly stashed away at the Funeral Home. Here, families remained in contact with the deceased until the burial. Somehow they've accepted Ben's empty presence.*

Molly set a plate and cup of tea on the table in front of Becca. "It's important for us to be nourished as well, Delphi."

She set beside her and picked up a chicken leg, taking a healthy bite. Becca toyed with her food. "I wonder if Harry will be able to rest."

"He'll sleep soundly now, dear."

"Molly, O'Shay, did you spike his tea?"

"Only a little, dear, just a tad."

"Ah ha, just like you did mine on my first night at your place. It's not appropriate to medicate someone without their consent."

"Eat your chicken, dear. There's cake as well."

It was a sober ride back to Becca's house. Thad spoke little, and Becca lost herself in thought...*So, they're having only a graveside service...They want a song...How can I sing over a tiny grave without breaking down...I might have to read scripture...what scripture? I know...I'll use the one Thad read last night...Matthew, chapter nineteen...Jesus said to allow children to come to him... I remember ...Reverend Tate used that at the service in my house...when we dedicated the Farris children...*

"I'll help dig the grave in the morning; I won't be dropping in to feed your horses. Sarah can help you." Thad looked into her face. "Delphi, you're exhausted. Promise me you'll spend the rest of the day relaxing."

Dig the grave...I never thought how that happens...someone has to dig the grave...In these times it must be family and friends.

"Charlie said the funeral will be at three-o-clock. The funeral dinner will be directly after at The Redwood Hotel. Everyone will bring in food. No cooking will be necessary. There's nothing else you'll need to worry about. You can sleep this afternoon."

I must have the girls ready for pictures in the morning.... I'll need to read the scripture to prepare... I'll need to talk to the little girls...mentally prepare them for the burial...

Thad directed the horse to pull in as near to the gate as possible. He got out and assisted Becca. As they walked into the house, he glanced around for Annie.

"Where's your grandmother, Sarah?"

"She's feeding the children, shall I get her?"

"Please tell her that Delphi must relax for rest of the day."

He's getting terribly bossy. When I feel up to it, I must line him out on that.

Thad continued. "Will you take care of the chores this evening and in the morning? I wouldn't want Delphi to expose her wounds to uncleanness in the barn and chicken house. It could cause Lock Jaw."

Lock Jaw?

Thad escorted Becca to her room. She collapsed on the bed. He kissed her gently.

"I'll be here to take you and the Farris girls to the funeral. Hannah shouldn't be out with her wounds. Perhaps she can look after the babe for that time."

Becca took his hand. "Who will set with the body tonight?

"I promised Harry that I would."

"Thad you're worried about me, but you're getting no rest at all."

She moved to the far side of the bed. "Stretch out and take a short nap, at least."

Thad lay down beside her, being careful to keep his shoes off the bed. She snuggled up to him, and he put an arm around her. *It feels so comfortable...so right...Tomorrow was the day Delphi and I planned to exchange bodies... I'll be at the cemetery but not for that reason... I wonder if she'll be there...or if she's accepting that we can't do this yet...* Becca fell into a deep sleep. Several hours later, she awoke when Sarah brought her supper. Thad was gone.

66

"Remember that your children are not your own, but are lent to you by the Creator."

—Mohawk Tribal Proverb

Becca thought about the journal...*I must remind Delphi that the transition will need to be postponed as I told her when we spoke... I fear she wishes to push the issue...she's not happy...*After eating supper she did the best she could with a sponge bath...*I'll be so glad when these hands are completely healed...*She slipped into her nightgown and returned to bed. Sleep followed before she gave the journal another thought.

The long rest ended when her eyes popped open before dawn. Remembering all she had to do, she got up, struggled into her dressing gown and sneaked past the other bedrooms. She went first to the kitchen and started coffee. Sitting at the table with the Bible, she read the nineteenth chapter of Matthew.

> **"Then were there brought unto him little children that he should put his hands on them, and pray: and the disciples rebuked them. But Jesus said,**

"Suffer little children, and forbid them not, to come unto me: for of such is the kingdom of heaven." And he laid his hands on them, and departed thence."

She thought through what she would say...What can I say to comfort Ben's parents? What could I possibly say to help Harry?

Annie walked in and moved close to Becca. She peered into her face with her failing eyesight. "Are you ill?"

Becca smiled. "No, I just couldn't sleep any longer."

The woman examined her hands. She retrieved her basket of cactus and sliced them into thin pieces, placing the slices on Becca's wounds. She wrapped them tightly enough for the moisture to remain against the healing areas. Annie poured a cup of coffee, and refilled Becca's cup. She sat down and appeared to wait for Becca to initiate conversation.

"Have you ever been photographed, Annie?

The woman frowned. She doesn't understand. Becca pointed to the picture in the Bible of Jesus blessing the children. She tried to sign the action of a camera and pointed to her. Annie shook her head and took a drink of her coffee.

Becca explained her plan to have the Farris girls photographed. She also told her about the funeral in the afternoon. She wanted Annie to understand all the coming and going that would fill the day.

"I plan to have Hannah's photo taken. I'd like to have one made of us, Thad and me, as well. Would it be alright to take Sarah's photo?"

Annie was thoughtful. "Ask her."

"I would like one of you and Sara together."

She shook her head. "Not my ways." She rose and moved to the stove. She began the process of making oatmeal. "Many things to do... must start..."

"Thank you, Annie; I rely on you so much."

After the girls were fed, dressing them up was everyone's focus. Sara ironed the frocks, Hannah styled their hair. Becca sat them at the table with pieces of her stationary and pencils. "Draw pictures for Momma and Papa." *That should keep them busy for a while.*

Hannah was excited about having her first portrait ever. They planned how it could be done in the chair. At mid morning Thad arrived. He was dirty, sweaty and tired.

"Everything's ready. Doc's with the Farris family and the grave is prepared. Charley took the coffin over. They did good work on it. The carpenter even carved Benjamin on the top."

"Thad, you're exhausted. We'll get you something to eat and then you must sleep for a while."

"I'm here to beg for a bath. I need to change clothing. I have my suit in the buggy."

"That can be done, though you may have to draw your own water from the well. We're all a bit maimed."

As the water heated, Thad devoured a plateful of fried eggs and potatoes. Becca sat and watched him eat heartily.

"The photographer will be here soon. I thought about having our picture taken after the little girls, but you're so tired. We'll do it another time."

Thad placed his fork on his plate, and wiped his mouth with his napkin. "I'd really like that. A bath will restore my vigor."

At one-o-clock Thad, Becca, and the Farris girls rode to the Farris house in Becca's new carriage. Bonnie and Dublin appeared to be happy to be out and active. Becca watched as Doc and Molly took charge. They decided that Sybil, Harry and children would ride in Becca's large carriage with Thad and Becca. Next Charley would take the coffin, containing Ben, in his wagon. Pallbarriers would ride in the wagon. Third in line was Doc in his small buggy. Molly rode with him.

Along the way, mourners joined to walk behind, as everyone proceeded to the cemetery. Mr. and Mrs. Leng were there, becoming the first walkers to join the procession. When they arrived, the solemn group surrounded the open grave. Thad gently held Becca's arm as she approached the front end of the simple wooded coffin. He opened the Bible to the marked page, and held it in front of her.

A sea breeze blew through her hair. It was comforting. Her nerves made her miserable in more ways than she could count. Hannah had pulled her corset tighter than usual for the photo. The black velvet dress was heavy. The cape she wore to hide the fancy bodice was hot.

She glanced at the family. They stood in a line. Their quiet weeping caused tears to bubble up in her eyes; she wiped them with her glove. Just then she saw him...*Reverend...you just couldn't stay away...you're probably here to see me fall on my face...you'd love that...*I wasn't' surprised to see Grace among the walking mourners, but Harry asked you to stay away.

He stopped at an appropriate distance. The family couldn't observe him from their position. The annoyance she felt at Titus Walker put her emotions under control. Taking a deep breath, she sang the song, *Jesus Loves the Little Children*.

"*I see you've found ways to use my voice, though I've never sang that song before.*"

Go away, Delphi, scat...this is a funeral.

"*I have something to tell you.*"

Scram, unless you want your spirit to get misplaced in the child's body that's in that coffin, you'd better get back to my body.

Thad pushed the Bible closer, assuming she couldn't see from the held position. She read the passage. Then she looked at the group.

"Several weeks ago, Mr. and Mrs. Farris sought to baptize their children. They did this because they are good people and want to do the right thing by them. Now, I won't go into the difficulties they encountered, this is not the time or place for that."

The Reverend hung his head. "The important thing is that they didn't allow any hindrance to stop them. Just as these parents in the scripture, they pushed their children toward Jesus. A good Christian woman, Mrs. O'Shay, saw what needed to be done. And little Ben, his baby brother, and his sisters received their blessings because of good parenting and Christian community."

Reverend Walker took his handkerchief from his pocket and wiped his eyes.

"None of us knew that Ben's time would be so short when we had that little service. I think what we can learn is that none of us can know how long we have on earth. We should treat one another with the love, tolerance, and kindness that we would if we knew it was our last day, or theirs. Ben is not in pain or fear. I've had an experience, and though I can't explain it now, death is not to be feared. Ben is alright. Jesus said to allow children to come to him. Ben is with him."

Harry and Sybil had stopped crying and were watching her attentively.

"I'm going to dismiss in short a prayer. I ask all of you to pray for the comfort of this family and for healing of their broken hearts." She said a short prayer hoping her lack of practice didn't show.

Thad whispered in her ear. "Ashes to ashes"

Everyone stood quietly as though they expected more. "Ashes to ashes," he repeated...*What in heaven's name is he talking about?*

"You're suppose to pick up dirt, say ashes to ashes, dust to dust, and toss the soil on the coffin..."

Delphi, why are you still here?

"Do as I instructed...it's not over until you do..."

Thad had scooped up a small amount of sandy dirt and held it over the coffin.

"Ashes to ashes, dust to dust," she said.

Thad tossed it on the wooden top with its lettering, Benjamin.

"Amen," the mourners said jointly.

The pallbarriers slowly lowered the little coffin into the ground with ropes. It made a sick sounding thud when it reached the bottom. Harry stepped forward and took a shovel that was stuck in a heap of dirt. He scooped up some, and dropped it on the wooden box. The sound of it made Becca shudder. Sybil started to cry. Other sniffles were heard among the observers. Another scoop crashed on the wood, making a hollow noise. Becca whispered to Thad,

"He shouldn't have to do this. Can't this be done later? He'll destroy what's left of his back."

"*Haven't you ever attended a funeral before?*" Delphi hissed in her ear.

Not like this...

"It is customary for those close to the deceased to cover him. When he tires, someone else will offer..."

Delphi, why are you still here? You're taking a big chance on allowing my body to die.

Charley stepped up and tapped Harry on the shoulder. Harry shook his head and shoveled all the faster. Thad handed Becca the Bible and move toward him.

"Permit me to help you, my friend."

Again, Harry shook his head. Tears ran down his cheeks and his nose had desperate need for a handkerchief. Another scoop went into the grave. A black suit moved up behind Harry. Becca raised her eyes and gasped. Titus Walker placed a long arm around Harry's shoulder. His other hand took grip of the tool's handle.

"It's my turn, Harry. I feel God calling me to carry your grief. Please suffer me to minister to Ben in this hour."

Harry relinquished the shovel, returning to stand with his family. The girls wrapped little arms around his legs, and Sybil buried her face in his chest. Becca didn't know how long they stood by the grave. She forgot about the squeezing corset, the hot cape and the itchy dress. Silence ruled the small crowd. Ocean waves crashed onto the shore. Gulls called out as they passed. The barking of seals could be faintly heard on the distant rocks. The only sound that held her attention was the crash of the soil's return to the opening in the ground. One shovelful at a time, a remorseful minister buried a small child.

Soon after the gathering arrived at the Redwood Hotel, rain began to fall softly. Thad delivered Becca and the Farris family, and then returned to her house to pick up Annie and the girls. He carried Hannah to the carriage, and then into the hotel parlor.

Becca couldn't believe the dishes and pans of food that arrived following the short gravesite service. A baked ham, mutton stew, fried chicken, glazed duck, and a platter of lobster was delivered by friend through the back door. Piles of mashed potatoes, baked beans, and fresh baked bread collected on a side table. Annie provided a large basket of fry bread. Apple and berry pies competed for attention.

Becca hurried to the kitchen to assist, but was chased out by Molly.

"You take those poor hands right out of here. Sit with the Farris family, dear. They need your encouragement."

Becca returned to the parlor, but there was no empty seating by the grieved family. She spotted a place on the velvet sofa at the end of the room. She sat quietly and observed others in the room. Besides the Farris family, Hannah, Thad, Charley O'Shay, Reverend Walker, and others filled the room. Conversation was guarded.

Annie and Sarah found things to do in the kitchen. Becca knew they felt more comfortable working that sitting among strangers. The meal was quiet and somber. People left shortly after eating. Many placed gold coins into a fruit jar Molly set by the entrance ... *Why does it have to be so difficult to know what to say at these times?*

"There's nothing to be said...nothing will bring back their child."

Delphi...you're back...I can't focus on you right now...I'm sorry I couldn't meet with you at the cemetery, but as you could see, something came up...please leave...

"Oui...but that's why I must speak with you...we have much to discuss...

I realize that...but I can't discuss matters with you while I'm involved with this crisis...I promise...we'll work on the transition as soon as I can..."

"That is the problème...Something's gone awry... I'm so aggrieved...my heart is broken...yours will be as well.

I promise to come to you when I get home...

"Delphi, dear, you seem so far away." Molly's voice drew Becca back to the moment at hand. Molly held a teapot.

"Would you like more tea, dear?"

"No, thank you, I've had plenty."

She glanced at Thad, who studied her intently. He gave a slight nod of his head in the direction of the Farris family. Becca looked over at them. Reverend Walker had pulled up a chair in front of Sybil and her husband. Becca, already unnerved by Delphi's intrusion, grew anxious. *No, Rev...you did good...don't mess it up...*She stood, walked over, and stood by Sybil. Titus looked up at her.

"I just apologized to Mr. and Mrs. Farris. I told them I regret my harsh reaction to their request. I asked their forgiveness."

Becca placed a hand on Sybil's shoulder. "That's kind of you, Reverend Walker. I'm sure they appreciate your apology and your help at the graveside. Now, they need time to work through their grief. Forgiveness can't be forced...they may need time."

Sybil placed her hand on Becca's gloved hand. "I forgive Reverend Walker, Becca. My husband will forgive as well...in time. For the present, Harry is trying to forgive himself."

Titus opened his mouth, glanced at Becca, and closed it just as fast. *Good job, Rev. No sermons right now...no pressure.*

Thad took the grieving family back to their home. The remaining stragglers seemed to linger longer than Becca felt necessary. Molly appeared to be exhausted, and Charley had clearly eaten his way to misery. She could hardly wait for Thad to return with her carriage.

Titus stood, smiled, and asked for everyone's attention. He looked like a child needing approval.

"The piano is ordered. It'll be here in two weeks, three at the most. We have a new choir director...Miss. Castile. Please talk with her about joining the choir for the Christmas Mass."

"Yes, and we have the book gathering at Delphi's next Friday evening," announced Hannah, excitement radiating in her voice.

The minister's eyebrows knitted over eyes that sparked for a short moment.

"Don't worry, Reverend. The book we'll read is history of the Iroquois." Becca hurriedly explained...*It's not accurate history about Native Americans, but as good as it gets in this century.*

"You're invited. But you must understand, the readers are in charge of leading the discussion," Becca offered.

He appeared to be playing ping-pong in his brain. He wanted approval since he felt the loss of it recently, but he also had strong beliefs about secular books.

"Yes, well...if it were a Bible study, I would most assuredly attend."

"We're going to read a bible passage at the beginning of each gathering, before we read the assigned book. If you join us, you may have that honor."

His face brightened. "Ahh, that's most encouraging, Miss Castile...a little of the word to protect the mind... yes, I would be honored."

"I'm so glad you accept. The scriptures we have chosen will include all that relate to the words of Jesus."

"Oh, but the Old Testament stories are inspiring and powerful."

"Yes, I'm sure you enjoy them. We'll be covering the ministry of Christ. Your assigned reading will be the Sermon on the Mount. Then, we'll discuss how we must apply his words to our daily lives. I'm so thrilled you'll be part of this."

Grace, finished with the kitchen tasks, entered the parlor and prompted her husband to take their leave.

"Your husband has agreed that the two of you will join us for the book gathering, Grace. I'll ask Thad to bring you The song of Hiawatha. You can start reading it."

The woman looked surprised. She glanced at her husband's face. The ping-pong game still rattled in his head.

"That's very good news," she said, "very good, indeed."

67

"A wise woman wishes to be no one's enemy; a wise woman refuses to be anyone's victim."

—Maya Angelou

As Thad drove Becca's carriage, filled with her adopted family members, back home. She snuggled next to him. " I appreciate your for helping me manage that funeral, Thad."

"How could I do less? You're my lady."

"Harry insists that he'll return to work tomorrow. So I'll be very busy all day," he explained.

"That's fine. We'll manage."

'Molly asked Sybil to work for her. This was before the accident. She needs her to take Hannah's place."

Thad looked at her. "Is it true Hannah will become Mrs. Leng's apprentice?"

"It seems so; Hannah does very nice work."

"Perhaps with so much sorting itself out...we can marry soon."

Oh dear...we always come back to this..."Thad, there's something I need to discuss with you before we can make those plans."

Thad frowned and focused his attention on Bonnie and Dublin. "So, Mr. Mackey spoke with you...I asked him to permit me to speak with you first."

"Mr. Mackey, the school manager? No, I haven't seen him since our discussion at the dance last summer."

"He stopped in to post a job in the paper. He asked me to find out if you're interested."

"What kind of job...teaching?"

"He hired a man from Fort Lincoln for this school term. It's the little school at the edge of town. It provides schooling for the farmers' children, and a few families who've moved here to be near their husbands at the Fort. The fellow he hired was mustered out from the Fort for a while. Seems he shot himself in the foot. He'll have to return before the school term is ended. I prefer that you decline. I want nothing to postpone our marriage."

"Take the job...you'll need it."

Delphi... how can you know I'll need it? Have you nothing better to do than to meddle in my affairs all day?

"No, I do not... My gold won't last you forever...Your friend...Tom... he wants to take over your life...don't give up your independence...I worked too hard for it..."

It's Thad, not Tom...I'll not allow him to take control of your gold, Delphi. I'm aware that you'll need it... I know I need to start earning for myself...but I can't commit to a job or a marriage...if we plan to transition...

"But...I need to tell you something..."

"Delphi!" Thad's address brought back her attention. "You're doing it again...drifting off as though in a trance...why do you do that?"

"I'm just very tired. I understand your feelings about the job. I don't wish to upset you. However, I do want to hear what Mr. Mackey has to say. I need to earn some money. I've spent a great deal."

Thad's body tensed. He shook his head. "As my wife you'll need to earn nothing. I'll earn what we need. Do you think I'm not capable of fulfilling my obligations as your spouse?"

"Of course you're capable. A short-term of teaching is no insult to you."

"It's frowned upon for a married woman to teach. Usually, only men or single women are hired. I'll agree to it only if it won't postpone our marriage."

"You'll agree to it??? Hmmm

"See, did I not warn you? Very soon he'll have you tethered to crying bébés... spending the gold as he desires... beating you if you oppose him."

Becca's head throbbed and her stomached churned. She couldn't remember being caught between two such demanding opinions.

"Get out of here!"

She hadn't meant to say it aloud. Thad jumped and so did the team. Dublin sprung forward, ears laid back. Bonnie increased her speed to keep pace. For several terrifying moments, Thad fought the run-away team. The passengers hung on for dear life. At last he got them stopped and wiped his forehead.

"What in Sam Hill did ya do that for?" he demanded.

"Sorry, thinking out loud."

He gave the horses time to calm. Annie had an arm around each girl. She didn't look pleased. On each side of her were faces with saucer sized eyes, one pair blue, and the other brown.

"Bad, bad spirit," Annie mumbled.

"Becca broke the tense silence. "If Mr. Mackey will agree to my teaching while married, I'll accept. If not, I'll decline." *I can deal with compromise.*

Thad gently prodded the horses with a light pop of the reins. They moved forward. Becca could see her house in the distance. Nothing ever looked more inviting.

"As you wish, Delphi, but as my wife, you'll need not earn a living. This will be only to amuse you."

I'm not going to allow myself to get into a power struggle with Thad now. I'll ride the wave and rest in harmony. As Mrs. Leng said, "If it is in my path, it'll work itself out. I need not leave a footprint." He's thinking as he's been brought up to believe and trying to do right.

Once they were in the house, Becca and Annie set about storing the food Molly had sent home with them. Thad took care of the horses and carriage. Sarah, never low on energy, grabbed her shoulder basket and headed for the woods. She planned to gather healing herbs for Annie, and a generous amount of calming tea bark and herbs for the Reverend's tea. Hannah retired on the mattress and was soon sleeping. The afternoon activity had exhausted her. As Thad walked out the kitchen door, Becca made a suggestion.

"Come upstairs and take a nap when you're finished at the barn. You haven't really slept for several nights. There's no reason for you to return to town, right away."

He smiled and nodded. After tucking a loaf of bread into the bread box Becca went to her room. She slipped out of the black velvet frock, tight shoes, and hated corset. She put on her dressing gown. Opening the window to the autumn breeze, she settled into her bed. She listened intently until she heard Thad's footsteps ascending the stairs. He tapped on the door before opening it. She patted the open side of the bed.

"Come and rest before you drop in your shoes."

Thad removed his suit jacket and laid it carefully across the back of the rocker. He took off his tie, stiff collar, cuffs, and cufflinks and set them on her bureau. Slipping out of his shoes, he placed them neatly under the bed. Becca watched his systematic ritual. It amused her that he was meticulous with tasks...*Not surprising...he does everything with an eye for perfection...He expects much from himself, but he has tremendous tolerance for others...unusual combination.*

She smiled at herself. Secretly, she would have liked him to remove all his clothing, but these were times of propriety. She knew Thad's self expectations and respect for her good name would prevent any sexual advances before marriage...*I'm sure that is motivating his attempts to expedite the wedding plans...I'll use this time to tell him about everything...he needs to know before entertaining any additional plans for his future.*

Thad covered Becca with the quilt and then lay on top of it, beside her. *Good grief, he's separating us with the quilt... I think they call this bundling ...like* these six yards of dressing gown, pantaloons, and bodice aren't enough... Now I feel like I'm in a cocoon.

"Thad, are you ready to listen to what I have to tell you?"

"Yes, my darling. My attention is entirely on you."

"Well...it all starts the day the Brother Jonathan sunk... I happened to be in a recreational boat with..."

She noticed his even breathing and turned to look at him. He was sound asleep...*Later...I guess...*

She reached for the journal on her bedside table. Opening it, she noted a new entry. It was two days old. Delphi wrote a few lines stating she was in Crescent City. She came with Beth to pick up Jonah... *Ok, that's not news...I knew they were coming...Delphi and I planned to meet at the cemetery for the transition...* She reported that she and Beth were checked into Surfside Motel...*I wonder where that setting is in this century.*

Delphi continued to say that they would spend some time enjoying the town. A visit to Ocean World, The Museum, Lighthouse, and a drive through the Redwoods were planned. Becca thought back to her first visit to Crescent City, before the accident. *The Museum was closed...* As she closed her eyes, she felt herself drifting ... spinning ....passing the tunnel that led to the light...and finally, in Beth's living room.

She looked around the room. Beth and her new fiancé were at one end. They demonstrated a video game to Jonah. She watched them. Beth looked so happy.

If this incident hadn't happened, my sister would have never met her soul mate. Because he was on patrol and rescued Phil and my body, he was led to her...Jonah, in Ike's body, brought back the chilling memory of the incident on the Lorelei. Rather that the scowl that had dominated Ike's face, Jonah wore an innocent expression...Because of this whole affair, this man will have opportunities he would have never had before. Actually, Ike living as Cain is a new man because of it.

Delphi's quality piano took up a large portion of the room. Student music and books were scattered over its top...*It looks like she's staying busy with music lessons. I wonder if Delphi has gained from the experience... or...offered something to this era... I doubt that she would think so...*Becca drifted to Delphi's bedroom. The women lay on her side, weeping into a Kleenex. Becca moved closer.

"I know that you're here...sniff, sniff."

Why are you crying? Are you in pain?

"Only my mind and heart...all is hopeless...I've nothing for which to live..."

What's happened Delphi...you know my time is limited...please make good use of it.

The distressed woman pulled herself up in a sitting position. "I've been trying to tell you... we went to the Museum. It was difficile...I could only see the exhibits on the first floor...The wheelchair ... sniff...Beth went upstairs."

Are you upset because of that? You'll walk again one day...you can visit the museum later.

"No! That's not it...sob... just listen... Upstairs there's a room with items of past residents of the town...Under a glass counter there's a journal....my journal."

Your journal...the one I write in?

"Oui...what other could it be? It's very worn and fragile...pages have fallen out. These loose papers are spread out so that they can be read...by visitors."

Delphi blew her nose and reached for another tissue. Becca tried to process what she had said.

"Beth wanted to take photos with her cell phone, but none are allowed. She could have shown me..."

So the entries we post now will someday be on display for the public? Oh dear! Is that why you're in this melt down... because our entries are laid out to the public?

"No, no, no...listen...There's a picture...several pictures. Delphi marries...she stays in Crescent city...has children...raises orphans..."

I'm trying to not interrupt, Delphi, but it beats the heck out of me why you're upset...

Delphi gave into sobbing. When she caught her breath she spurted, "That Delphi Castile is not me, she's you."

Becca waited to respond. She felt stunned. When it appeared Delphi was not offering more she asked. *How could you know that? The body in the pictures will look the same regardless of whose spirit is there.*

"The things reported...these aren't things I'd do...I'll never marry. This Delphi eventually travels to San Francisco. She marches in protests...for...what did Beth say? Oui... Women Suffering."

Women Suffrage?

"*Oui. That's what I say. There's no music school...nothing that I wished for or worked for...that tells me...it's you. The transition won't happen.*"

But...couldn't it be possible...you might do those things...maybe your thinking will change after the transition.

"*Beth read the pages...some of them were written years after these events...the hand writing is yours... not mine.*"

I see.

Delphi took a deep breath. "*Beth and I discussed it driving back to Portland. It either means that we will try it and fail, or chose to not make the attempt, or when we proceed, one of us will not survive. I would say that would be me.*"

Because of what appears to be Delphi's involvement in causes?

"*You've found purpose in this folly. Whenever I go to you... you're très occupé...er.. busy always... I spend time feeling sorry for myself...wanting change...wanting to escape.*"

You've had much more to deal with than I, Delphi...you've been very brave...recovery from a broken back is challenging...

"*But I need purpose...survival is about purpose. Those years I was with Lily...The abuse... the indignities...I always had purpose...to escape...that's why I survived. Other girls died of disease...procedures to rid them of unwanted babies...even murder. But I lived for my purpose.*"

Becca remained silent, pondering what her counter-part had just said.

Why did you nag me today...you insisted that I not marry Thad...that I take the job...

"*I thought if I turned you from the destiny we discovered in the museum... it might change the outcome...I've accepted it now...it is what it is...*"

It seems my future's laid out...but we'll work together to shape yours into whatever purpose you embrace..."*Delphi! Delphi!*"

A distant voice pulled at Becca. In a swish she was racing fast. The drifting, spinning, falling, tunnel and light were a quick blur. She became aware of her shoulders shaking. She opened her eyes. Thad's worried face peered into hers.

"I thought...you didn't seem to be breathing...I was scared mindless."

She put her arms around him.

"I'm here, Thad...I'm really here."

68

"No one can make you feel inferior without your consent."

—Eleanor Roosevelt

The next several days were restful. Restful only in that accidents and death did not occur. House cleaning, washing, and ironing took up the women's time. Becca's healing hands permitted her to do more each day. Sarah's hand and arm were well enough to work in anyway needed.

Hannah was nearly finished with the sewing for Mrs. Leng. She was excited for her mentor to pick up and evaluate her work. Mrs. Leng promised to attend the book gathering. She would bring more work for Hannah. Doc dropped off the crutches he prescribed, and Hannah occasionally stood with them, stretching out her burned legs.

When Annie was at rest, she worked on the baskets. Any spare time for Sarah was spent refurbishing her grandmother's healing herbs, and gathering reeds and sea grass for basket making. While in the forest, she sometimes snared a rabbit. While gathering reeds, she caught several fish. She gathered acorns, and Annie ground them to powder and made a crusty loaf.

In late afternoons, Thad left Harry in charge of closing The Print Shop and came to give Becca training with the horses. He was impressed at her success with Dublin. Becca dressed in her new riding clothes, and learned to ride with the sidesaddle. She offered a fair amount of grumbling, however.

Just as Doc had predicted, Warrior recovered a bit each day, and began to walk. His gait was gimpy but steady. Becca felt unusually content, but portions of her thinking were occupied with Delphi and her struggles in the other century.

Evenings were her favorite time. After supper and cleanup, when the house started to a chill, Thad built a small fire in the stove in the drawing room. Annie sat by the tea table and worked on a basket. Thad cleaned his Winchester or sharpened his knife. Hannah did her sewing. Sarah practiced the knitting Hannah had been teaching her, and Becca read aloud to them. She always read several chapters of one of the Gospels and they talked about the meaning of the scriptures. Then she read several chapters from a different book.

Occasionally Thad shared a story about his childhood in Kansas. Sarah sometimes told a traditional fable from her tribe. Annie interrupted and corrected if she failed to relate the tale accurately.

On Friday, five ladies came to the book gathering; Molly, Grace, Sybil, Mrs. Leng, and Mrs. Sanders, the store owner's wife. James arrived excited, but appeared disappointed seeing the Reverend there. Becca gave him a reassuring smile.

"Don't worry, he'll be fine." She whispered when she took his jacket.

Annie prepared two kettles of tea, one for the group and one for Titus Walker. She wrapped up a bundle of calming tea for Grace to take home with her. Becca opened the meeting by explaining how reading and discussion would transpire. She had written four rules in the front of each book that were now in everyone's hands...*I'm glad Thad suggested this...*

1. No interrupting.
2. There will be a 3 minute time limit for comments.
3. There will be no arguing with another's opinion. Disagree respectively with statements like, "In my opinion, or "As I see it."
4. All individuals and opinions will be respected.

"Everyone's beliefs, opinions, and feelings will be respected at these gatherings," she stressed. "We'll treat each other with courtesy. We allow free discussion and encourage open minds."

...these rules are primarily for the Rev. of course...

Titus managed to grace them with a long opening prayer, but he was agreeable to stick to his assigned passage, Matthew 5:.3-12, for the devotional reading. After he finished with reading, Becca pointed to the grandfather clock.

"We have twenty minutes to discuss what Pastor Walker read. Let's address what Jesus said about being merciful, those that mourn, the pure at heart, hunger for righteousness, and those who are persecuted. Remember, three minutes limit for speaking time. Who would like to be the first?"

The women looked baffled...*Perhaps they've never been asked to comment about scripture before...*Becca looked at the Reverend, expecting that he was more than anxious to lead the comments. He was holding his teacup out for Sarah to refill.

"I must say," began Sybil, "the wonderful help all of you gave us...earlier this week...that's what Jesus meant about merciful."

From there the conversation moved along in lively fashion. Titus offered nods of agreement to most comments. He appeared to be prepared to get wound up about the word righteousness, but the twenty minute limit ended. Sarah refilled his cup. They took turns reading The Song of Hiawatha. Becca guided the discussion. She pointed out rhyming pattern, meter, words and phrases that defined the setting, and the poet's ability to set the mood. Soon others were sorting it out and offering observations.

James and Titus entered into the conversation enthusiastically. Thad participated but took every opportunity to flirt with Becca. When opportunity presented itself, she whispered, "Behave!"

As guests prepared to leave, each complimented Becca for thinking of the book gathering.

"James has as much to do with it as I," she insisted.

Mrs. Sanders offered to host it at her house the following Friday. As Mrs. Leng left she smiled and commented. "This is good...help me learn... English better."

Becca walked Thad to the gate. "I'll be over tomorrow with Mr. Mackey. I want to be here when you confer about the school job. You're a smart woman, but I know your folly regarding money."

Right...just because I'm getting used to the gold system...

"He requested that you visit the school Monday. He thinks you should make acquaintance with the scholars, reconnoiter the situation."

He pulled her into an embrace...*I doubt that I'll ever become accustomed to people approaching Thad regarding my business decisions.*

"I agree", she responded as she hugged him. "I'd like to ride to the school, and prove to you that I've mastered Bonnie and that beastly saddle."

"Dublin will insist on following."

"I know."

Thad kissed her tenderly. Even in the chill, she felt warm from head to toe. "I'm glad you're at peace with Reverend Walker," Thad whispered between kisses. "We need him to perform the marriage."

Becca slept well and awoke excited about the interview. Annie was excited about her baskets. She had six completed and Mr. Leng took them all when he picked up his wife from the gathering. She tucked the gold coins into a small leather bag that always hung from her belt.

Becca hated accepting the two gold coins she held out to her, but she knew Annie wanted to be responsible. The grandmother also gave Sarah two coins for her part of the work. Hannah was also thrilled with her wages. She insisted on paying a gold coin for her board. Becca sat at her desk and wrote all the transactions in her ledger... *This will eventually end up in the Crescent City Museum, I suppose...* She decided to add the money to the grocery fund.

The parlor was neatly swept and dusted when Mr. Mackey arrived. Becca made raisin, oatmeal cookies to serve with coffee. Thad had been lovingly reprimanded several times for swiping them off the cooling rack. Hannah, Annie, and Sarah busied themselves in other parts of the house while the interview took place. Becca served cups of coffee from a china service that came with the house. She passed the platter of crisp cookies to each man, and then sat by Thad on the sofa.

Mr. Mackey smiled pleasantly as he began. "Thad tells me you two are planning to wed."

Becca glanced at Thad, wondering what else he may have shared. *I wish I had asked him so I don't contradict whatever he's said.*

"Yes, the plans are in the making." She smiled and took a sip of her coffee.

"It will be necessary to know the date you've set. Married women are discouraged from teaching, you know."

Mr. Mackey crunched down on the cookie. "Hmmm, this is quite good; you're marrying a fine cook, Thad."

"Why is that, Mr. Mackey?" Her violet-blue eyes focused on his.

"Well, married ladies belong in the home, of course. That's generally agreed upon."

Thad opened his mouth, but got Becca's elbow in his rib. He declined to comment.

"But wouldn't you agree, Sir, your priority is to provide a capable person to instruct the children you're hired to serve with an education?"

"Yes, that's part of..."

"So, that being your priority, I assume your concern will not be about my marriage status, but rather my ability to teach... would you like more coffee, Sir?"

"Yes, thank you." He held out his cup. "I'll return to the marriage question in a bit. What experiences have you in teaching, Miss. Castile?"

If you only knew ... four years college... a degree in Elementary Education...a semester student teaching... a year in my own classroom...two years softball coach for the parks...swim teacher for Red Cross...counselor at summer camp for the Deaf...

"I've taught in a private school. I was mentored for part of a year by a professional educator, and I have a teaching certificate."

She smiled...That's sums it up pretty well...

"A certificate... well that's impressive...from somewhere back East?"

"I earned it in the state of Oregon."

"Hmm, I wasn't aware Oregon issued teacher certificates..."

Darn...shouldn't have mentioned certificate...

"My year of teaching in Portland was successful."

"How many students were in your school?"

School? *Oh he means classroom...*

"I taught twenty-four students."

"Our school is small but draws from surrounding areas. It's possible have up to thirty scholars, ages seven to nineteen."

Nineteen...holy smokes...I hadn't thought about the age differences being so great.

"We prefer to hire men for this country school...discipline can be a problem with older chaps. Boys need a man when it's time for a thrashing."

Thad began to squirm on the sofa. Becca handed him a cookie. *He's suddenly worried about unruly nineteen year old male students, I'll bet.*

"I don't believe in thrashing children, and I should think young men of nineteen don't belong with children as young as seven. Perhaps split sessions would work better."

Mr. Mackey looked at her confused. "Split sessions?"

"You only have one school term a year for three to four months, right? I'd suggest a second term for those who are fourteen or older. It could be accelerated learning."

Mr. Mackey scratched his head then tugged at his handlebar mustache.

"That is a dandy plan, but we only have funds for one term. That leads us to discuss wages."

Thad sat up and leaned forward...*Down boy, please let me negotiate this.*

"I'm prepared to offer you seven dollars and fifty cents per month for the remaining three months of this term. That's the starting salary for a school marm."

"The teacher you have now...the one who shot himself in the foot...Is that what he receives?"

"No, of course not, salaries for school masters start at eighteen dollars."

"He receives twice the money, just because he's a man? Has he taught before?"

That's just stupid! Equal pay for equal work is only fair...wait...that's still an issue in the twenty-first century...I won't win that fight.

"No, I believe not."

"Has he had any training to be a teacher?"

"No, he came to us straight from the Fort. He does understand discipline. We had trouble last year with older chaps. This year they refuse to attend. He put the fear of God into them."

"What I hear you saying is that brutality is more valuable to you than an educated, experienced teacher."

The man was silent for a moment. "I'm not sure what you are asking, Miss. Castile. We'll need a teacher in a week. The Fort wants Sergeant Fitzgerald back at his post. The salary will be seven dollars and fifty cents per month. If you're interested, I'll hire you today."

"If I marry Thad before the end of the term, will I be dismissed?"

He was thoughtful. "No, I prefer to not have another change of staff during this term. You'll be allowed to finish the term."

He's more desperate for a teacher than he first let on. I'll push for more money...

"I know the money is there for paying Mr. Reynolds, had he stayed. I'll be doing the same work as he. Therefore, I won't accept the position for less than fourteen dollars per month. If I can't maintain discipline the first month, then I'll agree to accept the seven fifty."

...might as well pave the way for future women teachers...

Thad's countenance fell. After Mr. Mackey left, Becca snuggled up to Thad on the sofa...*I have to assure him he's still in charge...or appears to be.*

"It's only for three months, my dearest. If it prevents harmony for our home, I won't accept it for a second term. Three to four months out of a year isn't much time, and the money will help us get off to a good start. Do you feel I did well with the money bargaining?"

"I can't believe he agreed to that much. You must have bewitched him."

"Don't say that too loud. Some states in the Union have been known to hang people referred to as witches."

"Is that true? Well, no one had better ever try to hang my Delphi."

Suddenly, he looked at her with purpose. "You've wanted to tell me something for days. What is it?"

If I'm not going back...there's no reason to tell now... Annie, Doc and Mrs. Leng will keep my secret... Thad would never grasp the truth.

"Hmmm, it's slipped my mind...must not have been important."

Later in the afternoon, Becca and Thad saddled horses and rode through the woods. Thad rode Susie and Becca perched on Bonnie. As usual, Dublin tagged along. They came up on several elk.

"I wish I'd brought my gun," Thad commented.

"They're so beautiful!" *I'm glad you don't have your gun.*

"They are magnificent animals. But their herds are plentiful. One of them would feed your household, the Farris family, and whoever you wanted to offer meat, for a good while."

I suppose, but I don't want to watch one of these creatures die. There's no refrigeration...most of it would spoil..."How would we preserve the meat, Thad?"

"He looked at her curiously. "How did your family preserve meat?"

"I must not have paid attention." *Freezers and refrigerators...if only you knew what you're missing.*

"I'm sure you ate ham and bacon...smoked meat...meat in salt brine?"

Of course...*I'll ask someone else for details...getting a bit tired of looking ignorant to this man...no wonder he thinks I need protection and guidance.*

After returning, Thad demonstrated the skill of hitching the team to the carriage while stressing various safety precautions. They took a long ride during sunset so Becca could practice managing the team.

This is lots easier than learning to drive a car...especially one with a clutch... Now I can come and go as I like without waiting for a ride or escort.

69

"Books are the carriers of civilization. Without books, history is silent, literature dumb, science crippled, thought and speculation at a standstill...."

—Henry David Thoreau

Sunday morning the carriage was filled to capacity. Thad carried Hannah who still couldn't walk, even with crutches. She was weary of being homebound. Even Annie agreed to go. Having met women at the book gathering, she felt more comfortable. At the church, Thad whispered in her ear.

"Abe and I have an errand to tend. Do you feel comfortable about taking the carriage home alone?"

Becca was surprised. "You sound mysterious. To answer your question, I feel very competent with the team and carriage."

"Just don't do anything to startle the horses," he cautioned. "And if they ever startle...don't turn them sharply..."

"I know, Thad, we went over this several times..."

He smiled and squeezed her hand. Turning, he walked away in the direction of Abe's home. Becca's group found seating by Molly and Charley. The windows were opened and the late autumn breeze cooled the crowded area. After several hymns and a long prayer, Reverend Walker took his place behind the pulpit.

"Brothers and sisters, I have had a delightful opportunity to read a wonderful work. Once I began reading it, I couldn't put it down. He picked up The Song of Hiawatha, and flipped to a marked page.

Oh my goodness...don't tell me he's going to preach from that poem...well, it will be more interesting than his redundant sermons about hell and sin.

"I want to thank one of our new members...Miss Castile, for introducing me to this book."

*Member...I'm now a member...I didn't know that...*Becca was impressed at the skill the Reverend demonstrated in summarizing the story. *I'm not too excited about his spoiling the ending before the group can read it...but hey...he's loosening up, at least.*

The preacher's main focus was the arrival of the Christian missionaries in the final verses, but at least he had now endorsed a secular book...that indicated some enlightenment.

After the service, interested individuals approached Becca. They wanted information about the gatherings and the book. She told them when the next meeting would be, and directed them to James to order books.

The ride home was comfortable. The day was sunny and warm. The team responded to her commands as the women discussed the service. She felt brave and important like she did when her parents allowed her to take family car for a solo drive the first time. As she reined Bonnie and Dublin onto her property, Thad scurried around the side of the house to meet them. He assisted each of them from the carriage and carried Hannah into the house. As he carefully placed Hannah on the sofa, Becca noticed blood on his trousers. She gasped, placed a hand on her heart.

"What happened, Thad, is someone injured?"

"Come and see." He started toward the door. Becca followed, dreading what she might see. From a limb of the big elm tree in the back yard, there hung sections of a butchered animal.

She stared at it silently. Thad smiled proudly. "I put some hay in the area where we saw the elk. Abe and I went there and sure enough, there he was." Thad was giddy. "Oh," was all she could think to say.

"Annie knew we were hunting this morning," he continued excitedly. 'I wanted to surprise you. She knows how to dry and smoke meat like the Indians do. She said she'll teach you."

Oh she did, did she...nice of you to arrange that.

"She also will cure the hide. She'll teach you that as well. They're valuable. The cobbler is always looking for good leather."

I can't wait...

"For now, the meat needs to cool. Fresh meat can cause stomach ailments. Are you surprised?"

"Yes, I'm speechless. You'll get a lecture from the Reverend if he hears you've been hunting on what he considers the Sabbath."

"He'll be agreeable when I take him a roast."

He kissed her on the cheek. "After we visit the school tomorrow, you ladies can get started. With all of you working on it, you should get it finished before your first day of teaching."

It appears that this is falling into my role. He hunts...I butcher...On second though, I wouldn't want to be a part of the killing."

"All right but understand, Thad, I'll be working on lesson plans once I assess the classroom. That's going to take a lot of my time."

"What are lesson plans?"

"It's an important part of what teachers do...we plan out what we'll teach, what the goals and objectives will be, the methods we'll use, and the class work the students will complete, and we determine how we'll measure the outcomes. There's as much work to do outside the classroom as there is inside, teaching."

"I didn't know that."

"You're not alone."

Thad was thoughtful before making a suggestion. "Well, you'll only be doing that for three months, I'll try to be helpful here as much as I can, especially after we're married... I'm starved."

After supper, Thad helped Becca with chores. The evening wasn't cold and they decided to leave Dublin and Bonnie in the fenced area rather than locking them in the stalls. Thad and Becca completed their goodbye under a full moon.

"Soon I'll be staying and not leaving you at bedtime."

Tightening her shawl around her, she stood by the gate and watched him until she could no longer see his silhouette. She went to her room and read a chapter from a novel before extinguishing the lamp...*I hope I get good night's sleep. I want to be on top of my game when I visit school tomorrow...*

Leaving her window partially opened, she covered with only the sheet and quickly drifted off into a strange dream. Reverend Walker, a dead elk, and a live Hiawatha mingled in a senseless plot. A horrible scream jerked her to wakefulness. She froze as she listened in anticipation of a repeat of the terrible noise...*Did I hear that, or was it part of my dream?*

Just as she allowed herself to believe it was a dream, the wail again sliced the silent darkness. Becca flung her legs out of the bed, slipped into her moccasins, grabbed her dagger from the side table and rushed into the hall. She and Sarah collided as both of them headed for the stairs.

"It sounds like a woman in danger," she gasped.

"It's a mountain lion," replied Sarah. She carried her spear.

"Are you sure?"

"I know their cry. I've heard them before."

They scrambled down the stairs, holding up nightgowns to keep from tripping over the long ruffled skirts. Dashing to the backdoor Becca commented. "I wonder if it came for the chickens."

"The elk meat lured him," the girl answered knowingly as they reached the back door.

"Wait," Sarah, "I'm not sure we should go out there."

"I'm not going far; he's a distance from the house."

She opened the door. They stepped out to the back porch, and gazed over the property. Dublin whinnied and snorted. Both horses stood near the gates that opened to their stalls. Warrior stood on the old blanket he used for a bed, and growled.

"There, see under the tree where the elk quarters are hung." Sarah pointed.

Becca focused on the tree and saw the large cat-like form. He walked from behind the tree and then around it. He looked toward the house, not at the fresh meat.

"He's lame," said Sarah. "He's limping on his front paw. I'll bet he's an old one. He's looking for food that's simple to get."

"I feel bad for him, but I don't want him to get our winter meat."

"He'll get more than that. He'll break into your chickens and attack your horses. He can't hunt. Now he knows there are easy meals here."

"I wish I knew what to do."

"I can throw my spear, but it's too short to kill such a large animal. It might make him leave...for now."

"I prefer to not wound him," said Becca. "I'll be right back, keep an eye on him."

She ran back into the kitchen and grabbed the dishpan, a pancake flipper, the washboard, and a soup ladle. Hurrying back, she handed the dishpan and soup ladle to Sarah. Beat on this like a drum. Becca began dragging the pancake flipper up and down the wash board. The cat howled and moved back a few feet. Even with Warrior's feeble attempt at barking with his healing tongue and mouth, the cat did not run away.

"We can't do this all night," Becca grumbled.

Annie stepped out onto the porch. "What big, bad noise you make!"

"Grandmother, a mountain lion is circling the elk."

She said something to Sarah in their Native tongue. It must have been in regard to the direction of the animal which Annie could not see. Sarah took her grandmother's hand and held it out in the direction of the animal. Annie faced that direction and began a loud yodeling like noise from her throat. The cat turned and disappeared into the forest...*I don't blame him...that's one scary sound...*

"I should have remembered to do that." Sarah lamented.

"Delphi!" Hannah screamed from her temporary bed in the drawing room.

Becca rushed back in and put her arms around the girl. "It's all right, Hannah."

"I heard an awful sound, Delphi. I think it's a forest ghost."

"He's a mountain lion and he's gone, or you might be referring to Annie's yelping, she scared him away."

Sarah and Becca concluded they must take turns guarding against the lion. After gathering quilts and pillows on the back porch, they prepared for a long night of shifts. They both fell asleep huddled against the back door. That's where Thad found them at sun-up.

He shook Becca gently.

"Why are you sleeping out here, hiding from bedbugs?"

"Not funny," she grumbled. "We spent the night guarding your elk."

Thad laughed. "Sleeping all cuddled up together under a quilt... that's what you call guarding?"

Sarah climbed out from under the quilt, and headed for the outhouse. Thad picked up the spear and Becca's dagger while she folded the quilt.

"At least you were armed, though not adequately."

"I need coffee," Becca mumbled.

Over breakfast, Thad talked of his concerns about the mountain lion.

"I wanted to allow the meat to hang another day or two, but I'll take it down today. Annie, do you want to start cutting up meat?"

The old woman nodded. She filled all the coffee cups. Then she signed to Thad that she needed sharp knives.

"I'll sharpen them first thing," he agreed. "Harry agreed to open shop this morning. People will be bringing in news and ads. He's great with setting type, but his writing skills are poor. I have to write everything out for him. I'll write them up tonight"

"I heard Mrs. Farris tell Mrs. O'Shay that he only got to third grade," offered Hannah. "His Papa made all the boys work and earn money for the family. His papa was a sot."

"You mustn't gossip, Hannah." Thad prompted.

"I don't think Hannah is gossiping," defended Becca. "She's offering information that helps us understand Harry. The better way to say it is that his papa had a drinking problem." *Perhaps Harry has inherited his issues with alcohol.*

"I don't see a difference in that and what I said." Hannah protested.

"Neither do I." Thad chuckled.

Political and social correctness is not here yet, I've noticed... "Saying it my way provides information without sounding so...judgmental. Saying he has a problem is different than calling him a name...like a sot."

"They're both the same thing, Delphi. Everyone knows that."

Thad's face turned sober. "Either way, it created a lot of unnecessary pain for Harry."

He finished his coffee, and set the cup back on its saucer. "Speaking of unnecessary pain, it reminds me of the urgency to set our wedding date."

Thad stacked his knife and fork on his empty plate. "I'm worried about you ladies out here alone, and last night gives me more concern. Are you going to want a fancy affair or a simple one?"

I wish I could know what's written in the future journal concerning this. I wouldn't have to make decisions...

"Simple is fine. I have no idea how to plan a fancy wedding." *Not in this century, anyway.*

"Oh, but everyone will be aggrieved if they're not invited, Delphi." Hannah looked at her in dismay.

"All right then, it'll be opened to everyone, but just not fancy."

"You'll have to have a new dress. Every bride needs a new dress for her wedding."

"Maybe I should let you plan it, Hannah." Becca teased.

"I want a photograph taken," commented Thad.

"May I...or rather...Sarah and I, be your maids? Hannah asked. "You know...stand up there with you and all."

"Of course, I'd be honored for both of you to be my maids."

"Then we'll need new dresses, too." Hannah offered a mischievous smile.

"How long will it take to have Mrs. Leng make three new dresses?"

Thad's brows were knitted as new roadblocks threatened his timeline.

"Can't take more than a couple of weeks," answered Hannah. "I'll make all the buttonholes and sew the hems for her. I won't even charge."

Becca laughed. "That's noble of you, considering one of the dresses will be yours."

"I'm taking the liberty to set the date for three weeks from yesterday," said Thad.

"I'll catch up with the Reverend today, and the photographer. I'll also have Mrs. Leng come over to do the measurements with you ladies. I'll place an invitation in the paper as soon as I have the date set with Titus."

*I guess that takes care of it...*A combination of excitement and anxiety moved through Becca. Thad changed the subject.

"I'll sharpen knives for Annie while you get ready for your school visit. Mr. Mackey suggested we arrive first thing, while the teacher is getting started."

Wonder why Mr. Mackey told you and not me...it's my job. I feel like I'm being micro-managed...

When Becca came down from dressing; Annie had filled a large tub with water and was stirring in salt. The kitchen table was cleared; brown paper saved from shopping bundles covered it. A huge hunk of the elk lay ready for cutting. Hannah and Sarah sat close by, each holding a butcher knife.

"I wasn't excited about this at first, but now I'm sorry to miss out."

Thad laughed as he washed his hands in the basin. "You aren't missing out, my darling. There'll be plenty to do when we get back."

Becca and Thad mounted their horses. Becca, dressed in her blue ridding outfit, wore the green velvet cape from Delphi's carpet bag. She resisted the comfort of moccasins, and cramped her feet into the tight high-topped shoes.

The morning was damp and chilly. Fog had lifted, but the gray skies promised rain. Bonnie rode in close proximity to Thad's mare, while Dublin kept pace with her on the other side.

"I can't believe you tolerate that dumb gilding tagging along like a duckling."

"He's causing no problems," Becca defended. "He just wants to look after his lady like you plan to look out for me."

Thad smiled, "Geldings don't have ladies."

"Tell that to Dublin, I dare you."

"No, I have no need to be bitten by him again."

70

"There can be no keener revelation of a society's soul than the way in which it treats its children."

—Nelson Mandela

At the school, Thad tied the horses. Mr. Mackey stood outside waiting for them. A man, about thirty years of age, stepped out of the building and rang a large hand bell. Children who were playing at the side of the building, and children just arriving, scurried to the door. As they filled the building, Becca look at the structure.

It wasn't anything like the pictures she had seen of old schoolhouses. It was a simple design, possibly a former house. A chimney at one end assured her there was heat. Smoke circled out and into the fresh air. The west side had no windows... *I hope there's enough natural light inside*...Stepping into the entrance, she noted four windows on the east wall...*They planned it like this to block the cold ocean winds.*

Two rows of hooks, one on each side of the door, held coats, capes and hats. It was apparent that one row was for girls and the other for boys. A long table stood at the back. A bench provided seating on one side, facing the blackboard. Three boys and two girls took places there. Becca guessed their ages to be around ten to twelve. Each child had a slate and chalk. The slates were in poor condition. Two were cracked, held together only by the frames. Another one was only a half slate with a rough broken edge.

In front of the table was a mix matched row of desks. Ten children crowded into them. Two children sat at each desk, sharing one chair per desk. These children appeared to be seven to eight years old. Their slates were equally worn. At the front of the room, a small bench held four very small students. Six to seven years old was Becca's guess, and they had neither desk nor table. They held their slates or pieces of slate in their tiny laps.

A small table served as the teacher's desk. It was positioned closest to the stove and received maximum benefit of any heat the small wood burner might produce.

Mr. Fitzgerald called role. Becca noticed that someone had carefully painted the letters of the alphabet on the windowless wall... *They're beautiful cursive...Like calligraphy... but why so high?...They'll get kinks in their little necks trying to view them...the younger ones need to turn their heads around like owls to see them at all.*

Mr. Mackey introduced Becca, explained she would be taking over soon, and that she was here to acquaint herself with the class and procedures. He offered her the only remaining chair. Thad stood behind her. Mr. Fitzgerald nodded. He gave Becca an examining and lingering gaze that made her uncomfortable, even in her liberated mindset. She felt Thad tense behind her. The teacher turned and began writing math problems on the left side of board.

Thad leaned over and whispered. "I've seen him around. He's a bad egg. He is disrespectful of women..."

"Shhh."

The oldest children began working the math on their slates. Occasionally, one would sneak a glance and offer a shy smile. Next, the school master wrote a list of words on the center part of the board. The students in the center area began writing them on their slates. A bumping noise caused him to turn around.

"Clyde, stop making that infernal noise!"

Becca stood so that she could see which child bore the name Clyde. She slipped off the cape and hung it over the chair. The front bench held three girls and one boy. Mr. Fitzgerald began writing numbers on the remaining side of the board. These, Becca assumed were for the youngest students...*These children have been in school for over a month. This doesn't seem to be advancing them very much.*

The thumping began again.

"Clyde, come here!"

"Teacher," said the child next to him. "His feet doesn't touch the floor, he can't help his legs swinging."

Mr. Fitzgerald turned and faced the girl. He pointed his finger in her face and boomed. "Don't you dare speak to me unless I call on you."

She crumbled into tears. He walked to the table and picked up his pointing stick.

"Clyde, come to me, now! You may be new, but it's best you learn early that my classroom has no disruptions."

The little boy stepped forward. His face was ashen. Becca shot a look at Mr. Mackey who leaned against the wall. His arms were folded and he showed no expression of descent. She rushed forward.

"Hold out you hands, take your punishment like a man," the teacher demanded as he raised the stick high.

The boy bravely lifted his shaking little arms holding his palms up.

Suddenly, the classroom gasped as Becca sprung and grabbed the stick. She wrestled it from the man's grip. Thad hurriedly weaved his tall frame through the small spaces to reach her.

"Delphi, give it to me."

The teacher looked a Becca with eyes of rage.

"How dare you interfere with my discipline?"

"Discipline? This is abuse. What do you know of discipline? Was it self-discipline that caused you to shoot yourself in your stupid foot?"

There was some twittering among the older children.

"That was an accident! Miss. Castile, I'll not allow you to disrespect me in my classroom." His voice was unnecessarily loud.

"You had an accident, did you? And did anyone flog you for it?"

He was silent. "But you, a big adult were preparing to strike a very small child because of an accident?" Did it occur to you to place that wooden box over there under his feet so his legs wouldn't swing and thump against the bench? No. of course not, that takes thinking."

She turned to Clyde. "Go back to you seat, honey, no one is going to harm you while I'm here."

She turned back to the angry man who now was puffed up like a toad.

"Delphi," Thad hissed. "Give the stick to me."

"Now," Mr. Fitzgerald, you told this six-year old to take pain like a man. A good teacher models what he teaches. Let's have you show the class, Sir, how a man takes pain. Hold out your hands please, palms up."

"I will not," he shouted.

"There's no reason to yell, Mr. Fitzgerald. You're much larger and stouter than little Clyde. It won't harm you nearly as much as it would hurt him. Come now, be a man."

She raised the stick high and looked at him expectantly.

The man's face was dark red; he looked at Mr. Mackey who looked back in aghast.

"I will never permit a mere woman to strike me! Never!" he yelled. Mr. Mackey, I demand you get this unreasonable...Bit..."

He didn't have opportunity to complete his sentence. Thad's fist found its way to his mouth.

Mr. Mackey dismissed school for the day and for the remainder of the week. Mr. Fitzgerald, missing two front teeth, quit on the spot. He was last seen riding in the direction of the Fort Lincoln.

Thad and Becca returned home. Annie insisted on burning the deep gash in Thad's knuckles, insisting, "Bites are very bad... very bad."

Although Becca knew she was right, she left the room and collapsed on the sofa... *I don't know how she can do that...it makes me feel a need to vomit...*Thad came to the drawing room with his hand loosely bandaged. Sarah brought in calming tea. Hannah was full of questions. She could hardly allow Becca to finish one answer before beginning another. When the story was completely told, she commented.

"Pshaw, Delphi, the school master whipped youngun's every day when I went to school."

"He whipped little children for bumping the leg of a bench?" Delphi pressed.

"No, but we got whacked on our knuckles for missing spelling words, or not remembering a history date."

"When I was forced to work for the farmers who bought me, I was flogged for spilling food, not making their bed good enough, and for speaking my native language," added Sarah.

"Well, it's not happening when I'm in the room."

"Are you sure you still have the job?" asked Thad.

He sounds a little too hopeful..."

Mr. Mackey told me to be prepared to begin next Monday."

"Do you still wish to be a school marm?"

"Yes, for one term at least. I want to prove I can teach more effectively, and have better discipline than what's been done before. I'm going back to rearrange that room. The smallest children should be closer to warmth. I want a blackboard hung along the entire blank wall. I'll arrange for proper sized tables and benches to be built. I'll order some books from James. There's a need for more slates..."

"Sounds like you're going to be paying them for the privilege of teaching in their school, Delphi." Thad mumbled.

Poor Thad...he was hoping I'd back out now...not a chance ...

"Hannah and Sarah, I'd like you to come to school. I could use your help, and there's more that each of you could learn. Would you be willing ... for a few days a week at least?"

Thad set his cup on the tea table and stood up. "I have to get back to the shop. I've got writing to do, and I want to catch up with the Rev. and the photographer."

Nothing gets him distracted from his cause...guess we're alike in that regard...

After he left, Becca and the girls rejoined Annie in the kitchen. "Show me what to do," said Becca, tying on an apron.

She looked at what was already accomplished. Long thin strips of red dense meat lay submerged under salt water.

"How did you do this before, without a sack of salt?".

"Sea water," replied Sarah as she cut another chunk of elk off the hindquarter. "We can make salt."

Becca noticed a thick wooden stick hanging on the wall. Long brown strings were tied to it. Another stick was tied to their ends.

"What's that?"

"Sinew," answered Sarah. "The Grandmother removed it first. She's stretching and drying it. It'll be used for sewing moccasins and tying grass in baskets."

"And those bones, does she have plans for those?"

"She'll boil them and scrape out the marrow. It's good as a tonic. The rest of the broth makes a sticky substance to use with herbs for healing. I'll use some to oil my bow. She cooks with it too. She'll boil down the hoofs for a sticky paste."

"Ah, like glue. Maybe she'll share with me for the school." Becca picked up a knife.

Sarah demonstrated how to take a round piece of meat and peel around it in a spiral. It transformed into a long thin piece of meat.

"After we've finished cutting the meat, we'll build a small fire and hang the strips above it. We'll turn it frequently until it's dried through and through."

"What if it rains?" asked Hannah, as she dropped a finished piece into the salt water.

"We'd normally build a light shelter of branches and leaves, but Thad said he'd make a smoke house. He has loose lumber piled behind The Print Shop. We'll need it for smoking salmon soon."

Becca worked several hours and soon mastered the skill. Her mind busily sorted through her concerns...*I must find out what books and aids are available...I remember studying the development of American text books in college...I just need to bring this time period back to memory... I remember Webster, McGuffey, and the one curriculum designed to have older students help teach younger pupils...Who created it? That's a good idea in this situation...*

Her thoughts were interrupted. Hannah, practicing on the crutches, stood at the window. "Reverend Walker is here."

Becca jumped up and washed her hands. She took off the bloodstained apron and smoothed back her hair.

"Sarah, would you please make tea, Reverend Walker's favorite tea?"

The knock came at the door, and Warrior announced it with his pathetic attempt at barking. Becca opened it to greet the clergyman.

"Well, what a surprise. Thad was planning to search you out today."

"Indeed, I spoke with him before riding here. The wedding date is set. I stopped there to place an announcement in the paper for choir practice. Since your reading group is held on Friday evenings, I've determined Saturday afternoon will be assigned for choir practice. After the piano arrives, we'll have it at the church, but until then, I supposed you'd want it here. You have a piano, after all."

"That'll be fine. I'll ask Molly to come and accompany on the piano. It's a bit out of tune, I suspect. Come, have a seat in the parlor."

Titus Walker took off his hat and settled into a chair. He laid a thin stack of papers on the side table.

"I came to discuss the choir, Miss Castile."

Please call me Delphi. My last name will soon change, and your wife and I are on a first name basis.

"I will if you wish, Delphi. As you may know, I have great admiration for John Wesley. His life inspired my ministry to a great extent. The Reverend Wesley had a rule for everything...I like that... without rules, there's no discipline. "

Discipline...there's a word I'd prefer to not hear again today...wonder what he'll think where he hears about the incident at school.

Titus cleared his throat, and held up one of the papers to read. "Here are his rules for singing hymns."

"He had rules for that?"

"Yes, of course, singing is an offering to God. It must be done correctly."

Sarah brought in tea filled cups. She placed one by the Reverend and one by Becca. "I know you prefer it sugared, Sir, so I added it already."

"Why, thank you, young lady. You're very thoughtful." He took a sip then returned to the paper.

71

"Though we may not think alike, may we not all love alike?"

—John Wesley

"**N**ow, there are seven rules. I'll cover them with you and you will teach them to the choir. I'd like them memorized. Perhaps at the first practice, you can have them write copies."

Memorize? *No...that's not happening.*

"**Number one; learn these tunes before learning any others. I understand this to mean those chosen to sing at service. The members must commit to singing no other tunes than those planned for service.** Only when they have them down perfect, can they take part in any other singing."

And how am I suppose to police that, pray tell... even if I wanted to.

"**Number two; sing them exactly as they are written; without altering or mending. If you have learned them otherwise, unlearn them as soon as you can...** I think that's plainly said. I need not explain."

So Mr. Wesley didn't want anyone arranging the stuff he wrote... interesting... thumbs down on that one as well...

"Number three; sing strong, let not weakness hinder. It is a cross to you, take it up."

Right...we want the participants to suffer...that would really please God...

"Number four; sing lustily and with good courage. Beware of singing as if you are dead, or half asleep."

Lustily? I can't believe that word slipped out your mouth, Rev.

Titus drank half of his tea and then focused back on the paper.

"Number five; sing modestly. Do not bawl to be heard above others"

That's a good rule, though I prefer to call it blending.

"Number six; sing in time. Do not run ahead or stay behind the leading voices."

Well, duh...that's common sense...

"Number seven; sing spiritually. Please him more than yourself. Attend to the sense of what you sing. See that your heart is not carried off with the sound..."

If you're not listening to the sound...how will you know you are keeping the other six rules?

Titus emptied his cup. Sarah miraculously stepped in carrying a teapot and provided a refill.

"There, you see, Miss...Delphi...These are splendid rules."

"Thank you Reverend, I'll start preparing for Saturday's rehearsal. But tell me, what is it about Reverend Wesley that inspires you?"

Titus who had just taken a sip of tea held the cup and smiled.

"He was a fine man. I heard about him from my first employer and mentor. He taught me to read, using Wesley's sermons. I read his biography later and determined that I wanted to be just like him."

"So you've never read any writings except Wesley and the Bible?"

He took another drink. "I also read church history while in seminary, and now my reading includes, *The Songs of Hiawatha*, as you know."

No wonder he's warped... Wesley was a great leader of his day, but not assigned to be the only role model forever...

"He lived a hundred years ago, correct?"

The man nodded. "Yes and his words live on."

"But, unlike Christ, he wasn't perfect...don't you agree."

Titus set down his empty cup folded his hands and appeared to mull the question for a moment. "I suppose not, though I know of no offense attached to him."

Remembering the family vacation in Savannah, Becca collected her thoughts. She wanted to relate the story she heard there accurately.

"All of us have sinned, sometimes purposefully and sometimes neglectfully. Mr. Wesley did as well. I visited a church where he once preached. Would you like to hear a true story about him? I'm sure it wasn't in the biography you read."

Sarah refilled the pastor's cup again, and he sat forward prepared to listen.

"Savannah Georgia is a very old town, and it has a very old church. John Wesley visited the United States. He held mass several times in this church. The governor of Georgia lived in Savannah at the time. He had a beautiful, unmarried daughter."

Titus' enthusiastic expression changed to a worried one.

"No, it's not what you may have imagined, let me finish." Titus drank some tea. "As you know John Wesley never married. I would suppose his ministry, writing songs, sermons, and rules, took a great deal of time. However, when he was introduced to the governor's daughter, he was smitten. For the months he was in Savannah, he pursued her. She was a pampered young woman. She had no interest in marriage to a strict, rule-bound, traveling clergyman."

"She could have done much worse," Titus grumbled as he set his cup in its saucer.

"Perhaps, but when he suddenly proposed, she turned him down soundly. He was angry, hurt and disappointed. The following Sunday morning, he refused to serve her communion at mass. She was publically humiliated. To refuse her communion implied she had unrepentant sin. This could set gossip tongues wagging."

The Reverend looked at his hands. "I'm not sure I care to hear the rest of this story."

"Oh, but you must. Her father, the governor, heard what had happened and was irate. He hired killers to murder Mr. Wesley, or at least made the minister believe that he had."

"That's awful. He was unwise in what he did, but he didn't deserve to die."

"Yes, well honor and a good name caused more than one southern gentleman to kill or die. Mr. Wesley wasted no time in getting out of the country on the first boat back to England. It's my understanding that he never returned to these shores."

"That's the most disturbing story I've ever heard. He did so many great things...and to have an ugly blotch to undermine it all."

"But you see, Reverend, life is filled with lessons, not just ours, but the mistakes of others as well. That mistake was a ringer, to be sure. His anger and revenge hurt another person, caused talk in the area that wasn't positive about the church, and he could have lost his life. We must assume he repented and learned to never abuse his power as a clergyman again."

He looked into her face. "Why did you tell me this story?"

"So you can see him for what he was. John Wesley was a mere human just like you and me. He got some things right and some things wrong...just like you and me. In the seventeen hundreds he fulfilled his mission and walked his path. But this is one hundred and fifty years later. You have a mission and path...it's not his...it's yours."

"I'm not sure what you want me to draw from this."

"There's one life, sent by God, who is our example. His words will last through the centuries. These rules you just read to me were for a group of people who lived one hundred- fifty years ago. Our choir may need different instructions. They're in a different country, different time, and some are quite talented."

"We can modify them, if you like."

"I'm seeing this in a bigger picture than the choir, Reverend."

"The rules Christ gave us in his teachings; those are the only ones we need to govern our spiritual lives. He's the one to inspire you. Mr. Wesley was pointing to Christ, but many people end up focused on the pointer and not Christ."

"I see what you mean." He picked up the remaining papers. I was going to suggest you use Reverend Wesley's songs, but perhaps I should allow you liberty to decide."

Becca took the papers. "We'll use one Wesley hymn and one newer song each Sunday. That's good balance, don't you think?"

"Yes, I agree."

"The Lengs are here," announced Hannah.

The pastor stood. "I'll go now. I've other visits to make."

"Wait, I'll get some elk steaks for you and Grace."

As Titus left, Mrs. Leng entered. Mr. Leng lingered to tie the horse.

Becca led her to the drawing room, knowing Hannah would wish to be included.

"To what do we owe this wonderful surprise?"

Becca offered her the only upholstered chair in the room. Mrs. Leng smiled broadly. "Get vedy for wedding...need to pick dress..."

"It's thoughtful of you to come so soon. I plan to keep it simple."

The seamstress pulled two small china dolls from her carpet bag. She laid them on the side table, displaying two styles of wedding frocks. Hannah gasped.

"Oh, Delphi, the white one is lovely...please choose that one."

Sarah stepped forward and examined the white satin dress trimmed with delicate lace. She smiled approval.

"But it would be more practical to pick this one."

Becca picked up the doll with the dark blue velvet gown. It was trimmed at neck, cuffs and hem with broad strips of black satin.

"This dress would be suitable for church, attending plays, soirees', and special gatherings."

"Oh, but for a first wedding, the bride must wear white, Delphi. Everyone knows that."

It's not my first wedding...I'd feel silly wearing white...

"First wedding...do you expect me to have more than one?" She looked at Hannah with a teasing smile.

"Widows wear dark wedding dresses. Sometime brides with questionable reputations have no choice but wear blue...but you, Delphi, you must choose the white," Hannah insisted.

"Then when the wedding is over, what do I do with the dress? It's such a waste."

Hannah placed her hands on her hips and rolled her eyes. "You'll save it for your daughters, Delphi, everyone knows that."

"Sorry, Hannah, I'm leaning toward the blue. I wonder what Thad would want. He believes in careful spending."

"Which takes longer to make?" She asked Mrs. Leng.

The women shrugged. "Same time...no difference."

"Which is more expensive?"

"I sew it for free...my gift to you...the cloth, velvet...satin...cost same."

"That's very generous of you, Mrs. Leng, I didn't expect that, but I do appreciate it."

Hannah's arms were now folded across her chest. "There, now you see there's no reason for you to not have a proper wedding dress."

Becca's head began to ache. She realized she was hungry as well as over stimulated from all that had happened in the day.

"All right, the white one it shall be."

Mrs. Leng took two more dolls from the bag.

"Oooh!" Hannah squealed, causing all of them to jump. "Look Sarah, here are the maid choices."

Each of the two dolls wore very different frocks. One was dressed in dark green muslin with layers of ruffles and long sleeves that ended in wide lace. The other selection was more slim-lined in the front, while yards of gathers created a bustle on the back. It was made of light blue satin, trimmed in white lace and exposed a tiny bit of shoulder. Both girls immediately focused on it. "It's the color of the sky," commented Sarah, touching it gingerly.

"I've never had a satin dress before," murmured Hannah.

I wonder if that wide neckline will give the Reverend a stroke...well, doesn't matter, I'm out voted... It took Mrs. Leng an hour to measure the women. Becca insisted that Annie have a new dress as well.

"You will be there, as my grandmother," she coaxed.

Annie chose plain muslin in brown with black trim, and cloth-covered black buttons.

Mr. Leng loaded up Annie's baskets and the bundles of sewing Hannah had completed. He paid them for their work. New work was left for Hannah. They departed with a large elk roast in hand.

Becca went to the kitchen, poured herself a cup of coffee, and buttered a piece of cold fry bread. The others took their place at the table, and prepared to continue with the meat cutting.

"Since I'm already dressed for riding, I'm going to town. I need to pick up some things at The Mercantile, and get an order in to James. There's not much afternoon left," she explained.

Hurrying to the barn, she saddled Bonnie, and placed a halter on Dublin. As they cantered down the road she met Thad coming from town. He was using Abe's wagon and team. He pulled the horses to a stop.

"To where be the lady of the castle sojourning ?"

Becca laughed at his playfulness. "Just to The Mercantile, I won't be long. What do you have in the wagon?"

Silly question, I can see its lumber and poles.

"I'm going to get started on the smoke house before it gets dark. Please be back before sundown."

Becca tied both horses in from of the store. Several people looked at her curiously.

"See, Dublin," she whispered. "Your separation anxiety and insistence to come along brings extra attention to us."

Inside, she went straight over the James's corner. "Hello," he greeted. "I'll bet you need school books."

She sat down in a straight back chair beside the small table he used as a desk. "So you've heard I got the teaching position?"

He looked away and smiled. "Yes, I heard...you'll be a much better teacher than the scoundrel they had."

She lowered her voice. "Has it gotten around...my misadventure?"

He smiled more broadly. "Yes, Delphi...your misadventures always get around...it's a small town, after all. Don't be troubled, no one liked Fitzgerald. He's been known to pick fights at the saloons."

He leaned closer and whispered. "He's been heard to brag about his use of brothels...he's abusive."

"All I care about is his treatment of children...I found it unacceptable."

"Do you want to order something specifically?"

Becca took a list out of her purse. "I once studied about the development of school textbooks. After giving it a great deal of thought, I was able to remember these particular ones. I'll need supplies as well. I'll have you write down a copy of my list. If you can determine what's available and from where to get things, I'd be most obliged."

James opened a small ink well and dipped in his pen. He looked at her expectantly.

"New slates, at least two dozen...most will be for me, but I'd like you to have some on hand for new students that enter the term late. I expect some older boys to return."

James began writing in his decorative hand.

"I must get some writing hints from you, James. Your penmanship is flawless. Next, I'd like some maps. I have no idea what might be available. I want my students to understand what a big and diverse world we have."

"I need to learn about the geography of this era..."I'll need a Webster Dictionary for the classroom, and a set of The Scholar's Arithmetic Series by a writer named Adams. I'm sorry; I can't remember his first name."

James wrote dutifully.

"I want three complete sets of McGuffey Eclectic Series for reading and spelling," she added.

James looked up as he dipped his pen in ink. "You want three sets?

"Yes, they'll still have to share, but I need them to have access to books"."

"I'll also need The American First-Class Reader. It's by Murray and designed for older learners. It's also recommended for one room school houses. I'm going to use it to set up a mentoring plan with older students helping younger ones."

"James nodded and wrote down the title. "Is that all?"

"No, not yet, I'm interested in a Primer ...The Pestalozzian. It's by John Knaggy. It'll include teaching tools...a "kaleidoscope and blocks with the letters on them, as well as a frame in which to place them...have you seen these aids, James?"

He shook his head. "I look forward to seeing how you use them."

"Finally, in watching the Lengs use their abacus; I'm convinced it's must for teaching small children math. I'd like at least three of those."

"This is the largest order I've had from anyone. It'll be expensive."

"I know, but investing in children's education is the most important investment a person can make."

James blew on the list to dry the ink. "I'll send telegrams to several companies in San Francisco as well as Back East. I won't rest until I track them down for you."

"Thank you James, I knew I could count on you. I must pick up a few things from Mr. Sanders, and hurry home before it gets dark."

She stood up and pushed the chair under the table. James stood up politely. "I won't charge you for my profits. You'll only have to pay for the materials and shipping costs."

"That's thoughtful, James, but I fully intended for you to profit from this order."

"I'd like to invest in education, as well." He smiled as though embarrassed. "After all, the more educated these children become, the more books I can sell them."

It was a happy Becca who rode home as the sun started to sink into the sea...*I must take James a nice package of elk steaks.*

72

"What is life? It is the flash of a firefly in the night. It is the breath of a buffalo in the wintertime. It is the little shadow which runs across the grass and loses itself in the sunset."

—Crowfoot, Blackfoot Warrior

After a supper of elk steak, mashed potatoes, gravy, and cooked carrots, Becca retired to her room for a sponge bath and early bedtime. She opened the journal reluctantly. *I'm so happy; it's going to bum me to read that Delphi isn't...she may have not posted at all...* She was surprised to see several paragraphs hurriedly written. It was not dated, but Becca knew it was written since their contact.

> **Beth and I had a long conversation about my situation. I must acknowledge that not everything about life in this time is deplorable.** *Well, I must say, you're using very good English, Delphi.*
>
> **I like the clothing, it's quite comfortable. The cars are convenient, and the food is enticing. I'm growing quite fond of television. The toiletries or**

rather, cosmetics, are delightful. Your sister, I suppose I should now refer to her as my sister, tells me you preferred to not use them. *True, the less the better...*

I think that is regrettable as I have developed methods that enhance your features remarkably. I've allowed your hair to grow, and will go to a salon this week to have it styled. *Interesting, I must visit during daytime hours so I can see what you've done to me.*

I've agreed with Beth to pursue education. She has convinced me it is as important for a woman in these times as for a man was in my birth era. Tomorrow we will go to a place Beth calls Continuing Education. Although you completed a college education, I do not have your knowledge. We will tell them I lost memory in the accident. I will take tests on pornography. Then, we will know what classes I must take.

Wait...you can't mean that...what are you trying to say... proficiency...that's it. That's a great idea; just don't request a pornography test.

While there, we will enlist me for classes to learn about computer. I must learn to write with the alphabet keys and swim the sea for knowledge. *I assume you mean, surf the net.*

The lamp's glow grew dim. Glancing at it, Becca saw its fuel was nearly depleted...*We've all been too busy to refuel the lamps. I must do it tomorrow...*Picking up the pencil she wrote...

I think all your plans are marvelous.

The light was fading when Becca blew out the wick's tiny flame and nestled into her pillow. It seemed to her that only a moment had passed when a morning breeze blew across her face, waking her to the morning light.

She passed through the kitchen where Annie stood filling the coffeepot from the water bucket. "I'll bring in kindling, Annie."

Unlocking the backdoor, she passed through. Stepping off the back porch and heading to the wood pile she stopped in her tracks. The mountain lion lay under the same tree he had visited before. He watched her with interest but not in a threatening manner. She scooped up an armload of small pieces of wood, and hurried back into the house.

"Annie, the big cat's back."

Annie calmly went to the door and presented her loud throat call. The animal jumped, and loped away.

"I wish he'd go stalking somewhere else."

"Very old, he'll die soon," the old woman muttered.

Becca waited until after breakfast to feed the horses and release the chickens. She looked around in all directions, and determined that the animal was gone. After spending time with Bonnie and Dublin, she released them into the fenced area. Inside, she poured a cup of coffee as Sarah entered the kitchen. Hannah followed on the crutches. They each filled a bowl with hot oatmeal, and sat at the kitchen table.

"The Grandmother says we must do the washing today," said Sarah. She blew on the spoonful of steaming gruel.

"It won't take long," said Hannah cheerfully. "I can stand long enough to scrub on the washboard, and you can hang clothes on the line."

"Keep an eye out for the mountain lion," Becca cautioned. "I saw him again this morning."

"I'll keep my spear close by," replied Sarah.

Later, while cleaning her room, Becca strapped the dagger on her wrist. By ten AM, she had completed sweeping and dusting. Annie had pumpkin pies in the oven, and the girls were finishing up with the laundry. They enjoyed tea on the porch, and then moved on to their work. Annie and Sarah stretched the elk hide on the ground in the back yard.

"Grandmother believes the hide is calling the lion," explained Sarah.

"Becca sat in the porch rocker, writing lesson plans to use until her supplies arrived. Hannah sat in the porch swing, sewing buttonholes in a bodice for Mrs. Leng. Sarah shoveled ashes from the pile where stove ashes were emptied. Annie, on her knees, spread them over the hair side of the hide, making sure it was completely covered.

"What is she doing?" Becca asked, looking up from her writing.

"I can't possibly imagine," answered Hannah.

Sarah stepped up on the porch, hearing the exchange.

"She's treating the hide. The ashes will help remove the hair. It will also make the scent less appealing to the lion."

The native women then rolled the large skin into a long bundle, hair-side in. Sarah dug a hole to put it in, and they buried it. Becca watch curiously.

"We'll dig it up in four days," said Sarah. "Then, we'll scrape off what remains of the hair. We'll soak it in acorn tea over night, dry it in the sun, and pound it until it's soft. We can make moccasin soles, knife sheaths, belts, things to sell."

"I'm so glad nothing is wasted of that lovely animal." Becca commented.

She looked over her own work...*I have a spelling list for each level, and math lessons for the first day. I'll have the older students read Hiawatha and the younger ones look through Hannah's children's poem book. That'll give me an idea of their skill levels. At this rate I'll have a week of lesson plans before I start. I also must start planning for the church choir.*

"What are your plans for that?"

Delphi?

"Oui, who else talks to you in your head?"

I'm pleased you're here. I read your post and I proud of all you're planning to do.

"Oui, I read your hasty reply."

I'm sorry I couldn't write more, my lamp went out.

"I started to write in your journal, but I turned up here, so I'll tell you instead. I tested this morning. I did well on grammar and arithmetic... they called it math. I did quite awful on history and science."

Of course, you can't expect to pass a test on information you've never been provided.

"Beth arranged for remedy lessons... "

Remedial classes?

"Oui... in those two subjects...and I'm also beginning lessons with the computer tomorrow. After leaving the Education Office, I went to therapy. The Therapist is pleased. I will start in the pool this week. I don't know how to swim, but they think I do...since you did."

You'll learn quickly, and it'll be so good for your recovery.

"Now what will you teach the choir?"

I don't know...We'll just sing a song over and over until we learn it. I don't know notes very well...

"Do you know shaped notes?"

What's that?

"The little shapes of each note. It tells you the pitch, especially if there's no instrument, or if your singers can't read music."

I'm sorry, I'm not following...

Becca could imagine Delphi rolling her eyes.

"Do, re, mi, fa, sol, la, ti, do...Each note represents a pitch of one note in the scale... They've been written in sheet music and hymn books for several years or more...I'll write them in the journal. You'll then understand what you are seeing when you look at the music. If you assign the singers parts, they will carry the harmony by following the shapes. If some don't know them, you may need to spend a few sessions teaching them...."

Delphi?

Becca jumped up and hurried inside. She went directly to the piano and picked up the hymnbook. Opening it, she looked at the music staff.

What-da-you-know, they are shaped. Why did I not notice that before?

An old song, Doe, a deer, a female deer...ran through her mind...

I always wondered what that ridiculous song was about.

Becca went to the kitchen and scooped beans into a bowl, thankful that Annie had put them on to cook early in the day. She ate them as she gazed out the kitchen window. She spotted movement and thought it was the lion, but she wasn't sure. A shadowy form lurked around the inner edge of the woods. After lunch she changed into her riding attire, saddled Bonnie, harnessed Dublin and rode to town.

Her first stop was at the Mill. Tying the horses, she went inside.

"May I please speak to your manager?" she asked a young man who busily stacked rough-cut boards.

"Manager? You must be asking for my foreman."

He disappeared to the back of the large building. Soon he returned with an older man. "This is Claude Williams. He can answer your questions, Miss."

Becca introduced herself, explained her new position at the school, and related how poorly equipped the school was.

"James Randall invested in the town's children with his assistance in ordering text books. I'm hoping to find others interested as well. We need desks or tables. A bookshelf would be nice. What do you think you could do for our children, Mr. Williams?"

The man leaned against the wall and filled his pipe. He played around with lighting it, and Becca restrained her impatience.

"My grandchild attends the country school. I heard you ran that Fitzgerald off."

Becca caught her breath...*That got around really fast...maybe he liked the strong discipline.*

"Well, Sir, I wouldn't say I ran him off. He more or less just..."

"I'm glad he's gone. He was too much of a braggart to teach, in my way of thinking."

He puffed on his pipe. Becca stepped back to avoid the smoke.

"I figure I can come up with some lumber that's not going anywhere else. You need a bookcase?"

"Yes, and three long narrow tables in three different heights. We'll also need benches properly measured, and built to fit the tables."

"Do you have someone to build them?"

"No, I'll be searching out a carpenter next."

"My son Dan is handy with wood. He's a fisherman, but he has time off this time of year. Get your measurements to me for the tables, benches and bookcase. I'll ask him to build them. It shouldn't take him long."

"Thank you so much, Mr. Williams. I plan to report all donations in the paper... only if I have permission from the donors, of course."

The foreman emptied his pipe on the sawdust covered floor, and put it in his pocket. He looked at her and smiled.

"That's considerate of you, Ma'am. Give the Mill credit for donating the lumber, and give Dan recognition for the carpentry."

Back with Bonnie and Dublin, Becca took paper and a pencil from her saddlebag. She wrote the names and donations down... *I must be sure to get these all correct when putting them in the paper...*She rode on into town and stopped at The Print Shop. Inside, Harry stood behind the counter.

"Hello, Delphi, Thad is in the print room."

"Good afternoon, Harry, I want to put a small piece in the paper. I'll write it down, and you can determine how to post it."

She wrote a short paragraph stating that a few citizens had invested in the education of the children in the country school. She listed James, the Mill, and Daniel Williams. She also noted their contributions. She listed items still needed; blackboards, chalk, books, pencils, paper, bowls, cups, spoons and a large pot to cook hot lunches at school. She entitled it; Investing in our future, and ended it with; all interested in this investment, please contact Delphi Castile.

Thad entered the room. He wore his printer's apron splattered with ink. Flashing a big smile, he poured himself a cup of ink-black coffee.

"Would you like some?"

She shook her head...*I think he must accidently mix it with the ink.*

He took off the apron and hung it on a hook.

"I've got everything ready for Harry to print. I'll spend the rest of the day finishing up Annie's smoke house."

He pulled out a chair for Becca and another for himself. She sat with him at the small table. He took a sip of the brew.

"I think getting the meat smoking will discourage wild animals from coming around."

"I saw the big cat this morning."

He held his cup in mid air. "Did he come in close? I wish he'd show up when I'm there with my gun."

"No, he just sat under the tree. He didn't look threatening...he just watched me.

"Big cats are unpredictable. I won't rest until I've shot him."

"If he doesn't bother us, why shoot him? He's old and will die soon...Annie says so."

Thad set his cup down on the table. He looked seriously into Becca's eyes.

"It's one thing to take on a defeated dog and a contrary horse, but I won't tolerate a mountain lion...he can't be hanging around."

I guess I'll just have to have Annie keep him scared off when you're around with your Winchester...

When Becca got up to go, Thad left with her. Harry thanked her for the elk meat she had sent over, and mentioned that Sybil was looking forward to the book gathering. She and Thad rode back together, discussing plans for the wedding and future use of the smoke house.

Thad worked steadily as he finished the loosely built structure. He explained that space between the boards would allow smoke to pass through. The roof was tight and high with a stove pipe sticking out the top. A small fire would be kept burning until the meat was dry. They would hope for some rain free days.

"Abe and I bought a hog," he explained around the square nails he held in his mouth. I'll smoke it here. He'll use half of it for his establishment. We can have the rest."

He hammered in a nail. "There's nothing like good bacon and ham."

Becca looked past him. A shadowy form emerged from the tree line. She returned to the house and opened the pantry door. There was a bowl of dried elk scraps Annie had dried by the wood stove for Warrior. She filled her apron pocket, leaving plenty for her dog. She left by the front door and slipped around the side of the house so that Thad wouldn't notice her. Slowly, she made her way to the edge of the redwood tree line. The shadow had slinked farther back into the shadows. She could see the light of yellow eyes watching her. She laid the dried meat down on the ground.

"I know you're hungry. Thank you for not bothering my chickens and horses. You can't come near the house or Thad will shoot you."

I feel like a fool, talking to a wild creature that may be dangerous. This is a strange place...Ike and Cain...Delphi and me...it's so mystical...I can't help but feel something is strange about this lion..."

73

"The philosophy of the school room in one generation will be the philosophy of the government in the next."

—Abraham Lincoln

The remaining days of Becca's week went by fast. Delphi drew the shaped note scale in the journal as she promised. Becca practiced everyday, both singing the pitches and playing the scales. She was surprised how quickly she paired the sound of the tone and its shape in her memory. She planned how she would introduce it to the choir.

Thad made a make-shift blackboard by painting a large, wide, flat board with black paint. It wasn't as smooth as a slate board, but it would do until the one she ordered came in on the steamer. Meanwhile, she used it for choir practice.

James was successful with telegram communication. Her ordered curriculum would be in on the next steamer. A week of lessons was planned for the school. The school furniture was under construction. Donations were coming in, both requested items and gold coins. Becca set up a ledger to record all that came, and for what they were used.

Hannah now walked without her crutches. Her legs were horribly scarred, but she had escaped disability. She and Sarah agreed to attend school part time. Sarah would go on Tuesdays and Thursdays. Hannah would attend Wednesdays and Fridays. By alternating, Annie would never be alone.

Harry purchased lumber, and men from the church planned to pitch in, and attach a large room onto their small house. Reverend Walker was one of the volunteers. Eight-year-old Emily Farris would start school on Becca's first day to teach.

Mrs. Leng and Hannah focused on the wedding frocks. They would be ready in plenty of time. Becca was glad Hannah had persuaded her to wear the white gown.

The elk was now smoked, wrapped in cotton cloth, and stored in lard cans. There was plenty of meat to last until the pig was butchered.

Sunday afternoon she walked a ways into the woods with the journal. She wanted to check on Delphi. She had frightened Thad and Hannah when they discovered her coming out of the trance. This would provide her privacy. Finding a shady tree surrounded with soft moss, she sat down. Warrior lay beside her. Bringing the sharpened pencil from her apron pocket, Becca opened the journal, and flipped to the first blank page. She wrote about the success of the first choir rehearsal.

Before she could complete her entry, she was overcome with dizziness. The forest trees seemed to whirl around her. She heard Warrior whine and felt him lick her hand from which the journal had fallen. The caws of the crows, complaining about her presence, faded into the distance.

She regained stability in Beth's apartment. Beth and her mother sat on the sofa. Becca placed herself between them. She wished she could feel them, and they could feel her. Delphi, in her wheelchair, had a walker within her reach. Captain Gale, Beth's fiancée, sat on the piano bench. Phillip's parents, side-by-side on the loveseat, held each other and cried. A stranger sat in the middle of the room on an ottoman.

What's going on? I feel I've walked into a funeral. Delphi...I'm here...what's happened.

"Your husband is dead. *I think they expect me to cry...I can't produce tears I don't feel.*"

Becca felt stunned, she glanced around the room. Both her mother and Beth appeared stunned. Captain Gale looked thoughtful.

"Do they suspect foul play?" he asked.

"No," his body will be here tomorrow. As Phil's attorney, I'll assist you with arrangements, Mr. and Mrs. Cates. Rebecca isn't up to the demands of planning a funeral."

"My sister nearly died because of Philip Cates," Beth said tersely. "I don't know why you had everyone meet here for this news."

"They're still legally married," the attorney commented. "You, all of you, are Philip's only family."

Except for Tonya, I don't see her here weeping...

"They broke up within weeks of the boat wreck; I'm sure I told you."

Delphi, when did Phil die, and what caused his death?

"Over a week ago... he went pack-backing with several friends."

You mean backpacking? I never knew he liked doing that. Golf and sailing were his favorite sports.

"I don't know about that...I didn't even know he was away...it's not like we visited each other, after all."

"Captain Gale inquired. "Why did it take so long to find him? They must have planned out their trails?"

"Rogue River Siskiyou National Forest has over a million acres of wilderness. He and his friends became separated," the lawyer explained. "They continued to look for him rather than return to seek help. They had no cell service."

Becca's mother asked softly, "Do they think he fell to his death, or was he killed by an animal?"

Phil's mother sobbed. Becca felt sorrow for her. She held no hard feelings toward his parents.

"Decomposition prevents them from knowing for sure. Perhaps, after the autopsy they'll be able to tell us more. A wild animal definitely mauled him. Whether it was before death or after is not yet clear."

The elder Mr. Cates stood up. "I'm going to take my wife home. This has all been a terrible shock for her. Come, dear, enough for one day."

I hope the lawyer goes too. I want to talk with Delphi about this...no...wait...

Becca became aware of Warrior licking her face.

"Yuk!" She sat up from the slumped position her body had fallen.

Patting Warrior's head, she teased. "I think you need a toothbrush, your breath is awful."

Warrior's eyes were fixed on something behind her. Turning, her heart skipped a beat. Six yards away, lay the mountain lion. The information she had just heard rushed back to her memory...*I was stupid to feed this animal. Thad is right. Wild animals are unpredictable.*

She got up slowly, avoiding eye contact with the cat. "Come, Warrior, let's go."

Monday morning, Becca was up early. She was so excited; she could hardly swallow her breakfast.

"Do we have everything that's needed packed in the carriage?" Thad asked, helping himself to another scoop of hot cornmeal mush.

"Yes, it's been checked off my list. I have my lesson plans, pencils, new chalk that Mr. Sanders donated, and the news print paper you brought home. I have scissors."

I'll assign an older child to cut it into proper paper sizes to be used for tests and writing assignments.

Annie set a large bowl of chopped carrots, turnips, onions, and winter squash on the table. Beside it she laid a small cloth bundle of dried elk.

"Looks like I might need to ride over to the school around dinner time," teased Thad.

Becca smiled, "Some of the mothers volunteered to bring one-pot meals each week, so it won't always be my responsibility. Your wonderful story in the paper really inspired people, Thad. I appreciate it." Maybe school hot lunches will catch on...

He reached across the table and squeezed her hand. "It gratified me to write something for a change. Usually, I organize client ads or edit their news offerings. I think I may start writing a column every week."

Once the last of her bundles, pans and various other items were secured in the carriage, Thad assisted her to the driver's seat.

"I hope all goes well, dear. Don't tolerate disrespect from those older chaps."

The air was cold and crisp. She tightened her shawl...*I should have worn my cape. I will tomorrow...The fog lay like a thick curtain before her... I hope Dublin and Bonnie can see through fog better than I do...*

At the cross road she turned left away from town. The wagon road that eventually ended up at the Fort, led directly to the school. As she approached the entrance to property, she noted the lifting fog and narrow beams of sunlight creating a scene of silhouettes; the school, outhouse, and several trees. She wished she could photograph it. She positioned her carriage as closely as she could to the north side of the building. She reasoned it would be less handy for children who liked to climb and investigate. Leading her horses into the penned area, she admonished Dublin.

"There will be other horses and ponies. Don't you dare bite them!"

With arms loaded, she walked to the school house door. Setting down her bundles, she placed the large key in the lock. Sunbeams lightened the area of sandy, moist soil around the front step. Children's active feet had stomped out all greenery. Large paw prints were plainly visible. She stooped to examine them closer. *These are clearly prints of a feline...a large one...I wonder if it's the same lion that hides in my woods...There'd be no reason for him to wander here into the open spaces...nah... It's probably a different one...they're everywhere, after all.*

"Do you need help, Miss. Castile?"

She jumped and turned quickly. A teenaged boy stood quietly, holding his cap with both hands. She recognized him.

"You're the young man who ran an errand for me last summer, aren't you?"

He nodded and smiled, revealing a broken front tooth.

Becca casually ground her foot over the paw prints... *I can't have my male students abandoning school to go on a wild cat hunt...*

"I would be delighted to have your help. What's your name?"

"Jacob Bradley, most folks call me Jake."

"Well, Jake, unlock the door while I bring the rest of my supplies from the carriage. Then if you'd chop wood and start a fire, I'd be forever grateful."

Soon a fire was roaring in the small stove. Jake pumped a bucket of water from the well, and Becca started the stew cooking. She set a large water-filled pitcher on the small table near the door.

"Now, Jake, I've brought nails and a hammer. I need you to pound them in a line above the pitcher... On second thought; half of them should be at a lower level for the shorter children.

"We have pegs for the coats, Ma'am."

"These aren't for coats, they're for cups. Each child will have a personal cup."

Jake picked up the hammer and a square nail; he looked confused, but followed her directions.

"I mean no respect, Miss. Castile, but the dipper for drinking is hanging over there. We usually use a bucket for water."

"I understand, Jake, but that's how colds and illness spread. The separate cups will prevent sharing ger.... It'll be more sanitary. The pitcher has a lid to prevent bacti...uh...dust from collecting in the water."

As he hammered nails, Becca took a pile of cloth squares from her large basket. She, Annie, and the girls had cut them from several old sheets. She stacked them by the wash basin.

"What's that?' Jake asked.

"These are cloths for wiping hands. Once used, these will be dropped into this basket for washing."

"That's going to take some getting used to," the boy responded.

Becca swept as Jake moved the tables around at her request. They hung a donated clock over the blackboard. As the children arrived, she greeted them, writing their names and ages on one side of the board. Once everyone was seated, the room was quiet with expectation. Becca stood at the front and smiled.

"As all of you know, I'm Miss. Castile. I'll be your teacher through the remainder of the term. I am hopeful that by working together, we'll be so successful, I'll be asked back for the next term."

As she glanced over the faces and noted new ones who had not been there the day she visited...*Some who dropped out or were expelled must have heard of the teacher change...*

"For us to be successful there must be rules." She wrote the golden rule across the top of the board. After an open discussion about its meaning, they, summarized it into three rules; 1. Respect one another with words and actions. 2. Respect property, both school and personal. 3. Complete all class work to best of your ability.

Becca walked to the stove and stirred the soup; she added a cup of water.

"Now I want to discuss a few new procedures. After a week of getting to know one another, I'll pair an older child with each younger one. You will mentor one another."

She then explained the system for getting drinks and hand washing. They watched her in stunned silence. She wanted to giggle, but maintained a serious face...*I must appear to be in authority.*

An older boy raised his hand. She nodded her permission for him to speak. "What happens if someone breaks a rule?"

"The rule-breaker will correct his wrong with restitution. If a student damages property he or she will replace it before allowed back at school. If one of you hurts another, either with your words or actions, you'll be required to complete three helpful acts for the person you hurt."

"Who decides what those acts will be?" An older girl asked.

"That would be the injured party, of course."

The boy's hand shot up again. "What if the injured party chooses a favor that's really hard, or that takes a long time to carry out?"

"I would advise each one of you consider that before being harsh, unkind, or injurious to another person."

There was a low hum of discussion in the room. Becca allowed it for a few minutes before rapping her knuckles on the table top to bring order.

"Now we will discuss responsibilities."

She picked up a picture frame in which she had placed several layers of the empty newsprint. It worked like a clipboard. She explained that each child would have a daily task. Older boys would water horses, chop wood, keep the fire fed on cold days, pump fresh water from the well for drinking. Older girls would wash dishes, make the soup, and sweep at the end of the day...*This is falling into male and female roles which I don't like, but it's the time I'm in.*

"The smaller children will clean black boards, and dust desks and books."

After writing the names of those assigned with chores for the week, she pulled a crate from behind the teacher's table.

"Now, since you've had to sit quietly for this long, let's get some outdoor time."

From the box, she pulled jump ropes, balls, yoyos, and a rolling hoop.

"You have thirty minutes to work off the wiggles, and then we'll come in for some soup. Jake, you'll be in charge of keeping order during recess, today."

She sat at the teacher's table and transferred the names and ages from the board to a ledger...*This is going better than I had hoped. I'm sure it's some kind of honeymoon period.*

After the soup was eaten, and the bowls and spoons washed and put away, Becca tested for levels. She started with a few easy math problems having them solve them on the few available slates. She increased the difficulty of the equations with each trial. Soon, she had them divided into three groups. The same method was used for spelling and reading... *This isn't the best testing method, but with limited supplies, it'll have to do.*

74

"When we show our respect for other living things, they respond with respect for us."

—Arapaho Tribal Proverb

An hour before school ended for the day, Thad stopped by. He walked in quietly and surveyed the class. They worked quietly in small groups. A list on the board outlined the basics for a short story. The three groups were in teams, each writing a portion of the story. Thad smiled. He motioned Becca to come to the door.

"You have them as calm as lambs."

"Thank you, it's worked out well."

"I really need the carriage to take home more school donations. They're filling up The Print Shop. I thought I'd leave Susie with you to ride home. I'll take the carriage and team. It's my saddle, so go straight home so no one sees you riding straddle."

"Certainly, we can't have gossip," she said sarcastically.

After completing the writing assignment, Becca read their combined story. Laughter filled the room over the ridiculous outcome.

She ended the day by reading a few pages of Hiawatha and then released them. Each student knew what their task would be the following day.

As she locked the door, Harry arrived to pick up Emily. "Sybil said to tell you we'll bring a pot of beans and a pan of corn bread for tomorrow."

"Please express my appreciation to Sybil."

Becca mounted Thad's horse and settled into the saddle. She slowly rode from the property trail to the wagon road. Her thoughts sorted through the events of the day. It was exciting to have a classroom again.

Suddenly a gunshot rang out at the edge of the forest. Susie jumped and reared. She gripped her legs, thankful she wasn't on her side saddle. Her horse turned into a spin. She doubted if she could stay on, but held to the saddle horn with all her strength. From the corner of her eye, she saw a man in uniform. He was mounted on a horse, holding a pistol in his hand.

"Whoa, Susie, whoa..." She tried to soothe her with her voice... *Was he shooting at me?*

As her mount calmed, she patted her neck and looked back. A wild, piercing scream chilled her spine. From the branches above the soldier's head, dropped a mountain lion. Man and cat fell from the horse and rolled. The victim screamed in pain. Becca kicked Susie into a full run... *Should I go back? He'll kill that man...but the man may have been trying to kill me... I can't fight a lion...I do have a dagger...* She reigned to a stop and turned around. Susie balked.

"I don't blame you, he scares me too, but we can't leave a man to die."

As she came within range of the incident, she glanced around. No one was in sight. Man, horse and cat had disappeared... *Did I imagine it?*

She dismounted and walked to the area the cat had dropped. Holding the reins firmly, she talked calmly to the horse. She looked up in the trees... *nothing there... Looking at the ground, she saw several splatters of* blood...*I wonder if the cat dragged him into the woods...* She rode the rest of the way home in shock.

At supper, Thad said grace and immediately opened the subject of the mountain lion.

"Just before I left The Print Shop, Doc stopped by for a paper. He said that a lion mauled Fitzgerald. He was able to catch his horse, and ride into town for help. Doc treated him and planned to take him back to the barracks in the buggy."

He looked at Becca. "He's the teacher you scrapped with, remember?"

"I know who he is. Did he say what happened?" *It's interesting that he failed to mention he shot a gun, and frightened my horse? If I tell Thad that, he'll feel compelled to make a fight out of it to defend me.*

"He said he was just riding slowly along on his way to the Fort. He was near the school when the thing dropped out of a tree. He chewed him up a bit and ran off."

He was either threatening me or trying to frighten my horse so I'd be thrown. He must feel revengeful..."Why would a lion attack and run away?"

Thad buttered a roll. "I'm going to get a group of men and go after that cat. It distresses me to think it might have been you who was attacked. The cat is acting peculiar. A sick and disordered animal is dangerous."

Becca laid her napkin beside her plate. "Thad, Mr. Fitzgerald didn't tell the whole truth. I was riding down the wagon road, coming home. He moved out of the tree line and fired a shot. I don't know the reason; to scare the horse...to intimidate me? The mountain lion dropped on him after that. The cat probably felt threatened by the gunshot, but it gave me time to get away."

"Why didn't you tell me?"

"I just did tell you."

"You should have told me the moment I walked into this house." His voice sounded irritated.

"What does it matter when I told you? I told you."

"But, if I hadn't mentioned what Doc said, you wouldn't have told me. Would you?"

Annie slowly got up, and took her plate into the kitchen. Sarah and Hannah's eyes were wide open as they held their forks like statues.

"Thad, this is our family meal. There shouldn't be argument around the table. We'll talk about it later."

He dropped his napkin on his plate of uneaten food. "I can tolerate almost anything except lying."

Becca pushed her chair back and placed her hands on her hips. "You listen to me, Buster."

"Buster?"

"I did not lie! Delaying information was not a lie. How dare you to say that I did! You're dismissed. I'd like you to leave now."

"Dismissed? I'm not one of your students."

She jumped up, rushed through the kitchen and out the back door. Leaning against the porch post, she tried to calm her breathing... *It was such a perfect day until that idiot decided to shoot...for what ever reason.*

The sinking sun cast shadows over the backyard. The chickens slowly filed into their coop. Bonnie and Dublin stood by their stalls, wanting to be let in. A few caws of crows from the woods announced the forest bedtime. Movement caught her eye. The cat slinked between the trees.

What keeps you here? You need to move far, far away...

"Delphi, I'm sorry." Thad touched her shoulder. She turned around and maneuvered them around so that he wouldn't face the woods.

"The thought of that cat dropping on you, scared my socks off. And then when you said that rogue fired at you...I let my anger go. I'm not faulting you...I shouldn't have sounded so harsh."

"The acreage around my property is owned by me, correct?"

He looked at her, confusion on his face.

"Until we're married, this property is mine, and I will have no hunting or killing of animals on my property. Is that clear?"

He shook his head. "You're being unreasonable. Someone will eventually kill that cat...if not here...than somewhere else. He's off kilter "

"As long as it's not here...and it's not you...otherwise we're going to have a whale of a fight coming from me."

"What does it matter?"

"I don't know, but I feel that today, the cat may have saved my life. And even if Fitzgerald wasn't trying to kill me...he was up to something. He received his punishment from the mountain lion."

"We'll speak no more about the cat. Now assure me that I'm back in your good graces."

75

"Forgiveness says you are given another chance to make a new beginning."

—Desmond Tutu

She assured him that all was good, although her feelings felt more than a little ruffled. After walking him to the gate, she relaxed in the drawing room. Sarah brought her some tea.

"The grandmother said you should drink this to settle you. It's been a frightening day."

Becca took a sip of Annie's calming tea, heavily laced with honey.

"Thank you, Sarah. Are you going to school with me tomorrow?"

"Yes, tomorrow is ironing day, and Hannah doesn't trust me to not scorch the clothing."

Becca laughed. "Don't feel bad, she has never trusted me to iron either."

The wood stove crackled and the lamplights gave a golden glow. The women settled into favorite places for an evening of family time. Annie worked on a small basket, Hannah sewed, and Sarah cut pieces of scrap cloth for a quilt. Becca read aloud from the Bible. She read from Luke, chapter seven.

"This is a parable, she explained. It's a story Jesus told to teach a larger lesson. This one is about forgiveness."

She read about the indebtedness of two men. Each owed money to the same lender. One owed a large amount, and the other owed much less. Neither man had enough money to pay their loans. The lender chose to forgive both debts.

> **Then Jesus asked Simon, "Which debtor loved the lender more?" Simon answered that the man with the largest debt would love him more.**
>
> **Jesus then pointed out a woman who was forgiven of many sins. He concluded that this woman had done more than his own disciples to show her appreciation to Jesus. She recognized the greatness of her forgiveness.**
>
> **"He, who has been forgiven little, loves little."**

Becca glanced around the room. No one seemed to be particularly interested in her reading tonight. She pondered about the parable.

Is that true? Would a really evil person have the compassion to love God more after forgiveness than someone who had seldom sinned? Perhaps one who hasn't experienced feelings of heavy guilt doesn't feel the relief of forgiveness as one who has...maybe Jesus was telling Simon that his self-righteousness is more sinful than the woman's sin...

She remembered another parable she had read in the book of Matthew... *Where was that? It was about forgiveness...* She carefully turned the thin pages, stopping at Matthew, chapter eighteen. She read silently.

In this parable Jesus told a story of a king with two servants. One servant owed him money. When he demanded the servant pay or be imprisoned, the debtor begged for mercy. The king forgave the debt. The same debtor went to another servant who owed him less than he owed the king. He demanded to be paid. This man begged for mercy as well. However, the forgiven servant refused mercy for his debtor. He had the man put into prison. The king was angry saying, "I canceled your debt but you had no mercy on your fellow servant." The king withdrew his forgiveness, and put the harsh servant in prison...

Interesting...this teaches that to be forgiven, we must be willing to forgive...The other parable taught that those who have the most need for forgiveness are as close or closer to God's love as those who have few offences...How forgiving am I?... I've never been one to hold grudges...but do I really forgive?

Tuesday went well at school. Becca introduced Sarah as her adopted daughter, and placed her in the middle group. She was small for her age so she fit in. The students made no audible comments about the young native, but Becca noticed two older girls whispering in the back of the room. She walked to the board and pointed to the rule; **Respect one another.** They straightened in their seats, and focused on their slates.

On Wednesday Dan delivered the new tables and benches. The students assisted in rearranging the room. Becca looked forward to Saturday when the steamer would bring in some of her curriculum order and new slates. As she rode up to her gate on Bonnie, she noticed the Reverend's horse tied at her hitching post. She dismounted and tied Bonnie and Dublin. She hurried into the house...*I hope he's not bringing bad news...* She found him sitting alone in the parlor.

"Hello, Rev, didn't anyone offer you tea?"

"Yes, but I declined. I wanted to be here alone and think."

Is there no where to think at your house...?

She sat down in a chair opposite him as she waited for him to initiate conversation. He leaned over with elbows on his knees, rubbing his hands together. Then he raised his face to look at her.

"I think I'll quit the ministry."

"What? Does Grace know?"

"Yes, she's been crying all afternoon. She married me as a minister and can't imagine another life. She's a much better person in this life than am I."

Becca took a deep breath...*I honestly think you should quit...I'm not going to say that...it's not my decision...*"What would you do, Titus?"

He shrugged his shoulders, straightened up on the sofa, and toyed with the doily on the side table.

"I don't know, teach perhaps. Back East there are many schools where I could find a position."

"Why are you thinking like this? What brought you to this decision?"

He looked at his lap. "I'm a hypocrite."

Becca sat back and folded her hands. She remained silent while Titus fought to bring his emotions under control. Finally, he cleared his throat.

"I know ministers often speak of being called to the cloth. Others feel they were destined to the vocation...I can make neither claim."

He squirmed on the sofa and placed his arm over its back.

"Why did you decide to take up the ministry?"

"I admired the man who took me in when I was an angry, lost boy. Grace told me that she shared my story with you. That's why I feel comfortable in speaking with you about it."

"Did he persuade you to choose this vocation?"

"No, but I wanted to be like him, and he was a minister. He was flattered that I wished to follow in his footsteps. He raised the money for my one year of Seminary. He would have found a way to pay for the rest, had I remained there."

"Do you keep in touch?"

"He died during the war. I wish I could talk to him. Seminary was difficult for me. I learned to read late in childhood. He taught me reading and writing after I ran away from my stepfather. I had to work really hard to pass the courses in college. I was actually relieved to move into chaplain services for the Union Army. It gave me the creditability I needed, without all that tedious schooling."

"I see, but why do you feel like a hypocrite?"

The man before her took a deep breath. "I faced myself today and said, Titus, you do not like people. People make you angry."

Becca restrained a smile that insisted on forming on her lips. "I think we all feel that way at times."

"No, I feel that way all the time. As a child, the only people I was around were my mother and stepfather. I adored my mother. I hated the man who abused us both. I wanted to kill him, but before I grew old enough to get revenge, he died of consumption. I still blame him for my mother's death. It was unforgivable...but I also blame myself for not finding a way to help her escape."

Forgivable...forgive...forgive to be forgiven..."He, who has been forgiven little, loves little."

"After I met my mentor, I knew I wanted to be like him...not like my mean-spirited stepfather. However, my lack of compassion...it's not like him...it's like that evil man...I think he's somehow within me."

"Do you think it might be possible that your anger for your stepfather...and it's well deserved...could be the cause of your dislike for people...your impatience...what you refer to as lack of compassion?"

The man was silent; his hands that had lain on his lap were now held in tight fists.

Becca walked over to the bookshelf and picked up the Bible. She flipped it open to the parables she had been reading. She sat by him on the sofa, and placed the book on his lap.

"I know you've read this before, as had I. However, this week these parables ignited something in me. Please read these as though you are standing there in the very group to whom Jesus was speaking. Imagine he's talking to you."

Titus read both passages, slowly and with reverence. "You're pointing out to me that I must forgive my stepfather?"

"I believe you're in a fight with a dead man. You can't win or lose such a fight. That anger, combined with helplessness to resolve it, must influence your decisions and reactions. Continuous anger is poison to a person's brain and body. But that very evil man is holding you back, because you are allowing it. I think this scripture is telling us that to be forgiven, we must forgive. We must be forgiven to truly feel love."

"Yes...but how? It's not something one can just decide to do."

"Perhaps it is. In the story, the king chose to forgive, and he expected the servant to do likewise."

"Yes...it deserves some thought...it surely does."

"Besides, your ministry has not been in vain, Titus."

"Oh, but I fear it has...I've only pretended to be a man of the cloth...it's never been in my heart. As long as I could hold parishioners to rules, judgments, discipline, I could manage. But to lead from the heart, from feelings...I can't do that."

"Titus, I hadn't touched a Bible for at least three years. Because of you, I've been reading it."

Not for the right reasons ...rather for preparation to debate you...but reading, never-the-less...

His eyebrows raised in surprise.

"And another thing... Thad told me how you sat with him and read comforting Psalms during those long nights when he reacted to the memories of war and death. He credits you for his sanity."

"Is that true? I helped him that much?"

"Yes, and he'd be the first to tell you. I don't know if the ministry is right for you. If you decide it's not, I think you should feel free to do what makes you happy. But I hope you'll work out the anger issues ...the forgiveness... before making a final decision. I believe you do have compassion...it's just buried."

Titus Walker stood up. The slumped shoulders of his tall frame, revealed his physical and mental exhaustion.

"I'm going to spend a few days alone to think things through. You've shown me from where some of this bleak darkness comes, I believe. Will you please check on Grace while I'm away?"

"Of course, I shall call on her every day."

After walking her guest to the door and locking up, Becca went to her room. She was glad it was Friday. The day ahead had no demands. She glanced at the journal...*Do I dare open it? I'm too tired for time travel... I'd like to report to Delphi and Beth, regarding my success with the school...*She slowly lifted the paper sheets to the marked page...*Ahh...Delphi made an entry...I'm too curious not to read it...*

My Dear Friend, lost in time,

We're preparing for Phil's memorial service. Beth said that black clothing is not required for funerals anymore. However, I feel it's inappropriate not to do as I was taught. I purchased a black two-piece suit, and a smart hat with veil. It will hide my lack of tears. I can't cry for someone I never knew except in the knowledge that he caused all of our suffering...*People who knew Phil and me will wonder why I'm dressing so stylish...no one has ever seen me in a hat...except a baseball cap.*

Our attorney called today. Phil did not change the beneficiary in his life insurance. He also did not alter his will. Since he was opposing the divorce, he probable thought it would look bad for him, if he did.

Therefore, the million dollars is left to you. I can not pass it back one-hundred-fifty years; therefore I shall accept it for you. I hope that the relief of his meeting justice through natural ways over-rides any resentment you might have of me obtaining the inheritance.

Sincerely, Delphi

Becca picked up a pencil and wrote, **"Enjoy!"**

She closed the book, and sat on the side of her bed...*Delphi is a millionaire. Wow, who would have thought things would turn out like this? We couldn't get legal action against him...but like Delphi says, nature brought justice. I wonder if he had regrets... While lost in the mountains, did he think back about his evil plan to kill me, become wealthy, and marry Tonya? Did he see how cruel...how stupid it was? His greedy and selfish behavior changed the lives of Delphi, me, Jonah and Ike...even his own.*

She began to disrobe... Things worked out better for Ike. He's changed his ways... started a new life...escaped being murdered by the mobsters who were after him.

She slipped her cotton nightgown over her head... *Jonah benefited. Beth will always see that he's provided care. He'll receive training; have opportunity to reach his potential.*

She pulled down the covers and plumped her feather pillow... *Delphi has made out all right. She had to go through a painful recovery and rehabilitation, and there' more to come... but she's got money to fulfill her dreams...even if it is in a later era...she won't be shunned because of her checkered past, as she would have been here...*

She blew out the lamp flame, and slipped under the sheet and quilt.

They're all better off really...*am I better off?*

She turned on her side. A bright moon cast golden beams through the window. A breeze lifted the thin white curtain; making it flutter in the mellow light...*I was perfectly happy with my life until I learned of Philip's cheating... I loved our loft apartment, my kindergarten class...being near Beth, my sister and best friend...having Mom nearby...I can't say I'm any happier now...life is a bit more challenging...everything's a bit of a fight for what's right...what's fair...*

She pulled the covers over her shoulders...*I love Thad...but we're on different wave lengths...I'm not sure I'm the best match for him...I cause him so much trouble...I have no idea what my future holds...well except according to Delphi...the museum journal says I marry Thad....and live a long life.*

Tears flooded her eyes, and cascaded onto her pillow. She didn't know why they came. Was she homesick? Was she actually grieving Phil's horrible death? Maybe it was time to grieve the dream that died with his betrayal. She wiped the moisture from her face...*You made a mess of things for you and me, Phil! You never had to face up to it, but I'll live with the consequences for the rest of my life...It may take a very long time to forgive you...if ever.*

The next she knew, Hannah was shaking her. "Wake up, sleepy head. It's eight-o-clock already. Mrs. Leng brought our gowns over for a fitting."

76

"God moves in a mysterious way, His wonders to perform."

—William Cowper (Hymn Writer, 1731–1800).

Becca jumped up and washed her face, brushed her teeth, and combed her hair. Pulling it back, she tied it with a ribbon. Hurrying down the stairs, she saw Mrs. Leng in the parlor. She was drinking tea Hannah had served her. New frocks lay over the back of the sofa.

"Come into the drawing room," Becca invited. "Sorry I wasn't up."

Mrs. Leng smiled and followed her hostess. Several hours passed as each of them tried on the gowns. She pinned up the hems, and checked for any other adjustments that might be needed. The girls giggled and chattered through it all...*They sound exactly like teens in my own time...*

Once they were finished; they sat in the dinning room and enjoyed potato soup. Becca decided to seek some wisdom from these women she admired.

"Mrs. Leng, remember when I talked with you about my experience of exchanging bodies?"

Sarah and Annie showed no surprise, but Hannah shot her a questioning look. Her eyes were wide with interest... *I'll have to swear her to secrecy later.*

Mrs. Leng silently looked at her, waiting for her to continue.

Becca pushed a lock of wayward hair behind her ear. "You explained that you could easily believe what happened to me, and that my acceptance to what I can't control helps me find my path."

The woman nodded, "Yes."

"Well now I have another question." She toyed with her napkin. "There's a strange mountain lion that lingers here. He lives at the edge of the woods. He's never harmed anything on the property. The interesting thing is that he left tracks at the school, and he attacked a threatening man along the road home from the school. It's like he follows me."

"Spirit animal," murmured Annie, without looking up.

"Annie says that she believes certain people, who have developed strong spiritual power, can shape-shift." Becca explained to Mrs. Leng.

"Why?" asked Hannah, still staring intently at Becca.

"They do so to spy on people and places." Sarah explained calmly. "Or to discover helpful information, or warn people they care about. They may also be protectors."

"Vedy interesting," Mrs. Leng responded.

"What do you think? I know of no one who would do this to protect me. But it does seem like this cat is doing just that." She studied Mrs. Leng's face.

Mrs. Leng lay down the spoon and placed her hands in her lap. "Yes, I hear that... also...I believe... sad souls come back... need to make things right...need to mend bad deeds."

Becca pondered what she had said, trying to process it.

"What are all of you talking about?" persisted Hannah, her voice growing impatient.

"Just hush, and listen, Hannah," Becca said, frowning at the girl.

"So you're saying that someone who lived a very bad life may come back as an animal...like reincarnation? You believe we reincarnate when we die?"

"Not always...only some... some not ready...not learned about path...some need to make right."

"But not as an animal," Becca clarified.

"It is not we who choose...an animal...yes...maybe... can be animal...insect....what is needed..."

"Do you think the lion is a danger to me?"

Annie mumbled something in her language.

"The Grandmother says spirits harm you only if you fear them." Sarah related.

Mrs. Leng picked up her spoon. She looked at Becca. "If he need to hurt you...he would already..."

The subject was dropped by all but Hannah.

"What are you talking about? People can't become animals, everyone knows that, Delphi."

After Mrs. Leng left, Becca saddled Bonnie, and rode to check on Grace. She turned Dublin and Bonnie loose in the small pen by the parsonage. When she knocked on the door, Grace appeared and invited her in. The usually tidy woman looked unkempt. Her hair had not been combed. The wrinkled house dress appeared to have served as a nightgown. Her face was swelled from long bouts of crying. Becca placed her arms around her and held her tightly.o

"It's going to get better, Grace. The dark shadow that has stalked Titus since childhood will be taken down to size. He needs to sort this out. He feels all the pain of his childhood with childlike intensity."

They sat down in the simple parlor. Grace took a shaky breath.

"I can't imagine beginning our lives over."

"Grace, are you concerned about your husband's anger issues, or about him leaving the ministry?"

"He's always had anger...impatience...nerves. I gently restrain him. I cushion his life, apologize for his mishaps, I sooth his nerves..."

"Don't you think he would be happier if he resolved those issues? It would be a better marriage if you didn't have to intercede for his out bursts."

"I don't mind. I love him and...well...I like helping him."

"You feel he needs you? You feel soothing him...covering up for his temper...... it gives you meaning?"

Grace sat quietly, thinking. "Well, yes...but in marriage we should need one another...help each other."

"Grace, did you ever play those childhood games like...maybe hide and seek?"

"Yes, one child covers her eyes, another child hides, and the first searches for her."

"It has simple rules and that makes it work, right?"

Grace looked at her with questioning eyes.

"You and Titus have developed a game. He judges, reacts harshly, sets high expectations of others, and looses his temper. That's his part of the game. Then you, the other child, do your part. You sooth him, smooth over and make amends. Titus feels guilty for the behavior that reminds him of the stepfather. He shows you that he is grateful for what you've done. Is that how it works?"

Grace's eyes were down cast. "I...I guess so."

Becca patted her folded hands. "Grace, there isn't much, these days, to challenge a smart woman, I know. And women need purpose as much as men. But you have more to offer...more reasons to feel worthy than cleaning up after Titus's emotional messes."

"Like what?"

"I'm learning that I'm on a path. I can't see around every bend, but when I pass around it I see why things have happened. Let Titus find healing. Let him become who he was created to be. Allow yourself to be who you were created to be. If he leaves the ministry, it's no disgrace. It can be an adventure for both of you."

"Yes, I believe you are right."

"While your husband is taking this time, take some for you. Visit friends, stop by the school and see what we're doing. I'd love your input. Help me with choir. Dig up those talents you've buried while looking after Titus."

Grace smiled weakly. "I'll try."

Before Becca left, she persuaded Grace to bathe. She braded her hair and fastened it over her head. They had tea. As Grace walked her to the gate, she reached out for a hug.

"Delphi, I've always liked you, but today, I feel we're friends."

Saturday evening, Thad brought Becca's boxes home from the Steamer. Part of the curriculum, the slates, chalk, paper and pencils arrived. She spent all evening organizing, and planning lessons that would utilize them.

The next morning, Thad, Becca, and her household attended church. With the Reverend away, only singing and prayer time was held and church dismissed an hour earlier than usual. They went to the Redwood to have their Sunday dinner with the O'Shay's. Grace and Doc rounded out the gathering. Molly served a delicious venison roast and her usual blackberry pies.

In respect for Grace, questions and comments about Titus were avoided. However, Hannah wasted no time before blurting out her concerns about the mountain lion.

"Just hanging out the laundry scares me all to pieces."

"If it were me, I'd set some traps," declared Charley as he forked a second piece of meat.

Thad responded. "He'd be easy to shoot; he's the boldest wild cat I've ever been around."

"No one's going to shoot or trap him. He's ill, and he'll die soon from natural causes. That's why he's acting strange." Becca's voice revealed her irritation.

I *feel like choking Hannah for bringing this subject up. She knows Thad and I disagree about it.*

"The Grandmother says it's a spirit," Sarah offered, noticing Becca's discomfort and hoping to relieve it.

"Shaw, spirits aren't like that, they're ghost-like...invisible," scoffed Molly.

"Personally, I don't believe in spirits," commented Thad.

If only you knew who you are marrying Thad...That's why I'll never be able to explain this body switch situation...you're too practical...you'd never believe me...

"All I know, is that he could have attacked me on several occasions and didn't. When Fitzgerald fired a shot that frightened Susie and endangered me, the cat attacked him. He's safe while on my land...end of story."

Grace reached out and touched Becca's hand. "Perhaps he's an angel, dear. I've heard stories of angels taking on the form of animals. Why in the Old Testament an angel entered a prophet's donkey. He even talked to the prophet and prevented him from doing something that God didn't want him to do."

"Thank you Grace, I appreciate your suggesting another possibility. Now I wish we would change the subject. Is anyone interested in what I'm planning for the school?"

On Monday, Becca took her carriage to work. It contained the slates, books, supplies, and a pot filled with ingredients for chicken stew. She was pleased at the enthusiasm the students showed over the books and slates. Driving the carriage home, she planned how she would share every detail at the supper table. Walking through the drawing room to the kitchen, she noticed her wedding dress hanging from a hook. Hannah sat on a stool, hemming the yards of skirt.

"It's beautiful, Hannah, are you still glad I chose the gown? It's a lot of work."

The girl nodded, and tried to smile while holding several pins in her mouth. Becca entered the kitchen and grabbed her apron. "What can I do to help with supper?"

Annie pointed toward the boiled potatoes and Becca grabbed the mashing tool. Soon fried steaks, mashed potatoes and gravy adorned the dining room table. Becca looked out the window nervously.

"We won't start until Thad arrives."

An hour later, she relented. *It's not fair to hold a meal back from the others...I wonder what's happened...*The other women ate supper, but Becca sat on the porch watching the road...*Thad is never late. If he's injured, someone would have come to tell me...If his work held him up, he'd have sent a message with someone...this isn't like him...*

The sun was nearly set when she spotted a rider coming. She stood to get a better look. As the silhouette morphed into a recognizable image, she knew it was Thad. She breathed a sigh of relief. He halted his horse in front of the gate and slid off. As he took a few steps forward, she could see he was drunk.

"Thad, I've never seen you intoxicated before...what happened..."

He reached the porch and leaned against a supporting post. She searched his face. He was clearly angry.

"Why didn't you tell me the truth? You deceived me. That's the same as lying. You've made a mockery of my trust and feelings for you...why?"

"Thad, until you tell me what you're talking about, I can't explain."

A dented pan set in the yard. It was there to provide water for Warrior. Thad kicked it. It rolled into the fence.

Becca raised her voice. "You'll calm down and tell me your problem or you can leave and come back when you're sober."

He spun around. "Is that what you tell your customers?"

A sick feeling moved through Becca's core. "What customers?"

"Don't act innocent, I saw the tintype. I know what you are."

Oh no, I forgot about the photograph... I should have destroyed that stupid picture..."What tintype?

Thad dropped to a seated position on the porch. He took a jagged breath. "I left The Print Shop and went to talk to Abe about the hog."

"At his saloon?"

Thad nodded. "There were two men at the other end of the bar. One was Fitzgerald. The other, I've never seen before."

Becca sat beside him, waiting for him to continue.

"I was talking with Abe about standing up with me at the wedding. Those b'hoys kept laughing and making randy remarks. Abe glared at them, and then I noticed they were looking at me while laughing. I went on talking to Abe, but they kept it up. They appeared to be trying to start something. I walked over ready to fix their flint right off the reel when the strange chap held up a photograph."

Becca had held her breath throughout Thad's explanation. Feeingl nauseous, she forced herself to breathe.

"Fitzgerald grinned at me and said, "This fella spent the night with your lady. What-a-ya think of that?" Only he didn't call you a lady. I wanted to hit him right there, but I was so stunned at seeing you in that photograph, I froze."

Becca rushed in, "Thad, I swear I've never spent the night with that man. I'm sure he's the same thief who ransacked my room at the Redwood. He's probably trying to cause trouble for me because I stabbed him with my dagger. It was self defense; he threatened me with a gun."

Thad looked into her face. Even in the moonlight she could see the pain in his glazed eyes.

"Oh yes, he's the same man, alright. He said he did that to recover the gold bar and jewels you stole from him. I always wondered how you got so much gold, Delphi. You never explained it. Now it makes sense."

"Thad, I didn't steal that gold, and the picture looks like me, but it's not really."

"Then why was it in your room?" Thad stood up. He pushed his hands into his pocket and looked up at the moon for a few moments.

"I have always respected you. I've treated you like a lady. I wanted our marriage to be honorable in every way. Now I've learned you worked in San Francisco for that woman...Lilly? All this time you allowed me to believe you were from Louisiana...or was it Portland... a teacher..."

He shook his head and looked at her with an expression of disappointment and disgust.

"I could have handled the truth, Delphi. I might have had trouble with it at first, but I understand people make mistakes and change..."

He slowly walked toward the gate.

Becca ran after him. "Thad, I want to tell you the truth, but it'll be hard for you to believe. The real truth is not what you think, but it's very strange...let me explain."

He stopped and turned to face her. "You're told so many things... you're so good at lying; I wouldn't believe anything you told me now, Delphi."

Her legs crumbled beneath her, and she fell to her knees. A sob caught in her throat. She watched his shadowy form climb onto Susie. He turned his head and looked back at Delphi.

"I feel I should warn you. They're taking the tintype to the sheriff and school manager tomorrow. If they bring the law with them and claim the gold in my safe, I'll have to turn it over. They may even bring him here to claim the jewels he says you stole from him. The photograph is evidence that you've lived outside the law. Therefore, whatever they accuse you of, you'll have little defense. I know of no way to protect you, Delphi. If only you had told me the truth, I could have found a way to prevent this."

He rode into the darkness. Becca began to tremble. A small arm slipped around her. She turned her head, and looked into the face of Sarah.

77

"Character is like a tree, and reputation like a shadow. The shadow is what we think of it; the tree is the real thing."

—A<small>BRAHAM</small> L<small>INCOLN</small>

"Sarah, did you hear?" Becca sobbed.

"Yes, I heard."

"I didn't steal anything. That man who accuses me is a professional thief."

"Is there anything here that they can say you stole?"

"Yes, a bit of jewelry."

"Will you permit me to hide it?"

"Do what you like, throw in it the sea for all I care…it's cursed."

"Let's gather it now."

Sarah helped Becca to her feet. As they turned toward the house, Becca glanced at the tree line. Two large golden eyes reflected the moonlight.

"Sarah, the lion is here."

" I saw. Don't fear him."

The two went to Becca's room. After gathering the pieces of jewelry, Becca began placing the items in the carpetbag.

"No, wait, I have an idea." Sarah hurried from the room. She soon returned with a small leather bag.

Becca dropped the jewelry into it, and tied the leather strings. She handed it to Sarah. "Do nothing that will endanger you in any way, Sarah"

"I will need Bonnie."

"Can't you hide it here? I fear for you riding off in the night."

"It shouldn't be found on your property. I saw some of my people wrongly accused because of stolen items found near their lodges; they were placed there by evil men who accused them."

Soon Becca watched from the window as Sarah mounted Bonnie, bareback. She quietly headed for the forest with Dublin walking sleepily behind. Becca said a silent prayer for her protection. She returned to her room and disrobed. In her nightgown she picked up the journal. She hurriedly wrote.

Delphi,

I want to change back to our rightful times, NOW! I'm desperate. Your past has caught up with me. Please understand my panic.

She barely closed the book when Delphi's translucent glow appeared.

"What has caused you to be so vexed?"

Becca walked to her bed and climbed in. She didn't have the energy or strength to hold up her body any longer. She collapsed on her back.

That stupid picture you had made wearing only your pantaloons...the man who tried to rob me found it in the empty safe. He showed it to Thad. Now Thad wants nothing to do with me.

Tears rolled down her cheeks, took a turn, and filled her ears.

"I told you he would be trouble. He's not worth your tears. Good riddance, I'd say."

Good, let's change back, and you can tell him that.

"When I wanted to change, you said it wasn't safe. You said one or both of us might die. You said God..."

I know what I said... I've changed my mind, ok?

"I'm sorry that silly photograph Lilly forced me to take has caused you difficulty, but I am quite content now. This week my therapist will begin training me with a cane. If successful, I will give up the walker. Do you realize how close I am to having rehabilitated your body?"

I'm thankful to you for taking such good care of my body, Delphi. You not only took it from death to recovery, you've made it beautiful with your skill at hairstyling, makeup, and fashion...but I need it back. I can't live in this time...I don't want to be here.

"You were the strong one, I was the crybaby. Now you sound like a whimpering puppy. Stop it! You are clever. Remember? I saw the journal in the museum. You'll marry Thad, have children and enjoy a long life."

Yeah, well right now Thad has walked away...rode away, actually, and the Sheriff will give your gold to that thief. I'll be penniless. I'll lose my job at the school... I may even be sent to prison...

"My, my, what despair... you aren't thinking about this with any wisdom at all. Who has actually seen the gold and jewels?"

Hannah and Thad...no one else.

"Can they be trusted?"

Hannah is trustworthy, but I'm not sure about Thad now. He's so angry...

"Pooh on him...his male pride is ruffled...he'll get over it. So...you'll deny ever having the gold and jewels. You were fished out of the water with only the clothes on your back. Ask them how a tiny woman could possibly carry all that treasure through such a catastrophe. They'll feel foolish trying to explain that."

But, Delphi you did carry it...well eventually I did...I'm not a good liar...

"Becca, your problem is that you have always wanted to prove your strength and bravery. That's an advantage in your time, but not necessarily so in my time. Sometimes a woman must allow herself to appear weak, helpless, and vulnerable. That's how we survived in my time. Trust me...if you insist you don't have the strength or self-sufficiency to steal a valuable gold bar with a bag of jewels, and smuggle it pass Lilly, then keep it afloat in an angry sea, the authorities will believe you."

But, the picture...that's what's causing the most problems...I should have thrown it away, but it wasn't mine to destroy...I thought we would change back soon...then I forgot about it.

"It all seems so silly; they should see what I wear, or don't wear on a hot day now... Insist that it's not you...Tell them it was in the room when you got there...tell them anything, but never let them make you confess. It's not a lie, Becca. It really isn't you...and you really did find the photograph..."

That's true...maybe I can...Delphi?

Becca tossed in her bed trying to think through the dilemma before finally falling into a restless sleep. She was exhausted when rising to face the day. Through the day's responsibilities at school, she was glad Hannah was with her. The girl tended the cooking and small errands. Becca assigned each younger child to a mentor from the older group, and then distributed textbooks. She was fatigued beyond words when finally arriving home.

Dropping on a chair in the parlor, she thought about Thad. *I wonder what he's doing. I hope he hasn't told Harry about the picture and the claim that I'm a thief...wonder if the sheriff confiscated my gold from his safe...* She had dozed off, but was startled awake at the sound of a heavy step on the porch. Warrior, lying at her feet, raised his head and growled... *It can't be Thad....Warrior knows his sound and smell...Who?*

A heavy knock pounded the door. Becca stood, and straightened her hair as she rushed to answer it. She paused...*What if it's Fitzgerald, or the man who tried to rob me? My dagger is upstairs...*

The visitor repeated the knock. "Miss Castile, I know you're home, please permit me to talk with you."

She opened the door. Standing before her were Sheriff Carter and Mr. Mackey. Her stomach churned with anxiety.

May we come in, Miss Castile?" asked the school manager.

She stepped back, and held open the door. "Certainly, please have a seat. Would you like a cup of tea or coffee?"

"No, ma'am," replied the lawman. He sat on one end of the sofa, and Mr. Mackey sat on the other. Becca returned to the upholstered chair, and called Warrior to her......*can't have my dog biting either of these men...*

"To what do I owe this visit?" She forced calm into her voice.

The men looked at one another as though each wanted the other to speak first. Finally the sheriff directed his gaze at her.

"A man came to my office this morning with a complaint against you, ma'am."

"I'm not aware of having offended any one?"

"Are you acquainted with a man named Ned Baxter?"

"No, I've never heard that name, Sheriff."

"Well, he knows you, young lady. He has filed a report that you stole a gold bar and bag of jewels from him in San Francisco."

"He's either lying, or has mistaken me for someone. I've never lived in San Francisco. I grew up in Portland. I've never lived anywhere else before here."

"She did tell me she was from Portland." Mr. Mackey confirmed.

"Of course she did. Can you give me an address of a relative in Portland? Someone I could telegraph and verify to your claim."

"I wish I could. I have no relatives alive"... *at the present time*

"Surely, you can think of a friend." he persisted.

"Can you provide the name of a parent of one of your students... or a former teacher?" Mr. Mackey asked hopefully.

"The Brother Jonathan came to Crescent City from San Francisco. You were on it when it went down. That means you boarded there. Do you deny that as well?" The lawman persisted.

"Sheriff, I have no memory of being on that steamer, but I do remember growing up in Portland. I was raised to respect others and their property. I've never stolen or destroyed any property, ever. I will continue to insist on telling only the truth. If you believe I robbed that man, then you'll have to prove it."

"All I'll need to prove is that you're a liar, Miss. Castile. I can do that."

"Really?"

"Mr. Baxter has a photograph of you...a randy one, I must say... shameful. A San Francisco photographer's stamp is on the back as well as the establishment, Treasure by the Sea."

"I don't know of that establishment, and I certainly have never been there."

"It's my understanding that this house of ill repute was run by Lilly O' Kennan before being closed by the city officials."

Becca remained silent; watching her interrogator with what she hoped was a serene face.

"You are doing very well...stay calm."

Becca turned her head slightly. Her peripheral vision caught Delphi's shimmer...*He's not believing me...*

"He can't prove anything; he's trying to break you. Hold fast"

"Miss Castile?"

"Yes."

"You seem to have not heard my question. I asked if you ever worked for Lilly O' Kennan."

"No, I did not, nor did I ever meet her."

"I see. Mr. Mackey tells me you solicited quite a bit of money for the school. With this recent concern about your integrity, I must ask if you have records of how those funds were spent."

"What is he speaking of?"

Hush; don't talk to me unless you can help.

Becca went to her desk and retrieved her ledger. She opened it to the section where all donations were entered, and all items purchased listed. A few receipts from James were pinned to the page with a straight pin.

"Here it is. Every cent is accounted for."

Mr. Mackey looked over the sheriff's shoulder.

"That's very impressive, Miss Castile. I wish my bookkeeper was this thorough with my accounts."

Sheriff Carter handed the ledger back.

"Yes, I see no problem there. However, I had a complaint a few months ago. It concerned the theft of a dog and the destruction of a pistol. I didn't pursue it since it seemed trivial, at the time."

"You're speaking of your cousin and his dog fighting ring?"

The man didn't answer. Becca moved to the desk, returning with the handwritten receipt proving she had replaced the gun, and he had forfeited Warrior. After reading it, he nodded.

"That will suffice for that, I suppose. Now, if you'll allow me to search for the jewels and gold, perhaps we can conclude our visit."

"Don't allow it...he has no right..."

He'll find nothing...

"Search away, Sheriff, you'll find nothing stolen here."

Mr. Mackey appeared embarrassed as he fumbled with his hat, squirmed, and then wiped invisible dust from his shoes. The sheriff looked through her desk drawers, behind pictures for hidden safes, and wandered through the downstairs rooms. The school manager grew more nervous.

"Miss Castile, You've done a fine job these few weeks. I've heard only good reports from parents and students...however, due to these accusations; I must ask you to step down until all this can be cleared up."

Becca caught her breath. She had feared she might lose her job, but the reality shook her.

"Oh phooey with that silly old school, start your own academy in this house like I planned. You can put him out of business."

Carter entered the parlor after making the loop through the ground floor. "I'd like to see upstairs, now."

"I'll come along, Sheriff. I have house members to whose privacy I'm committed."

Up stairs, Carter quickly glanced though Hannah's room. Her meager possessions didn't draw his interest. Looking into Annie and Sarah's room, he fingered the native baskets, shell necklaces, and glanced around.

"Why are you keeping these injuns here?"

"These women are my friends and adopted family. I would appreciate if you keep your references to them respectful."

He shook his head in disbelief. "They belong on the reservation. They're all notorious thieves."

"You seem to suspect thievery a lot, don't you Sheriff?"

"Be cautious. You are winning this...don't anger him, be coy."

I'd like to rip off his lips...

"Is this your chamber, Miss Castile?"

"Yes, you may enter."

She followed him in. He opened the door of her wardrobe, looked into her hat boxes, and stooped to peek under her bed. He pulled out the carpetbag.

"Ah yes, this looks like the carpetbag Baxter described."

"Does it really? Perhaps that's because it looks like most carpetbags, don't you think?"

He opened it and peered into the empty satchel. "Where did you get this?"

"As I explained before, my memory is faint on some minor things before the accident. I don't remember where the bag was purchased. It was tied to me when I was rescued. It contained a few necessities."

The sheriff straightened. "I'll need to see what you had in this carpetbag."

"Not a problem."

Walking to her chest-of-drawers, she pulled out a corset, and pushed it into his hands. Before he could respond, she handed over pantaloons, garters, stockings. As she pulled a petticoat from the drawer, he pushed the undergarments back at her as if they were explosives.

"I was referring to a gold bar, coins and jewels."

Putting her hands on her hips, she raised her face to look into his eyes.

"Do you think a woman my size, would have floated long enough to be rescued if there were such heavy items in that bag? Sheriff, I'd have thought you could think that through."

She turned on her heel and left the room. He followed. They descended the stairs where Mr. Mackey stood waiting, still holding his hat.

Hannah stood looking out the window. She glanced at Becca and pointed to the outside…*Maybe Thad is here…*

78

"Reputation is what men and women think of us; character is what God and angels know of us."

—THOMAS PAINE

"I do have another question Miss Castile. I find it odd that a young woman surviving a shipwreck could purchase such a large house. Where did you get enough money for it?"

"Inheritance...you inherited it from me...it's the truth..."

"Inheritance, Sheriff, remember, I told you I don't have living parents"...*now.*

"Why did you buy a house this large? What were your plans? Perhaps you planned a whorehouse?"

"Now, Sheriff, there's no reason to use loose language." Mr. Mackey objected.

"Perhaps your reason for taking in Indian women was to begin your business with cheap harlots?"

Becca didn't have time to think. Her right hand landed a hard slap across the sheriff's face.

"You may insult me if you must, but you will not insult my friends!"

"Oh dear, that was not a wise thing to do...remember I advised you to appear helpless"

Not a chance...I'm just getting started...

"Well, hello, did I walk in on a gathering? Titus Walker's voice boomed.

Becca turned. Hannah stood by the opened door. The Reverend filled the opening. He removed his hat and walked in. Becca was surprised that he was dressed in his black jacket and clerical collar... *Perhaps he's not quitting the ministry after all.*

"O dear me... now the priest is after us too..."

"Hello, Sheriff, Mr. Mackey, I've been away a few days, and came by to pay a visit to my most cherished church member. What brings the two of you here?"

Mr. Mackey stood stone still. Sheriff Carter turned toward the minister, his face still red with anger from the assault.

"Mr. Mackey," Titus began. "How are things working out with the family? I prayed for you and Mrs. Mackey while at my retreat. I hope you've made things right with your wife. She is a devoted woman."

"Reverend, I don't think this is the time and place to discuss my marriage." Mackey's face turned white.

"Oh, I'm not discussing anything, just inquiring. Your secret is safe with me."

"And Sheriff, I prayed for you too. That little problem of bribed votes in your last election...I hope you got that mess ironed out. Honesty is so important for a lawman. I'm sure you've put everyone's mind at ease about that."

The sheriff looked around, then at his shoes, then at Mackey.

"I reckon we're finished here. We'll be going now."

"Wait," said Becca. "Are you finished with accusing me? Is this false complaint over?

"Who is accusing you and of what, pray tell." Titus demanded.

The pastor appeared shocked, but Becca could see it was pretended.

"What could this dear lady have done to cause you to accuse her? She was the first one in town to reach out and show concern to an impoverished family. Did you know that, Sheriff? She took in an injured orphan and ill old woman to save their lives. And Mr. Mackey can tell you what great things she's done for the sinking country school."

Both men appeared intensely uncomfortable.

"Do you find reason to accuse her, Sheriff?"

The lawman put on his hat. "No, I've found no evidence to back up the complaint. I'm leaving now."

Mr. Mackey started to meekly follow.

I'm sure you're looking forward to Miss Castile continuing her gifted teaching in the little school. Am I correct, Mr. Mackey?"

"Yes, her job is secure. I'm leaving as well."

"He's a very scary priest...but I think I like him..."

I never thought I'd appreciate that loud, bombastic voiced and pushy personality ... but today I do.

When the door was closed behind the retreating men, Becca threw herself into the Reverend's arms and sobbed.

"What are you doing? You can't behave so boldly with a priest! Even I would do no such thing"

Thanks for your help, Delphi. You may go...it's ok now...

"How did you know to come?"

She looked up into his smiling face. Pulling back, she wiped her eyes with the handkerchief he handed her.

"Sarah rode to the parsonage last night; left a little bundle in Grace's keeping, and told her what had happened. Grace knew where I was, and sent for me this morning. I hurried here to practice a little New Testament wisdom. I also wanted to tell you, I'm staying in the ministry. I found it."

"Found what?"

"The calling, I found it. You were right. My lack of forgiveness blinded me from everything else."

Another pounding at the door caused Becca's heart to jump. Hannah opened it, and James rushed in. He was breathless.

"Reverend, I'm so glad you're here. I think someone should be with Delphi."

"What's the matter, James?" Becca asked, panicked.

"Thad and that Baxter fella...they're getting ready to duel."

"What? Duel as in guns?" Becca gasped. "That's insane!"

The Reverend placed his hat on his head and turned toward the door. "Where are they, James?"

"They're meeting at the Lake." James gave a breathless reply. "I didn't know you were here Reverend. Perhaps you can reach them in time. I wanted to warn Delphi..."

Delphi had already run out the back door. She pulled up her skirts to give freedom to her feet. Calling to Bonnie, she rushed for a saddle. As she lifted it on to the back of her mare, Titus entered the barn.

"Delphi, I'll go. You stay here. Women are not permitted at duel challenges. I'll reason with them."

Becca didn't reply. She reserved her time and energy for the fast ride to the Lake. She arranged the saddle, reaching under Bonnie for the strap. Titus approached her.

"Delphi, if it's any assurance, I can testify to the fact that in most duels, the challengers miss their mark," he assured her.

Becca adjusted the stirrups. She was using the stride saddle, and Thad had used it last.

"I don't know why he's doing something so stupid. This mess isn't worth him dying over." She muttered.

"Dueling isn't about dying; it's about proving that you aren't afraid to die for honor. I don't agree with it either, but customs are hard to change," the minister explained.

James walked in at that moment. "Delphi, don't go. You'll prove to be a distraction. Thad's a great aim with any gun. He'll win this, I'm certain."

She led Bonnie out into the penned area, and beside a wooden crate she kept in place to use as stepping stool. She stepped on it to reach the stirrup.

"And if he loses, he's dead. If he wins he's murdered someone. How is that supposed to comfort me, James?"

She adjusted her skirts around her straddled position, and trotted Bonnie through the opened gate. Dublin followed, casting a wary eye at the men. Both men ran to their own mounts at the front of the house. Once on the road, Becca nudged Bonnie with her heels. The horse gleefully responded, more than ready for a run. Behind her Dublin, James and Titus attempted to keep up...*Thad can't die...the museum journal reports our marriage...but he could be seriously wounded...maimed...or kill Baxter. He's already troubled about the atrocities he witnessed in the war...what would killing a man do to his mental health?*

Suddenly from the corner of her eye, she saw a flash of light fawn color. The Reverend managed catch up, approaching her on the left side.

"There's a mountain lion keeping pace with us. He's four or five yards away, inside the woods."

"I know," she replied. "Don't worry about him." *for an old, lame animal, he's moving really fast.*

Before reaching the Lake, Titus called. "Delphi, slow down... halt. We must approach quietly. Our distraction might disadvantage one or both, and cause more harm than good."

Becca pulled back on Bonnie's reins. A shot rang out in the quiet woods. A large raven flew from the direction of the gunfire, scolding loudly.

"Oh no." She started to proceed.

Titus reached over, and covered her hand that held the reins. "Wait, Delphi, they always fire a test shot from each pistol to be sure they both work properly."

Another shot sounded, verifying Titus's knowledge of the ritual. The three dismounted, tied their horses to tree limbs. They crept in the direction they now knew the duelers to be.

As they reached the clearing, Becca couldn't believe her eyes. Fitzgerald stood on the sideline, a witness for Baxter no doubt. Thad and Baxter were positioned some distance from each other, and facing opposite directions. Abe stood on a large dead log, holding a white cloth above his head.

"I have to stop them." She started to run forward. Titus caught her and held her tightly.

"No, they're focused on shooting; you might cause one of them to accidently shoot you."

She started to sob. Then she saw him, the lion at the tree line. He was just out of Baxter's sight. He was crouched.

"What's he doing? This is so crazy...please, someone make it all stop."

Abe dropped the cloth. Both men quickly turned. Thad's gun discharged. She closed her eyes. Loud male voices could be heard exclaiming surprise and protests. Opening her eyes, she saw Thad still holding the pistol. Smoke spiraled from its barrel. Her gaze followed his. Baxter was on the ground. The cat was on top of him. Another shot rang out and the cat rolled over and lay limp. Becca looked around and saw Fitzgerald lowering his pistol...*He shot the lion... oh no...*

79

"Forgiveness is the fragrance that the violet sheds on the heel that has crushed it."

—MARK TWAIN

Breaking free from the minister who had now relaxed his arms in his own astonishment, she reached the limp form of the lion. Baxter scrambled to his feet. His face was clawed; blood ran from his upper arm. From the rip in his shirt sleeve, Becca could see it was from lion teeth and not a bullet wound.

She dropped down by the cat. He opened his golden eyes.

"I'm sorry they shot you. What were you thinking, jumping in the middle of things like that?"

Thad's placed his hand on her shoulder.

"I'm sorry your wild friend was shot, Delphi. I aimed for Baxter's arm, but missed when that cat jumped in. You wouldn't expect Fitzgerald not to also shoot to save Baxter from his attack."

"Thad's clearly won the challenge, he shot first," Abe loudly proclaimed. "You're lucky to be alive, Baxter. Now give him the tintype as agreed. The deal is, you leave town, right?"

Becca shut out the voices... *Let them resolve their honor issues. I have issues of my own.*

She leaned over and whispered into the ear of the large animal.

"I know who you are."

The cat expelled a soft moan.

"You found God's forgiveness, dying on that mountain, didn't you?"

The large amber eyes settled on her face.

"Go in peace, Phil. I forgive you." She petted the tawny head, and the cat released a jagged breath.

"You tried to stop this ridiculous fight...or maybe it was what you had to do so we could communicate...or maybe you needed to hear me forgive...or maybe I needed to hear me forgive..."

The golden eyes closed and she knew a spirit now moved to the light. Becca was aware of movement and voices around her. She felt numb as well as cold. Thad's warm topcoat settled over her shoulders. His firm grip tugged at her elbows.

"Come, Delphi. All is well. We have nothing more to worry about."

"I don't understand what you're talking about." Her voice revealed her emotion.

"I have the photograph. We'll burn it. We'll not speak of it again."

As he helped her to her feet, she turned and faced him. "That's what this is all about? You arranged a duel to get that stupid picture? Would you choose to live the rest of your life knowing you murdered someone just to get a stupid picture?"

"I had no intention of killing him, Delphi; I only planned to wing him. We agreed to only wound. My winning resulted in his turning over of the photograph, and leaving town without causing any further slander against your character."

"And if you lost, Thad, did you think of that? What would have been the outcome then?"

"Then Doc would patch me up, and Baxter would continue with his mischief. At least everyone would know I was willing to defend your honor."

Becca pushed the dissembled locks of hair from her face. Thad tried to pull her to him, but she backed away.

"I want to go home now. I've had enough of this day."

"Delphi, I'm regretful for my drunken rant the other night. Will you forgive me? I prefer we put all this to rest."

A lot of forgiveness happening tonight...

"Of course, I forgive you Thad. But you must promise to never participate in anything like this again."

He reached for her. She allowed his embrace. "I promise," he said softly.

"I also want you to come back to the house. We're going to have a meeting, you, me, the Rev, Doc, Annie, and Mrs. Leng. You're going to hear the real truth. You'll have a hard time believing it, but if you truly love me you will."

He walked with her to the wooded area where Bonnie waited. After asking Titus to come back to the house, she requested James to take messages to the Lengs and Doc. She and Thad rode back to the house in silence. Entering the house, Becca made a request of Hannah and Sarah.

"Would you please warm up some leftovers, and make a pot of coffee? I'll catch you up on all that's happened soon. No one is seriously hurt."

She found Annie in the drawing room. "Annie, the time has come to explain things to Thad. I'll need your support. Please speak English so Thad will understand some of this mystery."

When Thad returned from settling the horses in the barn, he found Becca sitting calmly in the parlor with Annie. The silver serving service sat on the tea table with steaming coffee. He sat on the end of the sofa. Together, they waited for the others to come.

After the guests arrived, everyone gathered in the drawing room. Sarah and Hannah had spread plates of food and hot creamed tea on the tea table. Thad moved the two upholstered chairs from the parlor to provide more seating. Everyone exchanged appropriate greetings and soon quieted. They sat expectantly for the news Becca would share with her fiancée. Thad sat beside Becca, insisting on holding her hand. Becca glanced around the group.

Titus looked directly at her. "I don't wish to be presumptuous, but with your permission, I'd like to begin this gathering with prayer."

"Certainly, Reverend," Becca responded, adding a weak smile... *Please don't wear everyone out with a long, long prayer.*

The pastor bowed his head. "Our Dear Heavenly Farther, Creator, and Guide, we thank you for this gathering of your children, all made in your image, and brothers and sisters of your great family."

That's different for Titus...he's being quite inclusive and respectful for the diversity that's represented here.

"First, we thank you for preserving the lives that were endangered this afternoon, and we pray you make us wiser in all future conflicts."

Great...I like that...

"Give us open ears and hearts as we continue with this meeting. Amen"

Amazing...his shortest prayer ever...and it was purposeful...

The Reverend looked at Becca as she straightened her posture. Taking a breath, she began.

"I have something to share with my future husband. It's most unusual, and at first I found it hard to believe. However, living the experience has made it my reality."

She turned her head, and looked into Thad's eyes.

"Please don't draw a conclusion until I've finished my story, and our friends can explain to you why they believe me."

He squeezed her hand. "I'll try my best."

"I was born in 1991 and died in the twenty-first century."

Thad's eyebrows knitted, but he made no attempt to comment.

"In that century, my name was Rebecca Cates. I was married to Philip Cates. People called me Becca. I was a teacher in Portland, and preparing to begin my second year of teaching. I'd just learned that my husband was having an affair with his assistant, Tonya."

She paused, giving Thad a chance to process what she had said.

"In the twenty-first century, money will have an inflated value compared to now, and will be handled very differently. Most people won't hold it in safes or in the form of gold bars or coins. They'll put it in banks, or invest it in business, or in the market, or prevent financial disaster by purchasing insurance. Phillip inherited his father's insurance business, and was doing very well, but he was greedy. He placed a million dollar life policy on me, and arranged my death."

Thad's knitted brows now lifted. His hazel eyes opened wide. He remained silent.

Doc cleared his throat. "Delphi, may I add something here?"

"Yes, of course."

Thad turned his attention to the doctor. "When I first called on Delphi...as we all refer to her...she insisted her name was Rebecca Cates. This was the morning after the Brother Jonathan's sinking. I have my notes from that visit."

He held the small notebook Becca remembered seeing him use during that visit. Adjusting his spectacles, he leaned into the lamplight and read from his notes.

"The patient believes that she had arrived from Portland, although the steamer she was on came from San Francisco. She insists her name is Rebecca Cates, and that she survived an attempted murder that was arranged by her husband."

He looked up from the notebook. "It sounded to me, at the time, like delirium caused by the horrid ordeal."

"How did he try to kill you, and where is he now?" Thad's voice revealed a touch of anger. Becca knew it came from his obsession to protect her.

"He's no longer living." *I'll put his mind to rest about that at least...*

"Anyway...he arranged to have me thrown overboard from a pleasure boat at the exact same place Brother Jonathan sunk...only one-hundred-fifty years later..."

Thad's eyebrows knitted again. Still holding her hand, he rubbed his temples with his other hand.

"I was fighting the waves, trying to survive when I saw the ship sinking. I grabbed a plank that floated my way. Soon after another woman crashed into me and grabbed onto the plank. We were hit by a big wave that knocked me unconscious...I believe it killed me. The next thing I knew, Tate and other crewmen pulled me into the life boat. The other woman was gone...at least I thought so...but I later realized I was in her body...or my spirit was.

80

"It is in pardoning that we are pardoned."

—Francis Of Assisi

"Shape shifting," said Annie.

Everyone looked at her in surprise. Annie seldom spoke, and rarely in English. "Shape shifting is strong medicine, can only happen to very strong spirits, and only with agreement of the Great Spirit."

Mrs. Leng nodded her head. "Spirit return... sometime necessary... person learn harmony... teach harmony...Creator decide who... not for man to question"

Doc pushed his glasses up again. "I must say, I believe Delphi. She has extraordinary knowledge regarding medicine...things that could only be learned by insight into a future time."

Thad looked into Becca's eyes. "So the other woman was Delphi Castile?"

"Yes, I soon learned that." She answered.

"When I gathered information from the few survivors," Doc continued," they identified her as Delphi Castile, one of the brothel girls. However, she had no memories of being on the ship when I talked with her on that first visit. Delphi Castile was French. This Delphi spoke no French...not even an accent was apparent."

Becca decided she must regain control of the narrative. "So... when I figured things out...as to what had happened...I thought I'd have to make the best of things. I found Delphi's journal. I read it to learn about who I would have to pretend to be."

"I was there when she found the journal," piped Hannah. "We opened the carpet bag together. I could see she was as surprised about what was in it as was I. She made me promise to not speak of it to others. I kept my promise." She smiled proudly at Becca.

Becca reached over to the small side table, and picked up the journal. She handed it to Thad.

"After our meeting, I want you to read all of this. You'll find entries with different penmanship, different voice, and you'll plainly see it's written by two different women."

He accepted the book from her.

"You'll read the sad story of a young teenage girl who set out to seek a career in music, and ended up enslaved in a brothel against her will. That's where the photograph was taken."

"Such a travesty... poor child," muttered Titus.

"Eventually, many years from now, society will no longer blame the victims of sex trafficking. They'll blame the evil people who run the disgusting operation, and the men who keep it in business, but it'll continue to be a problem, an illegal practice." Becca explained.

"The church should find ways to help those poor souls," commented Reverend Walker. He appeared to be lost in his thought, plotting new interventions.

Becca directed her attention to Thad. "You'll also read about how Delphi's spirit entered my much damaged body, and is now living in two-thousand-fifteen. You'll read how my ex-husband died. Later I'll explain the mystery of the mountain lion."

"What is it like then?" Thad looked up from the journal, and focused on her face. "What's it like in that century?"

"Some things are better...others, not so much. There'll be cars... they're horseless carriages...Airplanes... they're flying machines. People will ride in them clear across the ocean."

The silence in the room was eerie.

"Rather than bleeding people, doctors will put blood into patients. People can have damaged hearts replaced, as well as other vital organs. Many diseases will all but disappear due to immunization ... uh...that's a special medicine. New lethal ailments will develop."

Doc's face revealed his curiosity. He appeared to be bursting with questions.

The Reverend's brows knitted. "Well, I guess the Lord's return won't happen as soon as I thought. Will the dissenting religions cease their disagreements and unite?"

Becca shook her head. She looked at the pastor. "Some will merge while others split, causing more divisions. Some new ones will be invented. There'll continue to be some who think they own God, and have the only truth. There'll still be those who want the government to operate regarding their beliefs only. And bloody wars will be fought in disguise of religion... But...there'll continue to be other leaders that repeat the teaching of Jesus... tolerance... forgiveness... charity... love...inclusion."

"Will any of my people be alive?" Sarah asked.

Becca smiled at the girl. "Oh yes, Sarah, your people are indestructible. Treaties will continue to be made. Every single one will be broken, but the people will survive. They'll be an important part of American society and a rich part of its history."

"And slavery...the reason I fought in the war...the reason I'm lame...it won't return?" Thad ventured.

"Not in America, Thad, but slavery will continue in the world. The good news is that there will always be brave people tirelessly working to end it, just as some fair-minded individuals will continue to fight racism, poverty, and other inequalities."

"The church should take an active role in that," declared Titus, his brow again knitting in concentration.

"And some churches will," she smiled at her pastor. "Others who call themselves Christians will promote prejudice, resist enlightenment."

My, how he's changed...

"And war...with all that they'll discover...all that wisdom they will have then...they will end all war?" Thad looked at her anxiously.

She looked down, knowing her answer would disappoint him.

"No, my darling, the foundation of war is rooted in greed, and an unquenchable thirst for power. Those will always be a part of society. The war you just experienced will be nothing compared to what will follow. Wars will include many countries, bigger weapons, and a massive loss of life."

"And immigrants...like us? Mr. Leng inquired.

"People from other countries will continue to seek freedom and opportunity in America, since that's the foundation upon which it is built. But...there'll always be a struggle for acceptance... exploitation ... hate crimes committed against them. I'm sorry, Mr. Leng, prejudice to new-comers will always be held by some, but other's will take a stand against intolerance."

She found it difficult to look into his sad brown eyes, remembering how the history she knew recorded the brutal treatment toward Chinese American business owners. That was yet to come for the Lengs and their little Chinatown in the Crescent.

"Hopefully, the church will follow Christ's teachings...and intercede" Titus' bombastic tone sounded like he planned to will it so.

"Some religious leaders will, Titus....some will. There will always be some on the right side of history."

"Are we?" asked Doc. "Are we, at this time, on the right side of history?"

Becca glanced around the room...

There's the Lengs...sitting side-by-side and dressed partially in Oriental clothing and partly in American fashion...Hannah and Sarah sharing an upholstered chair...Doc, her friend and the first to believe her wild experience... his openness to science and knowledge... Annie, preserving the Native ways, language, and pride... but so willing to share it...Titus, with his new found calling, his restored love for humanity and zeal to minister...

Thad...loving, honest...always willing to fight for right... whether it is the savagery of slavery or her reputation....She smiled warmly.

"Yes, my friends. Having come from the future, I can assure you, all here are on the right side of history."

Thad grinned. "Then may I suggest we eat some of this food. I'm starving."

As they stood and prepared together plates, Titus placed his stovepipe hat on his head.

"If you will excuse me, I must have a visit with Harry. I have a sincere apology, explanation, and promise to offer him. I pray he will forgive me. "

"I pray that Harry will be able to forgive himself." Thad said softly.

"Yes, well, we will have to work on that as well, " the pastor promised.

Becca stood to walk Titus to the door. As she turned she saw Thad's warm smile.

"I'm befuddled trying to understand it all, Delphi. I do believe you, but it'll a take a spell to understand it."

"As well it should. I'm not sure I understand it all either."

When everyone had left, she slipped easily into his embrace and they shared a deep and lingering kiss.

"In a few days you'll be my wife. Life can go on from there, one long happy journey."

"Yes," she agreed, "I dare not imagine what adventures will be on that journey. "

"The journey is the reward."

—Tao Proverb

Vocabulary words and phrases of the 19th Century

All-overish: drunk, hung-over

Be-fuddled: To be confused about something

B'hoy: Could apply to an outlaw, thug or other mistrusted male.

Blood letting: A common medical practice of cutting a vain, bleeding the patient, and bandaging the wound. Used for a variety of complaints.

Brain Fever: any mental stress, otherwise not able to be diagnosed.

Chamber pot: an ornate bucket-like container, used for nighttime toilet calls before indoor plumbing. They were made from metal, porcelain or crockery.

"Cut a rug": term for doing something exceptionally well or in a way that impresses others, performance at one's best.

Fancy: When used as a verb it meant, to like and approve of, to want to desire.

Fuddy-duddy: One who believe he/herself to be better than everyone else.

Gangrene: A serious and lethal infection prevalent before antibiotics was developed. Treated by amputation.

Laudanum: a commonly used tranquilizer that was Opium based. It was easily obtained and not controlled.

"Honey-fuggled": Scammed, ripped-off, tricked, deceived

"Little end of the horn": Treated badly by fate, unlucky, short-changed.

Lock Jaw: 19th century word for Tetanus

Melancholies: Depression, sadness, grief

Mental illness and special needs: Medical terminology changes with time. The terms *Imbecile, Lunatic, and Moron* were at one time acceptable medical terms in this century.

Mrs. Winslow's Soothing Syrup: A common household medication. Popular with ladies for anxiety, nausea, and headaches, baby's colic and teething pain. It was sugary syrup mixed with Opium tincture

Notions: (1) Any item that a housewife might have on her list of necessities for shopping (2) an idea or opinion; a though being pondered.

Off the reel; right away, without hesitation can also refer to "flying off the handle with temper."

Poke: the name used to describe a sack or bag.

"Plumb streaked": extremely frightened or out of control with excitement.

Pshaw! Acceptable slang, not considered cussing. Used in the same way as; "Good Grief!" "Golly Gee!" or "Dang"...

Randy: inappropriate, off color, suggestive language. "randy remarks"

Rankles: To annoy or upset

Reconnoiter: to inspect, observe, or survey

Simpleton: A common reference at the time that referred to people with learning challenges.

Scythe: A long handled tool attached to a sharp blade, used from cutting grass, weeds, or harvesting hay.

Tote: The act of carrying; "Please allow me to tote your parcels."

http://mess1.homestead.com/Nineteenth_Century_Slang_Dictionary.pdf

Research

1. **Historical events regarding Brother Jonathan**
   Brothhttp://worldhistoryproject.org/1865//30/sinking-of-the-brother-johnathan, posting undated, retrieved by C.Silvers 7/27/2014
   http://acdwyer.com/stories/ss-brother-jonathan-shipwreck-treasure-page-1.php, 2008-1014, A.C Dwyer, retrieved by C.Silvers 7/4/2014, Copyright 2008–2014
   http://www.nytimes.com/1865/08/26/news/another-great-disaster-wreck- http://www.nytimes.com/1865/08/26/news/another-great-disaster--wreck-steamship-Brother., Published 8/26/1965, retrieved by Silvers 7/27/2014
   Dennis M. Powers, Treasure Ship, copyright 2006, Citadel press Books, Kensington Pub Corp, 850 3rd Ave, N.Y., NY/ http://www.localhistories.org/sanfrancisco.html

2. **Research about Crescent City**
   The History of Del Norte County, Ester Ruth Smith, copyright 1953, & Rachel Smith Tomini, copyright 1989, Eureka, California,
   Crescent City and Del Note County by Del Norte Historical Society, pub 2005, Arcadia Publishing
   Crescent City, A Walk through Time, self published by the students of Crescent Elk School
   Del Norte County, Then and Now, Complied by Lark Weston, Andra Goss, & Carol Byers

3. **Clothing a customs of dress**
   http://www.quilthistory.com/life.htm

4. **Information regarding Native American Medicine**
   http://www.soyouwanna.com/native-american-remedies-burns-3367.html, by Katherine Checkley, retrieved by C.Silvers, 10/4/2014

http://www.kumeyaay.info/southern_calif_indigenous_plants. html?http%3A//www.kumeyaay.info/california_native_plants/native_willow.html
Sea anemone as Native American Medicine: Ocean World, Crescent City California, Retrieved through interview by C. Silvers, 11/26.2014
http://bioexpedition.com/sea-anemone/ retrieved by C. Silvers, 11/29/2014
http://www.buzzle.com/articles/facts-about-sea-anemones.html retrieved by C. Silvers, 11/29/2014
http://animals.nationalgeographic.com/animals/invertebrates/sea-anemone/retrieved by C. Silvers, 11/29/2014

5. **Information regarding Religious African American leadership and history Episcopal-Methodist churches in the 19th century.**
Ministry School on line, The Methodist Church, http://www.u-s-istory.com/pages/h3800.html, retrieved by C. Silver, 12/29/2014
Free African Society (FAS), which Richard Allen, Absalom Jones, and other free blacks established in Philadelphia in 1787.

6. **John Wesley's Rules for Singing**
http://www.sneconline.org/article/188/departments-ministeries.the-singong-church/articles-from-the-september-2008-issue/john wesley-s-rules-for-singing-1761, retrieved by C. Silvers, 2/4/2015

7. **Education and textbook of the 19th century**
Webster to McGuffey: A sketch of American Literacy Textbooks. History of Reading News. Vol.XXV No.2 (2002:Spring) by Charles Monaghan- retrieved by C. Silvers, 2/4/2015, http://historyliteracy.org/scripts/search_display.php?Article_ID=182
Mrs. Leng's Tao religious beliefs
http://www.religionfacts.com/taoism/beliefs.htm-retrieved by c. silvers, 12/14

http://www.religionfacts.com/big_religion_chart.htm retrieved by c. silvers, 12/14
Becca's Injury and treatment
http://www.medicinenet.com/spinal_cord_injury_treatments_and_rehabilitation/
Native American history, customs and religions
http://are.as.wvu.edu/ruvolo.htm
http://www.california-indians.com/tolowa-indians/193
http://www.yuroktribe.org/
11. Quotes
http://www.brainyquotes.com/quotes/keywords
http://www.taoistic.com/taoquotes/taoquotes-02-nature-world.htm
http://www.legendsofamerica.com/na-proverbs.html

Made in the USA
Lexington, KY
16 July 2015